The Masque of Mañana

Robert Sheckley

Edited by Sharon L. Sbarsky

The NESFA Press
Post Office Box 809
Framingham, MA 01701
2005

FIRST EDITION
Second Printing
August, 2008

International Standard Book Number:
1-886778-60-4

Copyrights and First Appearances

Introduction by David Hartwell
The Accountant, *F&SF* Jul 1954
All the Things You Are, *Galaxy* Jul 1956
Bad Medicine, *Galaxy* Jul 1956
The Battle, *If* Sep 1954
Citizen in Space ["Spy Story"], *Playboy* Sep 1955
The Deaths of Ben Baxter, *Galaxy* Jul 1957
The Demons, *Fantasy Magazine* Mar 1953
Dukakis and the Aliens, *Alternate Presidents,* ed. Mike Resnick, Tor 1992
Early Model, *Galaxy* Aug 1956
Fool's Mate, *Astounding* Mar 1953
Ghost V, *Galaxy* Oct 1954
Gray Flannel Armor, *Galaxy* Nov 1957
Holdout, *F&SF* Dec 1957
The Language of Love, *Galaxy* May 1957
The Laxian Key, *Galaxy* Nov 1954
The Leech, *Galaxy* Dec 1952
The Lifeboat Mutiny, *Galaxy* Apr 1955
Milk Run, *Galaxy* Sep 1954
The Minimum Man, *Galaxy* Jun 1958
The Monsters, *F&SF* Mar 1953
The Native Problem, *Galaxy* Dec 1956
The Necessary Thing, *Galaxy* Jun 1955
Pilgrimage to Earth ["Love, Incorporated"], *Playboy* Sep 1956
The Prize of Peril, *F&SF* May 1958
Prospector's Special, *Galaxy* Dec 1959
Sarkanger, *Stardate* Jan/Feb 1986
Seventh Victim, *Galaxy* Apr 1953
Shall We Have a Little Talk?, *Galaxy* Oct 1965
Shape ["Keep Your Shape"], *Galaxy* Nov 1953
Skulking Permit, *Galaxy* Dec 1954
Something for Nothing, *Galaxy* Jun 1954
The Store of the Worlds ["The World of Heart's Desire"], *Playboy* Sep 1959
Squirrel Cage, *Galaxy* Jan 1955
The Skag Castle, *Fantastic Universe* Mar 1956
The Sweeper of Loray, *Galaxy* Apr 1959
A Thief in Time, *Galaxy* Jul 1954
A Ticket to Tranai, *Galaxy* Oct 1955
Triplication, *Playboy* May 1959
Untouched by Human Hands ["One Man's Poison"], *Galaxy* Dec 1953
What Is Life?, *Playboy* Dec 1976
A Wind Is Rising, *Galaxy* Jul 1957

Contents

The Masque of Mañana

ROBERT SHECKLEY

Robert Sheckley is the subject of a recent essay by Brian Aldiss, who says, "Whereas most writers of this kind of futuristic fairy tale will go to great lengths, by deploying ordinary language, and by methods of realism adapted from the mundane or everyday novel, to reassure us that their feet are on the ground, even if their heads are in galactic space, Sheckley's heart is with the Unbelievable. His main target is the Incredible. With one swing of his computer he hacks through the string which suspends our disbelief. It would crash down, were it not for the fact that there is no gravity in Sheckley's space." Sheckley is one of the important living SF writers, whose reputation is based primarily on the quality of his quirky, subversive, satirical short fiction, a body of work admired by everyone from Kingsley Amis, J. G. Ballard, and Harlan Ellison to Roger Zelazny (with whom he collaborated). And now, finally, he is the guest of honor at the World Science Fiction Convention, and this book of stories is published to commemorate the event.

I started reading Sheckley in the early 1950s in *Galaxy, F&SF,* and elsewhere. I bought his collections, starting with *Untouched by Human Hands* and *Citizen in Space,* those wonderful Ballantine paperbacks, and read them avidly. Later I bought the Ballantine hardcovers, and even later bought the cover painting for *Citizen in Space* from Richard Powers. I still have it and it is one of the chief ornaments of my art collection. I really like the AAA Ace Decontamination Agency stories ("Ghost V" may be the best of them, although "The Lifeboat Mutiny" is very fine as well. You might be pleasantly surprised if you can find a copy of the '50s radio adaptation on Dimension X, if I recall correctly. The sound track features fine musical jokes.). Those stories, with their twisty plots and good humor are in some ways the foundation of Sheckley's early popularity—his early mastery was in part a mastery of the plot twist. I think "The Prize of Peril" and "The Seventh Victim" are important SF stories, and I read the Sheckley stories and novels that in many ways just got better and better until the late 1960s (remember the novels *Mindswap* and *Dimension of Miracles?*) when they sort of stopped for a while. Not entirely, but almost.

I later learned that he had dropped out and gone to live on the island of Ibiza. He came back in the 1970s and published some things I don't find so memorable as the earlier stuff. He became the fiction editor of *Omni* in the early 1980s, got remarried at least once, left New York again, and ended up in Portland, Oregon for nearly twenty years mostly married to the writer Gail Dana, during which time he hit his stride again in short fiction, including publishing some stories I have included in my Year's Best anthologies over the last ten years. I regret that it hasn't been possible for NESFA to find room for some of them in this book, but, oh well, there should be another volume anyway.

He also wrote a series of three ironic detective novels about Hob Draconian, proprietor of the Alternative Detective Agency, an aging hippie who used to live on Ibiza and who wanders through criminal investigations, often hilariously, until the solution somehow works itself out around him. Do yourself a favor and read *Soma*, the third and final and best to date. Then you'll want to find the first two, *The Alternative Detective* and *Draconian New York*.

Now he lives in Red Hook, New York, a couple of hours north of New York City. He's still writing well, and still produces fiction today that is thought-provoking, memorable, and stylish. And satirical too—do notice that, because it is where the politics comes in.

As an ironic investigator of questions of identity and of the nature of reality, he is a peer of Philip K. Dick and Kurt Vonnegut. In an interview that has been up on the web for years at this writing (www.fantascienza.net/sfpeople/robert.sheckley) this exchange took place:

Delos: Why is there something, instead of there being nothing?

Sheckley: There isn't something. There's only nothing masquerading as something and looking very like Gerard Depardieu. That, by the way, is the real meaning of cyberspace.

I now interrupt this introduction for a short rant:

Robert Sheckley is one of the finest SF writers of the 20th century and beyond, and is still producing first-class work in short fiction and at novel length. There are present Grand Masters who have contributed less, and only a few who have contributed more to SF worldwide in the last sixty years.

The present fashion is to ignore the contributions of a writer unless they are novels, and that is a growing disaster and a betrayal of the history of SF achievement in the 20th century. Not just the SFWA, but fans in general are losing touch with SF literary history and many of the masterworks and fine writers of the past, but especially those whose finest achievements were short fiction.

Despite the efforts of NESFA Press and others, almost everybody is looking at novels as the measure of a writer's true quality. If this goes on without challenge, everyone from Damon Knight to Harlan Ellison, from Lucius Shepard to Ted Chiang will end up as second rank, and not worthy of Grand Master awards no matter how fine their stories. And to put it bluntly, there are a disproportionate number of excellent short story writers in the SF tradition, but not a lot of first class novelists. Better than half the present Grand Masters made a major part of their contribution to SF through their short stories, some, such as Fritz Leiber, were most important for their stories.

Never publishing a body of classic novels as a thumb rule for elimination from the main SF canon is the same kind of arbitrary literary politics as eliminating a writer from the canon because she or he only wrote SF. We ought not to forget this. And the point holds whether or not you care anything at all about genre awards.

End of rant.

Douglas Adams once said, when an interviewer asked what the difference was between Adams' writing and Sheckley's, that the difference is that Sheckley writes better. This speaks well of Adams as a writer of perception and taste. Like all great SF writers, and I do think Robert Sheckley is a great SF writer, Sheckley has a mastery of his individual style that other writers admire. Like, say, Terry Prachett, a good bit of the humor in Sheckley is embedded in the way the sentences are constructed and in the careful management of tone. Reading a bit of it aloud can be a help to appreciation—and I have heard readers and writers suddenly start to read a Sheckley sentence aloud in the middle of the evening at a convention party. Hey, Sheckley can still make me laugh out loud while I am reading, and that's a rare pleasure.

This is a collection of good, and some great, SF, by a great SF writer. Whether you are reading the stories for the first time, or going back to old favorites after too long away, I believe you are in for a treat.

And then tell your friends.

David G. Hartwell
Pleasantville, NY
April, 2005

The Leech

The leech was waiting for food. For millennia it had been drifting across the vast emptiness of space. Without consciousness, it had spent the countless centuries in the void between the stars. It was unaware when it finally reached a sun. Life-giving radiation flared around the hard, dry spore. Gravitation tugged at it.

A planet claimed it, with other stellar debris, and the leech fell, still dead-seeming within its tough spore case.

One speck of dust among many, the winds blew it around the Earth, played with it, and let it fall.

On the ground, it began to stir. Nourishment soaked in, permeating the spore case. It grew—and fed.

Frank Conners came up on the porch and coughed twice. "Say, pardon me, Professor," he said.

The long, pale man didn't stir from the sagging couch. His horn-rimmed glasses were perched on his forehead, and he was snoring very gently.

"I'm awful sorry to disturb you," Conners said, pushing back his battered felt hat. "I know it's your restin' week and all, but there's something damned funny in the ditch."

The pale man's left eyebrow twitched, but he showed no other sign of having heard.

Frank Conners coughed again, holding his spade in one purple-veined hand. "Didja hear me, Professor?"

"Of course I heard you," Micheals said in a muffled voice, his eyes still closed. "You found a pixie."

"A what?" Conners asked, squinting at Micheals.

"A little man in a green suit. Feed him milk, Conners."

"No, sir. I think it's a rock."

Micheals opened one eye and focused it in Conners' general direction.

"I'm awfully sorry about it," Conners said. Professor Micheals' resting week was a ten-year-old custom, and his only eccentricity. All winter Micheals taught anthropology, worked on half a dozen committees,

17

dabbled in physics and chemistry, and still found time to write a book a year. When summer came, he was tired.

Arriving at his worked-out New York State farm, it was his invariable rule to do absolutely nothing for a week. He hired Frank Conners to cook for that week and generally make himself useful, while Professor Micheals slept.

During the second week, Micheals would wander around, look at the trees and fish. By the third week he would be getting a tan, reading, repairing the sheds, and climbing mountains. At the end of four weeks, he could hardly wait to get back to the city.

But the resting week was sacred.

"I really wouldn't bother you for anything small," Conners said apologetically. "But that damned rock melted two inches off my spade."

Micheals opened both eyes and sat up. Conners held out the spade. The rounded end was sheared cleanly off. Micheals swung himself off the couch and slipped his feet into battered moccasins.

"Let's see this wonder," he said.

The object was lying in the ditch at the end of the front lawn, three feet from the main road. It was round, about the size of a truck tire, and solid throughout. It was about an inch thick, as far as he could tell, grayish black and intricately veined.

"Don't touch it," Conners warned.

"I'm not going to. Let me have your spade." Micheals took the spade and prodded the object experimentally. It was completely unyielding. He held the spade to the surface for a moment, then withdrew it. Another inch was gone.

Micheals frowned, and pushed his glasses tighter against his nose. He held the spade against the rock with one hand, the other held close to the surface. More of the spade disappeared.

"Doesn't seem to be generating heat," he said to Conners. "Did you notice any the first time?"

Conners shook his head.

Micheals picked up a clod of dirt and tossed it on the object. The dirt dissolved quickly, leaving no trace on the gray-black surface. A large stone followed the dirt and disappeared in the same way.

"Isn't that just about the damnedest thing you ever saw, Professor?" Conners asked.

"Yes," Micheals agreed, standing up again. "It just about is."

He hefted the spade and brought it down smartly on the object. When it hit, he almost dropped the spade. He had been gripping the handle rigidly, braced for a recoil. But the spade struck that unyielding surface and *stayed*. There was no perceptible give, but absolutely no recoil.

"Whatcha think it is?" Conners asked.

"It's no stone," Micheals said. He stepped back. "A leech drinks blood. This thing seems to be drinking dirt. And spades." He struck it a few more times, experimentally. The two men looked at each other. On the road, half a dozen Army trucks rolled past.

"I'm going to phone the college and ask a physics man about it," Micheals said. "Or a biologist. I'd like to get rid of that thing before it spoils my lawn."

They walked back to the house.

Everything fed the leech. The wind added its modicum of kinetic energy, ruffling across the gray-black surface. Rain fell, and the force of each individual drop added to its store. The water was sucked in by the all-absorbing surface.

The sunlight above it was absorbed, and converted into mass for its body. Beneath it, the soil was consumed, dirt, stones and branches broken down by the leech's complex cells and changed into energy. Energy was converted back into mass, and the leech grew.

Slowly, the first flickers of consciousness began to return. Its first realization was of the impossible smallness of its body.

It grew.

When Micheals looked the next day, the leech was eight feet across, sticking out into the road and up the side of the lawn. The following day it was almost eighteen feet in diameter, shaped to fit the contour of the ditch, and covering most of the road. That day the sheriff drove up in his Model A, followed by half the town.

"Is that your leech thing, Professor Micheals?" Sheriff Flynn asked.

"That's it," Micheals said. He had spent the past days looking unsuccessfully for an acid that would dissolve the leech.

"We gotta get it out of the road," Flynn said, walking truculently up to the leech. "Something like this, you can't let it block the road, Professor. The Army's gotta use this road."

"I'm terribly sorry," Micheals said with a straight face. "Go right ahead, Sheriff. But be careful. It's hot." The leech wasn't hot, but it seemed the simplest explanation under the circumstances.

Micheals watched with interest as the sheriff tried to shove a crowbar under it. He smiled to himself when it was removed with half a foot of its length gone.

The sheriff wasn't so easily discouraged. He had come prepared for a stubborn piece of rock. He went to the rumble seat of his car and took out a blowtorch and a sledgehammer, ignited the torch and focused it on one edge of the leech.

After five minutes, there was no change. The gray didn't turn red or even seem to heat up. Sheriff Flynn continued to bake it for fifteen minutes, then called to one of the men.

"Hit that spot with the sledge, Jerry."

Jerry picked up the sledgehammer, motioned the sheriff back, and swung it over his head. He let out a howl as the hammer struck unyieldingly. There wasn't a fraction of recoil.

In the distance they heard the roar of an Army convoy.

"Now we'll get some action," Flynn said.

Micheals wasn't so sure. He walked around the periphery of the leech, asking himself what kind of substance would react that way. The answer was easy—no substance. No *known* substance.

The driver in the lead jeep held up his hand, and the long convoy ground to a halt. A hard, efficient-looking officer stepped out of the jeep. From the star on either shoulder, Micheals knew he was a brigadier general.

"You can't block this road," the general said. He was a tall, spare man in suntans, with a sunburned face and cold eyes. "Please clear that thing away."

"We can't move it," Micheals said. He told the general what had happened in the past few days.

"It must be moved," the general said. "This convoy must go through." He walked closer and looked at the leech. "You say it can't be jacked up by a crowbar? A torch won't burn it?"

"That's right," Micheals said, smiling faintly.

"Driver," the general said over his shoulder. "Ride over it."

Micheals started to protest, but stopped himself. The military mind would have to find out in its own way.

The driver put his jeep in gear and shot forward, jumping the leech's four-inch edge. The jeep got to the center of the leech and stopped.

"I didn't tell you to stop!" the general bellowed.

"I didn't, sir!" the driver protested.

The jeep had been yanked to a stop and had stalled. The driver started it again, shifted to four-wheel drive, and tried to ram forward. The jeep was fixed immovably, as though set in concrete.

"Pardon me," Micheals said. "If you look, you can see that the tires are melting down."

The general stared, his hand creeping automatically toward his pistol belt. Then he shouted, "Jump, driver! Don't touch that gray stuff."

White-faced, the driver climbed to the hood of his jeep, looked around him, and jumped clear.

There was complete silence as everyone watched the jeep. First its tires melted down, and then the rims. The body, resting on the gray surface, melted, too.

The aerial was the last to go.

The general began to swear softly under his breath. He turned to the driver. "Go back and have some men bring up hand grenades and dynamite."

The driver ran back to the convoy.

"I don't know what you've got here," the general said. "But it's not going to stop a U.S. Army convoy."

Micheals wasn't so sure.

The leech was nearly awake now, and its body was calling for more and more food. It dissolved the soil under it at a furious rate, filling it in with its own body, flowing outward.

A large object landed on it, and that became food also. Then suddenly—

A burst of energy against its surface, and then another, and another. It consumed them gratefully, converting them into mass. Little metal pellets struck it, and their kinetic energy was absorbed, their mass converted. More explosions took place, helping to fill the starving cells.

It began to sense things—controlled combustion around it, vibrations of wind, mass movements.

There was another, greater explosion, a taste of *real* food! Greedily it ate, growing faster. It waited anxiously for more explosions, while its cells screamed for food.

But no more came. It continued to feed on the soil and on the Sun's energy. Night came, noticeable for its lesser energy possibilities, and then more days and nights. Vibrating objects continued to move around it.

It ate and grew and flowed.

Micheals stood on a little hill, watching the dissolution of his house. The leech was several hundred yards across now, lapping at his front porch.

Good-by, home, Micheals thought, remembering the ten summers he had spent there.

The porch collapsed into the body of the leech. Bit by bit, the house crumpled.

The leech looked like a field of lava now, a blasted spot on the green Earth.

"Pardon me, sir," a soldier said, coming up behind him. "General O'Donnell would like to see you."

"Right," Micheals said, and took his last look at the house.

He followed the soldier through the barbed wire that had been set up in a half-mile circle around the leech. A company of soldiers was on guard around it, keeping back the reporters and the hundreds of curious people who had flocked to the scene. Micheals wondered why he was still allowed inside. Probably, he decided, because most of this was taking place on his land.

The soldier brought him to a tent. Micheals stooped and went in. General O'Donnell, still in suntans, was seated at a small desk. He motioned Micheals to a chair.

"I've been put in charge of getting rid of this leech," he said to Micheals. Micheals nodded, not commenting on the advisability of giving a soldier a scientist's job.

"You're a professor, aren't you?"

"Yes. Anthropology."

"Good. Smoke?" The general lighted Micheals' cigarette. "I'd like you to stay around here in an advisory capacity. You were one of the first to see this leech. I'd appreciate your observations on—" he smiled—"the enemy."

"I'd be glad to," Micheals said. "However, I think this is more in the line of a physicist or a biochemist."

"I don't want this place cluttered with scientists," General O'Donnell said, frowning at the tip of his cigarette. "Don't get me wrong. I have the greatest appreciation for science. I am, if I do say so, a scientific soldier. I'm always interested in the latest weapons. You can't fight any kind of a war any more without science."

O'Donnell's sunburned face grew firm. "But I can't have a team of longhairs poking around this thing for the next month, holding me up. My job is to destroy it, by any means in my power, and at once. I am going to do just that."

"I don't think you'll find it that easy," Micheals said.

"That's what I want you for," O'Donnell said. "Tell me why and I'll figure out a way of doing it."

"Well, as far as I can figure out, the leech is an organic mass-energy converter, and a frighteningly efficient one. I would guess that it has a double cycle. First, it converts mass into energy, then back into mass for its body. Second, energy is converted directly into the body mass. How this takes place, I do not know. The leech is not protoplasmic. It may not even be cellular—"

"So we need something big against it," O'Donnell interrupted. "Well, that's all right. I've got some big stuff here."

"I don't think you understand me," Micheals said. "Perhaps I'm not phrasing this very well. *The leech eats energy.* It can consume the strength of any energy weapon you use against it."

"What happens," O'Donnell asked, "if it keeps on eating?"

"I have no idea what its growth-limits are," Micheals, said. "Its growth may be limited only by its food source."

"You mean it could continue to grow probably forever?"

"It could possibly grow as long as it had something to feed on."

"This is really a challenge," O'Donnell said, "That leech can't be totally impervious to force."

"It seems to be. I suggest you get some physicists in here. Some biologists also. Have them figure out a way of nullifying it."

The general put out his cigarette. "Professor, I cannot wait while scientists wrangle. There is an axiom of mine which I am going to tell you." He paused impressively. "Nothing is impervious to force. Muster enough force and anything will give. *Anything.*"

"Professor," the general continued, in a friendlier tone, "you shouldn't sell short the science you represent. We have, massed under North Hill, the greatest accumulation of energy and radioactive weapons ever assembled in one spot. Do you think your leech can stand the full force of them?"

"I suppose it's possible to overload the thing," Micheals said doubtfully. He realized now why the general wanted him around. He supplied the trappings of science, without the authority to override O'Donnell.

"Come with me," General O'Donnell said cheerfully, getting up and holding back a flap of the tent. "We're going to crack that leech in half."

After a long wait, rich food started to come again, piped into one side of it. First there was only a little, and then more and more. Radiations, vibrations, explosions, solids, liquids—an amazing variety of edibles. It accepted them all. But the food was coming too slowly for the starving cells, for new cells were constantly adding their demands to the rest.

The ever-hungry body screamed for more food, faster!

Now that it had reached a fairly efficient size, it was fully awake. It puzzled over the energy-impressions around it, locating the source of the new food massed in one spot.

Effortlessly it pushed itself into the air, flew a little way and dropped on the food. Its super-efficient cells eagerly gulped the rich radioactive substances. But it did not ignore the lesser potentials of metal and clumps of carbohydrates.

"The damned fools," General O'Donnell said. "Why did they have to panic? You'd think they'd never been trained." He paced the ground outside his tent, now in a new location three miles back.

The leech had grown to two miles in diameter. Three farming communities had been evacuated.

Micheals, standing beside the general, was still stupefied by the memory. The leech had accepted the massed power of the weapons for a while, and then its entire bulk had lifted in the air. The Sun had been blotted out as it flew leisurely over North Hill, and dropped. There should have been time for evacuation, but the frightened soldiers had been blind with fear.

Sixty-seven men were lost in Operation Leech, and General O'Donnell asked permission to use atomic bombs. Washington sent a group of scientists to investigate the situation.

"Haven't those experts decided yet?" O'Donnell asked, halting angrily in front of the tent. "They've been talking long enough."

"It's a hard decision," Micheals said. Since he wasn't an official member of the investigating team, he had given his information and left. "The physicists consider it a biological matter, and the biologists seem to think the chemists should have the answer. No one's an expert on this, because it's never happened before. We just don't have the data."

"It's a military problem," O'Donnell said harshly. "I'm not interested in what the thing is—I want to know what can destroy it. They'd better give me permission to use the bomb."

Micheals had made his own calculations on that. It was impossible to say for sure, but taking a flying guess at the leech's mass-energy absorption rate, figuring in its size and apparent capacity for growth, an atomic bomb *might* overload it—if used soon enough.

He estimated three days as the limit of usefulness. The leech was growing at a geometric rate. It could cover the United States in a few months.

"For a week I've been asking for permission to use the bomb," O'Donnell grumbled. "And I'll get it, but not until after those jackasses end their damned talking." He stopped pacing and turned to Micheals. "I am going to destroy the leech. I am going to smash it, if that's the last thing I do. It's more than a matter of security now. It's personal pride."

That attitude might make great generals, Micheals thought, but it wasn't the way to consider this problem. It was anthropomorphic of O'Donnell to see the leech as an enemy. Even the identification, "leech," was a humanizing factor. O'Donnell was dealing with it as he would any physical obstacle, as though the leech were the simple equivalent of a large army.

But the leech was not human, not even of this planet, perhaps. It should be dealt with in its own terms.

"Here come the bright boys now," O'Donnell said.

From a nearby tent a group of weary men emerged, led by Allenson, a government biologist.

"Well," the general asked, "have you figured out what it is?"

"Just a minute, I'll hack off a sample," Allenson said, glaring through red-rimmed eyes.

"Have you figured out some *scientific* way of killing it?"

"Oh, that wasn't too difficult," Moriarty, an atomic physicist, said wryly. "Wrap it in a perfect vacuum. That'll do the trick. Or blow it off the Earth with antigravity."

"But failing that," Allenson said, "we suggest you use your atomic bombs, and use them fast."

"Is that the opinion of your entire group?" O'Donnell asked, his eyes glittering.

"Yes."

The general hurried away. Micheals joined the scientists.

"He should have called us in at the very first," Allenson complained. "There's no time to consider anything but force now."

"Have you come to any conclusions about the nature of the leech?" Micheals asked.

"Only general ones," Moriarty said, "and they're about the same as yours. The leech is probably extraterrestrial in origin. It seems to have been in a spore-stage until it landed on Earth." He paused to light a pipe. "Incidentally, we should be damned glad it didn't drop in an ocean. We'd have had the Earth eaten out from under us before we knew what we were looking for."

They walked in silence for a few minutes.

"As you mentioned, it's a perfect converter—it can transform mass into energy, and any energy into mass." Moriarty grinned. "Naturally that's impossible and I have figures to prove it."

"I'm going to get a drink," Allenson said. "Anyone coming?"

"Best idea of the week," Micheals said. "I wonder how long it'll take O'Donnell to get permission to use the bomb."

"If I know politics," Moriarty said, "too long."

The findings of the government scientists were checked by other government scientists. That took a few days. Then Washington wanted to know if there wasn't some alternative to exploding an atomic bomb in the middle of New York State. It took a little time to convince them of the necessity. After that, people had to be evacuated, which took more time.

Then orders were made out, and five atomic bombs were checked out of a cache. A patrol rocket was assigned, given orders, and put under General O'Donnell's command. This took a day more.

Finally, the stubby scout rocket was winging its way over New York. From the air, the grayish-black spot was easy to find. Like a festered wound, it stretched between Lake Placid and Elizabethtown, covering Keene and Keene Valley, and lapping at the edges of Jay.

The first bomb was released.

It had been a long wait after the first rich food. The greater radiation of day was followed by the lesser energy of night many times, as the leech ate away the Earth beneath it, absorbed the air around it, and grew. Then one day—

An amazing burst of energy!

Everything was food for the leech, but there was always the possibility of choking. The energy poured over it, drenched it, battered it, and the leech grew frantically, trying to contain the titanic dose. Still small, it quickly reached its overload limit. The strained cells, filled to satiation,

were given more and more food. The strangling body built new cells at
lightning speed. And—

It held. The energy was controlled, stimulating further growth. More
cells took over the load, sucking in the food.

The next doses were wonderfully palatable, easily handled. The leech
overflowed its bounds, growing, eating, and growing.

That was a taste of real food! The leech was as near ecstasy as it had
ever been. It waited hopefully for more, but no more came.

It went back to feeding on the Earth. The energy, used to produce
more cells, was soon dissipated. Soon it was hungry again.

It would always be hungry.

O'Donnell retreated with his demoralized men. They camped ten miles
from the leech's southern edge, in the evacuated town of Schroon Lake.
The leech was over sixty miles in diameter now and still growing fast. It
lay sprawled over the Adirondack Mountains, completely blanketing everything from Saranac Lake to Port Henry, with one edge of it over
Westport, in Lake Champlain.

Everyone within two hundred miles of the leech was evacuated.

General O'Donnell was given permission to use hydrogen bombs,
contingent on the approval of his scientists.

"What have the bright boys decided?" O'Donnell wanted to know.

He and Micheals were in the living room of an evacuated Schroon
Lake house. O'Donnell had made it his new command post.

"Why are they hedging?" O'Donnell demanded impatiently.
"The leech has to be blown up quick. What are they fooling around for?"

"They're afraid of a chain reaction," Micheals told him. "A concentration of hydrogen bombs might set one up in the Earth's crust or in the
atmosphere. It might do any of half a dozen things."

"Perhaps they'd like me to order a bayonet attack," O'Donnell said
contemptuously.

Micheals sighed and sat down in an armchair. He was convinced that
the whole method was wrong. The government scientists were being
rushed into a single line of inquiry. The pressure on them was so great
that they didn't have a chance to consider any other approach but force—
and the leech thrived on that.

Micheals was certain that there were times when fighting fire with fire
was not applicable.

Fire. Loki, god of fire. And of trickery. No, there was no answer there.
But Micheals' mind was in mythology now, retreating from the unbearable present.

Allenson came in, followed by six other men.

"Well," Allenson said, "there's a damned good chance of splitting the Earth wide open if you use the number of bombs our figures show you need."

"You have to take chances in war," O'Donnell replied bluntly. "Shall I go ahead?"

Micheals saw, suddenly, that O'Donnell didn't care if he did crack the Earth. The red-faced general only knew that he was going to set off the greatest explosion ever produced by the hand of Man.

"Not so fast," Allenson said. "I'll let the others speak for themselves. "

The general contained himself with difficulty. "Remember," he said, "according to your own figures, the leech is growing at the rate of twenty feet an hour."

"And speeding up," Allenson added. "But *this* isn't a decision to be made in haste."

Micheals found his mind wandering again, to the lightning bolts of Zeus. That was what they needed. Or the strength of Hercules.

Or—

He sat up suddenly. "Gentlemen, I believe I can offer you a possible alternative, although it's a very dim one."

They stared at him.

"Have you ever heard of Antaeus?" he asked.

The more the leech ate, the faster it grew and the hungrier it became. Although its birth was forgotten, it did remember a long way back. It had eaten a planet in that ancient past. Grown tremendous, ravenous, it had made the journey to a nearby star and eaten that, replenishing the cells converted into energy for the trip. But then there was no more food, and the next star was an enormous distance away.

It set out on the journey, but long before it reached the food, its energy ran out. Mass, converted back to energy to make the trip, was used up. It shrank.

Finally, all the energy was gone. It was a spore, drifting aimlessly, in space.

That was the first time. Or was it? It thought it could remember back to a distant, misty time when the Universe was evenly covered with stars. It had eaten through them, cutting away whole sections, growing, swelling. And the stars had swung off in terror forming galaxies and constellations.

Or was that a dream?

Methodically, it fed on the Earth, wondering where the rich food was. And then it was back again but this time above the leech.

It waited, but the tantalizing food remained out of reach. It was able to sense how rich and pure the food was.

Why didn't it fall?

For a long time the leech waited, but the food stayed out of reach. At last, it lifted and followed.

The food retreated, up, up from the surface of the planet. The leech went after as quickly as its bulk would allow.

The rich food fled out, into space, and the leech followed. Beyond, it could sense an even richer source.

The hot, wonderful food of a sun!

O'Donnell served champagne for the scientists in the control room. Official dinners would follow, but this was the victory celebration.

"A toast," the general said, standing. The men raised their glasses. The only man not drinking was a lieutenant, sitting in front of the control board that guided the drone spaceship.

"To Micheals, for thinking of—what was it again, Micheals?"

"Antaeus." Micheals had been drinking champagne steadily, but he didn't feel elated. Antaeus, born of Ge, the Earth and Poseidon, the Sea. The invincible wrestler. Each time Hercules threw him to the ground, he arose refreshed.

Until Hercules held him in the air.

Moriarty was muttering to himself, figuring with slide rule, pencil, and paper. Allenson was drinking, but he didn't look too happy about it.

"Come on, you birds of evil omen," O'Donnell said, pouring more champagne. "Figure it out later. Right now, drink." He turned to the operator. "How's it going?"

Micheals' analogy had been applied to a spaceship. The ship, operated by remote control, was filled with pure radioactives. It hovered over the leech until, rising to the bait, it had followed. Antaeus had left his mother, the Earth, and was losing his strength in the air. The operator was allowing the spaceship to run fast enough to keep out of the leech's grasp, but close enough to keep it coming.

The spaceship and the leech were on a collision course with the Sun.

"Fine, sir," the operator said. "It's inside the orbit of Mercury now."

"Men," the general said, "I swore to destroy that thing. This isn't exactly the way I wanted to do it. I figured on a more personal way. But the important thing is the destruction. You will all witness it. Destruction is at times a sacred mission. This is such a time. Men, I feel wonderful."

"Turn the spaceship!" It was Moriarty who had spoken, His face was white. "Turn the damned thing!"

He shoved his figures at them.

They were easy to read. The growth-rate of the leech. The energy-consumption rate, estimated. Its speed in space, a constant. The energy it would receive from the Sun as it approached, an exponential curve. Its energy-absorption rate, figured in terms of growth, expressed as a hyped-up discontinuous progression.

The result—

"It'll consume the Sun," Moriarty said, very quietly.

The control room turned into a bedlam. Six of them tried to explain it to O'Donnell at the same time. Then Moriarty tried, and finally Allenson.

"Its rate of growth is so great and its speed so slow—and it will get so much energy—that the leech win be able to consume the Sun by the time it gets there. Or, at least, to live off it until it can consume it."

O'Donnell didn't bother to understand. He turned to the operator.

"Turn it," he said.

They all hovered over the radar screen, waiting.

The food turned out of the leech's path and streaked away. Ahead was a tremendous source, but still a long way off. The leech hesitated.

Its cells, recklessly expending energy, shouted for a decision. The food showed, tantalizingly near.

The closer source or the greater?

The leech's body wanted food *now.*

It started after it, away from the Sun.

The Sun would come next.

"Pull it out at right angles to the plane of the Solar System," Allenson said.

The operator touched the controls. On the radar screen, they saw a blob pursuing a dot. It had turned.

Relief washed over them. It had been close!

"In what portion of the sky would the leech be?" O'Donnell asked, his face expressionless.

"Come outside; I believe I can show you," an astronomer said. They walked to the door. "Somewhere in that section," the astronomer said, pointing.

"Fine. All right, Soldier," O'Donnell told the operator.

"Carry out your orders."

The scientists gasped in unison. The operator manipulated the controls and the blob began to overtake the dot. Micheals started across the room.

"Stop," the general said, and his strong, commanding voice stopped Micheals. "I know what I'm doing. I had that ship especially built."

The blob overtook the dot on the radar screen.

"I told you this was a personal matter," O'Donnell said. "I swore to destroy that leech. We can never have any security while it lives." He smiled. "Shall we look at the sky?"

The general strolled to the door, followed by the scientists.

"Push the button, Soldier!"

The operator did. For a moment, nothing happened. Then the sky lit up!

A bright star hung in space. Its brilliance filled the night, grew, and started to fade.

"What did you do?" Micheals gasped.

"That rocket was built around a hydrogen bomb," O'Donnell said, his strong face triumphant. "I set it off at the contact moment." He called to the operator again. "Is there anything showing on the radar?"

"Not a speck, sir."

"Men," the general said, "I have met the enemy and he is mine. Let's have some more champagne."

But Micheals found that he was suddenly ill.

It had been shrinking from the expenditure of energy, when the great explosion came. No thought of containing it. The leech's cells held for the barest fraction of a second, and then spontaneously overloaded.

The leech was smashed, broken up, destroyed. It was split into a thousand particles, and the particles were split a million times more.

The particles were thrown out on the wave front of the explosion, and they split further, spontaneously.

Into spores.

The spores closed into dry, hard, seemingly lifeless specks of dust, billions of them, scattered, drifting. Unconscious, they floated in the emptiness of space.

Billions of them, waiting to be fed.

THE DEMONS

Walking along Second Avenue, Arthur Gammet decided it was a rather nice spring day. Not too cold, just brisk and invigorating. A perfect day for selling insurance, he told himself. He stepped off the curb at Ninth Street. And vanished.

"Didja see that?" A butcher's assistant asked the butcher. They had been standing in front of their store, idly watching people go by.

"See what?" the butcher, a corpulent, red-faced man, replied.

"The guy in the overcoat. He disappeared."

"Yeh," the butcher said. "So he turned up Ninth, so what?"

The butcher's assistant hadn't seen Arthur turn up Ninth, down Ninth, or across Second. He had seen him disappear. But should he insist on it? You tell your boss he's wrong, so where does it get you? Besides, the guy in the overcoat probably *had* turned up Ninth. Where else could he have gone?

But Arthur Gammet was no longer in New York. He had thoroughly vanished.

Somewhere else, not necessarily on Earth, a being who called himself Neelsebub was staring at a pentagon. Within it was something he hadn't bargained for. Neelsebub fixed it with a bitter stare, knowing he had good cause for anger. He'd spent years digging out magic formulas, experimenting with herbs and essences, reading the best books on wizardry and witchcraft. He'd thrown everything into one gigantic effort, and what happened? The wrong demon appeared.

Of course, there were many things that might have gone amiss. The severed hand of the corpse—it just *might* have been the hand of a suicide, for even the best of dealers aren't to be trusted. Or the line of the pentagon might have been the least bit wavy; that was very significant. Or the words of the incantation might not have been in the proper order. Even one syllable wrongly intoned could have done it.

Anyhow, the damage was done. Neelsebub leaned one red-scaled shoulder against the huge bottle in back of him, scratching the other shoulder

31

with a dagger-like fingernail. As usual when perplexed, his barbed tail flicked uncertainly.

At least he had a demon of some sort.

But the thing inside the pentagon didn't look like any conventional kind of demon. Those loose folds of gray flesh, for example…But then, the historical accounts were notoriously inaccurate. Whatever kind of supernatural being it was, it would have to come across. Of that he was certain. Neelsebub folded his hooved feet under him more comfortably, waiting for the strange being to speak.

Arthur Gammet was still too stunned to speak. One moment he had been walking to the insurance office, minding his own business, enjoying the fine air of an early spring morning. He had stepped off the curb at Second and Ninth—and landed here. Wherever *here* was.

Swaying slightly, he made out, through the deep mist that filled the room, a huge red-scaled monster squatting on its haunches. Beside it was what looked like a bottle, but a bottle fully ten feet high. The creature had a barbed tail and was now scratching his head with it, glaring at Arthur out of little piggish eyes. Hastily, Arthur tried to step back, but was unable to move more than a step. He was inside a chalked area, he noticed, and for some reason was unable to step over the white lines.

"So," the red creature said, finally breaking the silence. "I've finally got you." These weren't the words he was saying; the sounds were utterly foreign. But somehow, Arthur was able to understand the thought behind the words. It wasn't telepathy, but rather as though he were translating a foreign language, automatically, colloquially.

"I must say I'm rather disappointed," Neelsebub continued when the captured demon in the pentagon didn't answer. "All our legends say that demons are fearful things, fifteen feet high, with wings and tiny heads and a hole in the chest that throws out jets of cold water."

Arthur Gammet peeled off his overcoat, letting it fall in a sodden heap at his feet. Dimly, he could appreciate the idea of demons being able to produce jets of cold water. The room was like a furnace. Already his gray tweed suit was a soggy, wrinkled mass of cloth and perspiration.

And with that thought came acceptance—of the red creature, the chalk lines he was unable to cross, the sweltering room—everything.

He had noticed in books, magazine and motion-pictures that a man, confronted by an odd situation, usually mouthed lines such as, "Pinch me, this can't be true," or, "Good God, I'm either dreaming, drunk, or crazy." Arthur had no intention of saying anything so palpably absurd. For one thing, he was sure the huge red creature wouldn't appreciate it; and for another, he knew he wasn't dreaming, drunk, or crazy. There were no words in Arthur Gammet's vocabulary for it, but he knew. A dream was one thing; this was another.

"The legends never mentioned being able to peel off your skin," Neelsebub said thoughtfully, looking at the overcoat at Arthur's feet. "Interesting."

"This is a mistake," Arthur said firmly. The experience he had had as an insurance agent stood him in good stead now. He was used to meeting all kinds of people, unraveling all kinds of snarled situations. This creature had, evidently, tried to raise a demon. Through nobody's fault he had gotten Arthur Gammet, and was under the impression that *he* was a demon. The error must be rectified at once.

"I am an insurance agent," he said. The creature shook its tremendous horned head. Its tail swished from side to side unpleasantly.

"Your other-world functions don't concern me in the slightest," Neelsebub growled. "I don't care, really, what species of demon you are."

"But I tell you I'm not a—"

"It won't work!" Neelsebub howled, glaring angrily at Arthur from the edge of the pentagon. "I know you're a demon. And I want *drast!*"

"Drast? I don't think—"

"I'm up to all your demoniac tricks," Neelsebub said, calming himself with obvious effort. "I know—and you know—that when a demon is conjured, he must grant one wish. I conjured you, and I want drast. Ten thousand pounds of it."

"Drast..." Arthur began uncomfortably, standing in the corner of the pentagon furthest from the tail-lashing monster.

"Drast, or voot, or hakatinny, or sup-der-oop. It's all the same thing."

It was speaking of money, Arthur Gammet realized. The slang terms had been unfamiliar, but there was no mistaking the sense behind them. Undoubtedly, drast was what passed for currency in its country.

"Ten thousand pounds isn't much," Neelsebub said with a cunning little smile. "Not for *you*. You ought to be glad I'm not one of those fools who ask for immortality."

Arthur was.

"And if I don't?" he asked.

"In that case," Neelsebub replied, a frown replacing the little smile, "I'll be forced to conjure you again—inside the bottle." Arthur looked at the green bottle, towering over Neelsebub's head. It was wide at its misty base, tapering to a slim neck. If the thing ever got him in, he would never be able to squeeze out through that neck. *If* the thing could get him in. And Arthur was fairly sure it could.

"Of course," Neelsebub said, his smile returning, more cunning than ever, "There's no reason for heroic measures. Ten thousand pounds of the old sup-der-oop isn't much for you. It'll make me rich, but all you have to do is wave your hand." He paused, his smile becoming ingratiating.

"You know," he went on softly, "I've really spent a long time on this. Read a lot of books, spent a pile of voot." His tail lashed the floor suddenly, like a bullet glancing off granite. "Don't try to put something over on me!" he shouted.

Arthur found that the force rising from the chalk extended as high as he could reach. Gingerly, he leaned against the invisible wall, and, finding that it supported his weight, rested against it.

Ten thousand pounds of drast, he thought. Evidently the creature was a sorcerer, from God-knows-where. Some other planet, perhaps. The creature had tried to conjure a wish-granting demon, and had gotten him. It wanted something from him—or else the bottle. All very unreasonable, but Arthur Gammet was beginning to suspect that most wizards were unreasonable people.

"I'll try to get your drast," Arthur said, feeling that he had to say something. "But I'll have to go back to the—ah—underworld to get it. That handwaving stuff is out."

"All right," the monster said to him, standing at the edge of the pentagon and leering in. "I trust you. But remember, I can call you any time I want. You can't get away, you know, so don't even try. By the way, my name is Neelsebub."

"Any relation to Beelzebub?" Arthur asked.

"Great-grandfather," Neelsebub replied, looking suspiciously at Arthur. "He was an army man. Unfortunately, he—" Neelsebub stopped abruptly, glaring angrily at Arthur. "But you demons know all about that! Begone! *And bring that drast!*"

Arthur Gammet vanished again.

He materialized on the corner of Second Avenue and Ninth Street, where he had first vanished. His overcoat was at his feet, his clothes filled with perspiration. He staggered for a moment to hold his balance—since he had been leaning against the wall of force when Neelsebub had vanished him—picked up his overcoat and hurried to his apartment. Luckily, there had been only a few people around. Two housewives gulped and walked quickly away. A nattily dressed man blinked four or five times, took a step forward as though he wanted to ask something, changed his mind and hurried off toward Eighth Street. The rest of the people either hadn't seen him or just didn't give a damn.

In his two-room apartment Arthur made one feeble attempt to dismiss the whole thing as a dream. Failing miserably, he began to outline his possibilities.

He could produce the drast. That is, perhaps he could if he found out what it was. The stuff Neelsebub considered valuable might be just about anything. Lead, perhaps, or iron. Even that would stretch his meagre earnings to the breaking-point.

He could notify the police. And be locked up in an asylum. Forget that one.

Or, he could not produce the drast—and spend the rest of his life in a bottle. Forget that one, too.

All he could do was wait until Neelsebub conjured him again, and find out then what drast was. Perhaps it was common dirt. He could get that from his uncle's farm in New Jersey, if Neelsebub could manage the transportation.

Arthur Gammet telephoned the office and told them he was ill, and that he expected to be ill for several days. After that he fixed a bite of food in his kitchenette, feeling quite proud of his good appetite. Not everyone faced with the strong possibility of being shut up in a bottle could have tucked away a meal that well. He tidied up the place, and changed into a light Palm Beach suit. It was four-thirty in the afternoon. He stretched out on the bed and waited. Along about nine-thirty he disappeared.

"Changed your skin again," Neelsebub commented. "Where's the drast?" His tail twitched eagerly as he hurried around the pentagon.

"It's not hidden behind me," Arthur said, turning to look at Neelsebub. "I'll have to have more information." He adopted a nonchalant pose, leaning against the invisible lines that radiated from the chalk. "And I'll have to have your promise that once I produce it you'll leave me alone."

"Of course," Neelsebub answered cheerfully. "I can only ask for one wish anyhow. Tell you what, I'll swear the great oath of Satanas. That's absolutely binding, you know."

"Satanas?"

"One of our early presidents," Neelsebub said with a reverential air. "My great grandfather Beelzebub served under him. Unfortunately—oh, well, you know all that."

Neelsebub swore the great oath of Satanas, and very impressive it was. The blue mists in the room were edged in red when he was done, and the outlines of the huge bottle shifted eerily in the dim light. Arthur was perspiring freely, even in his summer suit. He wished he were a cold-producing demon.

"That's it," Neelsebub said, standing erectly in the middle of the room, his tail looped around his wrist. There was a strange look in his eyes, a look of one recalling past glories.

"Now what sort of information do you want?" Neelsebub began pacing the floor in front of the pentagon, his tail dragging.

"Describe this drast to me."

"Well, it's soft, heavy—"

That could be lead.

"And yellow."

Gold.

"Hmm," Arthur said, staring at the bottle. "I don't suppose it's ever gray, is it? Or dark brown?"

"No. It's always yellow. With sometimes a reddish hue."

Still gold. Arthur contemplated the red-scaled monster in front of him, pacing up and down with ill-concealed eagerness. Ten thousand pounds of gold. That would come to…No, better not think of it. Impossible.

"I'll need a little time," Arthur said. "Perhaps sixty or seventy years. Tell you what, I'll call you as soon as—"

Neelsebub interrupted him with a huge roar of laughter. Arthur had tickled his rudimentary sense of humor, evidently, because Neelsebub was hugging his haunches, screaming with mirth.

"Sixty or seventy years!" Neelsebub shouted, and the bottle shook, and even the lines of the pentagon seemed to waver. "I'll give you sixty or seventy minutes! Or the bottle!"

"Now just a minute," Arthur said, from the far side of the pentagon. "I'll need a little—hold it!" He had just had an idea, and it was undeniably the best idea he had ever had. More, it was his own idea.

"I'll have to have the exact formula you used to get me," Arthur said. "Must check with the main office to be sure everything is in order."

The monster raved and swore, and the air turned black and purple; the bottle rang in sympathetic vibration with Neelsebub's voice, and the very room seemed to sway. But Arthur Gammet stood firm. He explained to Neelsebub, patiently, seven or eight times, that it would do no good to bottle him, since he would never get his gold that way. All he wanted was the formula, and certainly that wouldn't—

Finally he got it.

"And no tricks!" Neelsebub thundered finally, gesturing at the bottle with both hands and his tail. Arthur nodded feebly and reappeared in his room.

The next few days he spent in a frenzied search around New York. Some of the ingredients of the incantation were easy to fill—the sprig of mistletoe, for example, from a florist, and the sulphur. Graveyard mold was more difficult, as was a bat's left wing. What really had him stumped for a while was the severed hand of the murdered man. He finally procured one from a store that specialized in filling orders for medical students. He had the dealer's guarantee that the body to which the hand belonged had died a violent death. Arthur suspected that the dealer was trying to humor him, but there was really very little he could do about it.

Among other things, he bought a large bottle. It was surprisingly inexpensive. There were really compensations for living in New York, he decided. There seemed to be nothing—literally *nothing* one couldn't buy.

In three days he had all his materials, and at midnight of the third night he arranged them on the floor of his apartment. The light of a three-quarters full moon was shining in the window—the incantation had been vague as to what phase it should be—and everything seemed to be in order. Arthur drew the pentagon, lighted the candles, burned the incense, and started the chant. He figured that, by following directions carefully, he should be able to conjure Neelsebub. His one wish would be that Neelsebub leave him strictly alone. He couldn't see how that would fail.

The blue mists spread through the room as he mumbled the formula, and soon he could see something growing in the center of the pentagon.

"Neelsebub!" he cried. But it wasn't.

The thing in the pentagon was about fifteen feet high when the incantation was finished. It had to stoop almost to the ground to fit under Arthur's ceiling. It was a fearful-looking thing, with wings and a tiny head and a hole in its chest.

Arthur Gammet had conjured the wrong demon.

"What's all this?" the demon asked, shooting a jet of ice water out of his chest. The water splashed against the invisible walls of the pentagon and rolled to the floor. It must have been pure reflex, because Arthur's room was pleasantly cool.

"I want my one wish," Arthur said. The demon was blue and impossibly thin; his wings were vestigial stumps. They flapped once or twice against his bony chest before he answered.

"I don't know what you are or how you got me here," the demon said. "But it's clever. It's undeniably clever."

"Let's not chatter," Arthur replied nervously, wondering how soon Neelsebub was going to conjure him again. "I want ten thousand pounds of gold. Also known as drast, hakatinny, and the old sup-der-oop." At any moment, he thought, he might find himself inside a bottle.

"Well," the cold-producing demon said. "You seem to be laboring under the mistaken impression that I'm—"

"You have twenty-four hours,"

"I'm not a rich man," the cold-producing demon said. "Small businessman. But perhaps if you give me time—"

"Or the bottle," Arthur said. He pointed to the large bottle in one corner, then realized it would never hold fifteen feet of cold-producing demon.

"The next time I conjure you I'll have a bottle big enough," Arthur said. "I didn't think you'd be so tall."

"We have stories about people disappearing," the demon mused. "So *this* is what happens to them. The underworld. Don't suppose anyone would believe me, though."

"Get that drast," Arthur said. "Begone!"

The cold-producing demon was gone.

Arthur Gammet knew he could not afford more than twenty-four hours. Even that was probably cutting it too thin, he thought, because one could never tell when Neelsebub would decide he had had enough time. There was no telling what the red-scaled monster would do, if he were disappointed a third time. Arthur found that, toward the end of the day, he was clutching the steam pipe. A lot of good that would do if he were conjured! But it was nice to have something solid to grasp.

It was a shame also, he thought, to have to impose on the cold-producing demon that way. It was pretty obvious that the demon wasn't a real demon, any more than Arthur was. Well, he would never use the bottle on him. It would do no good if Neelsebub weren't satisfied.

Finally he mumbled the incantation again.

"You'll have to make your pentagon wider," the coldproducing demon said, stooping uncomfortably inside. "I haven't got room for—"

"Begone!" Arthur said, and feverishly rubbed out the pentagon. He sketched it again, this time using the area of the whole room. He lugged the bottle—the same one, since he hadn't found one fifteen feet high—into the kitchen, stationed himself in the closet, and went through the formula again. Once more the thick, twisting blue mists gathered.

"Now don't be hasty," the cold-producing demon said, from within the pentagon. "I haven't got the old sup-der-oop yet. There's a tie-up, and I can explain everything." He beat his wings to part the mist. Beside him was a bottle, fully ten feet high. Within it, green with rage, was Neelsebub. He seemed to be shouting, but the bottle was stoppered. No sound came through.

"Got the formula out of the library," the demon said, "Could have knocked me over when the thing worked. Always been a hard-headed businessman, you know. Don't like this supernatural stuff. But, you have to face facts. Anyhow, I got hold of this demon here—" He jerked a spidery arm at the bottle— "But he wouldn't come across. So I bottled him." The cold-producing demon heaved a deep sigh when Arthur smiled. It was like a reprieve.

"Now, I don't want you to bottle me," the cold-producing demon went on, "because I've got a wife and three kids. You know how it is.

Insurance slump and all that, I couldn't raise ten thousand pounds of drast with an army. But as soon as I persuade this demon here—"

"Never mind about the drast," Arthur said. "Just take the demon with you. Keep him in storage. Inside the bottle, of course."

"I'll do that," the blue-winged insurance man said. "And about that drast—"

"Forget it," Arthur said warmly. After all, insurance men have to stick together. "Handle fire and theft?"

"General accident is more my line," the insurance man said. "But you know, I've been thinking—"

Neelsebub raved and swore inside the bottle while the two insurance men discussed the intricacies of their profession.

FOOL'S MATE

The players met on the great, timeless board of space. The glittering dots that were the pieces swam in their separate patterns. In that configuration at the beginning, even before the first move was made, the outcome of the game was determined.

Both players saw, and knew which had won. But they played on.

Because the game had to be played out.

"Nielson!"

Lieutenant Nielson sat in front of his gunfire board with an idyllic smile on his face. He didn't look up.

"Nielson!"

The lieutenant was looking at his fingers with the stare of a puzzled child.

"Nielson! Snap out of it!" General Branch loomed sternly over him. "Do you hear me, Lieutenant?"

Nielson shook his head dully. He started to look at his fingers again, then his gaze was caught by the glittering array of buttons on the gunfire panel.

"Pretty," he said.

General Branch stepped inside the cubicle, grabbed Nielson by the shoulders, and shook him.

"Pretty things," Nielson said, gesturing at the panel. He smiled at Branch.

Margraves, second-in-command, stuck his head in the doorway. He still had sergeant's stripes on his sleeve, having been promoted to colonel only three days ago.

"Ed," he said, "the President's representative is here. Sneak visit."

"Wait a minute," Branch said, "I want to complete this inspection." He grinned sourly. It was one hell of an inspection when you went around finding how many sane men you had left.

"Do you hear me, Lieutenant?"

"Ten thousand ships," Nielson said. "Ten thousand ships—all gone!"

41

"I'm sorry," Branch said. He leaned forward and slapped Nielson smartly across the face.

The lieutenant started to cry.

"Hey, Ed—what about that representative?"

At close range, Colonel Margraves's breath was a solid essence of whiskey, but Branch didn't reprimand him. If you had a good officer left, you didn't reprimand him, no matter what he did. Also, Branch approved of whiskey. It was a good release, under the circumstances. Probably better than his own, he thought, glancing at his scarred knuckles.

"I'll be right with you. Nielson, can you understand me?"

"Yes, sir," the lieutenant said in a shaky voice. "I'm all right now, sir."

"Good," Branch said. "Can you stay on duty?"

"For a while," Nielson said. "But, sir—I'm not well, I can feel it."

"I know," Branch said. "You deserve a rest. But you're the only gunnery officer I've got left on this side of the ship. The rest are in the wards."

"I'll try, sir," Nielson said, looking at the gunfire panel again. "But I hear voices sometimes. I can't promise anything, sir."

"Ed," Margraves began again, "that representative—"

"Coming. Good boy, Nielson." The lieutenant didn't look up as Branch and Margraves left.

"I escorted him to the bridge," Margraves said, listing slightly to starboard as he walked. "Offered him a drink, but he didn't want one."

"All right," Branch said.

"He was bursting with questions," Margraves continued, chuckling to himself. "One of those earnest, tanned State Department men, out to win the war in five minutes flat. Very friendly boy. Wanted to know why I, personally, thought the fleet had been maneuvering in space for a year with no action."

"What did you tell him?"

"Said we were waiting for a consignment of zap guns," Margraves said. "I think he almost believed me. Then he started talking about logistics."

"Hmmm," Branch said. There was no telling what Margraves, half-drunk, had told the representative. Not that it mattered. An official inquiry into the prosecution of the war had been due for a long time.

"I'm going to leave you here," Margraves said. "I've got some unfinished business to attend to."

"Right," Branch said, since it was all he could say. He knew that Margraves's unfinished business concerned a bottle.

He walked alone to the bridge.

The President's representative was looking at the huge location screen. It covered one entire wall, glowing with a slowly shifting pattern of dots.

The thousands of green dots on the left represented the Earth fleet, separated by a black void from the orange of the enemy. As he watched, the fluid, three-dimensional front slowly changed. The armies of dots clustered, shifted, retreated, advanced, moving with hypnotic slowness.

But the black void remained between them. General Branch had been watching that sight for almost a year. As far as he was concerned, the screen was a luxury. He couldn't determine from it what was really happening. Only the CPC computers could, and they didn't need it.

"How do you do, General Branch?" the President's representative said, coming forward and offering his hand. "My name's Richard Ellsner."

Branch shook hands, noticing that Margraves's description had been pretty good. The representative was no more than thirty. His tan looked strange, after a year of pallid faces.

"My credentials," Ellsner said, handing Branch a sheaf of papers. The general skimmed through them, noting Ellsner's authorization as Presidential Voice in Space. A high honor for so young a man.

"How are things on Earth?" Branch asked, just to say something. He ushered Ellsner to a chair, and sat down himself.

"Tight," Ellsner said. "We've been stripping the planet bare of radioactives to keep your fleet operating. To say nothing of the tremendous cost of shipping food, oxygen, spare parts, and all the other equipment you need to keep a fleet this size in the field."

"I know," Branch murmured, his broad face expressionless.

"I'd like to start right in with the President's complaints," Ellsner said. "Just to get them off my chest."

"Go right ahead," Branch said.

"Now, then," Ellsner began, consulting a pocket notebook, "you've had the fleet in space for eleven months and seven days. Is that right?"

"Yes."

"During that time there have been light engagements, but no actual hostilities. You—and the enemy commander—have been content, evidently, to sniff each other like discontented dogs."

"I wouldn't use that analogy," Branch said, conceiving an instant dislike for the young man. "But go on."

"I apologize. It was an unfortunate, though inevitable, comparison. Anyhow, there has been no battle, even though you have a numerical superiority. Is that correct?"

"Yes."

"And you know the maintenance of this fleet strains the resources of Earth. The President would like to know why battle has not been joined."

"I'd like to hear the rest of the complaints first," Branch said. He tightened his battered fists, but, with remarkable self-control, kept them at his sides.

"Very well. The morale factor. We keep getting reports from you on the incidence of combat fatigue—crackup, in plain language. The figures are absurd! Thirty percent of your men seem to be under restraint. That's way out of line, even for a tense situation."

Branch didn't answer.

"To cut this short," Ellsner said, "I would like the answers to those questions. Then I would like your assistance in negotiating a truce. This war was ill-advised to begin with. It was none of the Earth's choosing. It seems to the President that, in view of the static situation, the enemy commander will be amenable to the idea."

Colonel Margraves staggered in, his face flushed. He had completed his unfinished business, adding another fourth to his half-drunk.

"What's this I hear about a truce?" he shouted.

Ellsner stared at him for a moment, then turned back to Branch.

"I suppose you will take care of this yourself. If you will contact the enemy commander, I will try to come to terms with him."

"They aren't interested," Branch said.

"How do you know?"

"I've been trying to negotiate a truce for six months. They want complete capitulation."

"But that's absurd," Ellsner said, shaking his head. "They have no bargaining point. The fleets are approximately the same size. There have been no major engagements. How can they—"

"Easily," Margraves roared, walking up to the representative and peering truculently in his face.

"General. This man is drunk," Ellsner got to his feet.

"Of course, you idiot! Don't you understand yet? *The war is lost!* Completely, irrevocably."

Ellsner turned angrily to Branch. The general sighed and stood up.

"That's right, Ellsner. The war is lost and every man in the fleet knows it. That's what's wrong with the morale. We're just hanging here, waiting to be blasted out of existence."

The fleets shifted and weaved. Thousands of dots floated in space, in twisted, random patterns.

Seemingly random.

The patterns interlocked, opened, and closed. Dynamically, delicately balanced, each configuration was a planned move on a hundred-thousand-mile front. The opposing dots shifted to meet the exigencies of the new pattern.

Where was the advantage? To the unskilled eye, a chess game is a meaningless array of pieces and positions. But to the players the game may already be won or lost.

The mechanical players who moved the thousands of dots knew who had won—and who had lost.

"Now let's all relax," Branch said soothingly. "Margraves, mix us a couple of drinks. I'll explain everything." The colonel moved to a well-stocked cabinet in a corner of the room.

"I'm waiting," Ellsner said.

"First, a review. Do you remember when the war was declared, two years ago? Both sides subscribed to the Holmstead Pact not to bomb home planets. A rendezvous was arranged in space, for the fleets to meet."

"That's ancient history," Ellsner said.

"It has a point. Earth's fleet blasted off, grouped, and went to the rendezvous." Branch cleared his throat.

"Do you know the CPCs? The Configuration-Probability Computers? They're like chess players, enormously extended. They arrange the fleet in an optimum attack-defense pattern, based on the configuration of the opposing fleet. So the first pattern was set."

"I don't see the need—" Ellsner started, but Margraves, returning with the drinks, interrupted him.

"Wait, my boy. Soon there will be a blinding light."

"When the fleets met, the CPCs calculated our probabilities of successful attack. They found we'd lose approximately eighty-seven percent of our fleet to sixty-five percent of the enemy's. If they attacked, they'd lose seventy-nine percent to our sixty-four. That was the situation as it stood then. By extrapolation, their *optimum* attack pattern—at that time—would net them a forty-five percent loss. Ours would have given us a seventy-two percent loss."

"I don't know much about the CPCs," Ellsner confessed. "My field's psych." He sipped his drink, grimaced, and sipped again.

"Think of them as chess players," Branch said. "They can estimate the loss probabilities for an attack at any given point of time, in any pattern. They can extrapolate the probable moves of both sides."

"That's why battle wasn't joined when we first met. No commander is going to annihilate his entire fleet like that."

"Well, then," Ellsner said, "why haven't you exploited your slight numerical superiority? Why haven't you gotten an advantage over them?"

"Ah!" Margraves cried, sipping his drink. "It comes, the light!"

"Let me put it in the form of an analogy," Branch said. "If you have two chess players of equally high skill, the game's end is determined when one of them gains an advantage. Once the advantage is there, there's nothing the other player can do, unless the first makes a mistake. If everything goes as it should, the game's end is predetermined. The turning point may come a few moves after the game starts, although the game itself could drag on for hours."

"And remember," Margraves broke in, "to the casual eye, there may be no apparent advantage. Not a piece may have been lost."

"That's what's happened here," Branch finished sadly. "The CPC units in both fleets are of maximum efficiency. But the enemy has an edge that they are carefully exploiting. And there's nothing we can do about it."

"But how did this happen?" Ellsner asked. "Who slipped up?"

"The CPCs have deduced the cause of the failure," Branch said. "The end of the war was inherent *in our takeoff formation.*"

"What do you mean?" Ellsner said, setting down his drink.

"Just that. The configuration the fleet was in, light-years away from battle, before we had even contacted their fleet. When the two met, they had an infinitesimal advantage of position. That was enough. Enough for the CPCs, anyhow."

"If it's any consolation," Margraves put in, "it was a fifty-fifty chance. It could just as well have been us with the edge."

"I'll have to find out more about this," Ellsner said. "I don't understand it all yet."

Branch snarled, "The war's lost. What more do you want to know?"

Ellsner shook his head.

"'Wilt snare me with predestination 'round,'" Margraves quoted, "'and then impute my fall to sin?'"

Lieutenant Nielson sat in front of the gunfire panel, his fingers interlocked. This was necessary, because Nielson had an almost overpowering desire to push the buttons.

The pretty buttons.

Then he swore, and sat on his hands. He had promised General Branch that he would carry on, and that was important. It was three days since he had seen the general, but he was determined to carry on. Resolutely he fixed his gaze on the gunfire dials.

Delicate indicators wavered and trembled. Dials measured distance and adjusted aperture to range. The slender indicators rose and fell as the ship maneuvered, lifting toward the red line, but never quite reaching it.

The red line marked emergency. That was when he would start firing, when the little black arrow crossed the little red line.

He had been waiting almost a year now for that little arrow. Little arrow. Little narrow. Little arrow. Little narrow.

Stop it.

That was when he would start firing.

Lieutenant Nielson lifted his hands into view and inspected his nails. Fastidiously he cleaned a bit of dirt out of one. He interlocked his fingers again and looked at the pretty buttons, the black arrow, the red line.

He smiled to himself. He had promised the general. Only three days ago.

So he pretended not to hear what the buttons were whispering to him.

"The thing I don't see," Ellsner said, "is why you can't do something about the pattern? Retreat and regroup, for example."

"I'll explain that," Margraves said. "It'll give Ed a chance for a drink. Come over here," He led Ellsner to an instrument panel. They had been showing Ellsner around the ship for three days, more to relieve their own tensions than for any other reason. The last day had turned into a fairly prolonged drinking bout.

"Do you see this dial?" Margraves pointed to one. The instrument panel covered an area four feet wide by twenty feet long. The buttons and switches on it controlled the movements of the entire fleet.

"Notice the shaded area. That marks the safety limit. If we use a forbidden configuration, the indicator goes over and all hell breaks loose."

"And what is a forbidden configuration?"

"The forbidden configurations are those that would give the enemy an attack advantage. Or, to put it another way, moves that change the attack-probability-loss picture sufficiently to warrant an enemy attack."

"So you can move only within strict limits?" Ellsner asked, looking at the dial.

"That's right. Out of the infinite number of possible formations, we can use only a few, if we want to play safe. It's like chess. Say you'd like to put a sixth-row pawn in your opponent's back row. But it would take two moves to do it. And after you move to the seventh row, your opponent has a clear avenue leading to checkmate.

"Of course, if the enemy advances too boldly, the odds are changed again, and *we* attack."

"That's our only hope," General Branch said. "We're praying they do something wrong. The fleet is in readiness for instant attack if our CPC shows that the enemy has overextended himself anywhere,"

"And that's the reason for the crackups," Ellsner said. "Every man in the fleet is on nerves' edge, waiting for a chance he's sure will never come. But having to wait anyhow. How long will this go on?"

"This moving and checking can go on for a little more than two years," Branch said. "Then they will be in the optimum formation for attack, with a twenty-eight percent loss probability to our ninety-three. They'll have to attack then, or the probabilities will start to shift back in our favor,"

"You poor devils," Ellsner said softly. "Waiting for a chance that's never going to come. Knowing you're going to be blasted out of space sooner or later."

"Oh, it's jolly," said Margraves, with an instinctive dislike for a civilian's sympathy.

Something buzzed on the switchboard, and Branch walked over and plugged in a line. "Hello? Yes. Yes...all right, Williams. Right." He unplugged the line.

"Colonel Williams has had to lock his men in their rooms," Branch said. "That's the third time this month. I'll have to get CPC to dope out a formation so we can take him out of the front." He walked to a side panel and started pushing buttons.

"And there it is," Margraves said. "What do you plan to do, Mr. Presidential Representative?"

The glittering dots shifted and deployed, advanced and retreated, always keeping a barrier of black space between them. The mechanical chess players watched each move, calculating its effect into the far future. Back and forth across the great chessboard the pieces moved.

The chess players worked dispassionately, knowing beforehand the outcome of the game. In their strictly ordered universe there was no possible fluctuation, no stupidity, no failure.

They moved. And knew. And moved.

"Oh, yes," Lieutenant Nielson said to the smiling room. "Oh, yes." And look at all the buttons, he thought, laughing to himself.

So stupid. Georgia.

Nielson accepted the deep blue of sanctity, draping it across his shoulders. Birdsong, somewhere.

Of course.

Three buttons red. He pushed them. Three buttons green. He pushed them. Four dials. Riverread.

"Oh-oh. Nielson's cracked."

"Three is for me," Nielson said, and touched his forehead with greatest stealth. Then he reached for the keyboard again. Unimaginable associations raced through his mind, produced by unaccountable stimuli.

"Better grab him. Watch out!"

Gentle hands surround me as I push two are brown for which is for mother, and one is high for all rest.

"Stop him from shooting off those guns!"

I am lifted into the air. I fly, I fly.

"Is there any hope for that man?" Ellsner asked, after they had locked Nielson in a ward.

"Who knows?" Branch said. His broad face tightened; knots of muscle pushed out his cheeks. Suddenly he turned, shouted, and swung his fist wildly at the metal wall. After it hit, he grunted and grinned sheepishly.

"Silly, isn't it? Margraves drinks. I let off steam by hitting walls. Let's go eat."

The officers ate separately from the crew. Branch had found that some officers tended to get murdered by psychotic crewmen. It was best to keep them apart.

During the meal, Branch suddenly turned to Ellsner.

"Boy, I haven't told you the entire truth. I said this would go on for two years? Well, the men won't last that long. I don't know if I can hold this fleet together for two more weeks."

"What would you suggest?"

"I don't know," Branch said. He still refused to consider surrender, although he knew it was the only realistic answer.

"I'm not sure," Ellsner said, "but I think there may be a way out of your dilemma." The officers stopped eating and looked at him.

"Have you got some superweapon for us?" Margraves asked. "A disintegrator strapped to your chest?"

"I'm afraid not. But I think you've been so close to the situation that you don't see it in its true light. A case of the forest for the trees."

"Go on," Branch said, munching methodically on a piece of bread.

"Consider the universe as the CPC sees it. A world of strict causality. A logical, coherent universe. In this world, every effect has a cause. Every factor can be instantly accounted for.

"That's not a picture of the real world. There *is no* explanation for everything, really. The CPC is built to see a specialized universe, and to extrapolate on the basis of that."

"So," Margraves said, "what would you do?"

"Throw the world out of joint," Ellsner said. "Bring in uncertainty. Add a human factor that the machines can't compute."

"How can you introduce uncertainty in a chess game?" Branch asked, interested in spite of himself.

"By sneezing at a crucial moment, perhaps. How could a machine compute that?"

"It wouldn't have to. It would just classify it as extraneous noise and ignore it."

"True." Ellsner thought for a moment. "This battle—how long will it take, once the actual hostilities are begun?"

"About six minutes," Branch told him. "Plus or minus twenty seconds."

"That confirms an idea of mine," Ellsner said. "The chess-game analogy is faulty. There's no real comparison."

"It's a convenient way of thinking of it," Margraves said.

"But it's an *untrue* way of thinking of it. Checkmating a king can't be equated with destroying a fleet. Nor is the rest of the situation like chess.

In chess you play by rules previously agreed upon by the players. In this game you can make up your own rules."

"This game has inherent rules of its own," Branch said.

"No," Ellsner said. "Only the CPCs have rules. How about this? Suppose you dispensed with the CPCs? Gave every commander his head, told him to attack on his own, with no pattern. What would happen?"

"It wouldn't work," Margraves told him. "The CPC can still total the picture, on the basis of planning ability of the average human. More than that, they can handle the attack of a few thousand second-rate calculators—humans—with ease. It would be like shooting clay pigeons."

"But you've *got* to try something," Ellsner pleaded.

"Now wait a minute," Branch said. "You can spout theory all you want. I know what the CPCs tell me, and I believe them. I'm still in command of this fleet, and I'm not going to risk the lives in my command on some harebrained scheme."

"Harebrained schemes sometimes win wars," Ellsner said.

"They usually lose them."

"The war is lost already, by your own admission."

"I can still wait for them to make a mistake."

"Do you think it will come?"

"No."

"Well, then?"

"I'm still going to wait."

The rest of the meal was completed in moody silence. Afterward, Ellsner went to his room.

"Well, Ed?" Margraves asked, unbuttoning his shirt.

"Well yourself," the general said. He lay down on his bed, trying not to think. It was too much. Logistics. Predetermined battles. The coming debacle. He considered slamming his fist against the wall, but decided against it. He was going to sleep.

On the borderline between slumber and sleep, he heard a click.

The door!

Branch jumped out of bed and tried the knob. Then he threw himself against it.

Locked.

"General, please strap yourself down. We are attacking." It was Ellsner's voice, over the intercom.

"I looked over that keyboard of yours, sir, and found the magnetic doorlocks. Mighty handy in case of a mutiny, isn't it?"

"You idiot!" Branch shouted. "You'll kill us all! That CPC—"

"I've disconnected our CPC," Ellsner said pleasantly. "I'm a pretty logical boy, and I think I know how a sneeze will bother them."

"He's mad," Margraves shouted to Branch. Together they threw themselves against the metal door.

Then they were thrown to the floor.

"All gunners—fire at will!" Ellsner broadcast to the fleet.

The ship was in motion. The attack was under way!

The dots drifted together, crossing the no-man's-land of space.

They coalesced! Energy flared, and the battle was joined.

Six minutes, human time. Hours for the electronically fast chess player. He checked his pieces for an instant, deducing the pattern of attack.

There was no pattern!

Half of the opposing chess player's pieces shot out into space, completely out of the battle. Whole flanks advanced, split, rejoined, wrenched forward, dissolved their formation, formed it again.

No pattern? There *had* to be a pattern. The chess player knew that everything had a pattern. It was just a question of finding it, taking the moves already made and extrapolating to determine what the end was supposed to be.

The end was—chaos!

The dots swept in and out, shot away at right angles to the battle, checked, and returned, meaninglessly.

What did it mean? the chess player asked himself with the calmness of metal. He waited for a recognizable configuration to emerge.

Watching dispassionately as his pieces were swept off the board.

"I'm letting you out of your room now," Ellsner called, "but don't try to stop me. I think I've won your battle."

The lock released. The two officers ran down the corridor to the bridge, determined to break Ellsner into little pieces.

Inside, they slowed down.

The screen showed the great mass of Earth dots sweeping over a scattering of enemy dots.

What stopped them, however, was Nielson, laughing, his hands sweeping over switches and buttons on the great master control board.

The CPC was droning the losses. "Earth—eighteen percent. Enemy—eighty-three. Eighty-four. Eighty-six. Earth, nineteen percent."

"Mate!" Ellsner shouted. He stood beside Nielson, a Stillson wrench clenched in his hand. "Lack of pattern. I gave their CPC something it couldn't handle. An attack with no apparent pattern. Meaningless configurations!"

"But what are they doing?" Branch asked, gesturing at the dwindling enemy dots.

"Still relying on their chess player," Ellsner said. "Still waiting for him to dope out the attack pattern in this madman's mind. Too much faith in machines, general. This man doesn't even know he's precipitating an attack."

...And push three that's for dad on the olive tree I always wanted to two two two Danbury fair with buckle shoe brown all brown buttons down and in, sin, eight red for sin—

"What's the wrench for?" Margraves asked.

"That?" Ellsner weighed it in his hand. "That's to turn off Nielson here, after the attack."

...And five and love and black, all blacks, fair buttons in I remember when I was very young at all push five and there on the grass ouch—

THE MONSTERS

Cordovir and Hun stood on the rocky mountaintop, watching the new thing happen. Both felt rather good about it. It was undoubtedly the newest thing that had happened for some time.

"By the way the sunlight glints from it," Hum said, "I'd say it is made of metal."

"I'll accept that," Cordovir said. "But what holds it up in the air?"

They both stared intently down to the valley where the new thing was happening. A pointed object was hovering over the ground. From one end of it poured a substance resembling fire.

"It's balancing on the fire," Hum said. "That should be apparent even to your old eyes."

Cordovir lifted himself higher on his thick tail, to get a better look. The object settled to the ground and the fire stopped.

"Shall we go down and have a closer look?" Hum asked.

"All right. I think we have time—wait! What day is this?"

Hum calculated silently, then said, "The fifth day of Luggat."

"Damn," Cordovir said. "I have to go home and kill my wife."

"It's a few hours before sunset," Hum said. "I think you have time to do both."

Cordovir wasn't sure. "I'd hate to be late."

"Well, then. You know how fast I am," Hum said. "If it gets late, I'll hurry back and kill her myself. How about that?"

"That's very decent of you." Cordovir thanked the younger man and together they slithered down the steep mountainside.

In front of the metal object both men halted and stood up on their tails.

"Rather bigger than I thought," Cordovir said, measuring the metal object with his eye. He estimated that it was slightly longer than their village, and almost half as wide. They crawled a circle around it, observing that the metal was tooled, presumably by human tentacles.

In the distance the smaller sun had set.

53

"I think we had better get back," Cordovir said, noting the cessation of light.

"*I* still have plenty of time." Hum flexed his muscles complacently.

"Yes, but a man likes to kill his own wife."

"As you wish." They started off to the village at a brisk pace.

In his house, Cordovir's wife was finishing supper. She had her back to the door, as etiquette required. Cordovir killed her with a single flying slash of his tail, dragged her body outside, and sat down to eat.

After meal and meditation he went to the Gathering. Hum, with the impatience of youth, was already there, telling of the metal object. He probably bolted his supper, Cordovir thought with mild distaste.

After the youngster had finished, Cordovir gave his own observations. The only thing he added to Hum's account was an idea: that the metal object might contain intelligent beings.

"What makes you think so?" Mishill, another elder, asked.

"The fact that there was fire from the object as it came down," Cordovir said, "joined to the fact that the fire stopped after the object was on the ground. Some being, I contend, was responsible for turning it off."

"Not necessarily," Mishill said. The village men talked about it late into the night. Then they broke up the meeting, buried the various murdered wives, and went to their homes.

Lying in the darkness, Cordovir discovered that he hadn't made up his mind as yet about the new thing. Presuming it contained intelligent beings, would they be moral? Would they have a sense of right and wrong? Cordovir doubted it, and went to sleep.

The next morning every male in the village went to the metal object. This was proper, since the functions of males were to examine new things and to limit the female population. They formed a circle around it, speculating on what might be inside.

"I believe they will be human beings," Hum's elder brother Esktel said. Cordovir shook his entire body in disagreement.

"Monsters, more likely," he said. "If you take in account—"

"Not necessarily," Esktel said. "Consider the logic of our physical development. A single focusing eye—"

"But in the great Outside," Cordovir said, "there may be many strange races, most of them non-human. In the infinitude—"

"Still," Esktel put in, "the logic of our—"

"As I was saying," Cordovir went on, "the chance is infinitesimal that they would resemble us. Their vehicle, for example. Would we build—"

"But on strictly logical grounds," Esktel said, "you can see—"

That was the third time Cordovir had been interrupted. With a single movement of his tail he smashed Esktel against the metal object. Esktel fell to the ground, dead.

"I have often considered my brother a boor," Hum said. "What were you saying?"

But Cordovir was interrupted again. A piece of metal set in the greater piece of metal squeaked, turned and lifted, and a creature came out.

Cordovir saw at once that he had been right. The thing that crawled out of the hole was twin-tailed. It was covered to its top with something partially metal and partially hide. And its color! Cordovir shuddered.

The thing was the color of wet, flayed flesh.

All the villagers had backed away, waiting to see what the thing would do. At first it didn't do anything. It stood on the metal surface, and a bulbous object that topped its body moved from side to side. But there were no accompanying body movements to give the gesture meaning. Finally, the thing raised both tentacles and made noises.

"Do you think it's trying to communicate?" Mishill asked softly.

Three more creatures appeared in the metal hole, carrying metal sticks in their tentacles. The things made noises at each other.

"They are decidedly not human," Cordovir said firmly. "The next question is, are they moral beings?" One of the things crawled down the metal side and stood on the ground. The rest pointed their metal sticks at the ground. It seemed to be some sort of religious ceremony.

"Could anything so hideous be moral?" Cordovir asked, his hide twitching with distaste. Upon closer inspection, the creatures were more horrible than could be dreamed. The bulbous object on their bodies just might be a head, Cordovir decided, even though it was unlike any head he had ever seen. But in the middle of that head! Instead of a smooth, characterful surface was a raised ridge. Two round indentures were on either side of it, and two more knobs on either side of that. And in the lower half of the head—if such it was—a pale, reddish slash ran across. Cordovir supposed this might be considered a mouth, with some stretching of the imagination.

Nor was this all, Cordovir observed. The things were so constructed as to show the presence of bone! When they moved their limbs, it wasn't a smooth, flowing gesture, the fluid motion of human beings. Rather, it was the jerky snap of a tree limb.

"God above," Gilrig, an intermediate-age male gasped. "We should kill them and put them out of their misery!" Other men seemed to feel the same way, and the villagers flowed forward.

"Wait!" one of the youngsters shouted. "Let's communicate with them, if such is possible. They might still be moral beings. The Outside is wide, remember, and anything is possible."

Cordovir argued for immediate extermination, but the villagers stopped and discussed it among themselves. Hum, with characteristic bravado, flowed up to the thing on the ground.

"Hello," Hum said.

The thing said something.

"I can't understand it," Hum said, and started to crawl back. The creature waved its jointed tentacles—if they were tentacles—and motioned at one of the suns. He made a sound.

"Yes, it is warm, isn't it?" Hum said cheerfully.

The creature pointed at the ground, and made another sound.

"We haven't had especially good crops this year," Hum said conversationally.

The creature pointed at itself and made a sound.

"I agree," Hum said. "You're as ugly as sin."

Presently the villagers grew hungry and crawled back to the village. Hum stayed and listened to the things making noises at him, and Cordovir waited nervously for Hum.

"You know," Hum said, after he rejoined Cordovir, "I think they want to learn our language. Or want me to learn theirs."

"Don't do it," Cordovir said, glimpsing the misty edge of a great evil.

"I believe I will," Hum murmured. Together they climbed the cliffs back to the village.

That afternoon Cordovir went to the surplus female pen and formally asked a young woman if she would reign in his house for twenty-five days. Naturally, the woman accepted gratefully.

On the way home, Cordovir met Hum, going to the pen.

"Just killed my wife," Hum said, superfluously, since why else would he be going to the surplus female stock?

"Are you going back to the creatures tomorrow?" Cordovir asked.

"I might," Hum answered, "if nothing new presents itself."

"The thing to find out is if they are moral beings or monsters."

"Right," Hum said, and slithered on.

There was a Gathering that evening, after supper. All the villagers agreed that the things were non-human. Cordovir argued strenuously that their very appearance belied any possibility of humanity. Nothing so hideous could have moral standards, a sense of right and wrong, and above all, a notion of truth.

The young men didn't agree, probably because there had been a dearth of new things recently. They pointed out that the metal object was obviously a product of intelligence. Intelligence axiomatically means standards of differentiation. Differentiation implies right and wrong.

It was a delicious argument. Olgolel contradicted Arast and was killed by him. Mavrt, in an unusual fit of anger for so placid an individual, killed the three Holian brothers and was himself killed by Hum, who was feeling pettish. Even the surplus females could be heard arguing about it, in their pen in a corner of the village.

Weary and happy, the villagers went to sleep.

The next few weeks saw no end of the argument. Life went on much as usual, though. The women went out in the morning, gathered food, prepared it, and laid eggs. The eggs were taken to the surplus females to be hatched. As usual, about eight females were hatched to every male. On the twenty-fifth day of each marriage, or a little earlier, each man killed his woman and took another.

The males went down to the ship to listen to Hum learning the language; then, when that grew boring, they returned to their customary wandering through hills and forests, looking for new things.

The alien monsters stayed close to their ship, coming out only when Hum was there.

Twenty-four days after the arrival of the non-humans, Hum announced that he could communicate with them, after a fashion.

"They say they come from far away," Hum told the village that evening. "They say that they are bisexual, like us, and that they are humans, like us. They say there are reasons for their different appearance, but I couldn't understand that part of it."

"If we accept them as humans," Mishill said, "then everything they say is true."

The rest of the villagers shook in agreement.

"They say that they don't want to disturb our life, but would be very interested in observing it. They want to come to the village and look around."

"I see no reason why not," one of the younger men said.

"No!" Cordovir shouted. "You are letting in evil. These monsters are insidious. I believe that they are capable of—telling an untruth!" The other elders agreed, but when pressed, Cordovir had no proof to back up this vicious accusation.

"After all," Sil pointed out, "just because they look like monsters, you can't take it for granted that they think like monsters as well."

"I can," Cordovir said, but he was outvoted.

Hum went on. "They have offered me—or us, I'm not sure which, various metal objects which they say will do various things. I ignored this breach of etiquette, since I considered they didn't know any better."

Cordovir nodded. The youngster was growing up. He was showing, at long last, that he had some manners.

"They want to come to the village tomorrow."

"No!" Cordovir shouted, but the vote was against him.

"Oh, by the way," Hum said, as the meeting was breaking up. "They have several females among them. The ones with the very red mouths are females. It will be interesting to see how the males kill them. Tomorrow is the twenty-fifth day since they came."

The next day the things came to the village, crawling slowly and laboriously over the cliffs. The villagers were able to observe the extreme brittleness of their limbs, the terrible awkwardness of their motions.

"No beauty whatsoever," Cordovir muttered. "And they all look alike."

In the village the things acted without any decency. They crawled into huts and out of huts. They jabbered at the surplus female pen. They picked up eggs and examined them. They peered at the villagers through black things and shiny things.

In midafternoon, Rantan, an elder, decided it was about time he killed his woman. So he pushed the thing who was examining his hut aside and smashed his female to death.

Instantly, two of the things started jabbering at each other, hurrying out of the hut.

One had the red mouth of a female.

"He must have remembered it was time to kill his own woman," Hum observed. The villagers waited, but nothing happened.

"Perhaps," Rantan said, "perhaps he would like someone to kill her for him. It might be the custom of their land."

Without further ado Rantan slashed down the female with his tail.

The male creature made a terrible noise and pointed a metal stick at Rantan. Rantan collapsed, dead.

"That's odd," Mishill said. "I wonder if that denotes disapproval?"

The things from the metal object—eight of them—were in a tight little circle. One was holding the dead female, and the rest were pointing the metal sticks on all sides. Hum went up and asked them what was wrong.

"I don't understand," Hum said, after he spoke with them. "They used words I haven't learned. But I gather that their emotion is one of reproach."

The monsters were backing away. Another villager, deciding it was about time, killed his wife who was standing in a doorway. The group of monsters stopped and jabbered at each other. Then they motioned to Hum.

Hum's body motion was incredulous after he had talked with them.

"If I understood right," Hum said, "They are ordering us not to kill any more of our women!"

"What!" Cordovir and a dozen others shouted.

"I'll ask them again." Hum went back into conference with the monsters who were waving metal sticks in their tentacles.

"That's right," Hum said. Without further preamble he flipped his tail, throwing one of the monsters across the village square. Immediately the others began to point their sticks while retreating rapidly.

After they were gone, the villagers found that seventeen males were dead. Hum, for some reason, had been missed.

"Now will you believe me!" Cordovir shouted. "The creatures told *a deliberate untruth!* They said they wouldn't molest us and then they proceed to kill seventeen of us! Not only an amoral act—but a *concerted death effort!*"

It was almost past human understanding.

"A deliberate untruth!" Cordovir shouted the blasphemy, sick with loathing. Men rarely discussed the possibility of anyone telling an untruth.

The villagers were beside themselves with anger and revulsion, once they realized the full concept of an *untruthful* creature. And, added to that was the monsters' concerted death effort!

It was like the most horrible nightmare come true. Suddenly it became apparent that these creatures didn't kill females. Undoubtedly they allowed them to spawn unhampered. The thought of that was enough to make a strong man retch.

The surplus females broke out of their pens and, joined by the wives, demanded to know what was happening. When they were told, they were twice as indignant as the men, such being the nature of women.

"Kill them!" the surplus females roared. "Don't let them change our ways. Don't let them introduce immorality!"

"It's true," Hum said sadly. "I should have guessed it."

"They must be killed at once!" a female shouted. Being surplus, she had no name at present, but she made up for that in blazing personality.

"We women desire only to live moral, decent lives, hatching eggs in the pen until our time of marriage comes. And then twenty-five ecstatic days! How could we desire more? These monsters will destroy our way of life. They will make us as terrible as they!"

"Now do you understand?" Cordovir screamed at the men. "I warned you, I presented it to you, and you ignored me! Young men must listen to old men in time of crisis!" In his rage he killed two youngsters with a blow of his tail. The villagers applauded.

"Drive them out," Cordovir shouted. "Before they corrupt us!"

All the females rushed off to kill the monsters.

"They have death-sticks," Hum observed. "Do the females know?"

"I don't believe so," Cordovir said. He was completely calm now. "You'd better go and tell them."

"I'm tired," Hum said sulkily. "I've been translating. Why don't you go?"

"Oh, let's both go," Cordovir said, bored with the youngster's adolescent moodiness. Accompanied by half the villagers they hurried off after the females.

They overtook them on the edge of the cliff that overlooked the object. Hum explained the death-sticks while Cordovir considered the problem.

"Roll stones on them," he told the females. "Perhaps you can break the metal of the object."

The females started rolling stones down the cliffs with great energy. Some bounced off the metal of the object. Immediately, lines of red fire came from the object and females were killed. The ground shook.

"Let's move back," Cordovir said. "The females have it well in hand, and this shaky ground makes me giddy."

Together with the rest of the males they moved to a safe distance and watched the action.

Women were dying right and left, but they were reinforced by women of other villages who had heard of the menace. They were fighting for their homes now, their rights, and they were fiercer than a man could ever be. The object was throwing fire all over the cliff, but the fire helped dislodge more stones which rained down on the thing. Finally, big fires came out of one end of the metal object.

A landslide started, and the object got into the air just in time. It barely missed a mountain; then it climbed steadily, until it was a little black speck against the larger sun. And then it was gone.

That evening, it was discovered that 53 females had been killed. This was fortunate since it helped keep down the surplus female population. The problem would become even more acute now, since seventeen males were gone in a single lump.

Cordovir was feeling exceedingly proud of himself. His wife had been gloriously killed in the fighting, but he took another at once.

"We had better kill our wives sooner than every twenty-five days for a while," he said at the evening Gathering. "Just until things get back to normal."

The surviving females, back in the pen, heard him and applauded wildly.

"I wonder where the things have gone," Hum said, offering the question to the Gathering.

"Probably away to enslave some defenseless race," Cordovir said.

"Not necessarily," Mishill put in and the evening argument was on.

SEVENTH VICTIM

Stanton Frelaine sat at his desk, trying to look as busy as an executive should at nine-thirty in the morning. It was impossible. He couldn't concentrate on the advertisement he had written the previous night, couldn't think about business. All he could do was wait until the mail came.

He had been expecting his notification for two weeks now. The government was behind schedule, as usual.

The glass door of his office was marked *Morger and Frelaine, Clothiers.* It opened, and E. J. Morger walked in, limping slightly from his old gunshot wound. His shoulders were bent; but at the age of seventy-three, he wasn't worrying much about his posture.

"Well, Stan?" Morger asked. "What about that ad?"

Frelaine had joined Morger sixteen years ago, when he was twenty-seven. Together they had built Protec-Clothes into a million-dollar concern.

"I suppose you can run it," Frelaine said, handing the slip of paper to Morger. If only the mail would come earlier, he thought.

"'Do you own a Protec-Suit?'" Morger read aloud, holding the paper close to his eyes. "'The finest tailoring in the world has gone into Morger and Frelaine's Protec-Suit, to make it the leader in men's fashions.'"

Morger cleared his throat and glanced at Frelaine. He smiled and read on.

"'Protec-Suit is the safest as well as the smartest. Every Protec-Suit comes with special built-in gun pocket, guaranteed not to bulge. No one will know you are carrying a gun—except you. The gun pocket is exceptionally easy to get at, permitting fast, unhindered draw. Choice of hip or breast pocket.' Very nice," Morger commented.

Frelaine nodded morosely.

"'The Protec-Suit Special has the fling-out gun pocket, the greatest modern advance in personal protection. A touch of the concealed button throws the gun into your hand, cocked, safeties off. Why not drop into the Protec-Store nearest you? *Why not be safe?*'"

"That's fine," Morger said. "That's a very nice, dignified ad." He thought for a moment, fingering his white mustache. "Shouldn't you mention that Protec-Suits come in a variety of styles, single and double-breasted, one- and two-button rolls, deep and shallow flares?"

"Right. I forgot."

Frelaine took back the sheet and jotted a note on the edge of it.

Then he stood up, smoothing his jacket over his prominent stomach. Frelaine was forty-three, a little overweight, a little bald on top. He was an amiable-looking man with cold eyes.

"Relax," Morger said. "It'll come in today's mail."

Frelaine forced himself to smile. He felt like pacing the floor, but instead sat on the edge of the desk.

"You'd think it was my first kill," he said with a deprecating smile.

"I know how it is," Morger said. "Before I hung up my gun, I couldn't sleep for a month, waiting for a notification. I know."

The two men waited. Just as the silence was becoming unbearable, the door opened. A clerk walked in and deposited the mail on Frelaine's desk.

Frelaine swung around and gathered up the letters. He thumbed through them rapidly and found what he had been waiting for—the long white envelope from ECB, with the official government seal on it.

"That's it!" Frelaine said, and broke into a grin. "That's the baby!"

"Fine." Morger eyed the envelope with interest, but didn't ask Frelaine to open it. It would be a breach of etiquette, as well as a violation of the law. No one was supposed to know a Victim's name except his Hunter. "Have a good hunt."

"I expect to," Frelaine replied confidently. His desk was in order—had been for a week. He picked up his briefcase.

"A good kill will do you a world of good," Morger said, putting his hand lightly on Frelaine's padded shoulder. "You've been keyed up."

"I know." Frelaine grinned again and shook Morger's hand.

"Wish I was a kid again," Morger said, glancing down at his crippled leg with wryly humorous eyes. "Makes me want to pick up a gun again."

The old man had been quite a Hunter in his day. Ten successful hunts had qualified him for the exclusive Tens Club. And, of course, in turn for each hunt, Morger had had to act as Victim, so he had twenty kills to his credit.

"I sure hope my Victim isn't anyone like you," Frelaine said, half in jest.

"Don't worry about it. What number will this be?"

"The seventh."

"Lucky seven. Go to it," Morger said. "We'll get you into the Tens yet."

Frelaine waved his hand and started out the door.

"Just don't get careless," warned Morger. "All it takes is a single slip and I'll need a new partner. If you don't mind, I like the one I've got now."

"I'll be careful," Frelaine promised.

Instead of taking a bus, Frelaine walked to his apartment. He wanted time to cool off. There was no sense in acting like a kid on his first kill.

As he walked, Frelaine kept his eyes strictly to the front. Staring at anyone was practically asking for a bullet, if the man happened to be serving as Victim. Some Victims shot if you just glanced at them. Nervous fellows. Frelaine prudently looked above the heads of the people he passed.

Ahead of him was a huge billboard, offering J. F. O'Donovan's services to the public.

"Victims!" the sign proclaimed in huge red letters. "Why take chances? Use an O'Donovan accredited Spotter. Let us locate your assigned killer. Pay *after* you get him!"

The sign reminded Frelaine. He would call Ed Morrow as soon as he reached his apartment.

He crossed the street, quickening his stride. He could hardly wait to get home now, to open the envelope and discover who his Victim was. Would he be clever or stupid? Rich, like Frelaine's fourth Victim, or poor, like the first and second? Would he have an organized Spotter service, or try to do it on his own?

The excitement of the chase was wonderful, coursing through his veins, quickening his heartbeat. From a block or so away, he heard gunfire. Two quick shots, and then a final one.

Somebody got his man, Frelaine thought. Good for him.

It was a superb feeling, he told himself. He was *alive* again.

At his one-room apartment, the first thing Frelaine did was to call Ed Morrow, his Spotter. The man worked as a garage attendant between calls.

"Hello, Ed? Frelaine."

"Oh, hi, Mr. Frelaine." He could see the man's thin, grease-stained face, grinning flat-lipped at the telephone.

"I'm going out on one, Ed."

"Good luck, Mr. Frelaine," Ed Morrow said. "I suppose you'll want me to stand by?"

"That's right. I don't expect to be gone more than a week or two. I'll probably get my notification of Victim Status within three months of the kill."

"I'll be standing by. Good hunting, Mr. Frelaine."

"Thanks. So long." He hung up. It was a wise safety measure to reserve a first-class Spotter. After his kill, it would be Frelaine's turn as Victim. Then, once again, Ed Morrow would be his life insurance.

And what a marvelous Spotter Morrow was! Uneducated—stupid, really. But what an eye for people! Morrow was a natural. His pale eyes could tell an out-of-towner at a glance. He was diabolically clever at rigging an ambush. An indispensable man.

Frelaine took out the envelope, chuckling to himself, remembering some of the tricks Morrow had turned for the Hunters. Still smiling, he glanced at the data inside the envelope.

Janet-Marie Patzig.

His Victim was a woman!

Frelaine stood up and paced for a few moments. Then he read the letter again. Janet-Marie Patzig. No mistake. A girl. Three photographs were enclosed, her address, and the usual descriptive data.

Frelaine frowned. He had never killed a woman.

He hesitated for a moment, then picked up the telephone and dialed ECB.

"Emotional Catharsis Bureau, Information Section," a man's voice answered.

"Say, look," Frelaine said. "I just got my notification and I pulled a girl. Is that in order?" He gave the clerk the girl's name.

"It's all in order, sir," the clerk replied after a minute of checking microfiles. "The girl registered with the board under her own free will. The law says she has the same rights and privileges as a man."

"Could you tell me how many kills she has?"

"I'm sorry, sir. The only information you're allowed is the Victim's legal status and the descriptive data you have received."

"I see." Frelaine paused. "Could I draw another?"

"You can refuse the hunt, of course. That is your legal right. But you will not be allowed another Victim until you have served. Do you wish to refuse?"

"Oh, no," Frelaine said hastily. "I was just wondering. Thank you."

He hung up and sat down in his largest armchair, loosening his belt. This required some thought.

Damn women, he grumbled to himself, always trying to horn in on a man's game. Why can't they stay home?

But they were free citizens, he reminded himself. Still, it just didn't seem *feminine.*

He knew that, historically speaking, the Emotional Catharsis Board had been established for men and men only. The board had been formed at the end of the Fourth World War—or Sixth, as some historians counted it.

At that time there had been a driving need for permanent, lasting peace. The reason was practical, as were the men who engineered it.

Simply—annihilation was just around the corner.

In the World Wars, weapons increased in magnitude, efficiency, and exterminating power. Soldiers became accustomed to them, less and less reluctant to use them.

But the saturation point had been reached. Another war would truly be the war to end all wars. There would be no one left to start another.

So this peace *had* to last for all time, but the men who engineered it were practical. They recognized the tensions and dislocations still present, the cauldrons in which wars are brewed. They asked themselves why peace had never lasted in the past.

"Because men like to fight," was their answer.

"Oh, no!" screamed the idealists.

But the men who engineered the peace were forced to postulate, regretfully, the presence of a need for violence in a large percentage of mankind.

Men aren't angels. They aren't fiends, either. They are just very human beings, with a high degree of combativeness.

With the scientific knowledge and the power they had at that moment, the practical men could have gone a long way toward breeding this trait out of the race. Many thought this was the answer.

The practical men didn't. They recognized the validity of competition, love of battle, courage in the face of overwhelming odds. These, they felt, were admirable traits for a race, and insurance toward its perpetuity. Without them, the race would be bound to retrogress.

The tendency toward violence, they found, was inextricably linked with ingenuity, flexibility, drive.

The problem, then: to arrange a peace that would last after they were gone. To stop the race from destroying itself, without removing the responsible traits.

The way to do this, they decided, was to rechannel man's violence. Provide him with an outlet, an expression.

The first big step was the legalization of gladiatorial events, complete with blood and thunder. But more was needed. Sublimations worked only up to a point. Then people demanded the real thing.

There is no substitute for murder.

So murder was legalized, on a strictly individual basis, and only for those who wanted it. The governments were directed to create Emotional Catharsis Boards.

After a period of experimentation, uniform rules were adopted. Anyone who wanted to murder could sign up at the ECB. After giving certain data and assurances, he would be granted a Victim.

Anyone who signed up to murder, under the government rules, had to take his turn a few months later as Victim—if he survived.

That, in essence, was the setup. The individual could commit as many murders as he wanted. But between one murder and the next, he had to be a Victim. If he successfully killed his Hunter, he could stop, or sign up for another murder.

At the end of ten years, an estimated one-third of the world's population had applied for at least one murder. The number slid to one-fourth, and stayed there.

Philosophers shook their heads, but the practical men were satisfied. War was where it belonged—in the hands of the individual.

Of course, there were ramifications to the game, and elaborations. Once its existence had been accepted, it became big business. There were services for Victim and Hunter alike.

The Emotional Catharsis Board picked the Victims' names at random. A Hunter was allowed two weeks in which to make his kill. This had to be done through his own ingenuity, unaided. He was given the name of his Victim, an address and a description, and was allowed to use a standard-caliber pistol. He could wear no armor of any sort.

The Victim was notified a week before the Hunter. He was told only that he was a Victim. He did not know the name of his Hunter.

He was allowed his choice of armor. He could hire Spotters. A Spotter couldn't kill; only Victim and Hunter could do that. But he could detect a stranger in town, or ferret out a nervous gunman.

The Victim could arrange any kind of ambush in his power to kill the Hunter.

There were stiff penalties for killing or wounding the wrong man, for no other murder was allowed. Grudge killings and gain killings were punishable by death.

The beauty of the system was that the people who wanted to kill could do so. Those who didn't—the bulk of the population—didn't have to.

At least there weren't any more big wars. Not even the imminence of one.

Just hundreds of thousands of small ones.

Frelaine didn't especially like the idea of killing a woman; but, she *had* signed up. It wasn't his fault. And he wasn't going to lose out on his seventh hunt.

He spent the rest of the morning memorizing the data on his Victim, then filed the letter.

Janet Patzig lived in New York. That was good. He enjoyed hunting in a big city, and he had always wanted to see New York. Her age wasn't given, but to judge from her photographs, she was in her early twenties.

Frelaine phoned for his jet reservations to New York, then took a shower. He dressed with care in a new Protec-Suit Special made for the occasion. From his collection he selected a gun, cleaned and oiled it, and fitted it into the fling-out pocket of the suit. Then he packed his suitcase.

A pulse of excitement was pounding in his veins. Strange, he thought, how each killing was a new thrill. It was something you just didn't tire of, the way you did of French pastry or women or drinking or anything else. It was always new and different.

Finally he looked over his books to see which he would take. His library contained all the good books on the subject. He wouldn't need any of his Victim books, such as L. Fred Tracy's *Tactics for the Victim,* with its insistence on a rigidly controlled environment, or Dr. Frisch's *Don't Think Like a Victim!*

He would be very interested in those in a few months, when he was a Victim again. Now he wanted hunting books.

Tactics for Hunting Humans was the standard and definitive work, but he had it almost memorized. *Development of the Ambush* was not adapted to his present needs.

He chose *Hunting in Cities* by Mitwell and Clark, *Spotting the Spotter* by Algreen, and *The Victim's Ingroup* by the same author.

Everything was in order. He left a note for the milkman, locked his apartment, and took a cab to the airport.

In New York he checked into a hotel in the midtown area, not too far from his Victim's address. The clerks were smiling and attentive, which bothered Frelaine. He didn't like to be recognized so easily as an out-of-town killer.

The first thing he saw in his room was a pamphlet on his bed table. *How to Get the Most Out of Your Emotional Catharsis,* it was called, with the compliments of the management. Frelaine smiled and thumbed through it.

Since it was his first visit to New York, he spent the afternoon just walking the streets in his Victim's neighborhood. After that, he wandered through a few stores.

Martinson and Black was a fascinating place. He went through their Hunter-Hunted room. There were lightweight bulletproof vests for Victims, and Richard Arlington hats, with bulletproof crowns.

On one side was a large display of a new .38-caliber sidearm. "Use the Malvern Strait-shot!" the ad proclaimed. "ECB approved. Carries a load of twelve shots. Tested deviation less than .001 inches per 1000 feet. Don't miss your Victim! Don't risk your life without the best! Be safe with Malvern!"

Frelaine smiled. The ad was good, and the small black weapon looked ultimately efficient. But he was satisfied with the one he had.

There was a special sale on trick canes, with concealed four-shot magazine, promising safety and concealment. As a young man, Frelaine had gone in heavily for novelties. But now he knew that the old-fashioned ways were usually best.

Outside the store, four men from the Department of Sanitation were carting away a freshly killed corpse. Frelaine regretted missing the take.

He ate dinner in a good restaurant and went to bed early. Tomorrow he had a lot to do.

The next day, with the face of his Victim before him, Frelaine walked through her neighborhood. He didn't look closely at anyone. Instead he moved rapidly, as though he were really going somewhere, the way an old Hunter should walk.

He passed several bars and dropped into one for a drink. Then he went on, down a side street off Lexington Avenue.

There was a pleasant sidewalk cafe there. Frelaine walked past it. And there she was! He could never mistake the face. It was Janet Patzig, seated at a table, staring into a drink. She didn't look up as he passed.

Frelaine walked to the end of the block. He turned the corner and stopped, hands trembling.

Was the girl crazy, exposing herself in the open? Did she think she had a charmed life?

He hailed a taxi and had the man drive around the block. Sure enough, she was just sitting there. Frelaine took a careful look.

She seemed younger than her pictures, but he couldn't be sure. He would guess her to be not much over twenty. Her dark hair was parted in the middle and combed above her ears, giving her a nun-like appearance. Her expression, as far as Frelaine could tell, was one of resigned sadness.

Wasn't she even going to make an attempt to defend herself? Frelaine paid the driver and hurried to a drugstore. Finding a vacant telephone booth, he called ECB.

"Are you sure that a Victim named Janet-Marie Patzig has been notified?"

"Hold on, sir." Frelaine tapped on the door while the clerk looked up the information. "Yes, sir. We have her personal confirmation. Is there anything wrong, sir?"

"No," Frelaine said. "Just wanted to check."

After all, it was no one's business if the girl didn't want to defend herself.

He was still entitled to kill her.

It was his turn.

He postponed it for that day, however, and went to a movie. After dinner he returned to his room and read the ECB pamphlet. Then he lay on his bed and glared at the ceiling.

All he had to do was pump a bullet into her. Just ride by in a cab and kill her.

She was being a very bad sport about it, he decided resentfully, and went to sleep.

The next afternoon, Frelaine walked by the cafe again. The girl was back, sitting at the same table. Frelaine caught a cab.

"Drive around the block very slowly," he told the driver.

"Sure," the driver said, grinning with sardonic wisdom.

From the cab, Frelaine watched for Spotters. As far as he could tell, the girl had none. Both of her hands were in sight upon the table. An easy, stationary target.

Frelaine touched the button of his double-breasted jacket. A fold flew open and the gun was in his hand. He broke it open and checked the cartridges, then closed it with a snap.

"Slowly now," he told the driver.

The taxi crawled by the cafe. Frelaine took careful aim, centering the girl in his sights. His finger tightened on the trigger.

"Damn it!" he said.

A waiter had passed by the girl. He didn't want to chance winging the wrong person.

"Around the block again," he told the driver.

The man gave him another grin and hunched down in his seat. Frelaine wondered if the driver would feel so happy if he knew that Frelaine was gunning for a woman.

This time there was no waiter around. The girl was lighting a cigarette, her mournful face intent on her lighter. Frelaine centered her in his sights, squarely above the eyes, and held his breath.

Then he shook his head and put the gun back in his pocket. The idiotic girl was robbing him of the full benefit of his catharsis.

He paid the driver and started to walk.

It's too easy, he told himself. He was used to a real chase. Most of the other six kills had been quite difficult. The Victims had tried every dodge. One had hired at least a dozen Spotters. But Frelaine had reached them all by altering his tactics to meet the situation.

Once he had dressed as a milkman, another time as a bill collector. The sixth Victim he had had to chase through the Sierra Nevadas. The man had clipped him, too. But Frelaine had done better.

How could he be proud of this one? What would the Tens Club say?

That brought Frelaine up with a start. He wanted to get into the club. Even if he passed up this girl, he would have to defend himself against a Hunter. If he survived, he would still be four hunts away from membership. At that rate he might never get in.

He began to pass the cafe again, but then, on impulse, stopped abruptly.

"Hello," he said.

Janet Patzig looked at him out of sad blue eyes, but said nothing.

"Say, look," he said, sitting down, "if I'm being fresh, just tell me and I'll go. I'm an out-of-towner. Here at a convention. And I'd just like someone feminine to talk to. If you'd rather I didn't—"

"I don't care," Janet Patzig said tonelessly.

"A brandy," Frelaine told the waiter. Janet Patzig's glass was still half-full.

Frelaine looked at the girl and he could feel his heart throbbing against his ribs. This was more like it—having a drink with your Victim!

"My name's Stanton Frelaine," he said, knowing it didn't matter.

"Janet."

"Janet what?"

"Janet Patzig."

"Nice to know you," Frelaine said in a perfectly natural voice. "Are you doing anything tonight, Janet?"

"I'm probably being killed tonight," she said quietly.

Frelaine looked at her carefully. Did she realize who he was? For all he knew, she had a gun leveled at him under the table.

He kept his hand close to the fling-out button.

"Are you a Victim?" he asked.

"You guessed it," she said sardonically. "If I were you, I'd stay out of the way. No sense getting hit by mistake."

Frelaine couldn't understand the girl's calm. Was she a suicide? Perhaps she just didn't care. Perhaps she wanted to die. "Haven't you got any Spotters?" he asked, with the right expression of amazement.

"No." She looked at him, full in the face, and Frelaine saw something he hadn't noticed before.

She was very lovely.

"I am a bad, bad girl," she said lightly. "I got the idea I'd like to commit a murder, so I signed for ECB. Then—I couldn't do it."

Frelaine shook his head, sympathizing with her.

"But I'm still in, of course. Even if I didn't shoot, I still have to take my turn as a Victim."

"But why don't you hire some Spotters?" he asked.

"I couldn't kill anyone," she said. "I just couldn't. I don't even have a gun."

"You've got a lot of courage," Frelaine said, "coming out in the open this way." Secretly he was amazed at her stupidity.

"What can I do?" she asked listlessly. "You can't hide from a Hunter. Not a real one. And I don't have enough money to make a good disappearance."

"Since it's in your own defense, I should think—" Frelaine began, but she interrupted.

"No. I've made up my mind on that. This whole thing is wrong, the whole system. When I had my Victim in the sights—when I saw how easily I could—I could—"

She pulled herself together quickly.

"Oh, let's forget it," she said, and smiled.

Frelaine found her smile dazzling.

After that, they talked of other things. Frelaine told her of his business, and she told him about New York. She was twenty-two, an unsuccessful actress.

They had supper together. When she accepted Frelaine's invitation to go to the Gladiatorials, he felt absurdly elated.

He called a cab—he seemed to be spending his entire time in New York in cabs—and opened the door for her. She started in. Frelaine hesitated. He could have pumped a shot into her at that moment. It would have been very easy.

But he held back. Just for the moment, he told himself.

The Gladiatorials were about the same as those held anywhere else, except that the talent was a little better. There were the usual historical events: swordsmen and netmen, duels with saber and foil.

Most of these, naturally, were fought to the death.

Then bullfighting, lion fighting, and rhino fighting, followed by the more modern events. Fights from behind barricades, with bow and arrow. Dueling on a high wire.

The evening passed pleasantly.

Frelaine escorted the girl home, the palms of his hands sticky with sweat. He had never found a woman he liked better. And yet, she was his legitimate kill.

He didn't know what he was going to do.

She invited him in and they sat together on the couch. The girl lighted a cigarette for herself with a large lighter, then settled back.

"Are you leaving soon?" she asked him.

"I suppose so," Frelaine said. "The convention is only lasting another day."

She was silent for a moment. "I'll be sorry to see you go." They were quiet for a while. Then Janet went to fix him a drink. Frelaine eyed her retreating back. Now was the time. He placed his hand near the button.

But the moment had passed for him, irrevocably. He wasn't going to kill her. You don't kill the girl you love.

The realization that he loved her was shocking. He'd come to kill, not to find a wife.

She came back with the drink and sat down opposite him, staring at emptiness.

"Janet," he said, "I love you."

She sat, just looking at him. There were tears in her eyes.

"You can't," she protested. "I'm a Victim. I won't live long enough to—"

"You won't be killed. I'm your Hunter."

She stared at him a moment, then laughed uncertainly.

"Are you going to kill me?" she asked.

"Don't be ridiculous," he said. "I'm going to marry you." Suddenly she was in his arms.

"Oh, Lord!" she gasped. "The waiting—I've been so frightened—"

"It's all over," he told her. "Think what a story it'll make for our kids. How I came to murder you and left marrying you."

She kissed him, then sat back and lighted another cigarette. "Let's start packing," Frelaine said. "I want—"

"Wait," Janet interrupted. "You haven't asked if *I* love *you.*"

"What?"

She was still smiling, and the cigarette lighter was pointed at him. In the bottom of it was a black hole. A hole just large enough for a .38-caliber bullet.

"Don't kid around," he objected, getting to his feet.

"I'm not being funny, darling," she said.

In a fraction of a second, Frelaine had time to wonder how he could ever have thought she was not much over twenty. Looking at her now— *really* looking at her—he knew she couldn't be much less than thirty. Every minute of her strained, tense existence showed on her face.

"I don't love you, Stanton," she said very softly, the cigarette lighter poised.

Frelaine struggled for breath. One part of him was able to realize detachedly what a marvelous actress she really was. She must have known all along.

Frelaine pushed the button, and the gun was in his hand, cocked and ready.

The blow that struck him in the chest knocked him over a coffee table. The gun fell out of his hand. Gasping, half conscious, he watched her take careful aim for the coup de grâce.

"Now I can join the Tens," he heard her say as she squeezed the trigger.

SHAPE

Pid the Pilot slowed the ship almost to a standstill. He peered anxiously at the green planet below.

Even without instruments, there was no mistaking it. Third from its sun, it was the only planet in this system capable of sustaining life. Peacefully it swam through its gauze of clouds.

It looked very innocent. And yet, something on this planet had claimed the lives of every expedition the Glom had sent.

Pid hesitated a moment before starting irrevocably down. He and his two crewmen were as ready now as they would ever be. Their compact Displacers were stored in body pouches, inactive but ready.

Pid wanted to say something to his crew, but wasn't sure how to put it.

The crew waited. Ilg the Radioman had sent the final message to the Glom planet. Ger the Detector read sixteen dials at once and reported, "No sign of alien activity." His body surfaces flowed carelessly.

Pid noticed the flow and knew what he had to say. Ever since they had left Glom, Shape-discipline had been disgustingly lax. The Invasion Chief had warned him; but still, he had to do something about it. It was his duty, since lower castes such as Radiomen and Detectors were notoriously prone to Shapelessness.

"A lot of hopes are resting on this expedition," he began slowly. "We're a long way from home now."

Ger the Detector nodded. Ilg the Radioman flowed out of his prescribed shape and molded himself comfortably to a wall.

"However," Pid said sternly, "Distance is no excuse for promiscuous shapelessness."

Ilg flowed hastily back into proper Radioman's shape.

"Exotic shapes will undoubtedly be called for," Pid went on. "And for that we have a special dispensation. But remember—any shape not assumed strictly in the line of duty is a device of The Shapeless One!"

Ger's body surfaces abruptly stopped flowing.

"That's all," Pid said, and flowed into his controls. The ship started down, so smoothly coordinated that Pid felt a glow of pride.

73

They were good workers, he decided. He just couldn't expect them to be as shape-conscious as a high-caste Pilot. Even the Invasion Chief had told him that.

"Pid," the Invasion Chief had said at their last interview, "We need this planet desperately."

"Yes sir," Pid had said, standing at full attention, never quivering from Optimum Pilot's Shape.

"One of you," the Chief said heavily, "must get through and set up a Displacer near an atomic power source. The army will be standing by at this end, ready to step through."

"We'll do it, Sir," Pid said.

"This expedition has to succeed," the Chief said, and his features blurred momentarily from sheer fatigue. "In strictest confidence, there's considerable unrest on Glom. The miner caste is on strike, for instance. They want a new digging shape. Say the old one is inefficient."

Pid looked properly indignant. The Mining Shape had been set down by the ancients fifty thousand years ago, together with the rest of the basic shapes. And now these upstarts wanted to change it!

"That's not all," the Chief told him. "We've uncovered a new Cult of Shapelessness. Picked up almost eight thousand Glom, and I don't know how many more we missed."

Pid knew that Shapelessness was a lure of The Shapeless One, the greatest evil that the Glom mind conceived of. But how, he wondered, did Glom fall for His lures?

The Chief guessed his question. "Pid," he said, "I suppose it's difficult for you to understand. Do you enjoy Piloting?"

"Yes sir," Pid said simply. *Enjoy* Piloting! It was his entire life! Without a ship, he was nothing.

"Not all Glom feel that way," the Chief said. "I don't understand it either. All my ancestors have been Invasion Chiefs, back to the beginning of time. So of course *I* want to be an Invasion Chief. It's only natural, as well as lawful. But the lower castes don't feel that way." He shook his body sadly.

"I've told you this for a reason," the Chief went on. "We Glom need more room. This unrest is caused purely by crowding. All our psychologists say so. Another planet to expand into will cure everything. So we're counting on you, Pid."

"Yes sir," Pid said, with a glow of pride.

The Chief rose to end the interview. Then he changed his mind and sat down again.

"You'll have to watch your crew," he said. "They're loyal, no doubt, but low-caste. And you know the lower castes."

Pid did indeed.

"Ger, your Detector, is suspected of harboring Alterationist tendencies. He was once fined for assuming a quasi-Hunter shape. Ilg has never had any definite charge brought against him. But I hear that he remains immobile for suspiciously long periods of time. Possibly, he fancies himself a Thinker."

"But sir," Pid protested, "If they are even slightly tainted with Alterationism or Shapelessness, why send them on this expedition?"

The Chief hesitated before answering. "There are plenty of Glom I could trust," he said slowly. "But those two have certain qualities of resourcefulness and imagination that will be needed on this expedition." He sighed. "I really don't understand why those qualities are usually linked with Shapelessness."

"Yes sir," Pid said.

"Just watch them."

"Yes sir," Pid said again, and saluted, realizing that the interview was at an end. In his body pouch he felt the dormant Displacer, ready to transform the enemy's power source into a bridge across space for the Glom hordes.

"Good luck," the chief said. "I'm sure you'll need it."

The ship dropped silently toward the surface of the enemy planet. Ger the Detector analyzed the clouds below and fed data into the Camouflage Unit. The Unit went to work. Soon the ship looked, to all outward appearances, like a cirrus formation.

Pid allowed the ship to drift slowly toward the surface of the mystery planet. He was in Optimum Pilot's Shape now, the most efficient of the four shapes allotted to the Pilot Caste. Blind, deaf, and dumb, an extension of his controls, all his attention was directed toward matching the velocities of the high-flying clouds, staying among them, becoming a part of them.

Ger remained rigidly in one of the two shapes allotted to Detectors. He fed data into the Camouflage Unit and the descending ship slowly altered into an alto-cumulus. There was no sign of activity from the enemy planet. Ilg located an atomic power source and fed the data to Pid. The Pilot altered course. He had reached the lowest level of clouds, barely a mile above the surface of the planet. Now his ship looked like a fat, fleecy cumulus.

And still there was no sign of alarm. The unknown fate that had overtaken twenty previous expeditions still had not showed itself.

Dusk crept across the face of the planet as Pid maneuvered near the atomic power installation. He avoided the surrounding homes and hovered over a clump of woods.

Darkness fell, and the green planet's lone moon was veiled in clouds.

One cloud floated lower.
And landed.

"Quick, everyone out!" Pid shouted, detaching himself from the ship's controls. He assumed the Pilot's Shape best suited for running and raced out of the hatch. Ger and Ilg hurried after him. They stopped fifty yards from the ship and waited.

Inside the ship a circuit closed. There was a silent shudder and the ship began to melt. Plastic dissolved, metal crumpled. Soon the ship was a great pile of junk and still the process went on. Big fragments broke into smaller fragments, and split, and split again.

Pid felt suddenly helpless, watching his ship scuttle itself. He was a Pilot, of the Pilot Caste. His father had been a Pilot, and his father before him, stretching back to the hazy past when the Glom had first constructed ships. He had spent his entire childhood around ships, his entire manhood flying them.

Now, shipless, he was naked in an alien world.

In a few minutes there was only a mound of dust to show where the ship had been. The night wind scattered it through the forest. And then there was nothing at all.

They waited. Nothing happened. The wind sighed and the trees creaked. Squirrels chirped and birds stirred in their nests.

An acorn fell to the ground.

Pid heaved a sigh of relief and sat down. The twenty-first Glom expedition had landed safely.

There was nothing to be done until morning, so Pid began to make plans. They had landed as close to the atomic power installation as they dared. Now they would have to get closer. Somehow, one of them had to get very near the reactor room, in order to activate the Displacer.

Difficult. But Pid felt certain of success. After all, the Glom were strong on ingenuity.

Strong on ingenuity, he thought bitterly, but terribly short of radioactives. That was another reason why this expedition was so important. There was little radioactive fuel left on any of the Glom worlds.

Ages ago, the Glom had spent their store of radioactives spreading throughout their neighbor worlds, occupying the ones that they could live on. Colonization barely kept up with the mounting birthrate. New worlds were constantly needed.

This particular world, discovered in a scouting expedition, was needed. It suited the Glom perfectly. But it was too far away. They didn't have enough fuel to mount a conquering space fleet.

Luckily, there was another way. A better way.

Over the centuries, the Glom scientists had developed the Displacer. A triumph of Identity Engineering, the Displacer allowed mass to be moved instantaneously between any two linked points.

One end was set up at Glom's sole atomic energy plant. The other end had to be placed in proximity to another atomic power source and activated. Diverted power then flowed through both ends, was modified, and modified again.

Then, through the miracle of Identity Engineering, the Glom could *step* through from planet to planet, or pour through in a great, overwhelming wave.

It was quite simple. But twenty expeditions had failed to set up the Earth-end Displacer.

What had happened to them was not known.

For no Glom ship had ever returned to tell.

Before dawn they crept through the woods, taking on the coloration of the plants around them. Their Displacers pulsed feebly, sensing the nearness of atomic energy.

A tiny, four-legged creature darted in front of them. Instantly, Ger grew four legs and a long, streamlined body and gave chase.

"Ger! Come back here." Pid howled at the Detector, throwing caution to the winds.

Ger overtook the animal and knocked it down. He tried to bite it, but he had neglected to grow teeth. The animal jumped free, and vanished into the underbrush. Ger thrust out a set of teeth and bunched his muscles for a leap.

"Ger!"

Reluctantly, the Detector turned away. He loped silently back to Pid.

"I was hungry," he said.

"You were not," Pid said sternly.

"Was," Ger mumbled, writhing with embarrassment.

Pid remembered what the Chief had told him. Ger certainly did have Hunter tendencies. He would have to watch him more closely.

"We'll have no more of that," Pid said. "Remember—the lure of Exotic Shapes is not sanctioned. Be content with the shape you were born to."

Ger nodded and melted back into the underbrush. They moved on.

At the extreme edge of the woods they could observe the atomic energy installation. Pid disguised himself as a clump of shrubbery and Ger formed himself into an old log. Ilg, after a moment's thought, became a young oak.

The installation was in the form of a long, low building, surrounded by a metal fence. There was a gate and guards in front of it.

The first job, Pid thought, was to get past that gate. He began to consider ways and means.

From the fragmentary reports of the survey parties, Pid knew that, in some ways, this race of Men were like the Glom. They had pets, as the Glom did, and homes and children, and a culture. The inhabitants were skilled mechanically, as were the Glom.

But there were terrific differences. The Men were of fixed and immutable forms, like stones or trees. And to compensate, their planet boasted a fantastic array of species, types and kinds. This was completely unlike Glom, which had only eight distinct forms of animal life.

And evidently, the Men were skilled at detecting invaders, Pid thought. He wished he knew how the other expeditions had failed. It would make his job much easier.

A Man lurched past them on two incredibly stiff legs. Rigidity was evident in his every move. Without looking, he hurried past.

"I know," Ger said, after the creature had moved away. "I'll disguise myself as a Man, walk through the gate to the reactor room, and activate my Displacer."

"You can't speak their language," Pid pointed out.

"I won't speak at all. I'll ignore them. Look." Quickly Ger shaped himself into a Man.

"That's not bad," Pid said.

Ger tried a few practice steps, copying the bumpy walk of the Man.

"But I'm afraid it won't work," Pid said.

"It's perfectly logical," Ger pointed out.

"I know. Therefore the other expeditions must have tried it. And none of them came back."

There was no arguing that. Ger flowed back into the shape of a log. "What, then?" he asked.

"Let me think," Pid said.

Another creature lurched past, on four legs instead of two. Pid recognized it as a Dog, a pet of Man. He watched it carefully.

The Dog ambled to the gate, head down, in no particular hurry. It walked through, unchallenged, and lay down in the grass.

"Hmm," Pid said.

They watched. One of the Men walked past and touched the Dog on the head. The Dog stuck out its tongue and rolled over on its side.

"I can do that," Ger said excitedly. He started to flow into the shape of a Dog.

"No, wait," Pid said. "We'll spend the rest of the day thinking it over. This is too important to rush into."

Ger subsided sulkily.

"Come on, let's move back," Pid said. He and Ger started into the woods. Then he remembered Ilg.

"Ilg?" he called softly.

There was no answer.

"Ilg!"

"What? Oh, yes," an oak tree said and melted into a bush. "Sorry. What were you saying?"

"We're moving back," Pid said. "Were you, by any chance, Thinking?"

"Oh, no," Ilg assured him. "Just resting."

Pid let it go at that. There was too much else to worry about.

They discussed it for the rest of the day, hidden in the deepest part of the woods. The only alternatives seemed to be Man or Dog. A Tree couldn't walk past the gates, since that was not in the nature of trees. Nor could anything else and escape notice.

Going as a Man seemed too risky. They decided that Ger would sally out in the morning as a Dog.

"Now get some sleep," Pid said.

Obediently his two crewmen flattened out, going immediately Shapeless. But Pid had a more difficult time.

Everything looked too easy. Why wasn't the atomic installation better guarded? Certainly the Men must have learned something from the expeditions they had captured in the past. Or had they killed them without asking any questions?

You couldn't tell what an alien would do.

Was that open gate a trap?

Wearily he flowed into a comfortable position on the lumpy ground. Then he pulled himself together hastily.

He had gone Shapeless!

Comfort had nothing to do with duty, he reminded himself, and firmly took a Pilot's Shape.

But Pilot's shape wasn't constructed for sleeping on damp, bumpy ground. Pid spent a restless night, thinking of ships and wishing he were flying one.

Pid awoke in the morning tired and ill-tempered. He nudged Ger.

"Let's get this over with," he said.

Ger flowed gaily to his feet.

"Come on, Ilg," Pid said angrily, looking around. "Wake up."

There was no reply.

"Ilg!" he called.

Still there was no reply.

"Help me look for him," Pid said to Ger. "He must be around here somewhere."

Together they tested every bush, tree, log, and shrub in the vicinity. But none of them was Ilg.

Pid began to feel a cold panic run through him. What could have happened to the Radioman?

"Perhaps he decided to go through the gate on his own," Ger suggested.

Pid considered the possibility. It seemed unlikely. Ilg had never shown much initiative. He had always been content to follow orders.

They waited. But mid-day came, and there was still no sign of Ilg.

"We can't wait any longer," Pid said, and they started through the woods. Pid wondered if Ilg *had* tried to get through the gates on his own. Those quiet types often concealed a foolhardy streak.

But there was nothing to show that Ilg had been successful. He would have to assume that the Radioman was dead or captured by the Men.

That left two of them to activate a Displacer.

And still he didn't know what had happened to the other expeditions.

At the edge of the woods, Ger turned himself into a facsimile of a Dog. Pid inspected him carefully.

"A little less tail," he said.

Ger shortened his tail.

"More ears."

Ger lengthened his ears.

"Now even them up." He inspected the finished product. As far as he could tell, Ger was perfect, from the tip of his tail to his wet, black nose.

"Good luck," Pid said.

"Thanks." Cautiously Ger moved out of the woods, walking in the lurching style of Dogs and Men. At the gate the guard called to him. Pid held his breath.

Ger walked past the Man, ignoring him. The Man started to walk over, and Ger broke into a run.

Pid shaped a pair of strong legs for himself, ready to dash if Ger was caught.

But the guard turned back to his gate. Ger stopped running immediately and strolled quietly toward the main gate.

Pid dissolved his legs with a sigh of relief.

But the main door was closed! Pid hoped the Radioman wouldn't try to open it. That was *not* in the nature of Dogs.

Another Dog came running toward Ger. Ger backed away from him. The Dog approached and sniffed. Ger sniffed back.

Then both of them ran around the building.

That was clever, Pid thought. There was bound to be a door in the rear.

He glanced up at the afternoon sun. As soon as the Displacer was activated, the Glom armies would begin to pour through. By the time the Men recovered from the shock, a million or more Glom troops would be here. With more following.

The day passed slowly, and nothing happened.

Nervously Pid watched the front of the plant. It shouldn't be taking so long, if Ger were successful.

Late into the night he waited. Men walked in and out of the installation, and Dogs barked around the gates. But Ger did not appear.

Ger had failed. Ilg was gone. Only he was left.

And *still* he didn't know what had happened.

By morning, Pid was in complete despair. He knew that the twenty-first Glom expedition to this planet was near the point of complete failure. Now it was all up to him.

He decided to sally out boldly in the shape of a Man. It was the only possibility left.

He saw that workers were arriving in great numbers, rushing through the gates. Pid wondered if he should try to mingle with them or wait until there was less commotion. He decided to take advantage of the apparent confusion and started to shape himself into a Man.

A Dog walked past the woods where he was hiding.

"Hello," the Dog said.

It was Ger!

"What happened?" Pid asked, with a sigh of relief. "Why were you so long? Couldn't you get in?"

"I don't know," Ger said, wagging his tail. "I didn't try."

Pid was speechless.

"I went hunting," Ger said complacently. "This form is ideal for Hunting, you know. I went out the rear gate with another Dog."

"But the expedition—your duty—"

"I changed my mind," Ger told him. "You know, Pilot, I never wanted to be a Detector."

"But you were *born* a Detector!"

"That's true," Ger said. "But it doesn't help. I always wanted to be a Hunter."

Pid shook his entire body in annoyance. "You can't," he said, very slowly, as one would explain to a Glomling. "The Hunter shape is forbidden to you."

"Not here it isn't," Ger said, still wagging his tail.

"Let's have no more of this," Pid said angrily. "Get into that installation and set up your Displacer. I'll try to overlook this heresy."

"I won't," Ger said. "I don't want the Glom here. They'd ruin it for the rest of us."

"He's right," an oak tree said.

"Ilg!" Pid gasped. "Where are you?"

Branches stirred. "I'm right here," Ilg said. "I've been Thinking."

"But—your caste—"

"Pilot," Ger said sadly, "Why don't you wake up? Most of the people on Glom are miserable. Only custom makes us take the caste-shape of our ancestors."

"Pilot," Ilg said, "All Glom are born Shapeless!"

"And being born Shapeless, all Glom should have Freedom of Shape," Ger said.

"Exactly," Ilg said. "But he'll never understand. Now excuse me. I want to Think." And the oak tree was silent.

Pid laughed humorlessly. "The Men will kill you off," he said. "Just as they killed off the rest of the expeditions."

"No one from Glom has been killed," Ger told him. "The other expeditions are right here."

"Alive?"

"Certainly. The Men don't even know we exist. That Dog I was Hunting with is a Glom from the nineteenth expedition. There are hundreds of us here, Pilot. We like it."

Pid tried to absorb it all. He had always known that the lower castes were lax in caste-consciousness. But this—this was preposterous!

This planet's secret menace was—freedom!

"Join us, Pilot," Ger said. "We've got a paradise here. Do you know how many species there are on this planet? An uncountable number! There's a shape to suit every need!"

Pid shook his head. There was no shape to suit *his* need. He was a Pilot.

But Men were unaware of the presence of the Glom. Getting near the reactor would be simple!

"The Glom Supreme Council will take care of all of you," he snarled, and shaped himself into a Dog. "I'm going to set up the Displacer myself."

He studied himself for a moment, bared his teeth at Ger, and loped toward the gate.

The Men at the gate didn't even look at him. He slipped through the main door of the building behind a man, and loped down a corridor.

The Displacer in his body pouch pulsed and tugged, leading him toward the reactor room.

He sprinted up a flight of stairs and down another corridor. There were footsteps around the bend and Pid knew instinctively that Dogs were not allowed inside the building.

He looked around desperately for a hiding place, but the corridor was bare. However, there were several overhead lights in the ceiling.

Pid leaped, and glued himself to the ceiling. He shaped himself into a lighting fixture and hoped that the Men wouldn't try to find out why he wasn't shining.

Men passed, running.

Pid changed himself into a facsimile of a Man, and hurried on.

He had to get closer.

Another Man came down the corridor. He looked sharply at Pid, started to speak, and then sprinted away.

Pid didn't know what was wrong, but he broke into a full sprint. The Displacer in his body pouch throbbed and pulsed, telling him he had almost reached the critical distance.

Suddenly a terrible doubt assailed his mind. *All the expeditions had deserted! Every single Glom!*

He slowed slightly.

Freedom of Shape...that was a strange notion. A disturbing notion.

And obviously a device of The Shapeless One, he told himself, and rushed on.

At the end of the corridor was a gigantic bolted door. Pid stared at it. Footsteps hammered down the corridor and Men were shouting.

What was wrong? How had they detected him? Quickly he examined himself and ran his fingers across his face.

He had forgotten to mold any features.

In despair he pulled at the door. He took the tiny Displacer out of his pouch, but the pulse beat wasn't quite strong enough. He had to get closer to the reactor.

He studied the door. There was a tiny crack running under it. Pid went quickly shapeless and flowed under, barely squeezing the Displacer through.

Inside the room he found another bolt on the inside of the door. He jammed it into place, and looked around for something to prop against the door.

It was a tiny room. On one side was a lead door, leading toward the reactor. There was a small window on another side, and that was all.

Pid looked at the Displacer. The pulse beat was right. At last he was close enough. Here the Displacer could work, drawing and altering the energy from the reactor.

All he had to do was activate it.

But they had all deserted, every one of them.

Pid hesitated. *All Glom are born Shapeless.* That was true. Glom children were amorphous, until old enough to be instructed in the caste-shape of their ancestors. But Freedom of Shape?

Pid considered the possibilities. To be able to take on any shape he wanted, without interference! On this paradise planet he could fulfill any ambition, become anything, do anything.

Nor would he be lonely. There were other Glom here as well, enjoying the benefits of Freedom of Shape.

The Men were beginning to break down the door. Pid was still uncertain.

What should he do? Freedom...

But not for him, he thought bitterly. It was easy enough to be a Hunter or a Thinker. But he was a Pilot. Piloting was his life and love. How could he do that here?

Of course, the Men had ships. He could turn into a Man, find a ship...

Never. Easy enough to become a Tree or a Dog. He could never pass successfully as a Man.

The Door was beginning to splinter from repeated blows.

Pid walked to the window to take a last look at the planet before activating the Displacer.

He looked—and almost collapsed from shock.

It was really true! He hadn't fully understood what Ger had meant when he said that there were species on this planet to satisfy every need. *Every* need! Even his!

Here he could satisfy a longing of the Pilot Caste that went even deeper than Piloting.

He looked again, then smashed the Displacer to the floor. The door burst open, and in the same instant he flung himself through the window.

The Men raced to the window and stared out. But they were unable to understand what they saw.

There was only a great white bird out there, flapping awkwardly but with increasing strength, trying to overtake a flight of birds in the distance.

UNTOUCHED BY HUMAN HANDS

Hellman plucked the last radish out of the can with a pair of dividers. He held it up for Casker to admire, then laid it carefully on the workbench beside the razor.

"Hell of a meal for two grown men," Casker said, flopping down in one of the ship's padded crash chairs.

"If you'd like to give up your share—" Hellman started to suggest.

Casker shook his head quickly. Hellman smiled, picked up the razor and examined its edge critically.

"Don't make a production out of it," Casker said, glancing at the ship's instruments. They were approaching a red dwarf, the only planet-bearing sun in the vicinity. "We want to be through with supper before we get much closer."

Hellman made a practice incision in the radish, squinting along the top of the razor. Casker bent closer, his mouth open. Hellman poised the razor delicately and cut the radish cleanly in half.

"Will you say grace?" Hellman asked.

Casker growled something and popped a half in his mouth. Hellman chewed more slowly. The sharp taste seemed to explode along his disused tastebuds.

"Not much bulk value," Hellman said.

Casker didn't answer. He was busily studying the red dwarf.

As he swallowed the last of his radish, Hellman stifled a sigh. Their last meal had been three days ago…if two biscuits and a cup of water could be called a meal. This radish, now resting in the vast emptiness of their stomachs, was the last gram of food on board ship.

"Two planets," Casker said. "One's burned to a crisp."

"Then we'll land on the other."

Casker nodded and punched a deceleration spiral into the ship's tape.

Hellman found himself wondering for the hundredth time where the fault had been. Could he have made out the food requisitions wrong when they took on supplies at Calao station? After all, he had been devoting most of his attention to the mining equipment. Or had the ground crew just forgotten to load those last precious cases?

85

He drew his belt in to the fourth new notch he had punched.

Speculation was useless. Whatever the reason, they were in a jam. Ironically enough, they had more than enough fuel to take them back to Calao. But they would be a pair of singularly emaciated corpses by the time the ship reached there.

"We're coming in now," Casker said.

And to make matters worse, this unexplored region of space had few suns and fewer planets. Perhaps there was a slight possibility of replenishing their water supply, but the odds were enormous against finding anything they could eat.

"Look at that place," Casker growled.

Hellman shook himself out of his reverie.

The planet was like a round gray-brown porcupine. The spines of a million needle-sharp mountains glittered in the red dwarf's feeble light. And as they spiraled lower, circling the planet, the pointed mountains seemed to stretch out to meet them.

"It can't be *all* mountains," Hellman said.

"It's not."

Sure enough, there were oceans and lakes, out of which thrust jagged island-mountains. But no sign of level land, no hint of civilization, or even animal life.

"At least it's got an oxygen atmosphere," Casker said.

Their deceleration spiral swept them around the planet, cutting lower into the atmosphere, braking against it. And still there was nothing but mountains and lakes and oceans and more mountains.

On the eighth run, Hellman caught sight of a solitary building on a mountain top. Casker braked recklessly, and the hull glowed red hot. On the eleventh run, they made a landing approach.

"Stupid place to build," Casker muttered.

The building was doughnut-shaped and fitted nicely over the top of the mountain. There was a wide, level lip around it, which Casker scorched as he landed the ship.

From the air, the building had merely seemed big. On the ground, it was enormous. Hellman and Casker walked up to it slowly. Hellman had his burner ready, but there was no sign of life.

"This planet must be abandoned," Hellman said almost in a whisper.

"Anyone in his right mind would abandon this place," Casker said. "There're enough good planets around, without anyone trying to live on a needle point."

They reached the door. Hellman tried to open it and found it locked. He looked back at the spectacular display of mountains.

"You know," he said, "when this planet was still in a molten state, it must have been affected by several gigantic moons that are now broken up. The strains, external and internal, wrenched it into its present spined appearance and—"

"Come off it," Casker said ungraciously. "You were a librarian before you decided to get rich on uranium."

Hellman shrugged his shoulders and burned a hole in the doorlock. They waited.

The only sound on the mountain top was the growling of their stomachs. They entered.

The tremendous wedge-shaped room was evidently a warehouse of sorts. Goods were piled to the ceiling, scattered over the floor, stacked haphazardly against the walls. There were boxes and containers of all sizes and shapes, some big enough to hold an elephant, others the size of thimbles.

Near the door was a dusty pile of books. Immediately, Hellman bent down to examine them.

"Must be food somewhere in here," Casker said, his face lighting up for the first time in a week. He started to open the nearest box.

"This is interesting," Hellman said, discarding all the books except one.

"Let's eat first," Casker said, ripping the top off the box. Inside was a brownish dust. Casker looked at it, sniffed, and made a face.

"Very interesting indeed," Hellman said, leafing through the book.

Casker opened a small can, which contained a glittering green slime. He closed it and opened another. It contained a dull orange slime.

"Hmm," Hellman said, still reading.

"Hellman! Will you kindly drop that book and help me find some food?"

"Food?" Hellman repeated, looking up. "What makes you think there's anything to eat here? For all you know, this could be a paint factory."

"It's a warehouse!" Casker shouted.

He opened a kidney-shaped can and lifted out a soft purple stick. It hardened quickly and crumpled to dust as he tried to smell it. He scooped up a handful of the dust and brought it to his mouth.

"That might be extract of strychnine," Hellman said casually.

Casker abruptly dropped the dust and wiped his hands.

"After all," Hellman pointed out, "granted that this is a warehouse—a cache, if you wish—we don't know what the late inhabitants considered good fare. Paris Green salad, perhaps, with sulphuric acid as dressing."

"All right," Casker said, "but we gotta eat. What're you going to do about all this?" He gestured at the hundreds of boxes, cans and bottles.

"The thing to do," Hellman said briskly, "is to make a qualitative analysis on four or five samples. We could start out with a simple titration, sublimate the chief ingredient, see if it forms a precipitate, work out its molecular makeup from—"

"Hellman, you don't know what you're talking about. You're a librarian, remember? And I'm a correspondence school pilot. We don't know anything about titrations and sublimations."

"I know," Hellman said, "but we should. It's the right way to go about it."

"Sure. In the meantime, though, just until a chemist drops in, what'll we do?"

"This might help us," Hellman said, holding up the book. "Do you know what it is?"

"No," Casker said, keeping a tight grip on his patience.

"It's a pocket dictionary and guide to the Helg language."

"Helg?"

"The planet we're on. The symbols match up with those on the boxes."

Casker raised an eyebrow. "Never heard of Helg."

"I don't believe the planet has ever had any contact with Earth," Hellman said. "This dictionary isn't Helg-English. It's Helg-Aloombrigian."

Casker remembered that Aloombrigia was the home planet of a small, adventurous reptilian race, out near the center of the Galaxy.

"How come you can read Aloombrigian?" Casker asked.

"Oh, being a librarian isn't a completely useless profession," Hellman said modestly. "In my spare time—"

"Yeah. Now how about—"

"Do you know," Hellman said, "the Aloombrigians probably helped the Helgans leave their planet and find another. They sell services like that. In which case, this building very likely *is* a food cache!"

"Suppose you start translating," Casker suggested wearily, "and maybe find us something to eat."

They opened boxes until they found a likely-looking substance. Laboriously, Hellman translated the symbols on it.

"Got it," he said. "It reads:—'USE SNIFFNERS—THE BETTER ABRASIVE.'"

"Doesn't sound edible," Casker said.

"I'm afraid not."

They found another, which read: VIGROOM! FILL ALL YOUR STOMACHS, AND FILL THEM RIGHT!

"What kind of animals do you suppose these Helgans were?" Casker asked.

Hellman shrugged his shoulders.

The next label took almost fifteen minutes to translate.

It read: ARGOSEL MAKES YOUR THUDRA ALL TIZZY. CONTAINS THIRTY ARPS OF RAMSTAT PULZ, FOR SHELL LUBRICATION.

"There must be *something* here we can eat," Casker said with a note of desperation.

"I hope so," Hellman replied.

At the end of two hours, they were no closer. They had translated dozens of titles and sniffed so many substances that their olfactory senses had given up in disgust.

"Let's talk this over," Hellman said, sitting on a box marked: VORMITASH—GOOD AS IT SOUNDS!

"Sure," Casker said, sprawling out on the floor. "Talk."

"If we could deduce what kind of creatures inhabited this planet, we'd know what kind of food they ate, and whether it's likely to be edible for us."

"All we do know is that they wrote a lot of lousy advertising copy."

Hellman ignored that. "What kind of intelligent beings would evolve on a planet that is all mountains?"

"Stupid ones!" Casker said.

That was no help. But Hellman found that he couldn't draw any inferences from the mountains. It didn't tell him if the late Helgans ate silicates or proteins or iodine-base foods or anything.

"Now look," Hellman said, "we'll have to work this out by pure logic— Are you listening to me?"

"Sure," Casker said.

"Okay. There's an old proverb that covers our situation perfectly: 'One man's meat is another man's poison.'"

"Yeah," Casker said. He was positive his stomach had shrunk to approximately the size of a marble.

"We can assume, first, that their meat is our meat."

Casker wrenched himself away from a vision of five juicy roast beefs dancing tantalizingly before him. "What if their meat is our *poison?* What then?"

"Then," Hellman said, "we will assume that their poison is our meat."

"And what happens if their meat *and* their poison are our poison?"

"We starve."

"All right," Casker said, standing up. "Which assumption do we start with?"

"Well, there's no sense in asking for trouble. This *is* an oxygen planet, if that means anything. Let's assume that we can eat some basic food of theirs. If we can't we'll start on their poisons."

"If we live that long," Casker said.

Hellman began to translate labels. They discarded such brands as ANDROGYNITES DELIGHT and VERBELL—FOR LONGER, CURLIER, MORE SENSITIVE ANTENNAE until they found a small gray box, about six inches by

three by three. It was called VALKORIN'S UNIVERSAL TASTE TREAT, FOR ALL
DIGESTIVE CAPACITIES.

"This looks as good as any," Hellman said. He opened the box.

Casker leaned over and sniffed. "No odor."

Within the box they found a rectangular, rubbery red block. It quiv-
ered slightly, like jelly.

"Bite into it," Casker said.

"Me?" Hellman asked. "Why not you?"

"You picked it."

"I prefer just looking at it," Hellman said with dignity. "I'm not too
hungry."

"I'm not either," Casker said.

They sat on the floor and stared at the jellylike block. After ten minutes, Hellman yawned, leaned back and closed his eyes.

"All right, coward," Casker said bitterly. "I'll try it. Just remember,
though, if I'm poisoned, you'll never get off this planet. You don't know
how to pilot."

"Just take a little bite, then," Hellman advised.

Casker leaned over and stared at the block. Then he prodded it with
his thumb.

The rubbery red block giggled.

"Did you hear that?" Casker yelped, leaping back.

"I didn't hear anything," Hellman said, his hands shaking. "Go ahead."

Casker prodded the block again. It giggled louder, this time with a
disgusting little simper.

"Okay," Casker said, "what do we try next?"

"Next? What's wrong with this?"

"I don't eat anything that giggles," Casker stated firmly.

"Now listen to me," Hellman said. "The creatures who manufactured
this might have been trying to create an esthetic sound as well as a pleasant
shape and color. That giggle is probably only for the amusement of the eater."

"Then bite into it yourself," Casker offered.

Hellman glared at him, but made no move toward the rubbery block.
Finally he said, "Let's move it out of the way."

They pushed the block over to a corner. It lay there giggling softly to
itself.

"Now what?" Casker said.

Hellman looked around at the jumbled stacks of incomprehensible
alien goods. He noticed a door on either side of the room.

"Let's have a look in the other sections," he suggested.

Casker shrugged his shoulders apathetically.

Slowly they trudged to the door in the left wall. It was locked and
Hellman burned it open with the ship's burner.

It was a wedge-shaped room, piled with incomprehensible alien goods. The hike back across the room seemed like miles, but they made it only slightly out of wind. Hellman blew out the lock and they looked in. It was a wedge-shaped room, piled with incomprehensible alien goods. "All the same," Casker said sadly and closed the door.

"Evidently there's a series of these rooms going completely around the building," Hellman said. "I wonder if we should explore them."

Casker calculated the distance around the building, compared it with his remaining strength, and sat down heavily on a long gray object.

"Why bother?" he asked.

Hellman tried to collect his thoughts. Certainly he should be able to find a key of some sort, a clue that would tell him what they could eat. But where was it?

He examined the object Casker was sitting on. It was about the size and shape of a large coffin, with a shallow depression on top. It was made of a hard, corrugated substance.

"What do you suppose this is?" Hellman asked.

"Does it matter?"

Hellman glanced at the symbol painted on the side of the object then looked them up in his dictionary.

"Fascinating," he murmured after a while.

"Is it something to eat?" Casker asked with a faint glimmering of hope.

"No. You are sitting on something called THE MOROG CUSTOM SUPER TRANSPORT FOR THE DISCRIMINATING HELGAN WHO DESIRES THE BEST IN VERTICAL TRANSPORTATION. It's a vehicle!"

"Oh," Casker said dully.

"This is important! Look at it! How does it work?"

Casker wearily climbed off the Morog Custom Super Transport and looked it over carefully. He traced four almost invisible separations on its four corners. "Retractable wheels, probably, but I don't see—"

Hellman read on. "It says to give it three amphus of high-gain Integor fuel, then a van of Tonder lubrication, and not to run it over three thousand Ruls for the first fifty mungus."

"Let's find something to eat," Casker said.

"Don't you see how important this is?" Hellman asked. "This could solve our problem. If we could deduce the alien logic inherent in constructing this vehicle, we might know the Helgan thought pattern. This, in turn, would give us an insight into their nervous systems, which would imply their biochemical makeup."

Casker stood still, trying to decide whether he had enough strength left to strangle Hellman.

"For example," Hellman said, "what kind of vehicle would be used in a place like this? Not one with wheels, since everything is up and down.

Anti-gravity? Perhaps, but what *kind* of anti-gravity? And why did the inhabitants devise a boxlike form instead—"

Casker decided sadly that he didn't have enough strength to strangle Hellman, no matter how pleasant it might be. Very quietly, he said, "Kindly stop making like a scientist. Let's see if there isn't *something* we can gulp down."

"All right," Hellman said sulkily.

Casker watched his partner wander off among the cans, bottles and cases. He wondered vaguely where Hellman got the energy and decided that he was just too cerebral to know when he was starving.

"Here's something," Hellman called out, standing in front of a large yellow vat.

"What does it say?" Casker asked.

"Little bit hard to translate. But rendered freely, it reads: MORISHILLE'S VOOZY, WITH LACTOECTO ADDED FOR A NEW TASTE SENSATION. EVERYONE DRINKS VOOZY. GOOD BEFORE AND AFTER MEALS, NO UNPLEASANT AFTER-EF-FECTS. GOOD FOR CHILDREN! THE DRINK OF THE UNIVERSE!"

"That sounds good," Casker admitted, thinking that Hellman might not be so stupid after all.

"This should tell us once and for all if their meat *is* our meat," Hellman said. "This Voozy seems to be the closest thing to a universal drink I've found yet."

"Maybe," Casker said hopefully, "maybe it's just plain water!"

"We'll see." Hellman pried open the lid with the edge of the burner.

Within the vat was a crystal-clear liquid.

"No odor," Casker said, bending over the vat.

The crystal liquid lifted to meet him.

Casker retreated so rapidly that he fell over a box. Hellman helped him to his feet and they approached the vat again. As they came near, the liquid lifted itself three feet into the air and moved toward them.

"What've you done now?" Casker asked, moving back carefully. The liquid flowed slowly over the side of the vat. It began to flow toward him.

"Hellman!" Casker shrieked.

Hellman was standing to one side, perspiration pouring down his face, reading his dictionary with a preoccupied frown.

"Guess I bumbled the translation," he said.

"Do something!" Casker shouted. The liquid was trying to back him into a corner.

"Nothing I can do," Hellman said, reading on. "Ah, here's the error. It doesn't say 'Everyone drinks Voozy.' Wrong subject. 'Voozy drinks *everyone.*' That tells us something! The Helgans must have soaked liquid in through their pores. Naturally, they would prefer to be drunk, instead of to drink."

Casker tried to dodge around the liquid, but it cut him off with a merry gurgle. Desperately he picked up a small bale and threw it at the Voozy. The Voozy caught the bale and drank it. Then it discarded that and turned back to Casker.

Hellman tossed another box. The Voozy drank this one and a third and fourth that Casker threw in. Then, apparently exhausted, it flowed back into its vat.

Casker clapped down the lid and sat on it, trembling violently.

"Not so good," Hellman said. "We've been taking it for granted that the Helgans had eating habits like us. But, of course, it doesn't necessarily—"

"No, it doesn't. No, sir, it certainly doesn't. I guess we can see that it doesn't. Anyone can see that it doesn't—"

"Stop that," Hellman ordered sternly. "We've no time for hysteria."

"Sorry." Casker slowly moved away from the Voozy vat.

"I guess we'll have to assume that their meat is our poison," Hellman said thoughtfully. "So now we'll see if their poison is our meat."

Casker didn't say anything. He was wondering what would have happened if the Voozy had drunk him.

In the corner, the rubbery block was still giggling to itself.

"Now here's a likely-looking poison," Hellman said, half an hour later.

Casker had recovered completely, except for an occasional twitch of the lips.

"What does it say?" he asked.

Hellman rolled a tiny tube in the palm of his hand.

"It's called Pvastkin's Plugger. The label reads: WARNING! HIGHLY DANGEROUS! PVASTKIN'S PLUGGER IS DESIGNED TO FILL HOLES OR CRACKS OF NOT MORE THAN TWO CUBIC VIMS. HOWEVER—THE PLUGGER IS NOT TO BE EATEN UNDER ANY CIRCUMSTANCES. THE ACTIVE INGREDIENT, RAMOTOL, WHICH MAKES PVASTKIN'S SO EXCELLENT A PLUGGER RENDERS IT HIGHLY DANGEROUS WHEN TAKEN INTERNALLY."

"Sounds great," Casker said. "It'll probably blow us sky-high."

"Do you have any other suggestions?" Hellman asked.

Casker thought for a moment. The food of Helg was obviously unpalatable for humans. So perhaps was their poison...but wasn't starvation better than this sort of thing?

After a moment's communion with his stomach, he decided that starvation was *not* better.

"Go ahead," he said.

Hellman slipped the burner under his arm and unscrewed the top of the little bottle. He shook it.

Nothing happened.

"It's got a seal," Casker pointed out.

Hellman punctured the seal with his fingernail and set the bottle on the floor. An evil-smelling green froth began to bubble out.

Hellman looked dubiously at the froth. It was congealing into a glob and spreading over the floor.

"Yeast, perhaps," he said, gripping the burner tightly.

"Come, come. Faint heart never filled empty stomach."

"I'm not holding *you* back," Hellman said.

The glob swelled to the size of a man's head.

"How long is that supposed to go on?" Casker asked.

"Well," Hellman said, "it's advertised as a Plugger. I suppose that's what it does—expands to plug up holes."

"Sure. But how *much?*"

"Unfortunately, I don't know how much two cubic vims are. But it can't go on much—"

Belatedly, they noticed that the Plugger had filled almost a quarter of the room and was showing no signs of stopping.

"We should have believed the label!" Casker yelled to him, across the spreading glob. "It *is* dangerous!"

As the Plugger produced more surface, it began to accelerate in its growth. A sticky edge touched Hellman and he jumped back.

"Watch out!"

He couldn't reach Casker, on the other side of the gigantic sphere of blob. Hellman tried to run around, but the Plugger had spread, cutting the room in half. It began to swell toward the walls.

"Run for it!" Hellman yelled, and rushed to the door behind him.

He flung it open just as the expanding glob reached him. On the other side of the room, he heard a door slam shut. Hellman didn't wait any longer. He sprinted through and slammed the door behind him.

He stood for a moment, panting, the burner in his hand. He hadn't realized how weak he was. That sprint had cut his reserves of energy dangerously close to the collapsing point. At least Casker had made it, too, though.

But he was still in trouble.

The Plugger poured merrily through the blasted lock, into the room. Hellman tried a practice shot on it, but the Plugger was evidently impervious…as, he realized, a good plugger should be.

It was showing no signs of fatigue.

Hellman hurried to the far wall. The door was locked, as the others had been, so he burned out the lock and went through.

How far could the glob expand? How much was two cubic vims? Two cubic miles, perhaps? For all he knew, the Plugger was used to repair faults in the crusts of planets.

In the next room, Hellman stopped to catch his breath. He remembered that the building was circular. He would burn his way through the remaining doors and join Casker. They would burn their way outside and...

Casker didn't have a burner!

Hellman turned white with shock. Casker had made it into the room on the right, because they had burned it open earlier. The Plugger was undoubtedly oozing into that room, through the shattered lock...and Casker couldn't get out! The Plugger was on his left, a locked door on his right!

Rallying his remaining strength, Hellman began to run. Boxes seemed to get in his way purposefully, tripping him, slowing him down. He blasted the next door and hurried on to the next. And the next. And the next.

The Plugger couldn't expand *completely* into Casker's room! Or could it?

The wedge-shaped rooms, each a segment of a circle, seemed to stretch before him forever, a jumbled montage of locked doors, alien goods, more doors, more goods. Hellman fell over a crate, got to his feet, and fell again. He had reached the limit of his strength and passed it. But Casker was his friend.

Besides, without a pilot, he'd never get off the place.

Hellman struggled through two more rooms on trembling legs and then collapsed in front of a third.

"Is that you, Hellman?" he heard Casker ask, from the other side of the door.

"You all right?" Hellman managed to gasp.

"Haven't much room in here," Casker said, "but the Plugger's stopped growing. Hellman, get me out of here!"

Hellman lay on the floor panting. "Moment," he said.

"Moment, hell!" Casker shouted. "Get me out. I've found water!"

"What? How?"

"Get me out of here!"

Hellman tried to stand up, but his legs weren't cooperating. "What happened?" he asked.

"When I saw that glob filling the room, I figured I'd try to start up the Super Custom Transport. Thought maybe it could knock down the door and get me out. So I pumped it full of high-gain Integor fuel."

"Yes?" Hellman said, still trying to get his legs under control.

"That Super Custom Transport is an animal, Hellman! And the Integor fuel is water! Now get me out!"

Hellman lay back with a contented sigh. If he had had a little more time, he would have worked out the whole thing himself by pure logic. But it was all very apparent now. The most efficient machine to go over those vertical, razor-sharp mountains would be an animal, probably with retractable suckers. It was kept in hibernation between trips; and if it drank water, the other products designed for it would be palatable, too.

Of course they still didn't know much about the late inhabitants, but undoubtedly...

"Burn down that door!" Casker shrieked, his voice breaking.

Hellman was pondering the irony of it all. If one man's meat—*and* his poison—are your poison, then try eating something else. So simple, really.

But there was one thing that still bothered him.

"How did *you* know it was an Earth-type animal?" he asked.

"Its breath, stupid! It inhales and exhales and smells as if it's eaten onions!" There was a sound of cans falling and bottles shattering. "Now hurry!"

"What's wrong?" Hellman asked, finally getting to his feet and poising the burner.

"The Custom Super Transport. It's got me cornered behind a pile of cases. Hellman, it seems to think that I'm *its* meat!"

SOMETHING FOR NOTHING

But had he heard a voice? He couldn't be sure. Reconstructing it a moment later, Joe Collins knew he had been lying on his bed, too tired even to take his waterlogged shoes off the blanket. He had been staring at the network of cracks in the muddy yellow ceiling, watching water drip slowly and mournfully through.

It must have happened then. Collins caught a glimpse of metal beside his bed. He sat up. There was a machine on the floor, where no machine had been.

In that first moment of surprise, Collins thought he heard a very distant voice say, "There! *That* does it!"

He couldn't be sure of the voice. But the machine was undeniably there.

Collins knelt to examine it. The machine was about three feet square and it was humming softly. The crackle-gray surface was featureless, except for a red button in one corner and a brass plate in the center. The plate said, CLASS-A UTILIZER, SERIES AA-1256432. And underneath, WARNING! THIS MACHINE SHOULD BE USED ONLY BY CLASS-A RATINGS!

That was all.

There were no knobs, dials, switches or any of the other attachments Collins associated with machines. Just the brass plate, the red button, and the hum.

"Where did you come from?" Collins asked. The Class-A Utilizer continued to hum. He hadn't really expected an answer. Sitting on the edge of his bed, he stared thoughtfully at the Utilizer. The question now was—what to do with it?

He touched the red button warily, aware of his lack of experience with machines that fell from nowhere. When he turned it on, would the floor open up? Would little green men drop from the ceiling?

But he had slightly less than nothing to lose. He pressed the button lightly.

Nothing happened.

97

"All right—*do* something," Collins said, feeling definitely let down. The Utilizer only continued to hum softly.

Well, he could always pawn it. Honest Charlie would give him at least a dollar for the metal. He tried to lift the Utilizer. It wouldn't lift. He tried again, exerting all his strength, and succeeded in raising one corner an inch from the floor. He released it and sat down on the bed, breathing heavily.

"You should have sent a couple of men to help me," Collins told the Utilizer. Immediately, the hum grew louder and the machine started to vibrate.

Collins watched, but still nothing happened. On a hunch, he reached out and stabbed the red button.

Immediately, two bulky men appeared, dressed in rough work-clothes. They looked at the Utilizer appraisingly. One of them said, "Thank God, it's the small model. The big ones is brutes to get a grip on."

The other man said, "It beats the marble quarry, don't it?"

They looked at Collins, who stared back. Finally the first man said, "Okay, Mac, we ain't got all day. Where you want it?"

"Who are you?" Collins managed to croak.

"The moving men. Do we look like the Vanizaggi Sisters?"

"But where do you come from?" Collins asked. "And *why?*"

"We come from the Powha Minnile Movers, Incorporated," the man said. "And we come because you wanted movers, that's why. Now, where you want it?"

"Go away," Collins said. "I'll call for you later."

The moving men shrugged their shoulders and vanished. For several minutes, Collins stared at the spot where they had been. Then he stared at the Class-A Utilizer, which was humming softly again.

Utilizer? He could give it a better name.

A Wishing Machine.

Collins was not particularly shocked. When the miraculous occurs, only dull, workaway mentalities are unable to accept it. Collins was certainly not one of those. He had an excellent background for acceptance.

Most of his life had been spent wishing, hoping, praying that something marvelous would happen to him. In high school, he had dreamed of waking up some morning with an ability to know his homework without the tedious necessity of studying it. In the army, he had wished for some witch or jinn to change his orders, putting him in charge of the day room, instead of forcing him to do close-order drill like everyone else.

Out of the army, Collins had avoided work, for which he was psychologically unsuited. He had drifted around, hoping that some fabulously wealthy person would be induced to change his will, leaving him Everything.

He had never really expected anything to happen. But he was prepared when it did.

"I'd like a thousand dollars in small unmarked bills," Collins said cautiously. When the hum grew louder, he pressed the button. In front of him appeared a large mound of soiled singles, five and ten dollar bills. They were not crisp, but they certainly were money.

Collins threw a handful in the air and watched it settle beautifully to the floor. He lay on his bed and began making plans.

First, he would get the machine out of New York—upstate, perhaps—some place where he wouldn't be bothered by nosy neighbors. The income tax would be tricky on this sort of thing. Perhaps, after he got organized, he should go to Central America, or...

There was a suspicious noise in the room.

Collins leaped to his feet. A hole was opening in the wall, and someone was forcing his way through.

"*Hey*, I didn't ask you anything!" Collins told the machine.

The hole grew larger, and a large, red-faced man was halfway through, pushing angrily at the hole.

At that moment, Collins remembered that machines usually have owners. Anyone who owned a wishing machine wouldn't take kindly to having it gone. He would go to any lengths to recover it. Probably, he wouldn't stop short of—

"Protect me!" Collins shouted at the Utilizer, and stabbed the red button.

A small, bald man in loud pajamas appeared, yawning sleepily. "Sanisa Leek, Temporal Wall Protection Service," he said, rubbing his eyes. "I'm Leek. What can I do for you?"

"Get him out of here!" Collins screamed. The red-faced man, waving his arms wildly, was almost through the hole.

Leek found a bit of bright metal in his pajamas pocket. The red-faced man shouted, "Wait! You don't understand! That man—"

Leek pointed his piece of metal. The red-faced man screamed and vanished. In another moment the hole had vanished too.

"Did you kill him?" Collins asked.

"Of course not," Leek said, putting away the bit of metal. "I just veered him back through his glommatch. He won't try *that* way again."

"You mean he'll try some other way?" Collins asked.

"It's possible," Leek said. "He could attempt a microtransfer, or even an animation." He looked sharply at Collins. "This is your Utilizer, isn't it?"

"Of course," Collins said, starting to perspire.

"And you're an A-rating?"

"Naturally," Collins told him. "If I wasn't, what would I be doing with a Utilizer?"

"No offense," Leek said drowsily, "just being friendly." He shook his head slowly. "How you A's get around! I suppose you've come back here to do a history book?"

Collins just smiled enigmatically.

"I'll be on my way," Leek said, yawning copiously. "On the go, night and day. I'd be better off in a quarry."

And he vanished in the middle of a yawn.

Rain was still beating against the ceiling. Across the airshaft, the snoring continued, undisturbed. Collins was alone again, with the machine.

And with a thousand dollars in small bills scattered around the floor, He patted the Utilizer affectionately. Those A-ratings had it pretty good. Want something? Just ask for it and press a button. Undoubtedly, the real owner missed it.

Leek had said that the man might try to get in some other way. What way?

What did it matter? Collins gathered up the bills, whistling softly. As long as he had the wishing machine, he could take care of himself.

The next few days marked a great change in Collins' fortunes. With the aid of the Powha Minnile Movers he took the Utilizer to upstate New York. There, he bought a medium-sized mountain in a neglected corner of the Adirondacks. Once the papers were in his hands, he walked to the center of his property, several miles from the highway. The two movers, sweating profusely, lugged the Utilizer behind him, cursing monotonously as they broke through the dense underbrush.

"Set it down here and scram," Collins said. The last few days had done a lot for his confidence.

The moving men sighed wearily and vanished. Collins looked around. On all sides, as far as he could see, was closely spaced forest of birch and pine. The air was sweet and damp. Birds were chirping merrily in the treetops, and an occasional squirrel darted by.

Nature! He had always loved nature. This would be the perfect spot to build a large, impressive house with swimming pool, tennis courts and, possibly, a small airport.

"I want a house," Collins stated firmly, and pushed the red button.

A man in a neat gray business suit and pince-nez appeared. "Yes, sir," he said, squinting at the trees, "but you really must be more specific. Do you want something classic, like a bungalow, ranch, split-level, mansion, castle, or palace? Or primitive, like an igloo or hut? Since you are an A, you could have something up-to-the-minute, like a semiface, an Extended New or a Sunken Miniature."

"Huh?" Collins said. "I don't know. What would you suggest?"

"Small mansion," the man said promptly. "They usually start with that."

"They do?"

"Oh, yes. Later, they move to a warm climate and build a palace." Collins wanted to ask more questions, but he decided against it. Everything was going smoothly. These people thought he was an A, and the true owner of the Utilizer. There was no sense in disenchanting them.

"You take care of it all," he told the man.

"Yes, sir," the man said. "I usually do."

The rest of the day, Collins reclined on a couch and drank iced beverages while the Maxima Olph Construction Company materialized equipment and put up his house.

It was a low-slung affair of some twenty rooms, which Collins considered quite modest under the circumstances. It was built only of the best materials, from a design of Mig of Degma, interior by Towige, a Mula swimming pool, and formal gardens by Vierien.

By evening, it was completed, and the small army of workmen packed up their equipment and vanished.

Collins allowed his chef to prepare a light supper for him. Afterward, he sat in his large, cool living room to think the whole thing over. In front of him, humming gently, sat the Utilizer.

Collins lighted a cheroot and sniffed the aroma. First of all, he rejected any supernatural explanations. There were no demons or devils involved in this. His house had been built by ordinary human beings, who swore and laughed and cursed like human beings. The Utilizer was simply a scientific gadget, which worked on principles he didn't understand or care to understand.

Could it have come from another planet? Not likely. They wouldn't have learned English just for him.

The Utilizer must have come from the Earth's future. But how?

Collins leaned back and puffed his cheroot. Accidents will happen, he reminded himself. Why couldn't the Utilizer have just *slipped* into the past? After all, it could create something from nothing, and that was much more complicated.

What a wonderful future it must be, he thought. Wishing machines! How marvelously civilized! All a person had to do was think of something. Presto! There it was. In time, perhaps, they'd eliminate the red button. Then there'd be no manual labor involved.

Of course, he'd have to watch his step. There was still the owner—and the rest of the A's. They would try to take the machine from him. Probably, they were a hereditary clique...

A movement caught the edge of his eye and he looked up. The Utilizer was quivering like a leaf in a gale.

Collins walked up to it, frowning blackly. A faint mist of steam surrounded the trembling Utilizer. It seemed to be overheating.

Could he have overworked it? Perhaps a bucket of water…

Then he noticed that the Utilizer was perceptibly smaller. It was no more than two feet square and shrinking before his eyes.

The owner! Or perhaps the A's! This must be the microtransfer that Leek had talked about. If he didn't do something quickly, Collins knew, his wishing machine would dwindle to nothingness and disappear.

"Leek Protection Service," Collins snapped. He punched the button and withdrew his hand quickly. The machine was very hot.

Leek appeared in a comer of the room, wearing slacks and a sports shirt, and carrying a golf club. "Must I be disturbed every time I—"

"*Do something!*" Collins shouted, pointing to the Utilizer, which was now only a foot square and glowing a dull red.

"Nothing I can do," Leek said. "Temporal wall is all I'm licensed for. You want the microcontrol people." He hefted his golf club and was gone.

"Microcontrol," Collins said, and reached for the button. He withdrew his hand hastily. The Utilizer was only about four inches on a side now and glowing a hot cherry red. He could barely see the button, which was the size of a pin.

Collins whirled around, grabbed a cushion and punched down.

A girl with horn-rimmed glasses appeared, notebook in hand, pencil poised. "With whom did you wish to make an appointment?" she asked sedately.

"Get me help fast!" Collins roared, watching his precious Utilizer grow smaller and smaller.

"Mr. Vergon is out to lunch," the girl said, biting her pencil thoughtfully. "He's de-zoned himself. I can't reach him."

"Who *can* you reach?"

She consulted her notebook. "Mr. Vis is in the Dieg Continuum and Mr. Elgis is doing field work in Paleolithic Europe. If you're really in a rush, maybe you'd better call Transferpoint Control. They're a smaller outfit, but—"

"Transferpoint Control. Okay—scram." He turned his full attention to the Utilizer and stabbed down on it with the scorched pillow. Nothing happened. The Utilizer was barely half an inch square, and Collins realized that the cushion hadn't been able to depress the almost invisible button.

For a moment Collins considered letting the Utilizer go. Maybe this was the time. He could sell the house, the furnishings, and still be pretty well off…

No! He hadn't wished for anything important yet! No one was going to take it from him without a struggle.

He forced himself to keep his eyes open as he stabbed the white-hot button with a rigid forefinger.

A thin, shabbily dressed old man appeared, holding something that looked like a gaily colored Easter egg. He threw it down. The egg burst and an orange smoke billowed out and was sucked directly into the infinitesimal Utilizer. A great billow of smoke went up, almost choking Collins. Then the Utilizer's shape started to form again. Soon, it was normal size and apparently undamaged. The old man nodded curtly.

"We're not fancy," he said, "but we're reliable." He nodded again and disappeared.

Collins thought he could hear a distant shout of anger.

Shakily, he sat down on the floor in front of the machine. His hand was throbbing painfully.

"Fix me up," he muttered through dry lips, and punched the button with his good hand.

The Utilizer hummed louder for a moment, then was silent. The pain left his scorched finger and, looking down, Collins saw that there was no sign of a burn—not even scar tissue to mark where it had been.

Collins poured himself a long shot of brandy and went directly to bed. That night, he dreamed he was being chased by a gigantic letter A, but he didn't remember it in the morning.

Within a week, Collins found that building his mansion in the woods had been precisely the wrong thing to do. He had to hire a platoon of guards to keep away sightseers, and hunters insisted on camping in his formal gardens.

Also, the Bureau of Internal Revenue began to take a lively interest in his affairs.

But, above all, Collins discovered he wasn't so fond of nature after all. Birds and squirrels were all very well, but they hardly ranked as conversationalists. Trees, though quite ornamental, made poor drinking companions.

Collins decided he was a city boy at heart.

Therefore, with the aid of the Powha Minnile Movers, the Maxima Olph Construction Corporation, the Jagton Instantaneous Travel Bureau, and a great deal of money placed in the proper hands, Collins moved to a small Central American republic. There, since the climate was warmer and income tax nonexistent, he built a large, airy, ostentatious palace.

It came equipped with the usual accessories—horses, dogs, peacocks, servants, maintenance men, guards, musicians, bevies of dancing girls, and everything else a palace should have. Collins spent two weeks just exploring the place.

Everything went along nicely for a while.

One morning Collins approached the Utilizer, with the vague intention of asking for a sports-car, or possibly a small herd of pedigreed cattle. He bent over the gray machine, reached for the red button...

And the Utilizer backed away from him.

For a moment, Collins thought he was seeing things, and he almost decided to stop drinking champagne before breakfast. He took a step forward and reached for the red button.

The Utilizer sidestepped him neatly and trotted out of the room.

Collins sprinted after it, cursing the owner and the A's. This was probably the animation that Leek had spoken about—somehow, the owner had managed to imbue the machine with mobility. It didn't matter. All he had to do was catch up, punch the button and ask for the Animation Control people.

The Utilizer raced down a hall, Collins close behind. An under-butler, polishing a solid gold doorknob, stared openmouthed.

"Stop it!" Collins shouted.

The under-butler moved clumsily into the Utilizer's path. The machine dodged him gracefully and sprinted toward the main door.

Collins pushed a switch and the door slammed shut.

The Utilizer gathered momentum and went right through it. Once in the open, it tripped over a garden hose, regained its balance and headed toward the open countryside.

Collins raced after it. If he could get just a little closer...

The Utilizer suddenly leaped into the air. It hung there for a long moment, then fell to the ground. Collins sprang at the button.

The Utilizer rolled out of his way, took a short run and leaped again. For a moment, it hung twenty feet above his head—drifted a few feet straight up, stopped, twisted wildly and fell.

Collins was afraid that, on a third jump, it would keep going up. When it drifted unwillingly back to the ground, he was ready. He feinted, then stabbed at the button. The Utilizer couldn't duck fast enough.

"Animation Control!" Collins roared triumphantly.

There was a small explosion, and the Utilizer settled down docilely. There was no hint of animation left in it.

Collins wiped his forehead and sat on the machine. Closer and closer. He'd better do some big wishing now, while he still had the chance.

In rapid succession, he asked for five million dollars, three functioning oil wells, a motion-picture studio, perfect health, twenty-five more dancing girls, immortality, a sports car and a herd of pedigreed cattle.

He thought he heard someone snicker. He looked around. No one was there.

When he turned back, the Utilizer had vanished.

He just stared. And, in another moment, *he* vanished.

When he opened his eyes, Collins found himself standing in front of a desk. On the other side was the large, red-faced man who had originally tried to break into his room. The man didn't appear angry. Rather, he appeared resigned, even melancholy.

Collins stood for a moment in silence, sorry that the whole thing was over. The owner and the A's had finally caught him. But it had been glorious while it lasted.

"Well," Collins said directly, "you've got your machine back. Now, what else do you want?"

"*My* machine?" the red-faced man said, looking up incredulously. "It's not my machine, sir. Not at all."

Collins stared at him. "Don't try to kid me, mister. You A-ratings want to protect your monopoly, don't you?"

The red-faced man put down his paper. "Mr. Collins," he said stiffly, "my name is Flign. I am an agent for the Citizens Protective Union, a non-profit organization, whose aim is to protect individuals such as yourself from errors of judgment."

"You mean you're not one of the A's?"

"You are laboring under a misapprehension, sir," Flign said with quiet dignity. "The A-rating does not represent a social group, as you seem to believe. It is merely a credit rating."

"A what?" Collins asked slowly.

"A credit rating." Flign glanced at his watch. "We haven't much time, so I'll make this as brief as possible. Ours is a decentralized age, Mr. Collins. Our businesses, industries and services are scattered through an appreciable portion of space and time. The utilization corporation is an essential link. It provides for the transfer of goods and services from point to point. Do you understand?"

Collins nodded.

"Credit is, of course, an automatic privilege. But, eventually, everything must be paid for."

Collins didn't like the sound of that. *Pay?* This place wasn't as civilized as he had thought. No one had mentioned paying. Why did they bring it up now?

"Why didn't someone stop me?" he asked desperately. "They must have known I didn't have a proper rating."

Flign shook his head. "The credit ratings are suggestions, not laws. In a civilized world, an individual has the right to his own decisions. I'm very sorry, sir." He glanced at his watch again and handed Collins the paper he had been reading.

"Would you just glance at this bill and tell me whether it's in order?"

Collins took the paper and read:

```
One Palace, with Accessories ..... Cr.  450,000,000
Services of Maxima Olph Movers ........... 111,000
122 Dancing Girls ......................... 122,000,000
Perfect Health ................................. 888,234,031
```

He scanned the rest of the list quickly. The total came to slightly better than eighteen billion Credits.

"Wait a minute!" Collins shouted. "I can't be held to this! The Utilizer just dropped into my room by accident!"

"That's the very fact I'm going to bring to their attention," Flign said. "Who knows? Perhaps they will be reasonable. It does no harm to try."

Collins felt the room sway. Flign's face began to melt before him.

"Time's up," Flign said. "Good luck."

Collins closed his eyes.

When he opened them again, he was standing on a bleak plain, facing a range of stubby mountains. A cold wind lashed his face and the sky was the color of steel.

A raggedly dressed man was standing beside him. "Here," the man said and handed Collins a pick.

"What's this?"

"This is a pick," the man said patiently. "And over there is a quarry, where you and I and a number of others will cut marble."

"Marble?"

"Sure. There's always some idiot who wants a palace," the man said with a wry grin. "You can call me Jang. We'll be together for some time."

Collins blinked stupidly. "How long?"

"You work it out," Jang said. "The rate is fifty credits a month until your debt is paid off."

The pick dropped from Collins' hand. They couldn't do this to him! The Utilization Corporation must realize its mistake by now! *They* had been at fault, letting the machine slip into the past. Didn't they realize that?

"It's all a mistake!" Collins said.

"No mistake," Jang said. "They're very short of labor. Have to go recruiting all over for it. Come on. After the first thousand years you won't mind it."

Collins started to follow Jang toward the quarry. He stopped.

"The first *thousand* years? I won't live that long!"

"Sure you will," Jang assured him. "You got immortality, didn't you?"

Yes, he had. He had wished for it, just before they took back the machine. Or had they taken back the machine *after* he wished for it? Collins remembered something. Strange, but he didn't remember seeing immortality on the bill Flign had showed him.

"How much did they charge me for immortality?" he asked.

Jang looked at him and laughed. "Don't be naïve, pal. You should have it figured out by now."

He led Collins toward the quarry. "Naturally, they give *that* away for nothing."

THE ACCOUNTANT

Mr. Dee was seated in the big armchair, his belt loosened, the evening papers strewn around his knees. Peacefully he smoked his pipe, and considered how wonderful the world was. Today he had sold two amulets and a philter; his wife was bustling around the kitchen, preparing a delicious meal; and his pipe was drawing well. With a sigh of contentment, Mr. Dee yawned and stretched.

Morton, his nine-year-old son, hurried across the living room, laden down with books.

"How'd school go today?" Mr. Dee called.

"Okay," the boy said, slowing down, but still moving toward his room.

"What have you got there?" Mr. Dee asked, gesturing at his son's tall pile of books.

"Just some more accounting stuff," Morton said, not looking at his father. He hurried into his room.

Mr. Dee shook his head. Somewhere, the lad had picked up the notion that he wanted to be an accountant. An accountant! True, Morton was quick with figures; but he would have to forget this nonsense. Bigger things were in store for him.

The doorbell rang.

Mr. Dee tightened his belt, hastily stuffed in his shirt and opened the front door. There stood Miss Greeb, his son's fourth-grade teacher.

"Come in, Miss Greeb," said Dee. "Can I offer something?"

"I have no time," said Miss Greeb. She stood in the doorway, her arms akimbo. With her gray, tangled hair, her thin, long-nosed face and red, runny eyes, she looked exactly like a witch. And this was as it should be, for Miss Greeb *was* a witch.

"I've come to speak to you about your son," she said.

At this moment Mrs. Dee hurried out of the kitchen, wiping her hands on her apron.

"I hope he hasn't been naughty," Mrs. Dee said anxiously.

Miss Greeb sniffed ominously. "Today I gave the yearly tests. Your son failed miserably."

"Oh, dear," Mrs. Dee said. "It's Spring. Perhaps—"

"Spring has nothing to do with it," said Miss Greeb. "Last week I assigned the Greater Spells of Cordus, section one. You know how easy *they* are. He didn't learn a single one."

"Hm," said Mr. Dee succinctly.

"In Biology, he doesn't have the slightest notion which are the basic conjuring herbs. Not the slightest."

"This is unthinkable," said Mr. Dee.

Miss Greeb laughed sourly. "Moreover, he has forgotten all the Secret Alphabet which he learned in third grade. He has forgotten the Protective Formula, forgotten the names of the ninety-nine lesser imps of the Third Circle, forgotten what little he knew of the Geography of Greater Hell. And what's more, he doesn't want to learn."

Mr. and Mrs. Dee looked at each other silently. This was very serious indeed. A certain amount of boyish inattentiveness was allowable—encouraged, even, for it showed spirit. But a child *had* to learn the basics if he ever hoped to become a full-fledged wizard.

"I can tell you right here and now," said Miss Greeb, "if this were the old days, I'd flunk him without another thought. But there are so few of us left."

Mr. Dee nodded sadly. Witchcraft had been steadily declining over the centuries. The old families died out, or were snatched by demoniac forces, or became scientists. And the fickle public showed no interest whatsoever in the charms and enchantments of ancient days.

Now only a scattered handful possessed the Old Lore, guarding it, teaching it in places like Miss Greeb's private school for the children of wizards. It was a heritage, a sacred trust.

"It's this accounting nonsense," said Miss Greeb. "I don't know where he got the notion." She stared accusingly at Dee. "And I don't know why it wasn't nipped in the bud."

Mr. Dee felt his cheeks grow hot.

"But I do know this. As long as Morton has *that* on his mind, he can't give his attention to Thaumaturgy."

Mr. Dee looked away from the witch's red eyes. It was his own fault. He should never have brought home that toy adding machine. And when he first saw Morton playing at double-entry bookkeeping, he should have burned the ledger.

But how could he have known it would grow into an obsession?

Mrs. Dee smoothed out her apron and said, "Miss Greeb, you know you have our complete confidence. What would you suggest?"

"All I can do I have done," said Miss Greeb. "The only remaining thing is to call up Boarbas, the Demon of Children. And that, naturally, is up to you."

"Oh, surely it's not that serious yet," Mr. Dee said quickly. "Calling up Boarbas is a serious measure."

"As I said, that's up to you," Miss Greeb said. "Call Boarbas or not, as you see fit. As things stand now, your son will never be a wizard." She turned and started to leave.

"Won't you stay for a cup of tea?" Mrs. Dee asked hastily.

"No, I must attend a Witches' Coven in Cincinnati," said Miss Greeb, and vanished in a puff of orange smoke.

Mr. Dee fanned the smoke with his hands and closed the door. "Phew," he said. "You'd think she'd use a perfumed brand."

"She's old-fashioned," Mrs. Dee murmured.

They stood beside the door in silence. Mr. Dee was just beginning to feel the shock. It was hard to believe that his son, his own flesh and blood, didn't want to carry on the family tradition. It couldn't be true!

"After dinner," Dee said finally, "I'll have a man-to-man talk with him. I'm sure we won't need any demoniac intervention."

"Good," Mrs. Dee said. "I'm sure you can make the boy understand." She smiled, and Dee caught a glimpse of the old witch-light flickering behind her eyes.

"My roast!" Mrs. Dee gasped suddenly, the witch-light dying. She hurried back to her kitchen.

Dinner was a quiet meal. Morton knew that Miss Greeb had been there, and he ate in guilty silence, glancing occasionally at his father. Mr. Dee sliced and served the roast, frowning deeply. Mrs. Dee didn't even attempt any small talk.

After bolting his dessert, the boy hurried to his room.

"Now we'll see," Mr. Dee said to his wife. He finished the last of his coffee, wiped his mouth, and stood up. "I am going to reason with him now. Where is my Amulet of Persuasion?"

Mrs. Dee thought deeply for a moment. Then she walked across the room to the bookcase. "Here it is," she said, lifting it from the pages of a brightly jacketed novel. "I was using it as a marker."

Mr. Dee slipped the amulet into his pocket, took a deep breath, and entered his son's room.

Morton was seated at his desk. In front of him was a notebook scribbled with figures and tiny, precise notations. On his desk were six carefully sharpened pencils, a soap eraser, an abacus, and a toy adding machine. His books hung precariously over the edge of the desk; there was *Money*, by Rimraamer, *Bank Accounting Practice*, by Johnson and Calhoun, *Ellman's Studies for the CPA*, and a dozen others.

Mr. Dee pushed aside a mound of clothes and made room for himself on the bed. "How's it going, son?" he asked in his kindest voice.

"Fine, Dad," Morton answered eagerly. "I'm up to Chapter Four in *Basic Accounting*, and I answered all the questions—"

"Son," Dee broke in, speaking very softly, "how about your regular homework?"

Morton looked uncomfortable and scuffed his feet on the floor.

"You know, not many boys have a chance to become wizards in this day and age."

"Yes sir, I know." Morton looked away abruptly. In a high, nervous voice he said, "But, Dad, I want to be an accountant. I really do, Dad."

Mr. Dee shook his head. "Morton, there's always been a wizard in our family. For eighteen hundred years, the Dees have been famous in supernatural circles."

Morton continued to look out the window and scuff his feet.

"You wouldn't want to disappoint me, would you, son?" Dee smiled sadly. "You know, anyone can be an *accountant*. But only a chosen few can master the Black Arts."

Morton turned away from the window. He picked up a pencil, inspected the point, and began to turn it slowly in his fingers.

"How about it, boy? Won't you work harder for Miss Greeb?"

Morton shook his head. "I want to be an accountant."

Mr. Dee contained his sudden rush of anger with difficulty. What was wrong with the Amulet of Persuasion? Could the spell have run down? He should have recharged it. Nevertheless, he went on.

"Morton," he said in a husky voice. "I'm only a Third Degree Adept, you know. My parents were very poor. They couldn't send me to The University."

"I know," the boy said in a whisper."

"I want you to have all the things I never had. Morton, you can be a First Degree Adept." He shook his head wistfully. "It'll be difficult. But your mother and I have a little put away, and we'll scrape the rest together somehow."

Morton was biting his lip and turning the pencil rapidly in his fingers.

"How about it, son? You know, as a First Degree Adept, you won't have to work in a store. You can be a Direct Agent of The Black One. A Direct Agent! What do you say, boy?"

For a moment, Dee thought his son was moved. Morton's lips were parted, and there was a suspicious brightness in his eyes. But then the boy glanced at his accounting books, his little abacus, his toy adding machine.

"I'm going to be an accountant," he said.

"We'll see!" Mr. Dee shouted, all patience gone. "You will *not* be an accountant, young man. You will be a wizard. It was good enough for the rest of your family, and by all that's damnable, it'll be good enough for you. You haven't heard the last of this, young man." And he stormed out of the room.

Immediately Morton returned to his accounting books.

Mr. and Mrs. Dee sat together on the couch, not talking. Mrs. Dee was busily knitting a wind-cord, but her mind wasn't on it. Mr. Dee stared moodily at a worn spot on the living room rug.

Finally, Dee said, "I've spoiled him. Boarbas is the only solution."

"Oh, no," Mrs. Dee said hastily. "He's so young."

"Do you want your son to be an accountant?" Mr. Dee asked bitterly. "Do you want him to grow up scribbling figures instead of doing The Black One's important work?"

"Of course not," said Mrs. Dee. "But Boarbas—"

"I know. I feel like a murderer already."

They thought for a few moments. Then Mrs. Dee said, "Perhaps his grandfather can do something. He was always fond of the boy."

"Perhaps he can," Mr. Dee said thoughtfully. "But I don't know if we should disturb him. After all, the old gentleman has been dead for three years."

"I know," Mrs. Dee said, undoing an incorrect knot in the wind-cord. "But it's either that or Boarbas."

Mr. Dee agreed. Unsettling as it would be to Morton's grandfather, Boarbas was infinitely worse. Immediately, Dee made preparations for calling up his dead father.

He gathered together the henbane, the ground unicorn's horn, and the hemlock. He added a morsel of dragon's tooth and put them all on the rug.

"Where's my wand?" he asked his wife.

"I put it in the bag with your golfsticks," she told him.

Mr. Dee got his wand and waved it over the ingredients. He muttered the three words of The Unbinding, and called out his father's name.

Immediately a wisp of smoke arose from the rug.

"Hello, Grandpa Dee," Mrs. Dee said.

"Dad, I'm sorry to disturb you," Mr. Dee said. "But my son—your grandson—refuses to become a wizard. He wants to be an—accountant."

The wisp of smoke trembled, then straightened out and described a character of the Old Language.

"Yes," Mr. Dee said. "We tried persuasion. The boy is adamant."

Again the smoke trembled and formed another character.

"I suppose that's best," Mr Dee said. "If you frighten him out of his wits once and for all, he'll forget this accounting nonsense. It's cruel—but it's better than Boarbas."

The wisp of smoke nodded, and streamed toward the boy's room. Mr. and Mrs. Dee sat down on the couch.

The door of Morton's room was slammed open, as though by a gigantic wind. Morton looked up, frowned, and returned to his books.

The wisp of smoke turned into a winged lion with the tail of a shark. It roared hideously, crouched, snarled, and gathered itself for a spring.

Morton glanced at it, raised both eyebrows, and proceeded to jot down a column of figures.

The lion changed into a three-headed lizard, its flanks reeking horribly of blood. Breathing gusts of fire, the lizard advanced on the boy.

Morton finished adding the column of figures, checked the result on his abacus, and looked at the lizard.

With a screech, the lizard changed into a giant gibbering bat. It fluttered around the boy's head, moaning and gibbering.

Morton grinned, and turned back to his books.

Mr. Dee was unable to stand it any longer. "Damn it," he shouted, "aren't you scared?"

"Why should I be?" Morton asked. "It's only Grandpa."

Upon the word, the bat dissolved into a plume of smoke. It nodded sadly to Mr. Dee, bowed to Mrs. Dee, and vanished.

"Good-bye, Grandpa," Morton called. He got up and closed his door.

"That does it," Mr. Dee said. "The boy is too cocksure of himself. We must call up Boarbas."

"No!" his wife said.

"What, then?"

"I just don't know anymore," Mrs. Dee said, on the verge of tears. "You *know* what Boarbas does to children. They're never the same afterward."

Mr. Dee's face was as hard as granite. "I know. It can't be helped."

"He's so young!" Mrs. Dee wailed. "It—it will be traumatic!"

"If so, we will use all the resources of modern psychology to heal him," Mr. Dee said soothingly. "He will have the best psychoanalysts money can buy. But the boy must be a wizard!"

"Go ahead, then," Mrs. Dee said, crying openly. "But please don't ask me to assist you."

How like a woman, Dee thought. Always turning into jelly at the moment when firmness was indicated. With a heavy heart he made the preparations for calling up Boarbas, Demon of Children.

First came the intricate sketching of the pentagon, the twelve-pointed star within it, and the endless spiral within that. Then came the herbs and essences—expensive items, but absolutely necessary for the conjuring. Then came the inscribing of the Protective Spell, so that Boarbas might not break loose and destroy them all. Then came the three drops of hippogriff blood—

"Where is my hippogriff blood?" Mr. Dee asked, rummaging through the living room cabinet.

"In the kitchen, in the aspirin bottle," Mrs. Dee said, wiping her eyes.

Dee found it, and then all was in readiness. He lighted the black candles and chanted the Unlocking Spell.

The room was suddenly very warm, and there remained only the Naming of the Name.

"Morton," Mr. Dee called. "Come here."

Morton opened the door and stepped out, holding one of his accounting books tightly, looking very young and defenseless.

"Morton, I am about to call up the Demon of Children. Don't make me do it, Morton."

The boy turned pale and shrank back against the door. But stubbornly he shook his head.

"Very well," Mr. Dee said. "BOARBAS!"

There was an earsplitting clap of thunder and a wave of heat, and Boarbas appeared, as tall as the ceiling, chuckling evilly.

"Ah!" cried Boarbas, in a voice that shook the room. "A little boy."

Morton gaped, his jaw open and eyes bulging.

"A naughty little boy," Boarbas said, and laughed. The demon marched forward, shaking the house with every stride.

"Send him away!" Mrs. Dee cried.

"I can't," Dee said, his voice breaking. "I can't do anything until he's finished."

The demon's great horned hands reached for Morton; but quickly the boy opened the accounting book. "Save me!" he screamed.

In that instant, a tall, terribly thin old man appeared, covered with worn pen points and ledger sheets, his eyes two empty zeros.

"Zico Pico Reel!" chanted Boarbas, turning to grapple with the newcomer. But the thin old man laughed and said, "A contract of a corporation which is *ultra vires* is not voidable only, but utterly void."

At these words, Boarbas was flung back, breaking a chair as he fell. He scrambled to his feet, his skin glowing red-hot with rage, and intoned the Demoniac Master-Spell: "VRAT, HAT, HO!"

But the thin old man shielded Morton with his body, and cried the words of Dissolution. "Expiration, Repeal, Occurrence, Surrender, Abandonment, and Death!"

Boarbas squeaked in agony. Hastily he backed away, fumbling in the air until he found The Opening. He jumped through this, and was gone.

The tall, thin old man turned to Mr. and Mrs. Dee, cowering in a corner of the living room. He said, "Know that I am The Accountant. And Know, Moreover, that this Child has signed a Compact with Me, to enter My Apprenticeship and be My Servant. And in return for Services Rendered, I, THE ACCOUNTANT, am teaching him the Damnation of Souls by means of ensnaring them in a cursed web of Figures, Forms, Torts and Reprisals; And behold, this is My Mark upon him!"

The Accountant held up Morton's right hand, and showed the ink smudge on the third finger.

He turned to Morton, and in a softer voice said, "Tomorrow, lad, we will consider some aspects of Income Tax Evasion as a Path to Damnation."

"Yes, *sir,*" Morton said eagerly.

And with another sharp look at the Dees, The Accountant vanished.

For long seconds there was silence. Then Dee turned to his wife.

"Well," Dee said, "if the boy wants to be an accountant *that* badly, I'm sure I'm not going to stand in his way."

A THIEF IN TIME

Thomas Eldridge was all alone in his room in Butler Hall when he heard the faint scraping noise behind him. It barely registered on his consciousness. He was studying the Holstead equations, which had caused such a stir a few years ago, with their hint of a non-Relativity universe. They were a disturbing set of symbols, even though their conclusions had been proved quite fallacious.

Still, if one examined them without preconceptions, they seemed to prove something. There was a strange relationship of temporal elements, with interesting force-applications. There was—he heard the noise again and turned his head.

Standing in back of him was a large man dressed in ballooning purple trousers, a little green vest, and a porous silver shirt. He was carrying a square black machine with several dials and he looked decidedly unfriendly.

They stared at each other. For a moment, Eldridge thought it was a fraternity prank. He was the youngest associate professor at Carvell Tech, and some student was always handing him a hard-boiled egg or a live toad during Hell Week.

But this man was no giggling student. He was at least fifty years old and unmistakably hostile.

"How'd you get in here?" Eldridge demanded. "And what do you want?"

The man raised an eyebrow. "Going to brazen it out, eh?"

"Brazen what out?" Eldridge asked, startled.

"This is Viglin you're talking to," the man said. "*Viglin*. Remember?"

Eldridge tried to remember if there were any insane asylums near Carvell. This Viglin looked like an escaped lunatic.

"You must have the wrong man," Eldridge said, wondering if he should call for help.

Viglin shook his head. "You are Thomas Monroe Eldridge," he said. "Born March 16, 1926, in Darien, Connecticut. Attended the University Heights College, New York University, graduating *cum laude*. Received a fellowship to Carvell last year, in early 1953. Correct so far?"

"All right, so you did a little research on me for some reason. It better be a good one or I call the cops."

"You always were a cool customer. But the bluff won't work. *I* will call the police."

He pressed a button on the machine. Instantly, two men appeared in the room. They wore light-weight orange and green uniforms, with metallic insignia on the sleeves. Between them they carried a black machine similar to Viglin's except that it had white stenciling on its top.

"Crime does not pay," Viglin said. "Arrest that thief!"

For a moment, Eldridge's pleasant college room, with its Gauguin prints, its untidy piles of books, its untidier hi-fi, and its shaggy little red rug, seemed to spin dizzily around him. He blinked several times, hoping that the whole thing had been induced by eyestrain. Or better yet, perhaps he had been dreaming.

But Viglin was still there, dismayingly substantial.

The two policemen produced a pair of handcuffs and walked forward.

"Wait!" Eldridge shouted, leaning against his desk for support. "What's this all about?"

"If you insist on formal charges," Viglin said, "you shall have them." He cleared his throat "Thomas Eldridge, in March, 1962, you invented the Eldridge Traveler. Then—"

"Hold on!" Eldridge protested. "It isn't 1962 yet, in case you didn't know."

Viglin looked annoyed. "Don't quibble. You *will* invent the Traveler in 1962, if you prefer that phrasing. It's all a matter of temporal viewpoint."

It took Eldridge a moment to digest this.

"Do you mean—you are from the future?" he blurted.

One of the policemen nudged the other. "What an act!" he said admiringly.

"Better than a groogly show," the other agreed, clicking his handcuffs.

"Of course we're from the future," Viglin said. "Where else would we be from? In 1962, you did—or will—invent the Eldridge Time Traveler, thus making time travel possible. With it, you journeyed into the first sector of the future, where you were received with highest honors. Then you traveled through the three sectors of Civilized Time, lecturing. You were a hero, Eldridge, an ideal. Little children wanted to grow up to be like you."

With a husky voice, Viglin continued. "We were deceived. Suddenly and deliberately, you stole a quantity of valuable goods. It was shocking! We had never suspected you of criminal tendencies. When we tried to arrest you, you vanished."

Viglin paused and rubbed his forehead wearily. "I was your friend, Tom, the first person you met in Sector One. We drank many a bowl of flox together. I arranged your lecture tour. And you robbed me."

His face hardened. "Take him, officers."

As the policemen moved forward, Eldridge had a good look at the black machine they shared. Like Viglin's, it had several dials and a row of push buttons. Stamped in white across the top were the words: ELDRIDGE TIME TRAVELER—PROPERTY OF THE EASKILL POLICE DEPT.

The policeman stopped and turned to Viglin. "You got the extradition papers?"

Viglin searched his pockets. "Don't seem to have them on me. But you *know* he's a thief!"

"Everybody knows that," the policeman said. "But we got no jurisdiction in a pre-contact sector without extradition papers."

"Wait here," Viglin said. "I'll get them." He examined his wristwatch carefully, muttered something about a half-hour gap, and pressed a button on the Traveler. Immediately, he was gone.

The two policemen sat down on Eldridge's couch and proceeded to ogle the Gauguins.

Eldridge tried to think, to plan, to anticipate. Impossible. He could not believe it. He refused to believe it. No one could make him believe—

"Imagine a famous guy like this being a crook," one of the policemen said.

"All geniuses are crazy," the other philosophized. "Remember the stuggie dancer who killed the girl? *He* was a genius, the readies said."

"Yeah." The first policeman lighted a cigar and tossed the burned match on Eldridge's shaggy little red rug.

All right, Eldridge decided, it was true. Under the circumstances, he had to believe. Nor was it so absurd. He had always suspected that he might be a genius.

But what had happened?

In 1962, he would invent a time machine.

Logical enough, since he was a genius.

And he would travel through the three sectors of Civilized Time.

Well, certainly, assuming he had a time machine. If there were three sectors, he would explore them.

He might even explore the uncivilized sectors.

And then, without warning, he became a thief....

No! He could accept everything else, but that was completely out of character. Eldridge was an intensely honest young man, quite above even petty dishonesties. As a student, he had never cheated at exams. As a man, he always paid his true and proper income tax, down to the last penny.

And it went deeper than that. Eldridge had no power drive, no urge for possessions. His desire had always been to settle in some warm, drowsy country, content with his books and music, sunshine, congenial neighbors, the love of a good woman.

So he was accused of theft. Even if he were guilty, what conceivable motive could have prompted the action?

What had happened to him in the future?

"You going to the scrug rally?" one of the cops asked the other.

"Why not? It comes on Malm Sunday, doesn't it?"

They didn't care. When Viglin returned, they would handcuff him and drag him to Sector One of the future. He would be sentenced and thrown into a cell.

All for a crime he was *going* to commit.

He made a swift decision and acted on it quickly.

"I feel faint," he said, and began to topple out of his chair.

"Look out—he may have a gun!" one of the policemen yelped.

They rushed over to him, leaving their time machine on the couch.

Eldridge scuttled around the other side of the desk and pounced on the machine. Even in his haste, he realized that Sector One would be an unhealthy place for him. So, as the policemen sprinted across the room, he pushed the button marked Sector Two.

Instantly, he was plunged into darkness.

When he opened his eyes, Eldridge found that he was standing ankle-deep in a pool of dirty water. He was in a field, twenty feet from a road. The air was warm and moist. The Time Traveler was clasped tightly under his arm.

He was in Sector Two of the future and it didn't thrill him a bit.

He walked to the road. On either side of it were terraced fields, filled with the green stalks of rice plants.

Rice? In New York State? Eldridge remembered that in his own time sector, a climatic shift had been detected. It was predicted that someday the temperate zones would be hot, perhaps tropical. This future seemed to prove the theory. He was perspiring already. The ground was damp, as though from a recent rain, and the sky was an intense, unclouded blue.

But where were the farmers? Squinting at the sun directly overhead, he had the answer.

At siesta, of course.

Looking down the road, he could see buildings half a mile away. He scraped mud from his shoes and started walking.

But what would he do when he reached the buildings? How could he discover what had happened to him in Sector One? He couldn't walk up to someone and say, "Excuse me, sir. I'm from 1954, a year you may have heard about. It seems that in some way or—"

No, that would never do.

He would think of something. Eldridge continued walking, while the sun beat down fiercely upon him. He shifted the Traveler to his other arm, then looked at it closely. Since he was going to invent it—no, already had—he'd better find out how it worked.

On its face were buttons for the first three sectors of Civilized Time. There was a special dial for journeying past Sector Three, into the Uncivilized Sectors. In one corner was a metal plate, which read: CAUTION: *Allow at least one half-hour between time jumps, to avoid cancellation.*

That didn't tell him much. According to Viglin, it had taken Eldridge eight years—from 1954 to 1962—to invent the Traveler. He would need more than a few minutes to understand it.

Eldridge reached the buildings and found that he was in a good-sized town. A few people were on the streets, walking slowly under the tropical sun. They were dressed entirely in white. He was pleased to see that styles in Section Two were so conservative that his suit could pass for a rustic version of their dress.

He passed a large adobe building. The sign in front read: PUBLIC READERY.

A library. Eldridge stopped. Within would undoubtedly be the records of the past few hundred years. There would be an account of his crime—if any—and the circumstances under which he had committed it.

But would he be safe? Were there any circulars out for his arrest? Was there an extradition between Sectors One and Two?

He would have to chance it. Eldridge entered, walked quickly past the thin, gray-faced librarian, and into the stacks.

There was a large section on time, but the most thorough one-volume treatment was a book called *Origins of Time Travel* by Ricardo Alfredex. The first part told how the young genius Eldridge had, one fateful day in 1954, received the germ of the idea from the controversial Holstead equations. The formula was really absurdly simple—Alfredex quoted the main propositions—but no one ever had realized it before. Eldridge's genius lay chiefly in perceiving the obvious.

Eldridge frowned at this disparagement. Obvious, was it?

He still didn't understand it. And *he* was the inventor!

By 1962, the machine had been built. It worked on the very first trial, catapulting its young inventor into what became known as Sector One.

Eldridge looked up and found that a bespectacled girl of nine or so was standing at the end of his row of books, staring at him. She ducked back out of sight. He read on.

The next chapter was entitled "Unparadox of Time." Eldridge skimmed it rapidly. The author began with the classic paradox of Achilles and the tortoise, and demolished it with integral calculus. Using this as a logical foundation, he went on to the so-called time paradoxes— killing one's great-great grandfather, meeting oneself, and the like. These held up no better than Zeno's ancient paradox. Alfredex went on to explain that all temporal paradoxes were the inventions of authors with a gift for confusion.

Eldridge didn't understand the intricate symbolic logic in this part, which was embarrassing, since *he* was cited as the leading authority.

The next chapter was called "Fall of the Mighty." It told how Eldridge had met Viglin, the owner of a large sporting-goods store in Sector One. They became fast friends. The businessman took the shy young genius under his wing. He arranged lecture tours for him. Then—

"I beg your pardon, sir," someone said. Eldridge looked up. The gray-faced librarian was standing in front of him. Beside her was the bespectacled little girl with a smug grin on her face.

"Yes?" Eldridge asked.

"Time Travelers are not allowed in the Readery," the librarian said sternly.

That was understandable, Eldridge thought. Travelers could grab an armload of valuable books and disappear. They probably weren't allowed in banks, either.

The trouble was, he didn't dare surrender this book.

Eldridge smiled, tapped his ear, and hastily went on reading.

It seemed that the brilliant young Eldridge had allowed Viglin to arrange all his contracts and papers. One day he found, to his surprise, that he had signed over all rights in the Time Traveler to Viglin, for a small monetary consideration. Eldridge brought the case to court. The court found against him. The case was appealed. Penniless and embittered, Eldridge embarked on his career of crime, stealing from Viglin—

"Sir!" the librarian said. "Deaf or not, you must leave at once. Otherwise I will call a guard."

Eldridge put down the book, muttered, "Tattle-tale," to the little girl, and hurried out of the Readery.

Now he knew why Viglin was so eager to arrest him. With the case still pending, Eldridge would be in a very poor position behind bars.

But why had he stolen?

The theft of his invention was an understandable motive, but Eldridge felt certain it was not the right one. Stealing from Viglin would not make him feel any better nor would it right the wrong. His reaction would be either to fight or to withdraw, to retire from the whole mess. Anything except stealing.

Well, he would find out. He would hide in Sector Two, perhaps find work. Bit by bit, he would—

Two men seized his arms from either side. A third took the Traveler away from him. It was done so smoothly that Eldridge was still gasping when one of the men showed a badge.

"Police," the man said. "You'll have to come with us, Mr. Eldridge."

"What for?" Eldridge asked.

"Robbery in Sectors One and Two."

So he had stolen here, too.

He was taken to the police station and into the small, cluttered office of the captain of police. The captain was a slim, balding, cheerful-faced man. He waved his subordinates out of the room, motioned Eldridge to a chair and gave him a cigarette.

"So you're Eldridge," he said.

Eldridge nodded morosely.

"Been reading about you ever since I was a little boy," the captain said nostalgically. "You were one of my heroes."

Eldridge guessed the captain to be a good fifteen years his senior, but he didn't ask about it. After all, *he* was supposed to be the expert on time paradoxes.

"Always thought you got a rotten deal," the captain said, toying with a large bronze paperweight. "Still, I couldn't understand a man like you stealing. For a while, we thought it might have been temporary insanity."

"Was it?" Eldridge asked hopefully.

"Not a chance. Checked your records. You just haven't got the potentiality. And that makes it rather difficult for me. For example, why did you steal *those* particular items?"

"What items?"

"Don't you remember?"

"I—I've blanked out," Eldridge said. "Temporary amnesia."

"Very understandable," the captain said sympathetically. He handed Eldridge a paper. "Here's the list."

ITEMS STOLEN BY
THOMAS MONROE ELDRIDGE

Taken from Viglin's Sporting Goods Store, Sector One: . Credits

4	Megacharge Hand Pistols	10,000
3	Lifebelts, Inflatable	100
5	Cans, Ollen's Shark Repellant	400

Taken from Alfghan's Specialty Shop, Sector One:

2	Microflex Sets, World Literature	1,000
5	Teeny-Tom Symphonic Tape Runs	2,650

Taken from Loorie's Produce Store, Sector Two:

4	Dozen Potatoes, White Turtle Brand	5
9	Packages, Carrot Seeds (Fancy)	6

Taken from Manori's Notions Store, Sector Two:

5	Dozen Mirrors, Silver-backed (hand size)	95
Total Value		14,256

"What does it mean?" the captain asked. "Stealing a million credits outright, I could understand, but why all that junk?"

Eldridge shook his head. He could find nothing meaningful in the list. The megacharge hand pistols sounded useful. But why the mirrors, lifebelts, potatoe,s and the rest of the things that the captain had properly called junk?

It just didn't sound like himself. Eldridge began to think of himself as two people. Eldridge I had invented time travel, been victimized, stolen some incomprehensible articles, and vanished. Eldridge II was himself, the person Viglin had found. He had no memory of the first Eldridge. But he had to discover Eldridge I's motives and/or suffer for his crimes.

"What happened after I stole these things?" Eldridge asked.

"That's what we'd like to know," the captain said. "All we know is, you fled into Sector Three with your loot."

"And then?"

The captain shrugged. "When we applied for extradition, the authorities told us you weren't there. Not that they'd have given you up. They're a proud, independent sort, you know. Anyhow, you'd vanished."

"Vanished? To where?"

"I don't know. You might have gone into the Uncivilized Sectors that lie beyond Sector Three."

"What are the Uncivilized Sectors?" Eldridge asked.

"We were hoping you would tell us," the captain said. "You're the only man who's explored beyond Sector Three."

Damn it, Eldridge thought, he was supposed to be the authority on everything he wanted to know!

"This puts me in a pretty fix," the captain remarked squinting at his paperweight.

"Why?"

"Well, you're a thief. The law says I must arrest you. However, I am also aware that you got a very shoddy deal. And I happen to know that you stole only from Viglin and his affiliates in both Sectors. There's a certain justice to it—unfortunately unrecognized by law."

Eldridge nodded unhappily.

"It's my clear duty to arrest you," the captain said with a deep sigh. "There's nothing I can do about it, even if I wanted to. You'll have to stand trial and probably serve a sentence of twenty years or so."

"*What?* For stealing rubbish like shark repellant and carrot seed? For stealing *junk?*"

"We're pretty rough on time theft," said the captain. "Temporal offense."

"I see," Eldridge said, slumping in his chair.

"Of course," said the captain thoughtfully, "if you should suddenly turn vicious, knock me over the head with this heavy paperweight, grab my personal Time Traveler—which I keep in the second shelf of that cabinet—and return to your friends in Sector Three, there would really be nothing I could do about it."

"Huh?"

The captain turned toward the window, leaving his paperweight within Eldridge's easy reach.

"It's really terrible," he commented, "the things one will consider doing for a boyhood hero. But, of course, you're a law-abiding man. You would never do such a thing and I have psychological reports to prove it."

"Thanks," Eldridge said. He lifted the paperweight and tapped the captain lightly over the head. Smiling, the captain slumped behind his desk. Eldridge found the Traveler in the cabinet, and set it for Sector Three. He sighed deeply and pushed the button.

Again he was overcome by darkness.

When he opened his eyes, he was standing on a plain of parched yellow ground. Around him stretched a treeless waste, and a dusty wind blew in his face. Ahead, he could see several brick buildings and a row of tents, built along the side of a dried-out gully. He walked toward them.

This future, he decided, must have seen another climatic shift. The fierce sun had baked the land, drying up the streams and rivers. If the trend continued, he could understand why the next future was Uncivilized. It was probably Unpopulated.

He was very tired. He had not eaten all day—or for several thousand years, depending on how you count. But that, he realized, was a false paradox, one that Alfredex would certainly demolish with symbolic logic.

To hell with logic. To hell with science, paradox, everything. He would run no farther. There had to be room for him in this dusty land. The people here—a proud, independent sort—would not give him up. They believed in justice, not the law. Here he would stay, work, grow old, and forget Eldridge I and his crazy schemes.

When he reached the village, he saw that the people were already assembled to greet him. They were dressed in long, flowing robes, like Arabian burnooses, the only logical attire for the climate.

A bearded patriarch stepped forward and nodded gravely at Eldridge. "The ancient sayings are true. For every beginning there is an ending."

Eldridge agreed politely. "Anyone got a drink of water?"

"It is truly written," the patriarch continued, "that the thief, given a universe to wander, will ultimately return to the scene of his crime."

"Crime?" Eldridge asked, feeling an uneasy tingle in his stomach.

"Crime," the patriarch repeated.

A man in the crowd shouted, "It's a stupid bird that fouls its own nest!" The people roared with laughter, but Eldridge didn't like the sound. It was cruel laughter.

"Ingratitude breeds betrayal," the patriarch said. "Evil is omnipresent. We liked you, Thomas Eldridge. You came to us with your strange machine, bearing booty, and we recognized your proud spirit. It made you one of us. We protected you from your enemies in the Wet Worlds. What did it matter to us if you had wronged them? Had they not wronged you? An eye for an eye!"

The crowd growled approvingly.

"But what did I do?" Eldridge wanted to know.

The crowd converged on him, waving clubs and knives. A row of men in dark blue cloaks held them off, and Eldridge realized that there were policemen even here.

"Tell me what I did," he persisted as the policemen took the Traveler from him.

"You are guilty of sabotage and murder," the patriarch told him.

Eldridge stared around wildly. He had fled a petty larceny charge in Sector One, only to find himself accused of it in Sector Two. He had retreated to Sector Three, where he was wanted for murder and sabotage.

He smiled amiably. "You know, all I ever really wanted was a warm drowsy country, books, congenial neighbors, and the love of a good—"

When he recovered, he found himself lying on packed earth in a small brick jail. Through a slitted window, he could see an insignificant strip of sunset. Outside the wooden door, someone was wailing a song.

He found a bowl of food beside him and wolfed down the unfamiliar stuff. After drinking some water from another bowl, he propped himself against the wall. Through his narrow window, the sunset was fading. In the courtyard, a gang of men were erecting a gallows.

"Jailor!" Eldridge shouted.

In a few moments, he heard the clump of footsteps.

"I need a lawyer," he said.

"We have no lawyers here," the man replied proudly. "Here we have justice." He marched off.

Eldridge began to revise his ideas about justice without law.

It was very good as an idea—but a horror as reality.

He lay on the floor and tried to think. No thoughts came. He could hear the workmen laughing and joking as they built the gallows. They worked late into the twilight.

In the early evening, Eldridge heard the key turn in his lock. Two men entered. One was middle-aged, with a small, well-trimmed beard. The other was about Eldridge's age, broad-shouldered, and deeply tanned.

"Do you remember me?" the middle-aged man asked.

"Should I?"

"You should. I was her father."

"And I was her fiancé," the young man said. He took a threatening step forward.

The bearded man restrained him. "I know how you feel, Morgel, but he will pay for his crimes on the gallows."

"Hanging is too good for him, Mr. Becker," Morgel argued. "He should be drawn, quartered, burned, and scattered to the wind."

"Yes, but we are a just and merciful people," Becker said virtuously.

"Whose father?" Eldridge asked. "Whose fiancé?"

The two men looked at each other.

"What did I do?" Eldridge asked.

Becker told him.

He had come to them from Sector Two, loaded with loot, Becker explained. The people of Sector Three accepted him. They were a simple folk, direct and quick-tempered, the inheritors of a wasted, war-torn Earth. In Sector Three, the minerals were gone, the soil had lost its fertility. Huge tracts of land were radioactive. And the sun continued to beat down, the glaciers melted, and the oceans continued to rise.

The men of Sector Three were struggling back to civilization. They had the rudiments of a manufacturing system and a few power installations. Eldridge had increased the output of these stations, given them a lighting system, and taught them the rudiments of sanitary processing. He continued his explorations into the Unexplored Sectors beyond Sector Three. He became a popular hero and the people of Sector Three loved and protected him.

Eldridge had repaid this kindness by abducting Becker's daughter.

This attractive young lady had been engaged to Morgel. Preparations were made for her marriage. Eldridge ignored all this and showed his true nature by kidnapping her one dark night and placing her in an infernal machine of his own making. When he turned the invention on, the girl vanished. The overloaded power lines blew out every installation for miles around.

Murder and sabotage!

But the irate mob had not been able to reach Eldridge in time. He had stuffed some of his loot into a knapsack, grabbed his Traveler and vanished.

"I did all that?" Eldridge gasped.

"Before witnesses," Becker said. "Your remaining loot is in the warehouse. We could deduce nothing from it."

With both men staring him full in the face, Eldridge looked at the ground.

Now he knew what he had done in Sector Three.

The murder charge was probably false, though. Apparently he had built a heavy-duty Traveler and sent the girl somewhere, without the intermediate stops required by the portable models. Not that anyone would believe him. These people had never heard of such a civilized concept as *habeas corpus.*

"Why did you do it?" Becker asked.

Eldridge shrugged his shoulders and shook his head helplessly.

"Didn't I treat you like my own son? Didn't I turn back the police of Sector Two? Didn't I feed you, clothe you? Why—*why*—did you do it?"

All Eldridge could do was shrug his shoulders and go on helplessly shaking his head.

"Very well," Becker said. "Tell your secret to the hangman in the morning."

He took Morgel by the arm and left.

If Eldridge had had a gun, he might have shot himself on the spot. All the evidence pointed to potentialities for evil in him that he had never suspected. He was running out of time. In the morning, he would hang.

And it was unfair, all of it. He was an innocent bystander, continually running into the consequences of his former—or later—actions. But only Eldridge I possessed the motives and knew the answers.

Even if his thefts were justified, why had he stolen potatoes, lifebelts, mirrors, and such?

What had he done with the girl?

What was he trying to accomplish?

Wearily, Eldridge closed his eyes and drifted into a troubled half-sleep.

He heard a faint scraping noise and looked up.

Viglin was standing there, a Traveler in his hands.

Eldridge was too tired to be very surprised. He looked for a moment, then said, "Come for one last gloat?"

"I didn't plan it this way," Viglin protested, mopping his perspiring face. "You must believe that. I never wanted you killed, Tom."

Eldridge sat up and looked closely at Viglin. "You did steal my invention, didn't you?"

"Yes," Viglin confessed. "But I was going to do the right thing by you. I would have split the profits."

"Then why did you steal it?"

Viglin looked uncomfortable. "You weren't interested in money at all."

"So you tricked me into signing over my rights?"

"If I hadn't, someone else would have, Tom. I was just saving you from your own unworldliness. I intended to cut you in—I swear it!" He wiped his forehead again. "But I never dreamed it would turn out like this."

"And then you framed me for those thefts," Eldridge said.

"What?" Viglin appeared to be genuinely surprised. "No, Tom. You *did* steal those things. It worked out perfectly for me—until now."

"You're lying!"

"Would I come here to lie? I've admitted stealing your invention. Why would I lie about anything else?"

"Then why did I steal?"

"I think you had some sort of wild scheme in the Uninhabited Sectors, but I don't really know. It doesn't matter. Listen to me now. There's no way I can call off the lawsuit—it's a temporal matter now—but I can get you out of here."

"Where will I go?' Eldridge asked hopelessly. "The cops are looking for me all through time."

"I'll hide you on my estate. I mean it: You can lie low until the statute of limitations has expired. They'd never think of searching my place for you."

"And the rights on my invention?"

"I'm keeping them," Viglin said, with a touch of his former confidence. "I can't turn them over to you without making myself liable for temporal action. But I *will* share them. And you *do* need a business partner."

"All right, let's get out of here," Eldridge said.

Viglin had brought along a number of tools, which he handled with suspicious proficiency. Within minutes, they were out of the cell and hiding in the dark courtyard.

"This Traveler's pretty weak," Viglin whispered, checking the batteries in his machine. "Could we possibly get yours?"

"It should be in the storehouse," Eldridge said.

The storehouse was unguarded and Viglin made short work of the lock. Inside, they found Eldridge II's machine beside Eldridge I's preposterous, bewildering loot.

"Let's go," Viglin said.

Eldridge shook his head.

"What's wrong?" asked Viglin, annoyed.

"I'm not going."

"Listen, Tom, I know there's no reason why you should trust me. But I really will give you sanctuary. I'm not lying to you."

"I believe you," Eldridge said. "Just the same, I'm not going back."

"What are you planning to do?"

Eldridge had been wondering about that ever since they had broken out of the cell. He was at the crossroads now. He could return with Viglin or he could go on alone.

There was no choice, really. He had to assume that he had known what he was doing the first time. Right or wrong, he was going to keep faith and meet whatever appointments he had made with the future.

"I'm going into the Uninhabited Sectors," Eldridge said. He found a sack and began loading it with potatoes and carrot seeds.

"You can't!" Viglin objected. "The first time, you ended up in 1954. You might not be so lucky this time. You might be canceled out completely."

Eldridge had loaded all the potatoes and the packages of carrot seeds. Next he slipped in the World Literature Sets, the lifebelts, the cans of shark repellant and the mirrors. On top of this he put the megacharge hand pistols.

"Have you any idea what you're going to do with that stuff?"

"Not the slightest," Eldridge said, buttoning the Symphonic Tape Runs inside his shirt. "But they must fit somewhere."

Viglin sighed heavily. "Don't forget, you have to allow half an hour between jumps or you'll get canceled. Have you got a watch?"

"No, I left it in my room."

"Take this one. Sportsman's Special." Viglin attached it to Eldridge's wrist. "Good luck, Tom. I mean that."

"Thanks."

Eldridge set the button for the farthest jump into the future he could make. He grinned at Viglin and pushed the button.

There was the usual moment of blackness, then a sudden icy shock. When Eldridge opened his eyes, he found that he was under water.

He found his way to the surface, struggling against the weight of the sack. Once his head was above water, he looked around for the nearest land.

There was no land. Long, smooth-backed waves slid toward him from the limitless horizon, lifted him and ran on, toward a hidden shore.

Eldridge fumbled in his sack, found the lifebelts and inflated them. Soon he was bobbing on the surface, trying to figure out what had happened to New York State.

Each jump into the future had brought him to a hotter climate. Here, countless thousands of years past 1954, the glaciers must have melted. A good part of the Earth was probably submerged.

He had planned well in taking the lifebelts. It gave him confidence for the rest of the journey. Now he would just have to float for half an hour, to avoid cancelation.

He leaned back, supported by his lifebelts, and admired the cloud formations in the sky.

Something brushed against him.

Eldridge looked down and saw a long black shape glide under his feet. Another joined it and they began to move hungrily toward him.

Sharks!

He fumbled wildly with the sack, spilling out the mirrors in his hurry, and found a can of shark repellant. He opened it, spilled it overboard, and an orange blotch began to spread on the blue-black water.

There were three sharks now. They swam warily around the spreading circle of repellant. A fourth joined them, lunged into the orange smear, and retreated quickly to clean water.

Eldridge was glad the future had produced a shark repellant that really worked.

In five minutes, some of the orange had dissipated. He opened another can. The sharks didn't give up hope, but they wouldn't swim into the tainted water. He emptied the cans every five minutes. The stalemate held through Eldridge's half-hour wait.

He checked his settings and tightened his grip on the sack.

He didn't know what the mirrors or potatoes were for, or why carrot seeds were critical. He would just have to take his chances.

He pressed the button and went into the familiar darkness. He found himself ankle-deep in a thick, evil-smelling bog. The heat was stifling and a cloud of huge gnats buzzed around his head.

Pulling himself out of the gluey mud, accompanied by the hiss and click of unseen life, Eldridge found firmer footing under a small tree. Around him was green jungle, shot through with riotous purples and reds.

Eldridge settled against the tree to wait out his half hour. In this future, apparently, the ocean waters had receded and the primeval jungle had sprung up. Were there any humans here? Were there any left on Earth? He wasn't at all sure. It looked as though the world was starting over.

Eldridge heard a bleating noise and saw a dull green shape move against the brighter green of the foliage. Something was coming toward him.

He watched. It was about twelve feet tall, with a lizard's wrinkled hide and wide splay feet. It looked amazingly like a small dinosaur.

Eldridge watched the big reptile warily. Most dinosaurs were herbivorous, he reminded himself, especially the ones that lived in swamps. This one probably just wanted to sniff him. Then it would return to cropping grass.

The dinosaur yawned, revealing a magnificent set of pointed teeth, and began to approach Eldridge with an air of determination.

Eldridge dipped into the sack, pushed irrelevant items out of the way, and grabbed a megacharge hand pistol.

This had better be it, he prayed, and fired.

The dinosaur vanished in a spray of smoke. There were only a few shreds of flesh and a smell of ozone to show where it had been. Eldridge looked at the megacharge hand pistol with new respect. Now he understood why it was so expensive.

During the next half hour, a number of jungle inhabitants took a lively interest in him. Each pistol was good for only a few firings—no surprise, considering their destructiveness. His last one began to lose its charge; he had to club off a pterodactyl with the butt.

When the half hour was over, he set the dial again, wishing he knew what lay ahead. He wondered how he was supposed to face new dangers with some books, potatoes, carrot seeds, and mirrors.

Perhaps there were no dangers ahead.

There was only one way to find out. He pressed the button.

He was on a grassy hillside. The dense jungle had disappeared. Now there was a breeze-swept pine forest stretching before him, solid ground underfoot, and a temperate sun in the sky.

Eldridge's pulse quickened at the thought that *this* might be his goal. He had always had an atavistic streak, a desire to find a place untouched by civilization. The embittered Eldridge I, robbed and betrayed, must have felt it even more strongly.

It was a little disappointing. Still, it wasn't too bad, he decided. Except for the loneliness. If only there were people—

A man stepped out of the forest. He was less than five feet tall, thickset, muscled like a wrestler and wearing a fur kilt. His skin was colored a medium gray. He carried a ragged tree limb, roughly shaped into a club.

Two dozen others came through the forest behind him.

They marched directly up to Eldridge.

"Hello, fellows," Eldridge said pleasantly. The leader replied in a guttural language and made a gesture with his open palm.

"I bring your crops blessings," Eldridge said promptly. "I've got just what you need." He reached into his sack and held up a package of carrot seeds. "Seeds! You'll advance a thousand years in civilization—"

The leader grunted angrily and his followers began to circle Eldridge. They held out their hands, palms up, grunting excitedly.

They didn't want the sack and they refused the discharged hand pistol. They had him almost completely circled now. Clubs were being hefted and he still had no idea what they wanted.

"Potato?" he asked in desperation.

They didn't want potatoes, either.

His time machine had two minutes more to wait. He turned and ran.

The savages were after him at once. Eldridge sprinted into the forest like a greyhound, dodging through the closely packed trees. Several clubs whizzed past him.

One minute to go.

He tripped over a root, scrambled to his feet and kept on running. The savages were close on his heels.

Ten seconds. Five seconds. A club glanced off his shoulder.

Time! He reached for the button—and a club thudded against his head, knocking him to the ground. When he could focus again, the leader of the savages was standing over his Time Traveler, club raised.

"Don't!" Eldridge yelled in panic.

But the leader grinned wildly and brought down the club. In a few seconds, he had reduced the machine to scrap metal.

Eldridge was dragged into a cave, cursing hopelessly. Two savages guarded the entrance. Outside, he could see a gang of men gathering wood. Women and children were scampering back and forth, laden down with clay containers. To judge by their laughter, they were planning a feast.

Eldridge realized, with a sinking sensation, that he would be the main dish.

Not that it mattered. They had destroyed his Traveler. No Viglin would rescue him this time. He was at the end of his road.

Eldridge didn't want to die. But what made it worse was the thought of dying without ever finding out what Eldridge I had planned.

It seemed unfair, somehow.

For several minutes, he sat in abject self-pity. Then he crawled farther back into the cave, hoping to find another way out.

The cave ended abruptly against a wall of granite. But he found something else.

An old shoe.

He picked it up and stared at it. For some reason, it bothered him, although it was a perfectly ordinary brown leather shoe, just like the ones he had on.

Then the anachronism struck him.

What was a manufactured article like a shoe doing back in this dawn age? He looked at the size and quickly tried it on. It fitted him exactly, which made the answer obvious—he must have passed through here on his first trip.

But why had he left a shoe?

There was something inside, too soft to be a pebble, too stiff to be a piece of torn lining. He took off the shoe and found a piece of paper wadded in the toe. He unfolded it and read in his own handwriting:

> *Silliest damned business—how do you address yourself? "Dear Eldridge"? All right, let's forget the salutation; you'll read this because I already have, and so, naturally, I'm writing it, otherwise you wouldn't be able to read it, nor would I have been.*
>
> *Look, you're in a rough spot. Don't worry about it, though. You'll come out of it in one piece. I'm leaving you a Time Traveler to take you where you have to go next.*
>
> *The question is: where do I go? I'm deliberately setting the Traveler before the half-hour lag it needs, knowing there will be a cancelation effect. That means the Traveler will stay here for you to use. But what happens to me?*

I think I know. Still, it scares me—this is the first cancelation I'll have experienced. But worrying about it is nonsensical; I know it has to turn out right because there are no time paradoxes.

Well, here goes. I'll push the button and cancel. Then the machine is yours.

Wish me luck.

Wish *him* luck! Eldridge savagely tore up the note and threw it away.

But Eldridge I had purposely canceled and been swept back to the future, which meant that the Traveler hadn't gone back with him! It must still be here!

Eldridge began a frantic search of the cave. If he could just find it and push the button, he could go on ahead. It *had* to be here!

Several hours later, when the guards dragged him out, he still hadn't found it.

The entire village had gathered and they were in a festive mood. The clay containers were being passed freely and two or three men had already passed out. But the guards who led Eldridge forward were sober enough.

They carried him to a wide, shallow pit. In the center of it was what looked like a sacrificial altar. It was decorated with wild colors and heaped around it was an enormous pile of dried branches.

Eldridge was pushed in and the dancing began.

He tried several times to scramble out, but was prodded back each time. The dancing continued for hours, until the last dancer had collapsed, exhausted.

An old man approached the rim of the pit, holding a lighted torch. He gestured with it and threw it into the pit.

Eldridge stamped it out. But more torches rained down, lighting the outermost branches. They flared brightly and he was forced to retreat inward, toward the altar.

The flaming circle closed, driving him back. At last, panting, eyes burning, legs buckling, he fell across the altar as the flames licked at him.

His eyes were closed and he gripped the knobs tightly—

Knobs?

He looked. Under its gaudy decoration, the altar was a Time Traveler—the same Traveler, past a doubt, that Eldridge I had brought here and left for him. When Eldridge I vanished, they must have venerated it as a sacred object.

And it *did* have magical qualities.

The fire was singeing his feet when he adjusted the regulator. With his finger against the button, he hesitated.

What would the future hold for him? All he had in the way of equipment was a sack of carrot seeds, potatoes, the symphonic runs, the microfilm volumes of world literature, and small mirrors.

But he had come this far. He would see the end. He pressed the button.

Opening his eyes, Eldridge found that he was standing on a beach. Water was lapping at his toes and he could hear the boom of breakers.

The beach was long and narrow and dazzlingly white. In front of him, a blue ocean stretched to infinity. Behind him, at the edge of the beach, was a row of palms. Growing among them was the brilliant vegetation of a tropical island.

He heard a shout.

Eldridge looked around for something to defend himself with. He had nothing, nothing at all. He was defenseless.

Men came running from the jungle toward him. They were shouting something strange. He listened carefully.

"Welcome! Welcome back!" they called out.

A gigantic brown man enclosed him in a bearlike hug. "You have returned!" he exclaimed.

"Why—yes," Eldridge said.

More people were running down to the beach. They were a comely race. The men were tall and tanned, and the women, for the most part, were slim and pretty. They looked like the sort of people one would like to have for neighbors.

"Did you bring them?" a thin old man asked, panting from his run to the beach.

"Bring what?"

"The carrot seeds. You promised to bring them. And the potatoes."

Eldridge dug them out of his pockets. "Here they are," he said.

"Thank you. Do you really think they'll grow in this climate? I suppose we could construct a—"

"Later, later," the big man interrupted. "You must be tired."

Eldridge thought back to what had happened since he had last awakened, back in 1954. Subjectively, it was only a day or so, but it had covered thousands of years back and forth and was crammed with arrests, escapes, dangers, and bewildering puzzles.

"Tired," he said. "Very."

"Perhaps you'd like to return to your own home?"

"My own?"

"Certainly. The house you built facing the lagoon. Don't you remember?"

Eldridge smiled feebly and shook his head.

"He doesn't remember!" the man cried.

"You don't remember our chess games?" another man asked.

"And the fishing parties?" a boy put in.

"Or the picnics and celebrations?"

"The dances?"

"And the sailing?"

Eldridge shook his head at each eager, worried question.

"All this was before you went back to your own time," the big man told him.

"Went back?" asked Eldridge. Here was everything he had always wanted. Peace, contentment, warm climate, good neighbors. He felt inside the sack and his shirt. And books and music, he mentally added to the list. Good Lord, no one in his right mind would leave a place like this! And that brought up an important question. "Why did I leave here?"

"Surely you remember *that!*" the big man said.

"I'm afraid not."

A slim, light-haired girl stepped forward. "You really don't remember coming back for me?"

Eldridge stared at her. "You must be Becker's daughter. The girl who was engaged to Morgel. The one I kidnapped."

"Morgel only *thought* he was engaged to me," she said. "And you didn't kidnap me. I came of my own free will."

"Oh, I see," Eldridge answered, feeling like an idiot. "I mean I think I see. That is—pleased to meet you," he finished inanely.

"You needn't be so formal," she said. "After all, we *are* married. And you *did* bring me a mirror, didn't you?"

It was complete now. Eldridge grinned, took out a mirror, gave it to her, and handed the sack to the big man. Delighted, she did the things with her eyebrows and hair that women always do whenever they see their reflections.

"Let's go home, dear," she said.

He didn't know her name, but he liked her looks. He liked her very much. But that was only natural.

"I'm afraid I can't right now," he replied, looking at his watch. The half hour was almost up. "I have something to do first. But I should be back in a very little while."

She smiled sunnily. "I won't worry. You said you would return and you did. And you brought back the mirrors and seed and potatoes that you told us you'd bring."

She kissed him. He shook hands all around. In a way, that symbolized the full cycle Alfredex had used to demolish the foolish concept of temporal paradoxes.

The familiar darkness swallowed Eldridge as he pushed the button on the Traveler.

He had ceased being Eldridge II.

From this point on, he was Eldridge I and he knew precisely where he was going, what he would do and the things he needed to do them. They all led to this goal and this girl, for there was no question that he would come back here and live out his life with her, their good neighbors, books and music, in peace and contentment.

It was wonderful, knowing that everything would turn out just as he had always dreamed.

He even had a feeling of affection and gratitude for Viglin and Alfredex.

THE BATTLE

Supreme General Fetterer barked "At ease!" as he hurried into the command room. Obediently his three generals stood at ease.

"We haven't much time," Fetterer said, glancing at his watch. "We'll go over the plan of battle again."

He walked to the wall and unrolled a gigantic map of the Sahara Desert.

"According to our best theological information, Satan is going to present his forces at these coordinates." He indicated the place with a blunt forefinger. "In the front rank there will be the devils, demons, succubi, incubi, and the rest of the ratings. Bael will command the right flank, Buer the left. His Satanic Majesty will hold the center."

"Rather medieval," General Dell murmured.

General Fetterer's aide came in, his face shining and happy with thought of the Coming.

"Sir," he said, "the priest is outside again."

"Stand at attention, soldier," Fetterer said sternly. "There's still a battle to be fought and won."

"Yes, sir," the aide said, and stood rigidly, some of the joy fading from his face.

"The priest, eh?" Supreme General Fetterer rubbed his fingers together thoughtfully. Ever since the Coming, since the knowledge of the imminent Last Battle, the religious workers of the world had made a complete nuisance of themselves. They had stopped their bickering, which was commendable. But now they were trying to run military business.

"Send him away," Fetterer said. "He knows we're planning Armageddon."

"Yes, sir," the aide said. He saluted sharply, wheeled, and marched out.

"To go on," Supreme General Fetterer said. "Behind Satan's first line of defense will be the resurrected sinners, and various elemental forces of evil. The fallen angels will act as his bomber corps. Dell's robot interceptors will meet them."

139

General Dell smiled grimly.

"Upon contact, MacFee's automatic tank corps will proceed toward the center of the line. MacFee's automatic tank corps will proceed toward the center," Fetterer went on, "supported by General Ongin's robot infantry. Dell will command the H-bombing of the rear, which should be tightly massed. I will thrust with the mechanized cavalry, here and here."

The aide came back, and stood rigidly at attention. "Sir," he said, "the priest refuses to go. He says he must speak with you."

Supreme General Fetterer hesitated before saying no. He remembered that this was the Last Battle, and that the religious workers *were* connected with it. He decided to give the man five minutes.

"Show him in," he said.

The priest wore a plain business suit, to show that he represented no particular religion. His face was tired but determined.

"General," he said, "I am a representative of all the religious workers of the world, the priests, rabbis, ministers, mullahs, and all the rest. We beg of you, General, to let us fight in the Lord's battle."

Supreme General Fetterer drummed his fingers nervously against his side. He wanted to stay on friendly terms with these men. Even he, the Supreme Commander, might need a good word, when all was said and done...

"You can understand my position," Fetterer said unhappily. "I'm a general. I have a battle to fight."

"But it's the Last Battle," the priest said. "It should be the people's battle."

"It is," Fetterer said. "It's being fought by their representatives, the military."

The priest didn't look at all convinced.

Fetterer said, "You wouldn't want to lose this battle, would you? Have Satan win?"

"Of course not," the priest murmured.

"Then we can't take any chances," Fetterer said. "All the governments agreed on that, didn't they? Oh, it would be very nice to fight Armageddon with the mass of humanity. Symbolic, you might say. But could we be certain of victory?"

The priest tried to say something, but Fetterer was talking rapidly.

"How do we know the strength of Satan's forces? We simply *must* put forth our best foot, militarily speaking. And that means the automatic armies, the robot interceptors and tanks, the H-bombs."

The priest looked very unhappy. "But it isn't *right*," he said. "Certainly you can find someplace in your plan for *people*?"

Fetterer thought about it, but the request was impossible. The plan of battle was fully developed, beautiful, irresistible. Any introduction of a gross human element would only throw it out of order. No living flesh could stand the noise of that mechanical attack, the energy potentials humming in the air, the all-enveloping firepower. A human being who came within a hundred miles of the front would not live to see the enemy."

"I'm afraid not," Fetterer said.

"There are some," the priest said sternly, "who feel that it was an error to put this in the hands of the military."

"Sorry," Fetterer said cheerfully. "That's defeatist talk. If you don't mind—" He gestured at the door. Wearily, the priest left.

"These civilians," Fetterer mused. "Well, gentlemen, are your troops ready?"

"We're ready to fight for Him," General MacFee said enthusiastically. "I can vouch for every automatic in my command. Their metal is shining, all relays have been renewed, and the energy reservoirs are fully charged. Sir, they're positively itching for battle!"

General Ongin snapped fully out of his daze. "The ground troops are ready, sir!"

"Excellent," General Fetterer said. "All other arrangements have been made. Television facilities are available for the total population of the world. No one, rich or poor, will miss the spectacle of the Last Battle."

"And after the battle—" General Ongin began, and stopped. He looked at Fetterer.

Fetterer frowned deeply. He didn't know what was supposed to happen after the battle. That part of it was, presumably, in the hands of the religious agencies.

"I suppose there'll be a presentation or something," he said vaguely.

"You mean we will meet—Him?" General Dell asked.

"Don't really know," Fetterer said. "But I should think so. After all— I mean, you know what I mean."

"But what should we wear?" General MacFee asked, in a sudden panic. "I mean what *does* one wear?"

"What do the angels wear?" Fetterer asked Ongin.

"I don't know," Ongin said.

"Robes, do you think?" General Dell offered.

"No," Fetterer said sternly. "We will wear dress uniform, without decorations."

The generals nodded. It was fitting.

And then it was time.

Gorgeous in their battle array, the legions of Hell advanced over the desert. Hellish pipes skirled, hollow drums pounded, and the great host moved forward.

In a blinding cloud of sand, General MacFee's automatic tanks hurled themselves against the satanic foe. Immediately, Dell's automatic bombers screamed overhead, hurling their bombs on the massed horde of the damned. Fetterer thrust valiantly with his automatic cavalry.

Into this melee advanced Ongin's automatic infantry, and metal did what metal could.

The hordes of the damned overflowed the front, ripping apart tanks and robots. Automatic mechanisms died, bravely defending a patch of sand. Dell's bombers were torn from the skies by the fallen angels, led by Marchocias, his griffin wings beating the air into a tornado.

The thin, battered line of robots held against gigantic presences that smashed and scattered them and struck terror into the hearts of television viewers in homes around the world. Like men, like heroes, the robots fought, trying to push back the forces of evil.

Astaroth shrieked a command, and Behemoth lumbered forward. Bael, with a wedge of devils behind him, threw a charge at General Fetterer's crumbling left flank. Metal screamed, electrons howled at the impact.

Supreme General Fetterer sweated and trembled, a thousand miles behind the firing line. But steadily, nervelessly, he guided the pushing of buttons and the throwing of levers.

His superb corps didn't disappoint him. Mortally damaged robots swayed to their feet and fought. Smashed, trampled, destroyed by the howling fiends, the robots managed to hold their line. Then the veteran Fifth Corps threw in a counterattack, and the enemy front was pierced.

A thousand miles behind the firing line, the generals guided the mopping-up operations.

"The battle is won," Supreme General Fetterer whispered, turning away from the television screen. "I congratulate you, gentlemen."

The generals smiled wearily.

They looked at each other, then broke into a spontaneous shout. Armageddon was won, and the forces of Satan had been vanquished.

But something was happening on their screens.

"Is that—is that—" General MacFee began, and then couldn't speak.

For the Presence was upon the battlefield, walking among the piles of twisted, shattered metal.

The generals were silent.

The Presence touched a twisted robot.

Upon the smoking desert, the robots began to move. The twisted, scored, fused metals straightened.

The robots stood on their feet again.

"MacFee." Supreme General Fetterer whispered. "Try your controls. Make the robots kneel or something."

The general tried, but his controls were dead.

The mutilated robots began to rise in the air. Around them were the angels of the Lord, and the robot tanks and soldiers and bombers floated upward, higher and higher.

"He's saving them!" Ongin cried hysterically. "He's saving the robots!"

"It's a mistake!" Fetterer said. "Quick. Send a messenger to—No! We will go in person!"

And quickly a ship was commanded, and quickly they sped to the field of battle. But by then it was too late, for Armageddon was over, and the robots gone, and the Lord and His host departed.

Milk Run

"We can't pass it up," Arnold was saying. "Millions in profits, small initial investment, immediate return. Are you listening?"

Richard Gregor nodded wearily. It was a very dull day in the offices of the AAA Ace Interplanetary Decontamination Service, exactly like every other day. Gregor was playing solitaire. Arnold, his partner, was at his desk, his feet propped on a pile of unpaid bills.

Shadows moved past their glass door, thrown by people going to Mars Steel, Neo-Roman Novelties, Alpha Dura Products, or any other offices on the same floor.

But nothing broke the dusty silence in AAA Ace.

"What are we waiting for?" Arnold demanded loudly. "Do we do it or don't we?"

"It's not our line," Gregor said. "We're planetary decontaminationists. Remember?"

"But no one wants a planet decontaminated," Arnold stated.

That, unfortunately, was true. After successfully cleansing Ghost V of imaginary monsters, AAA Ace had had a short rush of business. But then expansion into space had halted. People were busy consolidating their gains, building towns, plowing fields, constructing roads.

The movement would begin again. The human race would expand as long as there was anything to expand into. But, for the moment, business was terrible.

"Consider the possibilities," Arnold said. "Here are all these people on their bright, shiny new worlds. They need farm and food animals shipped from home—" he paused dramatically—"by us."

"We're not equipped to handle livestock," Gregor pointed out.

"We have a ship. What else do we need?"

"Everything. Mostly knowledge and experience. Transporting live animals through space is extremely delicate work. It's a job for experts. What would you do if a cow came down with hoof-and-mouth disease between here and Omega IV?"

145

Arnold said confidently, "We will ship only hardy, mutated species. We will have them medically examined. And I will personally sterilize the ship before they come on board."

"All right, dreamer," Gregor said. "Prepare yourself for the blow. The Trigale Combine does all animal shipping in this sector of space. They don't look kindly upon competitors—therefore, they have no competitors. How do you plan to buck them?"

"We'll undersell them."

"And starve."

"We're starving now," Arnold said.

"Starving is better than being 'accidentally' holed by a Trigale tug at the port of embarkation. Or finding that someone has loaded our water tanks with kerosene. Or that our oxygen tanks were never filled at all."

"What an imagination you have!" Arnold said nervously.

"Those figments of my imagination have already happened. Trigale wants to be alone in the field and it is. By accident, you might say, if you like gory gags."

Just then, the door opened. Arnold swung his feet off the desk and Gregor swept his cards into a drawer.

Their visitor was an outworlder, to judge by his stocky frame, small head and pale green skin. He marched directly up to Arnold.

"They'll be at the Trigale Central Warehouse in three days," he said.

"So soon, Mr. Vens?" Arnold asked.

"Oh, yes. Had to transport the Smags pretty carefully, but the Queels have been on hand for several days."

"Fine. This is my partner," Arnold said, turning to Gregor, who was blinking rapidly.

"Happy." Vens spook Gregor's hand firmly. "Admire you men. Free enterprise, competition—believe in it. You've got the route?"

"All taped," Arnold said. "My partner is prepared to blast off at any moment."

"I'll go directly to Vermoine II and meet you there. Good show."

He turned and left.

Gregor said slowly, "Arnold, what have you done?"

"I've been making us rich, that's what I've done," Arnold retorted.

"Shipping livestock?"

"Yes."

"In Trigale territory?"

"Yes."

"Let me see the contract."

Arnold produced it. It stated that the AAA Ace Planetary Decontamination (and Transportation) Service promised to deliver five Smags, five

Firgels and ten Queels to the Vermoine solar system. Pickup was to be made at the Trigale Central Warehouse, delivery to Main Warehouse, Vermoine II. AAA Ace also had the option of building its own warehouse.

Said animals were to arrive intact, alive, healthy, happy, productive, *et cetera*. There were heavy forfeiture clauses in event of loss of animals, their arrival unalive, unhealthy, unproductive, *et cetera*.

The document read like a temporary armistice between unfriendly nations.

"You actually signed this death warrant?" Gregor asked incredulously.

"Sure. All you have to do is pick up the beasts, pop over to Vermoine and drop them."

"*I?* And what will *you* be doing?"

"I'll be right here, backing you all the way," Arnold said.

"Back me aboard ship."

"No, no—impossible. I get deathly sick at the very sight of a Queel."

"And that's how I feel about this deal. Let's stick *your* neck out for a change."

"But I'm the research department," Arnold objected, perspiring freely. "We set it up that way. Remember?"

Gregor remembered, sighed, and shrugged his shoulders helplessly.

They began at once to put their ship in order. The hold was divided into three compartments, each to carry a separate species. All were oxygen breathers and all could sustain life at about seventy degrees Fahrenheit, so that was no problem. The correct foods were put on board.

In three days, when they were as ready as they would ever be, Arnold decided to accompany Gregor as far as the Trigale Central Warehouse.

It was an uneventful trip to Trigale, but Gregor landed on the approach platform with considerable trepidation. There were too many stories about the Combine for him to feel entirely at home in their stronghold. He had taken what precautions he could. The ship had been completely fueled and provisioned at Luna Station and no Trigale man would be allowed on board.

However, if the personnel of the station were worried about the battered old spaceship, they hid it nicely. The ship was dragged to the loading platform by a pair of tractors and squeezed in between two sleek Trigale express freighters.

Leaving Arnold in charge of loading, Gregor went inside to sign the manifests. A suave Trigale official produced the papers and looked on with interest as Gregor read them over.

"Loading Smags, eh?" the official inquired politely.

"That's right," Gregor said, wondering what a Smag looked like.

"Queels and Firgels, too," the official mused. "Shipping them all together. You've got a lot of courage, Mr. Gregor."

"I have? Why?"

"You know the old saying—'When you travel with Smags, don't forget your magnifying glass.'"

"I hadn't heard that one."

The official grinned amiably and shook Gregor's hand. "After this trip, you'll be able to make up your own sayings. The very best of luck, Mr. Gregor. Unofficially, of course."

Gregor smiled feebly and returned to the loading platform. The Smags, Firgels, and Queels were on board, each in their own compartment. Arnold had turned on the air, checked the temperature, and given them all a day's ration.

"Well, you're off," Arnold said cheerfully.

"I'm off, all right," Gregor admitted with no cheer whatever. He climbed aboard, ignoring a faint snicker from the watching crowd.

The ship was tractored to a blastoff strip and soon Gregor was in space, bound for a tiny warehouse circling in orbit around Vermoine II.

There was always plenty to do on the first day in space. Gregor checked his instruments, then went over the main drive and the tanks, pipes and wiring, to make sure nothing had broken loose in the blastoff. Then he decided to inspect his cargo. It was about time he found out what they looked like.

The Queels, in the forward starboard compartment, looked like immense snowballs. Gregor knew that they were prized for their wool, which commanded a top price everywhere.

Apparently they hadn't gotten used to free-fall, for their food was untouched. He left them banking clumsily off walls and ceiling and bleating plaintively for solid ground.

The Firgels were no problem at all. They were big, leathery lizards, whose purpose on a farm Gregor couldn't guess. At present, they were dormant and would remain so throughout the trip.

Aft, the five Smags barked merrily when they saw him. They were friendly, herbivorous mammals and they seem to enjoy free-fall very much.

Satisfied, Gregor floated back to the control room. It was a good beginning. Trigale hadn't bothered him and his animals were doing all right in space.

This trip might be just a milk run, he decided.

After testing his radio and control switches, Gregor set the alarm and turned in.

He awoke, eight hours later, unrefreshed and with a splitting headache. His coffee tasted like slag and he could barely focus on the instrument panel.

The effects of canned air, he decided, and radioed Arnold that all was well. But halfway through the conversation, he found he could hardly keep his eyes open.

"Signing off," he said, yawning deeply. "Stuffy in here. Going to take a nap."

"Stuffy?" Arnold asked, his voice very distant over the radio. "It shouldn't be. The air circulators—"

Gregor found that the controls were swaying drunkenly and beginning to go out of focus. He leaned against the panel and closed his eyes.

"Gregor!"

"Hmm?"

"*Gregor!* Check your oxygen content!"

Gregor propped one eye open long enough to read the dial. He found, to his amusement, that the carbon dioxide concentration had reached a level he had never seen before.

"No oxygen," he told Arnold. "I'll fix it after nap."

"Sabotage!" Arnold shouted. "Wake up, Gregor!"

With a gigantic effort, Gregor reached forward and turned on the emergency air tank. The blast of air sobered him. He stood up, swaying uncertainly, and splashed some water on his face.

"The animals!" Arnold was screaming. "See about the animals!"

Gregor turned on the auxiliary air supply for all three compartments and hurried down the corridor.

The Firgels were still alive and dormant. The Smags apparently hadn't even noticed the difference. Two of the Queels had passed out, but they were reviving. And, in their compartment, Gregor found out what had happened.

There was no sabotage. The ventilators in wall and ceiling, through which the ship's air circulated, were jammed shut with Queel wool. Tufts of fleece floated in the still air, looking like a slow-motion snowfall.

"Of course, of course," Arnold said, when Gregor reported by radio. "Didn't I warn you that Queels have to be sheared twice a week? No, I guess I forgot to. Here's what the book says: 'The Queel—*Queelis Tropicalis*—is a small, wool-bearing mammal, distantly related to the Terran Sheep. Queels are natives of Tensis V, but have been successfully introduced on other heavy-gravity planets. Garments woven of Queel wool are fireproof, insectproof, rotproof, and will last almost indefinitely, due to the metallic content in the wool. Queels should be sheared twice a week. They reproduce feemishly.'"

"No sabotage," Gregor commented.

"No sabotage, but you'd better start shearing those Queels," Arnold said.

Gregor signed off, found a pair of tin snips in his tool kit and went to work on the Queels. But the metallic wool simply blunted the cutting edges. It seemed that Queels had to be sheared with special hard-alloy tools.

He gathered as much of the floating wool as he could find, and cleared the ventilators again. After a last inspection, he went to have his supper.

His beef stew was filled with oily, metallic Queel wool.
Disgusted, he turned in.

When he awoke, he found that the creaking old ship was still holding a true course. Her main drive was operating efficiently and the outlook seemed much brighter, especially after he found that the Firgels were still dormant and the Smags were doing nicely.

But when Gregor inspected the Queels, he found that they hadn't touched a morsel of food since coming on board. It was serious now. He called Arnold for advice.

"Very simple," Arnold told him, after searching through several reference books. "Queels haven't any throat muscles. They rely on gravity to get food down. But in free-fall, there isn't any gravity, so they can't get the food down."

It was simple, Gregor knew, one of those little things you would never consider on Earth. But space, with its artificial environment, aggravated even the simplest problems.

"You'll have to spin ship to give them some gravity," Arnold said.

Gregor did some quick mental multiplication. "That'll use up a lot of power."

"Then the book says you can push the food down their throats by hand. You roll it up in a moist ball and reach in as far as the elbow and—"

Gregor signed off and activated the side jets. His feet settled to the floor and he waited anxiously.

The Queels began to feed with an abandon that would have done a Queel-farmer's heart good.

He would have to refuel at the Vermoine II space warehouse and that would bring up their operating expenses, for fuel was expensive in newly colonized systems. Still, there would be a good margin of profit left over.

He returned to normal ship's duties. The spaceship crawled through the immensity of space.

Feeding time came again. Gregor fed the Queels and went on to the Smag compartment. He opened the door and called out, "Come and get it!"

Nothing came.

The compartment was empty.

Gregor felt a curious sensation in his stomach. It was impossible. The Smags couldn't be gone. They were playing a joke on him, hiding somewhere.

But there was no place in the compartment for five large Smags to hide.

The trembling sensation was turning into a full-grown quiver. Gregor remembered the forfeiture clauses in event of loss, damage, *et cetera, et cetera.*

"Here, Smag! *Here, Smag!*" he shouted. There was no answer.

He inspected the walls, ceiling, door and ventilators, on the chance that the Smags had somehow bored through.

There were no marks.

Then he heard a faint noise near his feet. Looking down, he saw something scuttle past him.

It was one of his Smags, shrunken to about two inches in length. He found the others hiding in a corner, all just as small.

What had the Trigale official said? "When you travel with Smags, don't forget your magnifying glass."

There was no time for a good, satisfying shock reaction. Gregor closed the door carefully and sprinted to the radio.

"Very odd," Arnold said, after radio contact had been made. "Shrunken, you say? I'm looking it up right now. Hmm...You didn't produce artificial gravity, did you?"

"Of course. To let the Queels feed."

"Shouldn't have done that," Arnold said. "Queels are light-gravity creatures."

"How was I supposed to know?"

"When they're subjected to an unusual—for them—gravity, they shrink down to microscopic size, lose consciousness and die."

"But *you* told me to produce artificial gravity."

"Oh, no! I simply mentioned, in passing, that that was one way of making Queels feed. I suggested hand-feeding."

Gregor resisted an almost overpowering urge to rip the radio out of the wall. He said, "Arnold, the Smags are light-gravity animals. Right?"

"Right."

"And the Queels are heavy gravity. Did you know that when you signed the contract?"

Arnold gulped for a moment, then cleared his throat. "Well, that did seem to make it a bit more difficult. But it pays very well."

"Sure, if you can get away with it. What do I do now?"

"Lower the temperature," Arnold replied confidently. "Smags stabilize at the freezing point."

"Humans freeze at the freezing point," Gregor said. "All right, signing off."

Gregor put on all the extra clothes he could find and turned up the ship's refrigeration system. Within an hour, the Smags had returned to their normal size.

So far, so good. He checked the Queels. The cold seemed to stimulate them. They were livelier than ever and bleated for more food. He fed them.

After eating a ham-and-wool sandwich, Gregor turned in.

The next day's inspection revealed that there were now fifteen Queels on board. The ten original adults had given birth to five young. All were hungry.

Gregor fed them. He set it down as a normal hazard of transporting mixed groups of livestock. They should have anticipated this and segregated the beasts by sexes as well as species.

When he looked in on the Queels again, their number had increased to thirty-eight.

"Reproduced, did they?" Arnold asked via radio, his voice concerned.

"Yes. And they show no signs of stopping."

"Well, we should have expected it."

"Why?" Gregor demanded baffledly.

"I told you. Queels reproduce feemishly."

"I *thought* that's what you said. What does it mean?"

"Just what it sounds like," said Arnold, irritated. "How did you ever get through school? It's freezing-point parthenogenesis."

"That does it," Gregor said grimly. "I'm turning this ship around."

"You can't! We'll be wiped out!"

"At the rate those Queels are reproducing, there won't be room for me if I keep going. A Queel will have to pilot this ship."

"Gregor, don't get panicky. There's a perfectly simple answer."

"I'm listening."

"Increase the air pressure and moisture content. That'll stop them."

"Sure. And it'll probably turn the Smags into butterflies."

"There won't be any other effects."

Turning back was no solution, anyhow. The ship was near the halfway mark. Now he could get rid of the beasts just as quickly by delivering them.

Unless he dumped them all into space. It was a tempting though impractical thought.

With increased air pressure and moisture content, the Queels stopped reproducing. They numbered forty-seven now and Gregor had to spend most of his time clearing the ventilators of wool. A slow-motion, surrealistic snowstorm raged in the corridors and engine room, in the water tanks and under his shirt.

Gregor ate tasteless meals of food and wool, with pie and wool for dessert.

He was beginning to feel like a Queel.

But then a bright spot approached on his horizon. The Vermoine sun began glowing on his forward screen. In another day, he would arrive, deliver his cargo and be free to go home to his dusty office, his bills and his solitaire game.

That night, he opened a bottle of wine to celebrate the end of the trip. It helped get the taste of wool out of his mouth and he fell into bed, mildly and pleasantly tipsy.

But he couldn't sleep. The temperature was still dropping. Beads of moisture on the walls of the ship were solidifying into ice.

He had to have heat.

Let's see—if he turned on the heaters, the Smags would shrink. Unless he stopped the gravity. In which case, the forty-seven Queels wouldn't eat.

To hell with the Queels. He was getting too cold to operate the ship.

He brought the vessel out of its spin and turned on the heaters. For an hour, he waited, shivering and stamping his feet. The heaters merrily drained fuel from the engines, but produced no heat.

That was ridiculous. He turned them on full blast.

In another hour, the temperature had sunk below zero. Although Vermoine was now visible, Gregor didn't know if he could even control the ship for a landing.

He had just finished building a small fire on the cabin floor, using the ship's more combustible furnishings as fuel, when the radio spluttered into life.

"I was just thinking," Arnold said. "I hope you haven't been changing gravity and pressure too abruptly."

"What difference does it make?" Gregor asked distractedly.

"You might unstabilize the Firgels. Rapid temperature and pressure changes could take them out of their dormant state. You'd better check."

Gregor hurried off. He opened the door to the Firgel compartment, peered in and shuddered.

The Firgels were awake and croaking. The big lizards were floating around their compartment, covered with frost.

A blast of sub-zero air roared into the passageway. Gregor slammed the door and hurried back to the radio.

"Of course, they're covered with frost," Arnold said. "Those Firgels are going to Vermoine I. Hot place, Vermoine I—right near the sun. The Firgels are cold-fixers—best portable air-conditioners in the Universe."

"Why didn't you tell me this sooner?" Gregor demanded.

"It would have upset you. Besides, they would have stayed dormant if you hadn't started fooling with gravity and pressure."

"The Firgels are going to Vermoine I. What about the Smags?"

"Vermoine II. Tiny planet, not much gravity."

"And the Queels?"

"Vermoine III, of course."

"You idiot!" Gregor shouted. "You give me a cargo like that and expect me to balance it?" If Arnold had been in the ship at that moment,

Gregor would have strangled him. "Arnold," he said, very slowly, "no more schemes, no more ideas—promise?"

"Oh, all right," Arnold agreed. "No need to get peevish about it."

Gregor signed off and went to work, trying to warm the ship. He succeeded in boosting it to twenty-seven degrees Fahrenheit before the overworked heaters gave up.

By then, Vermoine II was dead ahead.

Gregor knocked on a piece of wood he hadn't burned and set the tape. He was punching a course for the Main Warehouse, in orbit around Vermoine II, when he heard an ominous grumbling noise. At the same time, half a dozen dials on the control panel flopped over to zero.

Wearily, he floated back to the engine room. His main drive was dead and it didn't take any special mechanical aptitude to figure out why.

Queel wool floated in the engine room's still air. Queel wool was in the bearings and in the lubricating system, clogging the cooling fans.

The metallic wool made an ideal abrasive for highly polished engine parts. It was a wonder the drive had held up this long.

He returned to the control room. He couldn't land the ship without the main drive. Repairs would have to be made in space, eating into their profits. Fortunately, the ship steered by rocket side jets. With no mechanical system to break down, he could still maneuver.

It would be close, but he could still make contact with the artificial satellite that served as the Vermoine warehouse.

"This is AAA Ace," he announced as he squeezed the ship into an orbit around the satellite. "Request permission to land."

There was a crackle of static. "Satellite speaking," a voice answered. "Identify yourself, please."

"This is the AAA Ace ship, bound to Vermoine II from Trigale Central Warehouse," Gregor elaborated. "My papers are in order." He repeated the routine request for landing privilege and leaned back in his chair.

It had been a struggle, but all his animals were alive, intact, healthy, happy, *et cetera, et cetera*. AAA Ace had made a nice little profit. But all he wanted now was to get out of this ship and into a hot bath. He wanted to spend the rest of his life as far from Queels, Smags, and Firgels as possible. He wanted...

"Landing permission refused."

"What?"

"Sorry, but we're full up at present. If you want to hold your present orbit, I believe we can accommodate you in about three months."

"Hold on!" Gregor yelped. "You can't do this! I'm almost out of food, my main drive is shot, and I can't stand these animals much longer!"

"Sorry."

"You can't turn me away," Gregor said hoarsely. "This is a public warehouse. You have to—"

"Public? I beg your pardon, sir. This warehouse is owned and operated by the Trigale Combine."

The radio went dead. Gregor stared at it for several minutes.

Trigale!

Of course they hadn't bothered him at their Central Warehouse. They had him by simply refusing landing privileges at their Vermoine warehouse.

And the hell of it was, they were probably within their rights.

He couldn't land on the planet. Bringing the ship down without a main drive would be suicide. And there was no other space warehouse in the Vermoine solar system.

Well, he had brought the animals *almost* to the warehouse. Certainly Mr. Vens would understand the circumstances and judge his intentions.

He contacted Vens on Vermoine II and explained the situation.

"Not *at* the warehouse?" Vens asked.

"Well, within fifty miles of the warehouse," Gregor said

"That really won't do. I'll take the animals, of course. They're mine. But there are forfeiture clauses in the event of incomplete delivery."

"You wouldn't invoke them, would you?" Gregor pleaded. "My intentions—"

"They don't interest me," Vens said. "Margin of profit and all that. We colonists need every little bit." He signed off.

Perspiring in the cold room, Gregor called Arnold and told him the news.

"It's unethical!" Arnold declared in outrage.

"But legal."

"I know, damn it. I have to have time to think."

"You'd better find something good," Gregor said.

"I'll call you back."

Gregor spent the next few hours feeding his animals, picking Queel wool out of his hair and burning more furniture on the deck of the ship. When the radio buzzed, he crossed his fingers before answering it.

"Arnold?"

"No, this is Vens."

"Listen, Mr. Vens," Gregor said, "if you'd just give us a little more time, we could work out this thing amicably. I'm sure—"

"Oh, you've got me over a barrel, all right," Vens snapped. "It's perfectly legal, too. I checked. Shrewd operation, sir, very shrewd operation. I'm sending a tug for the animals."

"But the forfeiture clause—"

"Naturally, I cannot invoke it." Vens signed off.

Gregor stared at the radio. Shrewd operation? What had Arnold done?
He called Arnold's office.

"This is Mr. Arnold's secretary," a young feminine voice answered.
"Mr. Arnold has left for the day."

"Left? Secretary? Is this the Arnold of AAA Ace? I've got the wrong
Arnold, haven't I?"

"No, sir, this is Mr. Arnold's office, of the AAA Ace Planetary Warehouse Service. Did you wish to place an order? We have a first-class warehouse in the Vermoine system, in an orbit near Vermoine II. We handle
light, medium and heavy gravity products. Personal supervision by our
Mr. Gregor. And I think you'll find that our rates are quite attractive."

So that was what Arnold had done—he had turned their ship into a
warehouse! On paper, at least. And their contract *did* give them the option of supplying their own warehouse. Clever!

But that nuisance Arnold could never leave well enough alone. Now
he wanted to go into the warehouse business!

"What did you say, sir?"

"I said this is the warehouse speaking. I want to leave a message for
Mr. Arnold."

"Yes, sir?"

"Tell Mr. Arnold to cancel all orders," Gregor said grimly. "His warehouse is coming home as fast as it can hobble."

GHOST V

"He's reading our sign now," Gregor said, his long bony face pressed against the peephole in the office door.

"Let me see," Arnold said.

Gregor pushed him back. "He's going to knock—no, he's changed his mind. He's leaving."

Arnold returned to his desk and laid out another game of solitaire. Gregor kept watch at the peephole.

They had constructed the peephole out of sheer boredom three months after forming their partnership and renting the office. During that time, the AAA Ace Planet Decontamination Service had had no business—in spite of being first in the telephone book. Planetary decontamination was an old, established line, completely monopolized by two large outfits. It was discouraging for a small new firm run by two young men with big ideas and a lot of unpaid-for equipment.

"He's coming back," Gregor called. *"Quick*—look busy and important!"

Arnold swept his cards into a drawer and just finished buttoning his lab gown when the knock came.

Their visitor was a short, bald, tired-looking man. He stared at them dubiously.

"You decontaminate planets?"

"That is correct, sir," Gregor said, pushing away a pile of papers and shaking the man's moist hand. "I am Richard Gregor. This is my partner, Doctor Frank Arnold."

Arnold, impressively garbed in a white lab gown and black horn-rimmed glasses, nodded absently and resumed his examination of a row of ancient, crusted test tubes.

"Kindly be seated, Mister—"

"Ferngraum."

"Mr. Ferngraum. I think we can handle just about anything you require," Gregor said heartily. "Flora or fauna control, cleansing atmosphere, purifying water supply, sterilizing soil, stability testing, volcano and earthquake control—anything you need to make a planet fit for human habitation."

Ferngraum still looked dubious. "I'm going to level with you. I've got a problem planet on my hands."

Gregor nodded confidently. "Problems are our business."

"I'm a freelance real-estate broker," Ferngraum said. "You know how it works—buy a planet, sell a planet, everyone makes a living. Usually I stick with the scrub worlds and let my buyers do their decontaminating. But a few months ago I had a chance to buy a real quality planet—took it right out from under the noses of the big operators."

Ferngraum mopped his forehead unhappily.

"It's a beautiful place," he continued with no enthusiasm whatsoever. "Average temperature of 71 degrees. Mountainous, but fertile. Waterfalls, rainbows, all that sort of thing. And no fauna at all."

"Sounds perfect," Gregor said. "Microorganisms?"

"Nothing dangerous."

"Then what's wrong with the place?"

Ferngraum looked embarrassed. "Maybe you heard about it. The government catalogue number is RJC-5. But everyone else calls it 'Ghost V.'"

Gregor raised an eyebrow. "Ghost" was an odd nickname for a planet, but he had heard odder. After all, you had to call them something. There were thousands of planet-bearing suns within spaceship range, many of them inhabitable or potentially inhabitable. And there were plenty of people from the civilized worlds who wanted to colonize them. Religious sects, political minorities philosophic groups—or just plain pioneers, out to make a fresh start.

"I don't believe I've heard of it," Gregor said.

Ferngraum squirmed uncomfortably in his chair. "I should have listened to my wife. But no—I was gonna be a big operator. Paid ten times my usual price for Ghost V and now I'm stuck with it."

"But what's *wrong* with it?" Gregor asked.

"It seems to be haunted," Ferngraum said in despair.

Ferngraum had radar-checked his planet, then leased it to a combine of farmers from Dijon VI. The eight-man advance guard landed and, within a day, began to broadcast garbled reports about demons, ghouls, vampires, dinosaurs and other inimical fauna.

When a relief ship came for them, all were dead. An autopsy report stated that the gashes, cuts and marks on their bodies could indeed have been made by almost anything, even demons, ghouls, vampires or dinosaurs, if such existed.

Ferngraum was fined for improper decontamination. The farmers dropped their lease. But he managed to lease it to a group of sun worshipers from Opal II.

The sun worshipers were cautious. They sent their equipment, but only three men accompanied it, to scout out trouble. The men set up camp, unpacked and declared the place a paradise. They radioed the home group to come at once—then, suddenly, there was a wild scream and radio silence.

A patrol ship went to Ghost V, buried the three mangled bodies and departed in five minutes flat.

"And that did it," Ferngraum said. "Now no one will touch it at any price. Space crews refuse to land on it. And I still don't know what happened."

He sighed deeply and looked at Gregor. "It's your baby, if you want it."

Gregor and Arnold excused themselves and went into the anteroom.

Arnold whooped at once, "We've got a job!"

"Yeah," Gregor said, "but what a job."

"We wanted the tough ones," Arnold pointed out. "If we lick this, we're established—to say nothing of the profit we'll make on a percentage basis."

"You seem to forget," Gregor said, "I'm the one who has to actually land on the planet. All you do is sit here and interpret my data."

"That's the way we set it up," Arnold reminded him. "I'm the research department—you're the troubleshooter. Remember?"

Gregor remembered. Ever since childhood, he had been sticking his neck out while Arnold stayed home and told him why he was sticking his neck out.

"I don't like it," he said.

"You don't believe in ghosts, do you?"

"No, of course not."

"Well, we can handle anything else. Faint heart ne'er won fair profit."

Gregor shrugged his shoulders. They went back to Ferngraum.

In half an hour, they had worked out their terms—a large percentage of future development profits if they succeeded, a forfeiture clause if they failed.

Gregor walked to the door with Ferngraum. "By the way, sir," he asked, "how did you happen to come to us?"

"No one else would handle it," Ferngraum said, looking extremely pleased with himself. "Good luck."

Three days later, Gregor was aboard a rickety space freighter, bound for Ghost V. He spent his time studying reports on the two colonization attempts and reading survey after survey on supernatural phenomena.

They didn't help at all. No trace of animal life had been found on Ghost V. And no proof of the existence of supernatural creatures had been discovered anywhere in the Galaxy.

Gregor pondered this, then checked his weapons as the freighter spiraled into the region of Ghost V. He was carrying an arsenal large enough to start a small war and win it.

If he could find something to shoot at...

The captain of the freighter brought his ship to within several thousand feet of the smiling green surface of the planet, but no closer. Gregor parachuted his equipment to the site of the last two camps, shook hands with the captain and 'chuted himself down.

He landed safely and looked up. The freighter was streaking into space as though the furies were after it.

He was alone on Ghost V.

After checking his equipment for breakage, he radioed Arnold that he had landed safely. Then, with drawn blaster, he inspected the sun worshipers' camp.

They had set themselves up at the base of a mountain, beside a small, crystal-clear lake. The prefabs were in perfect condition.

No storms had ever damaged them, because Ghost V was blessed with a beautifully even climate. But they looked pathetically lonely.

Gregor made a careful check of one. Clothes were still neatly packed in cabinets, pictures were hung on the wall and there was even a curtain on one window. In a corner of the room, a case of toys had been opened for the arrival of the main party's children.

A water pistol, a top and a bag of marbles had spilled onto the floor.

Evening was coming, so Gregor dragged his equipment into the prefab and made his preparations. He rigged an alarm system and adjusted it so finely that even a roach would set it off. He put up a radar alarm to scan the immediate area. He unpacked his arsenal, laying the heavy rifles within easy reach, but keeping a hand-blaster in his belt. Then, satisfied, he ate a leisurely supper.

Outside, the evening drifted into night. The warm and dreamy land grew dark. A gentle breeze ruffled the surface of the lake and rustled silkily in the tall grass.

It was all very peaceful.

The settlers must have been hysterical types, he decided. They had probably panicked and killed each other.

After checking his alarm system one last time, Gregor threw his clothes onto a chair, turned off the lights and climbed into bed. The room was illuminated by starlight, stronger than moonlight on Earth. His blaster was under his pillow. All was well with the world.

He had just begun to doze off when he became aware that he was not alone in the room.

That was impossible. His alarm system hadn't gone off. The radar was still humming peacefully.

Yet every nerve in his body was shrieking alarm. He eased the blaster out and looked around.

A man was standing in a comer of the room.

There was no time to consider how he had come. Gregor aimed the blaster and said, "Okay, raise your hands," in a quiet, resolute voice.

The figure didn't move.

Gregor's finger tightened on the trigger, then suddenly relaxed. He recognized the man. It was his own clothing, heaped on a chair, distorted by the starlight and his own imagination.

He grinned and lowered the blaster. The pile of clothing began to stir faintly. Gregor felt a faint breeze from the window and continued to grin.

Then the pile of clothing stood up, stretched itself and began to walk toward him purposefully.

Frozen to his bed, he watched the disembodied clothing, assembled roughly in manlike form, advance on him.

When it was halfway across the room and its empty sleeves were reaching for him, he began to blast.

And kept on blasting, for the rags and remnants slithered toward him as if filled with a life of their own. Flaming bits of cloth crowded toward his face and a belt tried to coil around his legs. He had to burn everything to ashes before the attack stopped.

When it was over, Gregor turned on every light he could find. He brewed a pot of coffee and poured in most of a bottle of brandy. Somehow, he resisted an urge to kick his useless alarm system to pieces. Instead, he radioed his partner.

"That's very interesting," Arnold said, after Gregor had brought him up to date. "Animation! Very interesting indeed."

"I hoped it would amuse you," Gregor answered bitterly. After several shots of brandy, he was beginning to feel abandoned and abused.

"Did anything else happen?"

"Not yet."

"Well, take care. I've got a theory. Have to do some research on it. By the way, some crazy bookie is laying five to one against you."

"Really?"

"Yeah. I took a piece of it."

"Did you bet for me or against me?" Gregor asked, worried.

"For you, of course," Arnold said indignantly. "We're partners, aren't we?"

They signed off and Gregor brewed another pot of coffee. He was not planning on any more sleep that night. It was comforting to know that Arnold had bet on him. But, then, Arnold was a notoriously bad gambler.

By daylight, Gregor was able to get a few hours of fitful sleep. In the early afternoon he awoke, found some clothes and began to explore the sun worshipers' camp.

Toward evening, he found something. On the wall of a prefab, the word *"Tgasklit"* had been hastily scratched. *Tgasklit.* It meant nothing to him, but he relayed it to Arnold at once.

He then searched his prefab carefully, set up more lights, tested the alarm system and recharged his blaster.

Everything seemed in order. With regret, he watched the sun go down, hoping he would live to see it rise again. Then he settled himself in a comfortable chair and tried to do some constructive thinking.

There was no animal life here—nor were there any walking plants, intelligent rocks or giant brains dwelling in the planet's core. Ghost V hadn't even a moon for someone to hide on.

And he couldn't believe in ghosts or demons. He knew that supernatural happenings tended to break down, under detailed examination, into eminently natural events. The ones that didn't break down—stopped. Ghosts just wouldn't stand still and let a non-believer examine them. The phantom of the castle was invariably on vacation when a scientist showed up with cameras and tape recorders.

That left another possibility. Suppose someone wanted this planet, but wasn't prepared to pay Ferngraum's price? Couldn't this someone hide here, frighten the settlers, kill them if necessary in order to drive down the price?

That seemed logical. You could even explain the behavior of his clothes that way. Static electricity, correctly used, could—

Something was standing in front of him. His alarm system, as before, hadn't gone off.

Gregor looked up slowly. The thing in front of him was about ten feet tall and roughly human in shape, except for its crocodile head. It was colored a bright crimson and had purple stripes running lengthwise on its body. In one claw, it was carrying a large brown can.

"Hello," it said.

"Hello," Gregor gulped. His blaster was on a table only two feet away. He wondered, would the thing attack if he reached for it?

"What's your name?" Gregor asked, with the calmness of deep shock.

"'I'm the Purple-striped Grabber," the thing said. "I grab things."

"How interesting." Gregor's hand began to creep toward the blaster.

"I grab things named Richard Gregor," the Grabber told him in its bright, ingenuous voice. "And I usually eat them in chocolate sauce." It held up the brown can and Gregor saw that it was labeled "Smig's Chocolate—An Ideal Sauce to Use with Gregors, Arnolds and Flynns."

Gregor's fingers touched the butt of the blaster. He asked, "Were you planning to eat me?"

"Oh, yes," the Grabber said.

Gregor had the gun now. He flipped off the safety catch and fired. The radiant blast cascaded off the Grabber's chest and singed the floor, the walls and Gregor's eyebrows.

"That won't hurt me," the Grabber explained. "I'm too tall."

The blaster dropped from Gregor's fingers. The Grabber leaned forward.

"I'm not going to eat you now," the Grabber said.

"No?" Gregor managed to enunciate.

"No. I can only eat you tomorrow, on May first. Those are the rules. I just came to ask a favor."

"What is it?"

The Grabber smiled winningly. "Would you be a good sport and eat a few apples? They flavor the flesh so wonderfully."

And, with that, the striped monster vanished.

With shaking hands, Gregor worked the radio and told Arnold everything that had happened.

"Hmm," Arnold said. "Purple-striped Grabber, eh? I think that clinches it. Everything fits."

"What fits? What is it?"

"First, do as I say. I want to make sure."

Obeying Arnold's instructions, Gregor unpacked his chemical equipment and laid out a number of test tubes, retorts and chemicals. He stirred, mixed, added and subtracted as directed and finally put the mixture on the stove to heat.

"Now," Gregor said, coming back to the radio, "Tell me what's going on."

"Certainly. I looked up the word 'Tgasklit.' It's Opalian. It means 'many-toothed ghost.' The sun worshipers were from Opal. What does that suggest to you?"

"They were killed by a home-town ghost," Gregor replied nastily. "It must have stowed away on their ship. Maybe there was a curse and—"

"Calm down," Arnold said. "There aren't any ghosts in this. Is the solution boiling yet?"

"No."

"Tell me when it does. Now let's take your animated clothing. Does it remind you of anything?"

Gregor thought. "Well," he said, "when I was a kid—no, that's ridiculous."

"Out with it," Arnold insisted.

"When I was a kid, I never left clothing on a chair. In the dark, it always looked like a man or a dragon or something. I guess everyone's had that experience. But it doesn't explain—"

"Sure it does! Remember the Purple-striped Grabber now?"

"No. Why should I?"

"Because you invented him! Remember? We must have been eight or nine, you and me and Jimmy Flynn. We invented the most horrible monster you could think of—he was our own personal monster and he only wanted to eat you or me or Jimmy—flavored with chocolate sauce. But only on the first of every month, when the report cards were due. You had to use the magic word to get rid of him."

Then Gregor remembered and wondered how he could ever have forgotten. How many nights had he stayed up in fearful expectation of the Grabber? It had made bad report cards seem very unimportant.

"Is the solution boiling?" Arnold asked.

"Yes," said Gregor, glancing obediently at the stove.

"What color is it?"

"A sort of greenish blue. No, it's more blue than—"

"Right. You can pour it out. I want to run a few more tests, but I think we've got it licked."

"Got *what* licked? Would you do a little explaining?"

"It's obvious. The planet has no animal life. There are no ghosts or at least none solid enough to kill off a party of armed men. Hallucination was the answer, so I looked for something that would produce it. I found plenty. Aside from all the drugs on Earth, there are about a dozen hallucination-forming gases in the *Catalogue of Alien Trace Elements*. There are depressants, stimulants, stuff that'll make you feel like a genius or an earthworm or an eagle. This particular one corresponds to Longstead 42 in the catalogue. It's a heavy, transparent, odorless gas, not harmful physically. It's an imagination stimulant."

"You mean I was just having hallucinations? I tell you—"

"Not quite that simple," Arnold cut in. "Longstead 42 works directly on the subconscious. It releases your strongest subconscious fears, the childhood terrors you've been suppressing. It animates them. And that's what you've been seeing."

"Then there's actually nothing here?" Gregor asked.

"Nothing physical. But the hallucinations are real enough to whoever is having them."

Gregor reached over for another bottle of brandy. This called for a celebration.

"It won't be hard to decontaminate Ghost V," Arnold went on confidently. "We can cancel the Longstead 42 with no difficulty. And then— we'll be rich, partner!"

Gregor suggested a toast, then thought of something disturbing. "If they're just hallucinations, what happened to the settlers?"

Arnold was silent for a moment. "Well," he said finally, "Longstead may have a tendency to stimulate the mortido—the death instinct. The settlers must have gone crazy. Killed each other."

"And no survivors?"

"Sure, why not? The last ones alive committed suicide or died of wounds. Don't worry about it. I'm chartering a ship immediately and coming out to run those tests. Relax. I'll pick you up in a day or two."

Gregor signed off. He allowed himself the rest of the bottle of brandy that night. It seemed only fair. The mystery of Ghost V was solved and they were going to be rich. Soon *he* would be able to hire a man to land on strange planets for him while *he* sat home and gave instructions over a radio.

He awoke late the next day with a hangover. Arnold's ship hadn't arrived yet, so he packed his equipment and waited. By evening, there was still no ship. He sat in the doorway of the prefab and watched a gaudy sunset, then went inside and made dinner.

The problem of the settlers still bothered him, but he determined not to worry about it. Undoubtedly there was a logical answer.

After dinner, he stretched out on a bed. He had barely closed his eyes when he heard someone cough apologetically.

"Hello," said the Purple-striped Grabber.

His own personal hallucination had returned to eat him. "Hello, old chap," Gregor said cheerfully, without a bit of fear or worry.

"Did you eat the apples?"

"Dreadfully sorry. I forgot."

"Oh, well." The Grabber tried to conceal his disappointment. "I brought the chocolate sauce." He held up the can.

Gregor smiled. "You can leave now," he said. "I know you're just a figment of my imagination. You can't hurt me."

"I'm not going to hurt you," the Grabber said. "I'm just going to eat you."

He walked up to Gregor. Gregor held his ground, smiling, although he wished the Grabber didn't appear so solid and undreamlike. The Grabber leaned over and bit his arm experimentally.

He jumped back and looked at his arm. There were toothmarks on it. Blood was oozing out—real blood—*his* blood.

The colonists had been bitten, gashed, torn and ripped.

At that moment, Gregor remembered an exhibition of hypnotism he had once seen. The hypnotist had told the subject he was putting a lighted cigarette on his arm. Then he had touched the spot with a pencil.

Within seconds, an angry red blister had appeared on the subject's arm, because he *believed* he had been burned. If your subconscious thinks you're dead, you're dead. If it orders the stigmata of toothmarks, they are there.

He didn't believe in the Grabber.

But his subconscious did.

Gregor tried to run for the door. The Grabber cut him off. It seized him in its claws and bent to reach his neck.

The magic word! What was it?

Gregor shouted, *"Alphoisto?"*

"Wrong word," said the Grabber. "Please don't squirm."

"Regnastikio!"

"Nope. Stop wriggling and it'll be over before you—"

"Voorshpellhappilo!"

The Grabber let out a scream of pain and released him. It bounded high into the air and vanished.

Gregor collapsed into a chair. That had been close. Too close. It would be a particularly stupid way to die—rent by his own death-desiring subconscious, slashed by his own imagination, killed by his own conviction. It was fortunate he had remembered the word. Now if Arnold would only hurry...

He heard a low chuckle of amusement.

It came from the blackness of a half-opened closet door, touching off an almost forgotten memory. He was nine years old again, and the Shadower—his Shadower—was a strange, thin, grisly creature who hid in doorways, slept under beds and attacked only in the dark.

"Turn out the lights," the Shadower said.

"Not a chance," Gregor retorted, drawing his blaster. As long as the lights were on, he was safe.

"You'd better turn them off."

"No!"

"Very well. Egan, Megan, Degan!"

Three little creatures scampered into the room. They raced to the nearest light bulb, flung themselves on it and began to gulp hungrily.

The room was growing darker.

Gregor blasted at them each time they approached a light. Glass shattered, but the nimble creatures darted out of the way.

And then Gregor realized what he had done. The creatures couldn't actually eat light. Imagination can't make any impression on inanimate matter. He had *imagined* that the room was growing dark and—

He had shot out his light bulbs! His own destructive subconscious had tricked him.

Now the Shadower stepped out. Leaping from shadow to shadow, he came toward Gregor.

The blaster had no effect. Gregor tried frantically to think of the magic word—and terrifiedly remembered that no magic word banished the Shadower.

He backed away, the Shadower advancing, until he was stopped by a packing case. The Shadower towered over him and Gregor shrank to the floor and closed his eyes.

His hands came in contact with something cold. He was leaning against the packing case of toys for the settlers' children. And he was holding a water pistol.

Gregor brandished it. The Shadower backed away, eyeing the weapon with apprehension.

Quickly, Gregor ran to the tap and filled the pistol. He directed a deadly stream of water into the creature.

The Shadower howled in agony and vanished.

Gregor smiled tightly and slipped the empty gun into his belt. A water pistol was the right weapon to use against an imaginary monster.

It was nearly dawn when the ship landed and Arnold stepped out. Without wasting any time, he set up his tests. By midday, it was done and the element definitely established as Longstead 42. He and Gregor packed up immediately and blasted off.

Once they were in space, Gregor told his partner every thing that had happened.

"Pretty rough," said Arnold softly, but with deep feeling.

Gregor could smile with modest heroism now that he was safely off Ghost V. "Could have been worse," he said.

"How?"

"Suppose Jimmy Flynn were here. There was a kid who could really dream up monsters. Remember the Grumbler?"

"All I remember is the nightmares it gave me," Arnold said.

They were on their way home. Arnold jotted down some notes for an article entitled "The Death Instinct on Ghost V: An Examination of Subconscious Stimulation, Hysteria, and Mass Hallucination in Producing Physical Stigmata." Then he went to the control room to set the autopilot.

Gregor threw himself on a couch, determined to get his first decent night's sleep since landing on Ghost V. He had barely dozed off when Arnold hurried in, his face pasty with terror.

"I think there's something in the control room," he said.

Gregor sat up. "There can't be. We're off the—"

There was a low growl from the control room.

"Oh, my God!" Arnold gasped. He concentrated furiously for a few seconds. "I know. I left the airlocks open when I landed. We're still breathing Ghost V air!"

And there, framed in the open doorway, was an immense gray creature with red spots on its hide. It had an amazing number of arms, legs, tentacles, claws and teeth, plus two tiny wings on its back. It walked slowly toward them, mumbling and groaning.

They both recognized it as the Grumbler.

Gregor dashed forward and slammed the door, in its face. "We should be safe in here," he panted. "That door is airtight. But how will we pilot the ship?"

"We won't," Arnold said. "We'll have to trust the robot pilot—unless we can figure out some way of getting that thing out of there."

They noticed that a faint smoke was beginning to seep through the sealed edges of the door.

"What's that?" Arnold asked, with a sharp edge of panic in his voice.

Gregor frowned. "You remember, don't you? The Grumbler can get into any room. There's no way of keeping him out."

"I don't remember anything about him," Arnold said. "Does he eat people?"

"No. As I recall, he just mangles them thoroughly."

The smoke was beginning to solidify into the immense gray shape of the Grumbler. They retreated into the next compartment and sealed the door. Within seconds, the thin smoke was leaking through.

"This is ridiculous," Arnold said, biting his lip. "To be hunted by an imaginary monster—wait! You've still got your water pistol, haven't you?"

"Yes, but—"

"Give it to me!"

Arnold hurried over to a water tank and filled the pistol. The Grumbler had taken form again and was lumbering toward them, groaning unhappily. Arnold raked it with a stream of water.

The Grumbler kept on advancing.

"Now it's all coming back to me," Gregor said. "A water pistol never could stop the Grumbler."

They backed into the next room and slammed the door. Behind them was only the bunkroom, with nothing behind that but the deadly vacuum of space.

Gregor asked, "Isn't there something you can do about the atmosphere?"

Arnold shook his head. "It's dissipating now. But it takes about twenty hours for the effects of Longstead to wear off."

"Haven't you any antidote?"

"No."

Once again the Grumbler was materializing, and neither silently nor pleasantly.

"How can we kill it?" Arnold asked. "There must be a way. Magic words? How about a wooden sword?"

Gregor shook his head. "I remember the Grumbler now," he said unhappily.

"What kills it?"

"'It can't be destroyed by water pistols, cap guns, firecrackers, sling-shots, stink bombs, or any other childhood weapon. The Grumbler is absolutely unkillable.'"

"That Flynn and his damned imagination! Why did we have to talk about him? How do you get rid of it then?"

"I told you. You don't. It just has to go away of its own accord."

The Grumbler was full size now. Gregor and Arnold hurried into the tiny bunkroom and slammed their last door.

"*Think,* Gregor," Arnold pleaded. "No kid invents a monster without a defense of some sort. *Think!*"

"The Grumbler cannot be killed," Gregor said.

The red-spotted monster was taking shape again. Gregor thought back over all the midnight horrors he had ever known. He *must* have done something as a child to neutralize the power of the unknown.

And then—almost too late—he remembered.

Under auto-pilot controls, the ship flashed Earthward with the Grumbler as complete master. He marched up and down the empty corridors and floated through steel partitions into cabins and cargo compartments, moaning, groaning and cursing because he could not get at any victim.

The ship reached the Solar System and took up an automatic orbit around the Moon.

Gregor peered our cautiously, ready to duck back if necessary. There was no sinister shuffling, no moaning or groaning, no hungry mist seeping under the door or through the walls.

"All clear," he called out to Arnold. "The Grumbler's gone."

Safe within the ultimate defense against night horrors—wrapped in the blankets that had covered their heads—they climbed out of their bunks.

"I told you the water pistol wouldn't do any good," Gregor said.

Arnold gave him a sick grin and put the pistol in his pocket. "I'm hanging onto it. If I ever get married and have a kid, it's going to be his first present."

"Not for any of mine," said Gregor. He patted the bunk affection-ately. "You can't beat blankets over the head for protection."

THE LAXIAN KEY

Richard Gregor was at his desk in the dusty office of the AAA Ace Interplanetary Decontamination Service. It was almost noon, but Arnold, his partner, hadn't shown up yet. Gregor was just laying out an unusually complicated game of solitaire. Then he heard a loud crash in the hall.

The door of AAA Ace opened, and Arnold stuck his head in.

"Banker's hours?" Gregor asked.

"I have just made our fortunes," Arnold said. He threw the door fully open and beckoned dramatically. "Bring it in, boys."

Four sweating workmen lugged in a square black machine the size of a baby elephant.

"There it is," Arnold said proudly. He paid the workmen, and stood, hands clasped behind his back, eyes half shut, surveying the machine.

Gregor put his cards away with the slow, weary motions of a man who has seen everything. He stood up and walked around the machine. "All right, I give up. What is it?"

"It's a million bucks, right in our fists," Arnold said.

"Of course. But *what* is it?"

"It's a Free Producer," Arnold said. He smiled proudly. "I was walking past Joe's Interstellar Junkyard this morning, and there it was, sitting in the window. I picked it up for next to nothing. Joe didn't even know what it was."

"I don't either," Gregor said. "Do you?"

Arnold was on his hands and knees, trying to read the instructions engraved on the front of the machine. Without looking up, he said, "You've heard of the planet Meldge, haven't you?"

Gregor nodded. Meldge was a third-rate little planet on the northern periphery of the galaxy, some distance from the trade routes. At one time, Meldge had possessed an extremely advanced civilization, made possible by the so-called Meldgen Old Science. The Old Science techniques had been lost ages ago, although an occasional artifact still turned up here and there.

"And this is a product of the Old Science?" Gregor asked.

"Right. It's a Meldgen Free Producer. I doubt if there are more than four or five of them in the entire universe. They're unduplicatable."

171

"What does it produce?" Gregor asked.

"How should I know?" Arnold asked. "Hand me the Meldge-English dictionary, will you?"

Keeping a stern rein on his patience, Gregor walked to the bookshelf. "You don't know what it produces—"

"Dictionary. Thank you. What does it matter what it produces? It's *free!* This machine grabs energy out of the air, out of space, the sun, anywhere. You don't have to plug it in, fuel, or service it. It runs indefinitely."

Arnold opened the dictionary and started to look up the words on the front of the Producer.

"Free Energy—"

"Those scientists were no fools," Arnold said, jotting down his translation on a pocket pad. "The Producer just grabs energy out of the air. So it really doesn't matter what it turns out. We can always sell it, and anything we get will be pure profit."

Gregor stared at his dapper little partner, and his long, unhappy face became sadder than ever.

"Arnold," he said, "I'd like to remind you of something. First of all, you are a chemist. I am an ecologist. We know nothing about machinery and less than nothing about complicated alien machinery."

Arnold nodded absently and turned a dial. The Producer gave a dry gurgle.

"What's more," Gregor said, retreating a few steps, "we are planetary decontaminationists. Remember? We have no reason to—"

The Producer began to cough unevenly.

"Got it now," Arnold said. "It says, 'The Meldgen Free Producer, another triumph of Glotten Laboratories. This Producer is Warranted Indestructible, Unbreakable, and Free of all Defects. No Power Hookup Is Required. To Start, Press Button One. To Stop, Use Laxian Key. Your Meldgen Free Producer comes with an Eternal Guarantee against Malfunction. If Defective in Any Way, Please Return at Once to Glotten Laboratories.'"

"Perhaps I didn't make myself clear," Gregor said. "We are planetary—"

"Don't be stodgy," Arnold said. "Once we get this thing working, we can retire. Here's Button One."

The machine began to clank ominously, then shifted to a steady purr. For long minutes, nothing happened.

"Needs warming up," Arnold said anxiously.

Then, out of an opening at the base of the machine, a gray powder began to pour.

"Probably a waste product," Gregor muttered. But the powder continued to stream over the floor for 15 minutes.

"Success!" Arnold shouted.

"What is it?" Gregor asked.

"I haven't the faintest idea. I'll have to run some tests." Grinning triumphantly, Arnold scooped some powder into a test tube and hurried over to his desk.

Gregor stood in front of the Producer, watching the gray powder stream out. Finally he said, "Shouldn't we turn it off until we find out what it is?"

"Of course not," Arnold said. "Whatever it is, it must be worth money." He lighted his bunsen burner, filled a test tube with distilled water, and went to work.

Gregor shrugged his shoulders. He was used to Arnold's harebrained schemes. Ever since they had formed AAA Ace, Arnold had been looking for a quick road to wealth. His shortcuts usually resulted in more work than plain old-fashioned labor, but Arnold was quick to forget that.

Well, Gregor thought, at least it kept things lively. He sat down at his desk and dealt out a complex solitaire.

There was silence in the office for the next few hours. Arnold worked steadily, adding chemicals, pouring off precipitates, checking the results in several large books he kept on his desk. Gregor brought in sandwiches and coffee. After eating, he paced up and down and watched the gray powder tumble steadily out of the machine.

The purr of the Producer grew steadily louder, and the powder flowed in a thick stream.

An hour after lunch Arnold stood up. "We are in!" he stated.

"What is that stuff?" Gregor asked, wondering if, for once, Arnold had hit on something.

"That stuff," Arnold said, "is Tangreese." He looked expectantly at Gregor.

"Tangreese, eh?"

"Absolutely."

"Then would you kindly tell me what Tangreese is?" Gregor shouted.

"I thought you knew. Tangreese is the basic food of the Meldgen people. An adult Meldgen consume several tons a year."

"Food, eh?" Gregor looked at the thick gray powder with new respect. A machine which turned out food steadily, 24 hours a day, might be a very good moneymaker. Especially if the machine never needed servicing, and cost nothing to run.

Arnold already had the telephone book open. "Here we are." He dialed a number. "Hello, Interstellar Food Corporation? Let me speak to the president. What? He isn't? The vice-president, then. This is important...Channels, eh? All right, here's the story. I am in a position to supply you with an almost unlimited quantity of Tangreese, the basic food of the Meldgen people. That's right. I knew you'd be interested. Yes, of course I'll hold on."

He turned to Gregor. "These corporations think they can push—yes?…Yes sir, that's right, sir. You *do* handle Tangreese, eh?…Fine splendid!"

Gregor moved closer, trying to hear what was being said on the other end. Arnold pushed him away.

"Price? Well, what is the fair market price?…Oh. Well, five dollars a ton isn't much, but I suppose—what? Five *cents* a ton? You're kidding! Let's be serious now."

Gregor walked away from the telephone and sank wearily into a chair. Apathetically he listened to Arnold saying, "Yes, yes. Well, I didn't know that…I see. Thank you."

Arnold hung up. "It seems," he said, "there's not much demand for Tangreese on Earth. There are only about 50 Meldgens here, and the cost of transporting it to the northern periphery is prohibitively high."

Gregor raised both eyebrows and looked at the Producer. Apparently it had hit its stride, for Tangreese was pouring out like water from a high-pressure hose. There was gray powder over everything in the room. It was half a foot deep in front of the machine.

"Never mind," Arnold said. "It must be used for something else." He returned to his desk and opened several more large books.

"Shouldn't we turn it off in the meantime?" Gregor asked.

"Certainly not," Arnold said. "It's *free,* don't you understand? It's making money for us."

He plunged into his books. Gregor began to pace the floor, but found it difficult wading through the ankle-deep Tangreese. He slumped into his chair, wondering why he hadn't gone into landscape gardening.

By early evening, gray dust filled the room to a depth of several feet. Several pens, pencils, a briefcase, and a small filing cabinet were already lost in it, and Gregor was beginning to shovel a path to the door, using a wastepaper basket as an improvised spade.

Arnold finally closed his books with a look of weary satisfaction. "There *is* another use."

"What?"

"Tangreese is used as a building material. After a few weeks' exposure to the air, it hardens like granite, you know."

"No, I didn't."

"Get a construction company on the telephone. We'll take care of this right now."

Gregor called the Toledo-Mars Construction Company and told a Mr. O'Toole that they were prepared to supply them with an almost unlimited quantity of Tangreese.

"Tangreese, eh?" O'Toole said. "Not too popular as a building material these days. Doesn't hold paint, you know."

"No, I didn't," Gregor said.

"Fact. Tell you what. Tangreese can be eaten by some crazy race. Why don't you—"

"We prefer to sell it as a building material," Gregor said.

"Well, I suppose we can buy it. Always some cheap construction going on. Give you 15 a ton for it."

"Dollars?"

"Cents."

"I'll let you know," Gregor said.

His partner nodded sagely when he heard the offer. "That's all right. Say this machine of ours produces ten tons a day, every day, year after year. Let's see…" He did some quick figuring with his slide rule. "That's almost 550 dollars a year. Won't make us rich, but it'll help pay the rent."

"But we can't leave it here," Gregor said, looking with alarm at the ever-increasing pile of Tangreese.

"Of course not. We'll find a vacant lot in the country and turn it loose. They can haul the stuff away any time they like."

Gregor called O'Toole and said they would be happy to do business.

"All right," O'Toole said. "You know where our plant is. Just truck the stuff in any old time."

"Us truck it in? I thought you—"

"At 15 cents a ton? No, we're doing you a favor just taking it off your hands. *You* truck it in."

"That's bad," Arnold said, after Gregor had hung up. "The cost of transporting it—"

"Would be far more than 15 cents a ton," Gregor said. "You'd better shut that thing off until we decide what to do."

Arnold waded up to the Producer. "Let me see," he said. "To turn it off, use the Laxian Key." He studied the front of the machine.

"Go ahead, turn it off." Gregor said.

"Just a moment."

"Are you going to turn it off or not?"

Arnold straightened up and gave an embarrassed little laugh. "It's not that easy."

"Why not?"

"We need a Laxian Key to turn it off. And we don't seem to have one."

The next few hours were spent in frantic telephone calls around the country. Gregor and Arnold contacted museums, research institutions, the archeological departments of colleges, and anyone else they could think of. No one had ever seen a Laxian Key or heard of one being found.

In depression, Arnold called Joe, the Interstellar Junkman, at his downtown penthouse.

"No, I ain't got no Laxian Key," Joe said. "Why you think I sold you the gadget so cheap?"

They put down the telephone and stared at each other. The Meldgen Free Producer was cheerfully blasting out its stream of worthless powder. Two chairs and a radiator had disappeared into it, and the gray Tangreese was approaching desk-top level.

"Nice little wage earner," Gregor said.

"We'll think of something."

"We?"

Arnold returned to his books and spent the rest of the night searching for another use for Tangreese. Gregor had to shovel the gray powder into the hall, to keep their office from becoming completely submerged.

The morning came, and the sun gleamed gaily on their windows through a film of gray dust. Arnold stood up and yawned.

"No luck?" Gregor asked.

"I'm afraid not."

Gregor waded out for coffee. When he returned, the building superintendent and two large red-faced policemen were shouting at Arnold.

"You gotta get every bit of that sand outa my hall!" the super screamed.

"Yes, and there's an ordinance against operating a factory in a business district," one of the red-faced policemen said.

"This isn't a factory," Gregor explained. "This is a Meldgen Free—"

"I say it's a factory," the policeman said. "And I say you gotta cease operation at once."

"That's our problem," Arnold said. "We can't seem to turn it off."

"Can't turn it off?" The policeman glared at them suspiciously. "You trying to kid me? I say you *gotta* turn it off."

"Officer, I swear to you—"

"Listen, wise guy, I'll be back in one hour. You get that thing turned off and this mess out of here, or I'm giving you a summons." The three men marched out.

Gregor and Arnold looked at each other, then at the Free Producer. The Tangreese was at desk-top level now and coming steadily.

"Damn it all," Arnold said, with a touch of hysteria, "there *must* be a way of working it out. There must be a market? It's free, I tell you. Every bit of this powder is free, free, free!"

"Steady," Gregor said, wearily scratching sand out of his hair.

"Don't you understand? When you get something free, in unlimited quantities, there has to be an application for it. And all this is free—"

The door opened, and a tall, thin man in a dark business suit walked in, holding a complex gadget in his hand.

"So *here* it is," the man said.

Gregor was struck by a sudden wild thought. "Is that a Laxian Key?" he asked.

"A what key? No, I don't suppose it is," the man said. "It is a drainometer."

"Oh," Gregor said.

"And it seems to have brought me the source of the trouble," the man said. "I'm Mr. Garstairs." He cleared sand from Gregor's desk, took a last reading on his drainometer and started to fill out a printed form.

"What's all this about?" Arnold asked.

"I'm from the Metropolitan Power Company," Garstairs said. "Starting around noon yesterday, we observed a sudden enormous drain on our facilities."

"And it's coming from here?" Gregor asked.

"From that machine of yours," Garstairs said. He completed his form, folded it, and put it in his pocket. "Thanks for your cooperation. You will be billed for this, of course." With some difficulty he opened the door, then turned and took another look at the Free Producer.

"It must be making something extremely valuable," he said, "to justify the expenditure of so much power. What is it? Platinum dust?"

He smiled, nodded pleasantly, and left.

Gregor turned to Arnold. "Free power, eh?"

"Well," Arnold said, "I guess it just grabs it from the nearest power source."

"So I see. Draws power out of the air, out of space, out of the sun. And out of the power company's lines, if they're handy."

"So it seems. But the basic principle—"

"To hell with the basic principle!" Gregor shouted. "We can't turn this damned thing off without a Laxian Key, no one's got a Laxian Key, we're submerged in worthless dust which we can't even afford to truck out, and we're probably burning up power like a sun gone nova!"

"There must be a solution," Arnold said sullenly.

"Yeah? Suppose you find it."

Arnold sat down where his desk had been and covered his eyes. There was a loud knock on the door, and angry voices outside.

"Lock the door," Arnold said.

Gregor locked it. Arnold thought for a few moments longer, then stood up.

"All is not lost," he said. "Our fortunes will still be made from this machine."

"Let's just destroy it," Gregor said. "Drop it in an ocean or something."

"No! I've got it now! Come on, let's get the spaceship warmed up."

The next few days were hectic ones for AAA Ace. They had to hire men, at exorbitant rates, to clear the building of Tangreese. Then came the problem of getting the machine, still spouting gray dust, into their space ship. But at last, everything was done. The Free Producer sat in the hold, rapidly filling it with Tangreese, and their ship was out of the system and moving fast on overdrive.

"It's only logical," Arnold explained later. "Naturally there's no market for Tangreese on Earth. Therefore there's no use trying to sell it on Earth. But on the planet Meldge—"

"I don't like it," Gregor said.

"It can't fail. It costs too much to transport Tangreese to Meldge. But we're moving our entire factory there. We can pour out a constant stream of the stuff."

"Suppose the market is low?" Gregor said.

"How low can it get? This stuff is like bread to Meldgens. It's their basic diet. How can we miss?"

After two weeks in space, Meldge hove in sight on their starboard bow. It came none too soon. Tangreese had completely filled the hold. They had sealed it off, but increasing pressure threatened to burst the sides of the ship. They had to dump tons of it everyday, but dumping took time, and there was a loss of heat and air in the process.

So they spiraled into Meldge with every inch of their ship crammed with Tangreese, low on oxygen and extremely cold.

As soon as they had landed, a large orange-skinned customs official came on board.

"Welcome," he said. "Seldom do visitors come to our important little planet. Do you expect to stay long?"

"Probably," Arnold said. "We're going to set up a business."

"Excellent!" the official said, smiling happily. "Our planet needs new blood, new enterprise. Might I enquire what business?"

"We're going to sell Tangreese, the basic food of—"

The official's face darkened. "You're going to sell what?"

"Tangreese. We have a Free Producer, and—"

The official pressed a button on a wrist dial. "I am sorry, you must leave at once."

"But we've got passports, clearance papers—"

"And we have laws. You must blast off immediately and take your Free Producer with you."

"Now look here," Gregor said, "there's supposed to be free enterprise on this planet."

"Not in the production of Tangreese there isn't."

Outside, a dozen army tanks rumbled onto the landing field and ringed themselves around the ship. The official backed out of the port and started down the ladder.

"Wait!" Gregor cried in desperation. "I suppose you're afraid of unfair competition. Well, take the Free Producer as our gift."

"No!" Arnold shouted.

"Yes! Just dig it out and take it. Feed your poor with it. Just raise a statue to us sometime."

A second row of army tanks appeared. Overhead, antiquated jet planes dipped low over the field.

"Get off this planet!" the official shouted. "Do you really think you can sell Tangreese on Meldge? Look around!"

They looked. The landing field was gray and powdery, and the buildings were the same unpainted gray. Beyond them stretched dull gray fields, to a range of low gray mountains.

On all sides, as far as they could see, everything was Tangreese gray.

"Do you mean," Gregor asked, "that the whole planet—"

"Figure it out for yourself," the official said, backing down the ladder. "The Old Science originated here, and there are always fools who have to tamper with its artifacts. Now get going. But if you ever find a Laxian Key, come back and name your price."

Skulking Permit

Tom Fisher had no idea he was about to begin a criminal career. It was morning. The big red sun was just above the horizon, trailing its small yellow companion. The village, tiny and precise, a unique white dot on the planet's green expanse, glistened under its two midsummer suns.

Tom was just waking up inside his cottage. He was a tall, tanned young man, with his father's oval eyes and his mother's easygoing attitude toward exertion. He was in no hurry; there could be no fishing until the fall rains, and therefore no real work for a fisher. Until fall, he was going to loaf and mend his fishing poles.

"It's supposed to have a red roof!" he heard Billy Painter shouting outside.

"Churches *never* have red roofs!" Ed Weaver shouted back.

Tom frowned. Not being involved, he had forgotten the changes that had come over the village in the last two weeks. He slipped on a pair of pants and sauntered out to the village square.

The first thing he saw when he entered the square was a large new sign, reading: NO ALIENS ALLOWED WITHIN CITY LIMITS. There were no aliens on the entire planet of New Delaware. There was nothing but forest, and this one village. The sign was purely a statement of policy.

The square itself contained a church, a jail and a post office, all constructed in the last two frantic weeks and set in a neat row facing the market. No one knew what to do with these buildings; the village had gone along nicely without them for over two hundred years. But now, of course, they had to be built.

Ed Weaver was standing in front of the new church, squinting upward. Billy Painter was balanced precariously on the church's steep roof, his blond mustache bristling indignantly. A small crowd had gathered.

"Damn it, man," Billy Painter was saying, "I tell you I was reading about it just last week. White roof, okay. Red roof, never."

"You're mixing it up with something else," Weaver said. "How about it, Tom?"

Tom shrugged, having no opinion to offer. Just then, the mayor bustled up, perspiring freely, his shirt flapping over his large paunch.

"Come down," he called to Billy. "I just looked it up. It's the Little Red *Schoolhouse,* not Churchhouse."

Billy looked angry. He had always been moody; all Painters were. But since the mayor made him chief of police last week, he had become downright temperamental.

"We don't have no little schoolhouse," Billy argued, half way down the ladder.

"We'll just have to build one," the mayor said. "We'll have to hurry, too." He glanced at the sky. Involuntarily the crowd glanced upward. But there was still nothing in sight.

"Where are the Carpenter boys?" the mayor asked. "Sid, Sam, Marv—where are you?"

Sid Carpenter's head appeared through the crowd. He was still on crutches from last month when he had fallen out of a tree looking for threstle's eggs; no Carpenter was worth a damn at tree-climbing.

"The other boys are at Ed Beer's Tavern," Sid said.

"Where else would they be?" Mary Waterman called from the crowd.

"Well, you gather them up," the mayor said. "They gotta build up a little schoolhouse, and quick. Tell them to put it up beside the jail." He turned to Billy Painter, who was back on the ground. "Billy, you paint that schoolhouse a good bright red, inside and out. It's very important."

"When do I get a police chief badge?" Billy demanded. "I read that police chiefs always get badges."

"Make yourself one," the mayor said. He mopped his, face with his shirttail. "Sure hot. Don't know why that inspector couldn't have come in winter...Tom! Tom Fisher! Got an important job for you. Come on, I'll tell you all about it."

He put an arm around Tom's shoulders and they walked to the mayor's cottage past the empty market, along the village's single paved road. In the old days, that road had been of packed dirt. But the old days had ended two weeks ago and now the road was paved with crushed rock. It made barefoot walking so uncomfortable that the villagers simply cut across each other's lawns. The mayor, though, walked on it out of principle.

"Now look, Mayor, I'm on my vacation—"

"Can't have any vacations now," the mayor said. "Not *now.* He's due any day." He ushered Tom inside his cottage and sat down in the big armchair, which had been pushed as close to the interstellar radio as possible.

"Tom," the mayor said directly, "how would you like to be a criminal?"

"I don't know," said Tom. "What's a criminal?"

Squirming uncomfortably in his chair, the mayor rested a hand on the radio for authority. "It's this way," he said, and began to explain.

Tom listened, but the more he heard, the less he liked. It was all the fault of that interstellar radio, he decided. Why hadn't it really been broken?

No one had believed it could work. It had gathered dust in the office of one mayor after another, for generations, the last silent link with Mother Earth. Two hundred years ago, Earth talked with New Delaware, and with Ford IV, Alpha Centauri, Nueva Espana, and the other colonies that made up the United Democracies' of Earth. Then all conversations stopped.

There seemed to be a war on Earth. New Delaware, with its one village, was too small and too distant to take part. They waited for news, but no news came. And then plague struck the village, wiping out three-quarters of the inhabitants.

Slowly the village healed. The villagers adopted their own ways of doing things. They forgot Earth.

Two hundred years passed.

And then, two weeks ago, the ancient radio had coughed itself into life. For hours, it growled and spat static, while the inhabitants of the village gathered around the mayor's cottage.

Finally words came out: "...hear me, New Delaware? Do you hear me?"

"Yes, yes, we hear you," the mayor said.

"The colony is still there?"

"It certainly is," the mayor said proudly.

The voice became stern and official. "There has been no contact with the Outer Colonies for some time, due to unsettled conditions here. But that's over, except for a little mopping up. You of New Delaware are still a colony of Imperial Earth and subject to her laws. Do you acknowledge the status?"

The mayor hesitated. All the books referred to Earth as the United Democracies. Well, in two centuries, names could change.

"We are still loyal to Earth," the mayor said with dignity.

"Excellent. That saves us the trouble of sending an expeditionary force. A resident inspector will be dispatched to you from the nearest point, to ascertain whether you conform to the customs, institutions and traditions of Earth."

"What?" the mayor asked, worried.

The stern voice became higher-pitched. "You realize, of course, that there is room for only one intelligent species in the Universe—Man! All others must be suppressed, wiped out, annihilated. We can tolerate no aliens sneaking around us. I'm sure you understand, General."

"I'm not a general. I'm a mayor."

"You're in charge, aren't you?"

"Yes, but—"

"Then you are a general. Permit me to continue. In this galaxy, there is no room for aliens. None! Nor is there room for deviant human cultures, which, by definition, are alien. It is impossible to administer an empire when everyone does as he pleases. There must be order, *no matter what the cost.*"

The mayor gulped hard and stared at the radio.

"Be sure you're running an Earth colony, General, with no radical departures from the norm, such as free will, free love, free elections, or anything else on the proscribed list. Those things are *alien,* and we're pretty rough on aliens. Get your colony in order, General. The inspector will call in about two weeks. That is all."

The village held an immediate meeting, to determine how best to conform with the Earth mandate. All they could do was hastily model themselves upon the Earth pattern as shown in their ancient books.

"I don't see why there has to be a criminal," Tom said.

"That's a very important part of Earth society," the mayor explained. "All the books agree on it. The criminal is as important as the postman, say, or the police chief. Unlike them, the criminal is engaged in antisocial work. He works *against* society, Tom. If you don't have people working *against* society, how can you have people working *for* it? There'd be no jobs for them to do."

Tom shook his head. "I just don't see it."

"Be reasonable, Tom. We have to have earthly things. Like paved roads. All the books mention that. And churches, and schoolhouses, and jails. And all the books mention crime."

"I won't do it," Tom said.

"Put yourself in my position," the mayor begged. "This inspector comes and meets Billy Painter, our police chief. He asks to see the jail. Then he says, 'No prisoners?' I answer, 'Of course not. We don't have any crime here.' 'No crime?' he says. 'But Earth colonies always have crime. You know that.' 'We don't,' I answer. 'Didn't even know what it was until we looked up the word last week,' 'Then why did you build a jail?' he asks me. 'Why did you appoint a police chief?'"

The mayor paused for breath. "You see? The whole thing falls through. He sees at once that we're not truly earthlike. We're faking it. We're *aliens!*"

"Hmm," Tom said, impressed in spite of himself.

"This way," the mayor went on quickly, "I can say, 'Certainly we've got crime here, just like on Earth. We've got a combination thief and murderer. Poor fellow had a bad upbringing and he's maladjusted. Our police chief has some clues, though. We expect an arrest within twenty-four hours. We'll lock him in the jail, then rehabilitate him.'"

"What's rehabilitate?" Tom asked.

"I'm not sure. I'll worry about that when I come to it. But now do you see how necessary crime is?"

"I suppose so. But why me?"

"Can't spare anyone else. And you've got narrow eyes. Criminals always have narrow eyes."

"They aren't *that* narrow. They're no narrower than Ed Weaver's—"

"Tom, please," the mayor said. "We're all doing our part. You want to help, don't you?"

"I suppose so," Tom repeated wearily.

"Fine. You're our criminal. Here, this makes it legal,"

He handed Tom a document. It read: SKULKING PERMIT. *Know all Men by these Presents that Tom Fisher is a Duly Authorized Thief and Murderer. He is hereby required to Skulk in Dismal Alleys, Haunt Places of Low Repute, and Break the Law.*

Tom read it through twice, then asked, "What law?"

"I'll let you know as fast as I make them up," the mayor said. "All Earth colonies have laws."

"But what do I *do?*"

"You steal. And kill. That should be easy enough." The mayor walked to his bookcase and took down ancient volumes entitled *The Criminal and his Environment, Psychology of the Slayer,* and *Studies in Thief Motivation.*

"These'll give you everything you need to know. Steal as much as you like. One murder should be enough, though. No sense overdoing it."

"Right," Tom nodded. "I guess I'll catch on."

He picked up the books and returned to his cottage.

It was very hot and all the talk about crime had puzzled and wearied him. He lay down on his bed and began to go through the ancient books.

There was a knock on his door.

"Come in," Tom called, rubbing his tired eyes.

Marv Carpenter, oldest and tallest of the red-headed Carpenter boys, came in, followed by old Jed Farmer. They were carrying a small sack.

"You the town criminal, Tom?" Marv asked.

"Looks like it."

"Then this is for you." They put the sack on the floor and took from it a hatchet, two knives, a short spear, a club and a blackjack.

"What's all that?" Tom asked, sitting upright.

"Weapons, of course," Jed Farmer said testily. "You can't be a real criminal without weapons."

Tom scratched his head. "Is that a fact?"

"You'd better start figuring these things out for yourself," Farmer went on in his impatient voice. "Can't expect us to do everything for you."

Marv Carpenter winked at Tom. "Jed's sore because the mayor made him our postman."

"I'll do my part," Jed said. "I just don't like having to write all those letters."

"Can't be too hard," Marv Carpenter said, grinning. "The postmen do it on Earth and they got a lot more people there. Gook luck, Tom."

They left.

Tom bent down and examined the weapons. He knew what they were; the old books were full of them. But no one had ever actually used a weapon on New Delaware. The only native animals on the planet were small, furry, and confirmed eaters of grass. As for turning a weapon on a fellow villager—why would anybody want to do that?

He picked up one of the knives. It was cold. He touched the point. It was sharp.

Tom began to pace the floor, staring at the weapons. They gave him a queer sinking feeling in the pit of his stomach. He decided he had been hasty in accepting the job.

But there was no sense worrying about it yet. He still had those books to read. After that, perhaps he could make some sense out of the whole thing.

He read for several hours, stopping only to eat a light lunch. The books were understandable enough; the various criminal methods were clearly explained, sometimes with diagrams. But the whole thing was unreasonable. What was the purpose of crime? Whom did it benefit? What did people get out of it?

The books didn't explain that. He leafed through them, looking at the photographed faces of criminals. They looked very serious and dedicated, extremely conscious of the significance of their work to society.

Tom wished he could find out what that significance was. It would probably make things much easier.

"Tom?" he heard the mayor call from outside.

"I'm in here, Mayor," Tom said.

The door opened and the mayor peered in. Behind him were Jane Farmer, Mary Waterman and Alice Cook.

"How about it, Tom?" the mayor asked.

"How about what?"

"How about getting to work?"

Tom grinned self-consciously. "I was going to," he said. "I was reading these books, trying to figure out—"

The three middle-aged ladies glared at him, and Tom stopped in embarrassment.

"You're taking your time reading," Alice Cook said.

"Everyone else is outside working," said Jane Farmer.

"What's so hard about stealing?" Mary Waterman challenged.

"It's true," the mayor told him. "That inspector might be here any day now and we don't have a crime to show him."

"All right, all right," Tom said.

He stuck a knife and a blackjack in his belt, put the sack in his pocket—
for loot—and stalked out.

But where was he going? It was mid-afternoon. The market, which was
the most logical place to rob, would be empty until evening. Besides, he
didn't want to commit a robbery in daylight. It seemed unprofessional.

He opened his skulking permit and read it through. *Required to Haunt
Places of Low Repute...*

That was it! He'd haunt a low repute place. He could form some plans
there, get into the mood of the thing. But unfortunately, the village didn't
have much to choose from.

There was the Tiny Restaurant, run by the widowed Ames sisters, there
was Jeff Hem's Lounging Spot, and finally there was Ed Beer's Tavern.

Ed's place would have to do.

The tavern was a cottage much like the other cottages in the village. It
had one big room for guests, a kitchen, and family sleeping quarters. Ed's
wife did the cooking and kept the place as clean as she could, considering
her ailing back. Ed served the drinks. He was a pale, sleepy-eyed man
with a talent for worrying.

"Hello, Tom," Ed said. "Hear you're our criminal."

"That's right," said Tom. "I'll take a perricola."

Ed Beer served him the nonalcoholic root extract and stood anxiously
in front of Tom's table. "How come you ain't out thieving, Tom?"

"I'm planning," Tom said. "My permit says I have to haunt places of
low repute. That's why I'm here."

"Is that nice?" Ed Beer asked sadly. "This is no place of low repute, Tom."

"You serve the worst meals in town," Tom pointed out.

"I know. My wife can't cook. But there's a friendly atmosphere here.
Folks like it."

"That's all changed, Ed. I'm making this tavern my headquarters."

Ed Beer's shoulders drooped. "Try to keep a nice place," he muttered.
"A lot of thanks you get." He returned to the bar.

Tom proceeded to think. He found it amazingly difficult. The more
he tried, the less came out. But he stuck grimly to it.

An hour passed. Richie Farmer, Jed's youngest son, stuck his head in
the door. "You steal anything yet, Tom?"

"Not yet," Tom told him, hunched over his table, still thinking.

The scorching afternoon drifted slowly by. Patches of evening became visible through the tavern's small, not too clean windows. A cricket
began to chirp outside, and the first whisper of night wind stirred the
surrounding forest.

Big George Waterman and Max Weaver came in for a glass of glava.
They sat down beside Tom.

"How's it going?" George Waterman asked.

"Not so good," Tom said. "Can't seem to get the hang of this stealing."

"You'll catch on," Waterman said in his slow, ponderous, earnest fashion. "If anyone could learn it, you can."

"We've got confidence in you, Tom," Weaver assured him.

Tom thanked them. They drank and left. He continued thinking, staring into his empty perricola glass.

An hour later, Ed Beer cleared his throat apologetically. "It's none of my business, Tom, but when *are* you going to steal something?"

"Right now," Tom said.

He stood up, made sure his weapons were securely in place, and strode out the door.

Nightly bartering had begun in the market. Goods were piled carelessly on benches, or spread over the grass on straw mats. There was no currency, no rate of exchange. Ten hand-wrought nails were worth a pail of milk or two fish, or vice versa, depending on what you had to barter and needed at the moment. No one ever bothered keeping accounts. That was one Earth custom the mayor was having difficulty introducing. As Tom Fisher walked down the square, everyone greeted him.

"Stealing now, huh, Tom?"

"Go to it, boy!"

"You can do it!"

No one in the village had ever witnessed an actual theft. They considered it an exotic custom of distant Earth and they wanted to see how it worked. They left their goods and followed Tom through the market, watching avidly.

Tom found that his hands were trembling. He didn't like having so many people watch him steal. He decided he'd better work fast, while he still had the nerve.

He stopped abruptly in front of Mrs. Miller's fruit-laden bench. "Tasty-looking geefers," he said casually.

"They're fresh," Mrs. Miller told him. She was a small and bright-eyed old woman. Tom could remember long conversations she had had with his mother, back when his parents were alive.

"They look very tasty," he said, wishing he had stopped somewhere else instead.

"Oh, they are," said Mrs. Miller. "I picked them just this afternoon."

"Is he going to steal now?" someone whispered.

"Sure he is. Watch him," someone whispered back. Tom picked up a bright green geefer and inspected it. The crowd became suddenly silent.

"Certainly looks very tasty," Tom said, carefully replacing the geefer.

The crowd released a long-drawn sigh.

Max Weaver and his wife and five children were at the next bench. Tonight they were displaying two blankets and a shirt. They all smiled shyly when Tom came over, followed by the crowd.

"That shirt's about your size," Weaver informed him. He wished the people would go away and let Tom work.

"Hmm," Tom said, picking up the shirt.

The crowd stirred expectantly. A girl began to giggle hysterically. Tom gripped the shirt tightly and opened his loot bag.

"Just a moment!" Billy Painter pushed his way through. He was wearing a badge now, an old Earth coin he had polished and pinned to his belt. The expression on his face was unmistakably official.

"What were you doing with that shirt, Tom?" Billy asked.

"Why...I was just looking at it."

"Just looking at it, huh?" Billy turned away, his hands clasped behind his back. Suddenly he whirled and extended a rigid forefinger. "I don't think you were just looking at it, Tom. I think you were planning on *stealing* it!"

Tom didn't answer. The tell-tale sack hung limply from one hand, the shirt from the other.

"As police chief," Billy went on, "I've got a duty to protect these people. You're a suspicious character. I think I'd better lock you up for further questioning."

Tom hung his head. He hadn't expected this, but it was just as well.

Once he was in jail, it would be all over. And when Billy released him, he could get back to fishing.

Suddenly the mayor bounded through the crowd, his shirt flapping wildly around his waist.

"Billy, what are you doing?"

"Doing my duty, Mayor. Tom here is acting plenty suspicious. The book says—"

"I know what the book says," the mayor told him. "I gave you the book. You can't go arresting Tom. Not yet."

"But there's no other criminal in the village," Billy complained.

"I can't help that," the mayor said.

Billy's lips tightened. "The book talks about preventive police work. I'm supposed to stop crime before it happens."

The mayor raised his hands and dropped them wearily. "Billy, don't you understand? This village *needs* a criminal record. You have to help, too."

Billy shrugged his shoulders. "All right, Mayor. I was just trying to do my job." He turned to go. Then he whirled again on Tom. "I'll still get you. Remember—Crime Does Not Pay." He stalked off.

"He's overambitious, Tom," the mayor explained. "Forget it. Go ahead and steal something. Let's get this job over with."

Tom started to edge away toward the green forest outside the village.

"What's wrong, Tom?" the mayor asked worriedly.

"I'm not in the mood any more," Tom said. "Maybe tomorrow night—"

"No, right now," the mayor insisted. "You can't go on putting it off. Come on, we'll all help you."

"Sure we will," Max Weaver said. "Steal the shirt, Tom. It's your size anyhow."

"How about a nice water jug, Tom?"

"Look at these skeegee nuts over here."

Tom looked from bench to bench. As he reached for Weaver's shirt, a knife slipped from his belt and dropped to the ground. The crowd clucked sympathetically.

Tom replaced it, perspiring, knowing he looked like a butterfingers. He reached out, took the shirt and stuffed it into the loot bag. The crowd cheered.

Tom smiled faintly, feeling a bit better. "I think I'm getting the hang of it."

"Sure you are."

"We knew you could do it."

"Take something else, boy."

Tom walked down the market and helped himself to a length of rope, a handful of skeegee nuts and a grass hat.

"I guess that's enough," he told the mayor.

"Enough for now," the mayor agreed, "This doesn't really count, you know. This was the same as people giving it to you. Practice, you might say."

"Oh," Tom said, disappointed.

"But you know what you're doing. The next time it'll be just as easy."

"I suppose it will."

"And don't forget that murder."

"Is it really necessary?" Tom asked.

"I wish it weren't," the mayor said. "But this colony has been here for over two hundred years and we haven't had a single murder. Not one! According to the records, all the other colonies had lots."

"I suppose we should have one," Tom admitted. "I'll take care of it." He headed for his cottage. The crowd gave a rousing cheer as he departed.

At home, Tom lighted a rush lamp and fixed himself supper. After eating, he sat for a long time in his big armchair. He was dissatisfied with himself. He had not really handled the stealing well. All day he had worried and hesitated. People had practically had to put things in his hands before he could take them.

A fine thief he was!

And there was no excuse for it. Stealing and murdering were like any other necessary jobs. Just because he had never done them before, just because he could see no sense to them, that was no reason to bungle them.

He walked to the door. It was a fine night, illuminated by a dozen nearby giant stars. The market was deserted again and the village lights were winking out.

This was the time to steal!

A thrill ran through him at the thought. He was proud of himself. That was how criminals planned and this was how stealing should be— skulking, late at night.

Quickly Tom checked his weapons, emptied his loot sack and walked out.

The last rush lights were extinguished. Tom moved noiselessly through the village. He came to Roger Waterman's house. Big Roger had left his spade propped against a wall. Tom picked it up. Down the block, Mrs. Weaver's water jug was in its usual place beside the front door. Tom took it. On his way home, he found a little wooden horse that some child had forgotten. It went with the rest.

He was pleasantly exhilarated, once the goods were safely home. He decided to make another haul.

This time he returned with a bronze plaque from the mayor's house, Marv Carpenter's best saw, and Jed Farmer's sickle.

"Not bad," he told himself. He *was* catching on. One more load would constitute a good night's work.

This time he found a hammer and chisel in Ron Stone's shed, and a reed basket at Alice Cook's house. He was about to take Jeff Hem's rake when he heard a faint noise. He flattened himself against a wall.

Billy Painter came prowling quietly along, his badge gleaming in the starlight. In one hand, he carried a short, heavy club; in the other, a pair of homemade handcuffs. In the dim light, his face was ominous. It was the face of a man who had pledged himself against crime, even though he wasn't really sure what it was.

Tom held his breath as Billy Painter passed within ten feet of him. Slowly Tom backed away.

The loot sack jingled.

"Who's there?" Billy yelled. When no one answered, he turned a slow circle, peering into the shadows. Tom was flattened against a wall again. He was fairly sure Billy wouldn't see him. Billy had weak eyes because of the fumes of the paint he mixed. All painters had weak eyes. It was one of the reasons they were moody.

"Is that you, Tom?" Billy asked, in a friendly tone. Tom was about to answer, when he noticed that Billy's club was raised in a striking position. He kept quiet.

"I'll get you yet!" Billy shouted.

"Well, get him in the morning!" Jeff Hem shouted from his bedroom window. "Some of us are trying to sleep."

Billy moved away. When he was gone, Tom hurried home and dumped his pile of loot on the floor with the rest. He surveyed his haul proudly. It gave him the sense of a job well done.

After a cool drink of glava, Tom went to bed, falling at once into a peaceful, dreamless sleep.

Next morning, Tom sauntered out to see how the little red schoolhouse was progressing. The Carpenter boys were hard at work on it, helped by several villagers.

"How's it coming?" Tom called out cheerfully.

"Fair," Mary Carpenter said. "It'd come along better if I had my saw."

"Your saw?" Tom repeated blankly.

After a moment, he remembered that *he* had stolen it last night. It hadn't seemed to belong to anyone then. The saw and all the rest had been objects to be stolen. He had never given a thought to the fact that they might be used or needed.

Marv Carpenter asked, "Do you suppose I could use the saw for a while? Just for an hour or so?"

"I'm not sure," Tom said, frowning. "It's legally stolen, you know."

"Of course it is. But if I could just borrow it—"

"You'd have to give it back."

"Well, naturally I'd give it back," Marv said indignantly. "I wouldn't keep anything that was legally stolen."

"It's in the house with the rest of the loot."

Marv thanked him and hurried after it.

Tom began to stroll through the village. He reached the mayor's house. The mayor was standing outside, staring at the sky.

"Tom, did you take my bronze plaque?" he asked.

"I certainly did," Tom said belligerently.

"Oh. Just wondering." The mayor pointed upward. "See it?"

Tom looked. "What?"

"Black dot near the rim of the small sun."

"Yes. What is it?"

"I'll bet it's the inspector's ship. How's your working coming?"

"Fine," Tom said, a trifle uncomfortably.

"Got your murder planned?"

"I've been having a little trouble with that," Tom confessed. "To tell the truth, I haven't made any progress on it at all."

"Come on in, Tom. I want to talk to you."

Inside the cool, shuttered living room, the mayor poured two glasses of glava and motioned Tom to a chair.

"Our time is running short," the mayor said gloomily. "The inspector may land any hour now. And my hands are full." He motioned at the interstellar radio. "*That* has been talking again. Something about a revolt on Deng IV and all loyal Earth colonies are to prepare for conscription, whatever that is. I never even heard of Deng IV, but I have to start worrying about it, in addition to everything else."

He fixed Tom with a stern stare. "Criminals on Earth commit dozens of murders a day and never even think about it. All your village wants of you is one little killing. Is that too much to ask?"

Tom spread his hands nervously. "Do you really think it's necessary?"

"You know it is," the mayor said. "If we're going earthly, we have to go all the way. This is the only thing holding us back. All the other projects are right on schedule."

Billy Painter entered, wearing a new official-blue shirt with bright metal buttons. He sank into a chair.

"Kill anyone yet, Tom?"

The mayor said, "He wants to know if it's *necessary.*"

"Of course it is," the police chief said. "Read any of the books. You're not much of a criminal if you don't commit a murder."

"Who'll it be, Tom?" the mayor asked.

Tom squirmed uncomfortably in his chair. He rubbed his fingers together nervously.

"Well?"

"Oh, I'll kill Jeff Hearn," Tom blurted.

Billy Painter leaned forward quickly. "Why?" he asked

"Why? Why *not?*"

"What's your motive?"

"I thought you just wanted a murder," Tom retorted. "Who said anything about a motive?"

"We can't have a fake murder," the police chief explained. "It has to be done right. And that means you have to have a proper motive."

Tom thought for a moment. "Well, I don't know Jeff well. Is that a good enough motive?"

The mayor shook his head. "No, Tom, that won't do. Better pick someone else."

"Let's see," Tom said. "How about George Waterman?"

"What's the motive?" Billy asked immediately.

"Oh...um...Well, I don't like the way George walks. Never did. And he's noisy sometimes."

The mayor nodded approvingly. "Sounds good to me. What do you say, Billy?"

"How am I supposed to deduce a motive like that?" Billy asked angrily. "No, that might be good enough for a crime of passion. But you're a legal criminal, Tom. By definition, you're cold-blooded, ruthless and cunning. You can't kill someone just because you don't like the way he walks. That's *silly.*"

"I'd better think this whole thing over," Tom said, standing up.

"Don't take too long," the mayor told him. "The sooner it's done, the better."

Tom nodded and started out the door.

"Oh, Tom!" Billy called. "Don't forget to leave clues. They're very important."

"All right," Tom said, and left.

Outside, most of the villagers were watching the sky. The black dot had grown immensely larger. It covered most of the smaller sun.

Tom went to his place of low repute to think things out. Ed Beer had apparently changed his mind about the desirability of criminal elements. The tavern was redecorated.

There was a large sign, reading: CRIMINAL'S LAIR. Inside, there were new, carefully soiled curtains on the windows, blocking the daylight and making the tavern truly a Dismal Retreat. Weapons, hastily carved out of soft wood, hung on one wall. On another wall was a large red splotch, an ominous-looking thing, even though Tom knew it was only Billy Painter's rootberry red paint.

"Come right in, Tom," Ed Beer said, and led him to the darkest corner in the room. Tom noticed that the tavern was unusually filled for the time of day. People seemed to like the idea of being in a genuine criminal's lair.

Tom sipped a perricola and began to think. He had to commit a murder.

He took out his skulking permit and looked it over. Unpleasant, unpalatable, something he wouldn't normally do, but he did have the legal obligation.

Tom drank his perricola and concentrated on murder. He told himself he was going to *kill* someone. He had to *snuff out a life.* He would make someone *cease to exist.*

But the phrases didn't contain the essence of the act. They were just words. To clarify his thoughts, he took big, redheaded Marv Carpenter as an example. Today, Marv was working on the schoolhouse with his borrowed saw. If Tom killed Marv—well, Marv wouldn't work any more.

Tom shook his head impatiently. He still wasn't grasping it. All right, here was Marv Carpenter, biggest and, many thought, the pleasantest of the Carpenter boys. He'd be planing down a piece of wood, grasping the plane firmly in his large freckled hands, squinting down the line he had drawn. Thirsty, undoubtedly, and with a small pain in his left shoulder that Jan Druggist was unsuccessfully treating.

That was Marv Carpenter.

Then—

Marv Carpenter sprawled on the ground, his eyes glaring open, limbs stiff, mouth twisted, no air going in or out his nostrils, no beat to his heart. Never again to hold a piece of wood in his large, freckled hands. Never again to feel the small and really unimportant pain in his shoulder that Jan Druggist was—

For just a moment, Tom glimpsed what murder really was. The vision passed, but enough of a memory remained to make him feel sick.

He could live with the thieving. But murder, even in the best interests of the village...

What would people think, after they saw what he had just imagined? How could he live with them? How could he live with himself afterward?

And yet he had to kill. Everybody in the village had a job and that was his.

But whom could he murder?

The excitement started later in the day when the interstellar radio was filled with angry voices.

"Call *that* a colony? Where's the capital?"

"This is it," the mayor replied.

"Where's your landing field?"

"I think it's being used as a pasture," the mayor said. "I could look up where it was. No ship has landed here in over—"

"The main ship will stay aloft then. Assemble your officials. I am coming down immediately."

The entire village gathered around an open field that the inspector designated. Tom strapped on his weapons and skulked behind a tree, watching.

A small ship detached itself from the big one and dropped swiftly down. It plummeted toward the field while the villagers held their breaths, certain it would crash. At the last moment, jets flared, scorching the grass, and the ship settled gently to the ground.

The mayor edged forward, followed by Billy Painter. A door in the ship opened, and four men marched out. They held shining metallic instruments that Tom knew were weapons. After them came a large, red-faced man dressed in black, wearing four bright medals. He was followed by a little man with a wrinkled face, also dressed in black. Four more uniformed men followed him.

"Welcome to New Delaware," the mayor said.

"Thank you, General," the big man said, shaking the mayor's hand firmly. "I am Inspector Delumaine. This is Mr. Grent, my political adviser."

Grent nodded to the mayor, ignoring his outstretched hand. He was looking at the villagers with an expression of mild disgust.

"We will survey the village," the inspector said, glancing at Grent out of the corner of his eye. Grent nodded. The uniformed guards closed around them.

Tom followed at a safe distance, skulking in true criminal fashion. In the village, he hid behind a house to watch the inspection.

The mayor pointed out, with pardonable pride, the jail, the post office, the church and the little red schoolhouse. The inspector seemed bewildered. Mr. Grent smiled unpleasantly and rubbed his jaw.

"As I thought," he told the inspector. "A waste of time, fuel and a battle cruiser. This place has nothing of value."

"I'm not so sure," the inspector said. He turned to the mayor. "But what did you build them for, General?"

"Why, to be earthly," the mayor said. "We're doing our best, as you can see."

Mr. Grent whispered something in the inspector's ear. "Tell me," the inspector asked the mayor, "how many young men are there in the village?"

"I beg your pardon?" the mayor said in polite bewilderment.

"Young men between the ages of fifteen and sixty," Mr. Grent explained.

"You see, General, Imperial Mother Earth is engaged in a war. The colonists on Deng IV and some other colonies have turned against their birthright. They are revolting against the absolute authority of Mother Earth."

"I'm sorry to hear that," the mayor said sympathetically.

"We need men for the space fleet," the inspector told him. "Good healthy fighting men. Our reserves are depleted—"

"We wish," Mr. Grent broke in smoothly, "to give all loyal Earth colonists a chance to fight for Imperial Mother Earth. We are sure you won't refuse."

"Oh, no," the mayor said. "Certainly not. I'm sure our young men will be glad—I mean they don't know much about it, but they're all bright boys. They can learn, I guess."

"You see?" the inspector said to Mr. Grent. "Sixty, seventy, perhaps a hundred recruits. Not such a waste after all."

Mr. Grent still looked dubious.

The inspector and his adviser went to the mayor's house for refreshment. Four soldiers accompanied them. The other four walked around the village, helping themselves to anything they found.

Tom hid in the woods nearby to think things over. In the early evening, Mrs. Ed Beer came furtively out of the village. She was a gaunt, grayish-blond middle-aged woman, but she moved quite rapidly in spite of her case of housemaid's knee. She had a basket with her, covered with a red checkered napkin.

"Here's your dinner," she said, as soon as she found Tom.

"Why…thanks," said Tom, taken by surprise, "You didn't have to do that."

"I certainly did. Our tavern is your place of low repute, isn't it? We're responsible for your well-being. And the mayor sent you a message."

Tom looked up, his mouth full of food. "What is it?"

"He said to hurry up with the murder. He's been stalling the inspector and that nasty little Grent man. But they're going to ask him. He's sure of it."

Tom nodded.

"When are you going to do it?" Mrs. Beer asked, cocking her head to one side.

"I mustn't tell you," Tom said.

"Of course you must. I'm a criminal's accomplice," Mrs. Beer leaned closer.

"That's true," Tom admitted thoughtfully. "Well, I'm going to do it tonight. After dark. Tell Billy Painter I'll leave all the fingerprints I can, and any other clues I think of."

"All right, Tom," Mrs. Beer said. "Good luck."

Tom waited for dark, meanwhile watching the village. He noticed that most of the soldiers had been drinking. They swaggered around as though the villagers didn't exist. One of them fired his weapon into the air, frightening all the small, furry grass-eaters for miles around.

The inspector and Mr. Grent were still in the mayor's house.

Night came. Tom slipped into the village and stationed himself in an alley between two houses. He drew his knife and waited.

Someone was approaching! He tried to remember his criminal methods, but nothing came. He knew he would just have to do the murder as best he could, and fast.

The person came up, his figure indistinct in the darkness.

"Why, hello, Tom." It was the mayor. He looked at the knife. "What are you doing?"

"You said there had to be a murder, so—"

"I didn't mean *me,*" the mayor said, backing away. "It can't be me."

"Why not?" Tom asked.

"Well, for one thing, somebody has to talk to the inspector. He's waiting for me. Someone has to show him—"

"Billy Painter can do that," said Tom. He grasped the mayor by the shirt front, raised the knife and aimed for the throat. "Nothing personal, of course," he added.

"Wait!" the mayor cried. "If there's nothing personal, then you have no motive!"

Tom lowered the knife, but kept his grasp on the mayor's shirt. "I guess I can think of one. I've been pretty sore about you appointing me criminal."

"It was the mayor who appointed you, wasn't it?"

"Well, sure—"

The mayor pulled Tom out of the shadows, into the bright starlight. "Look!"

Tom gaped. The mayor was dressed in long, sharply creased pants and a tunic resplendent with medals. On each shoulder was a double row of ten stars. His hat was thickly crusted with gold braid in the shape of comets.

"You see, Tom? I'm not the mayor any more. I'm a *General!*"

"What's that got to do with it? You're the same person, aren't you?"

"Not officially. You missed the ceremony this afternoon. The inspector said that since I was officially a general, I had to wear a general's uniform. It was a very friendly ceremony. All the Earthmen were grinning and winking at me and each other."

Raising the knife again, Tom held it as he would to gut a fish. "Congratulations," he said sincerely, "but you were the mayor when you appointed me criminal, so my motive still holds."

"But you wouldn't be killing the mayor! You'd be killing a general! And that's not murder!"

"It isn't?" Tom asked. "What is it then?"

"Why, killing a general is mutiny!"

"Oh." Tom put down the knife. He released the mayor. "Sorry."

"Quite all right," the mayor said. "Natural error. I've read up on it and you haven't, of course—no need to." He took a deep breath. "I'd better get back. The inspector wants a list of the men he can draft."

Tom called out, "Are you sure this murder is necessary?"

"Yes, absolutely," the mayor said, hurrying away. "Just not *me.*"

Tom put the knife back in his belt.

Not me, not me. Everyone would feel that way. Yet somebody had to be murdered. Who? He couldn't kill himself. That would be suicide, which wouldn't count.

He began to shiver, trying not to think of the glimpse he'd had of the reality of murder. The job had to be done.

Someone else was coming!

The person came nearer. Tom hunched down, his muscles tightening for the leap.

It was Mrs. Miller, returning home with a bag of vegetables.

Tom told himself that it didn't matter whether it was Mrs. Miller or anybody else. But he couldn't help remembering those conversations with his mother. They left him without a motive for killing Mrs. Miller.

She passed by without seeing him.

He waited for half an hour. Another person walked through the dark alley between the houses. Tom recognized him as Max Weaver.

Tom had always liked him. But that didn't mean there couldn't be a motive. All he could come up with, though, was that Max had a wife and five children who loved him and would miss him. Tom didn't want Billy Painter to tell him that that was no motive. He drew deeper into the shadow and let Max go safely by.

The three Carpenter boys came along. Tom had painfully been through that already. He let them pass. Then Roger Waterman approached.

He had no real motive for killing Roger, but he had never been especially friendly with him. Besides, Roger had no children and his wife wasn't fond of him. Would that be enough for Billy Painter to work on?

He knew it wouldn't be...and the same was true of all the villagers. He had grown up with these people, shared food and work and fun and grief with them. How could he possibly have a motive for killing any of them?

But he had to commit a murder. His skulking permit required it. He couldn't let the village down. But neither could he kill the people he had known all his life.

Wait, he told himself in sudden excitement. He could kill the inspector!

Motive? Why, it would be an even more heinous crime than murdering the mayor—except that the mayor was a general now, of course, and that would only be mutiny. But even if the mayor were still mayor, the inspector would be a far more important victim. Tom would be killing for glory, for fame, for notoriety. And the murder would show Earth how earthly the colony really was. They would say, "Crime is so bad on New Delaware that it's hardly safe to land there. A criminal actually killed our inspector on the very first day! Worst criminal we've come across in all space."

It would be the most spectacular crime he could commit, Tom realized, just the sort of thing a master criminal would do.

Feeling proud of himself for the first time in a long while, Tom hurried out of the alley and over to the mayor's house. He could hear conversation going on inside.

"...sufficiently passive population." Mr. Grent was saying, "Sheeplike, in fact."

"Makes it rather boring," the inspector answered. "For the soldiers especially."

"Well, what do you expect from backward agrarians? At least we're getting some recruits out of it." Mr. Grent yawned audibly. "On your feet, guards. We're going back to the ship."

Guards! Tom had forgotten about them. He looked doubtfully at his knife. Even if he sprang at the inspector, the guards would probably stop him before the murder could be committed. They must have been trained for just that sort of thing.

But if he had one of their own weapons...

He heard the shuffling of feet inside. Tom hurried back into the village.

Near the market, he saw a soldier sitting on a doorstep, singing drunkenly to himself. Two empty bottles lay at his feet and his weapon was slung sloppily over his shoulder.

Tom crept up, drew his blackjack and took aim.

The soldier must have glimpsed his shadow. He leaped to his feet, ducking the stroke of the blackjack. In the same motion, he jabbed with his slung rifle, catching Tom in the ribs, tore the rifle from his shoulder and aimed. Tom closed his eyes and lashed out with both feet.

He caught the soldier on the knee, knocking him over. Before he could get up, Tom swung the blackjack.

Tom felt the soldier's pulse—no sense killing the wrong man—and found it satisfactory. He took the weapon, checked to make sure he knew which button to push, and hastened after the Inspector.

Halfway to the ship, he caught up with them. The inspector and Grent were walking ahead, the soldiers straggling behind.

Tom moved into the underbrush. He trotted silently along until he was opposite Grent and the inspector. He took aim and his finger tightened on the trigger...

He didn't want to kill Grent, though. He was supposed to commit only one murder.

He ran on, past the inspector's party, and came out on the road in front of them. His weapon was poised as the party reached him.

"What's this?" the inspector demanded.

"Stand still," Tom said. "The rest of you drop your weapons and move out of the way."

The soldiers moved like men in shock. One by one they dropped their weapons and retreated to the underbrush. Grent held his ground.

"What are you doing, boy?" he asked.

"I'm the town criminal," Tom stated proudly. "I'm going to kill the inspector. Please move out of the way."

Grent stared at him. "Criminal? So that's what the mayor was prattling about."

"I know we haven't had any murder in two hundred years," Tom explained, "but I'm changing that right now. *Move out of the way!*"

Grent leaped out of the line of fire. The inspector stood alone, swaying slightly.

Tom took aim, trying to think about the spectacular nature of his crime and its social value. But he saw the inspector on the ground, eyes glaring open, limbs stiff, mouth twisted, no air going in or out the nostrils, no beat to the heart.

He tried to force his finger to close on the trigger. His mind could talk all it wished about the desirability of crime; his hand knew better.

"I can't!" Tom shouted.

He threw down the gun and sprinted into the underbrush.

The inspector wanted to send a search party out for Tom and hang him on the spot. Mr. Grent didn't agree. New Delaware was all forest. Ten thousand men couldn't have caught a fugitive in the forest, if he didn't want to be caught.

The mayor and several villagers came out, to find out about the commotion. The soldiers formed a hollow square around the inspector and Mr. Grent. They stood with weapons ready, their faces set and serious.

And the mayor explained everything. The village's uncivilized lack of crime. The job that Tom had been given. How ashamed they were that he had been unable to handle it.

"Why did you give the assignment to that particular man?" Mr. Grent asked.

"Well," the mayor said, "I figured if anyone could kill, Tom could. He's a fisher, you know. Pretty gory work."

"Then the rest of you would be equally unable to kill?"

"We wouldn't even get as far as Tom did," the mayor admitted sadly.

Mr. Grent and the inspector looked at each other, then at the soldiers. The soldiers were staring at the villagers with wonder and respect. They started to whisper among themselves.

"Attention!" the inspector bellowed. He turned to Grent and said in a low voice, "We'd better get away from here. Men in our armies who can't kill…"

"The morale," Mr. Grent said. He shuddered. "The possibility of infection. One man in a key position endangering a ship—perhaps a fleet—because he can't fire a weapon. It isn't worth the risk."

They ordered the soldiers back to the ship. The soldiers seemed to march more slowly than usual, and they looked back at the village. They whispered together, even though the inspector was bellowing orders.

The small ship took off in a flurry of jets. Soon it was swallowed in the large ship. And then the large ship was gone.

The edge of the enormous watery red sun was just above the horizon.

"You can come out now," the mayor called. Tom emerged from the underbrush, where he had been hiding, watching everything.

"I bungled it," he said miserably.

"Don't feel bad about it," Billy Painter told him. "It was an impossible job."

"I'm afraid it was," the mayor said, as they walked back to the village. "I thought that just possibly you could swing it. But you can't be blamed. There's not another man in the village who could have done the job even as well."

"What'll we do with these buildings?" Billy Painter asked, motioning at the jail, the post office, the church, and the little red schoolhouse.

The mayor thought deeply for a moment. "I know," he said. "We'll build a playground for the kids. Swings and slides and sandboxes and things."

"*Another* playground?" Tom asked.

"Sure. Why not?"

There was no reason, of course, why not.

"I won't be needing this any more, I guess," Tom said, handing the skulking permit to the mayor.

"No, I guess not," said the mayor. They watched him sorrowfully as he tore it up. "Well, we did our best. It just wasn't good enough."

"I had the chance," Tom muttered, "and I let you all down."

Billy Painter put a comforting hand on his shoulder. "It's not your fault, Tom. It's not the fault of any of us. It's just what comes of not being civilized for two hundred years. Look how long it took Earth to get civilized. Thousands of years. And we were trying to do it in two weeks."

"Well, we'll just have to go back to being uncivilized," the mayor said with a hollow attempt at cheerfulness.

Tom yawned, waved, went home to catch up on lost sleep.

Before entering, he glanced at the sky.

Thick, swollen clouds had gathered overhead and every one of them had a black lining. The fall rains were almost here. Soon he could start fishing again.

Now why couldn't he have thought of the inspector as a fish? He was too tired to examine that as a motive. In any case, it was too late. Earth was gone from them and civilization had fled for no one knew how many centuries more.

He slept very badly.

SQUIRREL CAGE

"The most beautiful farmland in the Galaxy—*ruined!*" the Seerian moaned. He was seven feet tall and colored a deep blue. Large tears rolled out of the lubrication duct on his neck and stained his expensive shirt. For fifteen minutes, he had been mumbling incoherently about his ruined farmland.

"Calm yourself, sir," Richard Gregor said, sitting erect and alert behind his ancient walnut desk. "The AAA Ace Interplanetary Decontamination Service can solve your problem for you."

"Could you tell us the nature of that problem, sir?" Arnold asked.

The Seerian was still choked with emotion. He dried his lubrication duct with a large handkerchief and stared earnestly at the two partners.

"Ruin!" he cried. "That's what I'm facing! The most beautiful farmland—"

"We understand, sir," Gregor said. "But what sort of ruin?"

"I own a farm in Bitter Lug, on the planet Seer," the Seerian said, quieting down with an effort. "I've planted eight hundred mulgs of land with catter, mow and barney. It will sprout inside of a month and the slegs will eat it all. I'll be ruined, destroyed, wiped out—"

"Slegs?" Arnold repeated.

"Rats, you would call them, of the species Alphyx Drex." The lubrication duct became moist at the thought and the Seerian hastily wiped it. "This year, there has been an infestation of slegs. My land is overrun with them. I've tried everything, but they multiply faster than I can kill them. Gentlemen, I will be fairly wealthy if I can harvest this crop. I will pay well if you can get rid of these beasts."

"I'm sure we can accommodate you," Gregor said. "Of course, there'll have to be a preliminary investigation. We like to know what we're getting into."

"That's what the other companies told me," the Seerian answered bitterly. "There just isn't time. I've invested everything in seed. It'll sprout in a few weeks and the slegs will wipe me out. They must be destroyed before the crop comes through."

Gregor's long, bony face became unhappy. He was a conservative operator and he didn't enjoy doing business this way. Because of Arnold's cockiness, AAA Ace had a habit of signing contracts with impossible conditions. Gregor resented it, but it was what came of running a planetary decontamination service on a shoestring. So far, they had been lucky. They were even beginning to show a mild profit. He didn't want to jeopardize that now and the gleam in his partner's eye made him apprehensive.

The Seerian seemed honest enough, but you could never tell. For all Gregor knew, these slegs were ten feet tall and armed with blasters. Stranger things had happened to AAA Ace.

"Have you had any trouble from slegs in the past?" Gregor asked.

"Of course. But they were no more a problem than the flying hangs, or the skegels, or the rotting mulch disease. They were a normal farming hazard."

"Why should they increase now?"

"How should I know?" the Seerian retorted impatiently. "Do you want the job or not?"

"We certainly do," Arnold said, "and we can start—"

"My partner and I must hold a conference first," Gregor cut in, and pulled Arnold into the hall.

Arnold was short, chubby, and incurably enthusiastic. His degree was in chemistry, but his interests lay everywhere. He had an enormous amount of odd information, culled from the several dozen technical journals he subscribed to, at considerable expense to AAA Ace.

For the most part, his knowledge was of little practical value. Few people cared why the natives of Deneb X were searching for an efficient method of racial suicide, or why nothing but winged life ever evolved on the Drei worlds.

Still, if you *wanted* to know, Arnold could tell you.

"I'd like to find out what we're getting into," Gregor said. "What is species Alphyx Drex?"

"They're rodents," Arnold answered promptly, "a little smaller than Earth rats and more timid. They're vegetarians, living on grains, grasses, and soft woods. Nothing unusual about them."

"Hmm. Suppose we find ten million of them?"

"Fine."

"Oh, stop it!"

"I'm serious! If he wanted every one of fifty rats destroyed, I wouldn't take the job. We could spend the rest of our lives hunting down the last five or six. What the Seerian needs is to have the sleg population reduced to its usual pre-epidemic proportions. That we can do and our contract will so state."

Gregor nodded. His partner could—very occasionally—show good business sense.

"But can we control them in time?" he asked.

"Absolutely. There are several modern rodent-control methods. Morganizing is one good way and the Tournier System is another. We'll be able to decimate the rat population in a matter of days."

"All right," Gregor said. "And we'll specify in the contract that we are dealing only with species Alphyx Drex. Then we'll know where we stand."

"Right."

They returned to the office. A contract was drawn up at once, giving AAA Ace a month to rid the farm of the greater number of its slegs. There was a bonus for every day before deadline that the work was completed, and forfeitures for every day past.

"I'm going on vacation until the whole thing is over," the Seerian said. "Do you really think you can save my crops?"

"Don't worry about it," Arnold assured him. "We have Morganizing equipment and we're taking Tournier System apparatus, just in case. Both are very effective."

"I know," the Seerian said. "I tried them. But perhaps I was doing something wrong. Good day and the very best of luck, gentlemen."

Gregor and Arnold stared at the door after the Seerian left.

The next day, they loaded their ship with a variety of manuals, poisons, traps, and other equipment guaranteed to make life difficult for rodents, and blasted off for Seer.

After four days of uneventful travel, Seer was a bright green beneath them. They descended and the coastline of Bitter Lug came into view. Finally they pinpointed their coordinates and touched down.

Barney Spirit, as the Seerian's farm was called, was a pretty place, with its neatly plowed fields and grassy meadows. The ancient shade trees were black and stately against the evening sky and twilight made the little reservoir a deep and translucent blue.

The signs of neglect and rodent infestation were everywhere. The great lawns were eaten bare in patches and the trees were drooping and un-kempt. Within the farmhouse, the marks of sleg teeth were on furniture, walls, even the big supporting beams.

"He's got his troubles, all right," Arnold said.

"*We've* got his troubles," Gregor corrected.

Their inspection of the farmhouse was accompanied by a continual squealing from slegs hiding just out of sight. As they approached a room, frantic scurryings began; but somehow the slegs vanished into their holes before the partners could see them.

It was too late to begin work, so Arnold and Gregor set up a variety of traps, to find out which would be most effective. They set up their sleeping bags and turned in.

Arnold could sleep through anything, but Gregor spent an extremely uncomfortable night. Battalions and regiments of slegs could be heard running across the floors, banging into tables, biting at the doors, and careening off the walls. Just as he was dozing off, an adventurous trio of slegs scampered across his chest. He brushed them off, burrowed lower into his sleeping bag, and managed to catch a few hours of fitful sleep.

In the morning, they inspected their traps and found every one of them empty.

They spent the next few hours dragging the ponderous Morganizing equipment from the ship, assembling it, and adjusting the trigger relays and lures. While Arnold was making the last fine adjustments, Gregor unloaded the Tournier System apparatus and ran the field wires around the farm house. They turned both on and sat back to await the slaughter.

Midday came; Seer's hot little sun hung directly overhead. The Morganizing equipment hummed and grumbled to itself. The Tournier wires flashed blue sparks.

Nothing happened.

The hours dragged by. Arnold read every available manual on rodent control. Gregor dug out a pack of tattered cards and morosely played solitaire. The equipment murmured and buzzed, exactly as its manufacturers guaranteed. Enough power was consumed to light a medium-sized village.

Not a single rodent corpse was produced.

By evening, it was apparent that slegs were not susceptible to Morganizing or Tournierizing. It was time for dinner and a conference.

"What could make them so elusive?" Gregor puzzled, sitting worriedly on a kitchen chair with a can of self-heating hash.

"A mutation," Arnold stated.

"Yeah, that could do it. Superior intelligence, adaptability…" Mechanically, Gregor ate his hash. All around the kitchen, he could hear the patter of countless little sleg feet, slipping in and out of holes, staying just out of sight.

Arnold opened an apple pie. "They *must* be a mutation, and a damned clever one. We'd better catch one quick and find out what we're up against."

But catching one was no easier than killing a thousand. The slegs stayed out of sight, ignoring traps, lures, snares, and doped bait.

At midnight, Arnold said, "This is ridiculous."

Gregor nodded abstractedly. He was putting the finishing touches on a new trap. It was a large sheet metal box with two sides left invitingly open. If a sleg were foolish enough to enter, a photo-electric cell closed the sides with the speed of a lightning bolt.

"Now we'll see," Gregor said. They left the box in the kitchen and went into the living room.

At two-thirty in the morning, the sides slammed shut.

They hurried in. Within the metal box, they could hear a frantic scurrying and squealing. Gregor turned on the lights and up-ended the box. Although he knew that no rat born could climb the polished sides of the trap, he withdrew the cover with great care, an inch at a time.

The squealing increased.

They eagerly peered into the trap, half prepared to see a rat in full soldier's uniform, waving a white flag.

They saw nothing. The box was empty.

"He couldn't have gotten out!" Arnold exclaimed.

"And he didn't gnaw through. Listen!"

Inside the box, the squealing continued, accompanied by frantic scratching sounds, as though a rat were trying to scramble up the sides of the trap.

Gregor put his hand in and felt cautiously around. *"Ouch!"* He jerked his hand back. There were two small tooth marks on his forefinger.

The noise within the empty box increased.

"We seem to have captured an invisible rat," Gregor said blankly.

The Seerian was vacationing at the Majestic Hotel, in the Catakinny Cluster. It took almost two hours to reach him by interstellar telephone.

Gregor started the conversation by shouting, "You never said anything about invisible slegs!"

"Didn't I?" the Seerian asked. "Careless of me. What about it?"

"It's a breach of contract, that's what!" Gregor yelled.

"Not at all. My lawyer, who happens to be vacationing with me, says that invisibility in animals comes under the classification of Natural Protective Coloration, and therefore need not be mentioned as a hazardous or unique condition. For legal purposes, the courts don't even admit a state of invisibility exists, as long as *some* means of detection is possible. They call it Relative Dimness and it is not allowed as permissible distress in an extermination contract."

Gregor was momentarily stunned.

"We poor farmers must protect ourselves, you know," the Seerian continued. "But I have perfect faith in your ability to cope. Good day."

"He's protected, all right," Arnold admitted, putting down the extension telephone. "If we clean out these invisible rats, he's got a bargain. If we don't, he collects forfeitures."

"Invisible or not," Gregor said, "Morganizing ought to work on them."

"But it doesn't," Arnold pointed out.

"I know. But why doesn't it work? Why don't traps work? Why doesn't the Tournierizing work?"

"Because the rats are invisible."

"That shouldn't matter. They still sniff like rats, don't they? They still hear like rats. They still think like—*or do they?*"

"Well," Arnold said, "if this invisibility is a true mutational change, it's possible that their sensory apparatus has changed, too."

Gregor frowned. "And a change in their sensory equipment would call for a change in our applied stimulus. Now all we need to know is how these slegs differ from the norm."

"Aside from their invisibility, you mean," Arnold said.

But how do you test the sensory apparatus of an invisible rat? Gregor began by constructing a maze out of the Seerian's choicer furniture. Its walls were designed to light up when an invisible sleg brushed by. In that way, the rodents' movements could be traced.

Arnold experimented with stains and dyes, searching for something that would return the slegs to visibility. One high-potency dye took momentary hold. A sleg appeared as though by magic, blinking slowly, his nose quivering. He looked at Arnold with maddening calm, then fearlessly turned his back. His rapid metabolic rate converted the dye almost immediately and he faded from view.

Gregor captured ten slegs and tried to run them through his maze. They were unbelievably uncooperative. Most of them refused to move at all. They sniffed disdainfully at the food he gave them, toyed with it a few moments, then ignored it. Even light electric shocks budged them only a few inches.

But the tests did give the answer to the failure of Morganizing and Tournierizing.

Like all large-scale extermination systems, they were based upon the concept of "normal" rodents. These normals could be tricked or scared into certain behavior patterns by stimulation of their hunger or fear drives. It was the norm among rodents that the systems destroyed.

Everything was fine as long as the norm represented a high percentage of the rodent population. But as the slegs had changed, their norm had changed, too. These slegs had adapted to invisibility.

They could no longer be panicked, for they had discovered that nothing chased them. And since they had no reason to flee, they could eat anywhere, at any time. Therefore, they were invariably well fed and in no mood to explore enticing smells, shapes or sounds.

Both Morganizing and Tournierizing *could* be adapted and *would* destroy slegs. But only a few. Only those rodents who had not adapted to invisibility—the unaverage ones. And this only served to reinforce the change in the others.

But what had happened to the natural enemies of the sleg, the forces acting to maintain an ecological balance? In order to find out, Gregor and Arnold made a frantic survey of the fauna of Bitter Lug.

Bit by bit, they reconstructed what must have happened.

The slegs had enemies on Seer—flying hangs, drigs, tree skurls, and omenesters. These unimaginative creatures had been unable to cope with the sudden change. For one thing, they were visual hunters, using smell only as an auxiliary. Although sleg scent was powerful in their nostrils, *seeing* was believing, not smelling. So they ate each other and left the slegs alone.

And the slegs increased and increased...

And AAA Ace could find nothing to check them.

"We're tackling this at the wrong end," Gregor said, after a fruitless week. "We should find out why they became invisible. Then we'd know how to deal with them."

"Mutation," Arnold insisted dogmatically.

"I don't believe it. No animal has ever mutated into invisibility. Why should the slegs be the first?"

Arnold shrugged his shoulders. "Consider the chameleon. There are insects that look like twigs. Others resemble leaves. Some fish can counterfeit the ocean bottom so perfectly—"

"Yes, yes," Gregor said impatiently, "that's camouflage. But invisibility—"

"Some kinds of jellyfish are transparent enough to be considered invisible," Arnold continued. "The hummingbird achieves it by dazzling speed. The shrew hides so well that few humans have ever seen one. All are moving toward invisibility."

"That's ridiculous. Nature equips each creature as best it can. But it never goes all the way by endowing one species with invulnerability from all others."

"You're being teleological," Arnold objected. "You're assuming that nature has some aim in mind, like the overseer of a garden. I maintain that it's a blind averaging process. Sure, the mean usually obtains, but there are bound to be extremes. Nature had to come up with invisibility eventually."

"Now *you're* being teleological. You're trying to tell me that the aim of camouflage is invisibility."

"It must be! Consider—"

"To hell with it," Gregor said wearily. "I'm not even sure what teleology is. We've been here ten days and we've captured some fifty rats, out of a population of several millions. Nothing works. Where do we go from here?"

They sat in silence. Outside, they could hear the scream of a flying hang as it dipped low over the fields.

"If only the slegs' natural enemies had some guts," Arnold said sadly.

"They're visual hunters. If they were—"

He stopped abruptly and stared at Arnold. Arnold looked puzzled for a moment. Then a slow light of comprehension dawned on his face.

"Of course!" he said.

Gregor lunged for the telephone and called Galactic Rapid Express. "Hello! Listen, this is a rush order…"

Galactic Rapid Express outdid themselves. Within two days, they deposited ten small boxes on the pocked lawn at Barney Spirit.

Gregor and Arnold brought the boxes inside and opened one. Out stepped a large, sleek, proud, yellow-eyed cat. She was of Earth stock, but her hunting capabilities had been improved with a Lyraxian strain.

She stared somberly at the two men and sniffed the air.

"Don't get your hopes too high," Gregor told Arnold as the cat stalked across the room. "This is outside all normal cat experience."

"Shh," Arnold said. "Don't distract her."

The cat stood, her head cocked delicately to one side, listening to several hundred invisible slegs amble disdainfully past her.

She wrinkled her nose and blinked several times.

"She doesn't like the setup," Gregor whispered.

"Who does?" Arnold whispered back.

The cat took a cautious step forward. She raised a forepaw, and then lowered it again.

"She isn't catching on," Gregor said regretfully. "Maybe if we tried terriers—"

The cat suddenly lunged. There was a wild squealing and she was gripping something invisible between her forepaws. She mewed angrily and bit. The squealing stopped.

But other squeals took its place and ratlike shrieks and rodent cries of terror. Gregor released four more cats, keeping the remaining five as his second team. Within minutes, the room sounded like a miniature abattoir. He and Arnold had to leave. The noise was nerve-shattering.

"Time for a celebration," Arnold said, opening one of the brandy bottles he had packed.

"Well," said Gregor, "it's a little early—"

"Not at all. The cats are at work, all's well with the world. By the way, remind me to order a few hundred more cats."

"Sure. But what if the slegs turn cautious again?"

"That's the beauty of it," Arnold said, pouring two stiff shots. "As long as the slegs are this way, they're meat for the cats. But if they revert to their old habits—if they become truly ratlike—we can use the Morganizer."

Gregor could find no argument. The slegs were caught between the cats and the Morganizer. Either way, the place should be back to normal in another week, in plenty of time for a sizable bonus.

"A toast to the Earth cat," Arnold proposed.

"I'll drink to that," Gregor said. "To the staunch, down-to-Earth, common-sense Earth cat."

"Invisible rats can't faze her."

"She eats 'em if they're there or not," Gregor said, listening to the sweet music of carnage going on throughout the farmhouse.

They drank quite a number of toasts to the various attributes of the Earth cat. Then they drank a solemn toast to Earth. After that, it seemed only proper to toast all the Earth-type suns, starting with Abaco.

Their brandy gave out when they reached Glostrea. Fortunately, the Seerian had a cellar well stocked with local wines.

Arnold passed out while proposing a toast to Wanlix. Gregor managed to last through Xechia. Then he laid his head on his arms and went to sleep.

They awoke late the next day with matching headaches, upset stomachs, and flashing pains in the joints. And just to make matters worse, not one of their staunch, down-to-Earth, common-sense Earth cats was to be found.

They searched the farmhouse. They looked in the barns, through the meadows, across the fields. They dug up sleg holes and peered into an abandoned well.

There was no sign of a cat—not even a wisp of fur.

On all sides, the slegs scampered merrily by, secure in their cloak of invisibility.

"Just when the cats were doing so well," Arnold mourned. "Do you suppose the slegs ganged up on them?"

"Not a chance," Gregor said. "It would be contrary to all sleg behavior. It's more reasonable to assume that the cats just wandered off."

"With all this food here?" Arnold asked. "Not a chance. It would be contrary to all cat behavior."

"Here, kitty, kitty!" Gregor called, for the last time. There was no answering meow, only the complacent squeals of a million careless slegs.

"We must find out what happened," Arnold said, walking to the boxes that housed their remaining five cats. "We'll try again. But this time we'll introduce a control element."

He removed a cat and fastened a belled collar around her neck. Gregor closed the outer doors of the farmhouse and they turned her loose.

She went to work with a vengeance and soon the chewed corpses of slegs began to appear, life—and invisibility—drained from them.

"This doesn't tell us anything," Arnold said.

"Keep on watching," Gregor told him.

After a while, the cat took a short nap, a sip of water and began again. Arnold started to doze off. Gregor watched, thinking dire thoughts.

Half of their month was now over, Gregor realized, and the sleg population was untouched. Cats could do the job; but if they gave up after a few hours, they would be too expensive to utilize. Would terriers do any better? Or would this happen to any—

He gaped suddenly and nudged Arnold. *"Hey!"* Arnold awoke with a groan and looked.

A moment ago, there had been an extremely busy cat. Now, abruptly, there was only a collar, suspended half a foot above the floor, its little bell tinkling merrily.

"She's become invisible!" Arnold cried. "But how? Why?"

"It must be something she ate," Gregor said wildly, watching the collar dart across the floor.

"All she's eaten is sleg."

They looked at each other with sudden comprehension.

"Then sleg invisibility is *not* mutational!" Gregor said. "I told you so all along. Not if it can be transmitted that way. The slegs must have eaten something, too!"

Arnold nodded. "I suspected it. I suppose, after the cat digests a certain amount of sleg, the stuff takes hold. The cat becomes invisible."

From the bedlam in the room, they could tell that the invisible cat was still devouring invisible slegs.

"They must all still be here," Gregor said. "But why didn't they answer when we called them?"

"Cats are pretty independent," Arnold suggested.

The bell tinkled. The collar, miraculously suspended half a foot above the floor, continued to dart back and forth among the ranks of sleg. Gregar realized that it didn't really matter if the cats couldn't be seen, as long as they continued working.

But while he watched, the tinkle of the bell stopped. The collar was motionless in the middle of the floor for a moment; then it disappeared.

Gregor continued staring at the spot where the collar had been. He was saying, very softly, "It didn't happen. It just didn't happen."

Unfortunately, he knew it had. The cat hadn't jumped, moved, advanced, or retreated.

The invisible cat had disappeared.

Although time was drawing short, they knew they would have to start at the beginning and find what was producing the invisibility. Arnold settled into his makeshift laboratory and began to test all substances around the farm. His eyes became red-rimmed and haggard from long hours of peering into a microscope and he jumped at the slightest sound.

Gregor continued to experiment with the cats. Before releasing number seven, he fitted a tiny radar reflector and radio signal emitter to her collar. She followed the identical pattern of cat number six—after several hours of hunting, she became invisible; shortly after that, she disappeared. Radar showed no trace of her and the radio signal had stopped abruptly.

He tried a more carefully controlled experiment. This time, he put cats eight and nine into separate cages and fed them weighed samples of sleg. They became invisible. He stopped feeding number eight, but continued with nine. Cat number nine disappeared like all the others, leaving no trace. Eight was still invisible, but present.

Gregor had a long argument with the Seerian over the interstellar telephone. The Seerian wanted AAA Ace to forfeit now, at only a small loss, and let one of the bigger companies move in. Gregor refused.

But after the talk, he wondered if he had done the right thing. The secrets at Barney Spirit were deep and involved, and might take him a lifetime to solve. Invisibility was bad enough. But the vanishing was much worse. It left so little to go on.

He was mulling this over when Arnold came in. His partner had a wild look in his eyes and his grin seemed almost demented.

"Look," he said to Gregor, holding out one hand, palm up.

Gregor looked. Arnold's hand was empty.

"What is it?" Gregor asked.

"Only the secret of invisibility, that's all it is," Arnold said with a cackle of triumph.

"But I can't see anything," Gregor answered cautiously, wondering how best to deal with a madman.

"Of course you can't. It's invisible." He laughed again.

Gregor moved back until he had put a table between them. Soothingly, he said, "Good work, old man. That hand of yours will go down in history. Now suppose you tell me all about it."

"Stop humoring me, you idiot," Arnold snapped, still holding out his open hand. "It's invisible, but it's there. Feel it."

Gregor reached out gingerly. In Arnold's hand was what felt like a bunch of coarse leaves.

"An invisible plant!" Gregor said.

"Exactly. *This* is the culprit."

Arnold had examined every substance on the farm without results. One day, he had been walking in front of the house. He had looked again at the bald spots on the pocked lawn. For the first time, it struck him how regularly they were spaced.

He bent down and examined one. It was bare, all right. The dirt showed through.

He touched the spot—and found that he was touching an invisible plant.

"As far as I can tell," Arnold said, "there's an invisible plant of no known species growing in each of those spots."

"But where did they come from?"

"Somewhere Man has never been," Arnold said positively. "I suppose that the progenitor of this species was floating in space, a microscopic spore. Finally it was drawn into the atmospheric orbit of Seer. It fell on the lawn at Barney Spirit, took root, blossomed, threw out seeds—and there we are. We know that slegs eat grasses and their sense of smell is relatively well developed. They probably found this stuff very tasty."

"But it's invisible!"

"That wouldn't bother a sleg. Invisibility is too sophisticated a concept for them."

"And you think all of them ate it?"

"No, not all. But those who did stood the best chance for survival. They were the ones the hangs and drigs didn't pick off. And they transmitted the taste to the next generation."

"And then the cats came in, ate the slegs and got enough of the substance to turn invisible. Fine. But why did they completely vanish?"

"That's obvious," Arnold said. "The slegs ate this plant as just a part of their normal diet. But the cats ate only sleg. They got an overdose."

"Why should an overdose make anything vanish? Vanish to where?"

"Maybe some day we'll find out. Right now, we have a job to do. We'll burn out all the plants. Once the slegs work the stuff out of their systems, they'll become visible again. Then the cats can go to work."

"I just hope it does the job," Gregor said dubiously.

They went to work with portable flamethrowers. The invisible plants were easy to spot, since they formed bare spots in the lush green lawns of Barney Spirit. In this instance, invisibility gave them an exceedingly low survival value.

By evening, Gregor and Arnold had burned every one of the plants into ashes.

The next morning, they examined the lawn and were disconcerted to find a new pattern of pock marks. New plants were growing in them, as copiously as before.

"No cause for alarm," Arnold said. "The first bunch must have seeded just before we destroyed them. This crop will be the last."

They spent another day destroying the plants, scorching the entire lawn for good measure. At dusk, a new shipment of cats arrived from Galactic Rapid Express. They kept them caged, waiting for the slegs to return to visibility.

In the morning, more invisible plants were growing on the scorched soil at Barney Spirit. AAA Ace held an emergency conference.

"It's a ridiculous idea," Gregor said.

"But it's the only way left," Arnold insisted.

Gregor shook his head stubbornly.

"What else can we do?" Arnold asked. "Do you have any ideas?"

"No."

"We're only a week from deadline. We'll probably lose part of our profits anyhow. But if we don't complete the job, we're out of business."

Arnold set a bowl of invisible plants on the table. "We have to find out where the cats go when they get an overdose."

Gregor stood up and began to pace the floor. "They might show up inside a sun, for all we know."

"That's a risk we have to take," Arnold said sternly.

"All right," Gregor sighed. "Go ahead."

"What?"

"I said go ahead."

"Me?"

"Who else? I'm not going to eat that stuff. This was your idea."

"But I can't," Arnold said, perspiring. "I'm the research end of this team. I have to stay here and—uh—collate data. Besides, I'm allergic to greens."

"I'll collate the data this time."

"But you don't know how! I have to work up a few new stains. My flow sheets are all messed up. I've got several solutions cooking in the stove, I'm running a pollenation test on—"

"You're breaking my heart," Gregor said wearily. "All right, I'll go. But this is absolutely the very last time."

"Right you are," Arnold quickly pulled a handful of invisible leaves from the bowl. "Here, eat this. That's it, take some more. What does it taste like?"

"Cabbage," Gregor mumbled, munching.

"I'm sure of one thing," Arnold said. "The effects can't last very long on a creature of your size. Your system should throw off the drug in a matter of hours. You'll reappear almost immediately."

Gregor suddenly became invisible except for his clothes.

"How do you feel?" Arnold asked.

"No different."

"Eat some more."

Gregor ate another double handful of leaves. And, suddenly, he was gone. Clothes and all, he had vanished.

"Gregor?" Arnold called anxiously.

"Are you anywhere around?" Arnold asked.

There was still no answer.

"He's gone," Arnold said out loud. "I didn't even wish him luck."

Arnold turned to his solutions boiling on the stove and lowered the flame under them. He worked for fifteen minutes, then stopped and stared around the room.

"Not that he should need any luck," Arnold said. "There can't be any real danger."

He prepared his dinner. Halfway through it, with a forkful of food poised in front of his mouth, he added, "I should have said good-bye."

Resolutely, he put all dark thoughts out of his mind and turned to his experiments. He labored all night and fell exhausted into bed at dawn. In the afternoon, after a hurried breakfast, he continued working.

Gregor had been gone over twenty-four hours.

The Seerian telephoned that evening and Arnold had to assure him that the slegs were nearly under control. It was just a matter of time.

After that, he read through his rodent manuals, straightened his equipment, rewired an armature in the Morganizer, played with a new idea for a sleg trap, burned a new crop of invisible plants, and slept again.

When he awoke, he realized that Gregor had been gone over seventy-two hours. His partner might never return.

"He was a martyr to science," Arnold said. "I'll raise a statue to him." But it seemed a very meager thing to do. He should have eaten the plant himself. Gregor wasn't much good in unusual situations. He had courage—no one could deny that—but not much adaptability.

Still, all the adaptability in the world wouldn't help you inside a sun, or in the vacuum of space, or—

He heard a noise behind him, and whirled eagerly, shouting, "Gregor!"

But it was not Gregor.

The creature who stood before Arnold was about four feet tall and had entirely too many limbs. His skin color appeared to be a grayish-pink, under a heavy layer of dirt. He was carrying a heavy sack. He wore a high peaked hat on his high peaked head, and not much else.

"You aren't Gregor, are you?" Arnold asked, too stunned to react properly.

"Of course not," the creature replied. "I'm Hem."

"Oh...Have you seen my partner, by any chance? His name is Richard Gregor. He's about a foot taller than I, thin and—"

"Of course I've seen him," Hem said. "Isn't he here?"

"No."

"That's odd. Hope nothing went wrong." He sat down and proceeded to scratch himself intently under three armpits.

Feeling giddy, Arnold asked, "Where do you come from?"

"From Oole, naturally," Hem said. "That's where we plant the scomp. And it comes out here."

"Just a moment." Arnold sat down heavily. "Suppose you start at the beginning."

"It's perfectly simple. For generations, we Oolens have planted the scomp. When the scomp is young, it disappears for a few weeks. Then the mature plant appears again in our fields and we harvest it and eat it."

"You're going too fast for me. Where did you say Oole is?"

"Gregor says Oole is in a parallel universe. I wouldn't know about that. He appeared in the middle of my fields about two months ago and taught me English. Then—"

"Two *months?*" Arnold echoed. He considered. "Different time framework, I suppose. Never mind. Go on."

"Do you have something to eat?" Hem asked. "Haven't eaten in three days. Couldn't, you know." Arnold handed him a loaf of bread and a jar of jam. "Well, when they opened the new North Territory," Hem said, "I put in an early bid. So I packed my animals, purchased three class B wives, and departed for my claim. Once there, I—"

"Stop!" Arnold begged. "What has this got to do with anything?"

"This is how it all happened. Don't interrupt."

Scratching his left shoulder with one hand while stuffing bread and jam in his mouth with two others, Hem explained, "I reached the new territory and planted scomp. It blossomed and disappeared, as always. But when it reappeared, most of it had been consumed by some creature. Well, farmers have to expect trouble, so I planted again. The next crop was still too poor to harvest. I was furious. I determined to continue planting. We pioneers are a determined lot, you understand. But I was just about to give up and return to civilization when your partner came—"

"Let me see if I understand so far," Arnold said, "You are from a universe parallel to ours. This scomp you plant grows in *two* universes, in order to complete its development."

"That's correct—at least it's how Gregor explained it to us."

"It seems an odd way to grow food."

"We like it," the Oolen said stiffly. He scratched behind all four knees. "Gregor says that our plants usually penetrate some uninhabited part of your universe. But this time, when I sowed in new territory, the scomp came up here."

"Aha!" Arnold cried.

"Aha? He didn't teach me that word. Anyhow, Gregor helped me. He told me I didn't have to abandon my land; I just had to use my other fields. Gregor assures me that there is no one-to-one spatial correspondence between parallel universes, whatever that means. And this is in payment for our other business."

Hem dropped the heavy sack on the floor. It made a loud clunk as it landed. Arnold opened it and peered inside.

The bars of yellow metal looked exactly like gold ingots.

Just then, the telephone rang. Arnold picked it up.

"Hello," Gregor said, from the other end. "Is Hem there yet?"

"Yes…"

"He explained it all, didn't he? About the parallel universe and how the scomp grows?"

"I think I understand," Arnold said. "But—"

"Now listen," Gregor continued. "Before, when we destroyed the plants, he sowed them again. Since his time is much longer than ours, they grew here overnight. But that's over. He's moving his fields. The next time you destroy the scomp, it'll stay destroyed. Wait a week, then turn the cats and the Morganizer loose."

Arnold shut his eyes tightly. Gregor had had two months to figure all this out. He hadn't. It was happening too fast for him.

"What about Hem?" he asked.

"He'll eat some scomp and go home. We had to starve it out of ourselves to get here."

"All right," Arnold said. "I think I—just a minute! *Where are you?*"

Gregor chuckled. "There's no one-to-one correspondence between parallel universes, you know. I was standing on the edge of the field when the scomp wore off. I came out on the planet Thule."

"But that's on the other side of the galaxy!" Gregor gasped.

"I know. I'll meet you back on Earth. Be sure to bring the gold."

Arnold hung up. Hem had gone.

It was only then that Arnold realized he hadn't asked Gregor what the other business was, the business that the Oolen had paid for in solid gold.

He found out later, when they were both back on Earth, in the offices of AAA Ace. The job was done. The slegs, returned to visibility, had been decimated by the cats and the Morganizer. Their contract was completed. They had to forfeit part of their profit, because the job ran two weeks overtime, but the loss was more than made good by the bars of Oolen gold.

"His fields were overrun with our cats," Gregor told Arnold. "They were scaring his livestock. I rounded them all up and we sold them to the Oole Central Zoo. They never saw anything like them. He and I split the take."

"Well," Arnold said, rubbing the back of his neck, "it all worked out for the best."

"It certainly did."

Gregor was ferociously scratching his shoulder. Arnold watched for a moment, then felt a strong itching sensation on his chest—in his hair—on his calf—everywhere.

Carefully, he reached down and probed with his fingernails.

"I guess we aren't quite through, though," Gregor said.

"Why?" Arnold asked, scratching at his left biceps. "What is this?"

"Hem wasn't the most hygienic of people and Oole was a pretty scrubby place."

"What is it?"

"I'm afraid I picked up a lot of lice," Gregor said. He scratched at his stomach. "Invisible lice, of course."

THE LIFEBOAT MUTINY

"Tell me the truth. Did you ever see sweeter engines?" Joe, the Interstellar Junkman asked. "And look at those servos!"

"Hmm," Gregor said judiciously.

"That hull," Joe said softly. "I bet it's five hundred years old, and not a spot of corrosion on it." He patted the burnished side of the boat affectionately. What luck, the pat seemed to say, that this paragon among vessels should be here just when AAA Ace needs a lifeboat.

"She certainly does seem rather nice," Arnold said, with the studied air of a man who has fallen in love and is trying hard not to show it. "What do you think, Dick?"

Richard Gregor didn't answer. The boat *was* handsome, and she looked perfect for ocean survey work on Trident. But you had to be careful about Joe's merchandise.

"They just don't build 'em this way any more," Joe sighed. "Look at the propulsion unit. Couldn't dent it with a trip-hammer. Note the capacity of the cooling system. Examine—"

"It *looks* good," Gregor said slowly. The AAA Ace Interplanetary Decontamination Service had dealt with Joe in the past, and had learned caution. Not that Joe was dishonest; far from it. The flotsam he collected from anywhere in the inhabited Universe worked. But the ancient machines often had their own ideas of how a job should be done. They tended to grow peevish when forced into another routine.

"I don't care if it's beautiful, fast, durable, or even comfortable," Gregor said defiantly. "I just want to be absolutely sure it's safe."

Joe nodded. "That's the important thing, of course. Step inside."

They entered the cabin of the boat. Joe stepped up to instrument panel, smiled mysteriously, and pressed a button.

Immediately Gregor heard a voice which seemed to originate in his head, saying, "I am Lifeboat 324-A. My purpose—"

"Telepathy?" Gregor interrupted.

"Direct sense recording," Joe said, smiling proudly. "No language barriers that way. I told you, they just don't build 'em this way any more."

"I am Lifeboat 324-A," the boat esped again. "My primary purpose is to preserve those within me from peril, and to maintain them in good health. At present, I am only partially activated."

"Could anything be safer?" Joe cried. "This is no senseless hunk of metal. This boat will look after you. This boat *cares!*"

Gregor was impressed, even though the idea of an emotional boat was somehow distasteful. But then, paternalistic gadgets had always irritated him.

Arnold had no such feelings. "We'll take it!"

"You won't be sorry," Joe said, in the frank and open tones that had helped make him a millionaire several times over.

Gregor hoped not.

The next day, Lifeboat 324-A was loaded aboard their spaceship and they blasted off for Trident.

This planet, in the heart of the East Star Valley, had recently been bought by a real-estate speculator. He'd found her nearly perfect for colonization. Trident was the size of Mars, but with a far better climate. There was no indigenous native population to contend with, no poisonous plants, no germ-borne diseases. And, unlike so many worlds, Trident had no predatory animals. Indeed, she had no animals at all. Apart from one small island and a polar cap, the entire planet was covered with water.

There was no real shortage of land; you could wade across several of Trident's seas. The land just wasn't heaped high enough.

AAA Ace had been commissioned to correct this minor flaw.

After landing on Trident's single island, they launched the boat. The rest of the day was spent checking and loading the special survey equipment on board. Early the next morning, Gregor prepared sandwiches and filled a canteen with water. They were ready to begin work.

As soon as the mooring lines were cast off, Gregor joined Arnold in the cabin. With a small flourish, Arnold pressed the first button.

"I am Lifeboat 324-A," the boat esped. "My primary purpose is to preserve those within me from peril, and to maintain them in good health. At present, I am only partially activated. For full activation, press button two."

Gregor pressed the second button.

There was a muffled buzzing deep in the bowels of the boat. Nothing else happened.

"That's odd," Gregor said. He pressed the button again. The muffled buzz was repeated.

"Sounds like a short circuit," Arnold said.

Glancing out the forward porthole, Gregor saw the shoreline of the island slowly drifting away. He felt a touch of panic. There was so much water here, and so little land. To make matters worse, nothing on the instrument panel resembled a wheel or tiller, nothing looked like a throttle or clutch. How did you operate a partially activated lifeboat?

"She must control telepathically," Gregor said hopefully. In a stern voice he said, "Go ahead slowly."

The little boat forged ahead.

"Now right a little."

The boat responded perfectly to Gregor's clear, although unnautical command. The partners exchanged smiles.

"Straighten out," Gregor said, "and full speed ahead!"

The lifeboat charged forward into the shining, empty sea.

Arnold disappeared into the bilge with a flashlight and a circuit tester. The surveying was easy enough for Gregor to handle alone. The machines did all the work, tracing the major faults in the ocean bottom, locating the most promising volcanoes, running the flow and buildup charts. When the survey was complete, the next stage would be turned over to a sub-contractor. He would wire the volcanoes, seed the faults, retreat to a safe distance and touch the whole thing off.

Then Trident would be, for a while, a spectacularly noisy place. And when things had quieted down, there would be enough dry land to satisfy even a real-estate speculator.

By mid-afternoon Gregor felt that they had done enough surveying for one day. He and Arnold ate their sandwiches and drank from the canteen. Later they took a short swim in Trident's clear green water.

"I think I've found the trouble," Arnold said. "The leads to the primary activators have been removed. And the power cable's been cut."

"Why would anyone do that?" Gregor asked.

Arnold shrugged. "Might have been part of the decommissioning. I'll have it right in a little while."

He crawled back into the bilge. Gregor turned in the direction of the island, steering telepathically and watching the green water foam merrily past the bow. At moments like this, contrary to all his previous experience, the Universe seemed a fine and friendly place.

In half an hour Arnold emerged, grease-stained but triumphant. "Try that button now," he said.

"But we're almost back."

"So what? Might as well have this thing working right."

Gregor nodded, and pushed the second button.

They could hear the faint click-click of circuits opening. Half a dozen small engines purred into life. A light flashed red, then winked off as the generators took up the load.

"That's more like it," Arnold said.

"I am Lifeboat 324-A," the boat stated telepathically. "I am now fully activated, and able to protect my occupants from danger. Have faith in me. My action-response tapes, both psychological and physical, have been prepared by the best scientific minds in all Drome."

"Gives you quite a feeling of confidence, doesn't it?" Arnold said.

"I suppose so," Gregor said. "But where is Drome?"

"Gentlemen," the lifeboat continued, "try to think of me, not as an unfeeling mechanism, but as your friend and comrade-in-arms. I understand how you feel. You have seen your ship go down, cruelly riddled by the implacable H'gen. You have—"

"What ship?" Gregor asked. "What's it talking about?"

"—crawled aboard me, dazed, gasping from the poisonous fumes of water; half-dead—"

"You mean that swim we took?" Arnold asked. "You've got it all wrong. We were just surveying—"

"—shocked, wounded, morale low," the lifeboat finished. "You are a little frightened, perhaps," it said in a softer mental tone. "And well you might be, separated from the Drome fleet and adrift upon an inclement alien planet. A little fear is nothing to be ashamed of, gentlemen. But this is war, and war is a cruel business. We have no alternative but to drive the barbaric H'gen back across space."

"There must be a reasonable explanation for all this," Gregor said. "Probably an old television script got mixed up in its response bank."

"We'd better give it a complete overhaul," Arnold said. "Can't listen to that stuff all day."

They were approaching the island. The lifeboat was still babbling about home and hearth, evasive action, tactical maneuvers, and the need for calm in emergencies like this. Suddenly it slowed.

"What's the matter?" Gregor asked.

"I am scanning the island," the lifeboat answered.

Gregor and Arnold glanced at each other. "Better humor it," Arnold whispered. To the lifeboat he said, "That island's okay. We checked it personally."

"Perhaps you did," the lifeboat answered. "But in modern, lightning-quick warfare, Drome senses cannot be trusted. They are too limited, too prone to interpret what they wish. Electronic senses, on the other hand, are emotionless, eternally vigilant, and infallible within their limits."

"But there isn't anything there!" Gregor shouted.

"I perceive a foreign spaceship," the lifeboat answered. "It has no Drome markings."

"It hasn't any enemy markings, either," Arnold answered confidently, since he had painted the ancient hull himself.

"No, it hasn't. But in war, we must assume that what is not ours is the enemy's. I understand your desire to set foot on land again. But I take into account factors that a Drome, motivated by his emotions, would overlook. Consider the apparent emptiness of this strategic bit of land; the unmarked spaceship put temptingly out for bait; the fact that our fleet is no longer in this vicinity; the—"

"All right, that's enough," Gregor was sick of arguing with a verbose and egoistic machine. "Go directly to that island. That's an order."

"I cannot obey that order," the boat said. "You are unbalanced from your harrowing escape from death—"

Arnold reached for the cutout switch, and withdrew his hand with a howl of pain.

"Come to your senses, gentlemen," the boat said sternly. "Only the decommissioning officer is empowered to turn me off. For your own safety, I must warn you not to touch any of my controls. You are mentally unbalanced. Later, when our position is safer, I will administer to you. Now my full energies must be devoted toward detection and escape from the enemy."

The boat picked up speed and moved away from the island in an intricate evasive pattern.

"Where are we going?" Gregor asked.

"To rejoin the Drome fleet!" the lifeboat cried so confidently that the partners stared nervously over the vast, deserted waters of Trident.

"As soon as I can find it, that is," the lifeboat amended.

It was late at night. Gregor and Arnold sat in a corner of the cabin, hungrily sharing their last sandwich. The lifeboat was still rushing madly over the waves, its every electronic sense alert, searching for a fleet that had existed five hundred years ago, upon an entirely different planet.

"Did you ever hear of these Dromes?" Gregor asked.

Arnold searched through his vast store of minutiae. "They were nonhuman, lizard-evolved creatures," he said. "Lived on the sixth planet of some little system near Capella. The race died out over a century ago."

"And the H'gen?"

"Also lizards. Same story." Arnold found a crumb and popped it into his mouth. "It wasn't a very important war. All the combatants are gone. Except this lifeboat, apparently."

"And us," Gregor reminded him. "We've been drafted as Drome soldiery." He sighed wearily. "Do you think we can reason with this tub?"

Arnold shook his head. "I don't see how. As far as this boat is concerned, the war is still on. It can only interpret data in terms of that premise."

"It's probably listening in on us now," Gregor said.

"I don't think so. It's not really a mind-reader. Its perception centers are geared only to thoughts aimed specifically at it."

"Yes siree," Gregor said bitterly, "they just don't build 'em this way any more." He wished he could get his hands on Joe, the Interstellar Junkman.

"It's actually a very interesting situation," Arnold said. "I may do an article on it for *Popular Cybernetics*. Here is a machine with nearly infallible apparatus for the perception of external stimuli. The percepts it receives are translated logically into action. The only trouble is, the logic is based upon no longer existent conditions. Therefore, you could say that the machine is the victim of a systematized delusional system."

Gregor yawned. "You mean the lifeboat is just plain nuts," he said bluntly.

"Nutty as a fruitcake. I believe paranoia would be the proper designation. But it'll end pretty soon."

"Why?" Gregor asked.

"It's obvious," Arnold said. "The boat's prime directive is to keep us alive. So he has to feed us. Our sandwiches are gone, and the only other food is on the island. I figure he'll have to take a chance and go back."

In a few minutes they could feel the lifeboat swinging, changing direction. It esped, "At present I am unable to locate the Drome fleet. Therefore, I am turning back to scan the island once again. Fortunately, there are no enemy in this immediate area. Now I can devote myself to your care with all the power of my full attention."

"You see?" Arnold said, nudging Gregor. "Just as I said. Now we'll reinforce the concept." He said to the lifeboat, "About time you got around to us. We're hungry."

"Yeah, feed us," Gregor demanded.

"Of course," the lifeboat said. A tray slid out of the wall. It was heaped high with something that looked like clay, but smelled like machine oil.

"What's that supposed to be?" Gregor asked.

"That is geezel," the lifeboat said. "It is the staple diet of the Drome peoples. I can prepare it in sixteen different ways."

Gregor cautiously sampled it. It tasted just like clay coated with machine oil.

"We can't eat that!" he objected.

"Of course you can," the boat said soothingly. "An adult Drome consumes five point three pounds of geezel a day, and cries for more."

The tray slid toward them. They backed away from it.

"Now listen," Arnold told the boat. "We are *not* Dromes. We're humans, an entirely different species. The war you think you're fighting ended five hundred years ago. We can't eat geezel. Our food is on that island."

"Try to grasp the situation. Your delusion is a common one among fighting men. It is an escape fantasy, a retreat from an intolerable situation. Gentlemen, I beg you, face reality!"

"You face reality!" Gregor screamed. "Or I'll have you dismantled bolt by bolt."

"Threats do not disturb me," the lifeboat esped serenely. "I know what you've been through. Possibly you have suffered some brain damage from your exposure to poisonous water."

"Poison?" Gregor gulped.

"By Drome standards," Arnold reminded him.

"If absolutely necessary," the lifeboat continued, "I am also equipped to perform physical brain therapy. It is a drastic measure, but there can be no coddling in time of war." A panel slid open, and the partners glimpsed shining surgical edges.

"We're feeling better already," Gregor said hastily. "Fine looking batch of geezel, eh, Arnold?"

"Delicious," Arnold said, wincing.

"I won a nationwide contest in geezel preparation," the lifeboat esped, with pardonable pride. "Nothing is too good for our boys in uniform. Do try a little."

Gregor lifted a handful, smacked his lips, and set it down on the floor. "Wonderful," he said, hoping that the boat's internal scanners weren't as efficient as the external ones seemed to be.

Apparently they were not. "Good," the lifeboat said. "I am moving toward the island now. And, I promise you, in a little while you will be more comfortable."

"Why?" Arnold asked.

"The temperature here is unbearably hot. It's amazing that you haven't gone into coma. Any other Drome would have. Try to bear it a little longer. Soon, I'll have it down to the Drome norm of twenty degrees below zero. And now, to assist your morale, I will play our national Anthem."

A hideous rhythmic screeching filled the air. Waves slapped against the sides of the hurrying lifeboat. In a few moments, the air was perceptibly cooler.

Gregor closed his eyes wearily, trying to ignore the chill that was spreading through his limbs. He was becoming sleepy. Just his luck, he thought, to be frozen to death inside an insane lifeboat. It was what came of buying paternalistic gadgets, high-strung, humanistic calculators, over-sensitive, emotional machines.

Dreamily he wondered where it was all leading to. He pictured a gigantic machine hospital. Two robot doctors were wheeling a lawnmower down a long white corridor. The Chief Robot Doctor was saying, "What's wrong with this lad?" And the assistant answered, "Completely out of his mind. Thinks he's a helicopter." "Aha!" the Chief said knowingly. "Flying fantasies! Pity. Nice looking chap." The assistant nodded. "Overwork did it. Broke his heart on crabgrass." The lawnmower stirred. "Now I'm an eggbeater!" he giggled.

"Wake up," Arnold said, shaking Gregor, his teeth chattering. "We have to do something."

"Ask him to turn on the heat," Gregor said groggily.

"Not a chance. Dromes live at twenty below. We are Dromes. Twenty below for us, and no back talk."

Frost was piled deep on the coolant tubes that traversed the boat. The walls had begun to turn white, and the portholes were frosted over.

"I've got an idea," Arnold said cautiously. He glanced at the control board, then whispered quickly in Gregor's ear.

"We'll try it," Gregor said. They stood up. Gregor picked up the canteen and walked stiffly to the far side of the cabin.

"What are you doing?" the lifeboat asked sharply.

"Going to get a little exercise," Gregor said. "Drome soldiers must stay fit, you know."

"That's true," the lifeboat said dubiously.

Gregor threw the canteen to Arnold.

Arnold chuckled synthetically and threw the canteen back to Gregor.

"Be careful with that receptacle," the lifeboat warned. "It is filled with a deadly poison."

"We'll be careful," Gregor said. "We're taking it back to headquarters." He threw the canteen to Arnold.

"Headquarters may spray it on the H'gen," Arnold said, throwing the canteen back.

"Really?" the lifeboat asked. "That's interesting. A new application of—"

Suddenly Gregor swung the canteen against the coolant tube. The tube broke and liquid poured over the floor.

"Bad shot, old man," Arnold said.

"How careless of me," Gregor cried.

"I should have taken precautions against internal accidents," the lifeboat esped gloomily. "It won't happen again. But the situation is very serious. I cannot repair the tube myself. I am unable to properly cool the boat."

"If you just drop us on the island—" Arnold began.

"Impossible!" the lifeboat said. "My first duty is to preserve your lives, and you could not live long in the climate of this planet. But I am going to take the necessary measures to ensure your safety."

"What are you going to do?" Gregor asked, with a sinking feeling in the pit of his stomach.

"There is no time to waste. I will scan the island once more. If our Drome forces are not present, we will go to the one place on this planet that can sustain Drome life."

"What place?"

"The southern polar cap," the lifeboat said. "The climate there is almost ideal—thirty below zero, I estimate."

The engines roared. Apologetically the boat added. "And, of course, I must guard against any further internal accidents."

As the lifeboat charged forward they could hear the click of the locks, sealing their cabin.

"Think!" Arnold said.

"I am thinking," Gregor answered. "But nothing's coming out."

"We must get off when he reaches the island. It'll be our last chance."

"You don't think we could jump overboard?" Gregor asked.

"Never. He's watching now. If you hadn't smashed the coolant tube, we'd still have a chance."

"I know," Gregor said bitterly. "You and your ideas."

"My ideas! I distinctly remember you suggesting it. You said—"

"It doesn't matter whose idea it was." Gregor thought deeply. "Look, we know his internal scanning isn't very good. When we reach the island, maybe we could cut his power cable."

"You wouldn't get within five feet of it," Arnold said, remembering the shock he had received from the instrument panel.

"Hmm." Gregor locked both hands around his head. An idea was beginning to form in the back of his mind. It was pretty tenuous, but under the circumstances...

"I am now scanning the island," the lifeboat announced.

Looking out the forward porthole, Gregor and Arnold could see the island, no more than a hundred yards away. The first flush of dawn was in the sky, and outlined against it was the scarred, beloved snout of their spaceship.

"Place looks fine to me," Arnold said.

"It sure does," Gregor agreed. "I'll bet our forces are dug in underground."

"They are not," the lifeboat said. "I scanned to a depth of a hundred feet."

"Well," Arnold said, "under the circumstances, I think we should examine a little more closely. I'd better go ashore and look around."

"It is deserted," the lifeboat said. "Believe me, my senses are infinitely more acute than yours. I cannot let you endanger your lives by going ashore. Drome needs her soldiers—especially sturdy, heat-resistant types like you."

"We like this climate," Arnold said.

"Spoken like a patriot!" the lifeboat said heartily. "I know how you must be suffering. But now I am going to the south pole, to give you veterans the rest you deserve."

Gregor decided it was time for his plan, no matter how vague it was. "That won't be necessary," he said.

"What?"

"We are operating under special orders," Gregor said. "We weren't supposed to disclose them to any vessel below the rank of super-dreadnaught. But under the circumstances—"

"Yes, under the circumstances," Arnold chimed in eagerly, "we will tell you."

"We are a suicide squad," Gregor said.

"Especially trained for hot climate work."

"Our orders," Gregor said, "are to land and secure that island for the Drome forces."

"I didn't know that," the boat said.

"You weren't supposed to," Arnold told it. "After all, you're only a lifeboat."

"Land us at once," Gregor said. "There's no time to lose."

"You should have told me sooner," the boat said. "I couldn't guess, you know." It began to move toward the island.

Gregor could hardly breathe. It didn't seem possible that the simple trick would work. But then, why not? The lifeboat was built to accept the word of its operators as the truth. As long as the 'truth' was consistent with the boat's operational premises, it would be carried out.

The beach was only fifty yards away now, gleaming white in the cold light of dawn.

Then the boat reversed its engines and stopped. "No," it said.

"No what?"

"I cannot do it."

"What do you mean?" Arnold shouted. "This is war! Orders—"

"I know," the lifeboat said sadly. "I am sorry. A different type of vessel should have been chosen for this mission. Any other type. But not a *life*boat."

"You must," Gregor begged. "Think of our country, think of the barbaric H'gen—"

"It is physically impossible for me to carry out your orders," the lifeboat told them. "My prime directive is to protect my occupants from harm. That order is stamped on my every tape, giving priority over all others. I cannot let you go to your certain death."

The boat began to move away from the island. "You'll be court-martialed for this!" Arnold screamed hysterically. "They'll decommission you."

"I must operate within my limitations," the boat said sadly. "If we find the fleet, I will transfer you to a killerboat. But in the meantime, I must take you to the safety of the south pole."

The lifeboat picked up speed, and the island receded behind them. Arnold rushed at the controls and was thrown flat. Gregor picked up the canteen and poised it, to hurl ineffectually at the sealed hatch. He stopped himself in mid-swing, struck by a sudden wild thought.

"Please don't attempt any more destruction," the boat pleaded. "I know how you feel, but—"

It was damned risky, Gregor thought, but the south pole was certain death anyhow.

He uncapped the canteen. "Since we cannot accomplish our mission," he said, "we can never again face our comrades. Suicide is the only alternative." He took a gulp of water and handed the canteen to Arnold.

"No! Don't!" the lifeboat shrieked. "That's *water!* It's a deadly poison—"

An electrical bolt leaped from the instrument panel, knocking the canteen from Arnold's hand.

Arnold grabbed the canteen. Before the boat could knock it again from his hand, he had taken a drink.

"We die for glorious Drome!" Gregor dropped to the floor. He motioned Arnold to lie still.

"There is no known antidote," the boat moaned. "If only I could contact a hospital ship…" Its engines idled indecisively. "Speak to me," the boat pleaded. "Are you still alive?"

Gregor and Arnold lay perfectly still, not breathing.

"Answer me!" the lifeboat begged. "Perhaps if you ate some geezel…" It thrust out two trays. The partners didn't stir.

"Dead," the lifeboat said. "Dead. I will read the burial service."

There was a pause. Then the lifeboat intoned, "Great Spirit of the Universe, take into your custody the souls of these, your servants. Although they died by their own hand, still it was in the service of their country, fighting for home and hearth. Judge them not harshly for their impious deed. Rather blame the spirit of war that inflames and destroys all Drome."

The hatch swung open. Gregor could feel a rush of cool morning air.

"And now, by the authority vested in me by the Drome Fleet, and with all reverence, I commend their bodies to the deep."

Gregor felt himself being lifted through the hatch to the deck. Then he was in the air, falling, and in another moment he was in the water, with Arnold beside him.

"Float quietly," he whispered.

The island was nearby. But the lifeboat was still hovering close to them, nervously roaring its engines.

"What do you think it's up to now?" Arnold whispered.

"I don't know," Gregor said, hoping that the Drome peoples didn't believe in converting their bodies to ashes.

The lifeboat came closer. Its bow was only a few feet away. They tensed. And then they heard it. The roaring screech of the Drome National Anthem.

In a moment it was finished. The lifeboat murmured, "Rest in peace," turned, and roared away.

As they swam slowly to the island, Gregor saw that the lifeboat was heading south, due south, to the pole, to wait for the Drome fleet.

The Necessary Thing

Richard Gregor was seated at his desk in the dusty offices of the AAA Ace Interplanetary Decontamination Service, staring wearily at a list. The list included some 2,305 separate items. Gregor was trying to remember what, if anything, he had left out.

Antiradiation salve? Vacuum flares? Water-purification kit? Yes, they were all there.

He yawned and glanced at his watch. Arnold, his partner, should have been back by now. Arnold had gone to order the 2,305 items and see them stowed safely aboard the spaceship. In a few hours, AAA Ace was scheduled to blast off on another job.

But had he listed everything important? A spaceship is an island unto itself, self-sufficient, self-sustaining. If you run out of beans on Dementia II, there is no store where you could buy more. No Coast Guard hurries out to replace the burned-out lining on your main drive. You have to have another lining on board, and the tools to replace it with, and the manuals telling you how. Space is just too big to permit much in the way of rescue operations.

Oxygen extractor? Extra cigarettes? It was like attaching jets to a department store, Gregor thought.

He pushed the list aside, found a pack of tattered cards, and laid out a hopeless solitaire of his own devising.

Minutes later, Arnold stepped jauntily in.

Gregor looked at his partner with suspicion. When the little chemist walked with that peculiar bouncing step, his round face beaming happily, it usually meant trouble for AAA Ace.

"Did you get the stuff?" Gregor asked.

"I did better than that," Arnold said proudly.

"We're supposed to blast off—"

"And blast we will," Arnold said. He sat down on the edge of his desk. "I have just saved us a considerable sum of money."

"Oh, no," Gregor sighed. "What have you done?"

"Consider," Arnold said impressively, "just consider the sheer waste in equipping the average expedition. We pack 2,305 items, just on the off chance we may need one. Our payload is diminished, our living space is cramped, and the stuff never gets used."

"Except for once or twice," Gregor said, "when it saves our lives."

"I took that into account," Arnold said. "I gave the whole problem careful study. And I was able to cut down the list considerably. Through a bit of luck, I found the one thing an expedition really needs. The necessary thing."

Gregor arose and towered over his partner. Visions of mayhem danced through his brain, but he controlled himself with an effort. "Arnold," he said, "I don't know what you've done. But you'd better get those 2,305 items on board and get them fast."

"Can't do it," Arnold said, with a nervous little laugh. "The money's gone. This thing will pay for itself, though."

"What thing?"

"The one really necessary thing. Come out to the ship and I'll show you."

Gregor couldn't get another word out of him. Arnold smiled mysteriously to himself on the long drive to Kennedy Spaceport. Their ship was already in a blast pit, scheduled for takeoff in a few hours.

Arnold swung the port open with a flourish. "There!" he cried. "Behold the answer to an expedition's prayers."

Gregor stepped inside. He saw a large and fantastic looking machine with dials, lights, and indicators scattered haphazardly over it.

"What is it?" Gregor asked.

"Isn't it a beauty?" Arnold patted the machine affectionately. "Joe the Interstellar Junkman happened to have it tucked away. I conned it out of him for a song."

That settled it, as far as Gregor was concerned. He had dealt with Joe the Interstellar Junkman before and had always come out on the disastrously short end of the deal. Joe's gadgets worked; but when, and how often, and with what kind of an attitude was something else again.

Gregor said sternly, "No gadget of Joe's is going into space with me again. Maybe we can sell it for scrap metal." He began to hunt around for a wrecking bar.

"Wait," Arnold begged. "Let me show you. Consider. We are in deep space. The main drive falters and fails. Upon examination, we find that a durraloy nut has worked its way off the number three pinion. We can't find the nut. What do we do?"

"We take a new nut from the two thousand three hundred and five items we've packed for emergencies just like this," Gregor said.

"Ah! But you didn't include any quarter-inch durraloy nuts!" Arnold said triumphantly. "I checked the list. What then?"

"I don't know," Gregor said. "You tell me."

Arnold stepped up to the machine and punched a button. In a loud, clear voice he said, "Durraloy nut, quarter-inch diameter."

The machine murmured and hummed. Lights flashed. A panel slid back, revealing a bright, freshly machined durraloy nut.

"*That's* what we do," Arnold said.

"Hmm," Gregor said, not particularly impressed. "So it manufactures nuts. What else does it do?"

Arnold pressed the button again. "A pound of fresh shrimp."

When he slid back the panel, the shrimp were there.

"I should have told it to peel them," Arnold said. "Oh well." He pressed the button. "A graphite rod, four feet long with a diameter of two inches."

The panel opened wider this time to let the rod come through.

"What else can it do?" Gregor asked.

"What else would you like?" Arnold said. "A small tiger cub? A model- A downdraft carburetor? A 25-watt light bulb or a stick of chewing gum?"

"Do you mean it'll turn out *anything?*" Gregor asked.

"Anything at all. It's a Configurator. Try it yourself."

Gregor tried and produced, in rapid succession, a pint of fresh water, a wristwatch, and a jar of cocktail sauce.

"Hmm," he said.

"See what I mean? Isn't this better than packing 2,305 items? Isn't it simpler and more logical to produce what you need when you need it?"

"It *seems* good," Gregor said. "But…"

"But what?"

Gregor shook his head. What indeed? He had no idea. It had simply been his experience that gadgets are never so useful, reliable, or consistent as they seem at first glance.

He thought deeply, then punched the button. "A transistor, series GE 1324E."

The machine hummed and the panel opened. There was the tiny transistor.

"Seems pretty good," Gregor admitted. "What are you doing?"

"Peeling the shrimp," Arnold said.

After enjoying a tasty shrimp cocktail, the partners received their clearance from the tower. In an hour, the ship was in space.

They were bound for Dennett IV, an average-sized planet in the Sycophax cluster. Dennett was a hot, steamy, fertile world, suffering from only one major difficulty: too much rain. It rained on Dennett a good nine tenths of the time, and when it wasn't raining, it was threatening rain.

This made it an easy job. The principles of climate control were well known, for many worlds suffered from similar difficulties. It would take only a few days for AAA Ace to interrupt and alter the pattern.

After an uneventful trip, Dennett came into view. Arnold relieved the automatic pilot and brought the ship down through thick cloud banks. They dropped through miles of pale gossamer mist. At last, mountaintops began to appear, and they found a level, barren gray plain.

"Odd color for a landscape," Gregor said.

Arnold nodded. With practiced ease he spiraled, leveled out, came down neatly above the plain, and, with his forces balanced, cut the drive.

"Wonder why there's no vegetation," Gregor mused.

In a moment they found out. The ship hung for a second, then dropped through the plain and fell another eight feet to the ground.

The plain, it seemed, was fog of a density only Dennett could produce.

Hastily they unbuckled themselves and tested various teeth, bones, and ligatures. Upon finding that nothing personal was broken, they checked their ship.

The impact had done the poor old spacecraft no good. The radio and automatic pilot were a complete loss. Ten stern plates had buckled, and, worst of all, some delicate components in the turn-drive control were shattered.

"We were lucky at that," Arnold said.

"Yes," Gregor said, peering through the blanketing fog. "But next time we use instruments."

"In a way I'm glad it happened," Arnold said. "Now you'll see what a lifesaver the Configurator is. Let's go to work."

They listed all the damaged parts. Arnold stepped up to the Configurator, pressed the button, and said, "A drive plate, five inches square, half inch in diameter, steel alloy 342."

The machine quickly turned it out.

"We need ten of them," Gregor said.

"I know." Again Arnold pushed the button. "Another one."

The machine did nothing.

"Probably have to give the whole command," Arnold said. He punched the button again and said, "Drive plate, five inches square, half inch in diameter, steel alloy 342."

The machine was silent.

"That's odd," Arnold said.

"Isn't it, though," Gregor said, with an odd sinking sensation in the pit of his stomach.

Arnold tried again, with no success. He thought deeply, then punched the button and said, "A plastic teacup."

The machine turned out a teacup of bright blue plastic.

"Another one," Arnold said. When the Configurator did nothing, Arnold asked for a wax crayon. The machine gave it to him. "Another wax crayon," Arnold said. The machine did nothing.

"That's interesting," Arnold said. "I suppose I should have thought of the possibility."

"What possibility?"

"Apparently the Configurator will turn out anything," Arnold said. "But only once." He experimented again, making the machine produce a number two pencil. It would do it once, but only once.

"That's fine," Gregor said. "We need nine more plates. And the turn-drive needs four identical parts. What are we going to do?"

"We'll think of something," Arnold said cheerfully.

"I hope so," Gregor said.

Outside the rain began. The partners settled down to think.

"Only one explanation," Arnold said, several hours later. "Pleasure principle."

"Huh?" Gregor said. He had been dozing, lulled by the soft patter of rain against the dented side of the spaceship.

"This machine must have some form of intelligence," Arnold said. "After all, it receives stimuli, translates it into action commands, and fabricates a product from a mental blueprint."

"Sure it does," Gregor said. "But only once."

"Yes. But *why* only once? That's the key to our difficulties. I think it must be a self-imposed limit, linked to a pleasure drive. Or perhaps a quasi-pleasure drive."

"I don't follow you," Gregor said.

"Look. The builders wouldn't have limited their machine in this way. The only possible explanation is this: When a machine is constructed on this order of complexity, it takes on quasi-human characteristics. It derives a quasi-humano-form pleasure from producing a new thing. But a thing is only new once. After that, the Configurator wants to produce something else."

Gregor slumped back into his apathetic half-slumber. Arnold went on talking. "Fulfillment of potential, that's what a machine wants. The Configurator's ultimate desire is to create everything possible. From its point of view, repetition would be a waste of time."

"That's the most suspect line of reasoning I've ever heard," Gregor said. "But assuming you're right, what can we do about it?"

"I don't know," Arnold said.

"That's what I thought."

For dinner that evening, the Configurator turned out a very credit-able roast beef. They finished with apple pie *à la machine,* with sharp cheese on the side. Their morale was improved considerably.

"Substitutions," Gregor said later, smoking a cigar *ex machina.* "That's what we'll have to try. Alloy 342 isn't the only thing we can use for the plates. There are plenty of materials that'll last until we get back to Earth."

The Configurator couldn't be tricked into producing a plate of iron or any of the ferrous alloys. They asked for and got a plate of bronze. But then the machine wouldn't give them copper or tin. Aluminum was acceptable, as was cadmium, platinum, gold and silver. A tungsten plate was an interesting rarity; Arnold wished he knew how the machine had cast it. Gregor vetoed plutonium, and they were running short of suitable metals. Arnold hit upon an extra tough ceramic as a good substitute. And the final plate was pure zinc.

The noble metals would tend to melt in the heat of space, of course; but with proper refrigeration, they might last as far as Earth. All in all it was a good night's work, and the partners toasted each other in an excellent, though somewhat oily, dry sherry.

The next day they bolted in the plates and surveyed their handiwork. The rear of the ship looked like a patchwork quilt.

"I think it's quite pretty," Arnold said.

"I just hope it'll hold up," Gregor said. "Now for the turn-drive components."

But that was a problem of a different nature. Four identical parts were missing: delicate, precisely engineered affairs of glass and wire. No substitutions were possible.

The machine turned out the first without hesitation. But that was all. By noon, both men were disgusted.

"Any ideas?" Gregor asked.

"Not at the moment. Let's take a break for lunch."

They decided that lobster salad would be pleasant, and ordered it on the machine. The Configurator hummed for a moment, but produced nothing.

"What's wrong now?" Gregor asked.

"I was afraid of this," Arnold said.

"Afraid of what? We haven't asked for lobster before."

"No," Arnold said, "but we did ask for shrimp. Both are shellfish. I'm afraid the Configurator is beginning to make decisions according to classes."

"You'd better break open a few cans then," Gregor said.

Arnold smiled feebly. "Well," he said, "after I bought the Configurator, I didn't think we'd have to bother—I mean—"

"No cans?"

"No."

They returned to the machine and asked for salmon, trout, and tuna, with no results. Then they tried roast pork, leg of lamb, and veal. Nothing.

"It seems to consider our roast beef last night as representative of all mammals," Arnold said. "This is interesting. We might be able to evolve a new theory of classes—"

"While starving to death," Gregor said. He tried roast chicken, and this time the Configurator came through without hesitation.

"Eureka!" Arnold cried.

"Damn!" Gregor said. "I should have asked for turkey."

The rain continued to fall on Dennett, and mist swirled around the spaceship's gaudy patchwork stem. Arnold began a long series of slide-rule calculations. Gregor finished off the dry sherry, tried unsuccessfully to order a case of Scotch, and started playing solitaire.

They ate a frugal supper on the remains of the chicken, and Arnold completed his calculations.

"It might work," he said.

"What might work?"

"The pleasure principle." He stood up and began to pace the cabin. "This machine has quasi-human characteristics. Certainly it possesses learning potential. I think we can teach it to derive pleasure from producing the same thing many times. Namely, the turn-drive components."

"It's worth a try," Gregor said.

Late into the night they talked to the machine. Arnold murmured persuasively about the joys of repetition. Gregor spoke highly of the esthetic values inherent in producing an artistic object like a turn-drive component, not once, but many times, each item an exact and perfect twin. Arnold murmured lyrically to the machine about the thrill, the supreme thrill of fabricating endlessly parts without end. Again and again, the same parts, produced of the same material, turned out at the same rate. Ecstasy! And, Gregor put in, so beautiful a concept philosophically, and so completely suited to the peculiar makeup and capabilities of a machine. As a conceptual system, he continued, Repetition (as opposed to mere Creation) closely approached the status of entropy, which, mechanically, was perfection.

By clicks and flashes, the Configurator showed that it was listening. And when Dennett's damp and pallid dawn was in the sky, Arnold pushed the button and gave the command for a turn-drive component.

The machine hesitated. Lights flickered uncertainly, indicators turned in a momentary hunting process. Uncertainty was manifest in every tube.

There was a click. The panel slid back. And there was another turn-drive component!

"Success!" Gregor shouted, and slapped Arnold on the back. Quickly he gave the order again. But this time the Configurator emitted a loud and emphatic buzz.

And produced nothing.

Gregor tried again. But there was no more hesitation from the machine, and no more components.

"What's wrong now?" Gregor asked.

"It's obvious," Arnold said sadly. "It decided to give repetition a try, just in case it had missed something. But after trying it, the Configurator decided it didn't like it."

"A machine that doesn't like repetition!" Gregor groaned. "It's inhuman!"

"On the contrary," Arnold said unhappily. "It's all too human."

It was suppertime, and the partners had to hunt for foods the Configurator would produce. A vegetable plate was easy enough, but not too filling. The machine allowed them one loaf of bread, but no cake. Milk products were out, as they had had cheese the other day. Finally, after an hour of trial and error, the Configurator gave them a pound of whale steak, apparently uncertain of its category.

Gregor went back to work, crooning the joys of repetition into the machine's receptors. A steady hum and occasional flashes of light showed that the Configurator was still listening.

Arnold took out several reference books and embarked on a project of his own. Several hours later he looked up with a shout of triumph.

"I knew I'd find it!"

Gregor looked up quickly. "What?"

"A substitute turn-drive control!" He pushed the book under Gregor's nose. "Look there. A scientist on Vednier II perfected this 50 years ago. It's clumsy, by modern standards, but it'll work. And it'll fit into our ship."

"But what's it made of?" Gregor asked.

"That's the best part of it. We can't miss! It's made of rubber!"

Quickly he punched the Configurator's button and read the description of the turn-drive control.

Nothing happened.

"You have to turn out the Vednier control!" Arnold shouted at the machine. "If you don't, you're violating your own principles!" He punched the button again and, enunciating with painful clarity, read the description again.

Nothing happened.

Gregor had a sudden terrible suspicion. He walked to the back of the Configurator, found what he had feared, and pointed it out to Arnold.

There was a manufacturer's plate bolted there. It read: *Class 3 Configurator. Made by Vednier Laboratories, Vednier II.*

"So they've already used it for that," Arnold said.

Gregor said nothing. There just didn't seem to be anything to say.

Mildew was beginning to form inside the spaceship, and rust had appeared on the steel plate in the stern. The machine still listened to the partners' hymn to repetition, but did nothing about it.

The problem of another meal came up. Fruit was out because of the apple pie, as were all meats, fish, milk products, and cereals. At last they dined sparsely on frog's legs, baked grasshoppers (from an old Chinese recipe), and filet of iguana. But now with lizards, insects, and amphibians used up, they knew that their machine-made meals were at an end.

Both men were showing signs of strain. Gregor's long face was bonier than ever. Arnold found traces of mildew in his hair. Outside, the rain poured ceaselessly, dripped past the portholes and into the moist earth. The spaceship began to settle, burying itself under its own weight.

For the next meal they could think of nothing.

Then Gregor conceived a final idea.

He thought it over carefully. Another failure would shatter their badly bent morale. But, slim though the chance of success might be, he had to try it.

Slowly he approached the Configurator. Arnold looked up, frightened by the wild light gleaming in his eyes.

"Gregor! What are you going to do?"

"I'm going to give this thing one last command," Gregor said hoarsely. With a trembling hand he punched the button and whispered his request.

For a moment, nothing happened. Then Arnold shouted, "Get back!"

The machine was quivering and shaking, dials twitching, lights flickering. Heat and energy indicators flashed through red into purple.

"What did you tell it to produce?" Arnold asked.

"I didn't tell it to produce anything," Gregor said. "I told it to *re*produce!"

The Configurator gave a convulsive shudder and emitted a cloud of black smoke. The partners coughed and gasped for air.

When the smoke cleared away the Configurator was still there, its paint chipped, and several indicators bent out of shape. And beside it, glistening with black machine oil, was a duplicate Configurator.

"You've done it!" Arnold cried. "You've saved us!"

"I've done more than that," Gregor said, with weary satisfaction. "I've made our fortunes." He turned to the duplicate Configurator, pressed its button and cried, "Reproduce yourself!"

Within a week, Arnold, Gregor and three Configurators were back in Kennedy Spaceport, their work on Dennett completed. As soon as they landed, Arnold left the ship and caught a taxi. He went first to Canal Street, then to midtown New York. His business didn't take long, and within a few hours he was back at the ship.

"Yes, it's all right," he called to Gregor. "I contacted several different jewelers. We can dispose of about 20 big stones without depressing the market. After that, I think we should have the Configurators concentrate on platinum for a while, and then—what's wrong?"

Gregor looked at him sourly. "Notice anything different?"

"Huh?" Arnold stared around the cabin, at Gregor, and at the Configurators. Then he noticed it.

There were four Configurators in the cabin, where there had been only three.

"You had them reproduce another?" Arnold said. "Nothing wrong with that. Just tell them to turn out a diamond apiece—"

"You still don't get it," Gregor said sadly. "Watch."

He pressed the button on the nearest Configurator and said, "A diamond."

The Configurator began to quiver.

"You and your damned pleasure principle," Gregor said. "Repetition! These damned machines are sex mad."

The machine shook all over, and produced—

Another Configurator.

CITIZEN IN SPACE

I'm really trouble now, more trouble than I ever thought possible. It's a little difficult to explain how I got into this mess, so maybe I'd better start at the beginning.

Ever since I graduated from trade school in 1991 I'd had a good job as sphinx valve assembler on the Starling Spaceship production line. I really loved those big ships, roaring to Cygnus and Alpha Centaurus and all the other places in the news. I was a young man with a future, I had friends, I even knew some girls.

But it was no good.

The job was fine, but I couldn't do my best work with those hidden cameras focused on my hands. Not that I minded the cameras themselves; it was the whirring noise they made. I couldn't concentrate.

I complained to Internal Security. I told them, look, why can't I have new, quiet cameras, like everybody else? But they were too busy to do anything about it.

Then lots of little things started to bother me. Like the tape recorder in my TV set. The F.B.I. never adjusted it right, and it hummed all night long. I complained a hundred times. I told them, look, nobody else's recorder hums that way. Why mine? But they always gave me that speech about winning the cold war, and how they couldn't please everybody.

Things like that make a person feel inferior. I suspected my government wasn't interested in me.

Take my Spy, for example. I was an 18-D Suspect—the same classification as the Vice-President—and this entitled me to part-time surveillance. But my particular Spy must have thought he was a movie actor, because he always wore a stained trench coat and a slouch hat, jammed over his eyes. He was a thin, nervous type, and he followed practically on my heels for fear of losing me.

Well, he was trying his best. Spying is a competitive business, and I couldn't help but feel sorry, he was so bad at it. But it was embarrassing, just to be associated with him. My friends laughed themselves

241

sick whenever I showed up with him breathing down the back of my neck. "Bill," they said, "is *that* the best you can do?" And my girl friends thought he was creepy.

Naturally, I went to the Senate Investigations Committee, and said, look, why can't you give me a *trained* Spy, like my friends have?

They said they'd see, but I knew I wasn't important enough to swing it.

All these little things put me on edge, and any psychologist will tell you it doesn't take something big to drive you bats. I was sick of being ignored, sick of being neglected.

That's when I started to think about Deep Space. There were billions of square miles of nothingness out there, dotted with too many stars to count. There were enough Earth-type planets for every man, woman and child. There had to be a spot for me.

I bought a Universe Light List, and a tattered Galactic Pilot. I read through the Gravity Tide Book, and the Interstellar Pilot Charts. Finally I figured I knew as much as I'd ever know.

All my savings went into an old Chrysler Star Clipper. This antique leaked oxygen along its seams. It had a touchy atomic pile, and spacewarp drives that might throw you practically anywhere. It was dangerous, but the only life I was risking was my own. At least, that's what I thought.

So I got my passport, blue clearance, red clearance, numbers certificate, space-sickness shots and deratification papers. At the job I collected my last day's pay and waved to the cameras. In the apartment, I packed my clothes and said good-bye to the recorders. On the street, I shook hands with my poor Spy and wished him luck.

I had burned my bridges behind me.

All that was left was final clearance, so I hurried down to the Final Clearance Office. A clerk with white hands and a sun lamp tan looked at me dubiously.

"Where did you wish to go?" he asked me.

"Space," I said.

"Of course. But where in space?"

"I don't know yet," I said. "Just space. Deep Space. Free Space."

The clerk sighed wearily. "You'll have to be more explicit than that, if you want a clearance. Are you going to settle on a planet in American Space? Or did you wish to emigrate to British Space? Or Dutch Space? Or French Space?"

"I didn't know *space* could be owned," I said.

"Then you don't keep up with the times," he told me, with a superior smirk. "The United States has claimed all space between coordinates 2XA and D2B, except for a small and relatively unimportant segment which is claimed by Mexico. The Soviet Union has coordinates 3DB to LO2—a very bleak region, I can assure you. And then there is the Belgian Grant, the Chinese Grant, the Ceylonese Grant, the Nigerian Grant—"

I stopped him. "Where is Free Space?" I asked.

"There is none."

"None at all? How far do the boundary lines extend?"

"To infinity," he told me proudly.

For a moment it fetched me up short. Somehow I had never considered the possibility of every bit of infinite space being owned. But it was natural enough. After all, *somebody* had to own it.

"I want to go into American Space," I said. It didn't seem to matter at the time, although it turned out otherwise.

The clerk nodded sullenly. He checked my records back to the age of five—there was no sense in going back any further—and gave me the Final Clearance.

The spaceport had my ship all serviced, and I managed to get away without blowing a tube. It wasn't until Earth dwindled to a pinpoint and disappeared behind me that I realized that I was alone.

Fifty hours out I was making a routine inspection of my stores, when I observed that one of my vegetable sacks had a shape unlike the other sacks. Upon opening it I found a girl, where a hundred pounds of potatoes should have been.

A stowaway. I stared at her, open-mouthed.

"Well," she said, "are you going to help me out? Or would you prefer to close the sack and forget the whole thing?"

I helped her out. She said, "Your potatoes are lumpy."

I could have said the same of her, with considerable approval. She was a slender girl, for the most part, with hair the reddish blond color of a flaring jet, a pert, dirt-smudged face and brooding blue eyes. On Earth, I would gladly have walked ten miles to meet her. In space, I wasn't so sure.

"Could you give me something to eat?" she asked. "All I've had since we left is raw carrots."

I fixed her a sandwich. While she ate, I asked, "What are you doing here?"

"You wouldn't understand," she said, between mouthfuls.

"Sure I would."

She walked to a porthole and looked out at the spectacle of stars—American stars, most of them—burning in the void of American space.

"I wanted to be free," she said.

"Huh?"

She sank wearily on my cot. "I suppose you'd call me a romantic," she said quietly. "I'm the sort of fool who recites poetry to herself in the black night, and cries in front of some absurd little statuette. Yellow autumn leaves make me tremble, and dew on a green lawn seems like the tears of all Earth. My psychiatrist tells me I'm a misfit."

She closed her eyes with a weariness I could appreciate. Standing in a potato sack for fifty hours can be pretty exhausting.

"Earth was getting me down," she said. "I couldn't stand it—the regimentation, the discipline, the privation, the cold war, the hot war, everything. I wanted to laugh in free air, run through green fields, walk unmolested through gloomy forests, sing—"

"But why did you pick on me?"

"You were bound for freedom," she said. "I'll leave, if you insist."

That was a pretty silly idea, out in the depths of space. And I couldn't afford the fuel to turn back.

"You can stay," I said.

"Thank you," she said very softly. "You *do* understand."

"Sure, sure," I said. "But we'll have to get a few things straight. First of all—" But she had fallen asleep on my cot, with a trusting smile on her lips.

Immediately I searched her handbag. I found five lipsticks, a compact, a phial of Venus V perfume, a paper-bound book of poetry, and a badge that read: *Special Investigator, FBI.*

I had suspected it, of course. Girls don't talk that way, but Spies always do.

It was nice to know my government was still looking out for me. It made space seem less lonely.

The ship moved into the depths of American Space. By working fifteen hours out of twenty-four, I managed to keep my spacewarp drive in one piece, my atomic piles reasonably cool, and my hull seams tight. Mavis O'Day (as my Spy was named) made all meals, took care of the light housekeeping, and hid a number of small cameras around the ship. They buzzed abominably, but I pretended not to notice.

Under the circumstances, however, my relations with Miss O'Day were quite proper.

The trip was proceeding normally—even happily—until something happened.

I was dozing at the controls. Suddenly an intense light flared on my starboard bow. I leaped backward, knocking over Mavis as she was inserting a new reel of film into her number three camera.

"Excuse me," I said.

"Oh, trample me anytime," she said.

I helped her to her feet. Her supple nearness was dangerously pleasant, and the tantalizing scent of Venus V tickled my nostrils.

"You can let me go now," she said.

"I know," I said, and continued to hold her. My mind inflamed by her nearness, I heard myself saying, "Mavis—I haven't known you very long, but—"

"Yes, Bill?" she asked.

In the madness of the moment I had forgotten our relationship of Suspect and Spy. I don't know what I might have said. But just then a second light blazed outside the ship.

I released Mavis and hurried to the controls. With difficulty I throttled the old Star Clipper to an idle, and looked around.

Outside, in the vast vacuum of space, was a single fragment of rock. Perched upon it was a child in a spacesuit, holding a box of flares in one hand and a tiny spacesuited dog in the other.

Quickly we got him inside and unbuttoned his spacesuit.

"My dog—" he said.

"He's all right, son," I told him.

"Terribly sorry to break in on you this way," the lad said.

"Forget it," I said. "What were you doing out there?"

"Sir," he began, in treble tones, "I will have to start at the start. My father was a spaceship test pilot, and he died valiantly, trying to break the light barrier. Mother recently remarried. Her present husband is a large, black-haired man with narrow, shifty eyes and tightly compressed lips. Until recently he was employed as a ribbon clerk in a large department store.

"He resented my presence from the beginning. I suppose I reminded him of my dead father, with my blond curls, large oval eyes and merry, outgoing ways. Our relationship smoldered fitfully. Then an uncle of his died (under suspicious circumstances) and he inherited holdings in British Space.

"Accordingly, we set out in our spaceship. As soon as we reached this deserted area, he said to mother, 'Rachel, he's old enough to fend for himself.' My mother said, 'Dirk, he's so young!' But soft-hearted, laughing mother was no match for the inflexible will of the man I would never call father. He thrust me into my spacesuit, handed me a box of flares, put Flicker into his own little suit, and said, 'A lad can do all right for himself in space these days.' 'Sir,' I said, 'there is no planet within two hundred light years.' 'You'll make out,' he grinned, and thrust me upon this spur of rock."

The boy paused for breath, and his dog Flicker looked up at me with moist oval eyes. I gave the dog a bowl of milk and bread, and watched the lad eat a peanut butter and jelly sandwich. Mavis carried the little chap into the bunk room and tenderly tucked him into bed.

I returned to the controls, started the ship again, and turned on the intercom.

"Wake up, you little idiot!" I heard Mavis say.

"Lemme sleep," the boy answered.

"Wake up! What did Congressional Investigation *mean* by sending you here? Don't they realize this is an FBI case?"

"He's been reclassified as a 10-F Suspect," the boy said. "That calls for full surveillance."

"Yes, but *I'm* here," Mavis cried.

"You didn't do so well on your last case," the boy said. "I'm sorry, ma'am, but Security comes first."

"So they send you," Mavis said, sobbing now. "A twelve-year-old child—"

"I'll be thirteen in seven months."

"A twelve-year-old child! And I've tried so hard! I've studied, read books, taken evening courses, listened to lectures—"

"It's a tough break," the boy said sympathetically. "Personally, I want to be a spaceship test pilot. At my age, this is the only way I can get in flying hours. Do you think he'll let me fly the ship?"

I snapped off the intercom. I should have felt wonderful. Two full-time Spies were watching me. It meant I was really someone, someone to be watched.

But the truth was, my Spies were only a girl and a twelve-year-old boy. They must have been scraping bottom when they sent those two.

My government was still ignoring me, in its own fashion.

We managed well on the rest of the flight. Young Roy, as the lad was called, took over the piloting of the ship, and his dog sat alertly in the co-pilot's seat. Mavis continued to cook and keep house. I spent my time patching seams. We were as happy a group of Spies and Suspect as you could find.

We found an uninhabited Earth-type planet. Mavis liked it because it was small and rather cute, with the green fields and gloomy forests she had read about in her poetry books. Young Roy liked the clear lakes, and the mountains, which were just the right height for a boy to climb.

We landed, and began to settle.

Young Roy found an immediate interest in the animals I animated from the Freezer. He appointed himself guardian of cows and horses, protector of ducks and geese, defender of pigs and chickens. This kept him so busy that his reports to the Senate became fewer and fewer, and finally stopped altogether.

You really couldn't expect any more from a Spy of his age.

And after I had set up the domes and force-seeded a few acres, Mavis and I took long walks in the gloomy forest, and in the bright green and yellow fields that bordered it.

One day we packed a picnic lunch and ate on the edge of a little waterfall. Mavis's unbound hair spread lightly over her shoulders, and there was a distant enchanted look in her blue eyes. All in all, she seemed extremely un-Spylike, and I had to remind myself over and over of our respective roles.

"Bill," she said after a while.

"Yes?" I said.

"Nothing." She tugged at a blade of grass.

I couldn't figure that one out. But her hand strayed somewhere near mine. Our fingertips touched, and clung.

We were silent for a long time. Never had I been so happy.

"Bill?"

"Yes?"

"Bill dear, could you ever—"

What she was going to say, and what I might have answered, I will never know. At that moment our silence was shattered by the roar of jets. Down from the sky dropped a spaceship.

Ed Wallace, the pilot, was a white-haired old man in a slouch hat and a stained trench coat. He was a salesman for Clear-Flo, an outfit that cleansed water on a planetary basis. Since I had no need for his services, he thanked me, and left.

But he didn't get very far. His engines turned over once, and stopped with a frightening finality.

I looked over his drive mechanism, and found that a sphinx valve had blown. It would take me a month to make him a new one with hand tools.

"This is terribly awkward," he murmured. "I suppose I'll have to stay here."

"I suppose so," I said.

He looked at his ship regretfully. "Can't understand how it happened," he said.

"Maybe you weakened the valve when you cut it with a hacksaw," I said, and walked off. I had seen the telltale marks.

Mr. Wallace pretended not to hear me. That evening I over heard his report on the interstellar radio, which functioned perfectly. His home office, interestingly enough, was not Clear-Flo, but Central Intelligence.

Mr. Wallace made a good vegetable farmer, even though he spent most of his time sneaking around with camera and notebook. His presence spurred Young Roy to greater efforts. Mavis and I stopped walking in the gloomy forest, and there didn't seem time to return to the yellow and green fields, to finish some unfinished sentences.

But our little settlement prospered. We had other visitors. A man and his wife from Regional Intelligence dropped by, posing as itinerant fruit pickers. They were followed by two girl photographers, secret representatives of the Executive Information Bureau, and then there was a young newspaper man, who was actually from the Idaho Council of Spatial Morals.

Every single one of them blew a sphinx valve when it came time to leave. I didn't know whether to feel proud or ashamed. A half-dozen agents were watching *me*—but every one of them was a second rater. And invariably, after a few weeks on my planet, they became involved in farmwork and their Spying efforts dwindled to nothing.

I had bitter moments. I pictured myself as a testing ground for novices, something to cut their teeth on. I was the Suspect they gave to Spies who were too old or too young, inefficient, scatterbrained, or just plain incompetent. I saw myself as a sort of half-pay retirement plan Suspect, a substitute for a pension.

But it didn't bother me too much. I did have a position, although it was a little difficult to define. I was happier than I had ever been on Earth, and my Spies were pleasant and cooperative people.

Our little colony was happy and secure.

I thought it could go on forever.

Then, one fateful night, there was unusual activity. Some important message seemed to be coming in, and all radios were on. I had to ask a few Spies to share sets, to keep from burning out my generator.

Finally all radios were turned off, and the Spies held conferences. I heard them whispering into the small hours. The next morning, they were all assembled in the living room, and their faces were long and somber. Mavis stepped forward as spokeswoman.

"Something terrible has happened," she said to me. "But first, we have something to reveal to you. Bill, none of us are what we seemed. We are all Spies for the government."

"Huh?" I said, not wanting to hurt any feelings.

"It's true," she said. "We've been Spying on you, Bill."

"Huh?" I said again. "Even you?"

"Even me," Mavis said unhappily.

"And now it's all over," Young Roy blurted out.

That shook me. *"Why?"* I asked.

They looked at each other. Finally Mr. Wallace, bending the rim of his hat back and forth in his calloused hands, said, "Bill, a resurvey has just shown that this sector of space is not owned by the United States."

"What country does own it?" I asked.

"Be calm," Mavis said. "Try to understand. This entire sector was overlooked in the international survey, and now it can't be claimed by any country. As the first to settle here, this planet, and several million miles of space surrounding it, belong to you, Bill."

I was too stunned to speak.

"Under the circumstances," Mavis continued, "we have no authorization to be here. So we're leaving immediately."

"But you can't!" I cried. "I haven't repaired your sphinx valves!"

"All Spies carry spare sphinx valves and hacksaw blades," she said gently.

Watching them troop out to their ships I pictured the solitude ahead of me. I would have no government to watch over me. No longer would I hear footsteps in the night, turn, and see the dedicated face of a Spy behind me. No longer would the whirr of an old camera soothe me at work, nor the buzz of a defective recorder lull me to sleep.

And yet, I felt even sorrier for them. Those poor, earnest, clumsy, bungling Spies were returning to a fast, efficient, competitive world. Where would they find another Suspect like me, or another place like my planet?

"Goodbye Bill," Mavis said, offering me her hand.

I watched her walk to Mr. Wallace's ship. It was only then that I realized that she was no longer *my* Spy.

"Mavis!" I cried, running after her. She hurried toward the ship. I caught her by the arm. "Wait. There was something I started to say in the ship. I wanted to say it again on the picnic."

She tried to pull away from me. In most unromantic tones I croaked, "Mavis, I love you."

She was in my arms. We kissed, and I told her that her home, was here, on this planet with its gloomy forests and yellow and green fields. Here with me.

She was too happy to speak.

With Mavis staying, Young Roy reconsidered. Mr. Wallace's vegetables were just ripening, and he wanted to tend them. And everyone else had some chore or other that he couldn't drop.

So here I am—ruler, king, dictator, president, whatever I want to call myself. Spies are beginning to pour in now from *every* country—not only America.

To feed all my subjects, I'll soon have to import food. But the other rulers are beginning to refuse me aid. They think I've bribed their Spies to desert.

I haven't, I swear it. They just come.

I can't resign, because I own this place. And I haven't the heart to send them away. I'm at the end of my rope.

With my entire population consisting of former government Spies, you'd think I'd have an easy time forming a government of my own. But no, they're completely uncooperative. I'm the absolute ruler of a planet of farmers, dairymen, shepherds and cattle raisers, so I guess we won't starve after all. But that's not the point. The point is: how in hell am I supposed to rule?

Not a single one of these people will Spy for me.

A Ticket to Tranai

One fine day in June, a tall, thin, intent, soberly dressed young man walked into the offices of the Transstellar Travel Agency. Without a glance, he marched past the gaudy travel poster depicting the Harvest Feast on Mars. The enormous photomural of dancing forests on Triganium didn't catch his eye. He ignored the somewhat suggestive painting of dawn-rites on Opiuchus II, and arrived at the desk of the booking agent.

"I would like to book passage to Tranai," the young man said.

The agent closed his copy of *Necessary Inventions* and frowned. "Tranai? Tranai? Is that one of the moons of Kent IV?"

"It is not," the young man said. "Tranai is a planet, revolving around a sun of the same name. I want to book passage there."

"Never heard of it." The agent pulled down a star catalog, a simplified star chart, and a copy of *Lesser Space Routes.*

"Well, now," he said finally. "You learn something new every day. You want to book passage to Tranai, Mister—"

"Goodman. Marvin Goodman."

"Goodman. Well, it seems that Tranai is about as far from Earth as one can get and still be in the Milky Way. *Nobody* goes there."

"I know. Can you arrange passage for me?" Goodman asked, with a hint of suppressed excitement in his voice.

The agent shook his head. "Not a chance. Even the non-skeds don't go that far."

"How close can you get me?"

The agent gave him a winning smile. "Why bother? I can send you to a world that'll have everything this Tranai place has, with the additional advantages of proximity, bargain rates, decent hotels, tours—"

"I'm going to Tranai," Goodman said grimly.

"But there's no way of getting there," the agent explained patiently. "What is it you expected to find? Perhaps I could help."

"You can help by booking me as far as—"

251

"Is it adventure?" the agent asked, quickly sizing up Goodman's un-athletic build and scholarly stoop. "Let me suggest Africanus II, a dawn-age world filled with savage tribes, sabertooths, man-eating ferns, quick-sand, active volcanoes, pterodactyls, and all the rest. Expeditions leave New York every five days and they combine the utmost in danger with absolute safety. A dinosaur head guaranteed or your money refunded."

"Tranai," Goodman said.

"Hmm." The clerk looked appraisingly at Goodman's set lips and uncompromising eyes. "Perhaps you are tired of the puritanical restrictions of Earth? Then let me suggest a trip to Almagordo III, the Pearl of the Southern Ridge Belt. Our ten day all-expense plan includes a trip through the mysterious Almagordian Casbah, visits to eight nightclubs (first drink on us), a trip to a zintal factory, where you can buy genuine zintal belts, shoes, and pocketbooks at phenomenal savings, and a tour through two distilleries. The girls of Almagordo are beautiful, vivacious, and refreshingly naïve. They consider the Tourist the highest and most desirable type of human being. Also—"

"Tranai," Goodman said. "How close can you get me?"

Sullenly the clerk extracted a strip of tickets. "You can take the *Constellation Queen* as far as Legis II and transfer to the *Galactic Splendor,* which will take you to Oumé. Then you'll have to board a local, which, after stopping at Machang, Inchang, Pankang, Lekung, and Oyster, will leave you at Tung-Bradar IV, if it doesn't break down en route. Then a non-sked will transport you past the Galactic Whirl (if it gets past) to Aloomsridgia, from which the mail ship will take you to Bellismoranti. I believe the mail ship is still functioning. That brings you about half way. After that, you're on your own."

"Fine," Goodman said. "Can you have my forms made out by this afternoon?"

The clerk nodded. "Mr. Goodman," he asked in despair, "just what sort of place is this Tranai supposed to be?"

Goodman smiled a beatific smile. "A utopia," he said.

Marvin Goodman had lived most of his life in Seakirk, New Jersey, a town controlled by one political boss or another for close to fifty years. Most of Seakirk's inhabitants were indifferent to the spectacle of corruption in high places and low, the gambling, the gang wars, the teenage drinking. They were used to the sight of their roads crumbling, their ancient water mains bursting, their power plants breaking down, their decrepit old buildings falling apart, while the bosses built bigger homes, longer swimming pools and warmer stables. People were used to it. But not Goodman.

A natural-born crusader, he wrote exposé articles that were never pub-lished, sent letters to Congress that were never read, stumped for honest

candidates who were never elected, and organized the League for Civic
Improvement, the People Against Gangsterism, the Citizen's Union for
an Honest Police Force, the Association Against Gambling, the Committee for Equal Job Opportunities for Women, and a dozen others.

Nothing came of his efforts. The people were too apathetic to care. The
politicoes simply laughed at him, and Goodman couldn't stand being
laughed at. Then, to add to his troubles, his fiancée jilted him for a noisy
young man in a loud sports jacket who had no redeeming feature other
than a controlling interest in the Seakirk Construction Corporation.

It was a shattering blow. The girl seemed unaffected by the fact that the
SCC used disproportionate amounts of sand in their concrete and shaved
whole inches from the width of their steel girders. As she put it, "Gee whiz,
Marvie, so what? That's how things are. You gotta be realistic."

Goodman had no intention of being realistic. He immediately repaired to Eddie's Moonlight Bar, where, between drinks, he began to
contemplate the attractions of a grass shack in the green hell of Venus.

An erect, hawk-faced old man entered the bar. Goodman could tell
he was a Spacer by his gravity-bound gait, his pallor, his radiation scars,
and his far-piercing gray eyes.

"A Tranai Special, Sam," the old spacer told the bartender.

"Coming right up, Captain Savage, sir," the bartender said.

"Tranai?" Goodman murmured involuntarily.

"Tranai," the captain said. "Never heard of it, did you, sonny?"

"No, sir," Goodman confessed.

"Well, sonny," Captain Savage said, "I'm feeling a mite wordy tonight,
so I'll tell you a tale of Tranai the Blessed, out past the Galactic Whirl."

The captain's eyes grew misty and a smile softened the grim line of his
lips.

"We were iron men in steel ships in those days. Me and Johnny
Cavanaugh and Frog Larsen would have blasted to hell itself for half a
load of terganium. Aye, and shanghaied Beelzebub for a wiper if we were
short of men. Those were the days when space scurvy took every third
man, and the ghost of Big Dan McClintock haunted the spaceways. Moll
Gann still operated the Red Rooster Inn out on Asteroid 342-AA, asking
five hundred Earth dollars for a glass of beer, and getting it too, there
being no other place within ten billion miles. In those days, the Scarbies
were still cutting up along Star Ridge and ships bound for Prodengum
had to run the Swayback Gantlet. So you can imagine how I felt, sonny,
when one fine day I came upon Tranai."

Goodman listened as the old captain limned a picture of the great days,
of frail ships against an iron sky, ships outward bound, forever outward,
to the far limits of the Galaxy.

And there, at the edge of the Great Nothing, was Tranai.

Tranai, where The Way had been found and men were no longer bound to The Wheel! Tranai the Bountiful, a peaceful, creative, happy society, not saints or ascetics, not intellectuals, but ordinary people who had achieved utopia.

For an hour, Captain Savage spoke of the multiform marvels of Tranai. After finishing his story, he complained of a dry throat. Space throat, he called it, and Goodman ordered him another Tranai Special and one for himself. Sipping the exotic, green-gray mixture, Goodman too was lost in the dream.

Finally, very gently, he asked, "Why don't you go back, Captain?"

The old man shook his head. "Space gout. I'm grounded for good. We didn't know much about modern medicine in those days. All I'm good for now is a landsman's job."

"What job do you have?"

"I'm a foreman for the Seakirk Construction Corporation," the old man sighed. "Me, that once commanded a fifty-tube clipper. The way those people make concrete...Shall we have another short one in honor of beautiful Tranai?"

They had several short ones. When Goodman left the bar, his mind was made up. Somewhere in the Universe, the *modus vivendi* had been found, the working solution to Man's old dream of perfection.

He could settle for nothing less.

The next day, he quit his job as designer at the East Coast Robot Works and drew his life savings out of the bank.

He was going to Tranai.

He boarded the *Constellation Queen* for Legis II and took the *Galactic Splendor* to Oumé. After stopping at Machang, Inchang, Pankang, Lekung, and Oyster—dreary little places—he reached Tung-Bradar IV. Without incident, he passed the Galactic Whirl and finally reached Bellismoranti, where the influence of Terra ended.

For an exorbitant fee, a local spaceline took him to Dvasta II. From there, a freighter transported him past Seves, Olgo, and Mi, to the double planet Mvanti. There he was bogged down for three months and used the time to take a hypnopedic course in the Tranaian language. At last he hired a bush pilot to take him to Ding.

On Ding, he was arrested as a Higastomeritreian spy, but managed to escape in the cargo of an ore rocket bound for g'Moree. At g'Moree, he was treated for frostbite, heat poisoning, and superficial radiation burns, and at last arranged passage to Tranai.

He could hardly believe it when the ship slipped past the moons Doé and Ri, to land at Port Tranai.

After the airlocks opened, Goodman found himself in a state of profound depression. Part of it was plain letdown, inevitable after a journey such as his. But more than that, he was suddenly terrified that Tranai might turn out to be a fraud.

He had crossed the Galaxy on the basis of an old spaceman's yarn. But now it all seemed less likely. Eldorado was a more probable place than the Tranai he expected to find.

He disembarked. Port Tranai seemed a pleasant enough town. The streets were filled with people and the shops were piled high with goods. The men he passed looked much like humans anywhere. The women were quite attractive.

But there was something strange here, something subtly yet definitely wrong, something *alien*. It took a moment before he could puzzle it out.

Then he realized that there were at least ten men for every woman in sight. And stranger still, practically all the women he saw apparently were under eighteen or over thirty-five.

What had happened to the nineteen-to-thirty-five age group? Was there a taboo on their appearing in public? Had a plague struck them?

He would just have to wait and find out.

He went to the Idrig Building, where all Tranai's governmental functions were carried out, and presented himself at the office of the Extraterrestrials Minister. He was admitted at once.

The office was small and cluttered, with strange blue blotches on the wallpaper. What struck Goodman at once was a high-powered rifle complete with silencer and telescopic sight, hanging ominously from one wall. He had no time to speculate on this, for the minister bounded out of his chair and vigorously shook Goodman's hand.

The minister was a stout, jolly man of about fifty. Around his neck he wore a small medallion stamped with the Tranaian seal—a bolt of lightning splitting an ear of corn. Goodman assumed, correctly, that this was an official seal of office.

"Welcome to Tranai," the minister said heartily. He pushed a pile of papers from a chair and motioned Goodman to sit down.

"Mister Minister—" Goodman began, in formal Tranaian.

"Den Melith is the name. Call me Den. We're all quite informal around here. Put your feet up on the desk and make yourself at home. Cigar?"

"No, thank you," Goodman said, somewhat taken back. "Mister— ah—Den, I have come from Terra, a planet you may have heard of."

"Sure I have," said Melith. "Nervous, hustling sort of place, isn't it? No offense intended, of course."

"Of course. That's exactly how I feel about it. The reason I came here—" Goodman hesitated, hoping he wouldn't sound too ridiculous.

"Well, I heard certain stories about Tranai. Thinking them over now, they seem preposterous. But if you don't mind, I'd like to ask you—"

"Ask anything," Melith said expansively. "You'll get a straight answer."

"Thank you. I heard that there has been no war of any sort on Tranai for four hundred years."

"Six hundred," Melith corrected. "And none in sight."

"Someone told me that there is no crime on Tranai."

"None whatsoever."

"And therefore no police force or courts, no judges, sheriffs, marshals, executioners, truant officers, or government investigators. No prisons, reformatories, or other places of detention."

"We have no need of them," Melith explained, "since we have no crime."

"I have heard," said Goodman, "that there is no poverty on Tranai."

"None that I ever heard of," Melith said cheerfully. "Are you sure you won't have a cigar?"

"No, thank you." Goodman was leaning forward eagerly now. "I understand that you have achieved a stable economy without resorting to socialistic, communistic, fascistic, or bureaucratic practices."

"Certainly," Melith said.

"That yours is, in fact, a free enterprise society, where individual initiative flourishes and governmental functions are kept to an absolute minimum."

Melith nodded. "By and large, the government concerns itself with minor regulatory matters, care of the aged, and beautifying the landscape."

"Is it true that you have discovered a method of wealth distribution without resorting to governmental intervention, without even taxation, based entirely upon individual choice?" Goodman challenged.

"Oh, yes, absolutely."

"Is it true that there is no corruption in any phase of the Tranaian government?"

"None," Melith said. "I suppose that's why we have a hard time finding men to hold public office."

"Then Captain Savage was right!" Goodman cried, unable to control himself any longer. "This is utopia!"

"We like it," Melith said.

Goodman took a deep breath and asked, "May I stay here?"

"Why not?" Melith pulled out a form. "We have no restrictions on immigration. Tell me, what is your occupation?"

"On Earth, I was a robot designer."

"Plenty of openings in that." Melith started to fill in the form. His pen emitted a blob of ink. Casually, the minister threw the pen against the wall, where it shattered, adding another blue blotch to the wallpaper.

"We'll make out the paper some other time," he said. "I'm not in the mood now." He leaned back in his chair. "Let me give you a word of advice. Here on Tranai, we feel that we have come pretty close to utopia, as you call it. But ours is not a highly organized state. We have no complicated set of laws. We live by observance of a number of unwritten laws, or customs, as you might call them. You will discover what they are. You would be advised—although certainly not ordered—to follow them."

"Of course I will," Goodman exclaimed. "I can assure you, sir, I have no intention of endangering any phase of your paradise."

"Oh, I wasn't worried about *us,*" Melith said with an amused smile. "It was your own safety I was considering. Perhaps my wife has some further advice for you."

He pushed a large red button on his desk. Immediately there was a bluish haze. The haze solidified, and in a moment Goodman saw a handsome young woman standing before him.

"Good morning, my dear," she said to Melith.

"It's afternoon," Melith informed her. "My dear, this young man came all the way from Earth to live on Tranai. I gave him the usual advice. Is there anything else we can do for him?"

Mrs. Melith thought for a moment, then asked Goodman, "Are you married?"

"No, ma'am," Goodman answered.

"In that case, he should meet a nice girl," Mrs. Melith told her husband. "Bachelordom is not encouraged on Tranai, although certainly not prohibited. Let me see…How about that cute Driganti girl?"

"She's engaged," Melith said.

"Really? Have I been in stasis *that* long? My dear, it's not too thoughtful of you."

"I was busy," Melith said apologetically.

"How about Mihna Vensis?"

"Not his type."

"Janna Vley!"

"Perfect!" Melith winked at Goodman. "A most attractive little lady." He found a new pen in his desk, scribbled an address and handed it to Goodman. "My wife will telephone her to be expecting you tomorrow evening."

"And do come around for dinner some night," said Mrs. Melith.

"Delighted," Goodman replied, in a complete daze.

"It's been nice meeting you," Mrs. Melith said. Her husband pushed the red button. The blue haze formed and Mrs. Melith vanished.

"Have to close up now," said Melith, glancing at his watch. "Can't work overtime—people might start talking. Drop in some day and we'll make out those forms. You really should call on Supreme President Borg, too, at the National Mansion. Or possibly he'll call on you. Don't let the old fox put anything over on you. And don't forget about Janna." He winked roguishly and escorted Goodman to the door.

In a few moments, Goodman found himself alone on the sidewalk. He had reached utopia, he told himself, a real, genuine, sure-enough utopia.

But there were some very puzzling things about it.

Goodman ate dinner at a small restaurant and checked in at a nearby hotel. A cheerful bellhop showed him to his room, where Goodman stretched out immediately on the bed. Wearily he rubbed his eyes, trying to sort out his impressions.

So much had happened to him, all in one day! And so much was bothering him. The ratio of men to women, for example. He had meant to ask Melith about that.

But Melith might not be the man to ask, for there were some curious things about him. Like throwing his pen against the wall. Was that the act of a mature, responsible official? And Melith's wife...

Goodman knew that Mrs. Melith had come out of a derrsin stasis field; he had recognized the characteristic blue haze. The derrsin was used on Terra, too. Sometimes there were good medical reasons for suspending all activity, all growth, all decay. Suppose a patient had a desperate need for a certain serum, procurable only on Mars. Simply project the person into stasis until the serum could arrive.

But on Terra, only a licensed doctor could operate the field. There were strict penalties for its misuse.

He had never heard of keeping one's wife in one.

Still, if all the wives on Tranai *were* kept in stasis, that would explain the absence of the nineteen-to-thirty-five age group and would account for the ten-to-one ratio of men to women.

But what was the reason for this technological purdah?

And something else was on Goodman's mind, something quite insignificant, but bothersome all the same.

That rifle on Melith's wall.

Did he hunt game with it? Pretty big game, then. Target practice? Not with a telescopic sight. Why the silencer? Why did he keep it in his office?

But these were minor matters, Goodman decided, little local idiosyncrasies which would become clear when he had lived a while on Tranai. He couldn't expect immediate and complete comprehension of what was, after all, an alien planet.

He was just beginning to doze off when he heard a knock at his door.

"Come in," he called.

A small, furtive, gray-faced man hurried in and closed the door behind him. "You're the man from Terra, aren't you?"

'That's right."

"I figured you'd come here," the little man said, with a pleased smile. "Hit it right the first time. Going to stay on Tranai?"

"I'm here for good."

"Fine," the man said. "How would you like to become Supreme President?"

"Huh?"

"Good pay, easy hours, only a one-year term. You look like a public-spirited type," the man said sunnily. "How about it?"

Goodman hardly knew what to answer. "Do you mean," he asked incredulously, "that you offer the highest office in the land so casually?"

"What do you mean, *casually?*" the little man spluttered. "Do you think we offer the Supreme Presidency to just anybody? It's a great honor to be asked."

"I didn't mean—"

"And you, as a Terran, are uniquely suited."

"Why?"

"Well, it's common knowledge that Terrans derive pleasure from ruling. We Tranians don't, that's all. Too much trouble."

As simple as that. The reformer blood in Goodman began to boil. Ideal as Tranai was, there was undoubtedly room for improvement. He had a sudden vision of himself as ruler of utopia, doing the great task of making perfection even better. But caution stopped him from agreeing at once. Perhaps the man was a crackpot.

"Thank you for asking me," Goodman said. "I'll have to think it over. Perhaps I should talk with the present incumbent and find out something about the nature of the work."

"Well, why do you think I'm here?" the little man demanded. "I'm Supreme President Borg."

Only then did Goodman notice the official medallion around the little man's neck.

"Let me know your decision. I'll be at the National Mansion." He shook Goodman's hand, and left.

Goodman waited five minutes, then rang for the bellhop. "Who was that man?"

"That was Supreme President Borg," the bellhop told him. "Did you take the job?"

Goodman shook his head slowly. He suddenly realized that he had a *great* deal to learn about Tranai.

The next morning, Goodman listed the various robot factories of Port Tranai in alphabetical order and went out in search of a job. To his amazement, he found one with no trouble at all, at the very first place he looked.

The great Abbag Home Robot Works signed him on after only a cursory glance at his credentials.

His new employer, Mr. Abbag, was short and fierce-looking, with a great mane of white hair and an air of tremendous personal energy.

"Glad to have a Terran on board," Abbag said. "I understand you're an ingenious people and we certainly need some ingenuity around here. I'll be honest with you, Goodman, I'm hoping to profit by your alien viewpoint. We've reached an impasse."

"Is it a production problem?" Goodman asked.

"I'll show you." Abbag led Goodman through the factory, around the Stamping Room, Heat-Treat, X-ray Analysis, Final Assembly and to the Testing Room. This room was laid out like a combination kitchen-living room. A dozen robots were lined up against one wall.

"Try one out," Abbag said.

Goodman walked up to the nearest robot and looked at its controls. They were simple enough; self-explanatory, in fact. He put the machine through a standard repertoire: picking up objects, washing pots and pans, setting a table. The robot's responses were correct enough, but maddeningly slow. On Earth, such sluggishness had been ironed out a hundred years ago. Apparently they were behind the times here on Tranai.

"Seems pretty slow," Goodman commented cautiously.

"You're right," Abbag said. "Damned slow. Personally, I think it's about right. But Consumer Research indicates that our customers want it slower still."

"Huh?"

"Ridiculous, isn't it?" Abbag asked moodily. "We'll lose money if we slow it down any more. Take a look at its guts."

Goodman opened the back panel and blinked at the maze of wiring within. After a moment, he was able to figure it out. The robot was built like a modern Earth machine, with the usual inexpensive high-speed circuits. But special signal delay relays, impulse-rejection units and step-down gears had been installed.

"Just tell me," Abbag demanded angrily, "how can we slow it down any more without building the thing a third bigger and twice as expensive? I don't know what kind of a disimprovement they'll be asking for next."

Goodman was trying to adjust his thinking to the concept of *disimproving* a machine.

On Earth, the plants were always trying to build robots with faster, smoother, more accurate responses. He had never found any reason to question the wisdom of this. He still didn't.

"And as if that weren't enough," Abbag complained, "the new plastic we developed for this particular model has catalyzed or some damned thing. Watch."

He drew back his foot and kicked the robot in the middle. The plastic bent like a sheet of tin. He kicked again. The plastic bent still further and the robot began to click and flash pathetically. A third kick shattered the case. The robot's innards exploded in spectacular fashion, scattering over the floor.

"Pretty flimsy," Goodman said.

"Not flimsy enough. It's supposed to fly apart on the first kick. Our customers won't get any satisfaction out of stubbing their toes on its stomach all day. But tell me, how am I supposed to produce a plastic that'll take normal wear and tear—we don't want these things falling apart accidentally—and still go to pieces when a customer wants it to?"

"Wait a minute," Goodman protested. "Let me get this straight. You purposely slow these robots down so they will irritate people enough to destroy them?"

Abbag raised both eyebrows. "Of course!"

"Why?"

"You *are* new here," Abbag said. "Any child knows that. It's fundamental."

"I'd appreciate it if you'd explain."

Abbag sighed. "Well, first of all, you are undoubtedly aware that *any* mechanical contrivance is a source of irritation. Human-kind has a deep and abiding distrust of machines. Psychologists call it the instinctive reaction of life to pseudo-life. Will you go along with me on that?"

Marvin Goodman remembered all the anxious literature he had read about machines revolting, cybernetic brains taking over the world, androids on the march, and the like. He thought of humorous little newspaper items about a man shooting his television set, smashing his toaster against the wall, "getting even" with his car. He remembered all the robot jokes, with their undertone of deep hostility.

"I guess I can go along on that," said Goodman.

"Then allow me to restate the proposition," Abbag said pedantically. "Any machine is a source of irritation. The better a machine operates, the stronger the irritation. So, by extension, a *perfectly operating* machine is a focal point for frustration, loss of self-esteem, undirected resentment—"

"Hold on there!" Goodman objected. "I won't go *that* far!"

"—and schizophrenic fantasies," Abbag continued inexorably. "But machines are necessary to an advanced economy. Therefore the best *human* solution is to have malfunctioning ones."

"I don't see that at all."

"It's obvious. On Terra, your gadgets work close to the optimum, producing inferiority feelings in their operators. But unfortunately you have a masochistic tribal taboo against destroying them. Result? Generalized anxiety in the presence of the sacrosanct and unhumanly efficient Machine, and a search for an aggression-object, usually a wife or friend. A very poor state of affairs. Oh, it's efficient, I suppose, in terms of robot-hour production, but very inefficient in terms of long-range health and well-being."

"I'm not sure—"

"The human is an anxious beast. Here on Tranai, we direct anxiety toward this particular point and let it serve as an outlet for a lot of other frustrations as well. A man's had enough—blam! He kicks hell out of his robot. There's an immediate and therapeutic discharge of feeling, a valuable—and valid—sense of superiority over mere machinery, a lessening of general tension, a healthy flow of adrenalin into the bloodstream, and a boost to the industrial economy of Tranai, since he'll go right out and buy another robot. And what, after all, has he done? He hasn't beaten his wife, suicided, declared a war, invented a new weapon, or indulged in any of the other more common modes of aggression-resolution. He has simply smashed an inexpensive robot which he can replace immediately."

"I guess it'll take me a little time to understand," Goodman admitted.

"Of course it will. I'm sure you're going to be a valuable man here, Goodman. Think over what I've said and try to figure out some inexpensive way of disimproving this robot."

Goodman pondered the problem for the rest of the day, but he couldn't immediately adjust his thinking to the idea of producing an inferior machine. It seemed vaguely blasphemous. He knocked off work at five-thirty, dissatisfied with himself, but determined to do better—or worse, depending on viewpoint and conditioning.

After a quick and lonely supper, Goodman decided to call on Janna Vley. He didn't want to spend the evening alone with his thoughts and he was in desperate need of finding something pleasant, simple and uncomplicated in this complex utopia. Perhaps this Janna would be the answer.

The Vley home was only a dozen blocks away and he decided to walk.

The basic trouble was that he had had his own idea of what utopia would be like and it was difficult adjusting his thinking to the real thing. He had imagined a pastoral setting, a planetful of people in small, quaint villages, walking around in flowing robes and being very wise and gentle and understanding. Children who played in the golden sunlight, young folk danced in the village square...

Ridiculous! He had pictured a tableau rather than a scene, a series of stylized postures instead of the ceaseless movement of life. Humans could never live that way, even assuming they wanted to. If they could, they would no longer be humans.

He reached the Vley house and paused irresolutely outside. What was he getting himself into now? What alien—although indubitably utopian—customs would he run into?

He almost turned away. But the prospect of a long night alone in his hotel room was singularly unappealing. Gritting his teeth, he rang the bell.

A red-haired, middle-aged man of medium height opened the door. "Oh, you must be that Terran fellow. Janna's getting ready. Come in and meet the wife."

He escorted Goodman into a pleasantly furnished living room and pushed a red button on the wall. Goodman wasn't startled this time by the bluish derrsin haze. After all, the manner in which Tranaians treated their women was their own business.

A handsome woman of about twenty-eight appeared from the haze. "My dear," Vley said, "this is the Terran, Mr. Goodman."

"So pleased to meet you," Mrs. Vley said. "Can I get you a drink?"

Goodman nodded. Vley pointed out a comfortable chair. In a moment, Mrs. Vley brought in a tray of frosted drinks and sat down.

"So you're from Terra," said Mr. Vley. "Nervous, hustling sort of place, isn't it? People always on the go?"

"Yes, I suppose it is," Goodman replied.

"Well, you'll like it here. We know how to live. It's all a matter of—"

There was a rustle of skirts on the stairs. Goodman got to his feet.

"Mr. Goodman, this is our daughter Janna," Mrs. Vley said.

Goodman noted at once that Janna's hair was the exact color of the supernova in Circe, her eyes were that deep, unbelievable blue of the autumn sky over Aigo II, her lips were the tender pink of a Scarsclott-Turner jet stream, her nose—

But he had run out of astronomical comparisons, which weren't suitable anyhow. Janna was a slender and amazingly pretty blond girl and Goodman was suddenly very glad he had crossed the Galaxy and come to Tranai.

"Have a good time, children," Mrs. Vley said.

"Don't come in too late," Mr. Vley told Janna.

Exactly as parents said on Earth to their children.

There was nothing exotic about the date. They went to an inexpensive night club, danced, drank a little, talked a lot. Goodman was amazed at their immediate *rapport*. Janna agreed with everything he said. It was refreshing to find intelligence in so pretty a girl.

She was impressed, almost overwhelmed, by the dangers he had faced in crossing the Galaxy. She had always known that Terrans were adventurous (though nervous) types, but the risks Goodman had taken passed all understanding.

She shuddered when he spoke of the deadly Galactic Whirl and listened wide-eyed to his tales of running the notorious Swayback Gantlet, past the bloodthirsty Scarbies who were still cutting up along Star Ridge and infesting the hell holes of Prodengum. As Goodman put it, Terrans were iron men in steel ships, exploring the edges of the Great Nothing.

Janna didn't even speak until Goodman told of paying five hundred Terran dollars for a glass of beer at Moll Gann's Red Rooster Inn on Asteroid 342-AA.

"You must have been very thirsty," she said thoughtfully.

"Not particularly," Goodman said. "Money just didn't mean much out there."

"Oh. But wouldn't it have been better to have saved it? I mean someday you might have a wife and children—" She blushed.

Goodman said coolly, "Well, that part of my life is over. I'm going to marry and settle down right here on Tranai."

"How *nice!*" she cried.

It was a most successful evening.

Goodman returned Janna to her home at a respectable hour and arranged a date for the following evening. Made bold by his own tales, he kissed her on the cheek. She didn't really seem to mind, but Goodman didn't try to press his advantage.

"Till tomorrow then," she said, smiled at him, and closed the door.

He walked away feeling light-headed. Janna! Janna! Was it conceivable that he was in love already? Why not? Love at first sight was a proven psycho-physiological possibility and, as such, was perfectly respectable. Love in utopia! How wonderful it was that here, upon a perfect planet, he had found the perfect girl!

A man stepped out of the shadows and blocked his path. Goodman noted that he was wearing a black silk mask which covered everything except his eyes. He was carrying a large and powerful-looking blaster, and it was pointed steadily at Goodman's stomach.

"Okay, buddy," the man said, "gimme all your money."

"What?" Goodman gasped.

"You heard me. Your money. Hand it over."

"You can't do this," Goodman said, too startled to think coherently. "There's no crime on Tranai!"

"Who said there was?" the man asked quietly. "I'm merely asking you for your money. Are you going to hand it over peacefully or do I have to club it out of you?"

"You can't get away with this! Crime does not pay!"

"Don't be ridiculous," the man said. He hefted the heavy blaster.

"All right. Don't get excited." Goodman pulled out his billfold, which contained all he had in the world, and gave its contents to the masked man.

The man counted it, and he seemed impressed. "Better than I expected. Thanks, buddy. Take it easy now."

He hurried away down a dark street.

Goodman looked wildly around for a policeman, until he remembered that there were no police on Tranai. He saw a small cocktail lounge on the corner with a neon sign saying Kitty Kat Bar. He hurried into it.

Inside, there was only a bartender, somberly wiping glasses.

"I've been robbed!" Goodman shouted at him.

"So?" the bartender said, not even looking up.

"But I thought there wasn't any crime on Tranai."

"There isn't."

"But I was *robbed.*"

"You must be new here," the bartender said, finally looking at him.

"I just came in from Terra."

"Terra? Nervous, hustling sort of—"

"Yes, yes," Goodman said. He was getting a little tired of that stereotype. "But how can there be no crime on Tranai if I was robbed?"

"That should be obvious. On Tranai, robbery is no crime."

"But robbery is *always* a crime!"

"What color mask was he wearing?"

Goodman thought for a moment. "Black. Black silk."

The bartender nodded. "Then he was a government tax collector."

"That's a ridiculous way to collect taxes," Goodman snapped.

The bartender set a Tranai Special in front of Goodman. "Try to see this in terms of the general welfare. The government has to have *some* money. By collecting it this way, we can avoid the necessity of an income tax, with all its complicated legal and legislative apparatus. And in terms of mental health, it's far better to extract money in a short, quick, painless operation than to permit the citizen to worry all year long about paying at a specific date."

Goodman downed his drink and the bartender set up another.

"But," Goodman said, "I thought this was a society based upon the concepts of free will and individual initiative."

"It is," the bartender told him. "Then surely the government, what little there is of it, has the same right to free will as any private citizen, hasn't it?"

Goodman couldn't quite figure that out, so he finished his second drink. "Could I have another of those? I'll pay you as soon as I can."

"Sure, sure," the bartender said good-naturedly, pouring another drink and one for himself.

Goodman said, "You asked me what color his mask was. Why?"

"Black is the government mask color. Private citizens wear white masks."

"You mean that private citizens commit robbery also?"

"Well, certainly! That's our method of wealth distribution. Money is equalized without government intervention, without even taxation, entirely in terms of individual initiative." The bartender nodded emphatically. "And it works perfectly, too. Robbery is a great leveler, you know."

"I suppose it is," Goodman admitted, finishing his third drink. "If I understand correctly, then, any citizen can pack a blaster, put on a mask, and go out and rob."

"Exactly," the bartender said. "Within limits, of course."

Goodman snorted. "If that's how it works, I can play that way. Could you loan me a mask? And a gun?"

The bartender reached under the bar. "Be sure to return them, though. Family heirlooms."

"I'll return them," Goodman promised. "And when I come back, I'll pay for my drinks."

He slipped the blaster into his belt, donned the mask and left the bar. If this was how things worked on Tranai, he could adjust all right. Rob him, would they? He'd rob them right back and then some!

He found a suitably dark street corner and huddled in the shadows, waiting. Presently he heard footsteps and, peering around the corner, saw a portly, well-dressed Tranaian hurrying down the street.

Goodman stepped in front of him, snarling, "Hold it, buddy."

The Tranaian stopped and looked at Goodman's blaster. "Hmmm. Using a wide-aperture Drog 3, eh? Rather an old fashioned weapon. How do you like it?"

"It's fine," Goodman said. "Hand over your—"

"Slow trigger action, though," the Tranaian mused. "Personally, I recommend a Mils-Sleeven needler. As it happens, I'm a sales representative for Sleeven Arms. I could get you a very good price on a trade-in—"

"Hand over your money," Goodman barked.

The portly Tranaian smiled. "The basic defect of your Drog 3 is the fact that it won't fire at all unless you release the safety lock." He reached out and slapped the gun out of Goodman's hand. "You see? You couldn't have done a thing about it." He started to walk away.

Goodman scooped up the blaster, found the safety lock, released it and hurried after the Tranaian.

"Stick up your hands," Goodman ordered, beginning to feel slightly desperate.

"No, no, my good man," the Tranaian said, not even looking back. "Only one try to a customer. Mustn't break the unwritten law, you know."

Goodman stood and watched until the man turned a corner and was gone. He checked the Drog 3 carefully and made sure that all safeties were off. Then he resumed his post.

After an hour's wait, he heard footsteps again. He tightened his grip on the blaster. This time he was going to rob and nothing was going to stop him.

"Okay, buddy," he said, "hands up!"

The victim this time was a short, stocky Tranaian, dressed in old workman's clothes. He gaped at the gun in Goodman's hand.

"Don't shoot, mister," the Tranaian pleaded.

That was more like it! Goodman felt a glow of deep satisfaction.

"Just don't move," he warned. "I've got all safeties off."

"I can see that," the stocky man said cringing. "Be careful with that cannon, mister. I ain't moving a hair."

"You'd better not. Hand over your money."

"Money?"

"Yes, your money, and be quick about it."

"I don't have any money," the man whined. "Mister, I'm a poor man. I'm poverty-stricken."

"There is no poverty on Tranai," Goodman said sententiously.

"I know. But you can get so close to it, you wouldn't know the difference. Give me a break, mister."

"Haven't you any initiative?" Goodman asked. "If you're poor, why don't you go out and rob like everybody else?"

"I just haven't had a chance. First the kid got the whooping cough and I was up every night with her. Then the derrsin broke down, so I had the wife yakking at me all day long. I say there oughta be a spare derrsin in every house! So she decided to clean the place while the derrsin generator was being fixed and she put my blaster somewhere and she can't remember where. So I was all set to borrow a friend's blaster when—"

"That's enough," Goodman said. "This is a robbery and I'm going to rob you of *something*. Hand over your wallet."

The man snuffled miserably and gave Goodman a worn billfold. Inside it, Goodman found one deeglo, the equivalent of a Terran dollar.

"It's all I got," the man snuffled miserably, "but you're welcome to it. I know how it is, standing on a drafty street corner all night—"

"Keep it," Goodman said, handing the billfold back to the man and walking off.

"Gee, thanks, mister!"

Goodman didn't answer. Disconsolately, he returned to the Kitty Kat Bar and gave back the bartender's blaster and mask. When he explained what had happened, the bartender burst into rude laughter.

"Didn't have any money! Man, that's the oldest trick in the books. Everybody carries a fake wallet for robberies—sometimes two or even three. Did you search him?"

"No," Goodman confessed.

"Brother, are you a greenhorn!"

"I guess I am. Look, I really will pay you for those drinks as soon as I can make some money."

"Sure, sure," the bartender said. "You better go home and get some sleep. You had a busy night."

Goodman agreed. Wearily he returned to his hotel room and was asleep as soon as his head hit the pillow.

He reported at the Abbag Home Robot Works and manfully grappled with the problem of disimproving automata. Even in unhuman work such as this, Terran ingenuity began to tell.

Goodman began to develop a new plastic for the robot's case. It was a silicone, a relative of the "silly putty" that had appeared on Earth a long while back. It had the desired properties of toughness, resiliency and long wear; it would stand a lot of abuse, too. But the case would shatter immediately and with spectacular effect upon receiving a kick delivered with an impact of thirty pounds or more.

His employer praised him for this development, gave him a bonus (which he sorely needed), and told him to keep working on the idea and, if possible, to bring the needed impact down to twenty-three pounds. This, the research department told them, was the average frustration kick.

He was kept so busy that he had practically no time to explore further the mores and folkways of Tranai. He did manage to see the Citizen's Booth. This uniquely Tranaian institution was housed in a small building on a quiet back street.

Upon entering, he was confronted by a large board, upon which was listed the names of the present officeholders of Tranai, and their titles. Beside each name was a button. The attendant told Goodman that, by pressing a button, a citizen expressed his disapproval of that official's acts. The pressed button was automatically registered in History Hall and was a permanent mark against the officeholder.

No minors were allowed to press the buttons, of course.

Goodman considered this somewhat ineffectual; but perhaps, he told himself, officials on Tranai were differently motivated from those on Earth.

He saw Janna almost every evening and together they explored the many cultural aspects of Tranai: the cocktail lounges and movies, the concert halls, the art exhibitions, the science museum, the fairs and festivals. Goodman carried a blaster and, after several unsuccessful attempts, robbed a merchant of nearly five hundred deeglo.

Janna was ecstatic over the achievement, as any sensible Tranaian girl would be, and they celebrated at the Kitty Kat Bar. Janna's parents agreed that Goodman seemed to be a good provider.

The following night, the five hundred deeglo—plus some of Goodman's bonus money—was robbed back, by a man of approximately the size and build of the bartender at the Kitty Kat, carrying an ancient Drog 3 blaster.

Goodman consoled himself with the thought that the money was circulating freely, as the system had intended.

Then he had another triumph. One day at the Abbag Home Robot Works, he discovered a completely new process for making a robot's case. It was a special plastic, impervious even to serious bumps and falls. The robot owner had to wear special shoes, with a catalytic agent imbedded in the heels. When he kicked the robot, the catalyst came in contact with the plastic case, with immediate and gratifying effect.

Abbag was a little uncertain at first; it seemed too gimmicky. But the thing caught on like wildfire and the Home Robot Works went into the shoe business as a subsidiary, selling at least one pair with every robot.

This horizontal industrial development was very gratifying to the plant's stockholders and was really more important than the original catalyst-plastic discovery. Goodman received a substantial raise in pay and a generous bonus.

On the crest of his triumphant wave, he proposed to Janna and was instantly accepted. Her parents favored the match; all that remained was to obtain official sanction from the government, since Goodman was still technically an alien.

Accordingly, he took a day off from work and walked down to the Idrig Building to see Melith. It was a glorious spring day of the sort that Tranai has for ten months out of the year, and Goodman walked with a light and springy step. He was in love, a success in business, and soon to become a citizen of utopia.

Of course, utopia could use some changes, for even Tranai wasn't quite perfect. Possibly he should accept the Supreme Presidency, in order to make the needed reforms. But there was no rush...

"Hey, mister," a voice said, "can you spare a deeglo?"

Goodman looked down and saw, squatting on the pavement, an unwashed old man, dressed in rags, holding out a tin cup.

"What?" Goodman asked.

"Can you spare a deeglo, brother?" the man repeated in a wheedling voice. "Help a poor man buy a cup of oglo? Haven't eaten in two days, mister."

"This is disgraceful! Why don't you get a blaster and go out and rob someone?"

"I'm too old," the man whimpered. "My victims just laugh at me."

"Are you sure you aren't just lazy?" Goodman asked sternly.

"I'm not, sir!" the beggar said. "Just look how my hands shake!"

He held out both dirty paws; they trembled.

Goodman took out his billfold and gave the old man a deeglo. "I thought there was no poverty on Tranai. I understood that the government took care of the aged."

"The government does," said the old man. "Look." He held out his cup. Engraved on its side was: GOVERNMENT AUTHORIZED BEGGAR, NUMBER DR-43241-3.

"You mean the government makes you do this?"

"The government *lets* me do it," the old man told him. "Begging is a government job and is reserved for the aged and infirm."

"Why, that's disgraceful."

"You must be a stranger here."

"I'm a Terran."

"Aha! Nervous, hustling sort of people, aren't you?"

"*Our* government does not let people beg," Goodman said.

"No? What do the old people do? Live off their children? Or sit in some home for the aged and wait for death by boredom? Not here, young man. On Tranai, every old man is assured of a government job, and one for which he needs no particular skill, although skill helps. Some apply for indoor work, within the churches and theatres. Others like the excitement of fairs and carnivals. Personally, I like it outdoors. My job keeps me out in the sunlight and fresh air, gives me mild exercise, and helps me meet many strange and interesting people, such as yourself."

"But *begging!*"

"What other work would I be suited for?"

"I don't know. But—but look at you! Dirty, unwashed, in filthy clothes—"

"These are my working clothes," the government beggar said. "You should see me on Sunday."

"You have other clothes?"

"I certainly do, and a pleasant little apartment, and a season box at the opera, and two Home Robots, and probably more money in the bank than you've seen in your life. It's been pleasant talking to you, young man, and thanks for your contribution. But now I must return to work and suggest you do likewise."

Goodman walked away, glancing over his shoulder at the government beggar. He observed that the old man seemed to be doing a thriving business.

But *begging!*

Really, that sort of thing should be stopped. If he ever assumed the Presidency—and quite obviously he should—he would look into the whole matter more carefully.

It seemed to him that there had to be a more dignified answer.

At the Idrig Building, Goodman told Melith about his marriage plans.

The immigrations minister was enthusiastic.

"Wonderful, absolutely wonderful," he said. "I've known the Vley family for a long time. They're splendid people. And Janna is a girl any man would be proud of."

"Aren't there some formalities I should go through?" Goodman asked. "I mean being an alien and all—"

"None whatsoever. I've decided to dispense with the formalities. You can become a citizen of Tranai, if you wish, by merely stating your intention verbally. Or you can retain Terran citizenship, with no hard feelings. Or you can do both—be a citizen of Terra *and* Tranai. If Terra doesn't mind, we certainly don't."

"I think I'd like to become a citizen of Tranai," Goodman said.

"It's entirely up to you. But if you're thinking about the Presidency, you can retain Terran status and still hold office. We aren't at all stuffy about that sort of thing. One of our most Successful Supreme Presidents was a lizard-evolved chap from Aquarella XI."

"What an enlightened attitude!"

"Sure, give everybody a chance, that's our motto. Now as to your marriage—any government employee can perform the ceremonies. Supreme President Borg would be happy to do it, this afternoon if you like." Melith winked. "The old codger likes to kiss the bride. But I think he's genuinely fond of you."

"This afternoon?" Goodman said. "Yes, I *would* like to be married this afternoon, if it's all right with Janna."

"It probably will be," Melith assured him. "Next, where are you going to live after the honeymoon? A hotel room is hardly suitable," He thought for a moment. "Tell you what—I've got a little house on the edge of town. Why don't you move in there, until you find something better? Or stay permanently, if you like it."

"Really," Goodman protested, "you're too generous—"

"Think nothing of it. Have you ever thought of becoming the next immigrations minister? You might like the work. No red tape, short hours, good pay— No? Got your eye on the Supreme Presidency, eh? Can't blame you, I suppose."

Melith dug in his pockets and found two keys. "This is for the front door and this is for the back. The address is stamped right on them. The place is fully equipped, including a brand-new derrsin field generator."

"A derrsin?"

"Certainly. No home on Tranai is complete without a derrsin stasis field generator."

Clearing his throat, Goodman said carefully, "I've been meaning to ask you—exactly what is the stasis field used for?"

"Why, to keep one's wife in," Melith answered. "I thought you knew."

"I did," said Goodman. "But *why?*"

"Why?" Melith frowned. Apparently the question had never entered his head. "Why does one do anything? It's the custom, that's all. And very logical, too. You wouldn't want a woman chattering around you all the time, night and day."

Goodman blushed, because ever since he had met Janna, he had been thinking how pleasant it would be to have her around him all the time, night and day.

"It hardly seems fair to the women," Goodman pointed out.

Melith laughed. "My dear friend, are you preaching the doctrine of equality of the sexes? Really, it's a completely disproved theory. Men and women just aren't the same. They're different, no matter what you've been told on Terra. What's good for men isn't necessarily—or even usually—good for women."

"Therefore you treat them as inferiors," Goodman said, his reformer's blood beginning to boil.

"Not at all. We treat them in a *different* manner from men, but not in an *inferior* manner. Anyhow, they don't object."

"That's because they haven't been allowed to know any better. Is there any law that requires me to keep my wife in the derrsin field?"

"Of course not. The custom simply suggests that you keep her *out* of stasis for a certain minimum amount of time every week. No fair incarcerating the little woman, you know."

"Of course not," Goodman said sarcastically. "Must let her live *some* of the time."

"Exactly," Melith said, seeing no sarcasm in what Goodman said. "You'll catch on."

Goodman stood up. "Is that all?"

"I guess that's about it. Good luck and all that."

"Thank you," Goodman said stiffly, turned sharply and left.

That afternoon, Supreme President Borg performed the simple Tranaian marriage rites at the National Mansion and afterward kissed the bride with zeal. It was a beautiful ceremony and was marred by only one thing.

Hanging on Borg's wall was a rifle, complete with telescopic sight and silencer. It was a twin to Melith's and just as inexplicable.

Borg took Goodman to one side and asked, "Have you given any further thought to the Supreme Presidency?"

"I'm still considering it," Goodman said. "I don't really want to hold public office—"

"No one does."

"—but there are certain reforms that Tranai needs badly. I think it may be my duty to bring them to the attention of the people."

"That's the spirit," Borg said approvingly. "We haven't had a really enterprising Supreme President for some time. Why don't you take office right now? Then you could have your honeymoon in the National Mansion with complete privacy."

Goodman was tempted. But he didn't want to be bothered by affairs of state on his honeymoon, which was all arranged anyhow. Since Tranai had lasted so long in its present near-utopian condition, it would undoubtedly keep for a few weeks more.

"I'll consider it when I come back," Goodman said.

Borg shrugged. "Well, I guess I can bear the burden a while longer. Oh, here." He handed Goodman a sealed envelope.

"What's this?"

"Just the standard advice," Borg said. "Hurry, your bride's waiting for you!"

"Come on, Marvin!" Janna called. "We don't want to be late for the spaceship!"

Goodman hurried after her, into the spaceport limousine.

"Good luck!" her parents cried.

"Good luck!" Borg shouted.

"Good luck!" added Melith and his wife, and all the guests.

On the way to the spaceport, Goodman opened the envelope and read the printed sheet within:

ADVICE TO A NEW HUSBAND

You have just been married and you expect, quite naturally, a lifetime of connubial bliss. This is perfectly proper, for a happy marriage is the foundation of good government. But you must do more than merely wish for it. Good marriage is not yours by divine right. A good marriage must be worked for!

Remember that your wife is a human being. She should be allowed a certain measure of freedom as her inalienable right. We suggest you take her out of stasis at least once a week. Too long in stasis is bad for her orientation. Too much stasis is bad for her complexion and this will be your loss as well as hers.

At intervals, such as vacations and holidays, it's customary to let your wife remain out of stasis for an entire day at a time, or even two or three days. It will do no harm and the novelty will do wonders for her state of mind.

Keep in mind these few common-sense rules and you can be assured of a happy marriage.

—By the Government
Marriage Council

Goodman slowly tore the card into little bits, and let them drop to the floor of the limousine. His reforming spirit was now thoroughly aroused. He had known that Tranai was too good to be true. Someone had to pay for perfection. In this case, it was the women.

He had found the first serious flaw in paradise.

"What was that, dear?" Janna asked, looking at the bits of paper.

"That was some very foolish advice," Goodman said. "Dear, have you ever thought—really thought—about the marriage customs of this planet of yours?"

"I don't think I have. Aren't they all right?"

"They are wrong, completely wrong. They treat women like toys, like little dolls that one puts away when one is finished playing. Can't you see that?"

"I never thought about it."

"Well, you can think about it now," Goodman told her, "because some changes are going to be made and they're going to start in our home."

"Whatever you think best, darling," Janna said dutifully. She squeezed his arm. He kissed her.

And then the limousine reached the spaceport and they got aboard the ship.

Their honeymoon on Doé was like a brief sojourn in a flawless paradise. The wonders of Tranai's little moon had been built for lovers, and for lovers only. No businessman came to Doé for a quick rest; no predatory bachelor prowled the paths. The tired, the disillusioned, the lewdly hopeful all had to find other hunting grounds. The single rule on Doé, strictly enforced, was two by two, joyous and in love, and in no other state admitted.

This was one Tranaian custom that Goodman had no trouble appreciating.

On the little moon, there were meadows of tall grass and deep, green forests for walking and cool, black lakes in the forests and jagged, spectacular mountains that begged to be climbed. Lovers were continually getting lost in the forests, to their great satisfaction; but not too lost, for one could circle the whole moon in a day. Thanks to the gentle gravity, no one could drown in the black lakes, and a fall from a mountaintop was frightening, but hardly dangerous.

There were, at strategic locations, little hotels with dimly lit cocktail lounges run by friendly, white-haired bartenders. There were gloomy caves which ran deep (but never too deep) into phosphorescent caverns glittering with ice, past sluggish underground rivers in which swam great luminous fish with fiery eyes.

The Government Marriage Council had considered these simple attractions sufficient and hadn't bothered putting in a golf course, swimming pool, horse track, or shuffleboard court. It was felt that once a couple desired these things, the honeymoon was over.

Goodman and his bride spent an enchanted week on Doé and at last returned to Tranai.

After carrying his bride across the threshold of their new home, Goodman's first act was to unplug the derrsin generator.

"My dear," he said, "up to now, I have followed all the customs of Tranai, even when they seemed ridiculous to me. But this is one thing I will not sanction. On Terra, I was the founder of the Committee for Equal Job Opportunities for Women. On Terra, we treat our women as equals, as companions, as partners in the adventure of life."

"What a strange concept," Janna said, a frown clouding her pretty face.

"Think about it," Goodman urged. "Our life will be far more satisfying in this companionable manner than if I shut you up in the purdah of the derrsin field. Don't you agree?"

"You know far more than I, dear. You've traveled all over the Galaxy, and I've never been out of Port Tranai. If you say it's the best way, then it must be."

Past a doubt, Goodman thought, she was the most perfect of women.

He returned to his work at the Abbag Home Robot Works and was soon deep in another disimprovement project. This time, he conceived the bright idea of making the robot's joints squeak and grind. The noise would increase the robot's irritation value, thereby making its destruction more pleasing and psychologically more valuable. Mr. Abbag was overjoyed with the idea, gave him another pay raise, and asked him to have the disimprovement ready for early production.

Goodman's first plan was simply to remove some of the lubrication ducts. But he found that friction would then wear out vital parts too soon. That naturally could not be sanctioned.

He began to draw up plans for a built-in squeak-and-grind unit. It had to be absolutely life-like and yet cause no real wear. It had to be inexpensive and it had to be small, because the robot's interior was already packed with disimprovements.

But Goodman found that small squeak-producing units sounded artificial. Larger units were too costly to manufacture or couldn't be fitted inside the robot's case. He began working several evenings a week, lost weight, and his temper grew edgy.

Janna became a good, dependable wife. His meals were always ready on time and she invariably had a cheerful word for him in the evenings and a sympathetic ear for his difficulties. During the day, she supervised the cleaning of the house by the Home Robots. This took less than an hour and afterward she read books, baked pies, knitted, and destroyed robots.

Goodman was a little alarmed at this, because Janna destroyed them at the rate of three or four a week. Still, everyone had to have a hobby. He could afford to indulge her, since he got the machines at cost.

Goodman had reached a complete impasse when another designer, a man named Dath Hergo, came up with a novel control. This was based upon a counter-gyroscopic principle and allowed a robot to enter a room at a ten-degree list. (Ten degrees, the research department said, was the most irritating angle of list a robot could assume.) Moreover, by employing a random-selection principle, the robot would *lurch*, drunkenly, annoyingly, at irregular intervals—never dropping anything, but always on the verge of it.

This development was, quite naturally, hailed as a great advance in disimprovement engineering. And Goodman found that he could center his built-in squeak-and-grind unit right in the lurch control. His name was mentioned in the engineering journals next to that of Dath Hergo.

The new line of Abbag Home Robots was a sensation. At this time, Goodman decided to take a leave of absence from his job and assume the Supreme Presidency of Tranai. He felt he owed it to the people. If Terran ingenuity and know-how could bring out improvements in disimprovements, they would do even better improving improvements. Tranai was a near-utopia. With his hand on the reins, they could go the rest of the way to perfection.

He went down to Melith's office to talk it over.

"I suppose there's always room for change," Melith said thoughtfully. The immigration chief was seated by the window, idly watching people pass by. "Of course, our present system has been working for quite some time and working very well. I don't know what you'd improve. There's no crime, for example—"

"Because you've legalized it," Goodman declared. "You've simply evaded the issue."

"We don't see it that way. There's no poverty—"

"Because everybody steals. And there's no trouble with old people because the government turns them into beggars. Really, there's plenty of room for change and improvement."

"Well, perhaps," Melith said. "But I think—" he stopped suddenly, rushed over to the wall and pulled down the rifle. "There he is!"

Goodman looked out the window. A man, apparently no different from anyone else, was walking past. He heard a muffled click and saw the man stagger, then drop to the pavement.

Melith had shot him with the silenced rifle.

"What did you do that for?" Goodman gasped

"Potential murderer," Melith said.

"What?"

"Of course. We don't have any out-and-out crime here, but, being human, we have to deal with the potentiality."

"What did he do to make him a potential murderer?"

"Killed five people," Melith stated.

"But—damn it, man, this isn't fair! You didn't arrest him, give him a trial, the benefit of counsel—"

"How could I?" Melith asked, slightly annoyed. "We don't have any police to arrest people with and we don't have any legal system. Good Lord, you didn't expect me to just let him go on, did you? Our definition of a murderer is a killer of ten and he was well on his way. I couldn't just sit idly by. It's my duty to protect the people. I can assure you, I made careful inquiries."

"It isn't just!" Goodman shouted.

"Who ever said it was?" Melith shouted back. "What has *justice* got to do with utopia?"

"Everything!" Goodman had calmed himself with an effort. "Justice is the basis of human dignity, human desire—"

"Now you're just using words," Melith said, with his usual good-natured smile. "Try to be realistic. We have created a utopia for *human beings,* not for saints who don't need one. We must accept the deficiencies of the human character, not pretend they don't exist. To our way of thinking, a police apparatus and a legal-judicial system all tend to create an atmosphere for crime and an acceptance of crime. It's better, believe me, not to accept the possibility of crime at all. The vast majority of the people will go along with you."

"But when crime does turn up as it inevitably does—"

"Only the potentiality turns up," Melith insisted stubbornly. "And even that is much rarer than you would think. When it shows up, we deal with it, quickly and simply."

"Suppose you get the wrong man?"

"We can't get the wrong man. Not a chance of it."

"Why not?"

"Because," Melith said, "anyone disposed of by a government official is, by definition and by unwritten law, a potential criminal."

Marvin Goodman was silent for a while. Then he said, "I see that the government has more power than I thought at first."

"It does," Melith said. "But not as much as you now imagine."

Goodman smiled ironically. "And is the Supreme Presidency still mine for the asking?"

"Of course. And with no strings attached. Do you want it?"

Goodman thought deeply for a moment. Did he really want it? Well, someone had to rule. Someone had to protect the people. Someone had to make a few reforms in this utopian madhouse.

"Yes, I want it," Goodman said.

The door burst open and Supreme President Borg rushed in. "Wonderful! Perfectly wonderful! You can move into the National Mansion today. I've been packed for a week, waiting for you to make up your mind."

"There must be certain formalities to go through—"

"No formalities," Borg said, his face shining with perspiration. "None whatsoever. All we do is hand over the Presidential Seal; then I'll go down and take my name off the rolls and put yours on."

Goodman looked at Melith. The immigration minister's round face was expressionless.

"All right," Goodman said.

Borg reached for the Presidential Seal, started to remove it from his neck—

It exploded suddenly and violently.

Goodman found himself staring in horror at Borg's red, ruined head. The Supreme President tottered for a moment, then slid to the floor.

Melith took off his jacket and threw it over Borg's head. Goodman backed to a chair and fell into it. His mouth opened, but no words came out.

"It's really a pity," Melith said. "He was so near the end of his term. I warned him against licensing that new spaceport. The citizens won't approve, I told him. But he was sure they would like to have two spaceports. Well, he was wrong."

"Do you mean—I mean—how—what—"

"All government officials," Melith explained, "wear the badge of office, which contains a traditional amount of tessium, an explosive you may have heard of. The charge is radio-controlled from the Citizens Booth. Any citizen has access to the Booth, for the purpose of expressing his disapproval of the government." Melith sighed. "This will go down as a permanent black mark against poor Borg's record."

"You let the people express their disapproval by blowing up officials?" Goodman croaked, appalled.

"It's the only way that means anything," said Melith. "Check and balance. Just as the people are in our hands, so we are in the people's hands."

"And *that's* why he wanted me to take over his term. Why didn't anyone tell me?"

"You didn't ask," Melith said, with the suspicion of a smile. "Don't look so horrified. Assassination is always possible, you know, on any planet, under any government. We try to make it a constructive thing. Under this system, the people never lose touch with the government, and the government never tries to assume dictatorial powers. And, since everyone knows he can turn to the Citizens Booth, you'd be surprised how sparingly it's used. Of course, there are always hotheads—"

Goodman got to his feet and started to the door, not looking at Borg's body.

"Don't you still want the Presidency?" asked Melith.

"No!"

"That's so like you Terrans," Melith remarked sadly. "You want responsibility only if it doesn't incur risk. That's the wrong attitude for running a government."

"You may be right," Goodman said. "I'm just glad I found out in time."

He hurried home.

His mind was in a complete turmoil when he entered his house. Was Tranai a utopia or a planetwide insane asylum? Was there much difference? For the first time in his life, Goodman was wondering if utopia was worth having. Wasn't it better to strive for perfection than to possess it? To have ideals rather than to live by them? If justice was a fallacy, wasn't the fallacy better than the truth?

Or was it? Goodman was a sadly confused young man when he shuffled into his house and found his wife in the arms of another man.

The scene had a terrible slow-motion clarity in his eyes. It seemed to take Janna forever to rise to her feet, straighten her disarranged clothing and stare at him open-mouthed. The man—a tall, good-looking fellow whom Goodman had never before seen—appeared too startled to speak. He made small, aimless gestures, brushing the lapel of his jacket, pulling down his cuffs.

Then, tentatively, the man smiled.

"Well!" Goodman said. It was feeble enough, under the circumstances, but it had its effect. Janna started to cry.

"Terribly sorry," the man murmured. "Didn't expect you home for hours. This must come as a shock to you. I'm terribly sorry."

The one thing Goodman hadn't expected or wanted was sympathy from his wife's lover. He ignored the man and stared at the weeping Janna.

"Well, what did you expect?" Janna screamed at him suddenly. "I had to! You didn't love me!"

"Didn't love you! How can you say that?"

"Because of the way you treated me."

"I loved you very much, Janna," he said softly.

"You didn't!" she shrilled, throwing back her head. "Just look at the way you treated me. You kept me around all day, every day, doing *housework, cooking, sitting.* Marvin, I could *feel* myself aging. Day after day, the same weary, stupid routine. And most of the time, when you came home, you were too tired to even notice me. All you could talk about was your stupid robots! I was being wasted, Marvin, *wasted!*"

It suddenly occurred to Goodman that his wife was unhinged. Very gently he said, "But, Janna, that's how life is. A husband and wife settle into a companionable situation. They age together side by side. It can't all be high spots—"

"But of course it can! Try to understand, Marvin. It can, on Tranai— for a woman!"

"It's impossible," Goodman said.

"On Tranai, a woman expects a life of enjoyment and pleasure. It's her right, just as men have their rights. She expects to come out of stasis and find a little party prepared, or a walk in the moonlight, or a swim, or a movie." She began to cry again. "But *you* were so smart. *You* had to change it. I should have known better than to trust a Terran."

The other man sighed and lighted a cigarette.

"I know you can't help being an alien, Marvin," Janna said.

"But I do want you to understand. Love isn't everything. A woman must be practical, too. The way things were going, I would have been an old woman while all my friends were still young."

"Still young?" Goodman repeated blankly.

"Of course," the man said. "A woman doesn't age in the derrsin field."

"But the whole thing is ghastly," said Goodman. "My wife would still be a young woman when I was old."

"That's just when you'd appreciate a young woman," Janna said.

"But how about you?" Goodman asked. "Would you appreciate an old man?"

"He still doesn't understand," the man said.

"Marvin, *try.* Isn't it clear yet? Throughout your life, you would have a young and beautiful woman whose only desire would be to please you. And when you died—don't look shocked, dear; everybody dies—when you died, I would still be young, and by law I'd inherit all your money."

"I'm beginning to see," Goodman said. "I suppose that's another accepted phase of Tranaian life—the wealthy young widow who can pursue her own pleasures."

"Naturally. In this way, everything is for the best for everybody. The man has a young wife whom he sees only when he wishes. He has his complete freedom and a nice home as well. The woman is relieved of all the dullness of ordinary living and, while she can still enjoy it, is well provided for."

"You should have told me," Goodman complained.

"I thought you knew," Janna said, "since you thought you had a better way. But I can see that you would never have understood, because you're so naïve—though I must admit it's one of your charms." She smiled wistfully. "Besides, if I told you, I would never have met Rondo."

The man bowed slightly. "I was leaving samples of Greah's Confections. You can imagine my surprise when I found this lovely young woman *out of stasis*. I mean it was like a storybook tale come true. One never expects old legends to happen, so you must admit that there's a certain appeal when they do."

"Do you love him?" Goodman asked heavily.

"Yes," said Janna. "Rondo cares for me. He's going to keep me in stasis long enough to make up for the time I've lost. It's a sacrifice on his part, but Rondo has a generous nature."

"If that's how it is," Goodman said glumly, "I certainly won't stand in your way. I am a civilized being, after all. You may have a divorce."

He folded his arms across his chest, feeling quite noble. But he was dimly aware that his decision stemmed not so much from nobility as from a sudden, violent distaste for all things Tranaian.

"We have no divorce on Tranai," Rondo said.

"No?" Goodman felt a cold chill run down his spine.

A blaster appeared in Rondo's hand. "It would be too unsettling, you know, if people were always swapping around. There's only one way to change a marital status."

"But this is revolting!" Goodman blurted, backing away. "It's against all decency!"

"Not if the wife desires it. And that, by the by, is another excellent reason for keeping one's spouse in stasis. Have I your permission, my dear?"

"Forgive me, Marvin," Janna said. She closed her eyes. "Yes!"

Rondo leveled the blaster. Without a moment's hesitation, Goodman dived head-first out the nearest window. Rondo's shot fanned right over him.

"See here!" Rondo called. "Show some spirit, man. Stand up to it!"

Goodman had landed heavily on his shoulder. He was up at once, sprinting, and Rondo's second shot scorched his arm. Then he ducked behind a house and was momentarily safe. He didn't stop to think about it. Running for all he was worth, he headed for the spaceport.

Fortunately, a ship was preparing for blastoff and took him to g'Moree. From there he wired to Tranai for his funds and bought passage to Higastomeritreia, where the authorities accused him of being a Ding spy. The charge couldn't stick, since the Dingans were an amphibious race, and Goodman almost drowned proving to everyone's satisfaction that he could breathe only air.

A drone transport took him to the double planet Mvanti, past Seves, Olgo, and Mi. He hired a bush pilot to take him to Bellismoranti, where the influence of Terra began. From there, a local spaceline transported him past the Galactic Whirl and, after stopping at Tung-Bradar IV, Oyster, Lekung, Pankang, and Inchang, arrived at Machang.

His money was now gone, but he was practically next door to Terra, as astronomical distances go. He was able to work his passage to Oumé, and from Oumé to Legis II. There the Interstellar Travelers Aid Society arranged a berth for him and at last he arrived back on Earth.

Goodman has settled down in Seakirk, New Jersey, where a man is perfectly safe as long as he pays his taxes. He holds the post of Chief Robotic Technician for the Seakirk Construction Corporation and has married a small, dark, quiet girl, who obviously adores him, although he rarely lets her out of the house.

He and old Captain Savage go frequently to Eddie's Moonlight Bar, drink Tranai Specials, and talk of Tranai the Blessed, where The Way has been found and Man is no longer bound to The Wheel. On such occasions, Goodman complains of a touch of space malaria—because of it, he can never go back into space, can never return to Tranai.

There is always an admiring audience on these nights.

Goodman has recently organized, with Captain Savage's help, the Seakirk League to Take the Vote from Women. They are its only members, but as Goodman puts it, when did that ever stop a crusader?

THE SKAG CASTLE

Within the offices of the AAA Ace Interplanetary Decontamination Service, a gloomy silence reigned. By the faint light that filtered through the dirty windows, Richard Gregor was playing a new form of solitaire. It involved three packs of cards, six jokers, a set of dice, and a slide rule. The game was extremely complicated, maddeningly difficult, and it always came out if you persisted long enough.

His partner, Mike Arnold, had swept his desk clear of its usual clutter of crusty test tubes and unpaid bills, and was now dozing fitfully on its stained surface.

Business couldn't have been worse.

There was a tentative knock on the door.

Quickly Gregor pushed his playing cards, dice, and slide rule into a drawer. Arnold rolled off his desk like a cat and flipped open Volume Two of Terkstiller's *Decontamination Modes on X-32* (Omega) *Worlds,* which he had been using for a pillow.

"Come in," Gregor called out.

The door opened and a girl entered. She was young, slender, dark-haired, and extremely pretty. Her eyes were gray, and they contained a hint of fear. Her lips were unsmiling.

She looked around the unkempt office. "Is this the AAA Ace?" she inquired tentatively.

"It certainly is," Gregor assured her. "Won't you sit down? We always keep the lights off. Much more restful, don't you think?"

And, he thought, quite necessary, since Con Mazda had shut off their power last week for nonpayment of a trifling bill.

"I suppose it is," the girl said, sitting in the cavernous client's chair. She surveyed the office again. "You people *are* planetary decontaminationists, aren't you? Not taxidermists or undertakers?"

"Don't let the office fool you," Arnold said. "We are the best, and the most reasonable. No planet too big, no asteroid too small."

"Maybe I've come to the right place after all," the girl said with a wan but enchanting smile. "You see, I don't have much money."

Gregor nodded sympathetically. AAA Ace's clients never had much money.

"But I do have a tiny little planet that needs decontaminating," the girl said. "It's the most wonderful place in the whole galaxy. But the job might be dangerous."

"Dangerous?" Arnold asked.

The girl nodded and glanced nervously at the door. "I don't even know if I'm safe here. Are you armed?"

Gregor found a rusty letter opener. Arnold hefted a bronze paperweight cast in the shape of the spaceship *Constitution*—a beautiful piece of workmanship.

Somewhat relieved, the girl went on. "I'm Myra Branch Ryan. I was on my little planet, minding my own business, when suddenly this Scarb appeared before me, leering horribly—"

"This what?"

"Perhaps I should start at the beginning," Myra Ryan said. "A few months ago my Uncle Jim died and left me a small planet and a Hemstet 4 spaceship. The planet is Coelle, in the Gelsors system. Uncle Jim bought the planet fifteen years ago for a vacation home. He had just gotten it into shape when he was called away on business. What with one thing and another, he never returned. Naturally I went out there as soon as I could."

Myra's face brightened as she remembered her first impressions.

"Coelle was very small but perfect. It had a complete air system, the best gravity money can buy, and an artesian well. Uncle Jim had planted several orchards, and berry bushes on the hillsides, and long grass everywhere. There was even a little lake.

"But Coelle's outstanding feature was the Skag Castle. Uncle Jim hadn't touched this, for the castle was old beyond belief. It was thought to have been built by the Skag Horde, who, according to legend, occupied the universe before the coming of man."

The partners nodded. Everyone had heard of the Skag Horde. A whole literature had sprung up around the scanty evidence of their existence. It was pretty well established that they had been reptile-evolved, and had mastered spaceflight. But legend went further than this. The Skag Horde was supposed to have known the Old Lore, a strange mixture of science and witchcraft. This, according to the legends, gave them powers beyond the conception of man, powers sprung from the evil counterforces of the universe.

Their disappearance, millennia before *Homo sapiens* descended from the treetops, had never been satisfactorily explained.

"I fell in love with Coelle," Myra continued, "and the old Skag Castle just made it perfect."

"But where does the decontaminating come in?" Gregor asked. "Were there natives on Coelle? Animals? Germs?"

"No, nothing like that," Myra said. "Here's what happened..."

She had been on her planet a week, exploring its groves and orchards, and wandering around the Skag Castle. Then, one evening, sitting in the castle's great library, she sensed something wrong. There was an unearthly stillness in the air, as though the planet were waiting for something to happen. Angrily she tried to shake off the mood. It was just nerves, she told herself. After she put a few more lights in the halls, and changed the blood-red draperies to something gayer...

Then she heard a dull rumbling noise, like the sound of a giant walking. It seemed to come from somewhere in the solid granite upon which the castle rested.

She stood completely still, waiting. The floor vibrated, a vase crept off a table and shattered on the flagstones. And then the Scarb appeared before her, leering horribly.

There was no mistaking it. According to legend, the Scarbs had been the wizard-scientists of the vanished Skag Horde—powerful reptiles dressed in cloaks of gray and purple. The creature that stood before Myra was over nine feet tall, with tiny atrophied wings and a horn growing from its forehead.

The Scarb said, "Earthwoman, go home!"

She almost fainted. The Scarb continued, "Know, rash human, that this planet of Coelle is the ancestral home of the Skag Horde, and this Castle is the original Skag Burrow. Here the spirit of the Skag still lives, through the intervention of Grad, Ieele, and other accursed powers of the universe. Quit this sacred planet at once, foolish human, or I, the Undead Scarb, will exact revenge."

And with that, it vanished.

"What did you do?" Gregor asked.

"Nothing," Myra said with a little laugh. "I just couldn't believe it. I thought I must have had an hallucination, and everything would be all right if I just got control of myself. Twice more that week I heard the underground noises. And then the Scarb appeared again. He said, 'You have been warned, Earthwoman. Now beware the wrath of the Undead Scarb!' After that, I got out as fast as I could."

Myra sniffed, took out a little handkerchief, and wiped her eyes.

"So you see," she said, "my little planet needs decontaminating. Or possibly exorcising."

"Miss Ryan," Gregor said very gently, "I don't mean to be insulting, but have you—ah—did you ever think of consulting a psychiatrist?"

The girl stood up angrily. "Do you think I'm crazy?"

"Not at all," Gregor said soothingly. "But remember, you yourself spoke of the possibility of hallucination. After all, a deserted planet, an ancient castle, these legends—which, by the way, have very little basis in fact—all would tend to—"

"You're right, of course," Myra said with a strange little smile. "But how do you explain this?" She opened her handbag and spilled three cans of film and a spool of magnetic tape onto Gregor's desk.

"I was able to *record* some of those hallucinations," she said.

The partners were momentarily speechless.

"Something is going on in that castle," Myra said earnestly. "It calls itself an Undead Scarb. Won't you get rid of it for me?"

Gregor groaned and rubbed his forehead. He hated to refuse anyone as beautiful as Miss Ryan, and they certainly could use the money. But this was not, in all honesty, a job for decontaminators. This looked like a psychic case, and psychic phenomena were notoriously tricky.

"Miss Ryan—" he began, but Arnold broke in.

"We would be delighted to take your case," he said. To Gregor he gave an I'll-explain-later wink.

"Oh, how wonderful!" Myra said. "How soon will you be ready?"

"As a rule," Arnold said, "we need a few weeks' notice. But for you—" He beamed fatuously. "For you, we are going to clear our calendar, postpone all other cases, and begin at once."

Gregor's long, sad face was unhappier than ever. "Perhaps you've forgotten," he told his partner, "Joe the Interstellar Junkman has our spaceship, due to a trifling bill we neglected to pay. I'm sorry, Miss Ryan—"

"Call me Myra," Myra said. "That's all right, my Hemstet 4 is fueled and ready to go."

"Then we'll leave tonight," Arnold said. "Have no fear, Myra. Your little planet is safe in our hands. We'll radio you as soon as—"

"Radio nothing," Myra said. "I'm going along. I wouldn't miss this for anything."

They arranged for Myra to obtain the clearances and meet them back at the office. As she walked to the door, Arnold said, "By the way, why did you ask if we were armed?"

She was silent for a moment. Then she said, "Since I came back to Terra, something's been following me. Something wearing gray and purple. I'm afraid it might be the Undead Scarb."

She closed the door gently behind her.

As soon as she was gone, Gregor shouted, "Have you gone completely out of your mind? Skags, Undead Scarbs—"

"She's beautiful," Arnold said dreamily.

"Are you listening to me? How are we supposed to decontaminate a haunted planet?"

"Coelle isn't haunted."

"What makes you think not?"

"Because the original Skag Burrow, according to the very best evidence, was on the planet Duerité, *not* on Coelle. A Skag ghost would know that. Ergo, what she saw was no ghost."

Gregor frowned thoughtfully.

"Mmm. You think someone wants to frighten her off Coelle?"

"Obviously," Arnold said.

"But the planet's been deserted for years. Why would someone take an interest in it now?"

"I'm going to find out."

"Sounds like a job for a detective," Gregor told him.

"Perhaps you've forgotten," Arnold said, "I am an honor graduate of the Hepburn School of Scientific Detection."

"That was only a six weeks' correspondence course."

"So what? Detection is simply the rational application of logic. Moreover, detection and decontamination are essentially the same thing. Decontamination just carries the process of detection to its logical conclusion."

"I hope you know what you're talking about," Gregor said. "What about this gray and purple creature that's been following Myra around?"

"No such thing. A case of overwrought nerves," Arnold diagnosed. "The poor girl needs someone to protect her. Me, for example."

"Yeah. But who's going to protect you?"

Arnold didn't bother answering, and the partners began to make their preparations.

II

They spent the rest of the day loading the Hemstet with various devices they had managed to keep out of hock. Gregor invested in a secondhand Steng needler. It seemed a good weapon against the more palpable forms of wizardry. After a quick dinner at the Milky Way Diner they started back to their office.

After they had walked several blocks, Arnold said, "I think we're being followed."

"You have overwrought nerves," Gregor diagnosed.

"He was in the diner, too," Arnold said. "And I'm sure I saw him at the spaceport."

Gregor glanced over his shoulder. Half a block behind he saw a man sauntering along and glancing idly into store windows, his attitude studiously casual.

The partners turned down a street. The man followed. They circled and returned to the avenue they had been on. The man was still there, keeping half a block between them.

"Have you noticed what he's wearing?" Arnold asked, wiping perspiration from his forehead.

Gregor looked again and saw that the man had on a gray suit and a purple tie—Skag colors.

"Hmm," Gregor said. "Do you suppose an Undead Scarb—if there were such a thing—could take on human form?"

"I'd hate to find out," Arnold said. "You'd better get that needler ready."

"I left it on the ship."

"That's just fine," Arnold said bitterly. "Just perfect. Someone—or some*thing*—is following us, probably with murderous intent, and you leave your blaster on the ship."

"Steady," Gregor said. "Maybe we can shake him."

They continued walking. Gregor looked back and saw that the man—or Scarb—was still there. He was walking more rapidly, closing the gap between them.

But coming down the street now was a taxi, its flag up.

They hailed it and climbed in. The man—or Scarb—looked around frantically for another cab, but there was none in sight. When they drove off he was standing on the curb, glaring at them, his purple tie slightly askew.

Myra Ryan was waiting for them at the office. She nodded when they told her about the follower.

"I warned you it might be dangerous," she said. "You can still back out, you know."

"What'll you do then?" Arnold asked.

"I'll go back to Coelle," Myra said. "No Skags are going to keep me off my planet."

"We're going," Arnold said, gazing tenderly at her. "You know we wouldn't desert you, Myra."

"Of course not," Gregor said wearily.

At that moment the door opened, and in walked a man wearing a gray suit and a purple tie.

"The Scarb!" Arnold gasped, and reached for his paperweight.

"That's no Scarb," Myra said calmly. "That's Ross Jameson. Hello, Ross."

Jameson was a tall, beautifully groomed man in his early thirties, with a handsome, impatient face and hard eyes.

"Myra," he said, "have you gone completely insane?"

"I don't think so, Ross," Myra said sweetly.

"Are you really going to Coelle with these charlatans?"

Gregor stepped forward. "Were you following us?"

"You're damned right I was," Jameson said belligerently.

"I don't know who you are," Gregor said, "but—"

"I'm Miss Ryan's fiancé," Jameson said, "and I'm not going to let her go through with this ridiculous project. Myra, from what you've told me, this planet of yours sounds dangerous. Why don't you forget about it and marry me?"

"I want to live on Coelle," Myra said in a dangerously quiet voice. "I want to live on my own little planet."

Jameson shook his head. "We've been through this a thousand times. Darling, you can't seriously expect me to give up my business and move to this little mudball with you. I've got my work—"

"And I've got my mudball," Myra said. "It's my very own mudball, and I want to live there."

"With the Skags?"

"I thought you didn't believe in that sort of thing," Myra said.

"I don't. But some trickery is going on, and I don't like to see you involved. It's probably that crazy hermit. There's no telling what he'll try next. Myra, won't you *please*—"

"No!" Myra said. "I'm going to Coelle!"

"Then I'm going with you,"

"You are not," Myra said coldly.

"I've already arranged it with my staff," Jameson said. "You'll need someone to protect you on that ridiculous planet, and you can't expect much from these two." He glared contemptuously at Gregor and Arnold.

"Maybe you didn't understand me," Myra said very quietly. "You are not coming, Ross."

Jameson's firm face sagged, and his eyes grew worried. "Myra," he said, "please let me come. If anything happened to you, I'd—I don't know what I'd do. Please, Myra?"

There was no doubting the sincerity in his voice. When Jameson dropped his commanding voice and lowered the imposing thrust of his shoulders, he became a very appealing young man, quite obviously in love.

Myra said softly, "All right, Ross. And—thanks."

Gregor cleared his throat loudly. "We blast off in two hours."

"Fine," Jameson said, taking Myra's arm. "We have time for a drink, dear."

Arnold said, "Pardon me, Mr. Jameson. How does it happen you are wearing gray and purple—the Skag Colors?"

"Are they?" Jameson asked. "Pure coincidence. I've owned this tie for years."

"And who is the hermit?"

"I thought you geniuses knew everything," Jameson said with a nasty grin. "See you at the ship."

After they had gone, a deep, gloomy silence hung over the office. Finally Arnold said, "So she's engaged."

"So it would seem," Gregor said. "But not married," he added sympathetically.

"No, she's not married," Arnold said, becoming cheerful again. "And Jameson is obviously the wrong man for her. I'm sure Myra wouldn't marry a liar."

"Of course she wouldn't marry a—Huh?"

"Didn't you notice? That purple tie he's 'owned for years' was brand new. I think we'll keep an eye on Mr. Jameson."

Gregor gazed at his partner with admiration. "That's a very clever observation."

"The process of detection," Arnold said sententiously, "is merely the accumulation of minute discrepancies and infinitesimal inconsistencies, which are immediately apparent to the trained eye."

Gregor and the trained eye put the office into order. At eleven o'clock they met Jameson and Myra at the ship, and without further incident they departed for Coelle.

III

Ross Jameson was president and chief engineer of Jameson Electronics, a small but growing concern he had inherited from his father. It was a great responsibility for so young a man, and Ross had adopted a brusque, overbearing manner to avoid any hint of indecisiveness. But whenever he was able to forget his exalted position he was a pleasant enough fellow, and a good sport in facing the many little discomforts of interstellar travel.

Myra's Hemstet 4 was old and hogged out of shape by repeated high-gravity takeoffs. The ship had developed a disconcerting habit of springing leaks in the most inaccessible places, which Arnold and Gregor had to locate and patch. The ship's astrogation system wasn't to be trusted either, and Jameson spent considerable time figuring out a way of controlling the automatics manually.

When Coelle's little sun was finally in sight and the ship was in its deceleration orbit, the four of them were able, for the first time, to share a meal together.

"What's the story on this hermit?" Gregor asked over coffee.

"You must have heard of him," Jameson said. "He calls himself Edward the Hermit, and he's written a book."

"The book is *Dreams on Kerma,*" Myra filled in. "It was a bestseller last year."

"Oh, *that* hermit," Gregor said, and Arnold nodded.

They had read the hermit's book, along with several thousand others, while sitting in their office waiting for business. *Dreams on Kerma* had been a sort of spatial Robinson Crusoe. Edward's struggles with his environment, and with himself, had made exciting reading. Because of his lack of scientific knowledge, the hermit had made many blunders. But he had persevered, and created a home for himself out of the virgin wilderness of the planet Kerma.

The young misanthrope's calm decision to give up the society of mankind and devote his life to the contemplation of nature and the universe—the Eternals, as he called them—had struck some responsive chord in millions of harried men and women. A few had been sufficiently inspired to seek out their own hermitages. Almost without exception they returned to Terra in six months or a year, sadder but wiser. Solitude, they discovered, made better reading than living.

"But what has he got to do with Coelle?" Arnold asked.

"Coelle is the second planet of the Gelsors system," Jameson said. "Kerma is the third planet, and the hermit is its only inhabitant."

Gregor said, "I still don't see—"

"I guess it was my fault," Myra said. "You see, the hermit's book inspired me. It was what decided me to live on Coelle, even if I had to do it alone." She threw Jameson a cutting glance. "Do you remember his chapter on the joy of possessing an entire planet? I can't describe what that did to me. I felt—"

"I still don't see the connection," Gregor said.

"I'm coming around to it," Myra said. "When I found out that Edward the Hermit and I were neighbors, astronomically speaking, I decided to speak to him. I just wanted to tell him how much his book meant to me. So I radioed him from Coelle."

"He has a radio?" Arnold asked,

"Of course," Myra said. "He keeps it so he can listen to the absurd voices of mankind, and laugh himself to sleep."

"Oh. Go on."

"Well, when he heard I was going to live on Coelle, he became furious. Said he couldn't stand having a human so close."

"That's ridiculous," Arnold said. "The planets are millions of miles apart."

"I told him that. But he started shouting and screaming at me. He said mankind wouldn't leave him alone. Real-estate brokers were trying to talk him into selling his mineral rights, and a travel agency was going to route its ships within ten thousand miles of the upper atmosphere of his planet. And then, to top it all, I come along and move in practically on his doorstep."

"And then he threatened her," Jameson said.

"I guess it was a threat," Myra said. "He told me to get out of the Gelsors system, or he wouldn't be responsible for what happened."

"Did he say *what* would happen?" Arnold asked.

"No. He just hinted it would be pretty extreme."

Jameson said, "I think it's apparent that the man's unbalanced. After the talk, these so-called Skag incidents began. There must be a connection."

"It's possible," Arnold said judiciously.

"I just can't believe it," Myra said, gazing pensively out a port. "His book was so beautiful. And his picture on the book jacket—he looked so soulful."

"Hah!" Jameson said. "Anyone who'd live alone on an empty planet *must* be off his rocker."

Myra gave him a venomous look. And then the radar alarm went off. They were about to land on Coelle…

The Skag Castle dominated Coelle. Built of an almost indestructible gray stone, the castle sprawled across the curved land like a prehistoric monster crouched over Lilliput. Its towers and battlements soared past the narrow limits of the planet's atmosphere and the uppermost spires were lost in haze. As they approached, the black slit windows seemed to stare menacingly at them.

"Cozy little place," Gregor commented.

"Isn't it wonderful?" Myra said. "Come on. I'll show you around."

The three men looked at the castle, then at each other.

"Just the ground floor," Arnold begged.

Myra wanted to show them *everything*. It wasn't every girl who became the owner of an alien birthplace, period house, and haunted castle, all rolled into one. But she settled for a few of the main attractions: the library—containing ten thousand Skag scrolls that no one could read—the Worship Chamber of Ieele, and the Grand Torture Room.

Dinner was prepared by the auto-cook Uncle Jim had thoughtfully installed, and later they had brandy on the terrace, under the stars. Myra gave them all bedrooms on the second floor, to avoid as much climbing as possible. They retired, planning to begin the investigation early in the morning.

The partners shared a bedroom the size of a small soccer field, with bronze death masks of Scarb princes leering from the wall. Arnold kicked off his shoes, flopped into bed, and was asleep immediately.

Gregor paced around for a few minutes, smoked a last cigarette, snapped off the light, and climbed into his bed. He was on the verge of sleep, when suddenly he sat upright. He thought he had heard a dull rumbling noise, like the sound of a giant walking underneath the castle. Nerves, he told himself.

Then the rumbling came again, the floor shook, and the death masks clattered angrily against the wall.

In another moment the noise had subsided.

"Did you hear it?" Gregor whispered.

"Of course I heard it," Arnold said crossly. "It almost shook me out of bed."

"What do you think?"

"It could be a form of poltergeist," Arnold answered, "although I doubt it. We'll explore the cellar tomorrow."

"I don't think this place has any cellar," Gregor said.

"It hasn't? Good! That would clinch it."

"What? What are you talking about?"

"I'll have to accumulate a bit more data before I can make a positive statement," Arnold said smugly.

"Have you any idea what you're talking about? Or are you just making it up as you go along? Because if—"

"Look!"

Gregor turned and saw a gray and purple light in one corner of the room. It pulsed weirdly, throwing fantastic shadows across the bronze death masks. Slowly it approached them. As it drew nearer they could make out the reptilian outlines of a Skag, and through him they could see the walls of the room.

Gregor fumbled under his pillow, found the needler, and fired. The charge went *through* the Skag, and pocked a neat three-inch groove in the stone wall.

The Skag stood before them, its cloak swirling, an expression of extreme disapproval on its face. And then, without a sound, it was gone.

As soon as he could move, Gregor snapped on the light. Arnold was smiling faintly, staring at the place where the Skag had been.

"Very interesting," Arnold said. "Very interesting indeed."

"What is?"

"Do you remember how Myra described the Undead Scarb?"

"Sure. She said it was nine feet tall, had little wings, and—oh, I think I see."

"Precisely," Arnold said. "This Skag or Scarb was no more than four feet in height, without wings."

"I suppose there could be two types," Gregor said dubiously. "But what bearing does this have on the underground noises? The whole thing is getting ridiculously complicated. Surely you must realize that."

"Complication is frequently a key to solution," Arnold said. "Simplicity alone is baffling. Complexity, on the other hand, implies the presence of a self-contradictory logic structure. Once the incomprehensibles are reconciled and the extraneous factors canceled, the murderer stands revealed in the glaring light of rational inevitability."

"What are you talking about?" Gregor shouted. "There wasn't any murder here!"

"I was quoting from Lesson Three in the Hepburn School for Scientific Detection Correspondence Course. And I know there was no murder. I was just speaking in general."

"But what do you think is going on?" Gregor asked.

"Something funny is going on," Arnold said. He smiled knowingly, turned over, and went to sleep.

294 ROBERT SHECKLEY

Gregor snapped out the light. Arnold's course, he remembered, had cost ten dollars plus a coupon from *Horror Crime Magazine*. His partner had certainly received his money's worth.

There were no further incidents that night.

IV

Bright and early in the morning, the partners were awakened by Myra pounding on their door.

"A spaceship is landing!" she called.

Hurriedly they dressed and came down, meeting Jameson on the stairs. Outside they saw that a small spacer had just put down, and its occupant was climbing out.

"More trouble," Jameson growled.

The new arrival hardly looked like trouble. He was middle-aged, short, and partially bald. He was dressed in a severely conservative business suit, and he carried a briefcase. His features were quiet and reserved.

"Permit me to introduce myself," he said. "I am Frank Olson, a representative of Transstellar Mining. My company is contemplating an expansion into this territory, to take advantage of the new Terra-to-Propexis space lane. I am doing the initial survey. We need planets upon which we can obtain mineral rights."

Myra shook her head. "Not interested. But why don't you try Kerma?" she asked with a sly smile.

"I just came from Kerma," Olson said. "I had what I considered a very attractive proposition for this Edward the Hermit fellow."

"I bet he booted you out on your ear," Gregor said.

"No, as a matter of fact, he wasn't there."

"*Wasn't there?*" Myra gasped. "Are you sure?"

"Reasonably so," Olson said. "His camp was deserted."

"Perhaps he went on a hike," Arnold said. "After all, he has an entire planet to wander over."

"I hardly think so. His big ship was gone, and a spaceship is hardly a suitable vehicle for wandering around a planet."

"Very clever deduction," Arnold said enviously.

"Not that it matters," Olson said. "I thought I'd ask him, just for the record." He turned to Myra. "You are the owner of this planet?"

"I am."

"Perhaps you would be interested in hearing our terms?"

"No!" Myra said.

"Wait," Jameson said. "You should at least hear him."

"I'm not interested," Myra said. "I'm not going to have anyone digging up *my* little planet."

"I don't even know if your planet has anything worth digging for," Olson said. "My company is simply trying to find out which planets are available."

"They'll never get this one," Myra said.

"Well, it isn't too important," Olson said. "There are many planets. Too many," he added with a sigh. "I won't disturb you people any longer. Thank you for your time." He turned, his shoulders slumping, and trudged back to his ship.

"Won't you stay for dinner?" Myra called impulsively. "You must get pretty tired eating canned food in that spaceship."

"I do," Olson said with a rueful smile. "But I really can't stay. I hate to make a blastoff after dark."

"Then stay until morning," Myra said. "We'd be glad to put you up."

"I wouldn't want to be any trouble—"

"I've got about two hundred rooms in there," Myra said, pointing at the Skag Castle. "I'm sure we can squeeze you in somewhere."

"You're very kind," Olson said. "I—I believe I will!"

"Hope you aren't nervous about Undead Scarbs," Jameson said.

"What?"

"This planet seems to be haunted," Arnold told him. "By the ghost or ghosts of an extinct reptilian race."

"Oh, come now," Olson said. "You're pulling my leg. Aren't you?"

"Not at all," Gregor said.

Olson grinned to show that no one was taking *him* in. "I believe I'll tidy up," he said.

"Dinner's at six," Myra said.

"I'll be there. And thank you again." He returned to his ship.

"Now what?" Jameson asked.

"Now we are going to do some searching," Arnold said. He turned to Gregor. "Bring the portable detector. And we'll need a few shovels."

"What are we looking for?" Jameson asked.

"You'll see when we find it," Arnold said. He smiled insidiously and added, "I thought *you* knew everything."

Coelle was a very small planet, and in five hours Arnold found what he was looking for. In a little valley there was a long mound. Near it, the detector buzzed gaily.

"We will dig here," Arnold said.

"I bet I know what it is," Myra told them. "It's a burial mound, isn't it? And when you've uncovered it, we'll find row upon row of Undead Scarbs, their hands crossed upon their chests, waiting for the full moon. And we'll put stakes through their hearts, won't we?"

Gregor's shovel clanged against something metallic.

"Is that the tomb?" Myra asked.

But when they had thrown aside more dirt, they saw that it was not a tomb. It was the top of a spaceship.

"What's *that* doing here?" Jameson asked.

"Isn't it apparent?" Arnold said. "The hermit is not on his own planet. We know his feelings about Coelle. Naturally he would be here."

"And naturally he wouldn't leave his spaceship in plain sight!" Gregor said.

"So he's here," Jameson said slowly. "But where? Where on the planet?"

"Almost undoubtedly he's somewhere in the Skag Castle," Arnold said.

Jameson turned in triumph to Myra. "You see? I told you it was that crazy hermit! Now we have to catch him."

"I don't think that will be necessary," Arnold said.

"Why not?"

"At the proper time, Edward the Hermit will appear," Arnold said coolly. And they couldn't get another word out of him.

That evening the auto-cook surpassed itself. Frank Olson was a little stiff at first; but he unbent over the brandy, and regaled them with stories of the planets he had touched upon in his search for mining properties. Jameson wanted to search the castle and drag the hermit out of his hiding place. Sullenly, he yielded when Arnold pointed out the impossibility of four people covering several hundred rooms and passageways.

Later they played bridge. Arnold's mind was elsewhere, however, and after he'd trumped his partner's perfectly good trick a second time, they all decided to call it a night.

V

An hour later, Arnold whispered across the bedroom, "Are you asleep?"

"No," Gregor whispered back.

"Get dressed, then, but leave your shoes off."

"What's up?"

"I think we are going to solve the mystery of Skag Castle tonight. Mind if I borrow your needler?"

Gregor gave it to him. They tiptoed out of the bedroom and down the great central staircase. They found a vantage point behind an enameled suit of Skag armor, from which they could watch without being seen. For half an hour there was silence.

Then they saw a shape at the top of the landing. Soundlessly it crept down the staircase and glided across the hall.

"Who is it?" Gregor whispered.

"Shh!" Arnold whispered back.

They followed the shape into the library. There it hesitated, as though uncertain what to do next.

At that moment the underground rumblings began, shattering the silence. The shape jerked abruptly, startled. A light appeared in its hand. By its feeble glow, the partners recognized Frank Olson.

With his tiny flashlight, Olson searched one library wall. Finally he pressed a panel. It slid back, revealing a small switchboard. Olson turned two dials. The underground noises stopped at once.

Wiping his forehead, Olson listened for several moments. Then he snapped off his light and crept noiselessly back to the hall, up the stairs, and into his bedroom.

Arnold pulled Gregor back behind the enameled armor.

"That ties it," Gregor said. "There's our Undead Scarb."

Arnold shook his head.

"Of course he is," Gregor said. "He must have planned this in order to frighten Myra off the planet. Then he could buy the mineral rights for next to nothing."

"Seems reasonable, doesn't it?" Arnold said. "But you've got a lot to learn about detection. In cases of this sort, what's reasonable is never right. The apparent solution is always wrong. Invariably!"

"Why look for complications that aren't there?" Gregor asked "We *saw* Olson go to that hidden switchboard. We *heard* the noises stop as soon as he touched the controls. Or was that pure coincidence?"

"No, there's a relationship."

"Hmm. Maybe Olson isn't a mining representative at all. Do you think someone hired him? Edward the Hermit, maybe? As a matter of fact, perhaps he *is* Edward the Hermit!"

"Shh," Arnold whispered. "Look!"

Gregor's eyes had become accustomed to the darkness. This time he recognized the man at once. It was Jameson, tiptoeing down the stairs.

Jameson walked to one side of the hall and turned on a small flashlight. By its light he found a panel in the wall, and pressed it. The panel slid back, revealing a small switchboard. Jameson breathed heavily and reached for the dials. Before he could touch them he heard a noise, and stepped quickly back.

A figure stepped out of the darkness. It was about six feet in height, and its face was hideous and reptilian. A long, spiked tail dragged behind it, and its fingers were webbed.

"I am the Undead Scarb!" it said to Jameson.

"Awk!" Jameson said, backing away.

"You must leave this planet," the Scarb said. "You must leave at once— or your life is forfeit!"

"Sure," Jameson said hastily. "Sure I will. Just stay away. We'll leave, Myra and I—"

"Not Miss Ryan. The Earthwoman has shown a reverent understanding for the Old Lore, and for the spirit of Skag. But you, Ross Jameson, have profaned the Sacred Burrow."

The Scarb moved closer, its webbed fingers splayed. Jameson backed into a wall, and suddenly pulled a blaster.

At that moment Arnold snapped on the lights. He shouted, "Don't shoot, Ross. You'd be arrested for murder." He turned to Gregor. "Now let's get a close look at this Scarb."

The Undead Scarb put one hand on top of his scaled head and pulled. The terrible head peeled off, revealing beneath it the youthful features of Edward the Hermit.

In a short time everyone was assembled in the great hall. Olson looked sleepy and disgruntled. He was fully dressed, as was Jameson. Myra was wearing a plaid wool bathrobe, and she was staring with interest at Edward the Hermit.

Edward looked younger than the picture on the jacket of his book. He had peeled off the rest of his Scarb disguise, and was wearing patched jeans and a gray sweatshirt. He was deeply tanned, his blond hair was cropped short, and he would have been good-looking if it weren't for the expression of fear and apprehension on his face.

After Arnold had summed up the events of the night, Myra was completely bewildered.

"It just doesn't make sense," she said. "Mr. Olson was turning Skag noises on and off, Ross had a switchboard, and Edward the Hermit was disguised as a Scarb. What's the explanation? Were they *all* trying to drive me from Coelle?"

"No," Arnold said. "Mr. Olson's part in this was purely accidental. Those underground noises weren't designed to frighten you. Were they, Mr. Olson?"

Olson smiled ruefully. "They certainly were not. As a matter of fact, I came here to stop them."

"I don't understand," Myra said.

"I'm afraid," Arnold said, "that Mr. Olson's company has been engaged in a bit of illegal mining." He smiled modestly. "Of course I recognized the characteristic sound of a Gens-Wilhem automatic oreblaster at once."

"I *told* them to install mufflers," Olson said. "Well, the full explanation is this. Coelle was surveyed seventeen years ago, and an excellent deposit of sligastrium was found. Transstellar Mining offered the then owner, James McKinney, a very good price for mineral rights. He refused, but after a short stay he left Coelle for good. A company official decided to extract a little ore anyhow, since this planet was so far out, and there were no local observers. You'd be surprised how common a practice that is."

"I think it's despicable," Myra said.

"Don't blame me," Olson said. "I didn't set up the operation."

"Then those underground noises—" Gregor said.

"Were merely the sounds of mining apparatus," Olson told them. "You caught us by surprise, Miss Ryan. We never really expected the planet to be inhabited again. I was sent, posthaste, to turn off the machines. Just half an hour ago I had my first opportunity."

"What if I hadn't asked you to stay overnight?" Myra asked.

"I would have faked a blown gasket or something." He sighed and sat down. "It was a pretty good operation while it lasted."

"That takes care of the noises," Jameson said. "The rest we know. This hermit came here, hid his spaceship, and disguised himself as a Scarb. He had already threatened Myra. Now he was going to frighten her into leaving Coelle."

"That's not true!" Edward shouted. "I—I was—"

"Was what?" Gregor asked.

The hermit clamped his mouth shut and turned away.

Arnold said, "*You* found that secret panel, Ross."

"Of course I did. You're not the only one who can detect. I knew there were no such things as Undead Scarbs and Skag ghosts. From what Myra told me, the whole thing sounded like an illusion to me, probably a modulated wave-pattern effect. So I looked around for a control board. I found it this afternoon."

"Why didn't you tell us?" Gregor asked.

"Because I consider you a pair of incompetents," Ross said contemptuously. "I came down this evening to catch the culprit in the act. And I did, too. I believe there are prison sentences for this sort of thing."

Everyone looked at Edward. The hermit's face had gone pale under its tan, but still he didn't speak.

Arnold walked to the control board and looked at the dials and switches. He pushed a button, and the great nine-foot figure of the Scarb appeared. Myra recognized it and gave a little gasp. Even now it was frightening. Arnold turned it off and faced Jameson.

"You were pretty careless," Arnold said quietly. "You really shouldn't have used company equipment for this. Every item here is stamped Jameson Electronics."

"That doesn't prove a thing," Jameson said. "Anyone can buy that equipment."

"Yes. But not everyone can use it." He turned to the hermit. "Edward, are you an engineer, by any chance?"

"Of course not," Edward said sullenly.

"We have no proof of that," Jameson said. "Just because he says he isn't—"

"We have proof," Gregor burst in. "The hermit's book! When his electric blanket broke down, he didn't know how to fix it. And remember

Chapter Six? It took him over a week to find out how to change a fuse in his auto-cook!"

Arnold said relentlessly, "The equipment's got your company's name on it, Ross. And I'll bet we find you've been absent from your office for considerable periods. The local spaceport will have any record of your taking out an interstellar ship. Or did you manage to hide all that?"

By Ross's face they could tell he hadn't. Myra said, "Oh, Ross."

"I did it for you, Myra," Jameson said. "I love you, but I couldn't live out here! I've got a company to think about, people depend on me..."

"So you tried to scare me off Coelle," Myra said.

"Doesn't that show how much I care for you?"

"That kind of caring I can live without," Myra said.

"But, Myra—"

"And that brings us to Edward the Hermit," Arnold said.

The hermit looked up quickly. "Let's just forget about me," he said. "I admit I was trying to scare Miss Ryan off her planet. It was stupid of me. I'll never bother her again in any way. Of course," he said, looking at Myra, "if you want to press charges—"

"Oh, no."

"I apologize again. I'll be going." The hermit stood up and started toward the door.

"Wait a minute," Arnold said. The expression on his face was painful. He hesitated, sighed fatalistically, and said. "Are you going to tell her, or shall I?"

"I don't know what you're talking about," Edward said. "I must leave now—"

"Not yet. Myra's entitled to the whole truth," Arnold said. "You're in love with her, aren't you?"

Myra stared at the hermit. Edward's shoulders drooped hopelessly.

"What is all this?" she asked. Edward looked angrily at Arnold. "I suppose you won't be satisfied until I've made an utter fool of myself. All right, here goes." He faced Myra. "When you radioed me and said you were going to live on Coelle, I was horrified. Everything started to go to pieces for me."

"But I was millions of miles away," Myra said.

"Yes. That was the trouble. You were so near—astronomically—and yet so far. You see, I was deathly sick of the whole hermit thing. I could stand it as long as no one was around, but once you came—"

"If you were tired of being a hermit," Myra said, "why didn't you leave?"

"My agent told me it would be literary suicide," the hermit said with a sickly attempt at a cynical grin. "You see, I'm a writer. This whole thing was a publicity stunt. I was to hermit a planet and write a book. Which I did. The book was a best-seller. My agent talked me into doing a second book. I couldn't leave until it was done. That would have ruined everything. But I was starving for a human face. And then you came."

"And you threatened me," Myra said.

"Not really. I said I wouldn't be responsible for the consequences. I was really referring to my sanity. For days after that I thought about you. Suddenly I realized I had to see you. Absolutely had to! So I came here, hid the ship—"

"And walked around dressed as a Scarb," Jameson sneered.

"Not at first," Edward said. "After I saw you, I guess—well, I guess I fell in love with you. I knew then that if you stayed on Coelle—practically next door, astronomically—I could find the strength to stay on Kerma and finish my book. But I saw that this Jameson fellow was trying to scare you off. So I decided to scare *him* off."

"Well," Myra said, "I'm glad we finally have met. I enjoyed your book so much."

"Did you?" Edward said, his face brightening.

"Yes. It inspired me to live on Coelle. But I'm sorry to hear it was all a fraud."

"It wasn't!" Edward cried. "The hermit thing was my agent's idea, but the book was perfectly genuine, and I did have all those experiences, and I *did* feel those things. I like being away from civilization, and I especially like having my own planet. The only thing wrong…"

"Yes?"

"Well, Kerma would be perfect if only I had one other person with me. Someone who understands, who feels as I do."

"I know just how you feel." Myra said.

They looked at each other. When Jameson saw that look, he moaned and put his head in his hands.

"Come on, friend," Olson said, dropping a sympathetic hand on Jameson's shoulder. "You're trumped. I'll give you a lift back to Earth."

Ross nodded vaguely, and started to the door with Olson. Olson said, "Say, I imagine you folks will be needing only one planet before long, huh?"

Myra blushed crimson. Edward looked embarrassed, then said in a firm voice, "Myra and I are going to get married. That is, if you'll have me, Myra. Will you marry me, Myra?"

She said yes in a very small voice.

"That's what I thought," Olson said. "So you won't be needing two planets. Would one of you care to lease your mineral rights? It'd be a nice little income, you know. Help to set up housekeeping."

Ross Jameson groaned and hurried out the door,

"Well," Edward said to Myra, "it isn't a bad idea, We'll be living on Kerma, so you might as well—"

"Just a minute," Myra said. "We are going to live on Coelle and no other place."

"No!" Edward said. "After all the work I've put into Kerma, I will not abandon it."

"Coelle has a better climate,"

"Kerma has a lighter gravity,"

Olson said, "When you get it figured out, you'll give Transstellar Mining first chance, won't you? For old times' sake?"

They both nodded, Olson shook hands with them and left.

Arnold said, "I believe that solves the mysteries of the Skag Castle. We'll be going now, Myra. We'll return your ship on drone circuit."

"I don't know how to thank you," Myra said.

"Perhaps you'll come to our wedding," Edward said.

"We'd be delighted."

"It'll be on Coelle, of course," Myra said.

"Kerma!"

When the partners left, the young couple were glaring angrily at each other.

VI

When they were at last in space, Terra-bound, Gregor said, "That was a very handsome job of detection."

"It was nothing," Arnold said modestly. "You would have figured it out yourself in a few months."

"Thanks. And it was very nice of you, speaking up for Edward the way you did."

"Well, Myra was a bit strong-minded for me," Arnold said. "And a trifle provincial. I am, after all, a creature of the great cities."

"It was still an extremely decent thing to do."

Arnold shrugged.

"The trouble is, how will Myra and Edward solve this planet problem? Neither seems the type to give in."

"Oh, that's as good as solved," Gregor said offhandedly.

"What do you mean?"

"Why it's obvious," Gregor said. "And it fills the one gaping hole in your otherwise logical reconstruction of events."

"What hole? What is it?"

"Oh, come now," Gregor said, enjoying his opportunity to the utmost. "It's apparent."

"I don't see it. Tell me."

"I'm sure you'll figure it out in a few months. Think I'll take a nap."

"Don't be that way," Arnold pleaded. "What is it?"

"All right. How tall was Jameson's electronic Scarb, the one that frightened Myra?"

"About nine feet."

"And how tall was Edward, disguised as a Scarb?"

"About six feet tall."

"And the Scarb we saw in our bedroom, the one we shot at—"

"Good Lord!" Arnold gasped. "That Scarb was only four feet tall. *We have one Scarb left over!*"

"Exactly. One Scarb that no one produced artificially, and that we can't account for—unless Coelle actually *is* haunted."

"I see what you mean," Arnold said thoughtfully. "They'll have to move to Kerma. But we didn't really fulfill our contract."

"We did enough," Gregor said. "We decontaminated three distinct species of Skag—produced by Jameson, Olson, and Edward. If they want a fourth species taken care of, that'll be a separate contract."

"You're right," Arnold said. "It's about time we became businesslike. And it's for their own good. Something has to make up their minds for them." He thought for a moment. "I suppose they'll leave Coelle to Transstellar Mining. Should we tell Olson that the planet is really haunted?"

"Certainly not," Gregor said. "He'd just laugh at us. Have you ever heard of ghosts frightening an automatic mining machine?"

ALL THE THINGS YOU ARE

There are regulations to govern the conduct of First Contact spaceships, rules drawn up in desperation and followed in despair, for what rule can predict the effect of any action upon the mentality of an alien people?

Jan Maarten was pondering this gloomily as he came into the atmosphere of Durell IV. He was a big, middle-aged man with thin ash-blond hair and a round, worried face. Long ago he had concluded that almost any rule was better than none. Therefore he followed his meticulously, but with an ever-present sense of uncertainty and human fallibility.

These were ideal qualifications for the job of First Contacter.

He circled the planet, low enough for observation, but not too low, since he didn't want to frighten the inhabitants. He noted the signs of a primitive-pastoral civilization and tried to remember everything he had learned in Volume Four, *Projected Techniques for First Contact on So-called Primitive-Pastoral Worlds,* published by the Department of Alien Psychology. Then he brought the ship down on a rocky, grass-covered plain, near a typical medium-sized village, but not *too* near, using the Silent Sam landing technique.

"Prettily done," commented Croswell, his assistant, who was too young to be bothered by uncertainties.

Chedka, the Eborian linguist, said nothing. He was sleeping, as usual.

Maarten grunted something and went to the rear of the ship to run his tests. Croswell took up his post at the viewport.

"Here they come," Croswell reported half an hour later. "About a dozen of them, definitely humanoid." Upon closer inspection, he saw that the natives of Durell were flabby, dead white in coloration, and deadpan in expression. Croswell hesitated, then added, "They're not too handsome."

"What are they doing?" Maarten asked.

"Just looking us over," Croswell said. He was a slender young man with an unusually large and lustrous mustache that he had grown on the long journey out from Terra. He stroked it with the pride of a man who has been able to raise a really good mustache.

"They're about twenty yards from the ship now," Croswell reported. He leaned forward, flattening his nose ludicrously against the port, which was constructed of one-way glass.

Croswell could look out, but no one could look in. The Department of Alien Psychology had ordered the change last year, after a Department ship had botched a first contact on Carella II. The Carellans had stared into the ship, become alarmed at something within, and fled. The Department still didn't know what had alarmed them, for a second contact had never been successfully established.

That mistake would never happen again.

"What now?" Maarten called.

"One of them's coming forward alone. Chief, perhaps. Or sacrificial offering."

"What is he wearing?"

"He has on a—a sort of—will you kindly come here and look for yourself?"

Maarten, at his instrument bank, had been assembling a sketchy profile of Durell. The planet had a breathable atmosphere, an equitable climate, and gravity comparable to that of Earth. It had valuable deposits of radioactives and rare metals. Best of all, it tested free of the virulent microorganisms and poisonous vapors that tended to make a Contacter's life feverishly short.

Durell was going to be a valuable neighbor to Earth, provided the natives were friendly—and the Contacters skillful.

Maarten walked to the viewport and studied the natives. "They are wearing pastel clothing. We shall wear pastel clothing."

"Check," said Croswell.

"They are unarmed. We shall go unarmed."

"Roger."

"They are wearing sandals. We shall wear sandals."

"To hear is to obey."

"I notice they have no facial hair," Maarten said with the barest hint of a smile. "I'm sorry, Ed, but that mustache—"

"Not my mustache!" Croswell yelped, quickly putting a protective hand over it.

"I'm afraid so."

"But, Jan, I've been six months raising it!"

"It has to go. That should be obvious."

"I don't see why," Croswell said indignantly.

"Because first impressions are *vital*. When an unfavorable first impression has been made, subsequent contacts become difficult, sometimes impossible. Since we know nothing about these people, conformity is our safest course. We try to look like them, dress in colors that are pleasing or at least acceptable to them, copy their gestures, interact within their framework of acceptance in every way—"

"All right, all right," Croswell said. "I suppose I can grow another on the way back."

They looked at each other; then both began laughing. Croswell had lost three mustaches in this manner.

While Croswell shaved, Maarten stirred their linguist into wakefulness. Chedka was a lemurlike humanoid from Eboria IV, one of the few planets where Earth maintained successful relations. The Eborians were natural linguists, aided by the kind of associative ability found in nuisances who supply words in conversation—only the Eborians were always right. They had wandered over a considerable portion of the Galaxy in their time and might have attained quite a place in it, were it not that they needed twenty hours' sleep out of twenty-four.

Croswell finished shaving and dressed in pale green coveralls and sandals. All three went through decontamination procedure. Then Maarten took a deep breath, uttered a silent prayer, and opened the port.

A low sigh went up from the crowd of Durellans, although the chief—or sacrifice—was silent. They were indeed humanlike, if one overlooked their pallor and the gentle, sheeplike blandness of their features—features upon which Maarten could read no trace of expression.

"Don't use any facial contortions," Maarten warned Croswell. Slowly they advanced until they were ten feet from the leading Durellan. Then Maarten said in a low voice, "We come in peace."

Chedka translated, then listened to the answer, which was so soft as to be almost indecipherable.

"Chief says welcome," Chedka reported in his economical English.

"Good, good," Maarten said. He took a few more steps forward and began to speak, pausing every now and then for translation. Earnestly, and with extreme conviction, he intoned Primary Speech BB-32 (for humanoid, primitive-pastoral, tentatively nonaggressive aliens).

Even Croswell, who was impressed by very little, had to admit it was a fine speech. Maarten said they were wanderers from afar, come out of the Great Nothingness to engage in friendly discourse with the gentle people of Durell. He spoke of green and distant Earth, so like this planet, and of the fine and humble people of Earth who stretched out hands in greeting. He told of the great spirit of peace and cooperation that emanated from Earth, of universal friendship, and of many other excellent things.

Finally he was done. There was a long silence.

"Did he understand it all?" Maarten whispered to Chedka.

The Eborian nodded, waiting for the chief's reply. Maarten was perspiring from the exertion, and Croswell couldn't stop nervously fingering his newly shaven upper lip.

The chief opened his mouth, gasped, made a little half-turn, and collapsed to the ground.

It was an embarrassing moment, and one not covered by any amount of theory.

The chief didn't rise; apparently it was not a ceremonial fall. As a matter of fact, his breathing seemed labored, like that of a man in a coma.

Under the circumstances, the Contact team could only retreat to their ship and await further developments.

Half an hour later a native approached the ship and conversed with Chedka, keeping a wary eye on the Earthmen and departing immediately.

"What did he say?" Croswell asked.

"Chief Moréri apologizes for fainting," Chedka told them. "He said it was inexcusably bad manners."

"Ah!" Maarten exclaimed. "His fainting might help us, after all— make him eager to repair his 'impoliteness.' Just as long as it was a fortuitous circumstance, unrelated to us—"

"Not," Chedka said.

"Not what?"

"Not unrelated," the Eborian said, curling up and going to sleep.

Maarten shook the little linguist awake. "What else did the chief say? How was his fainting related to us?"

Chedka yawned copiously. "The chief was very embarrassed. He faced the wind from your mouth as long as he could, but the alien odor—"

"My breath?" Maarten asked. "My *breath* knocked him out?" Chedka nodded, giggled unexpectedly, and went to sleep.

Evening came, and the long dim twilight of Durell merged imperceptibly into night. In the village, cooking fires glinted through the surrounding forest and winked out one by one. But lights burned within the spaceship until dawn. And when the sun rose, Chedka slipped out of the ship on a mission into the village. Croswell brooded over his morning coffee, while Maarten rummaged through the ship's medicine chest.

"It's purely a temporary setback," Croswell was saying hopefully. "Little things like this are bound to happen. Remember that time on Dingoforeaba VI—"

"It's little things that close planets forever," Maarten said.

"But how could anyone possibly guess—"

"I should have foreseen it," Maarten growled angrily. "Just because our breath hasn't been offensive anywhere else—here it is!"

Triumphantly he held up a bottle of pink tablets. "Absolutely guaranteed to neutralize any breath, even that of a hyena. Have a couple."

Croswell accepted the pills. "Now what?"

"Now we wait until—aha! What did he say?"

Chedka slipped through the entry port, rubbing his eyes. "The chief apologizes for fainting."

"We know that. What else?"

"He welcomes you to the village of Lannit at your convenience. The chief feels that this incident shouldn't alter the course of friendship between two peace-loving, courteous peoples."

Maarten sighed with relief. He cleared his throat and asked hesitantly, "Did you mention to him about the forthcoming—ah—improvement in our breaths?"

"I assured him it would be corrected," Chedka said, "although it never bothered *me.*"

"Fine, fine. We will leave for the village now. Perhaps you should take one of these pills?"

"There's nothing wrong with *my* breath," the Eborian said complacently.

They set out at once for the village of Lannit.

When one deals with a primitive-pastoral people, one looks for simple but highly symbolic gestures, since that is what they understand best. Imagery! Clear-cut and decisive parallels! Few words but many gestures! Those were the rules in dealing with primitive-pastorals.

As Maarten approached the village, a natural and highly symbolic ceremony presented itself. The natives were waiting in their village, which was in a clearing in the forest. Separating forest from village was a dry streambed, and across that bed was a small stone bridge.

Maarten advanced to the center of the bridge and stopped, beaming benignly on the Durellans. When he saw several of them shudder and turn away, he smoothed out his features, remembering his own injunction against facial contortions. He paused for a long moment.

"What's up?" Croswell asked, stopping in front of the bridge. In a loud voice, Maarten cried, "Let this bridge symbolize the link, now eternally forged, that joins this beautiful planet with—" Croswell called out a warning, but Maarten didn't know what was wrong. He stared at the villagers; they had made no movement.

"Get off the bridge!" Croswell shouted. But before Maarten could move, the entire structure had collapsed under him and he fell boneshakingly into the dry stream.

"Damnedest thing I ever saw," Croswell said, helping him to his feet. "As soon as you raised your voice, that stone began to pulverize. Sympathetic vibration, I imagine."

Now Maarten understood why the Durellans spoke in whispers.

He struggled to his feet, then groaned and sat down again. "What's wrong?" Croswell asked.

"I seem to have wrenched my ankle," Maarten said miserably. Chief Moréri came up, followed by twenty or so villagers, made a short speech, and presented Maarten with a walking stick of carved and polished black wood.

"Thanks," Maarten muttered, standing up and leaning gingerly on the cane. "What did he say?" he asked Chedka.

"The chief said that the bridge was only a hundred years old and in good repair," Chedka translated. "He apologizes that his ancestors didn't build it better."

"Hmm," Maarten said.

"And the chief says that you are probably an unlucky man."

He might be right, Maarten thought. Or perhaps Earthmen were just a fumbling race. For all their good intentions, population after population feared them, hated them, envied them, mainly on the basis of unfavorable first impressions.

Still, there seemed to be a chance here. What else could go wrong?

Forcing a smile, then quickly erasing it, Maarten limped into the village beside Moréri.

Technologically, the Durellan civilization was of a low order. A limited use had been made of wheel and lever, but the concept of mechanical advantage had been carried no further. There was evidence of a rudimentary knowledge of plane geometry and a fair idea of astronomy.

Artistically, however, the Durellans were adept and surprisingly sophisticated, particularly in woodcarving. Even the simplest huts had bas-relief panels, beautifully conceived and executed.

"Do you think I could take some photographs?" Croswell asked.

"I see no reason why not," Maarten said. He ran his fingers lovingly over a large panel carved of the same straight-grained black wood that formed his cane. The finish was as smooth as skin beneath his fingertips.

The chief gave his approval, and Croswell took photographs of Durellan home, market, and temple decorations.

Maarten wandered around, gently touching the intricate bas-reliefs, speaking with some of the natives through Chedka, and generally sorting out his impressions.

The Durellans, Maarten judged, were highly intelligent and had a potential comparable to that of *Homo sapiens*. Their lack of a defined technology was more the expression of a cooperation with nature than a flaw in their makeup. They seemed inherently peace-loving and non-aggressive—valuable neighbors for an Earth that, after centuries of confusion, was striving toward a similar goal.

This was going to be the basis of his report to the Second Contact Team. To this he hoped to be able to add, *A favorable impression seems to have been left concerning Earth. No unusual difficulties are to be expected.*

Chedka had been talking earnestly with Chief Moréri. Now, looking slightly more wide awake than usual, he came over and conferred with Maarten in a hushed voice. Maarten nodded, keeping his face expressionless, and went over to Croswell, who was snapping his last photographs.

"All ready for the big show?" Maarten asked. "What show?"

"Moréri is throwing a feast for us tonight," Maarten said. "Very big, very important feast. A final gesture of goodwill and all that." Although his tone was casual, there was a gleam of deep satisfaction in his eyes.

Croswell's reaction was more immediate. "Then we've made it! The contact is successful!"

Behind him, two natives shook at the loudness of his voice and tottered feebly away.

"We've made it," Maarten whispered, "if we watch our step. They're a fine, understanding people—but we *do* seem to grate on them a bit."

By evening, Maarten and Croswell had completed a chemical examination of the Durellan foods and found nothing harmful to humans. They took several more pink tablets, changed coveralls and sandals, and proceeded to the feast.

The first course was an orange-green vegetable that tasted like squash. Then Chief Moréri gave a short talk on the importance of intercultural relations. They were served a dish resembling rabbit, and Croswell was called upon to give a speech.

"Remember," Maarten whispered, *"whisper!"*

Croswell stood up and began to speak. Keeping his voice down and his face blank, he began to enumerate the many similarities between Earth and Durell, depending mainly on gestures to convey his message.

Chedka translated. Maarten nodded his approval. The chief nodded. The feasters nodded.

Croswell made his last points and sat down, Maarten clapped him on the shoulder. "Well done, Ed. You've got a natural gift for—what's wrong?"

Croswell had a startled and incredulous look on his face. "Look!"

Maarten turned. The chief and the feasters, their eyes open and staring, were still nodding.

"Chedka!" Maarten whispered. "Speak to them!"

The Eborian asked the chief a question. There was no response. The chief continued his rhythmic nodding.

"Those gestures!" Maarten said. "You must have hypnotized them!" He scratched his head, then coughed once, loudly. The Durellans stopped nodding, blinked, and began to talk rapidly and nervously among themselves.

"They say you've got some strong powers," Chedka translated at random. "They say that aliens are pretty queer people and they doubt that they can be trusted."

"What does the chief say?" Maarten asked.

"The chief believes you're all right. He is telling them that you meant no harm."

"Good enough. Let's stop while we're ahead."

He stood up, followed by Croswell and Chedka.

"We are leaving now," he told the chief in a whisper, "but we beg permission for others of our kind to visit you. Forgive the mistakes we have made; they were due only to ignorance of your ways."

Chedka translated, and Maarten went on whispering, his face expressionless, his hands at his sides; He spoke of the oneness of the Galaxy, the joys of cooperation, peace, the exchange of goods and art, and the essential solidarity of all human life.

Moréri, though still a little dazed from the hypnotic experience, answered that the Earthmen would always be welcome.

Impulsively, Croswell held out his hand. The chief looked at it for a moment, puzzled, then took it, obviously wondering what to do with it and why.

He gasped in agony and pulled his hand back. They could see deep burns blotched red against his skin.

"What could have—"

"Perspiration'" Maarten said. "It's an acid. Must have an almost instantaneous effect upon their particular makeup. Let's get out of here."

The natives were milling together and they had picked up some stones and pieces of wood. The chief, although still in pain, was arguing with them, but the Earthmen didn't wait to hear the results of the discussion. They retreated to their ship, as fast as Maarten could hobble with the help of his cane.

The forest was dark behind them and filled with suspicious movements. Out of breath, they arrived at the spaceship. Croswell, in the lead, sprawled over a tangle of grass and fell headfirst against the port with a resounding clang.

"Damn!" he howled in pain.

The ground rumbled beneath them, began to tremble and slide away.

"Into the ship!" Maarten ordered.

They managed to take off before the ground gave way completely.

"It must have been sympathetic vibration again," Croswell said, several hours later, when the ship was in space. "But of all the luck—to be perched on a rock fault!"

Maarten sighed and shook his head. "I really don't know what to do. I'd like to go back, explain to them, but—"

"We've overstayed our welcome," Croswell said.

"Apparently. Blunders, nothing but blunders. We started out badly, and everything we did made it worse."

"It is not what you *do,*" Chedka explained in the most sympathetic voice they had ever heard him use. "It's not your fault. It's what you *are.*"

Maarten considered that for a moment. "Yes, you're right. Our voices shatter their land, our expressions disgust them, our gestures hypnotize them, our breath asphyxiates them, our perspiration burns them. Oh, Lord!"

"Lord, Lord," Croswell agreed glumly. "We're living chemical factories—turning out only poison gas and corrosives."

"But that is not *all* you are," Chedka said. "Look."

He held up Maarten's walking stick. Along the upper part, where Maarten had handled it, long-dormant buds had burst into pink and white flowers, and their scent filled the cabin.

"You see?" Chedka said. "You are *this,* also."

"That stick was dead," Croswell mused. "Some oil in our skin, I imagine."

Maarten shuddered. "Do you suppose that all the carvings we touched—the huts—the temple—"

"I should think so," Croswell said.

Maarten closed his eyes and visualized it, the sudden bursting into bloom of the dead, dried wood.

"I think they'll understand," he said, trying very hard to believe himself. "It's a pretty symbol and they're quite an understanding people. I think they'll approve of—well, at least *some* of the things we are."

BAD MEDICINE

On May 2, 2103, Elwood Caswell walked rapidly down Broadway with a loaded revolver hidden in his coat pocket. He didn't want to use the weapon, but feared he might anyhow. This was a justifiable assumption, for Caswell was a homicidal maniac.

It was a gentle, misty spring day and the air held the smell of rain and blossoming dogwood. Caswell gripped the revolver in his sweaty right hand and tried to think of a single valid reason why he should not kill a man named Magnessen, who, the other day, had commented on how well Caswell looked.

What business was it of Magnessen's how he looked? Damned busybodies, always spoiling things for everybody...

Caswell was a choleric little man with fierce red eyes, bulldog jowls and ginger-red hair. He was the sort you would expect to find perched on a detergent box, orating to a crowd of lunching businessmen and amused students, shouting, "Mars for the Martians, Venus for the Venusians!"

But in truth, Caswell was uninterested in the deplorable social conditions of extraterrestrials. He was a jetbus conductor for the New York Rapid Transit Corporation. He minded his own business. And he was quite mad.

Fortunately, he knew this at least part of the time, with at least half of his mind.

Perspiring freely, Caswell continued down Broadway toward the 43rd Street branch of Home Therapy Appliances, Inc. His friend Magnessen would be finishing work soon, returning to his little apartment less than a block from Caswell's. How easy it would be, how pleasant, to saunter in, exchange a few words and...

No! Caswell took a deep gulp of air and reminded himself that he didn't *really* want to kill anyone. It was not right to kill people. The authorities would lock him up, his friends wouldn't understand, his mother would never have approved.

But these arguments seemed pallid, over-intellectual and entirely without force. The simple fact remained—he wanted to kill Magnessen.

Could so strong a desire be wrong? Or even unhealthy?

Yes, it could! With an agonized groan, Caswell sprinted the last few steps into the Home Therapy Appliances Store.

Just being within such a place gave him an immediate sense of relief. The lighting was discreet, the draperies were neutral, the displays of glittering therapy machines were neither too bland nor obstreperous. It was the kind of place where a man could happily lie down on the carpet in the shadow of the therapy machines, secure in the knowledge that help for any sort of trouble was at hand.

A clerk with fair hair and a long, supercilious nose glided up softly, but not too softly, and murmured, "May one help?"

"Therapy!" said Caswell.

"Of course, sir," the clerk answered, smoothing his lapels and smiling winningly. "That is what we are here for." He gave Caswell a searching look, performed an instant mental diagnosis, and tapped a gleaming white-and-copper machine.

"Now this," the clerk said, "is the new Alcoholic Reliever, built by IBM and advertised in the leading magazines. A handsome piece of furniture, I think you will agree, and not out of place in any home. It opens into a television set."

With a flick of his narrow wrist, the clerk opened the Alcoholic Reliever, revealing a 52-inch screen.

"I need—" Caswell began.

"Therapy," the clerk finished for him. "Of course. I just wanted to point out that this model need never cause embarrassment for yourself, your friends or loved ones. Notice, if you will, the recessed dial which controls the desired degree of drinking. See? If you do not wish total abstinence, you can set it to heavy, moderate, social or light. That is a new feature, unique in mechanotherapy."

"I am not an alcoholic," Caswell said, with considerable dignity. "The New York Rapid Transit Corporation does not hire alcoholics."

"Oh," said the clerk, glancing distrustfully at Caswell's bloodshot eyes. "You seem a little nervous. Perhaps the portable Bendix Anxiety Reducer—"

"Anxiety's not my ticket, either. What have you got for homicidal mania?"

The clerk pursed his lips. "Schizophrenic or manic-depressive origins?"

"I don't know," Caswell admitted, somewhat taken aback.

"It really doesn't matter," the clerk told him. "Just a private theory of my own. From my experience in the store, redheads and blonds are prone to schizophrenia, while brunettes incline toward the manic-depressive."

"That's interesting. Have you worked here long?"

"A week. Now then, here is just what you need, sir." He put his hand affectionately on a squat black machine with chrome trim.

"What's that?"

"That, sir, is the Rex Regenerator, built by General Motors. Isn't it handsome? It can go with any decor and opens up into a well-stocked bar. Your friends, family, loved ones need never know—"

"Will it cure a homicidal urge?" Caswell asked. "A *strong* one?"

"Absolutely. Don't confuse this with the little ten amp neurosis models. This is a hefty, heavy-duty, twenty-five amp machine for a really deep-rooted major condition."

"That's what I've got," said Caswell, with pardonable pride.

"This baby'll jolt it out of you. Big, heavy-duty thrust bearings! Oversize heat absorbers! Completely insulated! Sensitivity range of over—"

"I'll take it," Caswell said. "Right now. I'll pay cash."

"Fine! I'll just telephone Storage and—"

"This one'll do," Caswell said, pulling out his billfold. "I'm in a hurry to use it. I want to kill my friend Magnessen, you know."

The clerk clucked sympathetically. "You wouldn't want to do that…Plus five percent sales tax. Thank you, sir. Full instructions are inside."

Caswell thanked him, lifted the Regenerator in both arms and hurried out.

After figuring his commission, the clerk smiled to himself and lighted a cigarette. His enjoyment was spoiled when the manager, a large man impressively equipped with pince-nez, marched out of his office.

"Haskins," the manager said, "I thought I asked you to rid yourself of that filthy habit."

"Yes, Mr. Follansby, sorry, sir," Haskins apologized, snubbing out the cigarette. "I'll use the display Denicotinizer at once. Made rather a good sale, Mr. Follansby. One of the big Rex Regenerators."

"Really?" said the manager, impressed. "It isn't often we—wait a minute! You didn't sell the *floor model,* did you?"

"Why—why, I'm afraid I did, Mr. Follansby. The customer was in such a terrible hurry. Was there any reason—"

Mr. Follansby gripped his prominent white forehead in both hands, as though he wished to rip it off. "Haskins, I told you. I must have told you! That display Regenerator was a *Martian* model. For giving mechanotherapy to *Martians.* "

"Oh," Haskins said. He thought for a moment. "Oh."

Mr. Follansby stared at his clerk in grim silence.

"But does it really matter?" Haskins asked quickly. "Surely the machine won't discriminate. I should think it would treat a homicidal tendency even if the patient were not a Martian."

"The Martian race has never had the slightest tendency toward homicide. A Martian Regenerator doesn't even process the concept. Of course the Regenerator will treat him. It has to. *But what will it treat?*"

"Oh," said Haskins.

"That poor devil must be stopped before—you say he was *homicidal?* I don't know what will happen! Quick, what is his address?"

"Well, Mr. Follansby, he was in such a terrible hurry—"

The manager gave him a long, unbelieving look. "Get the police! Call the General Motors Security Division! Find him!"

Haskins raced for the door.

"Wait!" yelled the manager, struggling into a raincoat. "I'm coming, too."

Elwood Caswell returned to his apartment by taxicopter. He lugged the Regenerator into his living room, put it down near the couch and studied it thoughtfully.

"That clerk was right," he said after a while. "It *does* go with the room."

Esthetically, the Regenerator was a success.

Caswell admired it for a few more moments, then went into the kitchen and fixed himself a chicken sandwich. He ate slowly, staring fixedly at a point just above and to the left of his kitchen clock.

Damn you, Magnessen! Dirty no-good lying shifty-eyed enemy of all that's decent and clean in the world...

Taking the revolver from his pocket, he laid it on the table. With a stiffened forefinger, he poked it into different positions.

It was time to begin therapy.

Except that...

Caswell realized worriedly that he didn't want to lose the desire to kill Magnessen. What would become of him if he lost that urge? His life would lose all purpose, all coherence, all flavor and zest. It would be quite dull, really.

Moreover, he had a great and genuine grievance against Magnessen, one he didn't like to think about.

Irene!

His poor sister, debauched by the subtle and insidious Magnessen, ruined by him and cast aside. What better reason could a man have to take his revolver and...

Caswell finally remembered that he did not have a sister.

Now was *really* the time to begin therapy.

He went into the living room and found the operating instructions tucked into a ventilation louver of the machine. He opened them and read:

To Operate All Rex Model Regenerators:

1. Place the Regenerator near a comfortable couch. (A comfortable couch can be purchased as an additional accessory from any General Motors dealer.)

2. Plug in the machine.

3. Affix the adjustable contact-band to the forehead.

And that's all! Your Regenerator will do the rest! There will be no language bar or dialect problem, since the Regenerator communicates by Direct Sense Contact (Patent Pending). All you must do is cooperate.

Try not to feel any embarrassment or shame. Everyone has problems and many are worse than yours! Your Regenerator has no interest in your morals or ethical standards, so don't feel it is 'judging' you. It desires only to aid you in becoming well and happy.

As soon as it has collected and processed enough data, your Regenerator will begin treatment. You make the sessions as short or as long as you like. You are the boss! And of course you can end a session at any time.

That's all there is to it! Simple, isn't it? Now plug in your General Motors Regenerator and GET SANE!

"Nothing hard about that," Caswell said to himself. He pushed the Regenerator closer to the couch and plugged it in. He lifted the headband, started to slip it on, stopped.

"I feel so silly!" he giggled.

Abruptly he closed his mouth and stared pugnaciously at the black-and-chrome machine.

"So you think you can make me sane, huh?"

The Regenerator didn't answer.

"Oh, well, go ahead and try." He slipped the headband over his forehead, crossed his arms on his chest and leaned back.

Nothing happened. Caswell settled himself more comfortably on the couch. He scratched his shoulder and put the headband at a more comfortable angle. Still nothing. His thoughts began to wander.

Magnessen! You noisy, overbearing oaf, you disgusting—

"Good afternoon," a voice murmured in his head. "I am your mechanotherapist."

Caswell twitched guiltily. "Hello. I was just—you know, just sort of—"

"Of course," the machine said soothingly. "Don't we all? I am now scanning the material in your preconscious with the intent of synthesis, diagnosis, prognosis, and treatment. I find…"

"Yes?"

"Just one moment." The Regenerator was silent for several minutes. Then, hesitantly, it said, "This is beyond doubt a most unusual case."

"Really?" Caswell asked, pleased.

"Yes. The coefficients seem—I'm not sure…" The machine's robotic voice grew feeble. The pilot light began to flicker and fade.

"Hey, what's the matter?"

"Confusion," said the machine. "Of course," it went on in a stronger voice, "the unusual nature of the symptoms need not prove entirely baffling to a competent therapeutic machine. A symptom, no matter how bizarre, is no more than a signpost, an indication of inner difficulty. And *all* symptoms can be related to the broad mainstream of proven theory. Since the theory is effective, the symptoms must relate. We will proceed on that assumption."

"Are you sure you know what you're doing?" asked Caswell, feeling lightheaded.

The machine snapped back, its pilot light blazing. "Mechanotherapy today is an exact science and admits no significant errors. We will proceed with a word-association test."

"Fire away," said Caswell.

"House?"

"Home."

"Dog?"

"Cat."

"Fleefl?"

Caswell hesitated, trying to figure out the word. It sounded vaguely Martian, but it might be Venusian or even—

"Fleefl?" the Regenerator repeated.

"Marfoosh," Caswell replied, making up the word on the spur of the moment.

"Loud?"

"Sweet."

"Green?"

"Mother."

"Thanagoyes?"

"Patamathonga."

"Arrides?"

"Nexothesmodrastica."

"Chtheesnohelgnopteces?"

"Rigamaroo latasentricpropatria!" Caswell shot back. It was a collection of sounds he was particularly proud of. The average man would not have been able to pronounce them.

"Hmm," said the Regenerator. "The pattern fits. It always does."

"What pattern?"

"You have," the machine informed him, "a classic case of feem desire, complicated by strong dwarkish intentions."

"I do? I thought I was homicidal."

"That term has no referent," the machine said severely. "Therefore I must reject it as nonsense syllabification. Now consider these points: The feem desire is perfectly normal. Never forget that. But it is usually replaced at an early age by the hovendish revulsion. Individuals lacking in this basic environmental response—"

"I'm not absolutely sure I know what you're talking about," Caswell confessed.

"Please, sir! We must establish one thing at once. You are the patient. *I* am the mechanotherapist. You have brought your troubles to me for treatment. But you cannot expect help unless you cooperate."

"All right," Caswell said. "I'll try."

Up to now, he had been bathed in a warm glow of superiority. Everything the machine said had seemed mildly humorous. As a matter of fact, he had felt capable of pointing out a few things wrong with the mechanotherapist.

Now that sense of well-being evaporated, as it always did, and Caswell was alone, terribly alone and lost, a creature of his compulsions, in search of a little peace and contentment.

He would undergo anything to find them. Sternly he reminded himself that he had no right to comment on the mechanotherapist. These machines knew what they were doing and had been doing it for a long time. He would cooperate, no matter how outlandish the treatment seemed from his layman's viewpoint.

But it was obvious, Caswell thought, settling himself grimly on the couch, that mechanotherapy was going to be far more difficult than he had imagined.

The search for the missing customer had been brief and useless. He was nowhere to be found on the teeming New York streets and no one could remember seeing a red-haired, red-eyed little man lugging a black therapeutic machine.

It was all too common a sight.

In answer to an urgent telephone call, the police came immediately, four of them, led by a harassed young lieutenant of detectives named Smith.

Smith just had time to ask, "Say, why don't you people put tags on things?" when there was an interruption.

A man pushed his way past the policeman at the door. He was tall and gnarled and ugly, and his eyes were deep-set and bleakly blue. His clothes, unpressed and uncaring, hung on him like corrugated iron.

"What do you want?" Lieutenant Smith asked.

The ugly man flipped back his lapel, showing a small silver badge beneath. "I'm John Rath, General Motors Security Division."

"Oh…Sorry, sir," Lieutenant Smith said, saluting. "I didn't think you people would move in so fast."

Rath made a noncommittal noise. "Have you checked for prints, Lieutenant? The customer might have touched some other therapy machine."

"I'll get right on it, sir," Smith said. It wasn't often that one of the operatives from GM, GE, or IBM came down to take a personal hand. If a local cop showed he was really clicking, there just might be the possibility of an Industrial Transfer...

Rath turned to Follansby and Haskins, and transfixed them with a gaze as piercing and as impersonal as a radar beam. "Let's have the full story," he said, taking a notebook and pencil from a shapeless pocket.

He listened to the tale in ominous silence. Finally he closed his notebook, thrust it back into his pocket and said, "The therapeutic machines are a sacred trust. To give a customer the wrong machine is a betrayal of that trust, a violation of the Public Interest, and a defamation of the Company's good reputation."

The manager nodded in agreement, glaring at his unhappy clerk.

"A Martian model," Rath continued, "should never have been on the floor in the first place."

"I can explain that," Follansby said hastily. "We needed a demonstrator model and I wrote to the Company, telling them—"

"This might," Rath broke in inexorably, "be considered a case of gross criminal negligence."

Both the manager and the clerk exchanged horrified looks. They were thinking of the General Motors Reformatory outside of Detroit, where Company offenders passed their days in sullen silence, monotonously drawing microcircuits for pocket television sets.

"However, that is out of my jurisdiction," Rath said. He turned his baleful gaze full upon Haskins. "You are certain that the customer never mentioned his name?"

"No, sir. I mean yes, I'm sure," Haskins replied rattledly.

"Did he mention any names at all?"

Haskins plunged his face into his hands. He looked up and said eagerly, "Yes! He wanted to kill someone! A friend of his!"

"Who?" Rath asked, with terrible patience.

"The friend's name was—let me think—Magneton! That was it! Magneton! Or was it Morrison? Oh, dear..."

Mr. Rath's iron face registered a rather corrugated disgust. People were useless as witnesses. Worse than useless, since they were frequently misleading. For reliability, give him a robot every time.

"Didn't he mention *anything* significant?"

"Let me *think!*" Haskins said, his face twisting into a fit of concentration. Rath waited.

Mr. Follansby cleared his throat. "I was just thinking, Mr. Rath. About that Martian machine. It won't treat a Terran homicidal case as homicidal, will it?"

"Of course not. Homicide is unknown on Mars."

"Yes. But what will it do? Might it not reject the entire case as unsuitable? Then the customer would merely return the Regenerator with a complaint and we would—"

Mr. Rath shook his head. "The Rex Regenerator must treat if it finds evidence of psychosis. By Martian standards, the customer is a very sick man, a psychotic—*no matter what is wrong with him.*"

Follansby removed his pince-nez and polished them rapidly. "What will the machine do, then?"

"It will treat him for the Martian illness most analogous to his case. Feem desire, I should imagine, with various complications. As for what will happen once treatment begins, I don't know. I doubt whether anyone knows, since it has never happened before. Offhand, I would say there are two major alternatives: the patient may reject the therapy out of hand, in which case he is left with his homicidal mania unabated. Or he may accept the Martian therapy and reach a cure."

Mr. Follansby's face brightened. "Ah! A cure is possible!"

"You don't understand," Rath said. "He may effect a cure—*of his nonexistent Martian psychosis.* But to cure something that is not there is, in effect, to erect a gratuitous delusional system. You might say that the machine would work in reverse, producing psychosis instead of removing it."

Mr. Follansby groaned and leaned against a Bell Psychosomatica.

"The result," Rath summed up, "would be to convince the customer that he was a Martian. A *sane* Martian, naturally."

Haskins suddenly shouted, "I remember! I remember now! He said he worked for the New York Rapid Transit Corporation! I remember distinctly!"

"That's a break," Rath said, reaching for the telephone.

Haskins wiped his perspiring face in relief. "And I just remembered something else that should make it easier still."

"What?"

"The customer said he had been an alcoholic at one time. I'm sure of it, because he was interested at first in the IBM Alcoholic Reliever, until I talked him out of it. He had red hair, you know, and I've had a theory for some time about red-headedness and alcoholism. It seems—"

"Excellent," Rath said. "Alcoholism will be on his records. It narrows the search considerably."

As he dialed the NYRT Corporation, the expression on his craglike face was almost pleasant.

It was good, for a change, to find that a human *could* retain some significant facts.

"But surely you remember your goricae?" the Regenerator was saying.

"No," Caswell answered wearily.

"Tell me, then, about your juvenile experiences with the thorastrian fleep."

"Never had any."

"Hmm. Blockage," muttered the machine. "Resentment. Repression. Are you sure you don't remember your goricae and what it meant to you? The experience is universal."

"Not for me," Caswell said, swallowing a yawn.

He had been undergoing mechanotherapy for close to four hours and it struck him as futile. For a while, he had talked voluntarily about his childhood, his mother and father, his older brother. But the Regenerator had asked him to put aside those fantasies. The patient's relationships to an imaginary parent or sibling, it explained, were unworkable and of minor importance psychologically. The important thing was the patient's feelings—both revealed and repressed—toward his goricae.

"Aw, look," Caswell complained, "I don't even know what a goricae is."

"Of course you do. You just won't *let* yourself know."

"I don't know. Tell me."

"It would be better if you told me."

"How can I?" Caswell raged. "I don't know!"

"What do you *imagine* a goricae would be?"

"A forest fire," Caswell said. "A salt tablet. A jar of denatured alcohol. A small screwdriver. Am I getting warm? A notebook. A revolver—"

"These associations are meaningful," the Regenerator assured him. "Your attempt at randomness shows a clearly underlying pattern. Do you begin to recognize it?"

"What in hell is a goricae?" Caswell roared.

"The tree that nourished you during infancy, and well into puberty, if my theory about you is correct. Inadvertently, the goricae stifled your necessary rejection of the feem desire. This in turn gave rise to your present urge to dwark someone in a vlendish manner."

"No tree nourished me."

"You cannot recall the experience?"

"Of course not. It never happened."

"You are sure of that?"

"Positive."

"Not even the tiniest bit of doubt?"

"No! No goricae ever nourished me. Look, I can break off these sessions at any time, right?"

"Of course," the Regenerator said. "But it would not be advisable at this moment. You are expressing anger, resentment, fear. By your rigidly summary rejection—"

"Nuts," said Caswell, and pulled off the headband.

* * *

The silence was wonderful. Caswell stood up, yawned, stretched and massaged the back of his neck. He stood in front of the humming black machine and gave it a long leer.

"You couldn't cure me of a common cold," he told it.

Stiffly he walked the length of the living room and returned to the Regenerator.

"Lousy fake!" he shouted.

Caswell went into the kitchen and opened a bottle of beer. His revolver was still on the table, gleaming dully.

Magnessen! You unspeakable treacherous filth! You fiend incarnate! You inhuman, hideous monster! Someone must destroy you, Magnessen! Someone...

Someone? He himself would have to do it. Only he knew the bottomless depths of Magnessen's depravity, his viciousness, his disgusting lust for power.

Yes, it was his duty, Caswell thought. But strangely, the knowledge brought him no pleasure.

After all, Magnessen was his friend.

He stood up, ready for action. He tucked the revolver into his right-hand coat pocket and glanced at the kitchen clock. Nearly six-thirty. Magnessen would be home now, gulping his dinner, grinning over his plans.

This was the perfect time to take him.

Caswell strode to the door, opened it, started through, and stopped.

A thought had crossed his mind, a thought so tremendously involved, so meaningful, so far-reaching in its implications that he was stirred to his depths. Caswell tried desperately to shake off the knowledge it brought. But the thought, permanently etched upon his memory, would not depart.

Under the circumstances, he could do only one thing.

He returned to the living room, sat down on the couch and slipped on the headband.

The Regenerator said, "Yes?"

"It's the damnedest thing," Caswell said, "but do you know, I think I *do* remember my goricae!"

John Rath contacted the New York Rapid Transit Corporation by televideo and was put into immediate contact with Mr. Bemis, a plump, tanned man with watchful eyes.

"Alcoholism?" Mr. Bemis repeated, after the problem was explained. Unobtrusively, he turned on his tape recorder. "Among our employees?" Pressing a button beneath his foot, Bemis alerted Transit Security, Publicity, Intercompany Relations, and the Psychoanalysis Division.

This done, he looked earnestly at Rath. "Not a chance of it, my dear sir. Just between us, why does General Motors *really* want to know?"

Rath smiled bitterly. He should have anticipated this. NYRT and GM had had their differences in the past. Officially, there was cooperation between the two giant corporations. But for all practical purposes—

"The question is in terms of the Public Interest," Rath said.

"Oh, certainly," Mr. Bemis replied, with a subtle smile. Glancing at his tattle board, he noticed that several company executives had tapped in on his line. This might mean a promotion, if handled properly.

"The Public Interest of GM," Mr. Bemis added with polite nastiness. "The insinuation is, I suppose, that drunken conductors are operating our jetbuses and helis?"

"Of course not. I was searching for a single alcoholic predilection, an individual latency—"

"There's no possibility of it. We at Rapid Transit do not hire people with even the merest tendency in that direction. And may I suggest, sir, that you clean your own house before making implications about others?"

And with that, Mr. Bemis broke the connection.

No one was going to put anything over on *him*.

"Dead end," Rath said heavily. He turned and shouted, "Smith! Did you find any prints?"

Lieutenant Smith, his coat off and sleeves rolled up, bounded over. "Nothing usable, sir."

Rath's thin lips tightened. It had been close to seven hours since the customer had taken the Martian machine. There was no telling what harm had been done by now. The customer would be justified in bringing suit against the Company. Not that the money mattered much; it was the bad publicity that was to be avoided at all costs.

"Beg pardon, sir," Haskins said.

Rath ignored him. What next? Rapid Transit was not going to cooperate. Would the Armed Services make their records available for scansion by somatotype and pigmentation?

"Sir," Haskins said again.

"What is it?"

"I just remembered the customer's friend's name. It was Magnessen."

"Are you sure of that?"

"Absolutely," Haskins said, with the first confidence he had shown in hours. "I've taken the liberty of looking him up in the telephone book, sir. There's only one Manhattan listing under that name."

Rath glowered at him from under shaggy eyebrows. "Haskins, I hope you are not wrong about this. I sincerely hope that."

"I do too, sir," Haskins admitted, feeling his knees begin to shake.

"Because if you are," Rath said, "I will…Never mind. Let's go!"

By police escort, they arrived at the address in fifteen minutes. It was an ancient brownstone and Magnessen's name was on a second-floor door. They knocked.

The door opened and a stocky, crop-headed, shirt-sleeved man in his thirties stood before them. He turned slightly pale at the sight of so many uniforms, but held his ground.

"What is this?" he demanded.

"You Magnessen?" Lieutenant Smith barked.

"Yeah. What's the beef? If it's about my hi-fi playing too loud, I can tell you that old hag downstairs—"

"May we come in?" Rath asked. "It's important."

Magnessen seemed about to refuse, so Rath pushed past him, followed by Smith, Follansby, Haskins, and a small army of policemen. Magnessen turned to face them, bewildered, defiant and more than a little awed.

"Mr. Magnessen," Rath said, in the pleasantest voice he could muster, "I hope you'll forgive the intrusion. Let me assure you, it is in the Public Interest, as well as your own. Do you know a short, angry-looking, red-haired, red-eyed man?"

"Yes," Magnessen said slowly and warily.

Haskins let out a sigh of relief.

"Would you tell us his name and address?" asked Rath.

"I suppose you mean—hold it! What's he done?"

"Nothing."

"Then what you want him for?"

"There's no time for explanations," Rath said. "Believe me, it's in his own best interest, too. What is his name?"

Magnessen studied Rath's ugly, honest face, trying to make up his mind.

Lieutenant Smith said, "Come on, talk, Magnessen, if you know what's good for you. We want the name and we want it quick."

It was the wrong approach. Magnessen lighted a cigarette, blew smoke in Smith's direction and inquired, "You got a warrant, buddy?"

"You bet I have," Smith said, striding forward. "I'll warrant you, wise guy."

"Stop it!" Rath ordered. "Lieutenant Smith, thank you for your assistance. I won't need you any longer."

Smith left sulkily, taking his platoon with him.

Rath said, "I apologize for Smith's over-eagerness. You had better hear the problem." Briefly but fully, he told the story of the customer and the Martian therapeutic machine.

When he was finished, Magnessen looked more suspicious than ever. "You say he wants to kill *me?*"

"Definitely."

"That's a lie! I don't know what your game is, mister, but you'll never make me believe that. Elwood's my best friend. We been best friends since we was kids. We been in service together. Elwood would cut off his arm for me. And I'd do the same for him."

"Yes, yes," Rath said impatiently, "in a sane frame of mind, he would. But your friend Elwood—is that his first name or last?"

"First," Magnessen said tauntingly.

"Your friend Elwood is psychotic."

"You don't know him. That guy loves me like a brother. Look, what's Elwood really done? Defaulted on some payments or something? I can help out."

"You thickheaded imbecile!" Rath shouted. "I'm trying to save your life, and the life and sanity of your friend!"

"But how do I know?" Magnessen pleaded. "You guys come busting in here—"

"You must trust me," Rath said.

Magnessen studied Rath's face and nodded sourly. "His name's Elwood Caswell. He lives just down the block at number 341."

The man who came to the door was short, with red hair and red-rimmed eyes. His right hand was thrust into his coat pocket. He seemed very calm.

"Are you Elwood Caswell?" Rath asked. "The Elwood Caswell who bought a Regenerator early this afternoon at the Home Therapy Appliances Store?"

"Yes," said Caswell. "Won't you come in?"

Inside Caswell's small living room, they saw the Regenerator, glistening black and chrome, standing near the couch. It was unplugged.

"Have you used it?" Rath asked anxiously.

"Yes."

Follansby stepped forward. "Mr. Caswell, I don't know how to explain this, but we made a terrible mistake. The Regenerator you took was a Martian model—for giving therapy to Martians."

"I know," said Caswell.

"You do?"

"Of course. It became pretty obvious after a while."

"It was a dangerous situation," Rath said. "Especially for a man with your—ah—troubles." He studied Caswell covertly. The man seemed fine, but appearances were frequently deceiving, especially with psychotics. Caswell had been homicidal; there was no reason why he should not still be.

And Rath began to wish he had not dismissed Smith and his police-men so summarily. Sometimes an armed squad was a comforting thing to have around.

Caswell walked across the room to the therapeutic machine. One hand was still in his jacket pocket; the other he laid affectionately upon the Regenerator.

"The poor thing tried its best," he said. "Of course, it couldn't cure what wasn't there." He laughed. "But it came very near succeeding!"

Rath studied Caswell's face and said, in a trained, casual tone, "Glad there was no harm, sir. The Company will, of course, reimburse you for your lost time and for your mental anguish—"

"Naturally," Caswell said.

"—and we will substitute a proper Terran Regenerator at once."

"That won't be necessary."

"It *won't?*"

"No." Caswell's voice was decisive. "The machine's attempt at therapy forced me into a compete self-appraisal. There was a moment of absolute insight, during which I was able to evaluate and discard my homicidal intentions toward poor Magnessen."

Rath nodded dubiously. "You feel no such urge now?"

"Not in the slightest."

Rath frowned deeply, started to say something, and stopped. He turned to Follansby and Haskins. "Get that machine out of here. I'll have a few things to say to you at the store."

The manager and the clerk lifted the Regenerator and left.

Rath took a deep breath. "Mr. Caswell, I would strongly advise that you accept a new Regenerator from the Company, gratis. Unless a cure is effected in a proper mechanotherapeutic manner, there is always the dan-ger of a setback."

"No danger with me," Caswell said, airily but with deep conviction. "Thank you for your consideration, sir. And good night."

Rath shrugged and walked to the door.

"Wait!" Caswell called.

Rath turned. Caswell had taken his hand out of his pocket. In it was a revolver. Rath felt sweat trickle down his arms. He calculated the dis-tance between himself and Caswell. Too far.

"Here," Caswell said, extending the revolver butt-first. "I won't need this any longer."

Rath managed to keep his face expressionless as he accepted the re-volver and stuck it into a shapeless pocket.

"Good night," Caswell said. He closed the door behind Rath and bolted it.

At last he was alone.

Caswell walked into the kitchen. He opened a bottle of beer, took a deep swallow and sat down at the kitchen table. He stared fixedly at a point just above and to the left of the clock.

He had to form his plans now. There was no time to lose.

Magnessen! That inhuman monster who cut down the Caswell goricae! Magnessen! The man who, even now, was secretly planning to infect New York with the abhorrent feem desire! Oh, Magnessen, I wish you a long, long life, filled with the torture I can inflict on you. And to start with...

Caswell smiled to himself as he planned exactly how he would dwark Magnessen in a vlendish manner.

Early Model

The landing was almost a catastrophe. Bentley knew his coordination was impaired by the bulky weight on his back; he didn't realize how much until, at a crucial moment, he stabbed the wrong button. The ship began to drop like a stone. At the last moment, he overcompensated, scorching a black hole into the plain below him. His ship touched, teetered for a moment, then sickeningly came to rest.

Bentley had effected mankind's first landing on Tels IV.

His immediate reaction was to pour himself a sizable drink of strictly medicinal scotch.

When that was out of the way, he turned on his radio. The receiver was imbedded in his ear, where it itched, and the microphone was a surgically implanted lump in his throat. The portable sub-space set was self-tuning, which was all to the good, since Bentley knew nothing about narrowcasting on so tight a beam over so great a distance.

"All's well," he told Professor Sliggert over the radio. "It's an Earth-type planet, just as the survey reports said. The ship is intact. And I'm happy to report that I did not break my neck in the landing."

"Of course not," Sliggert said, his voice thin and emotionless through the tiny receiver. "What about the Protec? How does it feel? Have you become used to it yet?"

Bentley said, "Nope. It still feels like a monkey on my back."

"Well, you'll adjust," Sliggert assured him. "The Institute sends its congratulations and I believe the government is awarding you a medal of some sort. Remember, the thing now is to fraternize with the aborigines, and if possible to establish a trade agreement of some sort, any sort. As a precedent. We need this planet, Bentley."

"I know."

"Good luck. Report whenever you have a chance."

"I'll do that," Bentley promised and signed off.

He tried to stand up, but didn't make it on the first attempt. Then, using the handholds that had been conveniently spaced above the control

331

board, he managed to stagger erect. Now he appreciated the toll that no-weight extracts from a man's muscles. He wished he had done his exercises more faithfully on the long trip out from Earth.

Bentley was a big, jaunty young man, over six feet tall, widely and solidly constructed. On Earth, he had weighed two hundred pounds and had moved with an athlete's grace. But ever since leaving Earth, he'd had the added encumbrance of seventy-three pounds strapped irrevocably and immovably to his back. Under the circumstances, his movements resembled those of a very old elephant wearing tight shoes.

He moved his shoulders under the wide plastic straps, grimaced, and walked to a starboard porthole. In the distance, perhaps half a mile away, he could see a village, low and brown on the horizon. There were dots on the plain moving toward him. The villagers apparently had decided to discover what strange object had fallen from the skies breathing fire and making an uncanny noise.

"Good show," Bentley said to himself. Contact would have been difficult if these aliens had shown no curiosity. This eventuality had been considered by the Earth Interstellar Exploration Institute, but no solution had been found. Therefore it had been struck from the list of possibilities.

The villagers were drawing closer. Bentley decided it was time to get ready. He opened a locker and took out his linguascene, which, with some difficulty, he strapped to his chest. On one hip, he fastened a large canteen of water. On the other hip went a package of concentrated food. Across his stomach, he put a package of assorted tools. Strapped to one leg was the radio. Strapped to the other was a medicine kit.

Thus equipped, Bentley was carrying a total of 148 pounds, every ounce of it declared essential for an extraterrestrial explorer.

The fact that he lurched rather than walked was considered unimportant.

The natives had reached the ship now and were gathering around it, commenting disparagingly. They were bipeds. They had short thick tails and their features were human, but nightmare human. Their coloring was a vivid orange.

Bentley also noticed that they were armed. He could see knives, spears, lances, stone hammers, and flint axes. At the sight of this armament, a satisfied smile broke over his face. Here was the justification for his discomfort, the reason for the unwieldy seventy-three pounds which had remained on his back ever since leaving Earth.

It didn't matter what weapons these aboriginals had, right up to the nuclear level. They couldn't hurt him.

That's what Professor Sliggert, head of the Institute, inventor of the Protec, had told him.

Bentley opened the port. A cry of astonishment came from the Telians. His linguascene, after a few seconds' initial hesitation, translated the cries as, "Oh! Ah! How strange! Unbelievable! Ridiculous! Shockingly improper!"

Bentley descended the ladder on the ship's side, carefully balancing his 148 pounds of excess weight. The natives formed a semicircle around him, their weapons ready.

He advanced on them. They shrank back. Smiling pleasantly, he said, "I come as a friend." The linguascene barked out the harsh consonants of the Telian language.

They didn't seem to believe him. Spears were poised and one Telian, larger than the others and wearing a colorful headdress, held a hatchet in readiness.

Bentley felt the slightest tremor run through him. He was invulnerable, of course. There was nothing they could do to him as long as he wore the Protec. Nothing! Professor Sliggert had been certain of it.

Before takeoff, Professor Sliggert had strapped the Protec to Bentley's back, adjusted the straps and stepped back to admire his brainchild.

"Perfect," he had announced with quiet pride.

Bentley had shrugged his shoulders under the weight. "Kind of heavy, isn't it?"

"But what can we do?" Sliggert asked him. "This is the first of its kind, the prototype. I have used every weight-saving device possible— transistors, light alloys, printed circuits, pencil-power packs, and all the rest. Unfortunately, early models of any invention are invariably bulky."

"Seems as though you could have streamlined it a bit," Bentley objected, peering over his shoulder.

"Streamlining comes much later. First must be concentration, then compaction, then group-function, and finally styling. It's always been that way and it will always be. Take the typewriter. Now it is simply a keyboard, almost as flat as a briefcase. But the prototype typewriter worked with foot pedals and required the combined strength of several men to lift. Take the hearing aid, which actually shrank pounds through the various stages of its development. Take the linguascene, which began as a very massive, complicated electronic calculator weighing several tons—"

"Okay," Bentley broke in. "If this is the best you could make it, good enough. How do I get out of it?"

Professor Sliggert smiled.

Bentley reached around. He couldn't find a buckle. He pulled ineffectually at the shoulder straps, but could find no way of undoing them. Nor could he squirm out. It was like being in a new and fiendishly efficient straitjacket.

"Come on, Professor, how do I get it off?"

"I'm not going to tell you."

"Huh?"

"The Protec is uncomfortable, is it not?" Sliggert asked. "You would rather not wear it?"

"You're damned right."

"Of course. Did you know that in wartime, on the battlefield, soldiers have a habit of discarding essential equipment because it is bulky or uncomfortable? But we can't take chances on you. You are going to an alien planet, Mr. Bentley. You will be exposed to wholly unknown dangers. It is necessary that you be protected at all times."

"I know that," Bentley said. "I've got enough sense to figure out when to wear this thing."

"But do you? We selected you for attributes such as resourcefulness, stamina, physical strength—and, of course, a certain amount of intelligence. But—"

"Thanks!"

"But those qualities do not make you prone to caution. Suppose you found the natives seemingly friendly and decided to discard the heavy, uncomfortable Protec? What would happen if you had misjudged their attitude? This is very easy to do on Earth; think how much easier it will be on an alien planet!"

"I can take care of myself," Bentley said.

Sliggert nodded grimly. "That is what Atwood said when he left for Durabella II and we have never heard from him again. Nor have we heard from Blake, or Smythe, or Korishell. Can you turn a knife-thrust from the rear? Have you eyes in the back of your head? No, Mr. Bentley, you haven't—*but the Protec has!*"

"Look," Bentley had said, "believe it or not, I'm a responsible adult. I will wear the Protec at all times when on the surface of an alien planet. Now tell me how to get it off."

"You don't seem to realize something, Bentley. If only your life were at stake, we would let you take what risks seemed reasonable to you. But we are also risking several billion dollars' worth of spaceship and equipment. Moreover, this is the Protec's field test. The only way to be sure of the results is to have you wear it all the time. The only way to ensure *that* is by not telling you how to remove it. We want results. You are going to stay alive whether you like it or not."

Bentley had thought it over and agreed grudgingly. "I guess I might be tempted to take it off, if the natives were really friendly."

"You will be spared that temptation. Now do you understand how it works?"

"Sure," Bentley said. "But will it really do all you say?"

"It passed the lab tests perfectly."

"I'd hate to have some little thing go wrong. Suppose it pops a fuse or blows a wire?"

"That is one of the reasons for its bulk," Sliggert explained patiently. "Triple everything. We are taking no chance of mechanical failure."

"And the power supply?"

"Good for a century or better at full load. The Protec is perfect, Bentley! After this field test, I have no doubt it will become standard equipment for all extraterrestrial explorers." Professor Sliggert permitted himself a faint smile of pride.

"All right," Bentley had said, moving his shoulders under the wide plastic straps. "I'll get used to it."

But he hadn't. A man just doesn't get used to a seventy three-pound monkey on his back.

The Telians didn't know what to make of Bentley. They argued for several minutes, while the explorer kept a strained smile on his face. Then one Telian stepped forward. He was taller than the others and wore a distinctive headdress made of glass, bones and bits of rather garishly painted wood.

"My friends," the Telian said, "there is an evil here which I, Rinek, can sense."

Another Telian wearing a similar headdress stepped forward and said, "It is not well for a ghost doctor to speak of such things."

"Of course not," Rinek admitted. "It is not well to speak of evil in the presence of evil, for evil then grows strong. But a ghost doctor's work is the detection and avoidance of evil. In this work, we must persevere, no matter what the risk."

Several other men in the distinctive headdress, the ghost doctors, had come forward now. Bentley decided that they were the Telian equivalent of priests and probably wielded considerable political power as well.

"I don't think he's evil," a young and cheerful-looking ghost doctor named Huascl said.

"Of course he is. Just look at him."

"Appearances prove nothing, as we know from the time the good spirit Ahut M'Kandi appeared in the form of a—"

"No lectures, Huascl. All of us know the parables of Lalland. The point is, can we take a chance?"

Huascl turned to Bentley. "Are you evil?" the Telian asked earnestly.

"No," Bentley said. He had been puzzled at first by the Telians' intense preoccupation with his spiritual status. They hadn't even asked him where he'd come from, or how, or why. But then, it was not so strange. If an alien had landed on Earth during certain periods of religious zeal, the first question asked might have been, "Are you a creature of God or of Satan?"

"He says he's not evil," Huascl said.

"How would he know?"

"If he doesn't, who does?"

"Once the great spirit G'tal presented a wise man with three kdal and said to him—"

And on it went. Bentley found his legs beginning to bend under the weight of all his equipment. The linguascene was no longer able to keep pace with the shrill theological discussion that raged around him. His status seemed to depend upon two or three disputed points, none of which the ghost doctors wanted to talk about, since to talk about evil was in itself dangerous.

To make matters more complicated, there was a schism over the concept of the penetrability of evil, the younger ghost doctors holding to one side, the older to the other. The factions accused each other of rankest heresy, but Bentley couldn't figure out who believed what or which interpretation aided him.

When the sun drooped low over the grassy plain, the battle still raged. Then, suddenly, the ghost doctors reached an agreement, although Bentley couldn't decide why or on what basis.

Huascl stepped forward as spokesman for the younger ghost doctors.

"Stranger," he declared, "we have decided not to kill you."

Bentley suppressed a smile. That was just like a primitive people, granting life to an invulnerable being!

"Not yet, anyhow," Huascl amended quickly, catching a frown upon Rinek and the older ghost doctors. "It depends entirely upon you. We will go to the village and purify ourselves and we will feast. Then we win initiate you into the society of ghost doctors. No evil thing can become a ghost doctor; it is expressly forbidden. In this manner, we will detect your true nature."

"I am deeply grateful," Bentley said.

"But if you *are* evil, we are pledged to destroy evil. And if we must, we can!"

The assembled Telians cheered his speech and began at once the mile trek to the village. Now that a status had been assigned Bentley, even tentatively, the natives were completely friendly. They chatted amiably with him about crops, droughts, and famines.

Bentley staggered along under his equipment, tired, but inwardly elated. This was really a coup! As an initiate, a priest, he would have an unsurpassed opportunity to gather anthropological data, to establish trade, to pave the way for the future development of Tels IV.

All he had to do was pass the initiation tests. And not get killed, of course, he reminded himself, smiling.

It was funny how positive the ghost doctors had been that they *could* kill him.

The village consisted of two dozen huts arranged in a rough circle. Beside each mud-and-thatch hut was a small vegetable garden, and sometimes a pen for the Telian version of cattle. There were small green-furred animals roaming between the huts, which the Telians treated as pets. The grassy central area was common ground. Here was the community well and here were the shrines to various gods and devils. In this area, lighted by a great bonfire, a feast had been laid out by the village women.

Bentley arrived at the feast in a state of near-exhaustion, stooped beneath his essential equipment. Gratefully, he sank to the ground with the villagers and the celebration began.

First the village women danced a welcoming for him. They made a pretty sight, their orange skin glinting in the firelight, their tails swinging gracefully in unison. Then a village dignitary named Occip came over to him, bearing a full bowl.

"Stranger," Occip said, "you are from a distant land and your ways are not our ways. Yet let us be brothers! Partake, therefore, of this food to seal the bond between us, and in the name of all sanctity!"

Bowing low, he offered the bowl.

It was an important moment, one of those pivotal occasions that can seal forever the friendship between races or make them eternal enemies. But Bentley was not able to take advantage of it. As tactfully as he could, he refused the symbolic food.

"But it is purified!" Occip said.

Bentley explained that, because of a tribal taboo, he could eat only his own food. Occip could not understand that different species have different dietary requirements. For example, Bentley pointed out, the staff of life on Tels IV might well be some strychnine compound. But he did not add that even if he wanted to take the chance, his Protec would never allow it.

Nonetheless, his refusal alarmed the village. There were hurried conferences among the ghost doctors. Then Rinek came over and sat beside him.

"Tell me," Rinek inquired after a while, "what do you think of evil?"

"Evil is not good," Bentley said solemnly.

"Ah!" The ghost doctor pondered that, his tail flicking nervously over the grass. A small green-furred pet, a mog, began to play with his tail. Rinek pushed him away and said, "So you do not like evil."

"No."

"And you would permit no evil influence around you?"

"Certainly not," Bentley said, stifling a yawn. He was growing bored with the ghost doctor's tortuous examining.

"In that case, you would have no objection to receiving the sacred and very holy spear that Kran K'leu brought down from the abode of the Small Gods, the brandishing of which confers good upon a man."

"I would be pleased to receive it," said Bentley, heavy-eyed, hoping this would be the last ceremony of the evening.

Rinek grunted his approval and moved away. The women's dances came to an end. The ghost doctors began to chant in deep, impressive voices. The bonfire flared high.

Huascl came forward. His face was now painted in thin black and white stripes. He carried an ancient spear of black wood, its head of shaped volcanic glass, its length intricately although primitively carved.

Holding the spear aloft, Huascl said, "O Stranger from the Skies, accept from us this spear of sanctity! Kran K'leu gave this lance to Trin, our first father, and bestowed upon it a magical nature and caused it to be a vessel of the spirits of the good. Evil cannot abide the presence of this spear! Take, then, our blessings with it."

Bentley heaved himself to his feet. He understood the value of a ceremony like this. His acceptance of the spear should end, once and for all, any doubts as to his spiritual status. Reverently he inclined his head, Huascl came forward, held out the spear and—

The Protec snapped into action.

Its operation was simple, in common with many great inventions. When its calculator-component received a danger cue, the Protec threw a force field around its operator. This field rendered him invulnerable, for it was completely and absolutely impenetrable. But there were certain unavoidable disadvantages.

If Bentley had had a weak heart, the Protec might have killed him there and then, for its action was electronically sudden, completely unexpected and physically wrenching. One moment, he was standing in front of the great bonfire, his hand held out for the sacred spear. In the next moment, he was plunged into darkness.

As usual, he felt as though he had been catapulted into a musty, lightless closet, with rubbery walls pressing close on all sides. He cursed the machine's super-efficiency. The spear had not been a threat; it was part of an important ceremony. But the Protec, with its literal senses, had interpreted it as a possible danger.

Now, in the darkness, Bentley fumbled for the controls that would release the field. As usual, the force field interfered with his positional sense, a condition that seemed to grow worse with each subsequent use. Carefully he felt his way along his chest, where the button should have been, and located it at last under his right armpit, where it had twisted around to. He released the field.

The feast had ended abruptly. The natives were standing close together for protection, weapons ready, tails stretched stiffly out. Huascl, caught in the force field's range, had been flung twenty feet and was slowly picking himself up.

The ghost doctors began to chant a purification dirge, for protection against evil spirits. Bentley couldn't blame them.

When a Protec force field goes on, it appears as an opaque black sphere, some ten feet in diameter. If it is struck, it repels with a force equal to the impact. White lines appear in the sphere's surface, swirl, coalesce, vanish. And as the sphere spins, it screams in a thin, high-pitched wail.

All in all, it was a sight hardly calculated to win the confidence of a primitive and superstitious people.

"Sorry," Bentley said, with a weak smile. There hardly seemed anything else to say.

Huascl limped back, but kept his distance. "You cannot accept the sacred spear," he stated.

"Well, it's not exactly that," said Bentley. "It's just—well, I've got this protective device, kind of like a shield, you know? It doesn't like spears. Couldn't you offer me a sacred gourd?"

"Don't be ridiculous," Huascl said. "Who ever heard of a sacred gourd?"

"No, I guess not. But please take my word for it—I'm not evil. Really I'm not. I've just got a taboo about spears."

The ghost doctors talked among themselves too rapidly for the lingua scene to interpret it. It caught only the words "evil," "destroy," and "purification." Bentley decided his forecast didn't look too favorable.

After the conference, Huascl came over to him and said, "Some of the others feel that you should be killed at once, before you bring some great unhappiness upon the village. I told them, however, that you cannot be blamed for the many taboos that restrict you. We will pray for you through the night. And perhaps, in the morning, the initiation will be possible."

Bentley thanked him. He was shown to a hut and then the Telians left him as quickly as possible. There was an ominous hush over the village; from his doorway, Bentley could see little groups of natives talking earnestly and glancing covertly in his direction.

It was a poor beginning for cooperation between two races.

He immediately contacted Professor Sliggert and told him what had happened.

"Unfortunate," the professor said. "But primitive people are notoriously treacherous. They might have meant to kill you with the spear instead of actually handing it to you. Let you have it, that is, in the most literal sense."

"I'm positive there was no such intention," Bentley said. "After all, you have to start trusting people sometime."

"Not with a billion dollars' worth of equipment in your charge."

"But I'm not going to be able to *do* anything!" Bentley shouted. "Don't you understand? They're suspicious of me already. I wasn't able to accept their sacred spear. That means I'm very possibly evil. Now what if I can't pass the initiation ceremony tomorrow? Suppose some idiot starts to pick his teeth with a knife and the Protec saves me? All the favorable first impressions I built up will be lost."

"Good will can be regained," Professor Sliggert said sententiously. "But a billion dollars' worth of equipment—"

"—can be salvaged by the next expedition. Look, Professor, give me a break. Isn't there some way I can control this thing manually?"

"No way at all," Sliggert replied. "That would defeat the entire purpose of the machine. You might just as well not be wearing it if you're allowed to rely on your own reflexes rather than electronic impulses."

"Then tell me how to take it off."

"The same argument holds true—you wouldn't be protected at all times."

"Look," Bentley protested, "you chose me as a competent explorer. I'm the guy on the spot. I know what the conditions are here. Tell me how to get it off."

"No! The Protec must have a full field test. And we want you to come back alive."

"That's another thing," Bentley said. "These people seem kind of sure they can kill me."

"Primitive peoples always overestimate the potency of their strength, weapons, and magic."

"I know, I know. But you're certain there's no way they can get through the field? Poison, maybe?"

"Nothing can get through the field," Sliggert said patiently. "Not even light rays can penetrate. Not even gamma radiation. You are wearing an impregnable fortress, Mr. Bentley. Why can't you manage to have a little faith in it?"

"Early models of inventions sometimes need a lot of ironing out," Bentley grumbled. "But have it your way. Won't you tell me how to take it off, though, just in case something goes wrong?"

"I wish you would stop asking me that, Mr. Bentley. You were chosen to give Protec a *full* field test. That's just what you are going to do."

When Bentley signed off, it was deep twilight outside and the villagers had returned to their huts. Campfires burned low and he could hear the call of night creatures.

At that moment, Bentley felt very alien and exceedingly homesick.

He was tired almost to the point of unconsciousness, but he forced himself to eat some concentrated food and drink a little water. Then he unstrapped the tool kit, the radio, and the canteen, tugged defeatedly at the Protec, and lay down to sleep.

Just as he dozed off, the Protec went violently into action, nearly snapping his neck out of joint.

Wearily he fumbled for the controls, located them near his stomach, and turned off the field.

The hut looked exactly the same. He could find no source of attack.

Was the Protec losing its grip on reality, he wondered, or had a Telian tried to spear him through the window?

Then Bentley saw a tiny mog puppy scuttling away frantically, its legs churning up clouds of dust.

The little beast probably just wanted to get warm, Bentley thought. But of course it was alien. Its potential for danger could not be overlooked by the ever-wary Protec.

He fell asleep again and immediately began to dream that he was locked in a prison of bright red sponge rubber. He could push the walls out and out and out, but they never yielded, and at last he would have to let go and be gently shoved back to the center of the prison. Over and over, this happened, until suddenly he felt his back wrenched and awoke within the Protec's lightless field.

This time he had real difficulty finding the controls. He hunted desperately by feel until the bad air made him gasp in panic. He located the controls at last under his chin, released the field, and began to search groggily for the source of the new attack.

He found it. A twig had fallen from the thatch roof and had tried to land on him. The Protec, of course, had not allowed it.

"Aw, come on now," Bentley groaned aloud. "Let's use a little judgment!"

But he was really too tired to care. Fortunately, there were no more assaults that night.

Huascl came to Bentley's hut in the morning, looking very solemn and considerably disturbed.

"There were great sounds from your hut during the night," the ghost doctor said, "Sounds of torment, as though you were wrestling with a devil."

"I'm just a restless sleeper," Bentley explained.

Huascl smiled to show that he appreciated the joke.

"My friend, did you pray for purification last night and for release from evil?"

"I certainly did."

"And was your prayer granted?"

"It was," Bentley said hopefully. "There's no evil around me. Not a bit."

Huascl looked dubious. "But can you be sure? Perhaps you should depart from us in peace. If you cannot be initiated, we shall have to destroy you—"

"Don't worry about it," Bentley told him. "Let's get started."

"Very well," Huascl said, and together they left the hut.

The initiation was to be held in front of the great bonfire in the village square. Messengers had been sent out during the night and ghost doctors from many villages were there. Some had come as far as twenty miles to take part in the rites and to see the alien with their own eyes. The ceremonial drum had been taken from its secret hiding place and was now booming solemnly. The villagers watched, chattered together, laughed. But Bentley could detect an undercurrent of nervousness and strain.

There was a long series of dances. Bentley twitched worriedly when the last figure started, for the leading dancer was swinging a glass-studded club around his head. Nearer and nearer the dancer whirled, now only a few feet away from him, his club a dazzling streak.

The villagers watched, fascinated. Bentley shut his eyes, expecting to be plunged momentarily into the darkness of the force field.

But the dancer moved away at last and the dance ended with a roar of approval from the villagers.

Huascl began to speak. Bentley realized with a thrill of relief that this was the end of the ceremony.

"O brothers," Huascl said, "this alien has come across the great emptiness to be our brother. Many of his ways are strange and around him there seems to hang a strange hint of evil. And yet who can doubt that he means well? Who can doubt that he is, in essence, a good and honorable person? With this initiation, we purge him of evil and make him one of us."

There was dead silence as Huascl walked up to Bentley. "Now," Huascl said, "you are a ghost doctor and indeed one of us." He held out his hand.

Bentley felt his heart leap within him. He had won! He had been accepted! He reached out and clasped Huascl's hand.

Or tried to. He didn't quite make it, for the Protec, ever alert, saved him from the possibly dangerous contact.

"You damned idiotic gadget!" Bentley bellowed, quickly finding the control and releasing the field.

He saw at once that the fat was in the fire.

"Evil!" shrieked the Telians, frenziedly waving their weapons.

"Evil!" screamed the ghost doctors.

Bentley turned despairingly to Huascl.

"Yes," the young ghost doctor said sadly, "it is true. We had hoped to cure the evil by our ancient ceremonial. But it could not be. This evil must be destroyed! *Kill the devil!*"

A shower of spears came at Bentley. The Protec responded instantly. Soon it was apparent that an impasse had been reached. Bentley would remain for a few minutes in the field, then override the controls. The Telians, seeing him still unharmed, would renew their barrage and the Protec would instantly go back into action.

Bentley tried to walk back to his ship. But the Protec went on again each time he shut it off. It would take him a month or two to cover a mile, at that rate, so he stopped trying. He would simply wait the attackers out. After a while, they would find out they couldn't hurt him and the two races would finally get down to business.

He tried to relax within the field, but found it impossible. He was hungry and extremely thirsty. And his air was starting to grow stale.

Then Bentley remembered, with a sense of shock, that air had not gone through the surrounding field the night before. Naturally—nothing could get through. If he wasn't careful, he could be asphyxiated.

Even an impregnable fortress could fall, he knew, if the defenders were starved or suffocated out.

He began to think furiously. How long could the Telians keep up the attack? They would have to grow tired sooner or later, wouldn't they?

Or would they?

He waited as long as he could, until the air was all but unbreathable, then overrode the controls. The Telians were sitting on the ground around him. Fires had been lighted and food was cooking. Rinek lazily threw a spear at him and the field went on.

So, Bentley thought, they had learned. They were going to starve him out.

He tried to think, but the walls of his dark closet seemed to be pressing against him. He was growing claustrophobic and already his air was stale again.

He thought for a moment, then overrode the controls. The Telians looked at him coolly. One of them reached for a spear.

"Wait!" Bentley shouted. At the same moment, he turned on his radio.

"What do you want?" Rinek asked.

"Listen to me! It isn't fair to trap me in the Protec like this!"

"Eh? What's going on?" Professor Sliggert asked, through the ear receiver.

"You Telians know—" Bentley said hoarsely—"you know that you can destroy me by continually activating the Protec. I can't turn it off! I can't get out of it!"

"Ah'" said Professor Sliggert. "I see the difficulty. Yes."

"We are sorry," Huascl apologized. "But evil must be destroyed."

"Of course it must," Bentley said desperately. "But not me. Give me a chance. *Professor!*"

"This is indeed a flaw," Professor Sliggert mused, "and a serious one. Strange, but things like this, of course, can't show up in the lab, only in a full-scale field test. The fault will be rectified in the new models."

"Great! But I'm here now! How do I get this thing off?"

"I *am* sorry," Sliggert said. "I honestly never thought the need would arise. To tell the truth, I designed the harness so that you could not get out of it under any circumstances."

"Why, you lousy—"

"Please!" Sliggert said sternly. "Let's keep our heads. If you can hold out for a few months, we might be able—"

"I can't! The air! Water!"

"Fire!" cried Rinek, his face contorted. "By fire, we will chain the demon!"

And the Protec snapped on.

Bentley tried to think things out carefully in the darkness. He would have to get out of the Protec. But how? There was a knife in his tool kit. Could he cut through the tough plastic straps? He would have to!

But what then? Even if he emerged from his fortress, the ship was a mile away. Without the Protec, they could kill him with a single spear thrust. And they were pledged to, for he had been declared irrevocably evil.

But if he ran, he at least had a chance. And it was better to die of a spear thrust than to strangle slowly in absolute darkness.

Bentley turned off the field. The Telians were surrounding him with camp-fires, closing off his retreat with a wall of flame.

He hacked frantically at the plastic web. The knife slithered and slipped along the strap. And he was back in Protec.

When he came out again, the circle of fire was complete. The Telians were cautiously pushing the fires toward him, lessening the circumference of his circle.

Bentley felt his heart sink. Once the fires were close enough, the Protec would go on and stay on. He would not be able to override a continuous danger signal. He would be trapped within the field for as long as they fed the flames.

And considering how primitive people felt about devils, it was just possible that they would keep the fire going for a century or two.

He dropped the knife, used side-cutters on the plastic strap and succeeded in ripping it halfway through.

He was in Protec again.

Bentley was dizzy, half-fainting from fatigue, gasping great mouthfuls of foul air. With an effort, he pulled himself together. He couldn't drop now. That would be the end.

He found the controls, overrode them. The fires were very near him now. He could feel their warmth against his face. He snipped viciously at the strap and felt it give.

He slipped out of the Protec just as the field activated again. The force of it threw him into the fire. But he fell feet-first and jumped out of the flames without getting burned.

The villagers roared. Bentley sprinted away; as he ran, he dumped the linguascene, the tool kit, the radio, the concentrated food and the canteen. He glanced back once and saw that the Telians were after him.

But he was holding his own. His tortured heart seemed to be pounding his chest apart and his lungs threatened to collapse at any moment. But now the spaceship was before him, looming great and friendly on the flat plain.

He was going to just make it. Another twenty yards…

Something green flashed in front of him. It was a small, green-furred mog puppy. The clumsy beast was trying to get out of his way.

He swerved to avoid crushing it and realized too late that he should never have broken stride. A rock turned under his foot and he sprawled forward.

He heard the pounding feet of the Telians coming toward him and managed to climb on one knee.

Then somebody threw a club and it landed neatly on his forehead.

"Ar gwy dril?" a voice asked incomprehensibly from far off.

Bentley opened his eyes and saw Huascl bending over him. He was in a hut, back in the village. Several armed ghost doctors were at the doorway, watching.

"Ar dril?" Huascl asked again.

Bentley rolled over and saw, piled neatly beside him, his canteen, concentrated food, tools, radio and linguascene. He took a deep drink of water, then turned on the linguascene.

"I asked if you felt all right," Huascl said.

"Sure, fine," Bentley grunted, feeling his head. "Let's get it over with."

"Over with?"

"You're going to kill me, aren't you? Well, let's not make a production out of it."

"But we didn't want to destroy *you*," Huascl said. "We knew you for a good man. It was the devil we wanted!"

"Eh?" asked Bentley in a blank uncomprehending voice.

"Come, look."

The ghost doctors helped Bentley to his feet and brought him outside. There, surrounded by lapping flames, was the glowing great black sphere of the Protec.

"You didn't know, of course," Huascl said, "but there was a devil riding upon your back."

"Huh!" gasped Bentley.

"Yes, it is true. We tried to dispossess him by purification, but he was too strong. We had to force you, brother, to face that evil and throw it aside. We knew you would come through. And you did!"

"I see," Bentley said. "A devil on my back. Yes, I guess so."

That was exactly what the Protec would have to be, to them. A heavy, misshapen weight on his shoulders, hurling out a black sphere whenever they tried to purify it. What else could a religious people do but try to free him from its grasp?

He saw several women of the village bring up baskets of food and throw them into the fire in front of the sphere. He looked inquiringly at Huascl.

"We are propitiating it," Huascl said, "for it is a very strong devil, undoubtedly a miracle-working one. Our village is proud to have such a devil in bondage."

A ghost doctor from a neighboring village stepped up. "Are there more such devils in your homeland? Could you bring us one to worship?"

Several other ghost doctors pressed eagerly forward. Bentley nodded. "It can be arranged," he said.

He knew that the Earth-Tels trade was now begun. And at last a suitable use had been found for Professor Sliggert's Protec.

PILGRIMAGE TO EARTH

Alfred Simon was born on Kazanga IV, a small agricultural planet near Arcturus, and there he drove a combine through the wheatfields, and in the long, hushed evenings listened to the recorded love songs of Earth.

Life was pleasant enough on Kazanga, and the girls were buxom, jolly, frank, and acquiescent, good companions for a hike through the hills or a swim in the brook, staunch mates for life. But romantic—never! There was good fun to be had on Kazanga, in a cheerful, open manner. But there was no more than fun.

Simon felt that something was missing in this bland existence. One day he discovered what it was.

A vendor came to Kazanga in a battered spaceship loaded with books. He was gaunt, white-haired, and a little mad. A celebration was held for him, for novelty was appreciated on the outer worlds.

The vendor told them all the latest gossip: of the price war between Detroit II and III, and how fishing fared on Alana, and what the President's wife on Moracia wore, and how oddly the men of Doran V talked. And at last someone said, "Tell us of Earth."

"Ah!" said the vendor, raising his eyebrows. "You want to hear of the mother planet? Well, friends, there's no place like old Earth, no place at all. On Earth, friends, everything is possible, and nothing is denied."

"Nothing?" Simon asked.

"They've got a law against denial,". the vendor explained, grinning. "No one has ever been known to break it. Earth is *different*, friends. You folks specialize in farming? Well, Earth specializes in impracticalities such as madness, beauty, war, intoxication, purity, horror, and the like, and people come from light-years away to sample these wares."

"And love?" a woman asked.

"Why, girl," the vendor said gently, "Earth is the only place in the galaxy that still has love! Detroit II and III tried it and found it too expensive, you know, and Alana decided it was unsettling, and there was no time to import it on Moracia or Doran V. But as I said, Earth specializes in the impractical, and makes it pay."

"Pay?" a bulky farmer asked.

"Of course! Earth is old, her minerals are gone and her fields are barren. Her colonies are independent now, and filled with sober folk such as yourselves, who want value for their goods. So what else can old Earth deal in, except the nonessentials that make life worth living?"

"Were you in love on Earth?" Simon asked.

"That I was," the vendor answered with a certain grimness. "I was in love, and now I travel. Friends, these books…"

For an exorbitant price, Simon bought an ancient poetry book and, reading, dreamed of passion beneath the lunatic moon, of dawn glimmering whitely upon lovers' parched lips, of locked bodies on a dark beach, desperate with love and deafened by the booming surf.

And only on Earth was this possible! For, as the vendor told, Earth's scattered children were too hard at work wresting a living from alien soil. The wheat and corn grew on Kazanga, and the factories increased on Detroit II and III. The fisheries of Alana were the talk of the Southern Star Belt, and there were dangerous beasts on Moracia, and a whole wilderness to be won on Doran V. And this was good, and exactly as it should be.

But the new worlds were austere, carefully planned, sterile in their perfections. Something had been lost in the dead reaches of space, and only Earth knew love.

Therefore, Simon worked and saved and dreamed. And in his twenty-ninth year he sold his farm, packed all his clean shirts into a serviceable handbag, put on his best suit and a pair of stout walking shoes, and boarded the Kazanga-Metropole Flyer.

At last he came to Earth, where dreams *must* come true, for there is a law against their failure.

He passed quickly through Customs at Spaceport New York, and was shuttled underground to Times Square. There he emerged blinking into daylight, tightly clutching his handbag, for he had been warned about pickpockets, cutpurses, and other denizens of the city.

Breathless with wonder, he looked around.

The first thing that struck him was the endless array of theaters, with attractions in two dimensions, or three or four, depending upon your preference. And what attractions!

To the right of him a beetling marquee proclaimed: LUST ON VENUS! A DOCUMENTARY ACCOUNT OF SEX PRACTICES AMONG THE INHABITANTS OF THE GREEN HELL! SHOCKING! REVEALING!

He wanted to go in. But across the street was a war film. The billboard shouted, THE SUN BUSTERS! DEDICATED TO THE DAREDEVILS OF THE

SPACE MARINES! And farther down was a picture called TARZAN BATTLES THE SATURNIAN GHOULS!

Tarzan, he recalled from his reading, was an ancient ethnic hero of Earth.

It was all wonderful, but there was so much more! He saw little open shops where one could buy food of all worlds, and especially such native Terran dishes as pizza, hot dogs, spaghetti, and knishes. And there were stores that sold surplus clothing from the Terran spacefleets, and other stores that sold nothing but beverages.

Simon didn't know what to do first. Then he heard a staccato burst of gunfire behind him, and whirled.

It was only a shooting gallery, a long, narrow, brightly painted place with a waist-high counter. The manager, a swarthy fat man with a mole on his chin, sat on a high stool and smiled at Simon.

"Try your luck?"

Simon walked over and saw that, instead of the usual targets, there were four scantily dressed women at the end of the gallery, seated upon bullet-scored chairs. Each had a tiny bullseye painted on her forehead and above the heart.

"But do you fire real bullets?" Simon asked.

"Of course!" the manager said. "There's a law against false advertising on Earth. Real bullets and real gals! Step up and knock one off!"

One of the women called out, "Come on, sport! Bet you miss me!"

Another screamed, "He couldn't hit the broad side of a spaceship!"

"Sure he can!" another shouted. "Come on, sport!"

Simon rubbed his forehead and tried not to act surprised. After all, this was Earth, where anything was allowed as long as it was commercially feasible.

He asked, "Are there galleries where you shoot men, too?"

"Of course," the manager said. "But you ain't no pervert, are you?"

"Certainly not!"

"You an outworlder?"

"Yes. How did you know?"

"The suit. Always tell by the suit." The fat man closed his eyes and chanted, "Step up, step up and kill a woman! Get rid of a load of repressions! Squeeze the trigger and feel the old anger ooze out of you! Better than a massage! Better than getting drunk! Step up, step up and kill a woman!"

Simon asked one of the girls, "Do you stay dead when I kill you?"

"Don't be stupid," the girl said.

"But the shock—"

She shrugged her shoulders. "I could do worse."

Simon was about to ask how she could do worse, when the manager leaned over the counter, speaking confidentially.

"Look, buddy. Look what I got here."

Simon glanced over the counter and saw a compact submachine gun.

"For a ridiculously low price," the manager said, "I'll let you use the tommy. You can spray the whole place, shoot down the fixtures, rip up the walls. This drives a .45 slug, buddy, and it kicks like a mule. You really know you're firing when you fire the tommy."

"I am not interested," Simon said sternly.

"I've got a grenade or two," the manager said. "Fragmentation, of course. You could really—"

"No!"

"For a price," the manager said, "you can shoot *me* too, if that's how your tastes run, although I wouldn't have guessed it. What do you say?"

"No! Never! This is horrible!"

The manager looked at him blankly. "Not in the mood now? Okay. I'm open twenty-four hours a day. See you later, sport."

"Never!" Simon said, walking away.

"Be expecting you, lover!" one of the women called after him.

Simon went to a refreshment stand and ordered a small glass of cola-cola. He found that his hands were shaking. With an effort he steadied them and sipped his drink. He reminded himself that he must not judge Earth by his own standards. If people on Earth enjoyed killing people, and the victims didn't mind being killed, why should anyone object?

Or should they?

He was pondering this when a voice at his elbow said, "Hey, bub."

Simon turned and saw a wizened, furtive-faced little man in an over-size raincoat standing beside him.

"Out-of-towner?" the little man asked.

"I am," Simon said. "How did you know?"

"The shoes. I always look at the shoes. How do you like our little planet?"

"It's—confusing," Simon said carefully. "I mean, I didn't expect—well—"

"Of course," the little man said. "You're an idealist. One look at your honest face tells me that, my friend. You've come to Earth for a definite purpose. Am I right?"

Simon nodded. The little man said, "I know your purpose, my friend. You're looking for a war that will make the world safe for something, and you've come to the right place. We have six major wars running at all times, and there's never any wait for an important position in any of them."

"Sorry, but—"

"Right at this moment," the little man said impressively, "the down-trodden workers of Peru are engaged in a desperate struggle against a corrupt and decadent monarchy. One more man could swing the contest! *You, my friend, could be that man! You* could guarantee the socialist victory!"

Observing the expression on Simon's face, the little man said quickly, "But there's a lot to be said for an enlightened aristocracy. The wise old king of Peru (a philosopher-king in the deepest Platonic sense of the word) sorely needs your help. His tiny corps of scientists, humanitarians, Swiss guards, knights of the realm, and loyal peasants is sorely pressed by the foreign-inspired socialist conspiracy. A single man, now—"

"I'm not interested," Simon said.

"In China, the Anarchists—"

"No."

"Perhaps you'd prefer the Communists in Wales? Or the Capitalists in Japan? Or, if your affinities lie with a splinter group such as Feminists, Prohibitionists, Free Silverists, or the like, we could probably arrange—"

"I don't want a war," Simon said.

"Who could blame you!" the little man said, nodding rapidly. "War is hell. In that case, you've come to Earth for love."

"How did you know?" Simon asked.

The little man smiled modestly. "Love and war," he said, "are Earth's two staple commodities. We've been turning them both out in bumper crops since the beginning of time."

"Is love very difficult to find?" Simon asked.

"Walk uptown two blocks," the little man said briskly. "Can't miss it. Tell 'em Joe sent you."

"But that's impossible! You can't just walk out and—"

"What do you know about love?" Joe asked.

"Nothing."

"Well, we're experts on it."

"I know what the books say," Simon said. "Passion beneath the lunatic moon—"

"Sure, and bodies on a dark sea-beach desperate with love and deafened by the booming surf."

"You've read that book?"

"It's the standard advertising brochure. I must be going. Two blocks uptown. Can't miss it."

And with a pleasant nod, Joe moved into the crowd.

Simon finished his cola-cola and walked slowly up Broadway. His brow was knotted in thought but he was determined not to form any premature judgments.

When he reached Forty-fourth Street he saw a tremendous neon sign flashing brightly. It said LOVE, INC.

Smaller neon letters read *Open 24 Hours a Day!*

Beneath that the sign read *Up One Flight.*

Simon frowned, for a terrible suspicion had just crossed his mind. Still, he climbed the stairs and entered a small, tastefully furnished reception room. From there he was sent down a long corridor to a numbered room.

Within the room was a handsome gray-haired man who rose from behind an impressive desk and shook his hand, saying, "Well! How are things on Kazanga!"

"How did you know I was from Kazanga?"

"That shirt. I always look at the shirt. I'm Mr. Tate, and I'm here to serve you to the best of my ability. You are—"

"Simon, Alfred Simon."

"Please be seated, Mr. Simon. Cigarette? Drink? You won't regret coming to us, sir. We're the oldest love-dispensing firm in the business, and much larger than our closest competitor, Passion Unlimited. Moreover, our fees are more reasonable, and bring you an improved product. Might I ask how you heard of us? Did you see our full-page ad in the *Times?* Or—"

"Joe sent me," Simon said.

"Ah, he's an active one," Mr. Tate said, shaking his head playfully. "Well, sir, there's no reason to delay. You've come a long way for love, and love you shall have." He reached for a button on his desk, but Simon stopped him.

Simon said, "I don't want to be rude or anything, but—"

"Yes?" Mr. Tate said, with an encouraging smile.

"I don't understand this," Simon blurted out, flushing deeply, beads of perspiration standing out on his forehead. "I think I'm in the wrong place. I didn't come all the way to Earth just for…I mean, you can't really sell *love,* can you? Not *love!* I mean, then it isn't really *love,* is it?"

"But of course!" Mr. Tate said, half rising from his chair in astonishment. "That's the whole point! Anyone can buy sex. Good Lord, it's the cheapest thing in the universe, next to human life. But *love* is rare, *love* is special, *love* is found only on Earth. Have you read our brochure?"

"Bodies on a dark sea-beach?" Simon asked.

"Yes, that one. I wrote it. Gives something of the feeling, doesn't it? You can't get that feeling from just *anyone,* Mr. Simon. You can get that feeling only from someone who loves you."

Simon said dubiously, "It's not genuine love, though, is it?"

"Of course it is. If we were selling simulated love, we'd label it as such. The advertising laws on Earth are strict, I can assure you. Anything can be sold, but it must be labeled properly. That's ethics, Mr. Simon!"

Tate caught his breath, and continued in a calmer tone. "No sir, make no mistake. Our product is not a substitute. It is the exact selfsame feeling that poets and writers have raved about for thousands of years. Through the wonders of modern science we can bring this feeling to you at your convenience, attractively packaged, completely disposable, and for a ridiculously low price."

Simon said, "I pictured something more—spontaneous."

"Spontaneity has its charm," Mr. Tate agreed. "Our research labs are working on it. Believe me, there's nothing science can't produce, as long as there's a market for it."

"I don't like any of this," Simon said, getting to his feet. "I think I'll just go see a movie."

"Wait!" Mr. Tate cried. "You think we're trying to put something over on you. You think we'll introduce you to a girl who will act as though she loves you, but who in reality will not. Is that it?"

"I guess so," Simon said.

"But it just isn't so! It would be too costly, for one thing. For another, the wear and tear on the girl would be tremendous. And it would be psychologically unsound for her to attempt living a lie of such depth and scope."

"Then how do you do it?"

"By utilizing our understanding of science and the human mind."

To Simon, this sounded like doubletalk. He moved toward the door.

"Tell me something," Mr. Tate said. "You're a bright-looking young fellow. Don't you think you could tell real love from a counterfeit item?"

"Certainly."

"There's your safeguard! *You* must be satisfied, or don't pay us a cent."

"I'll think about it," Simon said.

"Why delay? Leading psychologists say that *real* love is a fortifier and a restorer of sanity, a balm for damaged egos, a restorer of hormone balance, and an improver of the complexion. The love we supply you has everything: deep and abiding affection, unrestrained passion, complete faithfulness, an almost mystic affection for your defects as well as your virtues, a pitiful desire to please, *and*—as a plus that only Love, Inc., can supply—that uncontrollable first spark, that blinding moment of love at first sight!"

Mr. Tate pressed a button. Simon frowned indecisively. The door opened, a girl stepped in, and Simon stopped thinking.

She was tall and slender, and her hair was brown with a sheen of red. Simon could have told you nothing about her face, except that it brought tears to his eyes. And if you asked him about her figure, he might have killed you.

"Miss Penny Bright," said Tate, "meet Mr. Alfred Simon." The girl tried to speak but no words came, and Simon was equally dumbstruck. He looked at her and *knew*. Nothing else mattered. To the depths of his heart he knew that he was truly and completely loved.

They left at once, hand in hand, and were taken by jet to a small white cottage in a pine grove overlooking the sea, and there they talked and laughed and loved, and later Simon saw his beloved wrapped in the sunset flame like a goddess of fire. And in blue twilight she looked at him with eyes enormous and dark, her known body mysterious again. The moon came up, bright and lunatic, changing flesh to shadow, and she wept and beat his chest with her small fists, and Simon wept too, although he did not know why. And at last dawn came, faint and disturbed, glimmering upon their parched lips and locked bodies, and nearby the booming surf deafened, inflamed, and maddened them.

At noon they were back in the offices of Love, Inc. Penny clutched his hand for a moment, then disappeared through an inner door.

"Was it real love?" Mr. Tate asked.

"Yes!"

"And was everything satisfactory?"

"Yes! It was love, it was the real thing! But why did she insist on returning?"

"Posthypnotic command," Mr. Tate said.

"What?"

"What did you expect? Everyone wants love, but few wish to pay for it. Here is your bill, sir."

Simon paid, fuming. "This wasn't necessary," he said. "Of course I would pay you for bringing us together. Where is she now? What have you done with her?"

"Please," Mr. Tate said soothingly. "Try to calm yourself."

"I don't want to be calm!" Simon shouted. "I want Penny!"

"That will be impossible," Mr. Tate said, with the barest hint of frost in his voice. "Kindly stop making a spectacle of yourself."

"Are you trying to get more money out of me?" Simon shrieked. "All right, I'll pay. How much do I have to pay to get her out of your clutches?" And Simon yanked out his wallet and slammed it on the desk.

Mr. Tate poked the wallet with a stiffened forefinger. "Put that back in your pocket," he said. "We are an old and respectable firm. If you raise your voice again, I shall have you ejected."

Simon calmed himself with an effort, put the wallet back in his pocket, and sat down. He took a deep breath and said very quietly. "I'm sorry."

"That's better," Mr. Tate said. "I will not be shouted at. However, if you are reasonable, I can be reasonable too. Now, what's the trouble?"

"The trouble?" Simon's voice started to lift. He controlled it and said, "She loves me."

"Of course."

"Then how can you separate us?"

"What has one thing to do with the other?" Mr. Tate asked. "Love is a delightful interlude, a relaxation, good for the intellect, for the ego, for the hormone balance, and for the skin tone. But one would hardly wish to *continue* loving, would one?"

"I would," Simon said. "This love was special, unique—"

"They all are," Mr. Tate said. "But as you know, they are all produced in the same way."

"What?"

"Surely you know something about the mechanics of love production?"

"No," Simon said. "I thought it was—natural."

Mr. Tate shook his head. "We gave up natural selection centuries ago, shortly after the Mechanical Revolution. It was too slow, and commercially infeasible. Why bother with it, when we can produce any feeling at will by conditioning and proper stimulation of certain brain centers? The result? Penny, completely in love with you! Your own bias in favor of her particular somatotype made it complete. We always throw in the dark sea-beach, the lunatic moon, the pallid dawn—"

"Then she could have been made to love anyone," Simon said slowly.

"Could have been *brought* to love anyone," Mr. Tate corrected.

"Oh, Lord, how did she get into this horrible work?" Simon asked.

"She came in and signed a contract in the usual way," Tate said. "It pays very well. And at the termination of the lease, we return her original personality—untouched! But why do you call the work horrible? There's nothing reprehensible about love."

"It wasn't love!" Simon cried.

"But it was! The genuine article! Unbiased scientific firms have made qualitative tests in comparison with the natural thing. In every case, *our* love tested out to more depth, passion, fervor, and scope."

Simon shut his eyes tightly, then opened them and said, "Listen to me. I don't care about your scientific tests. I love her, she loves me, that's all that counts. Let me speak to her! I want to marry her!"

Mr. Tate wrinkled his nose in distaste. "Come, come, man! You wouldn't want to *marry* a girl like that! But if it's marriage you're after, we deal in that too. I can arrange an idyllic and nearly spontaneous love-match for you with a guaranteed, government-inspected virgin—"

"No! I love Penny! At least let me speak to her!"

"That will be quite impossible," Mr. Tate said.

"Why?"

Mr. Tate pushed a button on his desk. "Why do you think? We've wiped out the previous indoctrination. Penny is now in love with someone else."

And then Simon understood. He had realized that even now Penny was looking at another man with that passion he had known, feeling for another man that complete and bottomless love which unbiased scientific firms had shown to be so much greater than the old-fashioned, commercially infeasible natural selection, and that upon that same dark sea-beach mentioned in the advertising brochure—

He lunged for Tate's throat. Two attendants, who had entered the office a few moments earlier, caught him and led him to the door.

"Remember!" Tate called. "This in no way invalidates your own experience."

Hellishly enough, Simon knew that what Tate said was true.

And then he found himself on the street.

At first all he desired was to escape from Earth, where the commercial impracticalities were more than a normal man could afford. He walked very quickly, and his Penny walked beside him, her face glorified with love for him, and him, and him, and you, and you.

And of course he came to the shooting gallery.

"Try your luck?" the manager asked.

"Set 'em up," said Alfred Simon.

The Native Problem

Edward Danton was a misfit. Even as a baby, he had shown pre-antisocial leanings. This should have been sufficient warning to his parents, whose duty it was to take him without delay to a competent prepubescent psychologist. Such a person could have discovered what lay in Danton's childhood to give him these contra-group tendencies. But Danton's parents, doubtless dramatizing problems of their own, thought the child would grow out of it.

He never did.

In school, Danton got barely passing grades in Group Acculturation, Sibling Fit, Values Recognition, Folkways Judgment, and other subjects a person must know in order to live serenely in the modern world. Because of his lack of comprehension, Danton could never live serenely in the modern world.

It took him a while to find this out.

From his appearance, one would never have guessed Danton's basic lack of Fit. He was a tall, athletic young man, green-eyed, easygoing. There was a certain something about him that intrigued the girls in his immediate affective environment. In fact, several paid him the highest compliment at their command, which was to consider him as a possible husband.

But even the flightiest girl could not ignore Danton's lacks. He was liable to weary after only a few hours of Mass Dancing, when the fun was just beginning. At Twelve-Hand Bridge, Danton's attention frequently wandered and he would be forced to ask for a recount of the bidding, to the disgust of the other eleven players. And he was impossible at Subways.

He tried hard to master the spirit of that classic game. Locked arm in arm with his teammates, he would thrust forward into the subway car, trying to take possession before another team could storm in the opposite doors.

His group captain would shout, "Forward, men! We're taking this car to Rockaway!" And the opposing group captain would scream back, "Never! Rally, boys! It's Bronx Park or bust!"

357

Danton would struggle in the close-packed throng, a fixed smile on his face, worry lines etched around his mouth and eyes. His girlfriend of the moment would say, "What's wrong, Edward? Aren't you having fun?"

"Sure I am," Danton would reply, gasping for breath.

"But you aren't!" the girl would cry, perplexed. "Don't you realize, Edward, that this is the way our ancestors worked off their aggressions? Historians say that the game of Subways averted an all-out hydrogen war. We have those same aggressions and we too must resolve them in a suitable social context."

"Yeah, I know," Edward Danton would say. "I really do enjoy this. I—oh, Lord!"

For at that moment a third group would come pounding in, arms locked, chanting, "Canarsie, Canarsie, Canarsie!"

In that way he would lose another girlfriend, for there was obviously no future in Danton. Lack of Fit can never be disguised. It was obvious that Danton would never be happy in the New York suburbs, which stretched from Rockport, Maine, to Norfolk, Virginia—nor in any other suburbs, for that matter.

Danton tried to cope with his problems, in vain. Other strains started to show. He began to develop astigmatism from the projection of advertisements on his retina, and there was a constant ringing in his ears from the sing-swoop ads. His doctor warned that symptom analysis would never rid him of these psychosomatic ailments. No, what had to be treated was Danton's basic neurosis, his antisociality. But this Danton found impossible to deal with.

And so his thoughts turned irresistibly to escape. There was plenty of room for Earth's misfits out in space.

During the last two centuries, millions of psychotics, neurotics, psychopaths, and cranks of every kind and description had gone outward to the stars. The early ones had the Mikkelsen Drive to power their ships, and spent twenty or thirty years chugging from star system to star system. The newer ships were powered by GM subspatial torque converters, and made the same journey in a matter of months.

The stay-at-homes, being socially adjusted, bewailed the loss of anyone, but they welcomed the additional breeding room.

In his twenty-seventh year, Danton decided to leave Earth and take up pioneering. It was a tearful day when he gave his breeding certificate to his best friend, Al Trevor.

"Gee, Edward," Trevor said, turning the precious little certificate over and over in his hands, "you don't know what this means to Myrtle and me. We always wanted two kids. Now, because of you—"

"Forget it," said Danton. "Where I'm going, I won't need any breeding permit. As a matter of fact, I'll probably find it impossible to breed," he added, the thought having just struck him.

"But won't that be frustrating for you?" Al asked, solicitous, as always, for his friend's welfare.

"I guess so. Maybe after a while, though, I'll find a girl pioneer. And in the meantime, there's always sublimation."

"True enough. What substitute have you selected?"

"Vegetable gardening. I might as well be practical."

"You might as well," Al said. "Well, boy, good luck, boy."

Once the breeding certificate was gone, the die was cast. Danton plunged boldly ahead. In exchange for his Birthright, the government gave him unlimited free transportation and two years' basic equipment and provisions.

Danton left at once.

He avoided the more heavily populated areas, which were usually in the hands of rabid little groups.

He wanted no part of a place like Korani II, for instance, where a giant calculator had instituted a reign of math.

Nor was he interested in Heil V, where a totalitarian population of 342 was earnestly planning ways and means of conquering the galaxy.

He skirted the Farming Worlds—dull, restrictive places given to extreme health theories and practices.

When he came to Hedonia, he considered settling on that notorious planet. But the men of Hedonia were said to be short-lived, although no one denied their enjoyment while they *did* live.

Danton decided in favor of the long haul, and journeyed on.

He passed the Mining Worlds—somber, rocky places sparsely populated by gloomy, bearded men given to sudden violence. And he came at last to the New Territories. These unpeopled worlds were past Earth's farthest frontier. Danton scanned several before he found one with no intelligent life whatever.

It was a calm and watery place, dotted with sizable islands, lush with jungle greenery, and fertile with fish and game. The ship's captain duly notarized Danton's claim to the planet, which Danton called New Tahiti. A quick survey showed a large island superior to the rest. Here he was landed, and here he proceeded to set up his camp.

There was much to be done at first. Danton constructed a house out of branches and woven grass, near a white and gleaming beach. He fashioned a fishing spear, several snares, and a net. He planted his vegetable garden and was gratified to see it thrive under the tropical sun, nourished by warm rains that fell every morning between seven and seven-thirty.

All in all, New Tahiti was a paradisiacal place, and Danton should have been very happy there. But there was one thing wrong.

The vegetable garden, which he had thought would provide first-class sublimation, proved a dismal failure. Danton found himself thinking about women at all hours of the day and night, and spending long hours crooning to himself—love songs, of course—beneath a great orange tropical moon.

This was unhealthy. Desperately he threw himself into other recognized forms of sublimation; painting came first, but he rejected it to keep a journal, abandoned that and composed a sonata, gave that up and carved two enormous statues out of a local variety of soapstone, completed them, and tried to think of something else to do.

There was nothing else to do. His vegetables took excellent care of themselves; being of Earth stock, they completely choked out all alien growths. Fish swam into his nets in copious quantities, and meat was his whenever he bothered to set a snare. He found again that he was thinking of women at all hours of the day and night—tall women, short women, white women, black women, brown women.

The day came when Danton found himself thinking favorably of Martian women, something no Terran had succeeded in doing before. Then he knew that something drastic had to be done.

But what? He had no way of signaling for help, no way of getting off New Tahiti. He was gloomily contemplating this when a black speck appeared in the sky to seaward.

He watched as it slowly grew larger. He was barely able to breathe for fear it would turn out to be a bird or a huge insect. But the speck continued to increase in size, and soon he could see pale jets, flaring and ebbing.

A spaceship had come! He was alone no longer!

The ship took a long, slow, cautious time landing. Danton changed into his best *pareu*, a South Seas garment he had found peculiarly well adapted to the climate of New Tahiti. He washed, combed his hair carefully, and watched the ship descend.

It was one of the ancient Mikkelsen Drive ships. Danton had thought that all of them were long retired from active service. But this ship, it was apparent, had been traveling for a long while. The hull was dented and scored, hopelessly archaic, yet with a certain indomitable look about it. Its name, proudly lettered on the bow, was *The Hutter People*.

When people come in from deep space, they are usually starved for fresh food. Danton gathered a great pile of fruit for the ship's passengers and had it tastefully arranged by the time *The Hutter People* had landed ponderously on the beach.

A narrow hatch opened and two men stepped out. They were armed with rifles and dressed in black from head to toe. Warily they looked around them.

Danton sprinted over. "Hey, welcome to New Tahiti! Boy, am I glad to see you folks! What's the latest news from—"

"Stand back!" shouted one of the men. He was in his fifties, tall and impossibly gaunt, his face seamed and hard. His icy blue eyes seemed to pierce Danton like an arrow; his rifle was leveled at Danton's chest. His partner was younger, barrel-chested, broad-faced, short, and very powerfully built.

"Something wrong?" Danton asked, stopping.

"What's your name?"

"Edward Danton."

"I'm Simeon Smith," the gaunt man said, "military commander of the Hutter people. This is Jedekiah Franker, second-in-command. How come you speak English?"

"I've always spoken English," said Danton. "Look, I—"

"Where are the others? Where are they hiding?"

"There aren't any others. Just me." Danton looked at the ship and saw the faces of men and women at every port. "I gathered this stuff for you folks." He waved his hand at the mound of fruit. "Thought you might want some fresh goods after being so long in space."

A pretty girl with short, tousled blond hair appeared in the hatchway. "Can't we come out now, Father?"

"No!" Simeon said. "It's not safe. Get inside, Anita."

"I'll watch from here, then," she said, staring at Danton with frankly curious eyes.

Danton stared back, and a faint and unfamiliar tremor ran through him.

Simeon said, "We accept your offering. We will not, however, eat it."

"Why not?" Danton reasonably wanted to know.

"Because," said Jedekiah, "we don't know what poisons you people might try to feed us."

"Poisons? Look, let's sit down and talk this over."

"What do you think?" Jedekiah asked Simeon.

"Just what I expected," the military leader said. "Ingratiating, fawning, undoubtedly treacherous. His people won't show themselves. Waiting in ambush, I'll bet. I think an object lesson would be in order."

"Right," said Jedekiah, grinning. "Put the fear of civilization into them." He aimed his rifle at Danton's chest.

"Hey!" Danton yelped, backing away.

"But, Father," said Anita, "he hasn't done anything yet."

"That's the whole point. Shoot him and he won't do anything. The only good native is a dead native."

"This way," Jedekiah put in, "the rest will know we mean business."

"It isn't right!" Anita cried indignantly. "The Council—"

"—isn't in command now," Jedekiah said. "Anyhow, an alien landfall constitutes an emergency. During such times, the military is in charge. We'll do what we think is best. Remember Lan II!"

"Hold on now," Danton said. "You've got this all wrong. There's just me, no others, no reason to—"

A bullet kicked up sand near his left foot. He sprinted for the protection of the jungle. Another bullet whined close, and a third cut a twig near his head as he plunged into the underbrush.

"There!" he heard Simeon roar. "That ought to teach them a lesson!"

Danton kept on running until he had put half a mile of jungle between himself and the pioneer ship.

He ate a light supper of the local vegetables and breadfruit, and tried to figure out what was wrong with the Hutters. Were they insane? They had seen that he was an Earthman, alone and unarmed, obviously friendly. Yet they had fired at him—as an object lesson. A lesson for whom? For the dirty natives, whom they wanted to teach a lesson...

That was it! Danton nodded emphatically to himself. The Hutters must have thought he was a native, an aboriginal, and that his tribe was lurking in the bush, waiting for a chance to massacre the new arrivals! It wasn't too rash an assumption, really. Here he was on a distant planet, without a spaceship, wearing only a loincloth and tanned a medium bronze. He was probably just what they thought a native should look like on a wilderness planet like this!

"But where," Danton asked himself, "do they think I learned English?"

The whole thing was ridiculous. He started walking back to the ship, sure he could clear up the misunderstanding in a few minutes. But after a couple of yards, he stopped.

Evening was approaching. Behind him, the sky was banked in white and gray clouds. To seaward, a deep blue haze advanced steadily on the land. The jungle was filled with ominous noises, which Danton had long ago found to be harmless. But the new arrivals might not think so.

These people were trigger-happy, he reminded himself. No sense barging in on them too fast and inviting a bullet.

So he moved cautiously through the tangled jungle growth, a silent, tawny shape blending into the jungle browns and greens. When he reached the vicinity of the ship, he crawled through the dense undergrowth until he could peer down on the sloping beach.

The pioneers had finally come out of their ship. There were several dozen men and women and a few children. All were dressed in heavy black cloth and were perspiring in the heat. They had ignored his gift of local fruit. Instead, an aluminum table had been spread with the spaceship's monotonous provisions.

On the periphery of the crowd, Danton saw several men with rifles and ammunition belts. They were evidently on guard, keeping close watch on the jungle and glancing apprehensively overhead at the darkening sky.

Simeon raised his hands. There was immediate silence.

"Friends," the military leader orated, "we have come at last to our long-awaited home! Behold, here is a land of milk and honey, a place of bounty and abundance. Was it not worth the long voyage, the constant danger, the endless search?"

"Yes, brother!" the people responded.

Simeon held up his hands again for silence. "No civilized man has settled upon this planet. We are the first, and therefore the place is ours. But there are perils, my friends! Who knows what strange monsters the jungle hides?"

"Nothing larger than a chipmunk," Danton muttered to himself. "Why don't they ask me? I'd tell them."

"Who knows what leviathan swims in the deep?" Simeon continued. "We *do* know one thing: There is an aboriginal people here, naked and savage, undoubtedly cunning, ruthless, and amoral, as aboriginals always are. Of these we must beware. We will live in peace with them, if they will let us. We will bring to them the fruits of civilization and the flowers of culture. They may profess friendship, but always remember this, friends: no one can tell what goes on in a savage heart. Their standards are not ours; their morals are not ours. We cannot trust them; we must be forever on guard. And if in doubt, *we* must shoot first! Remember Lan II!"

Everybody applauded, sang a hymn, and began their evening meal. As night fell, searchlights came on from the ship, making the beach as bright as day. The sentries paced up and down, shoulders hunched nervously, rifles ready.

Danton watched the settlers shake out their sleeping bags and retire under the bulge of the ship. Even their fear of sudden attack couldn't force them to spend another night inside the ship, when there was fresh air to breathe outside.

The great orange moon of New Tahiti was half hidden by high-flying night clouds. The sentries paced and swore, and moved closer together for mutual comfort and protection. They began firing at the jungle sounds and blasting at shadows.

Danton crept back into the jungle. He retired for the night behind a tree, where he would be safe from stray bullets. This evening had not seemed the time for straightening things out. The Hutters were too jumpy. It would be better, he decided, to handle the matter by daylight, in a simple, straightforward, reasonable fashion.

The trouble was, the Hutters hardly seemed reasonable.

In the morning, though, everything looked more promising. Danton waited until the Hutters had finished their breakfast, then strolled into view at the edge of the beach.

"Halt!" everyone of the sentries barked.

"That savage is back!" called a settler.

"Mummy," cried a little boy, "don't let the nasty bad man eat me!"

"Don't worry, dear," the boy's mother said. "Your father has a rifle for shooting savages."

Simeon rushed out of the spaceship and glared at Danton. "All right, you! Come forward!"

Danton stepped gingerly across the beach, his skin tingling with nervous expectation. He walked to Simeon, keeping his empty hands in sight.

"I am the leader of these people," Simeon said, speaking very slowly, as if to a child. "I the big chief fella. You big fella chief your people?"

"There's no need to talk that way," Danton said. "I can hardly understand you. I told you yesterday that I haven't any people. There's just me."

Simeon's hard face grew white with anger. "Unless you're honest with me, you're going to regret it. Now—where is your tribe?"

"I'm an Earthman," Danton yelled. "Are you deaf? Can't you hear how I talk?"

A stooped little man with white hair and great horn-rimmed glasses came over with Jedekiah. "Simeon," the little man said, "I don't believe I have met our guest."

"Professor Baker," said Simeon, "this savage here claims he's an Earthman and he says his name is Edward Danton."

The professor glanced at Danton's *pareu*, his tanned skin and callused feet. "You are an Earthman?" he asked Danton.

"Of course,"

"Who carved those stone statues up the beach?"

"I did," Danton said, "but it was just therapy. You see—"

"Obviously primitive work. That stylization, those noses—"

"It was accidental. Look, a few months ago I left Earth in a spaceship—"

"How was it powered?" Professor Baker asked.

"By a GM subspatial torque converter." Baker nodded, and Danton went on, "Well, I wasn't interested in places like Korani or Heil V, and Hedonia seemed too rich for my blood. I passed up the Mining Worlds and the Farming Worlds, and had the government ship drop me here. The planet's registered as New Tahiti, in my name. But I was getting pretty lonely, so I'm glad you folks came."

"Well, Professor?" Simeon said. "What do you think?"

"Amazing," Baker murmured. "Truly amazing. His grasp of colloquial English bespeaks a fairly high level of intelligence, which points up a phenomenon frequently met with in savage societies, namely an unusually well-developed power of mimicry. Our friend Danta (as his original. uncorrupted name must have been) will probably be able to tell us many tribal legends, myths, songs, dances—"

"But I'm an Earthman!"

"No, my poor friend," the professor corrected gently, "you are not. Obviously you have *met* an Earthman. Some trader, I daresay, stopping for repairs."

Jedekiah said, "There's evidence that a spaceship once landed here briefly."

"Ah," said Professor Baker, beaming. "Confirmation of my hypothesis."

"That was the government ship," Danton explained. "It dropped me off here."

"It is interesting to note," said Professor Baker in his lecturing voice, "how his almost plausible story lapses into myth at various crucial points. He claims that the ship was powered by a 'GM subspatial torque converter'—which is nonsense syllabification, since the only deep-space drive is the Mikkelsen. He claims that the journey from Earth was made in a matter of months (since his untutored mind cannot conceive of a journey lasting years), although we know that no space drive, even theoretically, can achieve that."

"It was developed after you people left Earth," Danton said. "How long have you been gone?"

"The Hutter spaceship left Earth one hundred and twenty years ago," Baker replied condescendingly. "We are mostly fourth and fifth generation. Note also," Baker said to Simeon and Jedekiah, "his attempt to think up plausible place-names. Words such as Kornai, Heil, Hedonia appeal to his sense of onomatopoeia. That there are no such places doesn't disturb him."

"There are!" Danton said indignantly.

"Where?" Jedekiah challenged. "Give me the coordinates."

"How should I know? I'm no navigator. I think Heil was near Boötes, or maybe it was Cassiopeia. No, I'm pretty sure it was Boötes—"

"I'm sorry, friend," said Jedekiah. "It may interest you to know that I'm the ship's navigator. I can show you the star atlases and charts. Those places aren't on them."

"Your charts are a hundred years out of date!"

"Then so are the stars," Simeon said. "Now, Danta, where is your tribe? Why do they hide from us? What are they planning?"

"This is preposterous," Danton protested. "What can I do to convince you? I'm an Earthman. I was born and raised—"

"That's enough," Simeon cut in. "If there's one thing we Hutters won't stand for, it's backtalk from natives. Out with it, Danta. *Where are your people?*"

"There's only me," Danton insisted.

"Tight-mouthed?" Jedekiah gritted. "Maybe a taste of the black-snake whip—"

"Later, later," Simeon said. "His tribe'll come around for handouts. Natives always do. In the meantime, Danta, you can join that work gang over there."

"No, thanks," said Danton. "I'm going back to—"

Jedekiah's fist lashed out, catching Danton on the side of the jaw. He staggered, barely keeping his footing.

"The chief said *no backtalk!*" Jedekiah roared. "Why are you natives always so bone-lazy? You'll be paid as soon as we unload the beads and calico. Now get to work."

That seemed to be the last word on the subject. Dazed and unsure, much like millions of natives before him on a thousand different worlds, Danton joined the long line of colonists passing goods out of the ship.

By late afternoon the unloading was done and the settlers were relaxed on the beach. Danton sat apart from them, trying to think his situation through. He was deep in thought when Anita came to him with a canteen of water.

"Do *you* think I'm a native?" he asked.

She sat down beside him and said, "I really don't see what else you could be. Everyone knows how fast a ship can travel."

"Times have changed since your people left Earth. They weren't in space all that time, were they?"

"Of course not. The Hutter ship went to H'gastro I, but it wasn't fertile enough, so the next generation moved to Ktedi. But the corn mutated and almost wiped them out, so they went to Lan II. They thought that would be a permanent home."

"What happened?"

"The natives," said Anita sadly. "I guess they were friendly enough at first, and everyone thought the situation was well in hand. Then, one day, we were at war with the entire native population. They only had spears and things, but there were too many of them, so the ship left again and we came here."

"Hmm," Danton said. "I see why you're so nervous about aboriginals."

"Well, of course. While there's any possibility of danger, we're under military rule. That means my father and Jedekiah. But as soon as the emergency is past, our regular Hutter government takes over."

"Who runs that?"

"A council of Elders," Anita said, "men of goodwill, who detest violence. If you and your people are really peaceable—"

"I haven't any people," Danton said wearily.

"—then you'll have every opportunity to prosper under the rule of the Elders."

They sat together and watched the sunset. Danton noticed how the wind stirred her hair, blowing it silkily across her forehead, and how the afterglow of the sun outlined and illuminated the line of her cheek and lip. He shivered and told himself it was the sudden chill of evening. And Anita, who had been talking animatedly about her childhood, found difficulty in completing her sentences, or even keeping her train of thought.

After a while, their hands strayed together. Their fingertips touched and clung. For a long time they said nothing at all. And at last, gently and lingeringly, they kissed.

"What the hell is going on here?" a loud voice demanded.

Danton looked up and saw a burly man standing over him, his powerful head silhouetted black against the moon, his fists on his hips.

"Please, Jedekiah," Anita said. "Don't make a scene."

"Get up," Jedekiah ordered Danton in an ominously quiet voice. "Get up on your feet."

Danton stood up, his hands half-clenched into fists, waiting.

"You," Jedekiah said to Anita, "are a disgrace to your race and to the whole Hutter people. Are you crazy? You can't mess around with a dirty native and still keep any self-respect." He turned to Danton. "And you gotta learn something and learn it good. *Natives don't fool with Hutter women!* I'm going to impress that little lesson on you right here and now."

There was a brief scuffle, and Jedekiah found himself sprawled on his back.

"Help!" Jedekiah shouted. *"The natives are revolting!"*

An alarm bell in the spaceship began to peal. Sirens wailed. The women and children, long trained for such an emergency, trooped back into the spaceship. The men were issued rifles, machine guns, and hand grenades, and began to advance on Danton.

"It's just man to man," Danton called out. "We had a disagreement, that's all. There's no natives or anything. Just me."

The foremost Hutter commanded, "Anita, quick, get back!"

"I didn't see any natives," the girl said staunchly. "And it wasn't really Danta's fault—"

"Get back!"

She was pulled out of the way. Danton dived into the bushes before the machine guns opened up.

He crawled on all fours for fifty yards, then broke into a dead run.

Fortunately the Hutters did not pursue him. They were interested only in guarding their ship and holding their beachhead and a narrow stretch of jungle. Danton heard gunfire throughout the night, and loud shouts and frantic cries.

"There goes one!"

"Quick, turn the machine gun! They're behind us!"

"There! There! I got one!"

"No, he got away. There he goes...But look, up in the tree!"

"Fire, man, fire!"

All night, Danton listened as the Hutters repulsed the attacks of imaginary savages.

Toward dawn the firing subsided. Danton estimated that a ton of lead had been expended, hundreds of trees decapitated, acres of grass trampled into mud. The jungle stank of cordite.

He fell into a fitful slumber.

At midday he awakened and made a meal for himself of bananas and mangoes. Then he decided to think things over.

But no thoughts came. His mind was filled with Anita and with grief over her loss.

All that day he wandered disconsolately through the jungle, and in the late afternoon he heard again the sound of someone moving through the underbrush.

He turned to go deeper into the island. Then he heard someone calling his name.

"Danta! Danta! Wait!"

It was Anita. Danton hesitated, not sure what to do. She might have decided to leave her people, to live in the green jungle with him. But more realistically, she might have been sent out as a decoy, leading a party of men to destroy him. How could he know where her loyalties lay?

"Danta! Where are you?"

Danton reminded himself that there could never be anything between them. Her people had shown what they thought of natives. They would always distrust him, forever try to kill him...

"Please, Danta!"

Danton shrugged and walked toward her voice.

They met in a little clearing. Anita's hair was disheveled and her dark clothing was torn by the jungle briars, but for Danton there could never be a lovelier woman. For an instant he believed that she had come to join him, flee with him.

Then he saw armed men fifty yards behind her.

"It's all right," Anita said. "They're not going to kill you. They just came along to guard me."

"Guard you? From *me?*" Danton laughed hollowly.

"They don't know you as I do," Anita said. "At the Council meeting today, I told them the truth."

"You did?"

"Of course. That fight wasn't your fault, and I told everybody so. I told them you fought only to defend yourself. And Jedekiah lied. No pack of natives attacked him. There was only you, and I told them this."

"Good girl," Danton said fervently. "Did they believe you?"

"I think so. I explained that the native attack came later."

Danton groaned. "Look, how could there be a native attack when there aren't any natives?"

"But there are," Anita said. "I heard them shouting."

"Those were your own people," Danton said desperately. If he couldn't convince this one girl, how could he possibly persuade the rest of the Hutters?

And then he had it. It was a very simple proof, but its effect would have to be overwhelming.

"You really believe there was a full-scale native attack," Danton stated.

"Of course."

"How many natives?"

"I heard that you outnumbered us by at least ten to one."

"And we were armed?"

"You certainly were."

"Then how," Danton asked triumphantly, "do you account for the fact that *not a single Hutter was wounded!*"

She stared at him, wide-eyed. "But, Danta dear, many of the Hutters were wounded, some seriously. It's a wonder no one was killed in all that fighting!"

Danton felt as though the ground had been kicked out from under him. For a terrifying minute he believed her. Perhaps he did have a tribe, hundreds of bronzed savages like himself, hidden in the jungle, waiting...

"That trader who taught you English," Anita said, "must have been a very unscrupulous character. It's against interstellar law, you know, to sell firearms to natives."

"Firearms?"

"Certainly. You couldn't use them very accurately, of course. But Simeon said that sheer firepower—"

"I suppose all your casualties were from gunshot wounds."

"Yes. The men didn't let you get close enough to use knives and spears."

"I see," Danton said. His proof was utterly demolished. But he felt enormously relieved at having regained his sanity. The disorganized Hutter soldiery had ranged around the jungle, firing at everything that moved. It was more than a wonder that some of them hadn't been killed. It was a miracle.

"But I explained that they couldn't blame you," said Anita. "You were attacked first and your own people must have thought you were in danger. The Elders thought this was probable."

"Nice of them," Danton said.

"They want to be reasonable. After all, they realize that natives are human beings just like ourselves."

"Are you sure of that?" Danton asked with feeble irony.

"Of course. The Elders held a big meeting on native policy and decided it once and for all. We're setting aside a thousand acres as a reservation for you and your people. That should be plenty of room, shouldn't it? The men are putting up the boundary posts now. You'll live peacefully in your reservation and we'll live in our own part of the island."

"*What?*" Danton said.

"And to seal the pledge," Anita continued, "the Elders asked you to accept this." She handed him a roll of parchment.

"What is it?"

"It's a peace treaty, declaring the end of the Hutter-New Tahitian war, and pledging our respective peoples to eternal amity."

Numbly, Danton accepted the parchment. He saw that the men who had accompanied Anita were setting red-and-black striped posts into the ground. They sang as they worked, happy to have reached a solution to the native problem so quickly and easily.

"But don't you think," Danton asked, "that perhaps—ah—assimilation might be a better solution?"

"I suggested it," Anita said, blushing.

"You did? You mean that you would—"

"Of course I would," said Anita, not looking at him. "I think the amalgamation of two strong races would be a fine and wonderful thing. And, Danta, what wonderful stories and legends you could have told the children!"

"I could have showed them how to fish and hunt," Danton said, "and which plants are edible, and things like that."

"And all your colorful tribal songs and dances." Anita sighed. "It would have been wonderful. I'm sorry, Danta."

"But something must be possible! Can't I talk to the Elders? Isn't there anything I can do?"

"Nothing," Anita said. "I'd run away with you, Danta, but they'd track us down, no matter how long it took."

"They'd never find us," Danton promised.

"Perhaps. I'd be willing to take the chance."

"Darling!"

"But I can't. Your poor people, Danta! The Hutters would take hostages, kill them if I wasn't returned."

"I don't have any people! I don't, damn it!"

"It's sweet of you to say that," Anita said tenderly. "But lives cannot be sacrificed just for the love of two individuals. You must tell your people not to cross the boundary lines, Danta. They'll be shot. Good-bye, and remember, it is best to live in the path of peace."

She hurried away from him. Danton watched her go, angry at her noble sentiments, which separated them for no reason at all, yet loving her for the love she showed his people. That his people were imaginary didn't matter. It was the thought that counted.

At last he turned and walked deep into the jungle.

He stopped by a still pool of black water, overhung with giant trees and bordered by flowering ferns, and here he tried to plan the rest of his life. Anita was gone; all commerce with human beings was gone. He didn't need any of them, he told himself. He had his reservation. He could replant his vegetable garden, carve more statues, compose more sonatas, start another journal...

"To hell with that!" he shouted to the trees. He didn't *want* to sublimate any longer. He wanted Anita and he wanted to live with humans. He was tired of being alone.

What could he do about it?

There didn't seem to be anything. He leaned back against a tree and stared at New Tahiti's impossibly blue sky. If only the Hutters weren't so superstitious, so afraid of natives, so...

And then it came to him, a plan so absurd, so dangerous...

"It's worth a try," Danton said to himself, "even if they kill me."

He trotted off toward the Hutter boundary line.

A sentry saw him as he neared the vicinity of the spaceship, and leveled his rifle. Danton raised both arms.

"Don't fire! I have to speak with your leaders!"

"Get back on your reservation," the sentry warned. "Get back or I'll shoot."

"I have to speak to Simeon," Danton stated, holding his ground.

"Orders is orders," said the sentry, taking aim.

"Just a minute." Simeon stepped out of the ship, frowning deeply. "What is all this?"

"That native came back," the sentry said. "Shall I pop him, sir?"

"What do you want?" Simeon asked Danton.

"I have come here to bring you," Danton roared, *"a declaration of war!"*

That woke up the Hutter camp. In a few minutes, every man, woman, and child had gathered near the spaceship. The Elders, a council of old men distinguished by their long white beards, were standing to one side.

"You accepted the peace treaty," Simeon pointed out.

"I had a talk with the other chiefs of the island," Danton said, stepping forward. "We feel the treaty is not fair. New Tahiti is ours. It belonged to our fathers and to our fathers' fathers. Here we have raised our children, sown our corn, and reaped the breadfruit. We will not live on the reservation!"

"Oh, Danta!" Anita cried, appearing from the spaceship. "I asked you to bring peace to your people!"

"They wouldn't listen," Danton said. "All the tribes are gathering. Not only my own people, the Cynochi, but the Drovati, the Lorognasti, the Retellsmbroichi and the Vitelli. Plus, naturally, their sub-tribes and dependencies."

"How many are you?" Simeon asked.

"Fifty or sixty thousand. Of course, we don't all have rifles. Most of us will have to rely on more primitive weapons, such as poisoned arrows and darts."

A nervous murmur arose from the crowd.

"Many of us will be killed," Danton said stonily. "We do not care. Every New Tahitian will fight like a lion. We are a thousand to your one. We have cousins on the other islands who will join us. No matter what the cost in human life and misery, we will drive you into the sea. I have spoken."

He turned and started back into the jungle, walking with stiff dignity.

"Shall I pop him now, sir?" the sentry begged.

"Put down that rifle, you fool!" Simeon snapped. "Wait, Danta! Surely we can come to terms. Bloodshed is senseless."

"I agree," Danton said soberly.

"What do you want?"

"Equal rights!"

The Elders went into an immediate conference. Simeon listened to them, then turned to Danton.

"That may be possible. Is there anything else?"

"Nothing," Danton said. "Except, naturally, an alliance between the ruling clan of the Hutters and the ruling clan of the New Tahitians, to seal the bargain. Marriage would be best."

After going into conference again, the Elders gave their instructions to Simeon. The military chief was obviously disturbed. The cords stood out on his neck, but with an effort he controlled himself, bowed his agreement to the Elders, and marched up to Danton.

"The Elders have authorized me," he said, "to offer you an alliance of blood brotherhood. You and I, representing the leading clans of our peoples, will mingle our blood together in a beautiful and highly symbolic ceremony, then break bread, take salt—"

"Sorry," Danton said. "We New Tahitians don't hold with that sort of thing. It has to be marriage."

"But, damn it all, man—"

"That is my last word."

"We'll never accept! Never!"

"Then it's war," Danton declared, and walked into the jungle.

He was in a mood for making war. But how, he asked himself, does a single native fight against a spaceship full of armed men?

He was brooding on this when Simeon and Anita came to him through the jungle.

"All right," Simeon said angrily. "The Elders have decided. We Hutters are sick of running from planet to planet. We've had this problem before and I suppose we'd just go somewhere else and have it again. We're sick and tired of the whole native problem, so I guess,"—he gulped hard, but manfully finished the sentence—"we'd better assimilate. At least that's what the Elders think. Personally, I'd rather fight."

"You'd lose," Danton assured him, and at that moment he felt he could take on the Hutters singlehanded and win.

"Maybe so," Simeon admitted. "Anyhow, you can thank Anita for making the peace possible."

"Anita? Why?"

"Why, man, she's the only girl in the camp who'd marry a naked, dirty, heathen savage!"

And so they were married, and Danta, now known as the White Man's Friend, settled down to help the Hutters conquer their new land. They, in turn, introduced him to the marvels of civilization. He was taught Twelve-Hand Bridge and Mass Dancing. And soon the Hutters built their first Subway—for a civilized people must release their aggressions—and that game was shown to Danta, too.

He tried to master the spirit of the classic Earth pastime, but it was obviously beyond the comprehension of his savage soul. Civilization stifled him, so Danta and his wife moved across the planet, always following the frontier, staying far from the amenities of civilization.

Anthropologists came frequently to visit him. They recorded all the stories he told his children, the ancient and beautiful legends of New Tahiti—tales of sky gods and water demons, fire sprites and woodland nymphs, and how Katamandura was ordered to create the world out of nothingness in just three days, and what his reward for this was, and what Jevasi said to Hootmenlati when they met in the underworld, and the strange outcome of this meeting.

The anthropologists noted similarities between these legends and certain legends of Earth, and several ingenious theories were put forth. And they were interested in the great soapstone statues on the main island of New Tahiti, weird and haunting colossi that no viewer could forget, clearly the work of a pre-New Tahitian race, of whom no trace could ever be found.

But most fascinating of all for the scientific workers was the problem of the New Tahitians themselves. Those happy, laughing, bronzed savages—bigger, stronger, handsomer, and healthier than any other race—had melted away at the coming of the white man. Only a few of the older Hutters could remember meeting them in any numbers, and their tales were considered none too reliable.

"My people?" Danta would say when questioned. "Ah, they could not stand the white man's diseases, the white man's mechanical civilization, the white man's harsh and repressive ways. They are in a happier place now, in Valhoola beyond the sky. And someday I shall go there too."

And white men, hearing this, experienced strangely guilty feelings and redoubled their efforts to show kindness to Danta, the Last Native.

THE LANGUAGE OF LOVE

Jefferson Toms went into an auto-café one afternoon after classes, to drink coffee and study. He sat down, philosophy texts piled neatly before him, and saw a girl directing the robot waiters. She had smoky gray eyes and hair the color of a rocket exhaust. Her figure was slight but sweetly curved and, gazing at it, Toms felt a lump in his throat and a sudden recollection of autumn, evening, rain, and candlelight.

This was how love came to Jefferson Toms. Although he was ordinarily a very reserved young man, he complained about the robot service in order to meet her. When they did meet, he was inarticulate, overwhelmed by feeling. Somehow, though, he managed to ask her for a date.

The girl, whose name was Doris, was strangely moved by the stocky, black-haired young student, for she accepted at once. And then Jefferson Toms's troubles began.

He found love delightful, yet extremely disturbing, in spite of his advanced studies in philosophy. But love was a confusing thing even in Toms's age, when spaceliners bridged the gaps between the worlds, disease lay dead, war was inconceivable, and just about anything of any importance had been solved in an exemplary manner.

Old Earth was in better shape than ever before. Her cities were bright with plastic and stainless steel. Her remaining forests were carefully tended bits of greenery where one might picnic in perfect safety, since all beasts and insects had been removed to sanitary zoos that reproduced their living conditions with admirable skill.

Even the climate of Earth had been mastered. Farmers received their quota of rain between three and three-thirty in the morning, people gathered at stadiums to watch a program of sunsets, and a tornado was produced once a year in a special arena as part of the World Peace Day Celebration.

But love was as confusing as ever, and Toms found this distressing.

He simply could not put his feelings into words. Such expressions as "I love you," "I adore you," "I'm crazy about you" were overworked and inadequate. They conveyed nothing of the depth and fervor of his emotions.

375

Indeed, they cheapened them, since every stereo, every second-rate play was filled with similar words. People used them in casual conversation and spoke of how much they *loved* pork chops, *adored* sunsets, were *crazy about* tennis.

Every fiber of Toms's being revolted against this. Never, he swore, would he speak of his love in terms used for pork chops. But he found, to his dismay, that he had nothing better to say.

He brought the problem to his philosophy professor. "Mr. Toms," the professor said, gesturing wearily with his glasses, "ah—*love,* as it is commonly called, is not an operational area with us as yet. No significant work has been done in this field, aside from the so-called Language of Love of the Tyanian race."

This was no help. Toms continued to muse on love and think lengthily of Doris. In the long, haunted evenings on her porch, when the shadows from the trellis vines crossed her face, revealing and concealing it, Toms struggled to tell her what he felt. And since he could not bring himself to use the weary commonplaces of love, he tried to express himself in extravagances.

"I feel about you," he would say, "the way a star feels about its planet."

"How immense!" she would answer, immensely flattered at being compared to anything so cosmic.

"That's not what I meant," Toms amended. "The feeling I was trying to express was more—well, for example, when you walk, I am reminded of—"

"Of a what?"

"A doe in a forest glade," Toms said, frowning.

"How charming!"

"It wasn't intended to be charming. I was trying to express the awkwardness inherent in youth, and yet—"

"But, honey," she said, "I'm not awkward. My dancing teacher—"

"I didn't mean *awkward.* But the essence of awkwardness is—is—"

"I understand," she said.

But Toms knew she didn't.

So he was forced to give up extravagances. Soon he found himself unable to say anything of any importance to Doris, for it was not what he meant, nor even close to it.

The girl became concerned at the long, moody silences that developed between them.

"Jeff," she would urge, "surely you can say *something!*" Toms shrugged his shoulders.

"Even if it isn't absolutely what you mean."

Toms sighed.

"Please," she cried, "say anything at all! I can't stand this!"

"Oh, hell—"

"Yes?" she breathed, her face transfigured.

"That wasn't what I meant," Toms said, relapsing into his gloomy silence.

At last he asked her to marry him. He was willing to admit that he "loved" her—but he refused to expand on it. He explained that a marriage must be founded upon truth or it is doomed from the start. If he cheapened and falsified his emotions at the beginning, what could the future hold for them?

Doris found his sentiments admirable, but refused to marry him.

"You must *tell* a girl that you love her," she declared. "You have to tell her a hundred times a day, Jefferson, and even then it's not enough."

"But I do love you!" Toms protested. "I mean to say I have an emotion corresponding to—"

"Oh, stop it!"

In this predicament, Toms thought about the Language of Love and went to his professor's office to ask about it.

"We are told," his professor said, "that the race indigenous to Tyana II had a specific and unique language for the expression of sensations of love. To say 'I love you' was unthinkable for Tyanians. They would use a phrase denoting the exact kind and class of love they felt at that specific moment, and used for no other purpose."

Toms nodded, and the professor continued. "Of course, developed with this language was, necessarily, a technique of lovemaking quite incredible in its perfection. We are told that it made all ordinary techniques seem like the clumsy pawing of a grizzly in heat." The professor coughed in embarrassment.

"It is precisely what I need!" Toms exclaimed.

"Ridiculous," said the professor. "The technique might be interesting, but your own is doubtless sufficient for most needs. And the language, by its very nature, can be used with only one person. To learn it impresses me as wasted energy."

"Labor for love," Toms said, "is the most worthwhile work in the world, since it produces a rich harvest of feeling."

"I refuse to stand here and listen to bad epigrams. Mr. Toms, why all this fuss about love?"

"It is the only perfect thing in this world," Toms answered fervently. "If one must learn a special language to appreciate it, one can do no less. Tell me, is it far to Tyana II?"

"A considerable distance," his professor said, with a thin smile. "And an unrewarding one, since the race is extinct."

"Extinct! But why! A sudden pestilence? An invasion?"

"It is one of the mysteries of the galaxy," his professor said somberly.

"Then the language is lost!"

"Not quite. Twenty years ago, an Earthman named George Varris went to Tyana and learned the Language of Love from the last survivors of the race." The professor shrugged. "I never considered it sufficiently important to read his report."

Toms looked up Varris in the *Interspatial Explorers' Who's Who* and found that he was credited with the discovery of Tyana, had wandered around the frontier planets for a time, but at last had returned to deserted Tyana, to devote his life to investigating every aspect of its culture.

After learning this, Toms thought long and hard. The journey to Tyana was a difficult one, time-consuming and expensive. Perhaps Varris would be dead before he got there, or unwilling to teach him the language. Was it worth the gamble?

"Is *love* worth it?" Toms asked himself, and knew the answer.

So he sold his ultra-fi, his memory recorder, his philosophy texts, and several stocks his grandfather had left him, and booked passage to Cranthis IV, which was the closest he could come to Tyana on a scheduled spaceway. And after all his preparations had been made, he went to Doris.

"When I return," he said, "I will be able to tell you exactly how much— I mean the particular quality and class of—I mean, Doris, when I have mastered Tyanian Technique, you will be loved as no woman has ever been loved!"

"Do you mean that?" she asked, her eyes glowing.

"Well," Toms said, "the term 'loved' doesn't quite express it. But I mean something very much like it."

"I will wait for you, Jeff," she said. "But—please don't be too long."

Jefferson Toms nodded, blinked back his tears, clutched Doris inarticulately, and hurried to the spaceport.

Within the hour, he was on his way.

Four months later, after considerable difficulties, Toms stood on Tyana, on the outskirts of the capital city. Slowly he walked down the broad, deserted main thoroughfare. On either side of him, noble buildings soared to dizzy heights. Peering inside one, Toms saw complex machinery and gleaming switchboards. With his pocket Tyana-English dictionary, he was able to translate the lettering above one of the buildings.

It read: COUNSELING FOR STAGE-FOUR LOVE PROBLEMS.

Other buildings were much the same, filled with calculating machinery, switchboards, ticker tapes, and the like. He passed THE INSTITUTE FOR RESEARCH INTO AFFECTION DELAY, stared at the two-hundred-story HOME FOR THE EMOTIONALLY RETARDED, and glanced at several others. Slowly the awesome, dazzling truth dawned upon him.

Here was an entire city given over to the research and aid of love.

He had no time for further speculation. In front of him was the gigantic GENERAL LOVE SERVICES BUILDING. And out of its marble hallway stepped an old man.

"Who the hell are you?" the old man asked.

"I am Jefferson Toms, of Earth. I have come here to learn the Language of Love, Mr. Varris."

Varris raised his shaggy white eyebrows. He was a small, wrinkled old man, stoop-shouldered and shaky in the knees. But his eyes were alert and filled with a cold suspicion.

"Perhaps you think the language will make you more attractive to women," Varris said. "Don't believe it, young man. Knowledge has its advantages, of course. But it has distinct drawbacks, as the Tyanians discovered."

"What drawbacks?" Toms asked.

Varris grinned, displaying a single yellow tooth. "You wouldn't understand, if you don't already know. It takes knowledge to understand the limitations of knowledge."

"Nevertheless," Toms said, "I want to learn the language."

Varris stared at him thoughtfully. "But it is not a simple thing, Toms. The Language of Love, and its resultant technique, is every bit as complex as brain surgery or the practice of corporation law. It takes work, much work, and a talent as well."

"I will do the work. And I'm sure I have the talent."

"Most people think that," Varris said, "and most of them are mistaken. But never mind, never mind. It's been a long time since I've had any company. We'll see how you get on, Toms."

Together they went into the General Services Building, which Varris called his home. They went to the Main Control Room, where the old man had put down a sleeping bag and set up a camp stove. There, in the shadow of the giant calculators, Toms's lessons began.

Varris was a thorough teacher. In the beginning, with the aid of a portable Semantic Differentiator, he taught Toms to isolate the delicate apprehension one feels in the presence of a to-be-loved person, to detect the subtle tensions that come into being as the potentiality of love draws near.

These sensations, Toms learned, must never be spoken of directly, for frankness frightens love. They must be expressed in simile, metaphor, and hyperbole, half-truths and white lies. With these, one creates an atmosphere and lays a foundation for love. And the mind, deceived by its own predisposition, thinks of booming surf and raging sea, mournful black rocks and fields of green corn.

"Nice images," Toms said admiringly.

"Those were samples," Varris told him. "Now you must learn them all."

So Toms went to work memorizing great long lists of natural wonders, to what sensations they were comparable, and at what stage they appeared in the anticipation of love. The language was thorough in this regard. Every state or object in nature for which there was a response in love-anticipation had been catalogued, classified, and listed with suitable modifying adjectives.

When Toms had memorized the list, Varris drilled him in perceptions of love. Toms learned the small, strange things that make up a state of love. Some were so ridiculous that he had to laugh.

The old man admonished him sternly. "Love is a serious business, Toms. You seem to find some humor in the fact that love is frequently predisposed by wind speed and direction."

"It seems foolish," Toms admitted.

"There are stranger things than that," Varris said, and mentioned another factor.

Toms shuddered. "*That* I can't believe. It's preposterous. Everyone knows—"

"If everyone knows how love operates, why hasn't someone reduced it to a formula? Murky thinking, Toms, murky thinking is the answer, and an unwillingness to accept cold facts. If you cannot face them—"

"I can face anything," Toms said, "if I have to. Let's continue."

As the weeks passed, Toms learned the words that express the first quickening of interest, shade by shade, until an attachment is formed. He learned what that attachment really is, and the three words that express it. This brought him to the rhetoric of sensation, where the body becomes supreme.

Here the language was specific instead of allusive, and dealt with feelings produced by certain words and, above all, by certain physical actions.

A startling little black machine taught Toms the thirty-eight separate and distinct sensations that the touch of a hand can engender, and he learned how to locate that sensitive area, no larger than a dime, which exists, just below the right shoulder blade.

He learned an entirely new system of caressing, which caused impulses to explode—and even implode—along the nerve paths and to shower colored sparks before the eyes.

He was also taught the social advantages of conspicuous desensitization.

He learned many things about physical love that he had dimly suspected, and still more things that *no one* had suspected.

It was intimidating knowledge. Toms had imagined himself to be at least an adequate lover. Now he found that he knew nothing, nothing at all, and that his best efforts had been comparable to the play of amorous hippopotami.

"But what else could you expect?" Varris asked. "Good lovemaking, Toms, calls for more study, more sheer intensive labor than any other acquired skill. Do you still wish to learn?"

"Definitely!" Toms said. "Why, when I'm an expert on lovemaking, I'll—I can—"

"That is no concern of mine," the old man stated. "Let's return to our lessons."

Next, Toms learned the Cycles of Love. Love, he discovered, is dynamic, constantly rising and falling, and doing so in definite patterns. There are fifty-two major patterns, three hundred and six minor patterns, four general exceptions, and nine specific exceptions.

Toms learned them better than his own name.

He acquired the uses of the Tertiary Touch. And he never forgot the day he was taught what a bosom *really* was like.

"But I can't say that!" Toms objected, appalled.

"It's true, isn't it?" Varris insisted.

"No! I mean—yes, I suppose it is. But it's unflattering."

"So it seems. But examine, Toms. Is it *actually* unflattering?"

Toms examined and found the compliment that lies beneath the insult, and so he learned another facet of the Language of Love.

Soon he was ready for the study of the Apparent Negations. He discovered that for every degree of love, there is a corresponding degree of hate, which is in itself a form of love. He came to understand how valuable hate is, how it gives substance and body to love, and how even indifference and loathing have their place in the nature of love.

Varris gave him a ten-hour written examination, which Toms passed with superlative marks. He was eager to finish, but Varris noticed that a slight tic had developed in his student's left eye and that his hands had a tendency to shake.

"You need a vacation," the old man informed him.

Toms had been thinking this himself. "You may be right," he said, with barely concealed eagerness. "Suppose I go to Cythera V for a few weeks."

Varris, who knew Cythera's reputation, smiled cynically. "Eager to try out your new knowledge?"

"Well, why not? Knowledge is to be used."

"Only after it's mastered."

"But I *have* mastered it! Couldn't we call this field work? A thesis, perhaps?"

"No thesis is necessary," Varris said.

"But, damn it all," Toms exploded, "I should do a little experimentation! I should find out for myself how all this works. Especially Approach 33-CV. It sounds fine in theory, but I've been wondering how it works out in actual practice. There's nothing like direct experience, you know, to reinforce—"

"Did you journey all this way to become a super-seducer?" Varris asked; with evident disgust.

"Of course not," Toms said. "But a little experimentation wouldn't—"

"Your knowledge of the mechanics of sensation would be barren unless you understand love, as well. You have progressed too far to be satisfied with mere thrills."

Toms, searching his heart, knew this to be true. But he set his jaw stubbornly. "I'd like to find out *that* for myself, too."

"You may go," Varris said, "but don't come back. No one will accuse me of loosing a callous scientific seducer upon the galaxy."

"Oh, all right. To hell with it. Let's get back to work."

"No. Look at yourself! A little more unrelieved studying, young man, and you will lose the capacity to make love. And wouldn't that be a sorry state of affairs?"

Toms agreed that it would certainly be.

"I know the perfect spot," Varris told him, "for relaxation from the study of love."

They entered the old man's spaceship and journeyed five days to a small unnamed planetoid. When they landed, the old man took Toms to the bank of a swift-flowing river, where the water ran fiery red, with green diamonds of foam. The trees that grew on the banks of that river, were stunted, and strange, and colored vermilion. Even the grass was unlike grass, for it was orange and blue.

"How alien!" gasped Toms.

"It is the least human spot I've found in this humdrum corner of the galaxy," Varris explained. "And believe me, I've done some looking."

Toms stared at him, wondering if the old man was out of his mind. But soon he understood what Varris meant.

For months he had been studying human reactions and human feelings, and surrounding it all was the now suffocating feeling of soft human flesh. He had immersed himself in humanity, studied it bathed in it, eaten and drunk and dreamed it. It was a relief to be here, where the water ran red, and the trees were stunted and strange and vermilion, and the grass was orange and blue, and there was no reminder of Earth.

Toms and Varris separated, for even each other's humanity was a nuisance. Toms spent his days wandering along the river edge, marveling at the flowers that moaned when he came near them. At night, three wrinkled moons played tag with each other, and the morning sun was different from the yellow sun of Earth.

At the end of a week, refreshed and renewed Toms and Varris returned to G'cel, the Tyanian city dedicated to the study of love.

Toms was taught the five hundred and six shades of Love Proper, from the first faint possibility to the ultimate feeling, which is so powerful that only five men and one woman have experienced it, and the strongest of them survived less than an hour.

Under the tutelage of a bank of small, interrelated calculators, he studied the intensification of love.

He learned all of the thousand different sensations of which the human body is capable, and how to augment them, and how to intensify them until they become unbearable, and how to make the unbearable bearable, and finally pleasurable, at which point the organism is not far from death.

After that, he was taught some things that have never been put into words and, with luck, never will be.

"And that," Varris said one day, "is everything."

"Everything?"

"Yes, Toms. The heart has no secrets from you. Nor, for that matter, has the soul, or the mind, or the viscera. You have mastered the Language of Love. Now return to your young lady."

"I will!" cried Toms. "At last she will know!"

"Drop me a postcard," Varris said. "Let me know how you're getting on."

"I'll do that," Toms promised. Fervently he shook his teacher's hand and departed for Earth.

At the end of the long trip, Jefferson Toms hurried to Doris's home. Perspiration beaded his forehead, and his hands were shaking. He was able to classify the feeling as Stage Two Anticipatory Tremors, with mild masochistic overtones. But that didn't help—this was his first fieldwork and he was nervous. Had he mastered *everything?*

He rang the bell.

She opened the door and Toms saw that she was more beautiful than he had remembered, her eyes smoky gray and misted with tears, her hair the color of a rocket exhaust, her figure slight but sweetly curved. He felt again the lump in his throat and sudden memories of autumn, evening, rain, and candlelight.

"I'm back," he croaked.

"Oh, Jeff," she said, very softly.

Toms simply stared, unable to say a word.

"It's been so long, Jeff, and I kept wondering if it was all worth it. Now I know."

"You—know?"

"Yes, my darling! I waited for you! I'd wait a hundred years, or a thousand! I love you, Jeff!"

She was in his arms.

"Now tell me, Jeff," she said. *"Tell me!"*

And Toms looked at her, and felt, and sensed, searched his classifications, selected his modifiers, checked and double-checked. And after much searching, and careful selection, and absolute certainty, and allowing for his present state of mind, and not forgetting to take into account climatic conditions, phases of the moon, wind speed and direction, sunspots, and other phenomena that have their due effect upon love, he said:

"My dear, I am rather fond of you."

"Jeff! Surely you can say more than that! The Language of Love—"

"The Language is damnably precise," Toms said wretchedly. "I'm sorry, but the phrase 'I am rather fond of you' expresses precisely what I feel."

"Oh, Jeff!"

"Yes," he mumbled.

"Oh, damn you, Jeff!"

There was, of course, a painful scene and a very painful separation. Toms took to traveling.

He held jobs here and there, working as a riveter at Saturn-Lockheed, a wiper on the Helg-Vinosce Trader, a farmer for a while on a kibbutz on Israel IV. He bummed around the Inner Dalmian System for several years, living mostly on handouts. Then, at Novilocessile, he met a pleasant, brown-haired girl, courted her, and, in due course, married her and set up housekeeping.

Their friends say that the Tomses are tolerably happy, although their home makes most people uncomfortable. It is a pleasant enough place; but the rushing red river nearby makes people edgy. And who can get used to vermilion trees, and orange-and-blue grass, and moaning flowers, and three wrinkled moons playing tag in the alien sky?

Toms likes it, though, and Mrs. Toms is, if nothing else, a flexible young lady.

Toms wrote a letter to his philosophy professor on Earth, saying that he had solved the problem of the demise of the Tyanian race, at least to his own satisfaction. The trouble with scholarly research, he wrote, is the inhibiting effect it has upon action. The Tyanians, he was convinced, had been so preoccupied with the science of love that after a while they just didn't get around to making any.

And eventually he sent a short postcard to George Varris. He simply said that he was married, having succeeded in finding a girl for whom he felt "quite a substantial liking."

"Lucky devil," Varris growled, after reading the card. "'Vaguely enjoyable' was the best I could ever find."

THE DEATHS OF BEN BAXTER

Edwin James, the Chief Programmer of Earth, had seated himself upon a little three-legged stool in front of the Probabilities Calculator. He was a small, spare man, impressively ugly, dwarfed by the great control board which soared a hundred feet above him.

The steady hum of the machine, the slow drift of lights across the face of the panel, brought a sense of security which he recognized as false, but which soothed him all the same. He had just started to doze off when the pattern of lights changed.

He sat up with a start and rubbed his face. A paper tape inched from a slot in the panel. The Chief Programmer tore it off and scanned it. He nodded sourly to himself and walked quickly out of the room.

Fifteen minutes later, he entered the meeting room of the World Planning Council. Summoned there by his order, the five representatives of the Federated Districts of Earth were seated around the long table, waiting for him.

There was a new member this year, Roger Beatty, from the Americas. He was tall and angular and his bushy brown hair was just beginning to thin on top. He appeared eager, earnest, and ill at ease. He was reading a procedural handbook and taking short, quick sniffs from his oxygen inhaler.

James knew the other members well. Lan Il from Pan-Asia, looking as small, wrinkled, and indestructible as ever, was engaged in intense conversation with large, blond Dr. Sveg from Europe. Miss Chandragore, beautiful and sleek, was playing her inevitable game of chess with Aaui of Oceania.

James turned up the room's oxygen supply and the members gratefully put away their inhalers.

"Sorry to keep you waiting," James said, taking his seat at the head of the table. "The current prediction just came through."

He took a notebook from his pocket and opened it.

"At our last meeting, we selected Alternate Probability Line 3B3CC, which began in the year 1832. The factor we were selecting for was the life of Albert

Levinsky. In the Main Historic Line, Levinsky died in 1935 of an automobile accident. By switching into Alternate Probability Line 3B3CC, Levinsky avoided this accident and lived to the age of sixty-two, completing his work. The result now, in our own time, is the opening up of Antarctica."

"What about side-effects?" asked Janna Chandragore.

"Those are discussed in the paper you will be given later. Briefly, though, 3B3CC adhered closely to the Historic Main Line. All important events remained constant. There were, of course, some effects which the prediction did not cover. They include an oil-well explosion in Patagonia, a flu epidemic in Kansas, and an increase in smog over Mexico City."

"Have all injured parties been compensated?" Lan Il wanted to know.

"They have. And the colonization of Antarctica is already begun."

The Chief Programmer unfolded the paper tape he had taken from the Probabilities Calculator.

"But now we face a dilemma. As predicted, the Historic Main Line leads into unpleasant complications. But there are no good alternate lines to switch into!"

The members murmured to each other.

James said, "Let me explain the situation." He walked to a wall and pulled down a large chart. "The crisis-point occurs on April 12, 1959, and our problem centers around an individual named Ben Baxter. The circumstances are as follows..."

Events, by their very nature, evoke alternate possibilities, each of which produces its own continuum of history. In other spatial-temporal worlds, Spain lost at Lepanto, Normandy at Hastings, England at Waterloo.

Suppose Spain had lost at Lepanto...

Spain did, disastrously. And Turkish sea power, invincible, swept the Mediterranean of European shipping. Ten years later, a Turkish fleet conquered Naples and paved the way for the Moorish invasion of Austria...

In another time and space, that is.

This speculation became observable fact after the development of temporal selection and displacement. By 2103, Oswald Meyner and his associates were able to show the theoretical possibility of Switching from the Historic Main Line—so named for convenience—to alternate lines. Within definite limits, however.

It would be impossible, for example, to Switch into a past where William of Normandy lost the battle of Hastings. The world developing from that event would be too different, alien in every way. Switching was found possible only into closely adjacent lines.

The theoretical possibility became a practical necessity in 2213. In that year, the Sykes-Raborn Calculator at Harvard predicted the complete sterilization of Earth's atmosphere by the accretion of radioactive by-products. The process was irreversible and inevitable. It could be stopped only in the past, where the poisoning had begun.

The first Switch was made with the newly developed Adams-Holt-Maartens Selector. The World Planning Council chose a line which involved the early death of Vassily Ouchenko (and the obliteration of his erroneous radiation damage theories.) A large part of the subsequent poisoning was avoided, although at the cost of seventy-three lives—descendants of Ouchenko for whom no Switchparents could be found.

After that, there was no turning back. Line Switching became as necessary to the world as disease prevention.

But the process had its limitations. A time had to come when no available line would be usable, when all futures looked unfavorable.

When that happened, the Planning Council was prepared to use more direct means.

"And those are the consequences for us," Edwin James concluded. "That is the outcome if we allow the Main Historic Line to continue."

Lan Il said, "Meaning that you predict serious trouble for Earth, Mr. Programmer."

"With regret, I do."

The Programmer poured himself a glass of water and turned a page in his notebook.

"Our pivotal point is Ben Baxter, who dies on April 12, 1959. He must live at least another ten years for his work to have the desired effect upon world events. In that time, Ben Baxter will purchase Yellowstone National Park from the government. He will continue to maintain it as a park, but will farm the trees. This enterprise will be highly successful. He will buy other great tracts of land in North and South America. The Baxter heirs will be lumber kings for the next two hundred years and will own huge standings throughout the world. Due to their efforts, there will be great forests in the world, up to and including our own time. But if Baxter dies—"

James gestured wearily. "With Baxter dead, the forests will be cut before the governments of the world are fully aware of the consequences. Then comes the great blight of '03, which the few remaining woodlands cannot withstand. And at last the present, with the natural carbon-dioxide-oxygen cycle disrupted by the destruction of the trees, with all combustion devices banned, with oxygen inhalers a necessity merely to survive."

"We've started the forests again," Aaui said.

"It will be hundreds of years before they have grown to any significant size, even with forced growing methods. In the meantime, the balance may become further upset. *That* is the importance of Ben Baxter to us. He holds the key to the air we breathe!"

"Very well," said Dr. Sveg. "The Main Line, in which Baxter dies, is clearly unusable. But there are Alternates—"

"Many," James said. "As usual, most of them cannot be selected. Counting the Main Line, we have a total of three choices. But, unfortunately, each of them results in the death of Ben Baxter on April 12, 1959."

The Programmer wiped his forehead. "To be more specific, *Ben Baxter dies on the afternoon of April 12, 1959, as a result of a business meeting with a man named Ned Brynne.*"

The new member, Roger Beatty, cleared his throat nervously. "This event takes place in all three probability worlds?"

"Yes. In every one of them, Brynne is the cause of Baxter's death."

Dr. Sveg came ponderously to his feet. "Formerly, this Council has avoided any direct interference with the existing lines of probability. But this situation seems to call for interference."

The council members nodded their agreement.

"Let's get down to cases," said Aaui. "For the good of Earth, can this Ned Brynne be Switched Out?"

"No," replied the Programmer. "Brynne himself plays a vital role in our future. He has an option on almost a hundred square miles of forest. He needs Baxter's backing to purchase it. If Brynne could be kept from that meeting with Baxter—"

"How?" asked Beatty.

"Take your pick," James suggested. "Threats, persuasion, bribery, kidnapping—any means short of murder. We have three worlds to work in. If we can restrain Brynne in just one of them, our problem is solved."

"What would be our best method?" asked Aaui.

"Try several, a different one in each probability world," said Miss Chandragore. "Our chances would be best that way. Shall we go ourselves?"

"We are best suited for the job," Edwin James said. "We know the factors involved. And politics gives one a certain skill in improvising—which will be sorely needed in this job. Each team will be absolutely on its own. There is no way for them to check on each other's progress across the time lines."

"Each team then," Dr. Sveg summed up, "will have to assume that the other teams fail."

"Probably with good reason," James said wryly. "Let's organize the teams and select our methods."

I

On the morning of April 12, 1959, Ned Brynne awakened and washed and dressed. At 1:30 that afternoon, he had an appointment with Ben Baxter, president of Baxter Industries. Brynne's entire future hinged upon the outcome of that meeting. If he could get the backing of the gigantic Baxter enterprises, and do so on favorable terms...

Brynne was a tall, darkly handsome man of thirty-six. There was a hint of fanatic pride in his carefully bland eyes, a suggestion of unreasoning stubbornness in his tightly held mouth. His movements had the controlled strength of a man who is constantly watching and judging himself.

He was almost ready to leave. He tucked a swagger stick under his arm and slipped a copy of Somerset's *American Peerage* into his jacket pocket. He was never without that infallible guide.

Finally he fixed to his lapel the golden sunburst decoration of his station. Brynne was a Chamberlain, second class, and properly proud of the fact. Some people thought him too young for so exalted a position. But they had to agree that Brynne carried the prerogatives and requirements of his office with a dignity quite beyond his years.

He locked his apartment and walked to the elevator. There was a small crowd waiting, mostly commoners, but two Equerries as well. All made way for him when the elevator came.

"Pleasant day, Chamberlain Brynne," the operator said as the car started down.

Brynne inclined his head an inch in the usual response to a commoner. He was deep in thought about Ben Baxter. But at the corner of his eye, he noticed one of the occupants of the car, a tall, strongly built fellow with golden-brown Polynesian features and tilted dark eyes. Brynne wondered what a man like that was doing in his apartment building. He knew the other tenants by sight, although their lower status naturally made them unworthy of his recognition.

The elevator reached the lobby and Brynne forgot about the Polynesian fellow. He had a lot on his mind today. There were some problems connected with Ben Baxter, problems he hoped to resolve before the meeting. He strode outside, into a dismal gray April morning, and decided to go to the Prince Charles Coffee Shop for a late breakfast.

It was 10:25 A.M.

"What do you think?" Aaui asked.

"Looks like a tough customer," said Roger Beatty. He inhaled deeply, savoring the rich air. It was a delightful luxury, breathing all the oxygen he wanted. In his time even the very wealthy turned down the oxygen tanks at night.

They were following half a block behind Brynne. There was no losing Brynne's tall, swaggering figure, even in New York's morning rush.

"He looked at you in the elevator," Beatty said.

"I know." Aaui grinned. "Give him something to worry about."

"He doesn't look like a worrying type," Beatty said. "I wish we had more time."

Aaui shrugged. "This was the closest we could come to the event. Our next choice would have been eleven years ago. And we would still have to wait until now before taking direct action."

"At least we'd know something about Brynne. He doesn't look as though he'll frighten easily."

"No, he doesn't," Aaui admitted. "But that's the course of action we selected."

They continued to follow, noticing how the crowds parted to make way for Brynne, who marched straight ahead, not looking to right or left. Then it happened.

Brynne, his attention turned inward, collided with a portly, florid-faced man, who wore in his lapel the dazzling purple and silver medallion of a First Order Crusader.

"Can't you watch where you're going, imbecile?" the Crusader barked.

Brynne noticed the man's rank, swallowed and muttered, "I beg your pardon, sir."

The Crusader wasn't so easily placated. "Do you make a habit of bumping into your betters, sirrah?"

"I do not," Brynne said, his face growing red, fighting hard to restrain his rage. A crowd of commoners had gathered to watch. They ringed the brilliantly dressed men, grinning and nudging each other.

"Then suppose you watch yourself!" the portly Crusader roared. "Stop cluttering the streets like a sleepwalker, before you are taught a lesson in manners!"

Brynne said, with deadly quiet, "Sir, if you feel the necessity of giving me such a lesson, I should be pleased to meet you at a place of your choosing, with such weapons as you elect—"

"*Me?* Meet *you?*" the Crusader asked incredulously.

"My rank permits it, sir."

"Your rank? You're a good five degrees beneath me, you simple idiot! Enough of this or I'll send my servants—who outrank you—to teach you a lesson in manners. I'll remember your face, young man. Now get out of my way!"

And with that, the Crusader pushed past him and stalked away.

"Coward!" said Brynne, his face a mottled red. But he said it softly, and the commoners noticed. Brynne turned to them, his hands tightening on his swagger stick. Grinning cheerfully, the crowd broke up.

Beatty said, "Dueling is permitted here?"

Aaui nodded. "The legal precedent came in 1804, when Alexander Hamilton killed Aaron Burr in a duel."

"I guess we'd better get to work," Beatty said. "But I wish we had more equipment."

"We took all we could carry. Let's get on with it."

Inside the Prince Charles Coffee Shop, Brynne sat at a table far in the rear. His hands were trembling; with an effort, he controlled them. Damn that First Order Crusader! Lousy, overbearing blowhard! But would he accept a duel? No, of course not. Had to hide behind the privileges of his station.

Rage was rising in Brynne, black and ominous. He should have killed the man and the blazes with the consequences! The blazes with everything! No man could step on him that way...

Stop it, he told himself. There was nothing he could do about it. He had to think about Ben Baxter and the all important meeting. Looking at his watch, he saw it was nearly eleven o'clock. In two and a half hours, he would be in Baxter's office and—

"Your order, sir?" a waiter asked him.

"Hot chocolate, toast, and a poached egg."

"French fries?"

"If I wanted French fries, I'd have told you!" Brynne shouted.

The waiter went pale, gulped, said, "Yes, sir, sorry, sir," and hurried off.

Now, Brynne thought, I'm reduced to yelling at commoners. Control—I must get myself under control.

"Ned Brynne!"

Brynne started and looked around. He had distinctly heard someone whisper his name. But there was no one within twenty feet of him.

"Brynne!"

"What is this?" Brynne muttered in unwilling reply. "Who's speaking?"

"You're nervous, Brynne, losing control of yourself. You need a rest, a vacation, a change."

Brynne went dead white under his tan and looked around the cafe. It was almost empty. There were three old ladies near the front. Beyond them he could see two men, talking together earnestly.

"Go home, Brynne, and get some rest. Take some time off while you can."

"I have an important business appointment," Brynne said, his voice shaky.

"Business before sanity," the voice pointed out mockingly.

"Who's talking to me?"

"What makes you think someone is talking to you?" the voice asked silkily.

"You mean I'm talking to myself?"

"You should know."

"Your egg, sir," the waiter said.

"What?" Brynne roared.

The waiter stepped hastily back, slopping hot chocolate into the saucer. "Sir?" he quavered.

"Don't creep around that way, idiot."

The waiter looked at Brynne incredulously, deposited the food and fled. Brynne stared after him suspiciously.

"You are in no condition to see anyone," the voice told him. *"Go home, get into bed, take a pill, sleep, heal!"*

"But what's the matter? Why?"

"Because your sanity is at stake! This external voice is your mind's last frantic attempt at stability. You can't afford to ignore this warning, Brynne!"

"It can't be true!" protested Brynne. "I'm sane. I'm—"

"Beg pardon, sir," said a voice at his elbow.

Brynne whirled, prepared to chastise this further intrusion on his privacy. He saw the blue uniform of a policeman looming over him. The man was wearing the white shoulder epaulets of a Noble Lieutenant.

Brynne swallowed hard and said, "Anything wrong, Officer?"

"Sir, the waiter and manager tell me you are talking to yourself and threatening violence."

"Preposterous," snapped Brynne.

"It's true! It's true! You're going crazy!" the voice screamed in his head.

Brynne stared at the great square bulk of the policeman. Surely he heard the voice! But apparently the Noble Lieutenant didn't, for he continued to look somberly down at him.

"It's not true," Brynne said, feeling secure in staking his word against a commoner's.

"I heard you myself," the Noble Lieutenant said.

"Well, sir, it's this way," Brynne began, choosing his words with care. "I was—"

The voice shrieked in his head, *"Tell him to go to hell, Brynne! Who's he to question you? Who's anyone to question you? Hit him! Blast him! Kill him! Destroy him!"*

Brynne said, through the barrage of noise in his head, "I was talking to myself, perfectly true, Officer. I frequently think out loud. It helps me to organize my thoughts."

The Noble Lieutenant gave a half nod. "But you offered violence, sir, at no provocation."

"No provocation! I ask you, sir, are cold eggs no provocation? Are limp toast and spilled chocolate no provocation?"

The waiter, called over, insisted, "Those eggs were hot—"

"They were not and that is all. I do not expect to sit here and argue a point of fact with a commoner."

"Quite right," the Noble Lieutenant said, nodding emphatically now. "But might I ask you, sir, to curb your anger somewhat, even though it may be perfectly justified? Not too much can be expected of commoners, after all."

"I know," Brynne agreed. "By the way, sir—the purple edging on your epaulets—are you related to O'Donnel of Moose Lodge, by any chance?"

"My third cousin on my mother's side," said the Noble Lieutenant, looking intently now at Brynne's sunburst medallion. "My son has entered the Chamberlain Halls as a probationary. A tall boy named Callahan."

"I will remember the name," Brynne promised.

"The eggs were hot!" said the waiter.

"Don't dispute the word of a gentleman," ordered the officer. "It could get you into serious trouble. Pleasant day to you, sir." The Noble Lieutenant saluted and left.

Brynne paid and left shortly after him. He deposited a sizable tip for the waiter, but determined never to come into the Prince Charles again.

"Resourceful fellow," Aaui said bitterly, putting the tiny microphone back in his pocket. "For a moment, I thought we had him."

"We would have, if he'd had any latent doubts about his sanity. Well, now for something more direct. Got the equipment?"

Aaui took two pairs of brass knuckles out of his pocket and handed one to Beatty.

"Try not to lose it," he said. "We're supposed to return it to the Primitive Museum."

"Right. It fits over the fist, doesn't it? Oh, yes, I see."

They paid and hurried out.

Brynne decided to take a stroll along the waterfront to quiet his nerves. The sight of the great ships lying calm and steadfast in their berths never failed to soothe him. He walked steadily along, trying to reason out what had happened to him.

Those voices in his head...

Was he really losing his grip? An uncle on his mother's side had spent his last years in an institution. Involutional melancholia. Was there some explosive hidden factor at work in him?

He stopped and looked at the bow of a great ship. The *Theseus*.

Where was it going? Italy, perhaps. He thought of blue skies, brilliant sunshine, wine, and relaxation. Those things would never be his. Work, frantic effort, that was the life he had set for himself. Even if it meant losing his mind, he would continue to labor under the iron-gray skies of New York.

But why, he asked himself. He was moderately well off. His business could take care of itself. What was to stop him from boarding that ship, dropping everything, spending a year in the sun?

Excitement stirred in him as he realized that *nothing* was stopping him. He was his own man, a determined, strong man. If he had the guts to succeed in business, he also had the guts to leave it, to drop everything and go away

"To hell with Baxter!" he said to himself.

His sanity was more important than anything. He *would* board that ship, right now, wire his associates from sea, tell them—

Two men were walking toward him down the deserted street. He recognized one by his golden-brown Polynesian features.

"Mr. Brynne?" inquired the other, a rangy fellow with a shock of brown hair.

"Yes?" said Brynne.

Without warning, the Polynesian threw both arms around him, pinning him, and the shock-haired man swung at him with a fist that glinted golden!

Brynne's keyed-up nerves reacted with shattering speed. He had been a Knight Rampant during the Second World Crusade. Now, years later, all the reaction patterns were still there. He ducked the shock-haired man's blow and drove his elbow into the Polynesian's stomach. The man grunted and his grip relaxed for a second. Brynne broke free.

He chopped at the Polynesian with the back of his hand, hitting the nerve trunk in the throat. The man went down, gasping for breath. At the same time, the shock-haired man was on him, raining brass-knuckled blows.

Brynne lashed out, missed, caught a solid punch in the solar plexus. He fought for air. Blackness began edging into the periphery of his vision. He was hit again and went down, fighting for consciousness. Then his opponent made a mistake.

The shock-haired man tried to finish him with a kick, but he didn't know how to kick. Brynne caught his foot and jerked. Off balance, the man crashed to the pavement, striking his head.

Brynne staggered to his feet, breathing hard. The Polynesian was sprawled in the road, his face purple, making feeble swimming movements with his arms and legs. The other man lay motionless, blood seeping slowly through his hair.

He should report this incident to the police, Brynne thought. But suppose he had killed the shock-haired man? He would be held on a manslaughter charge, at least. And the Noble Lieutenant would report his earlier irrational behavior.

He looked around. No one had witnessed the incident. It was best to simply walk away. Let his assailants report it, if they wanted to.

Things were falling into place now. These men must have been hired by one of his many business competitors, men who were also trying for an affiliation with Ben Baxter. Even the voice in his head might have been a clever trick.

Well, let them try to stop him! Still breathing heavily, he began walking toward Ben Baxter's office.

All thoughts of a cruise to Italy were gone now.

"Are you all right?" a voice asked from somewhere up above.

Beatty returned slowly to consciousness. For a short, alarmed while, he thought he had a fractured skull. But, touching it gently, he decided it was still in one piece, "What did he hit me with?" he asked.

"The pavement, I think," Aaui said. "Sorry I couldn't help. He put me out of action pretty early."

Beatty sat up, clutching his aching head. "What a fighter!"

"We underestimated him," said Aaui. "He must have had some kind of training. Do you think you can walk?"

"I think so," Beatty said, letting Aaui help him to his feet. "What time is it?"

"Nearly one o'clock. His appointment's at one-thirty. Maybe we can stop him at Baxter's office."

In five minutes, they caught a taxi and sped to Baxter's building.

The receptionist was young and pretty, and she stared at them open-mouthed. They had managed to clean up some of the damage in the taxi, but what remained looked pretty bad. Beatty had an improvised bandage over his head and Aaui's complexion bordered on green.

"What do you want?" the receptionist asked.

"I believe Mr. Baxter has a one-thirty appointment with Mr. Brynne," said Aaui in his most businesslike tone.

"Yes—"

The wall clock read one-seventeen. Aaui said, "We must see Mr. Brynne before he goes in. It's very urgent. So if you don't mind, we'll wait here for him."

"You can wait," the girl said. "But Mr. Brynne has already gone in."

"But it isn't one-thirty yet!"

"Mr. Brynne was early. Mr. Baxter decided to see him at once."

"I must speak to him," Aaui said.

"I have orders not to disturb them." The girl looked frightened and her finger hovered over a button on her desk.

Aaui knew that the button would probably summon help. A man like Baxter would have protection near at all times. The meeting was taking place now, and he didn't dare interfere. Perhaps his actions had changed

the course of events. It seemed likely. The Brynne in that office was a
different man, a man altered by his adventures of the morning.

"It's all right," Aaui said to the receptionist. "We'll just sit here and wait."

Ben Baxter was short, solid, bull-chested. He was totally bald and his
eyes, behind gold pince-nez, were expressionless. His business suit was
severe, and affixed to the lapel was the small ruby-and-pearls emblem of
the Wall Street House of Lords.

For half an hour, Brynne had talked, spread papers on Baxter's desk,
quoted figures, mentioned trends, predicted movements. He was perspiring anxiously now, waiting for a word out of Baxter.

"Hmm," said Ben Baxter.

Brynne waited. His temples were pounding with a steady, dull ache
and he was having trouble with the tight knots in his stomach. It was
years since he had fought in anger; he wasn't used to it. He hoped he
could control himself until the meeting was over.

"The terms you request," said Baxter, "are just short of preposterous."

"Sir?"

"Preposterous was the word, Mr. Brynne. You are, perhaps, hard of
hearing?"

"No," said Brynne.

"Excellent. These terms you present might be suitable for negotiation
between two companies of equal holdings. But such is not the case, Mr.
Brynne. It amounts to presumption that a company of your size should
offer such terms to Baxter Enterprises."

Brynne's eyes narrowed. He had heard about Baxter's reputation for
in-fighting. This was not personal insult, he reminded himself. It was the
kind of business maneuver that he himself had often used. It must be
dealt with as such.

"Let me point out," Brynne said, "the key nature of this forest area I
have an option on. With sufficient capitalization, we could extend the
holding enormously, to say nothing—"

"Hopes, dreams, promises," Baxter sighed. "You *may* have something
worth while. As yet, it is inadequately demonstrated."

This is business, Brynne reminded himself. He does want to back
me—I can tell. I expected to come down in the bargaining. Naturally. All
he's doing is beating down the terms. Nothing personal…

But too much had happened to Brynne in one day. The red-faced
Crusader, the voice in the restaurant, his short-lived dream of freedom,
the fight with the two men—he knew he couldn't take much more.

"Suppose, Mr. Brynne," said Baxter, "you make a more reasonable offer.
One in keeping with the modest and subsidiary status of your holdings."

He's testing me, Brynne thought. But it was too much. He was as nobly born as Baxter; how dare the man treat him this way?

"Sir," he said through numb lips. "I take exception."

"Eh?" said Baxter, and Brynne thought he glimpsed amusement in the cold eyes. "What do you take exception to?"

"Your statements, sir, and the manner in which you say them. I suggest you apologize."

Standing up stiffly, Brynne waited. His head was pounding inhumanly now and his stomach refused to unknot itself.

"I see nothing for which to apologize, sir," said Baxter. "And I see no reason to deal with a man who cannot keep personalities out of a business discussion."

He's right, Brynne thought. *I'm the one who should apologize.* But he could not stop. Desperately he said, "I warn you—apologize sir!"

"We can do no business this way," said Baxter. "And frankly, Mr. Brynne, I had hoped to do business with you. I will try to speak in a reasonable manner, if you will try to react in an equally reasonable manner. I ask you to withdraw your request for an apology and let us get on."

"I can't!" Brynne said, wishing passionately he could. "Apologize, sir!"

Baxter stood up, short and powerfully built. He stepped out from behind the desk, his face dark with anger. "Get out of here then, you insolent young dog! Get out or I'll have you thrown out, you hot-headed fool! Get out!"

Brynne, wishing to apologize, thought of the red-faced Crusader, the waiter, his two assailants. Something snapped in him. He lashed out with all his strength, the weight of his body behind the blow.

It caught Baxter full in the neck and slammed him against the desk. Eyes glazed, Baxter slumped to the floor.

"I'm sorry!" Brynne cried. "I apologize! I apologize!"

He knelt beside Baxter. "Are you all right, sir? I'm truly sorry. I apologize…"

A part of his mind, coldly functioning, told him that he had been caught in an unresolvable ambivalence. His need for action had been as strong as his need to apologize. And so he had solved the dilemma by trying to do both things, in the usual ambivalent muddle. He had struck—*then* apologized.

"Mr. Baxter?" he called in alarm.

Ben Baxter's features were congested and blood drooled from a corner of his mouth. Then Brynne noticed that Baxter's head lay at a queer angle from his body.

"Oh…" Brynne said.

He had served three years with the Knights Rampant. It was not the first broken neck he had seen.

II

On the morning of April 12, 1959, Ned Brynne awakened and washed and dressed. At 1:30 that afternoon, he had an appointment with Ben Baxter, the president of Baxter Industries. Brynne's entire future hinged upon the outcome of that meeting. If he could get the backing of the gigantic Baxter Enterprises, and do so on favorable terms...

Brynne was a tall, darkly handsome man of thirty-six. There was a hint of deep gentleness in his carefully bland eyes, a suggestion of uncompromising piety in his expressive mouth. His movements had the loose grace of an unselfconscious man.

He was almost ready to leave. He tucked a prayer stick under his arm and slipped a copy of Norsted's *Guide to the Gentle Way* into his pocket. He was never without that infallible guide.

Finally he fixed to his lapel the silver moon decoration of his station. Brynne was a Restrainer, second class, of the Western Buddhist Congregation, and he allowed himself a carefully restrained pride over the fact. Some people thought him too young for lay-priestly duties. But they had to agree that Brynne carried the prerogatives and requirements of his office with a dignity quite beyond his years.

He locked his apartment and walked to the elevator. There was a small crowd waiting, mostly Western Buddhists, but two Lamaists as well. All made way for him when the elevator came.

"Pleasant day, Brother Brynne," the operator said as the car started down.

Brynne inclined his head an inch in the usual modest response to a member of the flock. He was deep in thought about Ben Baxter. But at the corner of his eye, he noticed one of the occupants of the car, a slim, beautiful, black-haired woman with a piquant golden face. Indian, Brynne thought, wondering what a woman like that was doing in his apartment building. He knew the other tenants by sight, though, of course, he would not be sufficiently immodest to recognize them.

The elevator reached the lobby and Brynne forgot about the Indian woman. He had a lot on his mind today. There were some problems connected with Ben Baxter, problems he hoped to resolve before the meeting. He stepped outside, into a dismal gray April morning, and decided to go to the Golden Lotus Coffee Shop for a late breakfast.

It was 10:25 A.M.

"I could stay here and breathe this air forever!" said Janna Chandragore.

Lan Il smiled faintly. "Perhaps we can breathe it in our own age. How does he seem to you?"

"Smug and over-righteous," she said. They were following half a block behind Brynne. There was no losing Brynne's tall, stooped figure, even in New York's morning rush.

"He absolutely *stared* at you in the elevator," said Lan Il.

"I know." She smiled. "He's rather nice-looking, don't you think?"

Lan Il raised both eyebrows, but didn't comment. They continued to follow, noticing how the crowds parted out of respect for Brynne's rank. Then it happened.

Brynne, his attention turned inward, collided with a portly, florid-faced man who wore the yellow robe of a Western Buddhist priest.

"My apologies for violating your meditation, Young Brother," said the priest.

"My fault entirely, Father," Brynne said. "For it is written, 'Youth should know its footsteps.'"

The priest shook his head. "In youth," he said, "resides the dream of the future; and age must make way."

"Age is our guide and signposts along the Way," Brynne objected humbly but insistently. "The writings are clear on the point."

"If you accept age," said the priest, his lips tightening slightly, "then accept the dictum of age: youth must forge ahead! Kindly do not contradict me, Dear Brother."

Brynne, his eyes carefully bland, bowed deeply. The priest bowed in return and the men continued their separate ways.

Brynne walked more quickly, his hands tight on his prayer stick. Just like a priest—using his age as a support for arguments in favor of youth. There were some strange contradictions in Western Buddhism, but Brynne did not care to think about them at the moment.

He went into the Golden Lotus Coffee Shop and sat down at a table far in the rear. He fingered the intricate carvings on his prayer stick and felt anger wash away from him. Almost immediately, he regained that serene and unruffled union of mind with emotions so vital to the Gentle Way.

Now was the time to think about Ben Baxter. After all, a man had to perform his temporal duties as well as his religious ones. Looking at his watch, he saw it was nearly eleven o'clock. In two and a half hours, he would be in Baxter's office and—

"Your order, sir?" a waiter asked him.

"A glass of water and some dried fish, if you please," said Brynne.

"French fries?"

"Today is Visya. It is not allowed," Brynne murmured softly.

The waiter went pale, gulped, said, "Yes, sir, sorry, sir," and hurried off.

I shouldn't have made him feel ridiculous, thought Brynne. I should simply have refused the French fries. Should I apologize to the man?

He decided it would simply embarrass him. Resolutely Brynne put the thought out of his mind and concentrated on Ben Baxter. With Baxter's power behind the forest area Brynne had optioned, and its potential, there was no telling—

He became conscious of a disturbance at a nearby table. He turned and saw a golden-featured woman weeping bitterly into a tiny lace handkerchief. She was the woman he had seen earlier in his apartment building. With her was a small, wizened old man, who was trying in vain to console her.

As the woman wept, she cast a despairing glance at Brynne. There was only one thing a Restrainer could do under the circumstances.

He walked over to their table. "Excuse the intrusion," he said. "I couldn't help notice your distress. Perhaps you are strangers in the city. Can I help?"

"We are past help!" the woman wailed.

The old man shrugged his shoulders fatalistically.

Brynne hesitated, then sat down at their table. "Tell me," he begged. "No problem is unsolvable. It is written that there is a path through all jungles and a trail over the steepest mountains."

"Truly spoken," the old man assented. "But sometimes the feet of Man cannot reach the trail's end."

"At such times," Brynne replied, "each helps each and the deed is done. Tell me your trouble. I will serve you in any way I can."

In actual fact, this was more than a Restrainer was required to do. Total service was the obligation of higher-ranking priests. But Brynne was swept away by the woman's need and beauty, and the words were out before he could consider them.

"'In the heart of a young man is strength,'" quoted the old man, "'and a staff for weary arms.' But tell me, sir, are you a believer in religious toleration?"

"Absolutely!" said Brynne. "It is one of the essential tenets of Western Buddhism."

"Very well. Then know, sir, that my daughter Janna and I are from Lhagrama in India, where we serve the Daritria Incarnation of the Cosmic Function. We came here to America hoping to found a small temple. Unfortunately, the schismatics of the Marii Incarnation have arrived before us. My daughter must return to her home. But our lives are threatened momentarily by these Marii fanatics, who are sworn to stamp out the Daritria faith."

"But your lives can't be in danger here!" Brynne exclaimed. "Not in the heart of New York."

"Here more than anywhere else," said Janna. "For crowds are cloak and mask to the assassin."

"I shall not live long in any event," the old man said with serene unconcern. "I must remain here and complete my work. It is so written. But I wish my daughter to return safely to her home."

"I won't go without you!" Janna cried.

"You will do as you are told!" the old man said.

Janna looked meekly away from his steely black eyes. The old man turned to Brynne.

"Sir, this afternoon a ship sails for India. My daughter needs a man, a strong, true man, to guide and protect her, to bring her home. My fortune must go to the man who performs this sacred duty for me."

"I can hardly believe this," said Brynne, suddenly struck with doubt. "Are you sure—"

As if in answer, the old man pulled a small chamois bag from his pocket and spilled its contents on the tablecloth. Brynne was not an expert in gems, though he had had some dealings with them as a religious-instruction officer in the Second World Jehad. Still, he was sure he recognized the true fire of ruby, sapphire, diamond, and emerald.

"They are yours," said the old man. "Take them to a jewelry store. When their authenticity is verified, perhaps you will believe the rest of my story. Or if these are not sufficient proof—"

From another pocket, he pulled a thick billfold and handed it to Brynne. Opening it, Brynne saw that it was stuffed with high-denomination bills.

"Any bank will verify *their* authenticity," said the old man. "No, please, I insist. Keep it all. Believe me, it is only a portion of what I would like to bestow upon you for rendering me this sacred trust."

It was overwhelming. Brynne tried to remind himself that the gems could conceivably be clever fakes and the bills could be superb forgeries. But he knew they were not. They were real. And if this wealth, so casually given, was real, then didn't the rest of the story have to be true?

It would not be the first time a miraculous fairy-tale adventure happened in real life. Wasn't the *Book of Golden Replies* filled with similar incidents?

He looked at the beautiful, sorrowful, golden-featured woman. A great desire came over him to bring joy to those exquisite features, to make that tragic mouth smile. And in the way she looked at him, Brynne perceived more than simply the interest one gives to a protector.

"Sir!" cried the old man. "Is it possible that you might—that you might consider—"

"I'll do it!" said Brynne.

The old man clasped Brynne's hand. Janna simply looked at him, but he had the sensation of being enfolded into a warm embrace.

"You must leave at once," the old man said briskly. "Come, there's no time to lose. Even now, the enemy lurks in the shadows."

"But my clothes—"

"Unimportant. I will provide you with a wardrobe."

"—and friends, business appointments. Wait! Hold on a minute!"

Brynne took a deep breath. Haroun-al-Rashid adventures were all very well, but they had to be undertaken in a reasonable fashion.

"I have a business appointment this afternoon," Brynne said. "I must keep it. After that, I'm completely at your service. "

"The danger to Janna is too great!" cried the old man.

"You'll both be perfectly safe, I assure you. You can even accompany me there. Or better yet, I've got a cousin on the police force. I'm sure I can arrange for a bodyguard—"

Janna turned her beautiful sad face away from him. The old man said, "Sir, the ship sails at one P.M.—at one precisely."

"Those ships leave every day or so," Brynne pointed out. "Let's catch the next one. This appointment is very important. Crucial, you might say. I've worked for years to arrange it. And it's not just me. I have a business, employees, associates. For their sake, I have to keep that appointment."

"Business before life," the old man said bitterly.

"You'll be all right," Brynne assured him. "It is written, you know, that the beast of the jungle shies from the tread—"

"I know what is written. The word of death is painted large upon my forehead, and upon my daughter's, unless you aid us now. She will be on the *Theseus* in stateroom 2A. The next stateroom, 3A, will be yours. The ship sails at one this afternoon. If you value her life, sir, you will be there."

The old man and his daughter stood up, paid and left, ignoring Brynne's pleas for reason. As she went out the door, Janna turned for a moment and gazed at him.

"Your dried fish, sir," said the waiter. He had been hovering near waiting for a chance to serve it.

"To hell with it!" Brynne shouted. "Oh, sorry, sorry," he said in dismay to the shocked waiter. "No fault of yours."

He paid, leaving a sizable tip for the waiter, and hurried out. He had a lot of thinking to do.

"All the energy expended on that one scene," Lan Il complained, "has probably cost me ten years of my life."

"You loved every minute of it," said Janna Chandragore.

"True, true," Lan Il admitted, nodding vigorously. He sipped a glass of wine that a steward had brought to the stateroom. "The question now is—will he give up his appointment with Baxter and come?"

"He does seem to like me," Janna said.

"Which shows his excellent taste."

She inclined her head mockingly. "But really, that story! Was it necessary to make it so—so outrageous?"

"Absolutely necessary. Brynne is a strong and dedicated man, but he has his romantic streak. Nothing less than a fairy tale to match his gaudiest dream could pull him from duty's path."

"Perhaps even a fairy tale won't," Janna said thoughtfully.

"We'll see," said Lan Il. "Personally, I believe he will come."

"I don't."

"You underestimate your attractiveness and acting ability, my dear. Wait and see."

"I have no choice," said Janna, settling back in an arm chair.

The desk clock read 12:42.

Brynne decided to take a stroll along the waterfront to quiet his nerves. The sight of the great ships lying calm and steadfast in their berths never failed to soothe him. He walked steadily along, trying to reason out what had happened to him.

That magnificent sorrowful girl…

But what about his duty, the labor of faithful employees, to be culminated and completed this afternoon at the desk of Ben Baxter?

He stopped and looked at the bow of a great ship. The *Theseus.*

He thought of India, its blue skies, brilliant sunshine, wine, relaxation. Those things would never be his. Work, frantic effort, that was the life he had set for himself. Even if it meant losing the most beautiful woman in the world, he would continue to labor under the iron-gray skies of New York.

But why, he asked himself touching the chamois bag in his pocket. He was moderately well off. His business could take care of itself. What was to stop him from boarding that ship, dropping everything, spending a year in the sun?

Excitement stirred in him as he realized that *nothing* was stopping him. He was his own man, a strong, determined man. If he had the faith and will to succeed in business, he also had the faith and will to leave it, drop everything, and follow his heart.

"To hell with Baxter!" he said to himself. The girl's safety was more important than anything. He *would* board that that ship, and right now, wire his associates from sea, tell them—

The decision was made. He whirled and marched to the gangplank and resolutely climbed it.

An officer on deck the smiled and said, "Name, sir?"

"Ned Brynne."

"Brynne, Brynne." The officer checked his list. "I don't seem to—Oh, yes, right here. Yes, Mr. Brynne. You're on A deck, cabin 3. Let me wish you a most pleasant trip."

"Thank you," Brynne said, glancing at his watch. It read a quarter to one.

"By the way," he said to the officer, "what time does the ship sail?"

"At four-thirty sharp, sir."

"Four-thirty? Are you sure?"

"Quite sure, Mr. Brynne."

"But I was told you sailed at one o'clock."

"That was the original time, sir. But sailing time is often advanced a few hours. We'll easily make it up at sea."

Four-thirty! Yes, he had enough time! He could go back, see Ben Baxter and still return in time to catch the ship! Both problems were solved!

Murmuring a blessing to a mysterious but benevolent fate, Brynne turned and sprinted down the gangplank. He was fortunate enough to catch a taxi at once.

Ben Baxter was short, solid, bull-chested. He was totally bald and his eyes, behind gold pince-nez, were expressionless. His business suit was severe and affixed to the lapel was the small ruby-and-pearls emblem of the Humble Servitors of Wall Street.

For half an hour, Brynne had talked, mentioned trends, predicted movements. He was perspiring anxiously now, waiting for a word out of Baxter.

"Hmm," said Ben Baxter.

Brynne waited. His pulse was pounding heavily and his empty stomach was beginning to churn. Half his mind was on the *Theseus,* sailing soon. He wanted to end this meeting and get aboard.

"The merger terms you request," said Baxter, "are quite satisfactory."

"Sir?" breathed Brynne.

"Satisfactory, I said. Haven't got trouble with your hearing, have you, Brother Brynne?"

"Not for news like that," said Brynne, grinning.

"Our affiliation," Baxter said, smiling, "promises a great future for us both. I'm a direct man, Brynne, and I want to tell you this directly: I like the way you've handled the surveys and data and I like the way you've handled this meeting. Moreover, I like you personally. I am most happy about this and believe our association will prosper."

"I sincerely believe so, sir."

They shook hands and both men stood up.

"My lawyers will draw up the papers," Baxter said, "in accordance with this discussion. You should have them by the end of the week."

"Excellent." Brynne hesitated, wondering if he should tell Baxter he was going to India. He decided not to. It would be simple to arrange for receipt of the papers on the *Theseus* and he could carry out the final details by long-distance telephone. He wouldn't be gone too long, any-how—just long enough to see the girl safely home; then he would fly back.

They exchanged a few more pleasantries, shook hands again and Brynne turned to leave.

"That's a fine-looking prayer stick," Baxter said.

"Eh? Oh, yes," said Brynne. "I got it from Sinkiang just this week. They make the finest prayer sticks there, in my unworthy opinion."

"I know. May I look at it?"

"Of course. Please be careful, though. It opens rather fast."

Baxter took the intricately carved prayer stick and pressed the handle. A blade shot out of the other end, narrowly grazing his leg.

"It *is* fast!" Baxter said. "Fastest I've seen."

"Did you cut yourself?"

"A mere scratch. Beautiful damascene work on that blade." They talked for a few minutes about the threefold significance of the knife blade in Western Buddhism and of recent developments in the Western Buddhist spiritual center in Sinkiang. Then Baxter carefully closed the prayer stick and returned it to Brynne.

"A truly beautiful thing. Good day again, Dear Brother Brynne, and—"

Baxter halted in mid-sentence. His mouth was open and he seemed to be staring at a point just in back of Brynne's head.

Brynne turned, but nothing was there except the wall. When he turned back, Baxter's features were congested and a light froth had gathered at the corners of his mouth.

"Sir!" cried Brynne.

Baxter tried to speak, but couldn't. He took two tottering steps for-ward and collapsed to the floor.

Brynne rushed to the receptionist's office. "Call a doctor! Quick! Quick!" he shouted to the frightened girl. Then he rushed back to Baxter.

He was looking at the first American case of the mutated disease that was to be called the Sinkiang Plague. Transmitted on a hundred contaminated prayer sticks, it would go through New York like a flash fire, leaving a million dead in its wake. Within the week the symptoms of Sinkiang Plague would be better known than those of measles.

But Brynne was looking at the first casualty.

With horror, he stared at the hard, brilliant apple-green shine of Baxter's hands and face.

III

On the morning of April 12, 1959, Ned Brynne awakened and washed and dressed. At 1:30 that afternoon, he had an appointment with Ben Baxter, the president of Baxter Industries. Brynne's entire future hinged upon the outcome of that meeting. If he could get the backing of the gigantic Baxter Enterprises and do so on favorable terms…

Brynne was a tall, darkly handsome man of thirty-six. There was a hint of thoughtfulness in his carefully bland eyes, a look of reason and willingness to compromise in his relaxed mouth. His movements had the careless surety of a man who knows his place in the world.

He was almost ready to leave. He tucked an umbrella under his arm and slipped a paperbound copy of *Murder on the Metro* into his pocket. He was never without a good mystery of some sort.

Finally he fixed to his lapel the small onyx pin of a Commodore of the Ocean Cruising Club. Some people thought him too young for such an honor. But they had to agree that Brynne carried the prerogatives and requirements of his office with a dignity quite beyond his years.

He locked his apartment and walked to the elevator. There was a small crowd waiting, mostly shopkeepers, but two businessmen as well.

"Pleasant day, Mr. Brynne," the operator said as the car started down.

"Hope so," Brynne said, deep in thought about Ben Baxter. At the corner of his eye, he noticed one of the occupants of the car, a great blond Viking of a man, talking to a tiny, half-bald fellow. Brynne wondered what they were doing in his apartment building. He knew most of the tenants by sight, though he hadn't lived in the building long enough to get acquainted with them.

The elevator reached the lobby and Brynne forgot about the Viking. He had a lot on his mind today. There were some problems connected with Ben Baxter, problems he hoped to resolve before the meeting. He stepped outside, into a dismal gray April morning, and decided to go to Childs' for breakfast.

It was 10:25 A.M.

"What do you think?" asked Dr. Sveg.

"He looks ordinary enough," said Edwin James. "He even looks reasonable. We'll find out."

They were following half a block behind Brynne. There was no losing Brynne's tall, erect figure, even in New York's morning rush.

"I am certainly not one to advocate violence," said Dr. Sveg. "But this time—why don't we knock him over the head and be done with it?"

"That method was selected by Aaui and Beatty. Miss Chandragore and Lan Il decided to try bribery. We are committed to a course of reason."

"But suppose he can't be reasoned with, what then?"

James shrugged his shoulders.

"I don't like it," Dr. Sveg said.

Following half a block behind, they saw Brynne collide with a portly, florid-faced businessman.

"Sorry," said Brynne.

"Sorry," said the portly businessman.

They exchanged perfunctory nods and went on. Brynne went into Childs' and sat down at an empty table in the rear. Now was the time to think of Ben Baxter and of what the best approach would be—

"Your order, sir?" a waiter asked him.

"Scrambled eggs, toast, coffee," Brynne said.

"French fries?"

"No, thanks."

The waiter hurried off. Brynne concentrated on Ben Baxter. With Baxter's financial and political backing of the forest deal, there was no telling—

"Excuse me, sir," a voice said. "May we talk to you?" Brynne looked up and saw the blond man and his small friend whom he had seen in the elevator.

"What about?"

"A matter of the utmost urgency, sir," said the small man. Brynne glanced at his watch. It was almost 11:00. He had two and a half hours before his meeting with Baxter.

"Sure, sit down," he invited. "What's on your mind?"

The men looked at each other and exchanged embarrassed smiles. Finally the small man cleared his throat.

"Mr. Brynne," he said, "I am Edwin James. This is my associate, Dr. Sveg. We have a preposterous-sounding story to tell, which I hope you will hear to the end without interruptions. After that, we have certain proofs that may or may not convince you of the story's authenticity."

Brynne frowned, wondering what kind of crackpots he had met. But both men were well dressed, quietly spoken.

"Sure, go ahead," Brynne said.

An hour and twenty minutes later, Brynne was saying, "Wow! That's quite a little yarn!"

"I know," Dr. Sveg said apologetically. "Our proofs—"

"—are impressive. Let me see that first gadget again."

Sveg handed it to him. Brynne stared reverently at the small, shining object.

"Boys, if a thing that size can really turn out heat or cold in those quantities—the electrical corporations would give a couple of billion to get it!"

"It is a product of our technology," said Chief Programmer James, "as are the other gadgets. With the exception of the motrifier, they are all straight-line developments, refinements of present trends."

"And that thallasator. Nice, simple, inexpensive way of extracting fresh water from salt." He looked at the two men. "It is possible, of course, that these items are a hoax."

Dr. Sveg raised both eyebrows.

"But I'm not exactly untrained in science. Even if they're a hoax, they'd have to be every bit as advanced as the real thing. I guess you've sold me. Men from the future! Well, well!"

"Then you accept what we say about you?" James asked.

"And about Ben Baxter and time-line selection?"

"Well..." Brynne thought hard. "Tentatively."

"Will you cancel your appointment with Baxter?"

"I don't know."

"Sir?"

"I said I don't know. You've got a lot of nerve," Brynne said angrily. "I've worked like a galley slave, driving toward this goal. This meeting is the biggest chance I've ever had or ever will have. And you ask me to give up all that because of some nebulous prediction—"

"The prediction isn't nebulous," James said. "It is very explicit and most precise."

"Look, there's more involved than just me. I have a business, employees, associates, stockholders. I have to keep this meeting for their sake, too."

"Mr. Brynne," said Sveg, "consider the larger issues at stake!"

"Yeah, sure," Brynne said sourly. "How about those other teams you talked about? Maybe I've been stopped in some other probability world."

"You haven't."

"How do you know?"

"I couldn't say so to the teams," Chief Programmer James said, "but the probability of their success was vanishingly small—just as the probability of *my* success with you is small, statistically."

"Hell," said Brynne, "you guys come dropping out of the future and casually ask a man to change his entire life. You haven't got the right!"

"If you could postpone the appointment for a single day," Dr. Sveg suggested, "that might—"

"You don't postpone appointments with Ben Baxter. Either you keep the one he's given you or you wait—maybe forever—until he gives you another." Brynne stood up. "Look, I don't know what I'm going to do. I've heard you, I more or less believe you, but I just don't know. I'll have to make up my own mind."

Dr. Sveg and James also stood up.

"That is your privilege," said Chief Programmer James. "Goodbye. I hope you make the right decision, Mr. Brynne."

They shook hands. Brynne hurried out.

Dr. Sveg and James watched him go. Sveg said, "What do you think? It looks favorable, doesn't it? Don't you think so?"

"I can't guess," James said. "The possibility of altering events within a time-line is never favorable. I honestly have no idea of what he's going to do."

Dr. Sveg shook his head, then sniffed. "Some air, eh?"

"Quite," said Chief Programmer James.

Brynne decided to take a stroll along the waterfront to quiet his nerves. The sight of the great ships lying calm and steadfast in their berths never failed to soothe him. He walked steadily along, trying to reason out what had happened to him.

That ridiculous story...

In which he believed.

But what about his duty, the years spent working his way up to optioning that huge forest tract, its tremendous possibilities to be culminated and completed this afternoon at the desk of Ben Baxter?

He stopped and looked at the bow of a great ship. The *Theseus*...

He thought of the Caribbean, its blue skies, brilliant sunshine, wine, relaxation. Those things would never be his. Work, frantic effort, that was the life he had set for himself. No matter what the loss, he would continue to work under the iron-gray skies of New York.

But why, he asked himself. He was moderately well off. His business could take care of itself. What was to stop him from boarding that ship, dropping everything, spending a year in the sun?

Excitement stirred in him as he realized that *nothing* was stopping him. He was his own man, a strong, determined man. If he had the guts to succeed in business, he also had the guts to leave it, drop everything, and follow his heart.

And in that way, the ridiculous damned future would be safe.

"To hell with Ben Baxter!" he said to himself.

But he didn't mean it.

The future was just too uncertain, too far away. This whole thing might well be an elaborate hoax, arranged by a business competitor.

Let the future take care of itself!

Ned Brynne turned abruptly away from the *Theseus*. He had to hurry to make his appointment with Baxter on time.

In Baxter's building, riding up in the elevator, Brynne tried not to think. It was enough simply to act. He got off at the 16th floor and walked up to the receptionist.

"My name is Brynne. I have an appointment with Mr. Baxter."

"Yes, Mr. Brynne. Mr. Baxter is expecting you. You can go right in."

Brynne didn't move. A wave of doubt flooded his mind and he thought of the future generations, whose chances he was damaging by his act. He thought of Dr. Sveg and Chief Programmer Edwin James, earnest, well-meaning men. They wouldn't ask him to make such a sacrifice unless it was absolutely essential.

And he considered one thing more—

Among those future generations would be descendants of his own.

"You may go in, sir," the girl said.

Abruptly, something snapped in Brynne's mind.

"I've changed my mind," he said, in a voice he hardly recognized. "I'm canceling the appointment. Tell Baxter I'm sorry—about everything."

He turned, before he could change his mind, and ran down sixteen flights of stairs.

In the meeting room of the World Planning Council, the five representatives of the Federated Districts of Earth were seated around a long table, waiting for Edwin James. He entered, a small man, impressively ugly.

"Reports," he said.

Aaui, looking somewhat the worse for wear, told about their attempt at violence and its result. "Perhaps," he concluded, "if we had been conditioned to use more violence—faster—we could have stopped him."

"And perhaps not," said Beatty, who looked considerably worse than Aaui.

Lan Il reported the partial success and total failure of his mission with Miss Chandragore. Brynne had agreed to accompany them to India, even if it meant giving up the meeting with Baxter. Unfortunately, Brynne had found himself able to do both things.

Lan Il ended with several philosophical comments about the shockingly flexible schedules of steamship companies.

Chief Programmer James stood up. "The future we were selecting for was one in whose past Ben Baxter lived to complete his work of buying forests. That, unfortunately, is not to be. Our best line, under the circumstances, is the Main Historic Line, in which Dr. Sveg and I bent our efforts."

"You haven't reported yet," Miss Chandragore said. "What happened?"

"Reason," said Edwin James, "and an appeal to the intelligence seem to be the best operating procedures. After due thought, Brynne decided not to keep his appointment with Ben Baxter. But—"

Ben Baxter was short, solid, bull-chested. He was totally bald and his eyes, behind gold pince-nez, were expressionless. His business suit was severe and affixed to the lapel was the small ruby-and-pearls emblem of the Wall Street Club.

He had been sitting motionless for half an hour now, thinking about figures, trends, movements.

His buzzer sounded.

"Yes, Miss Cassidy?"

"Mr. Brynne was here. He just left."

"What do you mean?"

"I really don't understand it, Mr. Baxter. He came up and said he wanted to cancel his appointment."

"What did he say? Repeat it exactly, Miss Cassidy."

"He said he had an appointment with you and I said he could go right in. And he stood there looking at me very strangely, frowning. He seemed angry and upset. I told him again he could go in. Then he said—"

"Word for word now, Miss Cassidy."

"Yes, sir. He said, 'I've changed my mind. I'm canceling the appointment. Tell Baxter I'm sorry—for everything.'"

"That's all he said?"

"Every last word, Mr. Baxter."

"And then?"

"He turned and hurried downstairs."

"Stairs?"

"Yes, Mr. Baxter. He didn't wait for the elevator."

"I see."

"Is there anything else, Mr. Baxter?"

"No, nothing else, Miss Cassidy. Thank you."

Ben Baxter turned off the intercom and slumped wearily behind his desk.

So Brynne knew!

It was the only possible explanation. Word must have gotten out somehow, somewhere. He had thought it was safely hidden for another day, at least. But there must have been a leak.

Baxter smiled grimly to himself. He couldn't blame Brynne, though the man should at least have talked to him. But perhaps not. Maybe it was best this way.

But *how* had he found out? Who had broken the news to him that the Baxter industrial empire was hollow, decaying, crumbling at the foundations?

If only the news could have been concealed for another day, another few hours! He would have signed with Brynne. A fresh venture would have pumped new blood into the Baxter holdings. By the time people found out, he would once again have had a solid base from which to operate.

Brynne knew and had been scared off. That meant every one knew.

There was no holding things together now. The wolves would be at him. His friends, his wife, his partners and all the little people who had depended upon him...

Well, he had decided years ago what to do in this eventuality.

Without hesitation, Baxter opened his desk drawer and took out a small bottle. He extracted two white tablets.

He had always lived by his own rules. Now was the time to die by them.

Ben Baxter popped the pills into his mouth. In two minutes, he slumped forward on the desk.

His death precipitated the great stock market crash of '59.

A WIND IS RISING

Outside, a wind was rising. But within the station, the two men had other things on their minds. Clayton turned the handle of the water faucet again and waited. Nothing happened.

"Try hitting it," said Nerishev.

Clayton pounded the faucet with his fist. Two drops of water came out. A third drop trembled on the spigot's lip, swayed, and fell.

"That does it," Clayton said bitterly. "That damned water pipe is blocked again. How much water we got in storage?"

"Four gallons—assuming the tank hasn't sprung another leak," said Nerishev. He stared at the faucet, tapping it with long, nervous fingers. He was a big, pale, bearded man, fragile-looking in spite of his size. He didn't look like the type to operate an observation station on a remote and alien planet. But the Advance Exploration Corps had discovered, to its regret, that there was no "type" for that kind of work.

Nerishev was a competent biologist and botanist. Although chronically nervous, he had surprising reserves of calm. He was the sort of man who needs an occasion to rise to. This, if anything, made him suitable to pioneer a planet like Carella I.

"I suppose somebody should go out and unblock the water pipe," said Nerishev, not looking at Clayton.

"I suppose so," Clayton said, pounding the faucet again. "But it's going to be murder out there. Listen to it!"

Clayton was a short man, bull-necked, red-faced, powerfully constructed. This was his third tour of duty as a planetary observer.

He had tried other jobs in the Advance Exploration Corps, but none suited him. PEP—Primary Extraterrestrial Penetration—faced him with too many unpleasant surprises. It was work for daredevils and madmen. But Base Operations was much too tame and restricting.

He liked the work of a planetary observer, though. His job was to sit tight on a planet newly opened by the PEP boys and checked out by a drone camera crew. All he had to do on this planet was stoically endure discomfort and skillfully keep himself alive. After a year of this, the relief ship would remove him and note his report. On the basis of the report, further action would or would not be taken.

Before each tour of duty, Clayton dutifully promised his wife that this would be the last. After *this* tour, he was going to stay on Earth and work on the little farm he owned. He promised...

But at the end of each rest leave, Clayton journeyed out again, to do the thing for which he was best suited: staying alive through skill and endurance.

But this time he had had it. He and Nerishev had been eight months on Carella. The relief ship was due in another four months. If he came through alive, he was going to quit for good.

"Just listen to that wind," Nerishev said.

Muffled, distant, it sighed and murmured around the steel hull of the station like a zephyr, a summer breeze.

That was how it sounded to them inside the station, separated from the wind by three inches of steel plus a soundproofing layer.

"It's rising," Clayton said. He walked over to the windspeed indicator. According to the dial, the gentle-sounding wind was blowing at a steady eighty-two miles an hour—

A light breeze on Carella.

"Man, oh, man!" Clayton said. "I don't want to go out there. Nothing's worth going out there."

"It's your turn," Nerishev pointed out.

"I know. Let me complain a little first, will you? Come on, let's get a forecast from Smanik."

They walked the length of the station, their heels echoing on the steel floor, past compartments filled with food, air supplies, instruments, extra equipment. At the far end of the station was the heavy metal door of the receiving shed. The men slipped on air masks and adjusted the flow.

"Ready?" Clayton asked.

"Ready."

They braced themselves, gripping handholds beside the door. Clayton touched the stud. The door slid away and a gust of wind shrieked in. The men lowered their heads and butted into the wind, entering the receiving shed.

The shed was an extension of the station, some thirty feet long by fifteen feet wide. It was not sealed, as was the rest of the structure. The walls were built of openwork steel, with baffles set in. The wind could pass through this arrangement, but slowed down, controlled. A gauge told them it was blowing thirty-four miles an hour within the shed.

It was a damned nuisance, Clayton thought, having to confer with the natives of Carella in a gale. But there was no other way. The Carellans, raised on a planet where the wind never blew at less than seventy miles an hour, couldn't stand the "dead air" within the station. Even with the oxygen content cut down to the Carellan norm, the natives couldn't make the adjustments. Within the station, they grew dizzy and apprehensive. Soon they began strangling, like a man in a vacuum.

Thirty-four miles an hour of wind was a fair compromise point for human and Carellan to meet.

Clayton and Nerishev walked down the shed. In one corner lay what looked like a tangle of dried-out octopi. The tangle stirred and waved two tentacles ceremoniously.

"Good day," said Smanik.

"Good day," Clayton said. "What do you think of the weather?"

"Excellent," said Smanik.

Nerishev tugged at Clayton's sleeve. "What did he say?" he asked, and nodded thoughtfully when Clayton translated for him. Nerishev lacked Clayton's gift for language. Even after eight months, the Carellan tongue was still an undecipherable series of clicks and whistles to him.

Several more Carellans came up to join the conversation. They all looked like spiders or octopi, with their small centralized bodies and long, flexible tentacles. This was the optimum survival shape on Carella, and Clayton sometimes envied it. He was forced to rely absolutely on the shelter of the station; but the Carellans lived directly in their environment.

Often he had seen a native walking against a tornado-force wind, seven or eight limbs hooked into the ground and pulling, other tentacles reaching out for further grips. He had seen them rolling down the wind like tumbleweed, their tentacles curled around them, wickerwork-basket fashion. He thought of the gay and audacious way they handled their land ships, scudding merrily along on the wind…

Well, he thought, they'd look damned silly on Earth.

"What is the weather going to be like?" he asked Smanik.

The Carellan pondered the question for a while, sniffed the wind, and rubbed two tentacles together.

"The wind may rise a shade more," he said finally. "But it will be nothing serious."

Clayton wondered. "Nothing serious" for a Carellan could mean disaster for an Earthman. Still, it sounded fairly promising.

He and Nerishev left the receiving shed and closed the door.

"Look," said Nerishev, "if you'd like to wait—"

"Might as well get it over with," Clayton said.

Here, lighted by a single dim overhead bulb, was the smooth, glittering bulk of the Brute. That was the nickname they had given to the vehicle specially constructed for transportation on Carella.

The Brute was armored like a tank and streamlined like a spheric section. It had vision slits of shatterproof glass, thick enough to match the strength of its steel plating. Its center of gravity was low; most of its twelve tons were centered near the ground. The Brute was sealed. Its heavy diesel engine, as well as all necessary openings, were fitted with special dustproof covers. The Brute rested on its six fat tires, looking, in its immovable bulk, like some prehistoric monster.

Clayton got in, put on crash helmet and goggles, and strapped himself into the padded seat. He revved up the engine, listened to it critically, then nodded.

"Okay," he said, "the Brute's ready. Get upstairs and open the garage door."

"Good luck," said Nerishev. He left.

Clayton went over the instrument panel and made sure that all the Brute's special gadgets were in working order. In a moment he heard Nerishev's voice coming in over the radio.

"I'm opening the door."

"Right."

The heavy door slid back and Clayton drove the Brute outside.

The station had been set up on a wide, empty plain. Mountains would have offered some protection from the wind, but the mountains on Carella were in a constant restless state of building up and breaking down. The plain presented dangers of its own, however. To avert the worst of those dangers, a field of stout steel posts had been planted around the station. The closely packed posts pointed outward, like ancient tank traps, and served the same purpose.

Clayton drove the Brute down one of the narrow, winding channels that led through the field of posts. He emerged, located the pipeline, and started along it. On a small screen above his head, a white line flashed into view. The line would show any break or obstruction in the pipeline.

A wide, rocky, monotonous desert stretched before him. An occasional low bush came into sight. The wind was directly behind him, blanketed by the sound of the diesel.

He glanced at the windspeed indicator. The wind of Carella was blowing at ninety-two miles an hour.

He drove steadily along, humming to himself under his breath. From time to time he heard a crash. Pebbles, propelled by the hurricane wind, were cannonading against the Brute. They shattered harmlessly against the thick armor.

"Everything all right?" Nerishev asked over the radio.

"Fine," Clayton said.

In the distance he saw a Carellan land ship. It was about forty feet long, he judged, and narrow in the beam, skimming rapidly on crude wooden rollers. The ship's sails were made from one of the few leaf-bearing shrubs on the planet.

The Carellans waved their tentacles as they went past. They seemed to be heading toward the station.

Clayton turned his attention back to the pipeline. He was beginning to hear the wind now, above the roar of the diesel. The windspeed indicator showed that the wind had risen to ninety-seven miles an hour.

Somberly he stared through the sand-pocked slit-window. In the far distance were jagged cliffs, seen dimly through the dustblown air. More pebbles ricocheted off the hull and the sound rang hollowly through the vehicle. He glimpsed another Carellan land ship, then three more. They were tacking stubbornly into the wind.

It struck Clayton that a lot of Carellans were moving toward the station. He signaled to Nerishev on the radio.

"How are you doing?" Nerishev asked.

"I'm close to the spring and no break yet," Clayton reported. "Looks like a lot of Carellans heading your way."

"I know. Six ships are moored in the lee of the shed and more are coming."

"We've never had any trouble with the natives before," Clayton said slowly. "What does this look like?"

"They've brought food with them. It might be a celebration."

"Maybe. Watch yourself."

"Don't worry. You take care and hurry—"

"I've found the break! Speak to you later."

The break showed on the screen, glowing white, Peering out through the port, Clayton saw where a boulder had rolled across the pipeline, crushing it.

He brought the truck to a stop on the windward side of the pipe. The wind was blowing 113 miles an hour. Clayton slid out of the truck, carrying several lengths of pipe, some patches, a blowtorch, and a bag of tools. They were all tied to him, and he was secured to the Brute by a strong nylon rope.

Outside, the wind was deafening. It thundered and roared like breaking surf. He adjusted his mask for more oxygen and went to work.

Two hours later he had completed a fifteen-minute repair job. His clothing was shredded and his air extractor was completely clogged with dust.

He climbed back into the Brute, sealed the port, and lay on the floor, resting. The truck was starting to tremble in the wind gusts.

"Hello? Hello?" Nerishev called over the radio.

Wearily, Clayton climbed back into the driver's seat and acknowledged.

"Hurry back now, Clayton! No time to rest! The wind's up to 138! I think a storm is coming!"

A storm on Carella was something Clayton didn't even want to think about. They had experienced only one in eight months. During it, the winds had gone over 160 miles an hour.

He nosed the truck around and started back, driving directly into the wind. At full throttle, he found he was making very little progress. Three miles an hour was all the heavy diesel would do against the pressure of a 138-mile-an-hour wind.

He stared ahead through the slit-window. The wind, outlined by long streamers of dust and sand, seemed to be coming straight at him, funneled out of an infinitely wide sky to the tiny point of his window. Windborne rocks sailed at him, grew large, immense, and shattered against his window. He couldn't stop himself from ducking each time one came.

The heavy engine was beginning to labor and miss.

"Oh, baby," Clayton breathed, "don't quit now. Not now. Get Papa home. *Then* quit. Please!"

He figured he was about ten miles from the station, which lay directly upwind.

He heard a sound like an avalanche plummeting down a mountainside. It was made by a boulder the size of a house. Too big for the wind to lift, it was rolling at him from windward, digging a furrow in the rocky ground as it came.

Clayton twisted the steering wheel. The engine labored, and with infinite slowness the truck crept out of the boulder's path. Shaking, Clayton watched the boulder bearing down. With one hand he pounded on the instrument panel.

"Move, baby, move!"

Booming hollowly, the boulder rolled past at a good thirty miles an hour.

"Too close," Clayton said to himself. He tried to turn the Brute back into the wind, toward the station. The Brute wouldn't do it.

The diesel labored and whined, trying to turn the big truck into the wind. And the wind, like a solid gray wall, pushed the truck away.

The windspeed indicator stood at 159 miles an hour.

"How are you doing?" Nerishev asked over the radio.

"Just great! Leave me alone, I'm busy."

Clayton set his brakes, unstrapped, and raced back to the engine. He adjusted timing and mixture, and hurried back to the controls.

"Hey, Nerishev! That engine's going to conk out!"

It was a full second before Nerishev answered. Then, very calmly, he asked, "What's wrong with it?"

"Sand!" Clayton said. "Particles driven at 159 miles an hour—sand in the bearings, injectors, everything. I'm going to make all the distance I can."

"And then?"

"Then I'll try to sail her back," Clayton said. "I just hope the mast will take it."

He turned his attention to the controls. At windspeeds like this, the truck had to be handled like a ship at sea. Clayton picked up speed with the wind on his quarter, then came about and slammed into the wind.

The Brute made it this time and crossed over onto the other tack.

It was the best he could do, Clayton decided. His windward distance would have to be made by tacking. He edged toward the eye of the wind. But at full throttle, the diesel couldn't bring him much closer than forty degrees.

For an hour the Brute forged ahead, tacking back and forth across the wind, covering three miles to make two. Miraculously, the engine kept on running. Clayton blessed the manufacturer and begged the diesel to hold out a little while longer.

Through a blinding screen of sand, he saw another Carellan land ship. It was reefed down and heeled over precariously. But it forged steadily to windward and soon outdistanced him.

Lucky natives, Clayton thought—165 miles of wind was a sailing breeze to them!

The station, a gray half-sphere, came into sight ahead.

"I'm going to make it!" Clayton shouted. "Break out the rum, Nerishev! Papa's getting drunk tonight!"

The diesel chose that moment to break down for good.

Clayton swore violently as he set the brakes. What lousy luck! If the wind were behind him, he could roll in. But, of course, it had to be in front.

"What are you going to do now?" Nerishev asked.

"I'm going to sit here," Clayton said. "When the wind calms down to a hurricane, I'm going to walk home."

The Brute's twelve-ton mass was shaking and rattling in the wind blasts.

"You know," Clayton said, "I'm going to retire after this tour."

"That so! You really mean it?"

"Absolutely. I own a farm in Maryland, with frontage on Chesapeake Bay. You know what I'm going to do?"

"What?"

"I'm going to raise oysters. You see, the oyster—Hold it."

The station seemed to be drifting slowly upwind, away from him. Clayton rubbed his eyes, wondering if he was going crazy. Then he realized that in spite of its brakes, in spite of its streamlining, the truck was being pushed downwind, away from the station.

Angrily he shoved a button on his switchboard, releasing the port and starboard anchors. He heard the solid clunk of the anchors hitting the ground, heard the steel cables scrape and rattle. He let out a hundred and seventy feet of steel line, then set the winch brakes. The truck was holding again.

"I dropped the anchors," Clayton said.

"Are they holding?"

"So far." Clayton lighted a cigarette and leaned back in his padded chair. Every muscle in his body ached from tension. His eyelids twitched from watching the wind-lines converging on him. He closed his eyes and tried to relax.

The sound of the wind cut through the truck's steel plating, The wind howled and moaned, tugging at the truck, trying to find a hold on the smooth surface. At 169 miles an hour, the ventilator baffles blew out. He would be blinded, Clayton thought, if he weren't wearing sealed goggles, choked if he weren't breathing canned air. Dust swirled, thick and electric, within the Brute's cabin.

Pebbles, flung with the velocity of rifle bullets, splattered against the hull. They were striking harder now. He wondered how much more force they'd need before they started to pierce the armor plating.

At times like this, Clayton found it hard to maintain a commonsense attitude. He was painfully aware of the vulnerability of human flesh, appalled at the possibilities for violence in the Universe. What was he doing out here? Man's place was in the calm, still air of Earth.

"Are you all right?" Nerishev asked.

"Making out just great," Clayton said wearily. "How are things at the station?"

"Not so good. The whole structure's going into sympathetic vibration. Given enough time, the foundations could shatter."

"And they want to put a fuel station here!" Clayton said.

"Well, you know the problem. This is the only solid planet between Angarsa III and the South Ridge Belt. All the rest are gas giants."

"They better build their station in space."

"The cost—"

"Hell, man, it'll cost less to build another planet than to try to maintain a fuel base on this one," Clayton spat out a mouthful of dust. "I just want to get on that relief ship. How many natives at the station now?"

"About fifteen, in the shed."

"Any sign of violence?"

"No, but they're acting funny."

"How so?"

"I don't know," said Nerishev. "I just don't like it."

"Stay out of the shed, huh? You can't speak the language, anyhow, and I want you in one piece when I come back." He hesitated. "If I come back."

"You'll be fine," Nerishev said.

"Sure, I will. I—oh, Lord!"

"What's it? What's wrong?"

"Boulder coming down! Talk to you later!"

Clayton turned his attention to the boulder, a rapidly growing black speck to windward. It was heading directly toward his anchored and immobilized truck. He glanced at the windspeed indicator. Impossible— 174 miles an hour! And yet, he reminded himself, winds in the stratospheric jet stream on Earth blew at two hundred miles an hour.

The boulder, as large as a house, still growing as it approached, was rolling directly toward him.

"Swerve! Turn!" Clayton shouted at the boulder, pounding the instrument panel with his fist.

The boulder was coming at him, straight as a ruler line, rolling right down the wind.

With a yell of agony, Clayton touched a button, releasing both anchors at the cable end. There was no time to winch them in, even assuming the winch could take the strain. Still the boulder grew.

Clayton released the brakes.

The Brute, shoved by a wind of one hundred and seventy-eight miles an hour, began to pick up speed. Within seconds he was rolling downwind at thirty-eight miles an hour, watching through the rear-vision mirror as the boulder overtook him.

Clayton twisted the steering wheel hard to the left. The truck tilted over precariously, swerved, fishtailed on the hard ground, and tried to turn itself over. Clayton fought the wheel, trying to bring the Brute back to equilibrium. He thought: *I'm probably the first man who ever jibed a twelve-ton truck!*

The boulder, looking like a whole city block, roared past. The heavy truck teetered for a moment, then came to rest on its six wheels.

"Clayton! What happened? Are you all right?"

"Fine," Clayton gasped. "But I had to slip the cables. I'm running downwind."

"Can you turn?"

"Almost knocked her over, trying."

"How far can you run?"

Clayton stared ahead. In the distance he could make out the dramatic black cliffs that rimmed the plain.

"I got about fifteen miles to go before I pile into the cliffs. Not much time, at the speed I'm traveling." He locked his brakes. The tires began to scream and the brake linings smoked furiously. But the wind, at one hundred and eighty-three miles an hour, didn't even notice the difference. His speed over the ground had gone up to forty-four miles an hour.

"Try sailing her out!" Nerishev said.

"She won't take it."

"Try, man! What else can you do? The wind's hit one hundred and eighty-five here. The whole station's shaking! Boulders are tearing up the whole post defense. I'm afraid some boulders are going to get through and flatten—"

"Stow it," Clayton said. "I got troubles of my own."

"I don't know if the station will stand! Clayton, listen to me. Try the—"

The radio suddenly went dead.

Clayton banged it a few times, then gave up. His speed over the ground had reached forty-nine miles an hour. The cliffs were already looming large before him.

"So all right," Clayton said. "Here we go." He released his last anchor. At the end of two hundred and fifty feet of steel cable, it slowed him to thirty miles an hour. The anchor was breaking and ripping through the ground like a jet-propelled plow.

Then Clayton turned on the sail mechanism. The sail was final insurance in case the engine failed. On Carella, a man could never walk home from a stranded vehicle.

The mast, a short, powerful steel pillar, extruded through a gasketed hole in the roof. Magnetic shrouds and stays snapped into place. From the mast fluttered a sail of link-woven metal. For a mainsheet, there was a three-part, flexible steel cable working through a winch.

The sail was only a few square feet in area. But it could drive a twelve-ton truck with brakes locked and an anchor dug in at the end of two hundred and fifty feet of line—

Easily—with the wind blowing one hundred and eighty-five miles an hour.

Clayton winched in the mainsheet, taking the wind behind his quarter. But the course wasn't good enough. He winched the sail in still more and turned closer to the wind.

With the super-hurricane on his beam, the ponderous truck heeled over, lifting one entire side into the air. Clayton released a few feet of mainsheet. The metal-link sail screamed and chattered as the wind whipped at it.

Driving now with just the sail's leading edge, Clayton was able to keep the truck on its feet and make good a course to windward.

In the rear-vision mirror he could see the black, jagged cliffs behind him. They were his lee shore, his coast of wrecks. But he was sailing out of the trap. Foot by foot, he was pulling away.

"That's my baby!" Clayton shouted to the battling Brute. His sense of victory snapped almost at once, for he heard an earsplitting clang and something whizzed past his head. At one hundred and eighty-seven miles an hour, pebbles were piercing the truck's armor plating. It was the Carellan equivalent of a machine-gun barrage.

Desperately he clung to the steering wheel. He could hear the sail tearing itself apart. It was made out of the toughest flexible alloys available, but it wasn't going to hold up for long. The short, thick mast, supported by six heavy cables, was whipping like a light fishing rod.

His brake linings were worn out, and his speed over the ground came up to fifty-seven miles an hour.

He was too tired to think. He steered, his hands locked to the wheel, his slitted eyes glaring ahead into the storm.

The sail ripped with a scream. The tatters flogged for a moment, then brought the mast down. Wind gusts were approaching one hundred and ninety miles an hour.

The wind was now driving him back toward the cliffs. At one hundred and ninety-two miles an hour of wind, the Brute was lifted bodily, thrown for a dozen yards, slammed back on its wheels. A front tire blew, then two rear ones. Clayton put his head on his arms and waited for the end.

Suddenly the Brute stopped short. Clayton was flung forward. His safety belt checked him for a moment, then snapped. He banged against the instrument panel and fell back, dazed and bleeding.

He lay on the floor, half conscious, trying to figure out what had happened. Slowly he pulled himself back into the seat, foggily aware that he hadn't broken any limbs. His stomach was one great bruise. His mouth was bleeding.

At last, looking in the rear-vision mirror, he saw what had happened. The emergency anchor, trailing at the end of two hundred and fifty feet of steel cable, had caught in a deep outcropping of rock. A fouled anchor had brought him up short, less than half a mile from the cliffs. He was saved—

For the moment, at least.

But the wind hadn't given up. The one-hundred-and-ninety-three-mile-an-hour wind lifted the truck bodily and slammed it down again and again. The steel cable hummed like a taut guitar string. Clayton wrapped his arms and legs around the seat. He couldn't hold on much longer. And if he let go, the madly leaping Brute would smear him over the walls like toothpaste—

If the cable didn't part first and send the truck hurtling into the cliffs.

He held on. At the top of one swing, he caught a glimpse of the windspeed indicator. The sight of it sickened him. He was through, finished, done for. How could he be expected to hold on through the force of a one hundred and eighty-seven-mile-an-hour wind? It was too much.

One hundred and eighty-seven miles an hour? That meant that the wind was falling!

As he watched, the dial hand slowly crept down. At one hundred and sixty miles an hour, the truck stopped slamming and lay quietly at the end of its anchor line. At one hundred and fifty-three, the wind veered—a sure sign that the blow was nearly over.

When it had dropped to one hundred and forty-two miles an hour, Clayton allowed himself the luxury of passing out.

Carellan natives came out for him later in the day. Skillfully they maneuvered two big land ships up to the Brute, fastened on their long vines—which tested out stronger than steel—and towed the derelict truck back to the station.

They brought him into the receiving shed, and Nerishev carried him into the station's dead air.

"You didn't break anything except a couple of teeth," said Nerishev. "But there isn't an unbruised inch on you."

"We came through it," Clayton said.

"Just. Our boulder defense is completely flattened. The station took two direct hits from boulders and barely contained them. I've checked the foundations; they're badly strained. Another blow like that—"

"—and we'd make out somehow. Us Earth lads, we come through! That was the worst in eight months. Four months more, and the relief ship comes! Buck up, Nerishev. Come with me."

"Where are we going?"

"I want to talk to that damned Smanik!"

They came into the shed. It was filled to overflowing with Carellans. Outside, in the lee of the station, several dozen land ships were moored.

"Smanik!" Clayton called. "What's going on here?"

"It is the Festival of Summer," Smanik said. "Our great yearly holiday."

"Hm. What about that blow? What did you think of it?"

"I would classify it as a moderate gale," said Smanik. "Nothing dangerous, but somewhat unpleasant for sailing."

"Unpleasant! I hope you get your forecasts a little more accurate in the future."

"One cannot always outguess the weather," Smanik said. "It is regrettable that my last forecast should be wrong."

"Your *last?* How come?"

"These people," Smanik said, gesturing around him, "are my entire tribe. We have celebrated the Festival of Summer. Now summer is ended and we must go away."

"Where to?"

"To the caverns in the far west. They are two weeks' sail from here. We will live in the caverns for three months. In that way, we will find safety."

Clayton had a sudden sinking feeling in his stomach. "Safety from what, Smanik?"

"I told you. Summer is over. We need safety now from the winds—
the powerful storm winds of winter."

"What is it?" Nerishev said.

"Just a moment." Clayton thought quickly of the super-hurricane he
had just passed through, which Smanik had classified as a moderate and
harmless gale. He thought of their immobility, the ruined Brute, the
strained foundations of the station, the flattened boulder barrier, the relief ship four months away. "Could we go with you in the land ships,
Smanik, and take refuge in the caverns?"

"Of course," said Smanik hospitably.

"No, we couldn't," Clayton answered himself. "We'd need extra oxygen, our own food, a water supply—"

"What's the matter?" Nerishev asked. "What did he say to make you
look like that?"

"He says the *really* big winds are just coming," Clayton replied. The
two men looked at each other.

Outside, a wind was rising.

GRAY FLANNEL ARMOR

The means which Thomas Hanley selected to meet the girl who later became his wife is worthy of note, particularly by anthropologists, sociologists, and students of the bizarre. It serves, in its humble way, as an example of one of the more obscure mating customs of the late 20th century. And since this custom had an impact upon modern American industry, Hanley's story has considerable importance.

Thomas Hanley was a tall, slim young man, conservative in his tastes, moderate in his vices, and modest to a fault. His conversation with either sex was perfectly proper, even to the point of employing the verbal improprieties suitable to his age and station. He owned several gray flannel suits and many slim neckties with regimental stripes. You might think you could pick him out of a crowd because of his horn-rimmed glasses, but you would be wrong. That wasn't Hanley. Hanley was the other one.

Who would believe that, beneath this meek, self-effacing, industrious, conforming exterior beat a wildly romantic heart? Sadly enough, anyone would, for the disguise fooled only the disguised.

Young men like Hanley, in their gray flannel armor and horn-rimmed visors, are today's knights of chivalry. Millions of them roam the streets of our great cities, their footsteps firm and hurried, eyes front, voices lowered, dressed to the point of invisibility. Like actors or bewitched men, they live their somber lives, while within them the flame of romance burns and will not die.

Hanley daydreamed continually and predictably of the swish and thud of swinging cutlasses, of great ships driving toward the sun under a press of sail, of a maiden's eyes, dark and infinitely sad, peering at him from behind a gossamer veil. And, predictably still, he dreamed of more modern forms of romance.

But romance is a commodity difficult to come by in the great cities. This fact was recognized only recently by our more enterprising businessmen. And one night, Hanley received a visit from an unusual sort of salesman.

Hanley had returned to his one-room apartment after a harried Friday at the office. He loosened his tie and contemplated, with a certain melancholy, the long weekend ahead. He didn't want to watch the boxing on television and he had seen all the neighborhood movies. Worst of all, the girls he knew were uninteresting and his chances for meeting others were practically nil.

He sat in his armchair as the deep blue twilight spread over Manhattan, and speculated on where he might find an interesting girl, and what he would say if he found one, and—

His doorbell rang.

As a rule, only peddlers or solicitors for the Firemen's Fund called on him unannounced. But tonight he could welcome even the momentary pleasure of turning down a peddler. So he opened the door and saw a short, dapper, flashily dressed little man beaming at him.

"Good evening, Mr. Hanley," the little man said briskly. "I'm Joe Morris, a representative of the New York Romance Service, with its main office in the Empire State Building and branches in all the boroughs, Westchester, and New Jersey. We're out to serve lonely people, Mr. Hanley, and that means you. Don't deny it! Why else would you be sitting home on a Friday night? You're lonely and it's our business and our pleasure to serve you. A bright, sensitive, good-looking young fellow like yourself needs girls, nice girls, pleasant, pretty, understanding girls—"

"Hold on," Hanley said sternly. "If you run some sort of a fancy call girl bureau—"

He stopped, for Joe Morris had turned livid. The salesman's throat swelled with anger and he turned and started to leave.

"Wait!" said Hanley. "I'm sorry."

"I'll have you know, sir, I'm a family man," Joe Morris said stiffly. "I have a wife and three children in the Bronx. If you think for a minute I'd associate myself with anything underhanded—"

"I'm really sorry." Hanley ushered Morris in and gave him the armchair. Mr. Morris immediately regained his brisk and jovial manner.

"No, Mr. Hanley," he said, "the young ladies I refer to are not—ah—professionals. They are sweet, normal, romantically inclined young girls. But they are lonely. There are many lonely girls in our city, Mr. Hanley."

Somehow, Hanley had thought the condition applied only to men. "Are there?" he asked.

"There are. The purpose of the New York Romance Service," said Morris, "is to bring young people together under suitable circumstances."

"Hmm," Hanley said. "I take it then you run a sort of—if you'll pardon the expression—a sort of Friendship Club?"

"Not at all! Nothing like it! My dear Mr. Hanley, have you ever attended a Friendship Club?"

Hanley shook his head.

"You should, sir," said Morris. "Then you could really appreciate our Service. Friendship Clubs! Picture, if you will, a barren hall, one flight up in the cheaper Broadway area. At one end, five musicians in frayed tuxedos play, with a dreary lack of enthusiasm, the jittery songs of the day. Their thin music echoes disconsolately through the hall and blends with the screech of traffic outside. There is a row of chairs on either side of the hall, men on one side, women on the other. All are acutely embarrassed by their presence there.

"They cling to a wretched nonchalance, nervously chain-smoking cigarettes and stamping out the butts on the floor. From time to time, some unfortunate gets up his courage to ask for a dance and, stiffly, he moves his partner around the floor, under the lewd and cynical eyes of the rest. The master of ceremonies, an overstuffed idiot with a fixed and ghastly smile, hurries around, trying to inject some life into the corpse of the evening. But to no avail."

Morris paused for breath. "That is the anachronism known as the Friendship Club—a strained, nervous, distasteful institution better suited to Victorian times than to our own. At the New York Romance Service, we have done what should have been done years ago. We have applied scientific precision and technological know-how to a thorough study of the factors essential to a successful meeting between the sexes."

"What are those factors?" Hanley inquired.

"The most vital ones," said Morris, "are spontaneity and a sense of fatedness."

"Spontaneity and fate seem to be contradictory terms," Hanley pointed out.

"Of course. Romance, by its very nature, must be composed of contradictory elements. We have graphs to prove it."

"Then you sell romance?" Hanley asked dubiously.

"The very article! The pure and pristine substance itself! Not sex, which is available to everyone. Not love—no way of guaranteeing permanency and therefore commercially impracticable. We sell *romance,* Mr. Hanley, the missing ingredient in modern society, the spice of life, the vision of all the ages!"

"That's very interesting," Hanley said. But he questioned the validity of Morris's claims. The man might be a charlatan or he might be a visionary. Whatever he was, Hanley doubted whether he could sell *romance.* Not the real thing. Not the dark and fitful visions which haunted Hanley's days, and nights.

He stood up. "Thank you, Mr. Morris. I'll think over what you've said. Right now, I'm in rather a rush, so if you wouldn't mind—"

"But, sir! Surely you can't afford to pass up *romance!*"

"Sorry, but—"

"Try our system for a few days, absolutely free of charge," Mr. Morris said. "Here, put this is your lapel." He handed Hanley something that looked like a small transistor radio with a tiny video eye.

"What's this?" Hanley asked.

"A small transistor radio with a tiny video eye."

"What does it do?"

"You'll see. Just give it a try. We're the country's biggest firm specializing in romance, Mr. Hanley. We aim to stay that way by continuing to fill the needs of millions of sensitive young American men and women. Remember—romances sponsored by our firm are fated, spontaneous, esthetically satisfying, physically delightful, and morally justifiable."

And with that, Joe Morris shook Hanley's hand and left.

Hanley turned the tiny transistor radio in his hand. It had no buttons or dials. He fastened it to the lapel of his jacket. Nothing happened.

He shrugged his shoulders, tightened his tie and went out for a walk.

It was a clear, cool night. Like most nights in Hanley's life, it was a perfect time for romance. Around him lay the city, infinite in its possibilities and rich in promise. But the city was devoid of fulfillment. He had walked these streets a thousand nights, with firm step, eyes front, ready for anything. And nothing had ever happened.

He passed apartment buildings and thought of the women behind the high, blank windows, looking down, seeing a lonely walker on the dark streets and wondering about him, thinking…

"Nice to be on the roof of a building," a voice said. "To look down on the city."

Hanley stopped short and whirled around. He was completely alone. It took him a moment to realize that the voice had come from the tiny transistor radio.

"What?" Hanley asked.

The radio was silent.

Look down on the city, Hanley mused. The radio was suggesting he look down on the city. Yes, he thought, it would be nice.

"Why not?" Hanley asked himself, and turned toward a building.

"Not that one," the radio whispered.

Hanley obediently passed by the building and stopped in front of the next.

"This one?" he queried.

The radio didn't answer. But Hanley caught the barest hint of an approving little grunt.

Well, he thought, you had to hand it to the Romance Service. They seemed to know what they were doing. His movements were as nearly spontaneous as any guided movements could be.

Entering the building, Hanley stepped into the self-service elevator and punched for the top floor. From there, he climbed a short flight of stairs to the roof. Once outside, he began walking toward the west side of the building.

"Other side," whispered the radio.

Hanley turned and walked to the other side. There he looked out over the city, at the orderly rows of street lights, white and faintly haloed. Dotted here and there were the reds and greens of traffic lights, and the occasional colored blotch of an electric sign. His city stretched before him, infinite in its possibilities, rich in promise, devoid of fulfillment.

Suddenly he became aware of another person on the roof, staring raptly at the spectacle of lights.

"Excuse me," said Hanley. "Didn't mean to intrude."

"You didn't," the person said, and Hanley realized he was talking to a woman.

We are strangers, Hanley thought. A man and a woman who meet by accident—or fate—on a dark rooftop overlooking the city. He wondered how many dreams the Romance Service had analyzed, how many visions they had tabulated, to produce something as perfect as this.

Glancing at the girl, he saw that she was young and lovely. Despite her outward composure, he sensed how the rightness of this meeting, the place, the time, the mood stirred her as it did him.

He thought furiously, but could find nothing to say, No words came to him and the moment was drifting away.

"The lights," prompted his radio.

"The lights are beautiful," said Hanley, feeling foolish.

"Yes," murmured the girl. "Like a great carpet of stars, or spearpoints in the gloom."

"Like sentinels," said Hanley, "keeping eternal vigil in the night." He wasn't sure if the idea was his or if he was parroting a barely perceptible voice from the radio.

"I often come here," said the girl.

"I never come here," Hanley said.

"But tonight..."

"Tonight I had to come. I knew I would find you."

Hanley felt that the Romance Service needed a script writer. Such dialogue, in broad daylight, would be ridiculous. But now, on a high rooftop overlooking the city, with lights flashing below and the stars very close overhead, it was the most natural conversation in the world.

"I do not encourage strangers," said the girl, taking a step toward him. "But—"

"I am no stranger," Hanley said, moving toward her.

The girl's pale blonde hair glinted with starlight. Her lips parted. She looked at him, her features transfigured by the mood, the atmosphere, and the soft, flattering light

They stood face to face and Hanley could smell her faint perfume and the fragrance of her hair. His knees became weak and confusion reigned within him.

"Take her in your arms," the radio whispered.

Automatonlike, Hanley held out his arms. The girl entered them with a little sigh. They kissed—simply, naturally, inevitably, and with a mounting and predictable passion.

Then Hanley noticed the tiny jeweled transistor radio on the girl's lapel. In spite of it, he had to admit that the meeting was not only spontaneous and fateful, but enormously pleasant as well.

Dawn was touching the skyscrapers when Hanley returned to his apartment and tumbled, exhausted, into bed. He slept all day and awoke toward evening, ravenously hungry. He ate dinner in a neighborhood bar and considered the events of the previous night.

It had been wild, perfect and wonderful, all of it—the meeting on the roof and, later, her warm and darkened apartment; and at last his departure at dawn, with her drowsy kiss still warm on his mouth. But despite all this, Hanley was disturbed.

He couldn't help feeling a little odd about a romantic meeting set up and sponsored by transistor radios, which cued lovers into the proper spontaneous yet fated responses. It was undoubtedly clever but something about it seemed wrong.

He visualized a million young men in gray flannel suits and striped regimental ties, roaming the streets of the city in response to the barely heard commands of a million tiny radios. He pictured the radio operators at their central two-way videophone switchboard—earnest, hard-working people, doing their night's work at romance, then buying a newspaper and taking a subway home to the husband or wife and kids.

This was distasteful. But he had to admit that it was better than no romance at all. These were modern times. Even romance had to be put on a sound organizational basis or get lost in the shuffle.

Besides, Hanley thought, was it really so strange? In medieval times, a witch gave a knight a charm, which led him to an enchanted lady. Today, a salesman gave a man a transistor radio, which did the same thing and probably a lot faster.

Quite possibly, he thought, there has never been a truly spontaneous and fated romance. Perhaps the thing always requires a middleman.

Hanley cast further thoughts out of his mind. He paid for his dinner and went out for a walk.

This time, his firm and hurried steps led him into a poorer section of the city. Here garbage cans lined the sidewalks, and from the dirty tenement windows came the sound of a melancholy clarinet, and the shrill voices of women raised in argument. A cat, striped and agate-eyed, peered at him from an alleyway and darted out of sight.

Hanley shivered, stopped, and decided to return to his own part of the city.

"Why not walk on?" the radio urged him, speaking very softly, like a voice in his head.

Hanley shivered again and walked on.

The streets were deserted now and silent as a tomb. Hanley hurried past gigantic windowless warehouses and shuttered stores. Some adventures, it seemed to him, were not worth the taking. This was hardly a suitable locale for romance. Maybe he should ignore the radio and return to the bright, well-ordered world he knew.

He heard a sound of scuffling feet. Glancing down a narrow alley, he saw three wrestling figures. Two were men and the third, trying to break free, was a girl.

Hanley's reaction was instantaneous. He tensed to sprint away and find a policeman, preferably two or three. But the radio stopped him.

"You can handle them," the radio said.

Like hell I can, Hanley thought. The newspapers were full of stories about men who thought they could handle muggers. They usually had plenty of time to brood over their fistic shortcomings in a hospital.

But the radio urged him on. And touched by a sense of destiny, moved by the girl's plaintive cries, Hanley removed his horn-rimmed glasses, put them in their case, put the case into a hip pocket, and plunged into the black maw of the alley.

He ran full into a garbage can, knocked it over and reached the struggling group. The muggers hadn't noticed him yet. Hanley seized one by the shoulder, turned him and lashed out with his right fist. The man staggered back against the wall. His friend released the girl and went for Hanley, who struck out with both hands and his right foot.

The man went down, grumbling, "Take it easy, buddy."

Hanley turned back to the first mugger, who came at him like a wildcat. Surprisingly, the man's entire fusillade of blows missed and Hanley knocked him down with a single well-placed left.

The two men scrambled to their feet and fled. As they ran, Hanley could hear one complain to the other, "Ain't this a hell of a way to make a living?"

Ignoring this break in the script, Hanley turned to the girl. She leaned against him for support. "You came," she breathed.

"I had to," said Hanley, in response to a barely audible radio voice.

"I know," she murmured.

Hanley saw that she was young and lovely. Her black hair glinted with lamplight. Her lips parted. She looked at him, her features transfigured by the mood, the atmosphere, and the soft, flattering light.

This time, Hanley needed no command from the tiny radio to take her into his arms. He was learning the form and content of the romantic adventure and the proper manner of conducting a spontaneous yet fated affair.

They departed at once for her apartment. And as they walked, Hanley noticed a large jewel glittering in her black hair.

It wasn't until much later that he realized it was a tiny, artfully disguised transistor radio.

Next evening, Hanley was out again, walking the streets and trying to quiet a small voice of dissatisfaction within him. It had been a perfect night, he reminded himself, a night of tender shadows, soft hair brushing his eyes, and tears warm upon his shoulder. And yet...

The sad fact remained that this girl hadn't been his type, any more than the first girl had been. You simply can't throw strangers together at random and expect the fiery, quick romance to turn into love. Love has its own rules and enforces them rigidly.

So Hanley walked, and the conviction grew within him that tonight he was going to find love. For tonight the horned moon hung low over the city and a southern breeze carried the mingled scent of spice and nostalgia.

Aimlessly he wandered, for his transistor radio was silent. No command brought him to the little park at the river's edge and no secret voice urged him to approach the solitary girl standing there.

He stood near her and contemplated the scene. To his left was a great bridge, its girders faint and spidery in the darkness. The river's oily black water slid past, ceaselessly twisting and turning. A tug hooted and another replied, wailing like ghosts lost in the night.

His radio gave him no hint. So Hanley said, "Nice night."

"Maybe," said the girl, not turning. "Maybe not."

"The beauty is there," Hanley said, "if you care to see it."

"What a strange thing to say..."

"Is it?" Hanley asked, taking a step toward her. "Is it really strange? Is it strange that I'm here? And that you are here?"

"Perhaps not," the girl said, turning at last and looking into Hanley's face.

She was young and lovely. Her bronze hair glinted with moonlight and her features were transfigured by the mood, the atmosphere, and the soft, flattering light.

Her lips parted in wonder.

And then Hanley knew.

This adventure was truly fated and spontaneous! The radio had not guided him to this place, had not whispered cues and responses for him to murmur. And looking at the girl, Hanley could see no tiny transistor radio on her blouse or in her hair.

He had met his love, without assistance from the New York Romance Service! At last, his dark and fitful visions were coming true.

He held out his arms. With the faintest sigh, she came into them. They kissed, while the lights of the city flashed and mingled with the stars overhead, and the crescent moon dipped in the sky, and foghorns hooted mournful messages across the oily black river.

Breathlessly, the girl stepped back. "Do you like me?" she asked

"Like you!" exclaimed Hanley. "Let me tell you—"

"I'm so glad," said the girl, "because I am your Free Introductory Romance, given as a sample by Greater Romance Industries, with home offices in Newark, New Jersey. Only our firm offers romances which are truly spontaneous and fated. Due to our technological researches, we are able to dispense with such clumsy apparatus as transistor radios, which lend an air of rigidity and control where no control should be apparent. We are happy to have been able please you with this sample romance.

"But remember—this is only a sample, a taste, of what Greater Romance Industries, with branch offices all over world, can offer you. In this brochure, sir, several plans are outlined. You might be interested in the *Romance in Many Lands* package, or, if you are of an enterprising imagination perhaps the piquant *Romance through the Ages* package is for you. Then there is the regular City Plan and—"

She slipped a brightly illustrated pamphlet into Hanley's hand. Hanley stared at it, then at her. His fingers opened and the brochure fluttered to the ground.

"Sir, I trust we haven't offended you!" the girl cried. "These business-like aspects of romance are necessary, but quickly over. Then everything is purely spontaneous and fateful. You receive your bill each month in a plain unmarked envelope and—"

But Hanley had turned from her and was running down the street. As he ran, he plucked the tiny transistor radio from his lapel and hurled it into a gutter.

Further attempts at salesmanship were wasted on Hanley. He telephoned an aunt of his, who immediately and with twittering excitement arranged a date for him with a daughter of one of her oldest friends. They met in his aunt's over-decorated parlor and talked in halting sentences for three hours, about the weather, college, business, politics, and friends they might have in common. And Hanley's beaming aunt hurried in and out of the brightly lighted room, serving coffee and homemade cake.

Something about this stiff, formal, anachronistic setup must have been peculiarly right for the two young people. They progressed to regular dates and were married after a courtship of three months.

It is interesting to note that Hanley was among the last to find a wife in the old, unsure, quaint, haphazard, unindustrialized fashion. For the Service Companies saw at once the commercial potentialities of Hanley's Mode, graphed the effects of embarrassment upon the psyche, and even assessed the role of the Aunt in American Courtship.

And now one of the Companies' regular and most valued services is to provide bonded aunts for young men to call up, to provide these aunts with shy and embarrassed young girls, and to produce a proper milieu for all this in the form of a bright, over-decorated parlor, an uncomfortable couch, and an eager old lady bustling back and forth at meticulously unexpected intervals with coffee and homemade cake.

The suspense, they say, becomes almost overpowering.

HOLDOUT

The crew of a space ship must be friends. They must live harmoniously in order to achieve the split-second interaction that becomes necessary from time to time. In space, one mistake is usually enough.

It is axiomatic that even the best ships have their accidents; the mediocre ones don't survive.

Knowing this, it can be understood how Captain Sven felt when, four hours before blastoff, he was told that radioman Forbes would not serve with the new replacement.

Forbes hadn't met the new replacement yet, and didn't want to. Hearing about him was enough. There was nothing personal in this, Forbes explained. His refusal was on purely racial grounds.

"Are you sure of this?" Captain Sven asked, when his chief engineer came to the bridge with the news.

"Absolutely certain, sir," said engineer Hao. He was a small, flat-faced, yellow-skinned man from Canton. "We tried to handle it ourselves. But Forbes wouldn't budge."

Captain Sven sat down heavily in his padded chair. He was deeply shocked. He had considered racial hatred a thing of the remote past. He was as astonished at a real-life example of it as he would have been to encounter a dodo, a moa, or a mosquito.

"Racialism in this day and age!" Sven said. "Really, it's too preposterous. It's like telling me they're burning heretics in the village square, or threatening warfare with cobalt bombs."

"There wasn't a hint of it earlier," said Hao. "It came as a complete surprise."

"You're the oldest man on the ship," Sven said. "Have you tried reasoning him out of this attitude?"

"I've talked to him for hours," Hao said. "I pointed out that for centuries we Chinese hated the Japanese, and vice versa. If we could overcome our antipathy for the sake of the Great Co-operation, why couldn't he?"

"Did it do any good?"

"Not a bit. He said it just wasn't the same thing."

Sven bit off the end of a cigar with a vicious gesture, lighted it, and puffed for a moment. "Well, I'm damned if I'll have anything like this on *my* ship. I'll get another radioman!"

"That won't be too easy, sir," Hao said. "Not here."

Sven frowned thoughtfully. They were on Discaya II, a small outpost planet in the Southern Star Reaches. Here they had unloaded a cargo of machine parts, and taken on the Company-assigned replacement who was the innocent source of all the trouble. Discaya had plenty of trained men, but they were all specialists in hydraulics, mining, and allied fields. The planet's single radio operator was happy where he was, had a wife and children on Discaya, owned a house in a pleasant suburb, and would never consider leaving.

"Ridiculous, absolutely ridiculous," Sven said. "I can't spare Forbes, and I'll not leave the new man behind. It wouldn't be fair. Besides, the Company would probably fire me. And rightly, rightly. A captain should be able to handle trouble aboard his own ship."

Hao nodded glumly.

"Where is this Forbes from?"

"A farm near an isolated village in the mountain country of the Southern United States. Georgia, sir. Perhaps you've heard of it?"

"I think so," said Sven, who had taken a course in Regional Charactistics at Uppsala, to better fit himself for the job of captain. "Georgia produces peanuts and hogs."

"And men," Hao added. "Strong, capable men. You'll find Georgians working on all frontiers, out of all proportions to their actual numbers. Their reputation is unexcelled."

"I know all this," Sven grumbled. "And Forbes is an excellent man. But this racialism—"

"Forbes can't be considered typical," Hao said. "He was raised in a small, isolated community, far from the mainstream of American life. Similar communities all over the world develop and cling to strange folkways. I remember a village in Honan where—"

"I still find it hard to believe," Sven said, interrupting what promised to be a long dissertation on Chinese country life. "And there's simply no excuse for it. Every community everywhere has a heritage of some sort of racial feeling. But it's every individual's responsibility to rid himself of that when he enters the mainstream of Terran life. Others have. Why not Forbes? Why must he inflict his problems on us? Wasn't he taught anything about the Great Co-operation?"

Hao shrugged his shoulders. "Would you care to speak to him, Captain?"

"Yes. Wait, I'll speak to Angka first."

The chief engineer left the bridge. Sven remained deep in thought until he heard a knock at the door.

"Come in."

Angka entered. He was cargo foreman, a tall, splendidly proportioned man with skin the color of a ripe plum. He was a full-blooded Negro from Ghana, and a first-class guitar player.

"I assume," Sven said, "you know all about the trouble."

"It's unfortunate, sir," Angka said.

"Unfortunate? It's downright catastrophic! You know the risk involved in taking the ship up in this condition. I'm supposed to blast off in less than three hours. We can't sail without a radioman, and we need the replacement, too."

Angka stood impassively, waiting.

Sven flicked an inch of white ash from his cigar. "Now look, Angka, you must know why I called you here."

"I can guess, sir," Angka said, grinning.

"You're Forbes's best friend. Can't you do something with him?"

"I've tried, Captain, Lord knows I've tried. But you know Georgians."

"I'm afraid I don't."

"Good men, sir, but stubborn as mules. Once they've made up their minds, that's it. I've been talking to Forbes for two days about this. I got him drunk last night—strictly in line of duty, sir," Angka added hastily.

"It's all right. Go on."

"And I talked to him like I'd talk to my own son. Reminded him how good the crew got along. All the fun we'd had in all the ports. How good the Co-operation felt. Now look, Jimmy, I said to him, you keep on like this, you kill all that. You don't want that, do you, I asked him. He bawled like a baby, sir."

"But he wouldn't change his mind?"

"Said he *couldn't.* Told me I might as well quit trying. There was one and only one race in this galaxy he wouldn't serve with, and there was no sense talking about it. Said his pappy would spin in his grave if he were to do so."

"Is there any chance he'll change his mind?" Sven asked.

"I'll go on trying, but I don't think there's a chance."

He left. Captain Sven sat, his jaw cradled in one big hand. He glanced again at the ship's chronometer. Less than three hours before blastoff!

He lifted the receiver of the intercom and asked for a direct line to the spacefield tower. When he was in contact with the officer in charge he said, "I'd like to request permission to stay a few days longer."

"Wish I could grant it, Captain Sven," the officer said. "But we need the pit. We can only handle one interstellar ship at a time here. An ore boat from Calayo is due in five hours. They'll probably be short of fuel."

"They always are," Sven said.

"Tell you what we can do. If it's a serious mechanical difficulty, we could find a couple cranes, lower your ship to horizontal and drag it off the field. Might be quite a while before we could set it up again, though."

"Thanks, but never mind. I'll blast on schedule." He signed off. He couldn't allow his ship to become laid up like that. The Company would have his hide, not a doubt about it.

But there *was* a course of action he could take. An unpleasant one, but necessary. He got to his feet, discarded the dead cigar stump, and marched out of the bridge.

He came to the ship's infirmary. The doctor, in his white coat, was seated with his feet on a desk, reading a three-month-old German medical journal.

"Welcome, Cap. Care for a shot of strictly medicinal brandy?"

"I could use it," Sven said.

The young doctor poured out two healthy doses from a bottle marked *Swamp Fever Culture.*

"Why the label?" Sven asked.

"Discourages the men from sampling. They have to steal the cook's lemon extract." The doctor's name was Yitzhak Vilkin. He was an Israeli, a graduate of the new medical school at Beersheba.

"You know about the Forbes problem?" Sven asked.

"Everybody does."

"I wanted to ask you, in your capacity as medical officer aboard this ship: Have you ever observed any previous indications of racial hatred in Forbes?"

"Not one," Vilkin answered promptly.

"Are you sure?"

"Israelis are good at sensing that sort of thing. I assure you, it caught me completely by surprise. I've had some lengthy interviews with Forbes since, of course."

"Any conclusions?"

"He's honest, capable, straightforward, and slightly simple. He possesses some antiquated attitudes in the form of ancient traditions. The Mountain-Georgians, you know, have a considerable body of such customs. They've been much studied by anthropologists from Samoa and Fiji. Haven't you read *Coming of Age in Georgia?* Or *Folkways of Mountain-Georgia?*"

"I don't have time for such things," Sven said. "My time is pretty well occupied running this ship without me having to read up on the individual psychology of the entire crew."

"I suppose so, Cap," the doctor said. "Well, those books are in the ship's library, if you'd care to glance at them. I don't see how I can help you. Re-education takes time. I'm a medical officer anyhow, not a psychologist.

The plain fact is this: There is one race that Forbes will not serve with, one race which causes him to enact all his ancient racial hostilities. Your new man, by some mischance, happens to be from that race."

"I'm leaving Forbes behind," Sven said abruptly. "The communications officer can learn how to handle the radio. Forbes can take the next ship back to Georgia."

"I wouldn't recommend that."

"Why not?"

"Forbes is very popular with the crew. They think he's damned unreasonable, but they wouldn't be happy sailing without him."

"*More* disharmony," Sven mused. "Dangerous, very dangerous. But damn it, I can't leave the new man behind. I won't. It isn't fair! Who runs this ship, me or Forbes?"

"A very interesting question," Vilkin observed, and ducked quickly as the irate captain hurled his glass at him.

Captain Sven went to the ship's library, where he glanced over *Coming of Age in Georgia* and *Folkways of Mountain-Georgia*. They didn't seem to help much. He thought for a moment, and glanced at his watch. Two hours to blastoff! He hurried to the Navigation Room.

Within the room was Ks'rat. A native of Venus, Ks'rat was perched on a stool inspecting the auxiliary navigating instruments. He was gripping a sextant in three hands, and was polishing the mirrors with his foot, his most dexterous member. When Sven walked in the Venusian turned orange-brown to show his respect for authority, then returned to his habitual green.

"How's everything?" Sven asked.

"Fine," said Ks'rat. "Except for the Forbes problem, of course." He was using a manual soundbox, since Venusians had no vocal chords. At first, these sound boxes had been harsh and metallic; but the Venusians had modified them until now, the typical Venusian "voice" was a soft, velvety murmur.

"Forbes is what I came to see you about," said Sven. "You're non-Terran. As a matter of fact, you're non-human. I thought perhaps you could throw a new light on the problem. Something I may have overlooked."

Ks'rat pondered, then turned gray, his "uncertain" color. "I'm afraid I can't help much, Captain Sven. We never had any racial problems on Venus. Although you might consider the *sclarda* situation a parallel—"

"Not really," Sven said. "That was more a religious problem."

"Then I have no further ideas. Have you tried reasoning with the man?"

"Everyone else has."

"You might have better luck, Captain. As an authority symbol, you might tend to supplant the father symbol within him. With that advantage, try to make him aware of the true basis for his emotional reaction."

"There *is* no basis for racial hatred."

"Perhaps not in terms of abstract logic. But in human terms, you might find an answer and a key. Try to discover what Forbes fears. Perhaps if you can put him in better reality-contact with his own motives, he'll come around."

"I'll bear all that in mind," said Sven, with a sarcasm that was lost on the Venusian.

The intercom sounded the captain's signal. It was the first mate. "Captain! Tower wants to know whether you're blasting on schedule."

"I am," Sven said. "Secure the ship." He put down the phone.

Ks'rat turned a bright red. It was the Venusian equivalent of a raised eyebrow.

"I'm damned if I do and damned if I don't," Sven said. "Thanks for your advice. I'm going to talk to Forbes now."

"By the way," Ks'rat said, "of what race is the man?"

"What man?"

"The new man that Forbes won't serve with."

"How the hell should I know?" shouted Sven, his temper suddenly snapping. "Do you think I sit on the bridge inspecting a man's racial background?"

"It might make a difference."

"Why should it? Perhaps it's a Mongolian that Forbes won't serve with, or a Pakistani, or a New Yorker, or a Martian. What do I care what race his diseased, impoverished little mind picks on?"

"Good luck, Captain Sven," Ks'rat said as Sven hurried out.

James Forbes saluted when he entered the bridge, though it was not customary aboard Sven's ship. The radioman stood at full attention. He was a tall, slender youth, tow-headed, light-skinned, freckled. Everything about him looked pliant, malleable, complaisant. Everything except his eyes, which were dark blue and very steady.

Sven didn't know how to begin. But Forbes spoke first.

"Sir," he said, "I want you to know I'm mighty well ashamed of myself. You've been a good Captain, sir, the very best, and this has been a happy ship. I feel like a worthless no-account for doing this."

"Then you'll reconsider?" asked Sven, with a faint glimmer of hope.

"I wish I could, I really do. I'd give my right arm for you, Cap'n, or anything else I possess."

"I don't want your right arm. I merely want you to serve with the new man."

"That's the one thing I can't do," Forbes said sadly.

"Why in hell can't you?" Sven roared, forgetting his determination to use psychology.

"You just don't understand us Georgia mountain boys," Forbes said. "That's how my pappy, bless his memory, raised me. That poor little old man would spin in his grave if I went against his dying wish."

Sven stifled a curse and said, "You know the situation that leaves me in, Forbes. Do you have any suggestions?"

"Only one thing to do, sir. Angka and me'll leave the ship. You'll be better off short-handed than with an unco-operative crew, sir."

"Angka is leaving with you? Wait a minute! Who's *he* prejudiced against?"

"No one, sir. But him and me's been shipmates for close to five years now, ever since we met on the freighter *Stella*. Where one goes, the other goes."

A red light flickered on Sven's control board, indicating the ship's readiness for blastoff. Sven ignored it.

"I can't have both of you leaving the ship," Sven said. "Forbes, why won't you serve with the new man?"

"Racial reasons, sir," Forbes said tightly.

"Now listen closely. You have been serving under me, a Swede. Has that disturbed you?"

"Not at all, sir."

"The medical officer is an Israeli. The navigator is a Venusian. The engineer is Chinese. There are Russians, New Yorkers, Melanasians, Africans, and everything else in this crew. Men of all races, creeds, and colors. You have served with them."

"Of course I have. From earliest childhood us Mountain-Georgians expect to serve with all different races. It's our heritage. My pappy taught me that. But I will not serve with Blake."

"Who's Blake?"

"The new man, sir."

"Where's he from?" Sven asked wearily.

"Mountain-Georgia."

For a moment, Sven thought he hadn't heard right. He stared at Forbes, who stared nervously back.

"From the mountain country of Georgia?"

"Yes, sir. Not too far, I believe, from where I was born."

"This man Blake, is he white?"

"Of course, sir. White English-Scottish ancestry, same as me."

Sven had the sensation of discovering a new world, a world no civilized man had ever encountered. He was amazed to discover that weirder customs could be found on Earth than anywhere else in the galaxy.

He said to Forbes, "Tell me about the custom."

"I thought *everybody* knew about us Mountain-Georgians, sir. In the section I come from, we leave home at the age of sixteen and we don't come back. Our customs teach us to work with any race, live with any race...except our own."

"Oh," said Sven.

"This new man Blake is a white Mountain-Georgian. He should have looked over the roster and not signed for this ship. It's all his fault, really, and if he chooses to overlook the custom, I can't help that."

"But *why* won't you serve with your own kind?" Sven asked.

"No one knows, sir. It's been handed down from father to son for hundreds of years, ever since the Hydrogen War."

Sven stared at him closely, ideas beginning to form.

"Forbes, have you ever had any...feeling about Negroes?"

"Yes, sir."

"Describe it."

"Well sir, we Mountain-Georgians hold that the Negro is the white man's natural friend. I mean to say, whites can get along fine with Chinese and Martians and such, but there's something special about black and white—"

"Go on," Sven urged.

"Hard to explain it good, sir. It's just that—well, the, qualities of the two seem to mesh, like good gears. There's a special understanding between black and white."

"Did you know," Sven said gently, "that once, long ago, your ancestors felt that the Negro was a lesser human being? That they created laws to keep him from interacting with whites? And that they kept on doing this long after the rest of the world had conquered its prejudices? That they kept on doing it, in fact, right up to the Hydrogen War?"

"That's a lie, sir!" Forbes shouted. "I'm sorry, I don't mean to call you a liar, sir, but it just isn't true. Us Georgians have always—"

"I can prove it to you in history books and anthropological studies. I have several in the ship's library, if you'd care to look!"

"Yankee books!"

"I'll show you Southern books, too. It's true, Forbes, and it's nothing to be ashamed of. Education is a long, slow process. You have a great deal to be proud of in your ancestry."

"*If* this is true," Forbes said, very hesitantly, "then what happened?"

"It's in the anthropology book. You know, don't you, that Georgia was hit during the war by a hydrogen bomb meant for Norfolk?"

"Yes, sir."

"Perhaps you didn't know that the bomb fell in the middle of the so-called Black Belt. Many whites were killed. But almost the entire Negro population of that section of Georgia was wiped out."

"I didn't know that."

"Now, you must take my word that there had been race riots before the Hydrogen War, and lynchings, and a lot of bad feeling between white and black. Suddenly the Negroes were gone—dead. This created a considerable feeling of guilt among the whites, particularly in isolated communities. Some of the more superstitious whites believed that they had been spiritually responsible for this wholesale obliteration. And it hit them hard, for they were religious men."

"What would that matter, if they hated the Negroes?"

"They didn't, that's the whole point! They feared inter-marriage, economic competition, a change of hierarchy. But they didn't *hate* the Negroes. Quite the contrary. They always maintained, with considerable truth, that they liked the Negroes better than the 'liberal' Northerners did. It set up quite a conflict."

Forbes nodded, thinking hard.

"In an isolated community like yours, it gave rise to the, custom of working away from home, with any race except, their own. Guilt was at the bottom of it all."

Perspiration rolled down Forbes's freckled cheeks. "I can't believe it," he said.

"Forbes, have I ever lied to you?"

"No, sir."

"Will you believe me, then, when I swear to you that this is true?"

"I—I'll try, Captain Sven."

"Now you know the reason for the custom. Will you work with Blake?"

"I don't know if I can."

"Will you try?"

Forbes bit his lip and squirmed uncomfortably. "Captain, I'll try. I don't know if I can, but I'll try. And I'm doing it, for you and the men, not on account of what you said."

"Just try," Sven said. "That's all I ask of you."

Forbes nodded and hurriedly left the bridge. Sven immediately signaled the tower that he was preparing for blastoff.

Down in the crew's quarters, Forbes was introduced to the new man, Blake. The replacement was tall, black-haired, and obviously ill at ease.

"Howdy," said Blake.

"Howdy," said Forbes. Each made a tentative gesture toward a handshake, but didn't follow it through.

"I'm from near Pompey," said Forbes.

"I'm from Almira."

"Practically next door," Forbes said unhappily.

"Yeah, afraid so," Blake said.

They eyed each other in silence. After a long moment Forbes groaned, "I can't do it, I just can't." He began walk away.

Suddenly he stopped, turned and blurted out, "You all white?"

"Can't say as how I am," Blake replied. "I'm one-eighth Cherokee on my mother's side."

"Cherokee, huh?"

"That's right."

"Well, man, why didn't you say so in the first place? Knew a Cherokee from Altahatchie once, name of Tom Little Sitting Bear. Don't suppose you're kin to him?"

"Don't believe so," Blake said. "Never knew no Cherokees, myself."

"Well, it don't make no never-mind. They should a told me in the first place you was a Cherokee. Come on, I'll show you your bunk."

When the incident was reported to Captain Sven, several hours after blastoff, he was completely perplexed. How, he asked himself, could one-eighth Cherokee blood make a man a Cherokee? Wasn't the other seven-eighths more indicative?

He decided he didn't understand American Southerners at all.

THE PRIZE OF PERIL

Raeder lifted his head cautiously above the windowsill. He saw the fire-escape, and below it a narrow alley. There was a weather-beaten baby carriage in the alley and three garbage cans. As he watched, a black-sleeved arm moved from behind the furthest can, with something shiny in its fist. Raeder ducked down. A bullet smashed through the window above his head and punctured the ceiling, showering him with plaster.

Now he knew about the alley. It was guarded, just like the door.

He lay at full length on the cracked linoleum, staring at the bullet hole in the ceiling, listening to the sounds outside the door. He was a tall man with bloodshot eyes and a two-day stubble. Grime and fatigue had etched lines into his face. Fear had touched his features, tightening a muscle here and twitching a nerve there. The results were startling. His face had character now, for it was reshaped by the expectation of death.

There was a gunman in the alley and two on the stairs. He was trapped. He was dead.

Sure, Raeder thought, he still moved and breathed, but that was only because of death's inefficiency. Death would take care of him in a few minutes. Death would poke holes in his face and body, artistically dab his clothes with blood, arrange his limbs in some grotesque position of the graveyard ballet…

Raeder bit his lip sharply. He wanted to live. There had to be a way.

He rolled onto his stomach and surveyed the dingy cold-water apartment into which the killers had driven him. It was a perfect little one-room coffin. It had a door, which was watched, and a fire escape, which was watched. And it had a tiny windowless bathroom.

He crawled to the bathroom and stood up. There was a ragged hole in the ceiling, almost four inches wide. If he could enlarge it, crawl through into the apartment above…

He heard a muffled thud. The killers were impatient. They were beginning to break down the door.

He studied the hole in the ceiling. No use even considering it. He could never enlarge it in time.

They were smashing against the door, grunting each time they struck. Soon the lock would tear out, or the hinges would pull out of the rotting wood. The door would go down, and the two blank-faced men would enter, dusting off their jackets...

But surely someone would help him! He took the tiny television set from his pocket. The picture was blurred, and he didn't bother to adjust it. The audio was clear and precise.

He listened to the well-modulated voice of Mike Terry addressing his vast audience.

"...*terrible spot,*" *Terry was saying. "Yes, folks, Jim Raeder is in a truly terrible predicament. He had been hiding, you'll remember, in a third-rate Broadway hotel under an assumed name. It seemed safe enough. But the bellhop recognized him, and gave that information to the Thompson gang.*"

The door creaked under repeated blows. Raeder clutched the little television set and listened.

"*Jim Raeder just managed to escape from the hotel! Closely pursued, he entered a brownstone at one fifty-six West End Avenue. His intention was to go over the roofs. And it might have worked, folks, it just might have worked. But the roof door was locked. It looked like the end...But Raeder found that apartment seven was unoccupied and unlocked. He entered...*"

Terry paused for emphasis, then cried—"*and now he's trapped there, trapped like a rat in a cage! The Thompson gang is breaking down the door! The fire escape is guarded! Our camera crew, situated in a nearby building, is giving you a close-up now. Look, folks, just look! Is there no hope for Jim Raeder?*"

Is there no hope? Raeder silently echoed, perspiration pouring from him as he stood in the dark, stifling little bathroom, listening to the steady thud against the door.

"*Wait a minute!*" Mike Terry cried. "*Hang on, Jim Raeder, hang on a little longer. Perhaps there is hope! I have an urgent call from one of our viewers, a call on the Good Samaritan Line! Here's someone who thinks he can help you, Jim. Are you listening, Jim Raeder?*"

Raeder waited, and heard the hinges tearing out of rotten wood.

"*Go right ahead, sir,*" said Mike Terry. "*What is your name, sir?*"

"*Er—Felix Bartholemow.*"

"*Don't be nervous, Mr. Bartholemow. Go right ahead.*"

"*Well, okay. Mr. Raeder,*" said an old man's shaking voice, "*I used to live at one five six West End Avenue. Same apartment you're trapped in, Mr. Raeder—fact! Look, that bathroom has got a window, Mr. Raeder. It's been painted over, but it has got a—*"

Raeder pushed the television set into his pocket. He located the outlines of the window and kicked. Glass shattered, and daylight poured startling in. He cleared the jagged sill and quickly peered down.

Below was a long drop to a concrete courtyard.

The hinges tore free. He heard the door opening. Quickly Raeder climbed through the window, hung by his fingertips for a moment, and dropped.

The shock was stunning. Groggily he stood up. A face appeared at the bathroom window.

"Tough luck," said the man, leaning out and taking careful aim with a snub-nosed .38.

At that moment a smoke bomb exploded inside the bathroom.

The killer's shot went wide. He turned, cursing. More smoke bombs burst in the courtyard, obscuring Raeder's figure.

He could hear Mike Terry's frenzied voice over the TV set in his pocket. *"Now run for it!"* Terry was screaming. *"Run, Jim Raeder, run for your life. Run now, while the killers' eyes are filled with smoke. And thank Good Samaritan Sarah Winters, of three four one two Edgar Street, Brockton, Mass., for donating five smoke bombs and employing the services of a man to throw them!"* In a quieter voice, Terry continued. *"You've saved a man's life today, Mrs. Winters. Would you tell our audience how it—"* Raeder wasn't able to hear any more. He was running through the smoke-filled courtyard, past clotheslines, into the open street.

He walked down 63rd Street, slouching to minimize his height, staggering slightly from exertion, dizzy from lack of food and sleep.

"Hey, you!"

Raeder turned. A middle-aged woman was sitting on the steps of a brownstone, frowning at him.

"You're Raeder, aren't you? The one they're trying to kill?"

Raeder started to walk away.

"Come inside here, Raeder," the woman said.

Perhaps it was a trap. But Raeder knew that he had to depend upon the generosity and good-heartedness of the people. He was their representative, a projection of themselves, an average guy in trouble. Without them, he was lost. With them, nothing could harm him.

Trust in the people, Mike Terry had told him. They'll never let you down.

He followed the woman into her parlor. She told him to sit down and left the room, returning almost immediately with a plate of stew. She stood watching him while he ate, as one would watch an ape in the zoo eat peanuts.

Two children came out of the kitchen and stared at him. Three overalled men came out of the bedroom and focused a television camera on him. There was a big television set in the parlor. As he gulped his food, Raeder watched the image of Mike Terry and listened to the man's strong, sincere, worried voice.

"There he is, folks," Terry was saying. *"There's Jim Raeder now, eating his first square meal in two days. Our camera crews have really been working to cover this for you! Thanks, boys...Folks, Jim Raeder has been given a brief sanctuary by Mrs. Velma O'Dell, of three forty-three Sixty-Third Street. Thank you, Good Samaritan O'Dell! It's really wonderful how people from all walks of life have taken Jim Raeder to their hearts!"*

"You better hurry," Mrs. O'Dell said.

"Yes, ma'am," Raeder said.

"I don't want no gunplay in my apartment."

"I'm almost finished, ma'am."

One of the children asked. "Aren't they going to kill him?"

"Shut up," said Mrs. O'Dell.

"Yes, Jim," chanted Mike Terry. *"You'd better hurry. Your killers aren't far behind. They aren't stupid men, Jim. Vicious, warped, insane—yes! But not stupid. They're following a trail of blood—blood from your torn hand, Jim!"*

Raeder hadn't realized until now that he'd cut his hand on the windowsill.

"Here, I'll bandage that," Mrs. O'Dell said. Raeder stood up and let her bandage his hand. Then she gave him a brown jacket and a gray slouch hat.

"My husband's stuff," she said.

"He has a disguise, folks!" Mike Terry cried delightedly. *"This is something new! A disguise! With seven hours to go until he's safe!"*

"Now get out of here," Mrs. O'Dell said.

"I'm going, ma'am," Raeder said. "Thanks."

"I think you're stupid," she said. "I think you're stupid to be involved in this."

"Yes, ma'am."

"It just isn't worth it."

Raeder thanked her and left. He walked to Broadway, caught a subway to 59th Street, then an uptown local to 86th. There he bought a newspaper and changed for the Manhasset through-express.

He glanced at his watch. He had six and a half hours to go.

The subway roared under Manhattan. Raeder dozed, his bandaged hand concealed under the newspaper, the hat pulled over his face. Had he been recognized yet? Had he shaken the Thompson gang? Or was someone telephoning them now?

Dreamily he wondered if he had escaped death, or was he still a cleverly animated corpse, moving around because of death's inefficiency? (My dear, death is so *laggard* these days! Jim Raeder walked about for hours after he died and actually answered people's *questions* before he could be decently buried!)

Raeder's eyes snapped open. He had dreamed something...unpleasant. He couldn't remember what.

He closed his eyes again and remembered, with mild astonishment, a time when he had been in no trouble.

That was two years ago. He had been a big, pleasant young man working as a truck driver's helper. He had no talents. He was too modest to have dreams.

The tight-faced little truck driver had the dreams for him. "Why not try for a television show, Jim? I would if I had your looks. They like nice, average guys with nothing much on the ball. As contestants. Everybody likes guys like that. Why not look into it?"

So he had looked into it. The owner of the local television store had explained it further.

"You see, Jim, the public is sick of highly trained athletes with their trick reflexes and their professional courage. Who can feel for guys like that? Who can identify? People want to watch exciting things, sure, but not when some joker is making it his business for fifty thousand a year. That's why organized sports are in a slump. That's why the thrill shows are booming."

"I see," said Raeder.

"Six years ago, Jim, Congress passed the Voluntary Suicide Act. Those old senators talked a lot about free will and self-determinism at the time. But that's all crap. You know what the Act really means? It means the amateurs can risk their lives for the big loot, not just professionals. In the old days you had to be a professional boxer or footballer or hockey player if you wanted your brains beaten out legally for money. But now that opportunity is open to ordinary people like you, Jim."

"I see," Raeder said again.

"It's a marvelous opportunity. Take you. You're no better than anyone, Jim. Anything you can do, anyone can do. You're *average*. I think the thrill shows would go for you."

Raeder permitted himself to dream. Television shows looked like a sure road to riches for a pleasant young fellow with no particular talent or training. He wrote a letter to a show called *Hazard* and enclosed a photograph of himself.

Hazard was interested in him. The JBC network investigated, and found that he was average enough to satisfy the wariest viewer. His parentage and affiliations were checked. At last he was summoned to New York and interviewed by Mr. Moulain.

Moulain was dark and intense, and chewed gum as he talked. "You'll do," he snapped. "But not for *Hazard*. You'll appear on *Spills*. It's a half-hour daytime show on Channel Three."

"Gee," said Raeder.

"Don't thank me. There's a thousand dollars if you win or place second, and a consolation prize of a hundred dollars if you lose. But that's not important."

"No, sir."

"*Spills* is a little show. The JBC network uses it as a testing ground. First and second-place winners on *Spills* move on to *Emergency.* The prizes are much bigger on Emergency."

"I know they are, sir."

"And if you do well on *Emergency,* there are the first-class thrill shows, like *Hazard* and *Underwater Perils,* with their nationwide coverage and enormous prizes. And then comes the really big time. How far you go is up to you."

"I'll do my best sir," Raeder said.

Moulain stopped chewing gum for a moment and said, almost reverently, "You can do it, Jim. Just remember. You're the people, and the people can do anything."

The way he said it made Raeder feel momentarily sorry for Mr. Moulain, who was dark and frizzy-haired and pop-eyed, and was obviously not the people.

They shook hands. Then Raeder signed a paper absolving the JBC of all responsibility should he lose his life, limbs, or reason during the contest. And he signed another paper exercising his rights under the Voluntary Suicide Act. The law required this, and it was a mere formality.

In three weeks, he appeared on *Spills.*

The program followed the classic form of the automobile race. Untrained drivers climbed into powerful American and European competition cars and raced over a murderous twenty-mile course. Raeder was shaking with fear as he slid his big Maserati into the wrong gear and took off.

The race was a screaming, tire-burning nightmare. Raeder stayed back, letting the early leaders smash themselves up on the counterbanked hairpin turns. He crept into third place when a Jaguar in front of him swerved against an Alfa-Romeo and the two cars roared into a plowed field. Raeder gunned for second place on the last three miles, but couldn't find passing room. An S-curve almost took him, but he fought the car back on the road, still holding third. Then the lead driver broke a crankshaft in the final fifty yards, and Jim ended in second place.

He was now a thousand dollars ahead. He received four fan letters, and a lady in Oshkosh sent him a pair of argyles. He was invited to appear on *Emergency.*

Unlike the others, *Emergency* was not a competition-type program. It stressed individual initiative. For the show, Raeder was knocked out with a nonhabit-forming narcotic. He awoke in the cockpit of a small airplane, cruising on autopilot at ten thousand feet. His fuel gauge showed nearly empty. He had no parachute. He was supposed to land the plane. Of course, he had never flown before.

He experimented gingerly with the controls, remembering that last week's participant had recovered consciousness in a submarine, had opened the wrong valve, and had drowned.

Thousands of viewers watched spellbound as this average man, a man just like themselves, struggled with the situation just as they would do. Jim Raeder was *them*. Anything he could do, they could do. He was representative of *the people*.

Raeder managed to bring the ship down in some semblance of a landing. He flipped over a few times, but his seat belt held. And the engine, contrary to expectation, did not burst into flames.

He staggered out with two broken ribs, three thousand dollars, and a chance, when he healed, to appear on *Torero*.

At last, a first-class thrill show! *Torero* paid ten thousand dollars. All you had to do was kill a black Miura bull with a sword, just like a real, trained matador.

The fight was held in Madrid, since bullfighting was still illegal in the United States. It was nationally televised.

Raeder had a good cuadrilla. They liked the big, slow-moving American. The picadors really leaned into their lances, trying to slow the bull for him. The banderilleros tried to run the beast off his feet before driving in their banderillas. And the second matador, a mournful man from Algiceras, almost broke the bull's neck with fancy cape-work.

But when all was said and done, it was Jim Raeder on the sand, a red muleta clumsily gripped in his left hand, a sword in his right, facing a ton of black, blood-streaked, wide-horned bull.

Someone was shouting, "Try for the lung, *hombre*. Don't be a hero, stick him in the lung." But Jim only knew what the technical advisor in New York had told him: Aim with the sword and go in over the horns.

Over he went. The sword bounced off bone, and the bull tossed him over its back. He stood up, miraculously ungouged, took another sword and went over the horns again with his eyes closed. The god who protects children and fools must have been watching, for the sword slid in like a needle through butter, and the bull looked startled, stared at him unbelievingly, and dropped like a deflated balloon.

They paid him ten thousand dollars, and his broken collarbone healed in practically no time. He received twenty-three fan letters, including a passionate invitation from a girl in Atlantic City, which he ignored. And they asked him if he wanted to appear on another show.

He had lost some of his innocence. He was now fully aware that he had been almost killed for pocket money. The big loot lay ahead. Now he wanted to be almost killed for something worthwhile.

So he appeared on *Underwater Perils,* sponsored by Fairlady's Soap. In face mask, respirator, weighted belt, flippers and knife, he slipped into the warm waters of the Caribbean with four other contestants, followed by a cage-protected camera crew. The idea was to locate and bring up a treasure which the sponsor had hidden there.

Mask diving isn't especially hazardous. But the sponsor had added some frills for public interest. The area was sown with giant clams, moray eels, sharks of several species, giant octopuses, poison coral, and other dangers of the deep.

It was a stirring contest. A man from Florida found the treasure in a deep crevice, but a moray eel found him. Another diver took the treasure, and a shark took him. The brilliant blue-green water became cloudy with blood, which photographed well on color TV. The treasure slipped to the bottom, and Raeder plunged after it, popping an eardrum in the process. He plucked it from the coral, jettisoned his weighted belt and made for the surface. Thirty feet from the top he had to fight another diver for the treasure.

They feinted back and forth with their knives. The man struck, slashing Raeder across the chest. But Raeder, with the self-possession of an old contestant, dropped his knife and tore the man's respirator out of his mouth.

That did it. Raeder surfaced and presented the treasure at the standby boat. It turned out to be a package of Fairlady's Soap—"The Greatest Treasure of All."

That netted him twenty-two thousand dollars in cash and prizes, and three hundred and eight fan letters, and an interesting proposition from a girl in Macon, which he seriously considered. He received free hospitalization for his knife slash and burst eardrum, and injections for coral infection.

But best of all, he was invited to appear on the biggest of the thrill shows. *The Prize of Peril.*

And that was when the real trouble began...

The subway came to a stop, jolting him out of his reverie. Raeder pushed back his hat and observed, across the aisle, a man staring at him and whispering to a stout woman. Had they recognized him?

He stood up as soon as the doors opened, and glanced at his watch. He had five hours to go.

At the Manhasset station, he stepped into a taxi and told the driver to take him to New Salem.

"New Salem?" the driver asked, looking at him in the rear-vision mirror.

"That's right."

The driver snapped on his radio. "Fare to New Salem. Yep, that's right. *New Salem.*" They drove off. Raeder frowned, wondering if it had been a signal. It was perfectly usual for taxi drivers to report to their dispatchers, of course. But something about the man's voice…

"Let me off here," Raeder said.

He paid the driver and began walking down a narrow country road that curved through sparse woods. The trees were too small and too widely separated for shelter. Raeder walked on, looking for a place to hide.

There was a heavy truck approaching. He kept on walking, pulling his hat low on his forehead. But as the truck drew near, he heard a voice from the television set in his pocket. It cried, *"Watch out!"*

He flung himself into the ditch. The truck careened past, narrowly missing him, and screeched to a stop. The driver was shouting, "There he goes! Shoot, Harry, shoot!"

Bullets clipped leaves from the trees as Raeder sprinted into the woods.

"It's happened again!" Mike Terry was saying, his voice high-pitched with excitement. *"I'm afraid Jim Raeder let himself be lulled into a false sense of security. You can't do that, Jim! Not with your life at stake! Not with killers pursuing you! Be careful, Jim, you still have four and a half hours to go!"*

The driver was saying, "Claude, Harry, go around with the truck. We got him boxed."

"They've got you boxed, Jim Raeder!" Mike Terry cried. *"But they haven't got you yet! And you can thank Good Samaritan Susy Peters of twelve Elm Street, South Orange, New Jersey, for that warning shout just when the truck was bearing down on you. We'll have little Susy on stage in just a moment…Look, folks, our studio helicopter has arrived on the scene. Now you can see Jim Raeder running, and the killers pursuing, surrounding him…"*

Raeder ran through a hundred yards of woods and found himself on a concrete highway, with open woods beyond. One of the killers was trotting through the woods behind him. The truck had driven to a connecting road and was now a mile away, coming toward him.

A car was approaching from the other direction. Raeder ran into the highway, waving frantically. The car came to a stop.

"Hurry!" cried the blond young woman driving it.

Raeder dived in. The woman made a U-turn on the highway. A bullet smashed through the windshield. She stamped on the accelerator, almost running down the lone killer who stood in the way.

The car surged away before the truck was within firing range.

Raeder leaned back and shut his eyes tightly. The woman concentrated on her driving, watching for the truck in her rear-vision mirror.

"It's happened again!" cried Mike Terry, his voice ecstatic. *"Jim Raeder has been plucked again from the jaws of death, thanks to Good Samaritan Janice Morrow of four three three Lexington Avenue, New York City. Did*

you ever see anything like it, folks? The way Miss Morrow drove through a fusillade of bullets and plucked Jim Raeder from the mouth of doom! Later we'll interview Miss Morrow and get her reactions. Now, while Jim Raeder speeds away—perhaps to safety, perhaps to further peril—we'll have a short announcement from our sponsor. Don't go away! Jim's got four hours and ten minutes until he's safe: anything can happen!"

"Okay," the girl said. "We're off the air now. Raeder, what in the hell is the matter with you?"

"Eh?" Raeder asked. The girl was in her early twenties. She looked efficient, attractive, untouchable. Raeder noticed that she had good features, a trim figure. And he noticed that she seemed angry.

"Miss," he said, "I don't know how to thank you for—"

"Talk straight," Janice Morrow said. "I'm no Good Samaritan. I'm employed by the JBC network."

"So the program had me rescued!"

"Cleverly reasoned," she said.

"But why?"

"Look, this is an expensive show, Raeder. We have to turn in a good performance. If our rating slips, we'll all be in the street selling candy apples. And you aren't cooperating."

"What? Why?"

"Because you're terrible," the girl said bitterly. "You're a flop, a fiasco. Are you trying to commit suicide? Haven't you learned *anything* about survival?"

"I'm doing the best I can."

"The Thompsons could have had you a dozen times by now. We told them to take it easy, stretch it out. But it's like shooting a clay pigeon six feet tall. The Thompsons are cooperating, but they can only fake so far. If I hadn't come along, they'd have had to kill you—air-time or not."

Raeder stared at her, wondering how such a pretty girl could talk that way. She glanced at him, then quickly looked back to the road.

"Don't give me that look!" she said. "You chose to risk your life for money, buster. And plenty of money! You knew the score. Don't act like some innocent little grocer who finds the nasty hoods are after him. That's a different plot."

"I know," Raeder said.

"If you can't live well, at least try to die well."

"You don't mean that," Raeder said.

"Don't be too sure...You've got three hours and forty minutes until the end of the show. If you can stay alive, fine. The boodle's yours. But if you can't, at least try to give them a run for the money."

Raeder nodded, staring intently at her.

"In a few moments we're back on the air. I develop engine trouble, let you off. The Thompsons go all out now. They kill you when and if they can, as soon as they can. Understand?"

"Yes," Raeder said. "If I make it, can I see you some time?"

She bit her lip angrily. "Are you trying to kid me?"

"No. I'd like to see you again. May I?"

She looked at him curiously. "I don't know. Forget it. We're almost on. I think your best bet is the woods to the right. Ready?"

"Yes. Where can I get in touch with you? Afterward, I mean."

"Oh, Raeder, you aren't paying attention. Go through the woods until you find a washed-out ravine. It isn't much, but it'll give you some cover."

"Where can I get in touch with you?" Raeder asked again.

"I'm in the Manhattan telephone book." She stopped the car. "Okay, Raeder, start running."

He opened the door.

"Wait." She leaned over and kissed him on the lips. "Good luck, you idiot. Call me if you make it."

And then he was on foot, running into the woods.

He ran through birch and pine, past an occasional split-level house with staring faces at the big picture windows. Some occupant of those houses must have called the gang, for they were close behind him when he reached the washed-out little ravine. Those quiet, mannerly, law-abiding people didn't want him to escape, Raeder thought sadly. They wanted to see a killing. Or perhaps they wanted to see him *narrowly escape* a killing.

It came to the same thing, really.

He entered the ravine, burrowed into the thick underbrush and lay still. The Thompsons appeared on both ridges, moving slowly, watching for any movement. Raeder held his breath as they came parallel to him.

He heard the quick explosion of a revolver. But the killer had only shot a squirrel. It squirmed for a moment, then lay still.

Lying in the underbrush, Raeder heard the studio helicopter overhead. He wondered if any cameras were focused on him. It was possible. And if someone were watching, perhaps some Good Samaritan would help.

So looking upward, toward the helicopter, Raeder arranged his face in a reverent expression, clasped his hands and prayed. He prayed silently, for the audience didn't like religious ostentation. But his lips moved. That was every man's privilege.

And a real prayer was on his lips. Once, a lipreader in the audience had detected a fugitive *pretending* to pray, but actually just reciting multiplication tables. No help for that man!

Raeder finished his prayer. Glancing at his watch, he saw that he had nearly two hours to go.

And he didn't want to die. It wasn't worth it, no matter how much they paid! He must have been crazy, absolutely insane to agree to such a thing...

But he knew that wasn't true. And he remembered just how sane he had been.

One week ago, he had been on the *Prize of Peril* stage, blinking in the spotlight, and Mike Terry had shaken his hand.

"Now, Mr. Raeder," Terry had said solemnly, "do you understand the rules of the game you are about to play?"

Raeder nodded.

"If you accept, Jim Raeder, you will be a *hunted man* for a week. *Killers* will follow you, Jim. *Trained* killers, men wanted by the law for other crimes, granted immunity for this single killing under the Voluntary Suicide Act. They will be trying to kill *you*, Jim. Do you understand?"

"I understand," Raeder said. He also understood the two hundred thousand dollars he would receive if he could live out the week.

"I ask you again, Jim Raeder. We force no man to play for stakes of death."

"I want to play," Raeder said.

Mike Terry turned to the audience. "Ladies and gentlemen, I have here a copy of an exhaustive psychological test which an impartial psychological testing firm made on Jim Raeder at our request. Copies will be sent to anyone who desires them for twenty-five cents to cover the cost of mailing. The test shows that Jim Raeder is sane, well-balanced and fully responsible in every way." He turned to Raeder.

"Do you still want to enter the contest, Jim?"

"Yes, I do."

"Very well!" cried Mike Terry. "Jim Raeder, meet your would-be killers!"

The Thompson gang moved on stage, booed by the audience.

"Look at them, folks," said Mike Terry, with undisguised contempt. "Just look at them! Antisocial, thoroughly vicious, completely amoral. These men have no code but the criminal's warped code, no honor but the honor of the cowardly hired killer. They are doomed men, doomed by our society, which will not sanction their activities for long, fated to an early and unglamorous death."

The audience shouted enthusiastically.

"What have you to say, Claude Thompson?" Terry asked.

Claude, the spokesman of the Thompsons, stepped up to the microphone. He was a thin, clean-shaved man, conservatively dressed.

"I figure," Claude Thompson said hoarsely, "I figure we're no worse than anybody. I mean, like soldiers in a war: *they* kill. And look at the graft in government, and the unions. Everybody's got their graft."

That was Thompson's tenuous code. But how quickly, with what precision, Mike Terry destroyed the killer's rationalizations! Terry's questions pierced straight to the filthy soul of the man.

At the end of the interview, Claude Thompson was perspiring, mopping his face with a silk handkerchief and casting quick glances at his men.

Mike Terry put a hand on Raeder's shoulder. "Here is the man who has agreed to become your victim—if you can catch him."

"We'll catch him," Thompson said, his confidence returning.

"Don't be too sure," said Terry. "Jim Raeder has fought wild bulls—now he battles jackals. He's an average man. He's *the people*—who mean ultimate doom to you and your kind."

"We'll get him," Thompson said.

"And one thing more," Terry said, very softly. "Jim Raeder does not stand alone. The folks of America are for him. Good Samaritans from all corners of our great nation stand ready to assist him. Unarmed, defenseless, Jim Raeder can count on the aid and goodheartedness of *the people,* whose representative he is. So don't be too sure, Claude Thompson! The average men are for Jim Raeder—and there are a lot of average men!"

Raeder thought about it, lying motionless in the underbrush. Yes, *the people* had helped him. But they had helped the killers, too.

A tremor ran through him. He had chosen, he reminded himself. He alone was responsible. The psychological test had proved that.

And yet, how responsible were the psychologists who had given him the test? How responsible was Mike Terry for offering a poor man so much money? Society had woven the noose and put it around his neck, and he was hanging himself with it and calling it free will.

Whose fault?

"Aha!" someone cried.

Raeder looked up and saw a portly man standing near him.

The man wore a loud tweed jacket. He had binoculars around his neck and a cane in his hand.

"Mister," Raeder whispered, "please don't tell!"

"Hi!" shouted the portly man, pointing at Raeder with his cane. "Here he is!"

A madman thought Raeder. The damned fool must think he's playing Hare and Hounds.

"Right over here!" the man screamed.

Cursing, Raeder sprang to his feet and began running. He came out of the ravine and saw a white building in the distance. He turned toward it. Behind him he could still hear the man.

"That way, over there. Look, you fools, can't you see him yet?"

The killers were shooting again. Raeder ran, stumbling over uneven ground, past three children playing in a tree house.

"Here he is!" the children screamed. "Here he is!"

Raeder groaned and ran on. He reached the steps of the building and saw that it was a church.

As he opened the door, a bullet struck him behind the right kneecap. He fell, and crawled inside the church.

The television set in his pocket was saying, *"What a finish, folks, what a finish! Raeder's been hit! He's been hit, folks, he's crawling now, he's in pain, but he hasn't given up! NOT Jim Raeder!"*

Raeder lay in the aisle near the altar. He could hear a child's eager voice saying, "He went in there, Mr. Thompson. Hurry, you can still catch him!"

Wasn't a church considered a sanctuary? Raeder wondered.

Then the door was flung open, and Raeder realized that the custom was no longer observed. He gathered himself together and crawled past the altar, out of the back door of the church.

He was in an old graveyard. He crawled past crosses and stars, past slabs of marble and granite, past stone tombs and rude wooden markers. A bullet exploded on a tombstone near his head, showering him with fragments. He crawled to the edge of an open grave.

They had deceived him, he thought. All of those nice, average, normal people. Hadn't they said he was their representative? Hadn't they sworn to protect their own? But no, they loathed him. Why hadn't he seen it? Their hero was the cold, blank-eyed gunman, Thompson, Capone, Billy the Kid, Young Lochinvar, El Cid, Cuchulain, the man without human hopes or fears. They worshipped him, that dead, implacable robot gunman, and lusted to feel his foot in their face.

Raeder tried to move, and slid helplessly into the open grave.

He lay on his back, looking at the blue sky. Presently a black silhouette loomed above him, blotting out the sky. Metal twinkled. The silhouette slowly took aim.

And Raeder gave up all hope forever.

"Wait, Thompson!" roared the amplified voice of Mike Terry. The revolver wavered.

"It is one second past five o'clock! The week is up! JIM RAEDER HAS WON!"

There was pandemonium of cheering from the studio audience.

The Thompson gang, gathered around the grave, looked sullen.

"He's won, friends, he's won!" Mike Terry cried. *"Look, look on your screen! The police have arrived, they're taking the Thompsons away from their victim—the victim they could not kill. And all this is thanks to you, Good Samaritans of America. Look folks, tender hands are lifting Jim Raeder from the open grave that was his final refuge. Good Samaritan Janice Morrow is there. Could this be the beginning of a romance? Jim seems to have fainted,*

friends; they're giving him a stimulant. He's won two hundred thousand dollars! Now we'll have a few words from Jim Raeder!"

There was a short silence.

"That's odd," said Mike Terry. *"Folks, I'm afraid we can't hear from Jim just now. The doctors are examining him. Just one moment..."*

There was a silence. Mike Terry wiped his forehead and smiled.

"It's the strain, folks, the terrible strain. The doctor tells me... Well, folks, Jim Raeder is temporarily not himself. But it's only temporary! JBC is hiring the best psychiatrists and psychoanalysts in the country. We're going to do everything humanly possible for this gallant boy. And entirely at our own expense."

Mike Terry glanced at the studio clock. *"Well, it's about time to sign off, folks. Watch for the announcement of our next great thrill show. And don't worry, I'm sure that very soon we'll have Jim Raeder back with us."*

Mike Terry smiled, and winked at the audience. *"He's bound to get well, friends. After all, we're all pulling for him!"*

THE MINIMUM MAN

Everybody has his song, thought Anton Perceveral. A pretty girl is like a melody, and a brave spaceman like a flurry of trumpets. Wise old men on the Interplanetary Council make one think of richly blended woodwinds. There are geniuses whose lives are an intricate counterpoint endlessly embellished, and scum of the planets whose existence seems nothing more than the wail of an oboe against the inexorable pounding of a brass drum.

Perceveral thought about this, loosely gripping a razor blade and contemplating the faint blue veins in his wrist.

For if everybody has his song, his could be likened to a poorly conceived and miserably executed symphony of errors.

There had been muted horns of gladness at his birth. Bravely, to the sound of muffled drums, young Perceveral had ventured into school. He had excelled and been promoted to a small workshop class of five hundred pupils, where he could receive a measure of individual attention. The future had looked promising.

But he was congenitally unlucky. There was a constant series of small accidents with overturned inkwells, lost books, and misplaced papers. Things had a damnable propensity for breaking under his fingers; or sometimes his fingers broke under things. To make matters worse, he caught every possible childhood disease, including proto-Measles, Algerian Mumps, Impetigo, Foxpox, Green Fever, and Orange Fever.

These things in no way reflected upon Perceveral's native ability; but one needs more than ability in a crowded and competitive world. One needs considerable luck, and Perceveral had none. He was transferred to an ordinary class of ten thousand students, where his problems were intensified and his opportunities for catching disease expanded.

He was a tall, thin, bespectacled, good-hearted, hard-working young man whom the doctors early diagnosed as accident-prone, for reasons which defied their analysis. But whatever the reasons, the facts remained. Perceveral was one of those unhappy people for whom life is difficult to the point of impossibility.

Most people slip through the jungle of human existence with the facility of prowling panthers. But, for the Perceverals, the jungle is continually beset with traps, snares and devices, sudden precipices and unfordable streams, deadly fungus, and deadlier beasts. No way is safe. All roads lead to disaster.

Young Perceveral won his way through college in spite of his remarkable talent for breaking his leg on winding staircases, twisting his ankle on curbstones, fracturing his elbow in revolving doors, smashing his glasses against plate-glass windows, and all the rest of the sad, ludicrous, painful events which beset the accident-prone. Manfully he resisted the solace of hypochondria and kept trying.

Upon graduation from college, Perceveral took himself firmly in hand and tried to reassert the early clear theme of hope set by his stalwart father and gentle mother. With a ruffle of drums and a thrilling of chords, Perceveral entered the island of Manhattan, to forge his destiny. He worked hard to conquer his unhappy predisposition, and to stay cheerful and optimistic in spite of everything.

But his predisposition caught up with him. The noble chords dissolved into vague mutterings, and the symphony of his life degenerated to the level of opera-bouffé. Perceveral lost job after job in a snarl of broken voxwriters and smeared contracts, forgotten file cards and misplaced data sheets; in a mounting crescendo of ribs wrenched in the subway rush, ankles sprained on gratings, glasses smashed against unseen projections, and in a bout of illnesses which included Hepatitis Type J, Martian Flu, Venusian Flu, Waking Sickness, and Giggling Fever.

Perceveral still resisted the lure of hypochondria. He dreamed of space, of the iron-jawed adventurers advancing Man's frontier, of the new settlements on distant planets, of vast expanses of open land where, far from the hectic plastic jungles of Earth, a man could really find himself. He applied to the Planetary Exploration & Settlement Board, and was turned down. Reluctantly he pushed the dream aside and tried a variety of jobs. He underwent Analysis, Hypnotic Suggestion, Hypnotic Hypersuggestion, and Countersuggestion Removal—all to no avail.

Every man has his limits and every symphony has its end. Perceveral gave up hope at the age of thirty-four when he was fired, after three days, from a job he had sought for two months. That, as far as he was concerned, provided the final humorous off-key cymbal clash to something which probably shouldn't have been started in the first place.

Grimly he took his meager paycheck, accepted a last wary handshake from his former employer, and rode the elevator to the lobby. Already vague thoughts of suicide were crossing his mind in the form of truck wheels, gas pipes, tall buildings, and swift rivers.

The elevator reached the great marble lobby with its uniformed riot policemen and its crowds waiting admittance to the midtown streets. Perceveral waited on line, idly watching the Population Density Meter fluctuate below the panic line, until his turn came. Outside, he joined a compact body of people moving westward in the direction of his housing project.

Suicidal thoughts continued to flow through his mind, more slowly now, taking more definite forms. He considered methods and means until he reached home. There he disengaged himself from the crowd and slipped in through an entry port.

He struggled against a flood of children pouring through corridors, and reached his city-provided cubicle. He entered, closed and locked the door, and took a razor blade from his shaving kit. He lay down on the bed, propping his feet against the opposite wall, and contemplated the faint blue veins of his wrist.

Could he do it? Could he do it cleanly and quickly, without error and without regret? Or would he bungle this job, too, and be dragged screaming to a hospital, a ludicrous sight for the interns to snicker about?

As he was thinking, a yellow envelope was slipped under his door. It was a telegram, arriving pat on the hour of decision, with a melodramatic suddenness which Perceveral considered quite suspect. Still, he put down the razor blade and picked up the envelope.

It was from the Planetary Exploration & Settlement Board, the great organization that controlled every Earthman's movements in space. With trembling fingers, Perceveral opened the envelope and read:

Mr. Anton Perceveral
Temporary Housing Project 1993
District 43825, Manhattan 212, N.Y.

Dear Mr. Perceveral:

Three years ago you applied to us for a position in any off-Earth capacity. Regretfully we had to turn you down at that time. Your records have been kept on file, however, and have recently been brought up to date. I am happy to inform you that a position is immediately available for you, one which I consider well suited to your particular talents and qualifications. I believe this job will meet with your approval, carrying, as it does, a salary of $20,000 a year, all government fringe benefits, and an unexcelled opportunity for advancement.

Could you come in and discuss it with me?

Sincerely,
William Haskell
Asst. Placement Director
WH/ibm3dc

Perceval folded the telegram carefully and put it back in its envelope. His first feeling of intense joy vanished, to be replaced by a sense of apprehension.

What talents and qualifications did he have for a job commanding twenty thousand a year and benefits? Could they be confusing him with a different Anton Perceval?

It seemed unlikely. The Board just didn't do that sort of thing. And presuming that they knew him and his ill-starred past—what could they possibly want from him? What could *he* do that practically any man, woman, or child couldn't do better?

Perceval put the telegram in his pocket and replaced the razor blade in his shaving kit. Suicide seemed a little premature now. First he would find out what Haskell wanted.

At the headquarters of the Planetary Exploration & Settlement Board, Perceval was admitted at once to William Haskell's private office. The Assistant Placement Director was a large, blunt-featured, white-haired man who radiated a geniality which Perceval found suspicious.

"Sit down, sit down, Mr. Perceval," Haskell said. "Cigarette? Care for a drink? Awfully glad you could make it."

"Are you sure you have the right man?" Perceval asked.

Haskell glanced through a dossier on his desk. "Let's see Anton Perceval; age thirty-four; parents, Gregory James Perceval and Anita Swaans Perceval, Laketown, New Jersey. Is that right?"

"Yes," Perceval said. "And you have a job for me?"

"We have indeed."

"Paying twenty thousand a year and benefits?"

"Perfectly correct."

"Could you tell me what the job is?"

"That's what we're here for," Haskell said cheerfully. "The job I have in mind for you, Mr. Perceval, is listed in our catalogue as Extraterrestrial Explorer."

"I beg your pardon?"

"Extraterrestrial or alien-planet explorer," Haskell said. "The explorers, you know, are the men who make the first contacts on alien planets, the primary settlers who gather our essential data. I think of them as the Drakes and Magellans of this century. It is, I think you'll agree, an excellent opportunity."

Perceval stood up, his face a dull red. "If you're finished with the joke, I'll leave."

"Eh?"

"Me, an extraterrestrial explorer?" Perceval said with a bitter laugh. "Don't try to kid me. I read the papers. I know what the explorers are like."

"What are they like?"

"They're Earth's finest," Perceveral said. "The very best brains in the very best bodies. Men with trigger-quick reactions, able to tackle any problems, cope with any situation, adjust to any environment. Isn't that true?"

"Well," Haskell said, "it *was* true back in the early days of planetary exploration. And we have allowed that stereotype to remain in the public eye, to instill confidence. But that type of explorer is now obsolete. There are plenty of other jobs for men such as you describe. But not planetary exploration."

"Couldn't your supermen make the grade?" Perceveral asked with a faint sneer.

"Of course they could," Haskell said. "No paradox is involved here. The record of our early explorers is unsurpassed. Those men managed to survive on every planet where human survival was even remotely possible, against overwhelming odds, by sheer grit and tenacity. The planets called for their every resource and they rose to meet the challenge. They stand as an eternal monument to the toughness and adaptability of *Homo sapiens.*"

"Then why did you stop using them?"

"Because our problems on Earth changed," Haskell told him. "In the early days, the exploration of space was an adventure, a scientific achievement, a defense measure, a symbol. But that passed. Earth's overpopulation trend continued—explosively. Millions spilled into relatively empty lands like Brazil, New Guinea, and Australia. But the population explosion quickly filled them. In major cities, the population-panic-point was reached and produced the Weekend Riots. And the population, bolstered by geriatrics and a further sharp decrease in infant mortality, continued to grow."

Haskell rubbed his forehead. "It was a mess. But the ethics of population increase aren't my business. All we at the Board knew was, we had to have new land fast. We needed planets which—unlike Mars and Venus— would be rapidly self-supporting. Places to which we could siphon millions, while the scientists and politicians on Earth tried to straighten things out. We had to open these planets to colonization as rapidly as possible. And that meant speeding up the initial exploratory process."

"I know all that," Perceveral said. "But I still don't see why you stopped using the optimum explorer type."

"Isn't it obvious? We were looking for places where *ordinary* people could settle and survive. Our optimum explorer type was not ordinary. Quite the contrary, he almost approximated a new species. And he was no judge of *ordinary* survival conditions. For example, there are bleak, dreary, rain-swept little planets that the average colonist finds depressing to the point of insanity; but our optimum explorer is too sound to be disturbed by climatic monotony. Germs which devastate thousands give him, at most, a bad time for a while. Dangers which can push a colony to the brink of disaster, our optimum explorer simply evades. He can't assess these things in everyday terms. They simply don't touch him."

"I'm beginning to see," Perceveral said.

"Now the best way," Haskell said, "would have been to attack these planets in stages. First an explorer, then a basic research team, then a trial colony composed largely of psychologists and sociologists, then a research group to interpret the findings of the other groups, and so forth. But there's never enough time or money for all that. We need those colonies right now, not in fifty years."

Mr. Haskell paused and looked hard at Perceveral. "So, you see, we must have *immediate knowledge* as to whether a group of ordinary people could live and thrive on any new planet. That's why we changed our qualifications for explorers."

Perceveral nodded. "Ordinary explorers for ordinary people. There's just one thing, however."

"Yes?"

"I don't know how well you know my background…"

"Quite well," Haskell assured him.

"Then you might have noticed that I have certain tendencies toward—well, a certain accident-proneness. To tell you the honest truth, I have a hard time surviving right here on Earth."

"I know," Mr. Haskell said pleasantly.

"Then how would I make out on an alien planet? And why would you want me?"

Mr. Haskell looked slightly ill at ease. "Well, you stated our position wrongly when you said 'ordinary explorers for ordinary people.' It isn't that simple. A colony is composed of thousands, often millions of people, who vary considerably in their survival potentialities. Humanity and the law state that all of them must have a fighting chance. The people themselves must be reassured before they'll leave Earth. We must convince them—and the law—and ourselves—that even the weakest will have a chance for survival."

"Go on," Perceveral said.

"Therefore," Haskell said quickly, "some years ago we stopped using the optimum-survival explorer, and began using the minimum-survival explorer."

Perceveral sat for a while digesting this information. "So you want me because any place *I* can live in, *anyone* can live in."

"That more or less sums up our thinking on the problem," Hasken said, smiling genially.

"But what would *my* chances be?"

"Some of our minimum-survival explorers have done very well."

"And others?"

"There are hazards, of course," Haskell admitted. "And aside from the potential dangers of the planet itself, there are other risks involved in the very nature of the experiment. I can't even tell you what they are, since that would destroy our only control element on the minimum-survival test. I simply tell you that they are present."

"Not a very good outlook," Perceveral said.

"Perhaps not. But think of the rewards if you won through! You would, in effect, be the founding father of a colony! Your value as an expert would be immeasurable. You would have a permanent place in the life of the community. And equally important, you might be able to dispel certain insidious self-doubts concerning your place in the scheme of things."

Perceveral nodded reluctantly. "Tell me one thing. Your telegram arrived today at a particularly crucial moment. It seemed almost—"

"Yes, it was planned," Haskell said. "We've found that the people we want are most receptive when they've reached a certain psychological state. We keep close watch over the few who fit our requirements, waiting for the right moment to make our presentation."

"It might have been embarrassing if you'd been an hour later," Perceveral said.

"Or unfruitful if we'd been a day earlier." Haskell arose from behind his desk. "Would you join me for lunch, Mr. Perceveral? We can discuss final details over a bottle of wine."

"All right," Perceveral said. "But I'm not making any promises yet."

"Of course not," Haskell said, opening the door for him.

After lunch, Perceveral did some hard thinking. The explorer's job appealed to him strongly in spite of the risks. It was, after all, no more dangerous than suicide, and much better paying. The rewards were great if he won; the penalty for failure was no more than the price he had been about to pay for failure on Earth.

He hadn't done well in thirty-four years on Earth. The best he had shown were flashes of ability marred by a strong affinity for illness, accident, and blunder. But Earth was crowded, cluttered, and confused. Perhaps his accident proneness had been not some structural flaw in him but the product of intolerable conditions.

Exploration would give him a new environment. He would be alone, dependent only on himself, answerable only to himself. It would be tremendously dangerous—but what could be more dangerous than a glittering razor blade held in his own hand?

This would be the supreme effort of his life, the ultimate test. He would fight as he had never fought before to conquer his fatal tendencies.

And this time he would throw every ounce of strength and determination into the struggle.

He accepted the job. In the next weeks of preparation, he ate and drank and slept determination, hammered it into his brain and wove it between his nerves, mumbled it to himself like a Buddhist prayer, dreamed about it, brushed his teeth and washed his hands with it, meditated upon it until the monotonous refrain buzzed in his head waking and sleeping, and began slowly to act as a check and restraint upon action.

The day arrived when he was assigned a year's tour of duty upon a promising planet in the East Star Ridge. Haskell wished him luck and promised to stay in touch by L-phase radio. Perceveral and his equipment were put aboard the picket ship *Queen of Glasgow,* and the adventure was begun.

During the months in space, Perceveral continued to think obsessively of his resolve. He handled himself carefully in no-weight, watched his every movement and cross-checked his every motive. This continuous inspection slowed him down considerably; but gradually it became habitual. A set of new reflexes began to form, struggling to conquer the old reflex system.

But progress was spasmodic. In spite of his efforts, Perceveral caught a minor skin irritation from the ship's purification system, broke one of his ten pairs of glasses against a bulkhead, and suffered numerous headaches, backaches, skinned knuckles, and stubbed toes.

Still, he felt he had made progress, and his resolution hardened accordingly. And at last his planet came into view.

The planet was named Theta. Perceveral and his equipment were set down on a grassy, forested upland near a mountain range. The area had been pre-selected by air survey for its promising qualities. Water, wood, local fruits, and mineral-bearing ores were all nearby. The area could make an excellent colony site.

The ship's officers wished him luck, and departed. Perceveral watched until the ship vanished into a bank of clouds. Then he went to work.

First he activated his robot. It was a tall, gleaming, black multipurpose machine, standard equipment for explorers and settlers. It couldn't talk, sing, recite, or play cards like the more expensive models. Its only response was a headshake or a nod; dull companionship for the year ahead. But it was programmed to handle verbal work-commands of a considerable degree of complexity, to perform the heaviest labor, and to show a degree of foresight in problem situations.

With the robot's help, Perceveral set up his camp on the plain, keeping a careful check on the horizon for signs of trouble. The air survey had detected no signs of an alien culture, but you could never tell. And the nature of Theta's animal life was still uninvestigated.

He worked slowly and carefully, and the silent robot worked beside him. By evening, he had set up a temporary camp. He activated the radar alarm and went to bed.

He awoke just after dawn to the shrilling of the radar alarm bell. He dressed and hurried outside. There was an angry humming in the air, like the sound of a locust horde.

"Get two beamers," he told the robot, "and hurry back. Bring the binoculars, too."

The robot nodded and lurched off. Perceveral turned slowly, shivering in the gray dawn, trying to locate the direction of the sound. He scanned the damp plain, the green edge of forest, the cliffs beyond. Nothing moved. Then he saw, outlined against the sunrise, something that looked like a low dark cloud. The cloud was flying toward his camp moving very quickly against the wind.

The robot returned with the beamers. Perceveral took one and directed the robot to hold the other, awaiting orders to fire. The robot nodded, his eyecells gleaming dully as he turned toward the sunrise.

When the cloud swept nearer, it resolved into a gigantic flock of birds. Perceveral studied them through his binoculars. They were about the size of Terran hawks, but their darting, erratic flight resembled the flight of bats. They were heavily taloned and their long beaks were edged with sharp teeth. With all that lethal armament, they had to be carnivorous.

The flock circled them, humming loudly. Then, from all directions, with wings swept back and talons spread, they began to dive. Perceveral directed the robot to begin firing.

He and the robot stood back to back, blasting into the onslaught of birds. There was a whirling confusion of blood and feathers as battalions of birds were scythed out of the sky. Perceveral and the robot were holding their own, keeping the aerial wolf pack at a distance, even beating it back. Then Perceveral's beamer failed.

The beamers were supposed to be fully charged and guaranteed for seventy-five hours at full automatic. A beamer couldn't fail! He stood for a moment, stupidly clicking the trigger. Then he flung down the weapon and hurried to the supplies tent, leaving the robot to continue the fight alone.

He located his two spares and came out. When he rejoined the battle, he saw that the robot's beamer had stopped functioning. The robot stood erect, beating off the swarm of birds with his arms. Drops of oil sprayed from his joints as he flailed at the dense flock. He swayed, dangerously close to losing his balance, and Perceveral saw that some birds had evaded his swinging arms and were perched on his shoulders, pecking at his eyecells and kinesthetic antenna.

Perceveral swung up both beamers and began to cut into the swarm. One weapon failed almost immediately. He continued chopping with the last, praying it would retain its charge.

The flock, finally alarmed by its losses, rose and wheeled away, screaming and hooting. Miraculously unhurt, Perceveral and the robot stood knee-deep in scattered feathers and charred bodies.

Perceveral looked at the four beamers, three of which had failed him entirely. Then he marched angrily to the communications tent.

He contacted Haskell and told him about the attack of the birds and the failure of three beamers out of four. Red-faced with outrage, he denounced the men who were supposed to check an explorer's equipment. Then, out of breath, he waited for Haskell's apology and explanation.

"That," Haskell said, "was one of the control elements."

"Huh?"

"I explained it to you months ago," Haskell said. "We are testing for minimum-survival conditions. *Minimum,* remember? We have to know what will happen to a colony composed of people of varying degrees of proficiency. Therefore, we look for the lowest denominator."

"I know all that. But the beamers—"

"Mr. Perceveral, setting up a colony, even on an absolute minimum basis, is a fantastically expensive operation. We supply our colonists with the newest and best in guns and equipment, but we can't replace things that stop functioning or are used up. The colonists have to use irreplaceable ammunition, equipment that breaks and wears out, food stores that become exhausted or spoiled—"

"And that's what you've given me?" Perceveral asked.

"Of course. As a control, we have equipped you with the minimum of survival equipment. That's the only way we'll be able to predict how the colonists will make out on Theta."

"But it isn't fair! Explorers always get the best equipment!"

"No," Haskell said. "The old-style optimum-survival explorers did, of course. But we're testing for least potential, which must extend to equipment as well as to personality. I told you there would be risks."

"Yes, you did," Perceveral said. "But...All right. Do you have any other little secrets in store for me?"

"Not really," Haskell said, after a momentary pause. "Both you and your equipment are of minimum-survival quality. That about sums it up."

Perceveral detected something evasive in this answer, but Haskell refused to be more specific. They signed off and Perceveral returned to the chaos of his camp.

* * *

Perceveral and the robot moved their camp to the shelter of the forest for protection against further assaults by the birds. In setting up again, Perceveral noted that fully half of his ropes were badly worn, his electrical fixtures were beginning to burn out, and the canvas of his tents showed mildew. Laboriously he repaired everything, bruising his knuckles and skinning his palms. Then his generator broke down.

He sweated over it for three days, trying to figure out the trouble from the badly printed instruction book, written in German, that had been sent with the machine. Nothing seemed to be set up right in the generator and nothing worked. At last he discovered, by pure accident, that the book was meant for an entirely different model. He lost his temper at this and kicked the generator, almost breaking the little toe of his right foot.

Then he took himself firmly in hand and worked for another four days, figuring out the differences between his model and the model described, until he had the generator working again.

The birds found that they could plummet through the trees into Perceveral's camp, snatch food and be gone before the beamer could be leveled at them. Their attacks cost Perceveral a pair of glasses and a nasty wound on the neck. Laboriously he wove nets, and, with the robot's help, strung them in the branches above his camp.

The birds were baffled. Perceveral finally had time to check his food stores, and to discover that many of his dehydrated staples had been poorly processed, and others had become a host to an ugly airborne fungus. Either way, it added up to spoilage. Unless he took measures now, he would be short of food during the Thetan winter.

He ran a series of tests on local fruits, grains, berries, and vegetables. They showed several varieties to be safe and nourishing. He ate these, and broke into a spectacular allergy rash. Painstaking work with his medical kit gave him a cure for the allergy, and he set up a test to discover the guilty plant. But just as he was checking final results, the robot stamped in, upsetting test tubes and spilling irreplaceable chemicals.

Perceveral had to continue the allergy tests on himself, and to exclude one berry and two vegetables as unfit for his consumption.

But the fruits were excellent and the local grains made a fine bread. Perceveral collected seed, and, late in the Thetan spring, directed the robot to the tasks of plowing and planting.

The robot worked tirelessly in the new fields, while Perceveral did some exploring. He found pieces of smooth rock upon which characters had been scratched, and what looked like numbers, and even little stick-pictures of trees and clouds and mountains. Intelligent beings must have lived on Theta, he decided. Quite probably they still inhabited some parts of the planet. But he had no time to search for them.

When Perceveral checked his fields, he found that the robot had planted the seed inches too deep, in spite of his programmed instructions. That crop was lost, and Perceveral planted the next by himself.

He built a wooden shack and replaced the rotting tents with storage sheds. Slowly he made his preparations for survival through the winter. And slowly he began to suspect that his robot was wearing out.

The great black all-purpose machine performed its tasks as before. But the robot's movements were growing increasingly jerky and his use of strength was indiscriminate. Heavy jars splintered in his grip and farming implements broke when he used them. Perceveral programmed him for weeding the fields, but the robot's broad splay feet trampled the grain sprouts as his fingers plucked the weeds. When the robot went out to chop firewood, he usually succeeded in breaking the axe handle. The cabin shook when the robot entered, and the door sometimes left its hinges.

Perceveral wondered and worried about the robot's deterioration. There was no way he could repair it, for the robot was a factory-sealed unit, meant to be repaired only by factory technicians with special tools, parts and knowledge. All Perceveral could do was retire the robot from service. But that would leave him completely alone.

He programmed increasingly simple tasks into the robot and took more work upon himself. Still the robot continued to deteriorate. Then one evening, when Perceveral was eating his dinner, the robot lurched against the stove and sent a pot of boiling rice flying.

With his new-found survival talents, Perceveral flung himself out of the way and the boiling mess landed on his left shoulder instead of his face.

That was too much. The robot was dangerous to have around. After dressing his burn, Perceveral decided to turn the robot off and continue the work of survival alone. In a firm voice, he gave the Dormancy Command.

The robot simply glared at him and moved restlessly around the cabin, not responding to a robot's most basic command.

Perceveral gave the order again. The robot shook his head and began to stack firewood.

Something had gone wrong. He would have to turn the robot off manually. But there was no sign of the usual cut-out switch anywhere on the machine's gleaming black surface. Nevertheless, Perceveral took out his tool kit and approached the robot.

Amazingly, the robot backed away from him, arms raised defensively.

"Stand still!" Perceveral shouted.

The robot moved away until his back was against the wall. Perceveral hesitated, wondering what was going wrong. Machines weren't permitted to disobey orders. And the willingness to give up life had been carefully structured into all robotic devices.

He advanced on the robot, determined to turn him off somehow. The robot waited until he was close, then swung an armored fist at him. Perceval dodged out of the way and flung a wrench at the robot's kinesthetic antenna. The robot quickly retracted it and swung again. This time his armored fist caught Perceval in the ribs.

Perceval fell to the floor and the robot stood over him, his eyecells flaring red and his iron fingers opening and closing. Perceval shut his eyes and waited for the *coup de grâce*. But the machine turned and left the shack, smashing the lock as he went.

In a few minutes, Perceval heard the sound of firewood being cut and stacked—as usual.

With the aid of his medical kit, Perceval taped up his side. The robot finished work and came back for further instructions. Shakily, Perceval ordered him to a distant spring for water. The robot left, showing no further signs of aggression. Perceval dragged himself to the radio shack.

"You shouldn't have tried to turn him off," Haskell said, when he heard what had happened. "He isn't designed to be turned off. Wasn't that apparent? For your own safety, don't try it again."

"But what's the reason?"

"Because—as you've probably guessed by now—the robot acts as our quality-control over you."

"I don't understand," Perceval said. "Why do you need a quality-control?"

"Must I go through it all again?" Haskell asked wearily. "You were hired as a minimum-survival explorer. Not average. Not superior. *Minimum.*"

"Yes, but—"

"Let me continue. Do you recall how you were during your thirty-four years on Earth? You were continually beset by accident, disease, and general misfortune. That is what we wanted on Theta. But you've changed, Mr. Perceval."

"I've certainly *tried* to change."

"Of course," Haskell said. "We expected it. Most of our minimum-survival explorers change. Faced with a new environment and a fresh start, they get a grip on themselves such as they've never had before. But it's not what we're testing for, so we have to compensate for the change. Colonists, you see, don't always come to a planet in a spirit of self-improvement. And any colony has its careless ones, to say nothing of the aged, the infirm, the feeble-minded, the foolhardy, the inexperienced children, and so forth. Our minimum-survival standards are a guarantee that all of them will have a chance. Now are you beginning to understand?"

"I think so," Perceveral said.

"That's why we need a quality-control over you—to keep you from acquiring the average or superior survival qualities which we are *not* testing for."

"Therefore the robot," Perceveral said bleakly.

"Correct. The robot has been programmed to act as a check, a final control over your survival tendencies. He reacts to you, Perceveral. As long as you stay within a pre-selected range of general incompetence, the robot operates at par. But when you improve, become more skillful at survival, less accident-prone, the robot's behavior deteriorates. He begins to break the things that you should be breaking, to form the wrong decisions you should be forming—"

"That isn't fair!"

"Perceveral, you seem to feel that we're running some kind of sanitorium or self-aid program for your benefit. Well, we're not. We're interested only in getting the job that we bought and paid for. The job, let me add, which you chose as an alternative to suicide."

"All right!" Perceveral shouted. "I'm doing the job. But is there any rule that says I can't dismantle that damned robot?"

"No rule at all," Haskell said in a quieter voice, "if you can do it. But I earnestly advise you not to try. It's too dangerous. The robot will not allow himself to be deactivated."

"That's for me to decide, not him," Perceveral said, and signed off.

Spring passed on Theta, and Perceveral learned how to live with his robot. He ordered him to scout a distant mountain range, but the robot refused to leave him. He tried giving him no orders, but the black monster wouldn't stay idle. If no work was assigned, the robot assigned work to himself, suddenly bursting into action and creating havoc in Perceveral's field and sheds.

In self-defense, Perceveral gave him the most harmless task he could think of. He ordered the robot to dig a well, hoping he would bury himself in it. But, grimy and triumphant, the robot emerged every evening and entered the cabin, showering dirt into Perceveral's food, transmitting allergies, and breaking dishware and windows.

Grimly, Perceveral accepted the status quo. The robot now seemed the embodiment of that other, darker side of himself, the inept and accident-prone Perceveral. Watching the robot on his destructive rounds, he felt as though he were watching a misshapen portion of himself, a sickness cast into solid, living form.

He tried to shake free of this fantasy. But more and more the robot came to represent his own destructive urges cut loose from the life impulse and allowed to run rampant.

Perceveral worked, and his neurosis stalked behind him, eternally destructive, yet—in the manner of neuroses—protective of itself. His self-perpetuating malady lived with him, watched him while he ate and stayed close while he slept.

Perceveral did his work and became increasingly competent at it. He took what enjoyment he could from the days, regretted the setting of the sun, and lived through the horror of the nights when the robot stood beside his bed and seemed to wonder if now were the time for a summing-up. And in the morning, still alive, Perceveral tried to think of ways of disposing of his staggering, lurching, destructive neurosis.

But the deadlock remained until a new factor appeared to complicate matters.

It had rained heavily for several days. When the weather cleared, Perceveral walked out to his fields. The robot lumbered behind him, carrying the farming tools.

Suddenly a crack appeared in the moist ground under his feet. It widened, and the whole section he was standing on collapsed. Perceveral leaped for firm ground. He made it to the slope, and the robot pulled him up the rest of the way, almost yanking his arm from his socket.

When he examined the collapsed section of field, he saw that a tunnel had run under it. Digging marks were still visible. One side was blocked by the fall. On the other side, the tunnel continued deep into the ground.

Perceveral went back for his beamer and his flashlight. He climbed down one side of the hole and flashed his light into the tunnel. He saw a great furry shape retreat hastily around a bend. It looked like a giant mole.

At last he had met another species of life on Theta.

For the next few days, he cautiously probed the tunnels. Several times he glimpsed gray molelike shapes, but they fled from him into a labyrinth of passageways.

He changed his tactics. He went only a few hundred feet into the main tunnel and left a gift of fruit. When he returned the next day, the fruit was gone. In its place were two lumps of lead.

The exchange of gifts continued for a week. Then, one day when Perceveral was bringing more fruit and berries, a giant mole appeared, approaching slowly and with evident nervousness. He motioned at Perceveral's flashlight, and Perceveral covered the lens so that it wouldn't hurt the mole's eyes.

He waited. The mole advanced slowly on two legs, his nose wrinkling, his small wrinkled hands clasped to his chest. He stopped and looked at Perceveral with bulging eyes. Then he bent down and scratched a symbol in the dirt of the passageway.

Perceveral had no idea what the symbol meant. But the act itself implied language, intelligence and a grasp of abstractions. He scratched a symbol beside the mole's, to imply the same things.

An act of communication between alien races had begun. The robot stood behind Perceveral, his eyecells glowing, watching while the man and the mole searched for something in common.

Contact meant more labor for Perceveral. The fields and gardens still had to be tended, the repairs on equipment made and the robot watched; in his spare time, Perceveral worked hard to learn the mole's language. And the moles worked equally hard to teach him.

Perceveral and the moles slowly grew to understand each other, to enjoy each other's company, to become friends. Perceveral learned about their daily lives, their abhorrence of the light, their journeys through the underground caverns, their quest for knowledge and enlightenment. And he taught them what he could about Man.

"But what is the metal thing?" the moles wanted to know.

"A servant of Man," Perceveral told them.

"But it stands behind you and glares. It hates you, the metal thing. Do all metal things hate men?"

"Certainly not," Perceveral said. "This is a special case."

"It frightens us. Do all metal things frighten?"

"Some do. Not all."

"And it is hard to think when the metal thing stares at us, hard to understand you. Is it always like that with metal things?"

"Sometimes they do interfere," Perceveral admitted. "But don't worry, the robot won't hurt you."

The mole people weren't so sure. Perceveral made what excuses he could for the heavy, lurching, boorish machine, spoke of machinery's service to Man and the graciousness of life that it made possible. But the mole people weren't convinced and shrank from the robot's dismaying presence.

Nevertheless, after lengthy negotiations, Perceveral made a treaty with the mole people. In return for supplies of fresh fruits and berries, which the moles coveted but could rarely obtain, they agreed to locate metals for future colonists and find sources of water and oil. Furthermore, the colonists were granted possession of all the surface land of Theta and the moles were confirmed in their lordship of the underground.

This seemed an equitable distribution to both parties, and Perceveral and the mole chief signed the stone document with as much of a flourish as an incising tool would allow.

To seal the treaty, Perceveral gave a feast. He and the robot brought a great gift of assorted fruits and berries to the mole people. The gray-furred, soft-eyed moles clustered around, squeaking eagerly to each other.

The robot set down his baskets of fruit and stepped back. He slipped on a patch of smooth rock, flailed for balance, and came crashing down across one of the moles. Immediately he regained his balance and tried, with his clumsy iron hands, to help the mole up. But he had broken the creature's back.

The rest of the moles fled, carrying their dead companion with them. And Perceveral and the robot were left alone in the tunnel, surrounded by great piles of fruit.

That night, Perceveral thought long and hard. He was able to see the damnable logic of the event. Minimum-survival contacts with aliens should have an element of uncertainty, distrust, misunderstanding, and even a few deaths. His dealings with the mole people had gone altogether too smoothly for minimum requirements.

The robot had simply corrected the situation and had performed the errors which Perceveral should have made on his own.

But although he understood the logic of the event, he couldn't accept it. The mole people were his friends and he had betrayed them. There could be no more trust between them, no hope of cooperation for future colonists. Not while the robot clumped and stumbled down the tunnels.

Perceveral decided that the robot must be destroyed. Once and for all, he determined to test his painfully acquired skill against the destructive neurosis that walked continually beside him. And if it cost his life—well, Perceveral reminded himself, he had been willing to lose it less than a year ago, for much poorer reasons.

He re-established contact with the moles and discussed the problem with them. They agreed to help him, for even these gentle people had the concept of vengeance. They supplied some ideas which were surprisingly human, since the moles also possessed a form of warfare. They explained it to Perceveral and he agreed to try their way.

In a week, the moles were ready. Perceveral loaded the robot with baskets of fruit and led him into the tunnels, as though he were attempting another treaty.

The mole people weren't to be found. Perceveral and the robot journeyed deeper into the passageways, their flashlights probing ahead into the darkness. The robot's eyecells glowed red and he towered close behind Perceveral, almost at his back.

They came to an underground cavern. There was a faint whistle and Perceveral sprinted out of the way.

The robot sensed danger and tried to follow. But he stumbled, thwarted by his own programmed ineptness, and fruit scattered across the cavern floor. Then ropes dropped from the blackness of the cavern's roof and settled around the robot's head and shoulders.

He ripped at the tough fiber. More ropes settled around him, hissing in swift flight down from the roof. The robot's eyecells flared as he ripped the cords from his arms.

Mole people emerged from the passageways by the dozens. More lines snaked around the robot, whose joints spurted oil as he strained to break the strands. For minutes, the only sounds in the cavern were the hiss of flying ropes, the creak of the robot's joints, and the dry crack of breaking line.

Perceveral ran back to join the fight. They bound the robot closer and closer until his limbs had no room to gain a purchase. And still the ropes hissed through the air until the robot toppled over, bound in a great cocoon of rope with only his head and feet showing.

Then the mole people squeaked in triumph and tried to gouge out the robot's eyes with their blunt digging claws. But steel shutters slid over the robot's eyes. So they poured sand into his joints until Perceveral pushed them aside and attempted to melt the robot with his last beamer.

The beamer failed before the metal even grew hot. They fastened ropes to the robot's feet and dragged him down a passageway that ended in a deep chasm. They levered him over the side and listened while he bounced off the granite sides of the precipice, and cheered when he struck bottom.

The mole people held a celebration. But Perceveral felt sick. He returned to his shack and lay in bed for two days, telling himself over and over that he had not killed a man, or even a thinking being. He had simply destroyed a dangerous machine.

But he couldn't help remembering the silent companion who had stood with him against the birds, and had weeded his fields and gathered wood for him. Even though the robot had been clumsy and destructive, he had been clumsy and destructive in Perceveral's own personal way—a way that he, above all people, could understand and sympathize with.

For a while, he felt as though a part of himself had died. But the mole people came to him in the evenings and consoled him, and there was work to be done in the fields and sheds.

It was autumn, time for harvesting and storing his crops. Perceveral went to work. With the robot's removal, his own chronic propensity for accident returned briefly. He fought it back with fresh confidence. By the first snows, his work of storage and food preservation was done. And his year on Theta was coming to an end.

He radioed a full report to Haskell on the planet's risks, promises and potentialities, reported his treaty with the mole people, and recommended the planet for colonization. In two weeks, Haskell radioed back.

"Good work," he told Perceval. "The Board decided that Theta definitely fits our minimum-survival requirements. We're sending out a colony ship at once."

"Then the test is over?" Perceval asked.

"Right. The ship should be there in about three months. I'll probably take this batch out. My congratulations, Mr. Perceval. You're going to be the founding father of a brand-new colony!"

Perceval said, "Mr. Haskell, I don't know how to thank you—"

"Nothing to thank me for," Haskell said. "Quite the contrary. By the way, how did you make out with the robot?"

"I destroyed him," Perceval said. He described the killing of the mole and the subsequent events.

"Hmm," Haskell said.

"You told me there was no rule against it."

"There isn't. The robot was part of your equipment, just like the beamers and tents and food supplies. Like them, he was also part of your survival problems. You had a right to do anything you could about him."

"Then what's wrong?"

"Well, I just hope you really destroyed him. Those quality-control models are built to last, you know. They've got self-repair units and a strong sense of self-preservation. It's damned hard to really knock one out."

"I think I succeeded," Perceval said.

"I hope so. It would be embarrassing if the robot survived."

"Why? Would it come back for revenge?"

"Certainly not. A robot has no emotions."

"Well?"

"The trouble is this. The robot's purpose was to cancel out any gains you made in survival-quality. It did, in various destructive ways."

"Sure. So, if it comes back, I'll have to go through the whole business again."

"More. You've been separated from the robot for a few months now. If it's still functioning, it's been accumulating a backlog of accidents for you. All the destructive duties that it should have performed during those months—they'll all have to be discharged before the robot can return to normal duties. See what I mean?"

Perceval cleared his throat nervously. "And of course he would discharge them as quickly as possible in order to get back to regular operation."

"Of course. Now look, the ship will be there in about three months. That's the quickest we can make it. I suggest you make sure that robot is immobilized. We wouldn't want to lose you now."

"No, we wouldn't," Perceval said. "I'll take care of it at once."

He equipped himself and hurried to the tunnels. The mole people guided him to the chasm after he explained the problem. Armed with blow torch, hacksaw, sledge hammer and cold chisel, Perceval began a slow descent down the side of the precipice.

At the bottom, he quickly located the spot where the robot had landed. There, wedged between two boulders, was a complete robotic arm, wrenched loose from the shoulder. Further on, he found fragments of a shattered eyecell. And he came across an empty cocoon of ripped and shredded rope.

But the robot wasn't there.

Perceval climbed back up the precipice, warned the moles and began to make what preparations he could.

Nothing happened for twelve days. Then news was brought to him in the evening by a frightened mole. The robot had appeared again in the tunnels, stalking the dark passageways with a single eyecell glowing, expertly threading the maze into the main branch.

The moles had prepared for his coming with ropes. But the robot had learned. He had avoided the silent dropping nooses and charged into the mole forces. He had killed six moles and sent the rest into flight.

Perceval nodded briefly at the news, dismissed the mole and continued working. He had set up his defenses in the tunnels. Now he had his four dead beamers disassembled on the table in front of him. Working without a manual he was trying to interchange parts to produce One usable weapon.

He worked late into the night, testing each component carefully before fitting it back into the casing. The tiny parts seemed to float before his eyes and his fingers felt like sausages. Very carefully, working with tweezers and a magnifying glass, he began reassembling the weapon.

The radio suddenly blared into life.

"Anton?" Haskell asked. "What about the robot?"

"He's coming," said Perceval.

"I was afraid so. Now listen, I rushed through a priority call to the robot's manufacturers. I had a hell of a fight with them, but I got their permission for you to deactivate the robot, and full instructions on how to do it."

"Thanks," Perceval said. "Hurry up, how's it done?"

"You'll need the following equipment. A power source of two hundred volts delivered at twenty-five amps. Can your generator handle that?"

"Yes. Go on."

"You'll need a bar of copper, some silver wire and a probe made of some non-conductor such as wood. You set the stuff up in the following—"

"I'll never have time," Perceval said, "but tell me quickly."

His radio hummed loudly.

"Haskell!" Perceveral cried.

His radio went dead. Perceveral heard the sounds of breakage coming from the radio shack. Then the robot appeared in the doorway.

The robot's left arm and right eyecell were missing, but his self-repair units had sealed the damaged spots. He was colored a dull black now, with rust-streaks down his chest and flanks.

Perceveral glanced down at the almost-completed beamer. He began fitting the final pieces into place.

The robot walked toward him.

"Go cut firewood," Perceveral said, in as normal a tone as he could manage.

The robot stopped, turned, picked up the axe, hesitated, and started out the door.

Perceveral fitted in the final component, slid the cover into place and began screwing it down.

The robot dropped the axe and turned again, struggling with contradictory commands. Perceveral hoped he might fuse some circuits in the conflict. But the robot made his decision and launched himself at Perceveral.

Perceveral raised the beamer and pressed the trigger. The blast stopped the robot in mid-stride. His metallic skin began to glow a faint red.

Then the beamer failed again.

Perceveral cursed, hefted the heavy weapon and threw it at the robot's remaining eyecell. It just missed, bouncing off his forehead.

Dazed, the robot groped for him. Perceveral dodged his arm and fled from the cabin, toward the black mouth of the tunnel. As he entered, he looked back and saw the robot following.

He walked several hundred yards down the tunnel. Then he turned on a flashlight and waited for the robot.

He had thought the problem out carefully when he'd discovered that the robot had not been destroyed.

His first idea naturally was flight. But the robot, traveling night and day, would easily overtake him. Nor could be dodge aimlessly in and out of the maze of tunnels. He would have to stop and eat, drink, and sleep. The robot wouldn't have to stop for anything.

Therefore he had arranged a series of traps in the tunnels and had staked everything on them. One of them was bound to work. He was sure of it.

But even as he told himself this, Perceveral shivered, thinking of the accumulation of accidents that the robot had for him—the months of broken arms and fractured ribs; wrenched ankles, slashes, cuts, bites, infections, and diseases. All of which the robot would hound him into as rapidly as possible, in order to get back to normal routine.

He would never survive the robot's backlog. His traps *had* to work!
Soon he heard the robot's thundering footsteps. Then the robot appeared, saw him, and lumbered forward.

Perceveral sprinted down a tunnel, then turned into a smaller tunnel. The robot followed, gaining slightly.

When Perceveral reached a distinctive outcropping of rock, he looked back to gauge the robot's position. Then he tugged a cord he had concealed behind the rock.

The roof of the tunnel collapsed, releasing tons of dirt and rock over the robot.

If the robot had continued for another step, he would have been buried. But appraising the situation instantly, he whirled and leaped back. Dirt showered him, and small rocks bounced off his head and shoulders. But the main fall missed him.

When the last pebble had fallen, the robot climbed over the mound of debris and continued the pursuit.

Perceveral was growing short of wind. He was disappointed at the failure of the trap. But, he reminded himself, he had a better one ahead. The next would surely finish off the implacable machine.

They ran down a winding tunnel lit only by occasional flashes from Perceveral's flashlight. The robot began gaining again. Perceveral reached a straight stretch and put on a burst of speed.

He crossed a patch of ground that looked exactly like any other patch. But as the robot thundered over it, the ground gave way. Perceveral had calculated it carefully. The trap, which held under his weight, yielded at once under the robot's bulk.

The robot thrashed for a handhold. Dirt trickled through his fingers and he slid into the trap that Perceveral had dug—a pit with sloping sides that came together like a great funnel, designed to keep the robot immovably wedged at the bottom.

The robot, however, flung both his legs wide, almost at right angles to his body. His joints creaked as his heels bit into the sloping sides; they sagged under his weight, but held. He was able to stop himself before reaching the bottom, with both legs stiffly outspread and pressed into the soft dirt.

The robot's hand gouged deep handholds in the dirt. One leg retracted and found a foothold; then the other. Slowly the robot extricated himself, and Perceveral started running again.

His breath came short and hard now and he was getting a stitch in his side. The robot gained more easily, and Perceveral had to strain to stay ahead.

He had counted on those two traps. Now there was just one more left. A very good one, but risky to use.

Perceveral forced himself to concentrate in spite of a growing dizziness. The last trap had to be calculated carefully. He passed a stone marked in white and switched off his flashlight. He began counting strides, slowing until the robot was directly behind him, his fingers inches from his neck.

Eighteen—nineteen—twenty!

On the twentieth step, Perceveral flung himself head-first into the darkness. For seconds, he seemed to be floating in the air. Then he struck water in a flat, shallow dive, surfaced and waited.

The robot had been too close behind to stop. There was a tremendous splash as he hit the surface of the underground lake; a sound of furious splashings; and, finally, the sound of bubbles as the heavy robot sank beneath the surface.

When he heard that, Perceveral struck out for the opposite shore. He made it and pulled himself out of the icy water. For minutes, he lay shuddering on the slimy rocks. Then he forced himself to climb further ashore on hands and knees, to a cache where he had stored firewood, matches, whiskey, blankets, and clothes.

During the next hours, Perceveral dried himself, changed clothes and built a small fire. He ate and drank and watched the still surface of the underground lake. Days ago, he had tested with a hundred-foot line and found no bottom. Perhaps the lake was bottomless. More likely it fed into a swift-flowing underwater river that would pull the robot along for weeks and months. Perhaps...

He heard a faint sound in the water and trained his flashlight in its direction. The robot's head appeared, and then his shoulders and torso emerged.

The lake was very evidently not bottomless. The robot must have walked across the bottom and climbed the steep slope on the opposite side.

The robot began to climb the slimy rocks near shore. Perceveral wearily pulled himself to his feet and broke into a run.

His last trap had failed him and his neurosis was closing in for the kill. Perceveral headed toward a tunnel exit. He wanted the end to come in sunlight.

At a jolting dog-trot, Perceveral led the robot out of the tunnels toward a steep mountain slope. His breath felt like fire in his throat and his stomach muscles were knotted painfully. He ran with his eyes half-closed, dizzy from fatigue.

His traps had failed. Why hadn't he realized the certainty of their failure earlier? The robot was part of himself, his own neurosis moving to destroy him. And how can a man trick the trickiest part of himself? The right hand always finds out what the left hand is doing, and the cleverest of devices never fools the supreme fooler for long.

He had gone about the thing in the wrong way, Perceveral thought, as he began to climb the mountain slope. The way to freedom is not through deception. It is...

The robot clutched at his heel, reminding Perceveral of the difference between theoretical and practical knowledge. He pulled himself out of the way and bombarded the robot with stones. The robot brushed them aside and continued climbing.

Perceveral cut diagonally across the steep rock face. The way to freedom, he told himself, is not through deception. That was bound to fail. The way out is through *change!* The way out is through conquest, not of the robot, but of what the robot represented.

Himself!

He was feeling light-headed and his thoughts poured on unchecked. If, he insisted to himself, he could conquer his sense of kinship with the robot—then obviously the robot would no longer be *his* neurosis! It would simply be *a* neurosis, with no power over him.

All he had to do was lose his neurosis—even for ten minutes—and the robot couldn't harm him!

All sense of fatigue left him and he was flooded with a supreme and intoxicating confidence. Boldly, he ran across a mass of jumbled rocks, a perfect place for a twisted ankle or a broken leg. A year ago, even a month ago, he would infallibly have had an accident. But the changed Perceveral, striding like a demigod, traversed the rocks without error.

The robot, one-armed and one-eyed, doggedly took the accident upon himself. He tripped and sprawled at full length across the sharp rocks. When he picked himself up and resumed the chase, he was limping.

Completely intoxicated but minutely watchful, Perceveral came to a granite wall, and leaped for a fingerhold that was no more than a gray shadow above him. For a heart-stopping second, he dangled in the air. Then, as his fingers began to slip, his foot found a hold. Without hesitation, he pulled himself up.

The robot followed, his dry joints creaking loudly. He bent a finger out of commission making the climb that Perceveral should have failed.

Perceveral leaped from boulder to boulder. The robot came after him, slipping and straining, drawing near. Perceveral didn't care. The thought struck him that all his years of accident-proneness had gone into the making of this moment. The tide had turned now. He was at last what nature had intended him to be all along—an accident-*proof* man!

The robot crawled after him up a dazzling surface of white rock. Perceveral, drunk with supreme confidence, pushed boulders into motion and shouted to create an avalanche.

The rocks began to slide, and above him he heard a deep rumble. He dodged around a boulder, evaded the robot's outflung arm and came to a dead end.

He was in a small, shallow cave. The robot loomed in front of him, blocking the entrance, his iron fist pulled back.

Perceveral burst into laughter at the sight of the poor, clumsy, accident-prone robot. Then the robot's fist, driven by the full force of his body, shot out.

Perceveral ducked, but it wasn't necessary. The clumsy robot missed him anyhow, by at least half an inch. It was just the sort of mistake Perceveral had expected of the ridiculous accident-prone creature.

The force of the swing carried the robot outward. He fought hard to regain his balance, poised on the lip of the cliff. Any normal man or robot would have regained it. But not the accident-prone robot. He fell on his face, smashing his last eyecell, and began to roll.

Perceveral leaned out to accelerate the roll, then quickly crouched back inside the shallow cave. The avalanche completed the job for him, rolling a diminishing black dot down the dusty white mountainside and burying it under tons of stone.

Perceveral watched it all, chuckling to himself. Then he began to ask himself what, exactly, he had been doing.

And that was when he started to shake.

Months later, Perceveral stood by the gangplank of the colony ship *Cuchulain,* watching the colonists step down into Theta's midwinter sunshine. There were all types and kinds.

They had all come to Theta for a chance at a new life. Each of them was vitally important at least to himself, and each deserved a fighting chance at survival, no matter what his potentialities.

And he, Anton Perceveral, had scouted the minimum-survival requirements on Theta for these people; and had, in some measure, given hope and promise to the least capable among them—the incompetents who also wanted to live.

He turned away from the stream of pioneers and entered the ship by a rear ladder. He walked down a corridor and entered Haskell's cabin.

"Well, Anton," Haskell said, "how do they look to you?"

"They seem like a nice group," Perceveral said.

"They are. Those people consider you their founding father, Anton. They want you here. Will you stay?"

Perceveral said, "I consider Theta my home."

"Then it's settled. I'll just—"

"Wait," Perceveral said. "I'm not finished. I consider Theta my home. I want to settle here, marry, raise kids. But not yet."

"Eh?"

"I've grown pretty fond of exploring," Perceveral said. "I'd like to do some more of it. Maybe one or two more planets. Then I'll settle down on Theta."

"I was afraid you might want that," Haskell said unhappily.

"What's wrong with it?"

"Nothing. But I'm afraid we can't use you again as an explorer, Anton."

"Why not?"

"You know what we need. Minimum-survival personalities for staking out future colonies. You cannot by any stretch of the imagination be considered a minimum-survival personality any longer."

"But I'm the same man I always was!" Perceveral said. "Oh, sure, I improved on the planet. But you expected that and had the robot to compensate for it. And at the end—"

"Yes, what about that?"

"Well, at the end I just got carried away. I think I was drunk or something. I can't imagine how I acted that way."

"Still, that's how you did act."

"Yes. But look! Even with that, I barely survived the experience—the total experience on Theta! *Barely!* Doesn't, that prove I'm still a minimum-survival personality?"

Haskell pursed his lips and looked thoughtful. "Anton, you almost convince me. But I'm afraid you're indulging in a bit of word-juggling. In all honesty, I can't view you as minimum any longer. I'm afraid you'll just have to put up with your lot on Theta."

Perceveral's shoulders slumped. He nodded wearily, shook hands with Haskell and turned to go.

As he turned, the edge of his sleeve caught Haskell's inkstand, brushing it off the table. Perceveral lunged to catch it and banged his hand against the desk. Ink splattered over him. He fumbled again, tripped over a chair, fell.

"Anton," Haskell asked, "was that an act?"

"No," Perceveral said. "It wasn't, damn it."

"Hmm. Interesting. Now, Anton, don't raise your hopes too high, but maybe—I say just *maybe*—"

Haskell stared hard at Perceveral's flushed face, then burst into laughter.

"What a devil you are, Anton! You almost had me fooled. Now will you kindly get the hell out of here and join the colonists? They're dedicating a statue to you and I think they'd like to have you present."

Shamefaced, but grinning in spite of it, Anton Perceveral walked out to meet his new destiny.

THE SWEEPER OF LORAY

"Absolutely impossible," declared Professor Carver.

"But I saw it," said Fred, his companion and bodyguard. "Late last night, I saw it! They carried in this hunter—he had his head half ripped off—and they—"

"Wait," Professor Carver said, leaning forward expectantly.

They had left their spaceship before dawn, in order to witness the sunrise ceremonies in the village of Loray, upon the planet of the same name. Sunrise ceremonies, viewed from a proper distance, are often colorful and can provide a whole chapter for an anthropologist's book; but Loray, as usual, proved a disappointment.

Without fanfare, the sun rose, in answer to prayers made to it the preceding night. Slowly it hoisted its dull red expanse above the horizon, warming the topmost branches of the great rainforest that surrounded the village. And the natives slept on…

Not *all* the natives. Already the Sweeper was out, cleaning the debris between huts with his twig broom. He slowly shuffled along, human-shaped but unutterably alien. The Sweeper's face was a stylized blank, as though nature had drawn there a preliminary sketch of intelligent life. His head was strangely knobbed and his skin was pigmented a dirty gray.

The Sweeper sang to himself as he swept, in a thick, guttural voice. In only one way was the Sweeper distinguishable from his fellow Lorayans: painted across his face was a broad black band. This was his mark of station, the lowest possible station in that primitive society.

"Now then," Professor Carver said, after the sun had arisen without incident, "a phenomenon such as you describe could not exist. And it most especially could not exist upon a debased, scrubby little planet like this."

"I saw what I saw," Fred maintained. "I don't know from impossible, Professor. I saw it. You want to pass it up, that's up to you."

He leaned against the gnarly bole of a stabicus tree, folded his arms across his meager chest and glowered at the thatch-roofed village. They had been on Loray for nearly two months and Fred detested the village more each day.

He was an underweight, unlovely young man and he wore his hair in a bristling crewcut which accentuated the narrowness of his brow. He had accompanied the professor for close to ten years, had journeyed with him to dozens of planets, and had seen many strange and wonderful things. Everything he saw, however, only increased his contempt for the Galaxy at large. He desired only to return, wealthy and famous, or wealthy and unknown, to his home in Bayonne, New Jersey.

"This thing could make us rich," Fred accused. "And *you* want to pass it up."

Professor Carver pursed his lips thoughtfully. Wealth was a pleasant thought, of course. But the professor didn't want to interrupt his important scientific work to engage in a wild goose chase. He was now completing his great book, the book that would fully amplify and document the thesis that he had put forth in his first paper, "Color Blindness Among the Thang Peoples." He had expanded the thesis in his book, *Lack of Coordination in the Drang Race.* He had generalized it in his monumental *Intelligence Deficiencies Around the Galaxy,* in which he proved conclusively that intelligence among Non-Terrans decreases arithmetically as their planet's distance from Terra increases geometrically.

Now the thesis had come to full flower in Carver's most recent work, his unifying effort, which was to be titled *Underlying Causes of the Implicit Inferiority of Non-Terran Peoples.*

"If you're right—" Carver said.

"Look!" Fred cried. "They're bringing in another! See for yourself!"

Professor Carver hesitated. He was a portly, impressive, red-jowled man, given to slow and deliberate movement. He was dressed in a tropical explorer's uniform, although Loray was in a temperate zone. He carried a leather swagger stick, and strapped to his waist was a large revolver, a twin to the one Fred wore.

"If you're right," Carver said slowly, "it would indeed be, so to speak, a feather in the cap."

"Come on!" said Fred.

Four srag hunters were carrying a wounded companion to the medicine hut, and Carver and Fred fell in beside them. The hunters were visibly exhausted; they must have trekked for days to bring their friend to the village, for the srag hunts ranged deep into the rain forest.

"Looks done for, huh?" Fred whispered.

Professor Carver nodded. Last month he had photographed a srag, from a vantage point very high in a very tall, stout tree. He knew it for a large, ill-tempered, quick-moving beast, with a dismaying array of claws, teeth, and horns. It was also the only non-taboo meat-bearing animal on the planet. The natives had to kill srags or starve.

But the wounded man had not been quick enough with spear and shield, and the srag had opened him from throat to pelvis. The hunter had bled copiously, even though the wound had been hastily bound with dried grasses. Mercifully, he was unconscious.

"That chap hasn't a chance," Carver remarked. "It's a miracle he's stayed alive this long. Shock alone, to say nothing of the depth and extent of the wound—"

"You'll see," Fred said.

The village had suddenly come awake. Men and women, gray-skinned, knobby-headed, looked silently as the hunters marched toward the medicine hut. The Sweeper paused to watch. The village's only child stood before his parents' hut, and, thumb in mouth, stared at the procession. Deg, the medicine man, came out to meet the hunters, already wearing his ceremonial mask. The healing dancers assembled, quickly putting on their makeup.

"Think you can fix him, Doc?" Fred asked.

"One may hope," Deg replied piously.

They entered the dimly lighted medicine hut. The wounded Lorayan was laid tenderly upon a pallet of grasses and the dancers began to perform before him. Deg started a solemn chant.

"That'll never do it," Professor Carver pointed out to Fred, with the interested air of a man watching a steam shovel in operation. "Too late for faith healing. Listen to his breathing. Shallower, don't you think?"

"Absolutely," Fred said.

Deg finished his chant and bent over the wounded hunter. The Lorayan's breathing was labored. It slowed, hesitated...

"It is time!" cried the medicine man. He took a small wooden tube out of his pouch, uncorked it, and held it to the dying man's lips. The hunter drank. And then—

Carver blinked, and Fred grinned triumphantly. The hunter's breathing was becoming stronger. As they watched, the great gash became a line of scar tissue, then a thin pink mark, then an almost invisible white line.

The hunter sat up, scratched his head, grinned foolishly, and asked for something to drink, preferably intoxicating.

Deg declared a festival on the spot.

Carver and Fred moved to the edge of the rain forest for a conference. The professor walked like a man in a dream. His pendulous lower lip was thrust out and occasionally he shook his head.

"How about it?" Fred asked.

"It shouldn't be possible," said Carver dazedly. "No substance in nature should react like that. And you saw it work last night also?"

"Damned well right," Fred said. "They brought in this hunter—he had his head pulled half off. He swallowed some of that stuff and healed right before my eyes."

"Man's age-old dream," Carver mused. "A universal panacea!"

"We could get any price for stuff like that," Fred said.

"Yes, we could—as well as performing a duty to science," Professor Carver reminded him sternly. "Yes, Fred, I think we should obtain some of that substance."

They turned and, with firm strides, marched back to the village.

Dances were in progress, given by various members of the beast cults. At the moment, the Sathgohani, a cult representing a medium-sized deerlike animal, were performing. They could be recognized by the three red dots on their foreheads. Waiting their turn were the men of the Dresfeyxi and the Taganyes, cults representing other forest animals. The beasts adopted by the cults were taboo and there was an absolute injunction against their slaughter. Carver had been unable to discover the rationale behind this rule. The Lorayans refused to speak of it.

Deg, the medicine man, had removed his ceremonial mask. He was seated in front of his hut, watching the dancing. He arose when the Earthmen approached him.

"Peace!" he said.

"Sure," said Fred. "Nice job you did this morning."

Deg smiled modestly. "The gods answered our prayers."

"The gods?" said Carver. "It looked as though the serum did most of the work."

"Serum? Oh, the sersee juice!" Deg made a ceremonial gesture as he mentioned the name. "Yes, the sersee juice is the mother of the Lorayan people."

"We'd like to buy some," Fred said bluntly, ignoring Professor Carver's disapproving frown. "What would you take for a gallon?"

"I am sorry," Deg said.

"How about some nice beads? Mirrors? Or maybe a couple of steel knives?"

"It cannot be done," the medicine man asserted. "The sersee juice is sacred. It must be used only for holy healing."

"Don't hand me that," Fred said, a flush mounting his sallow cheek. "You gooks think you can—"

"We quite understand," Carver broke in smoothly. "We know about sacred things. Sacred things are sacred. They are not to be touched by profane hands."

"Are you crazy?" Fred whispered in English.

"You are a wise man," Deg said gravely. "You understand why I must refuse you."

"Of course. But it happens, Deg, I am a medicine man in my own country."

"Ah? I did not know this!"

"It is so. As a matter of fact, in my particular line, I am the highest medicine man."

"Then you must be a very holy man," Deg said, bowing his head.

"Man, he's holy!" Fred put in emphatically. "Holiest man you'll ever see around here."

"Please, Fred," Carver said, blinking modestly. He said to the medicine man, "It's true, although I don't like to hear about it. Under the circumstances, however, you can see that it would not be wrong to give me some sersee juice. On the contrary, it is your priestly duty to give me some."

The medicine man pondered for a long time while contrary emotions passed just barely perceptibly over his almost blank face. At last he said, "It may be so. Unfortunately, I cannot do what you require."

"Why not?"

"Because there is so little sersee juice, so terribly little. There is hardly enough for the village."

Deg smiled sadly and walked away.

Life in the village continued its simple, invariant way. The Sweeper moved slowly along, cleaning with his twig broom. The hunters trekked out in search of srags. The women of the village prepared food and looked after the village's one child. The priests and dancers prayed nightly for the sun to rise in the morning. Everyone was satisfied, in a humble, submissive fashion.

Everyone except the Earthmen.

They had more talks with Deg and slowly learned the complete story of the sersee juice and the troubles surrounding it.

The sersee bush was a small and sickly affair. It did not flourish in a state of nature. Yet it resisted cultivation and positively defied transplantation. The best one could do was to weed thoroughly around it and hope it would blossom. But most sersee bushes struggled for a year or two, then gave up the ghost. A few blossomed, and a few out of the few lived long enough to produce their characteristic red berries.

From the berry of the sersee bush was squeezed the elixir that meant life to the people of Loray.

"And you must remember," Deg pointed out, "how sparsely the sersee grows and how widely scattered it is. We must search for months, sometimes, to find a single bush with berries. And those berries will save the life of only a single Lorayan, or perhaps two at the most."

"Sad, very sad," Carver said. "But surely some form of intensive fertilization—"

"Everything has been tried."

"I realize," Carver said earnestly, "how important the sersee juice is to you. But if you could give us a little—even a pint or two—we could take it to Earth, have it examined, synthesized, perhaps. Then you could have all you need."

"But we dare not give any. Have you noticed how few children we have?" Carver nodded.

"There are very few births. Our life is a constant struggle against the obliteration of our race. Every man's life must be preserved until there is a child to replace him. And this can be done only by our constant and never-ending search for the sersee berries. And there are never enough," the medicine man sighed. "Never enough."

"Does the juice cure *everything?*" Fred asked.

"It does more than that. Those who have tasted sersee add fifty of our years to their lives."

Carver opened his eyes wide. Fifty years on Loray was roughly the equivalent of sixty-three on Earth.

The sersee was more than a healing agent, more than a regenerator. It was a longevity drug as well.

He paused to consider the prospect of adding another sixty years to his lifetime. Then he asked, "What happens if a man takes sersee again after fifty years?"

"We do not know," Deg told him. "No man would take it a second time while there is not enough."

Carver and Fred exchanged glances.

"Now listen to me carefully, Deg," Professor Carver said. He spoke of the sacred duties of science. Science, he told the medicine man, was above race, above creed, above religion. The advancement of science was above life itself. What did it matter, after all, if a few more Lorayans died? They would die eventually anyhow. The important thing was for Terran science to have a sample of sersee.

"It may be as you say," Deg said. "But my choice is clear. As a priest of the Sunniheriat religion, I have a sacred trust to preserve the lives of my people. I cannot go against this trust."

He turned and walked off. The Earthmen frustratedly returned to their spaceship.

After coffee, Professor Carver opened a drawer and took out the manuscript of *Underlying Causes for the Implicit Inferiority of Non-Terran Races.* Lovingly he read over the last chapter, the chapter that dealt with the specialized inferiorities of the Lorayan people. Then he put the manuscript away.

"Almost finished, Fred," he told his assistant. "Another week's work, two weeks at the most!"

"Um," Fred replied, staring at the village through a porthole.

"This will do it," Carver said. "This book will prove, once and for all, the natural superiority of Terrans. We have proven it by force of arms, Fred, and we have proven it by our technology. Now it is proven by the impersonal processes of logic."

Fred nodded. He knew the professor was quoting from the book's introduction.

"Nothing must interfere with the great work," Carver said. "You agree with that, don't you?"

"Sure," Fred said absent-mindedly. "The book comes first. Put the gooks in their place."

"Well, I didn't exactly mean that. But you know what I mean. Under the circumstances, perhaps we should forget about sersee. Perhaps we should just finish the job we started."

Fred turned and faced his employer. "Professor, how much do you expect to make out of this book?"

"Hm? Well, the last did quite well, you will remember. This book should do even better. Ten, perhaps twenty thousand dollars!" He permitted himself a small smile. "I am fortunate, you see, in my subject matter. The general public of Earth seems to be rather interested in it, which is gratifying for a scientist."

"Say you even make fifty thousand. Chicken feed! Do you know what we could make on a test tube of sersee?"

"A hundred thousand?" Carver said vaguely.

"Are you kidding? Suppose a rich guy was dying and we had the only thing to cure him. He'd give everything he owned! Millions!"

"I believe you're right," Carver agreed. "And it *would* be a valuable scientific advancement... But the medicine man unfortunately won't give us any."

"Buying isn't the only way." Fred unholstered his revolver and checked the chambers.

"I see, I see," Carver said, his red face turning slightly pale. "But have we the right?"

"What do *you* think?"

"Well, they *are* inferior. I believe I have proven that conclusively. You might indeed say that their lives don't weigh heavily in the scheme of things. Hm, yes—yes, Fred, we could save Terran lives with this!"

"We could save our own lives," Fred said. "Who wants to punk out ahead of time?"

Carver stood up and determinedly loosened his gun in its holster. "Remember," he told Fred, "we are doing this in the name of science, and for Earth."

"Absolutely, Professor," Fred said, moving toward the port, grinning.

They found Deg near the medicine hut. Carver said, without preamble, "We must have some sersee."

"But I explained to you," said the medicine man. "I told you why it was impossible."

"We gotta have it," Fred said. He pulled his revolver from its holster and looked ferociously at Deg.

"No."

"You think I'm kidding?" Fred asked. "You know what this weapon can do?"

"I have seen you use it."

"Maybe you think I won't use it on you."

"I do not care. You can have no sersee."

"I'll shoot," Fred warned, his voice rising angrily. "I swear to you, I'll shoot."

The villagers of Loray slowly gathered behind their medicine man. Gray-skinned, knobby-headed, they moved silently into position, the hunters carrying their spears, other villagers armed with knives and stones.

"You cannot have the sersee," Deg said.

Fred slowly leveled the revolver.

"Now, Fred," said Carver, "there's an awful lot of them. Do you really think—"

Fred's thin body tightened and his finger grew taut and white on the trigger. Carver closed his eyes.

There was a moment of dead silence. Then the revolver exploded. Carver warily opened his eyes.

The medicine man was still erect, although his knees were shaking. Fred was pulling back the hammer of the revolver. The villagers had made no sound. It was a moment before Carver could figure out what had happened. At last he saw the Sweeper.

The Sweeper lay on his face, his outstretched left hand still clutching his twig broom, his legs twitching feebly. Blood welled from the hole Fred had neatly drilled through his forehead.

Deg bent over the Sweeper, than straightened. "He is dead," the medicine man said.

"That's just the first," Fred warned, taking aim at a hunter.

"No!" cried Deg.

Fred looked at him with raised eyebrows.

"I will give it to you," Deg said. "I will give you all our sersee juice. Then you must go!"

He ran into the medicine hut and reappeared a moment later with three wooden tubes, which he thrust into Fred's hands.

"We're in business, Professor," Fred said. "Let's get moving!"

They walked past the silent villagers, toward their spaceship. Something bright flashed in the sunlight. Fred yipped and dropped his revolver. Professor Carver hastily scooped it up.

"One of those gooks cut me," Fred said. "Give me the revolver!"

A spear arced high and buried itself at their feet.

"Too many of them," said Carver. "Let's run for it!"

They sprinted to their ship with spears and knives singing around them, reached it safely and bolted the port.

"Too close," Carver said, panting for breath, leaning against the dogged port. "Have you got the serum?"

"I got it," said Fred, rubbing his arm. "Damn!"

"What's wrong?"

"My arm. It feels numb."

Carver examined the wound, pursed his lips thoughtfully, but made no comment.

"It's numb," Fred said. "I wonder if they poison those spears. "

"It's quite possible," Professor Carver admitted.

"They did!" Fred shouted. "Look, the cut is changing color already!"

The edges of the wound had a blackened, septic look.

"Sulfa," Carver said. "Penicillin, too. I wouldn't worry much about it, Fred. Modern Terran drugs—"

"—might not even touch this stuff. Open one of those tubes!"

"But, Fred," Carver objected, "we have so little of it. Besides—"

"To hell with that," Fred said. He took one of the tubes and uncorked it with his teeth.

"Wait, Fred!"

"Wait, nothing!"

Fred drained the contents of the tube and flung it down. Carver said testily, "I was merely going to point out that the serum should be tested before an Earthman uses it. We don't know how it'll react on a human. It was for your own good."

"Sure it was," Fred said mockingly. "Just look at how the stuff is reacting."

The blackened wound had turned flesh-colored again and was sealing. Soon there was a line of white scar tissue. Then even that was gone, leaving firm pink flesh beneath.

"Pretty good, huh?" Fred gloated, with a slight touch of hysteria. "It works, Professor, it works! Drink one yourself, pal, live another sixty years. Do you suppose we can synthesize this stuff? Worth a million, worth ten million, worth a billion. And if we can't, there's always good old Loray. We can drop back every fifty years or so for a refill. The stuff even tastes good, Professor. Tastes like—what's wrong?"

Professor Carver was staring at Fred, his eyes wide with astonishment.

"What's the matter?" Fred asked, grinning. "Ain't my seams straight? What you staring at?"

Carver didn't answer. His mouth trembled. Slowly he backed away.

"What the hell is wrong!" Fred glared at Carver. Then he ran to the spaceship's head and looked in the mirror.

"What's happened to me?"

Carver tried to speak, but no words came. He watched as Fred's features slowly altered, smoothed, became blank, rudimentary, as though nature had drawn there a preliminary sketch of intelligent life. Strange knobs were coming out on Fred's head. His complexion was changing slowly from pink to gray.

"I told you to wait," Carver sighed.

"What's happening?" asked Fred in a frightened whimper.

"Well," Carver said, "it must all be residual in the sersee. The Lorayan birth-rate is practically non-existent, you know. Even with the sersee's healing powers, the race should have died out long ago. Unless the serum had another purpose as well—the ability to change lower animal forms into the Lorayan form."

"That's a wild guess!"

"A working hypothesis based upon Deg's statement that sersee is the mother of the Lorayan people. I'm afraid that is the true meaning of the beast cults and the reason they are taboo. The various beasts must be the origins of certain portions of the Lorayan people, perhaps all the Lorayan people. Even the topic is taboo; there clearly is a deep-seated sense of inferiority about their recent step up from bestiality."

Carver rubbed his forehead wearily. "The sersee juice has," he continued, "we may hazard, a role-sharing in terms of the life of the race. We may theorize—"

"To hell with theory," Fred said, and was horrified to find that his voice had grown thick and guttural, like a Lorayan voice. "Professor, do something!"

"There's nothing I can do."

"Maybe Terran science—"

"No, Fred," Carver said quietly.

"What?"

"Fred, please try to understand. I can't bring you back to earth."

"What do you mean? You must be crazy!"

"Not at all. How can I bring you back with such a fantastic story? They would consider the whole thing a gigantic hoax."

"But—"

"Listen to me. No one would believe! They would consider, rather, that you were an unusually intelligent Lorayan. Your very presence, Fred, would undermine the whole thesis of my book!"

"You can't leave me," Fred said. "You just can't do that."

Professor Carver still had both revolvers. He stuck one in his belt and leveled the other.

"I am not going to endanger the work of a lifetime. Get out, Fred."

"No!"

"I mean it. Get out, Fred."

"I won't! You'll have to shoot me!"

"I will if I must," Carver assured him. "I'll shoot you and throw you out."

He took aim. Fred backed to the port, undogged it, opened it. The villagers were waiting quietly outside.

"What will they do to me?"

"I'm really sorry, Fred," Carver said.

"I won't go!" Fred shrieked, gripping the edges of the port with both hands.

Carver shoved him into the waiting hands of the crowd and threw the remaining tubes of sersee after him. Then, quickly, not wishing to see what was going to happen, he sealed the port.

Within an hour, he was leaving the planet's atmospheric limits.

When he returned to Earth, his book, *Underlying Causes of the Implicit Inferiority of Non-Terran Peoples,* was hailed as a milestone in comparative anthropology. But he ran into some difficulty almost at once.

A space captain named Jones returned to Earth and maintained that, on the planet Loray, he had discovered a native who was in every significant way the equal of a Terran. And he had tape recordings and motion pictures to prove it.

Carver's thesis seemed in doubt for some time, until Carver examined the evidence for himself. Then he pointed out, with merciless logic, that the so-called super-Lorayan, this paragon of Loray, this supposed equal of Terran humanity, occupied the lowest position in the Lorayan hierarchy, the position of Sweeper, clearly shown by the broad black stripe across his face.

The space captain admitted that this was true.

Why then, Carver thundered, was this Lorayan Superior not able, in spite of his so-called abilities, to reach any higher position in the debased society in which he dwelt?

The question silenced the space captain and his supporters, demolished the entire school, as a matter of fact. And the Carverian Doctrine of the Implicit Inferiority of Non-Terrans is now accepted by reasoning Terrans everywhere in the Galaxy.

TRIPLICATION

Oaxe II was a small, dusty, backward planet out near Orion. Its people were of Earth stock, and still adhered to Earth customs. Judge Abner Low was the sole source of justice upon the little planet. Most of his cases involved property lines and the ownership of pigs and geese, for the citizens of Oaxe II had little flair for crime.

But one day a spaceship landed containing the notorious Timothy Mont and his lawyer, who had come to Oaxe II for sanctuary and justice. And another spaceship came, containing three policemen and a Public Prosecutor.

The Public Prosecutor stated, "Your Honor, this fiend has perpetrated a heinous crime. Timothy Mont, Your Honor, *burned down an orphanage!* Furthermore, he pleaded before he fled. I have his signed confession."

Mont's lawyer, a pallid man with cold fish eyes, rose. "I request that you put aside sentence."

"I'll do no such thing," Judge Low said. "Burning an orphanage is a horrible crime."

"It is," the lawyer agreed, "in most places. But my client committed his act upon the planet Altira III. Is your Honor conversant with the customs of that planet?"

"No," said the judge.

"On Altira III," the lawyer said, "all orphans are trained in the art of assassination, for the purpose of reducing the population of neighboring planets. By burning the orphanage, my client saved thousands, perhaps millions of innocent lives. Therefore he must be considered a hero of the people."

"Is this true about Altira III?" the judge asked the court clerk.

The clerk looked up the facts in the Encyclopedia of Planetary Customs and Folklore, and found that it was indeed true.

Judge Low said, "Then I dismiss this case."

Mont and his lawyer left, and life droned peacefully on, on Oaxe II, disturbed only by an occasional lawsuit involving property lines, or the ownership of pigs and geese. But within a year Timothy Mont and his lawyer were back in court, with the Public Prosecutor following close behind them.

The charge again concerned the burning of an orphanage.

"However," the pale lawyer pointed out, "guilty though my client is, the court must remember that the orphanage in question was on the planet Deegra IV. As is well known, all orphans on Deegra IV are adopted into the torturer's guild, for the performance of certain abominable rites abhorred in all the civilized galaxy."

Finding this to be true, Judge Low again dismissed the case.

In 15 months, Timothy Mont and his lawyer were again in court, to stand trial on the same charge.

"Dear, dear," Judge Low said. "A reformer's zeal... Where did the crime take place?"

"On Earth," stated the Public Prosecutor.

"On *Earth?*" said the judge.

"I fear it is true," the lawyer said sadly. "My client is guilty."

"But what possible reason did he have this time?"

"Temporary insanity," the lawyer said promptly. "And I have 12 psychiatrists to prove it, and request a suspended sentence as provided under law for such circumstances."

The judge turned purple with wrath. "Timothy Mont, why did you do this?"

Before his lawyer could silence him, Mont stood up and said, "Because I *like* to burn orphanages!"

That day Judge Low passed a new law, one which has been noted throughout the civilized galaxy, and studied in such diversified places as Droma I and Aos X. Low's Law states that the defendant's lawyer shall serve concurrently whatever sentence is imposed upon his client.

Many consider this unfair. But the incidence of lawyers on Oaxe II has diminished remarkably.

Edmond Dritche, a tall, sallow, misanthropic scientist, had been brought to trial by the General Products Corporation for Downbeatedness, Group Disloyalty, and Negativism. These were serious charges, and they were substantiated by Dritche's colleagues. The magistrate had no choice but to discharge Dritche dishonorably. The usual jail sentence was waived in recognition of his 19 years of excellent work for General Products; but no other corporation would ever hire him.

Dritche, sallower and more misanthropic than ever, turned his back on General Products and its endless stream of automobiles, toasters, refrigerators, TV sets, and the like. He retired to his Pennsylvania farm and experimented in his basement laboratory.

He was sick of General Products and all it stood for, which was practically everything. He wanted to found a colony of people who thought as he did, felt as he did, looked like he did. His colony would be a utopia, and to hell with the rest of the cheerful, gadget-ridden world.

There was only one way to achieve this. Dritche and his wife Anna toiled night and day toward the great goal.

At last he met with success. He adjusted the unwieldy device he had built and turned the switch.

From the device stepped an exact Duplicate of Edmond Dritche.

Dritche had invented the world's first Duplicator.

He produced five hundred Dritches, then held a policy meeting. The five hundred pointed out that, for a successful colony, they needed wives.

Dritche 1 considered his own Anna a perfect mate. The five hundred Duplicates agreed, of course. So Dritche produced five hundred exact copies of her for the five hundred prototype Dritches, and the colony was founded.

Contrary to popular prediction, the Dritche colony did well at first. The Dritches enjoyed each other's company, never quarreled, and never wished for visitors. They comprised a satisfied little world in themselves. India sent a delegation to study their method, and Denmark wrote laws to ensure Duplication rights.

But, as in all other utopian attempts, the seeds of disaster were present in simple human frailty. First, Dritche 49 was caught in a compromising position with Mrs. Dritche 5. Then Dritche 37 fell suddenly and passionately in love with Anna 142. This in turn led to the uncovering of the secret love nest built by Dritche 10 for Anna 498, with the connivance of Anna 3.

In vain Dritche 1 pointed out that all were equal and identical. The erring couples told him he knew nothing about love, and refused to give up their new arrangements.

The colony might still have survived. But then it was found that Dritche 77 was maintaining a harem of eight Dritche women, Annas 12, 13, 77, 187, 303, 336, 489 and 500. These women declared him absolutely unique, and refused to leave him.

The end was in sight. It was hastened when Dritche 1's wife ran away with a reporter.

The colony disbanded, and Dritches 1, 19, 32 and 433 died of broken hearts.

It was probably just as well. Certainly the original Dritche could never have stood the shock of seeing his utopian Duplicator used to turn out endless streams of General Products automobiles, toasters, refrigerators, and the like.

Professor Bolton, the noted philosopher, left Earth to deliver a series of lectures at Mars University. He took his trusted robot valet Akka, a change of underwear, and eight pounds of notes. Aside from the crew, he was the only human passenger.

Somewhere near the Point of No Return, the ship sent out an emergency message: STARBOARD JETS BLOWING SHIP OUT OF CONTROL.

The citizens of Earth and Mars waited anxiously. Another message came: ENTIRE CREW KILLED BY FLASHBACK SHIP CRASHING IN ASTEROID BELT HELP BOLTON.

Rescue ships swept toward the area between Mars and Jupiter where the asteroids are strewn. They had a hazy fix from Bolton's last message; but the area to be searched was tremendous, and the chance of rescue was very small.

Three days later, this message was received: CANNOT SURVIVE MUCH LONGER ON ASTEROID I FACE DEATH WITH SERENE DIGNITY BOLTON.

Newspapers spoke of the indomitable spirit of this man, a modern-day Robinson Crusoe, struggling for life on an airless, foodless, waterless world, his supplies running low, ready—as he had taught in his books and lectures—to meet death with serene dignity.

The search was intensified.

The last message read: ALL SUPPLIES GONE SMILING DEATH AWAITS ME BOLTON.

Homing in on his final signal, a patrol boat located the asteroid and landed beside the gutted ship. They found the charred remains of the crew. And they found ample supplies of food, water and oxygen. But strangely, there was no sign of Bolton.

In the very rear of the ship they found Bolton's robot.

"The professor is dead," the robot said through rusted jaws. "I sent the last messages in his name, knowing you wouldn't come just for me."

"But how did he die?"

"With the greatest regret I killed him," the robot said grimly. "I can assure you that his death was painless."

"But *why* did you kill him? And where is his body?"

The robot tried to speak, but his corroded jaws refused to function. A squirt of oil brought him around.

"Lubrication," Akka said, "is a robot's greatest problem. Gentlemen, have you ever considered the problem of rendering a human body into its essential fats and oils without adequate equipment?"

The rescuers considered it with mounting horror, and the story was suppressed. But it was heard by the patrol ship's robot, who pondered it and passed it on to another robot, and then another.

Only now, since the triumphant revolt of the robot forces, can this inspiring saga of a robot's fight against space be openly told. Hail, Akka, our liberator!

The Store of the Worlds

Mr. Wayne came to the end of the long, shoulder-high mound of gray rubble, and there was the Store of the Worlds. It was exactly as his friends had described; a small shack constructed of bits of lumber, parts of cars, a piece of galvanized iron and a few rows of crumbling bricks, all daubed over with a watery blue paint.

Mr. Wayne glanced back down the long lane of rubble to make sure he hadn't been followed. He tucked his parcel more firmly under his arm; then, with a little shiver at his own audacity, he opened the door and slipped inside.

"Good morning," the proprietor said.

He, too, was exactly as described; a tall, crafty-looking old fellow with narrow eyes and a downcast mouth. His name was Tompkins. He sat in an old rocking chair, and perched on the back of it was a blue and green parrot. There was one other chair in the store, and a table. On the table was a rusted hypodermic.

"I've heard about your store from friends," Mr. Wayne said.

"Then you know my price," Tompkins said. "Have you brought it?"

"Yes," said Mr. Wayne, holding up his parcel. "But I want to ask first—"

"They always want to ask," Tompkins said to the parrot, who blinked. "Go ahead, ask."

"I want to know what really happens."

Tompkins sighed. "What happens is this. You pay me my fee. I give you an injection which knocks you out. Then, with the aid of certain gadgets which I have in the back of the store, I liberate your mind."

Tompkins smiled as he said that, and his silent parrot seemed to smile, too.

"What happens then?" Mr. Wayne asked.

"Your mind, liberated from its body, is able to choose from the countless probability-worlds which the Earth casts off in every second of its existence."

Grinning now, Tompkins sat up in his rocking chair and began to show signs of enthusiasm.

"Yes, my friend, though you might not have suspected it, from the moment this battered Earth was born out of the sun's fiery womb, it cast

505

off its alternate-probability worlds. Worlds without end, emanating from events large and small; every Alexander and every amoeba creating worlds, just as ripples will spread in a pond no matter how big or how small the stone you throw. Doesn't every object cast a shadow? Well, my friend, the Earth itself is four-dimensional; therefore it casts three-dimensional shadows, solid reflections of itself through every moment of its being. Millions, billions of Earths! An infinity of Earths! And your mind, liberated by me, will be able to select any of these worlds, and to live upon it for a while."

Mr. Wayne was uncomfortably aware that Tompkins sounded like a circus barker, proclaiming marvels that simply couldn't exist. But, Mr. Wayne reminded himself, things had happened within his own lifetime which he would never have believed possible. Never! So perhaps the wonders that Tompkins spoke of were possible, too.

Mr. Wayne said, "My friends also told me—"

"That I was an out-and-out fraud?" Tompkins asked.

"Some of them *implied* that," Mr. Wayne said cautiously. "But I try to keep an open mind. They also said—"

"I know what your dirty-minded friends said. They told you about the fulfillment of desire. Is that what you want to hear about?"

"Yes," said Mr. Wayne. "They told me that whatever I wished for— whatever I wanted—"

"Exactly," Tompkins said. "The thing could work in no other way. There are the infinite worlds to choose among. Your mind chooses, and is guided only by desire. Your deepest desire is the only thing that counts. If you have been harboring a secret dream of murder—"

"Oh hardly, hardly!" cried Mr. Wayne.

"—then you will go to a world where you *can* murder, where you can roll in blood, where you can outdo Sade or Caesar, or whoever your idol may be. Suppose it's power you want? Then you'll choose a world where you are a god, literally and actually. A bloodthirsty Juggernaut, perhaps, or an all-wise Buddha."

"I doubt very much if I—"

"There are other desires, too," Tompkins said. "All heavens and all hells. Unbridled sexuality. Gluttony, drunkenness, love, fame—anything you want."

"Amazing!" said Mr. Wayne.

"Yes," Tompkins agreed. "Of course, my little list doesn't exhaust all the possibilities, all the combinations and permutations of desire. For all I know you might want a simple, placid, pastoral existence on a South Seas island among idealized natives!"

"That sounds more like me," Mr. Wayne said, with a shy laugh.

"But who knows?" Tompkins asked. "Even you might not know what your true desires are. They might involve your own death."

"Does that happen often?" Mr. Wayne asked anxiously.

"Occasionally."

"I wouldn't want to die," Mr. Wayne said.

"It hardly ever happens," Tompkins said, looking at the parcel in Mr. Wayne's hands.

"If you say so…But how do I know all this is real? Your fee is extremely high, it'll take everything I own. And for all I know, you'll give me a drug and I'll just *dream!* Everything I own just for a—a shot of heroin and a lot of fancy words!"

Tompkins smiled reassuringly. "The experience has no drug-like quality about it. And no sensation of a dream, either."

"If it's *true,*" Mr. Wayne said, a little petulantly, "why can't I stay in the world of my desire for good?"

"I'm working on that," Tompkins said. "That's why I charge so high a fee; to get materials, to experiment. I'm trying to find a way of making the transition permanent. So far I haven't been able to loosen the cord that binds a man to his own Earth—and pulls him back to it. Not even the great mystics could cut that cord, except with death. But I still have my hopes."

"It would be a great thing if you succeeded," Mr. Wayne said politely.

"Yes it would!" Tompkins cried, with a surprising burst of passion. "For then I'd turn my wretched shop into an escape hatch! My process would be free then, free for everyone! Everyone would go to the Earth of their desires, the Earth that really suited them, and leave *this* damned place to the rats and worms—"

Tompkins cut himself off in mid-sentence, and became icy calm. "But I fear my prejudices are showing. I can't offer a permanent escape from the Earth yet; not one that doesn't involve death. Perhaps I never will be able to. For now, all I can offer you is a vacation, a change, a taste of another world and a look at your own desires. You know my fee. I'll refund it if the experience isn't satisfactory."

"That's good of you," Mr. Wayne said, quite earnestly. "But there's that other matter my friends told me about. The ten years off my life."

"That can't be helped," Tompkins said, "and can't be refunded. My process is a tremendous strain on the nervous system, and life-expectancy is shortened accordingly. That's one of the reasons why our so-called government has declared my process illegal."

"But they don't enforce the ban very firmly," Mr. Wayne said.

"No. Officially the process is banned as a harmful fraud. But officials are men, too. They'd like to leave this Earth, just like everyone else."

"The cost," Mr. Wayne mused, gripping his parcel tightly. "And ten years off my life! For the fulfillment of my secret desires…Really, I must give this some thought."

"Think away," Tompkins said indifferently.

All the way home Mr. Wayne thought about it. When his train reached Port Washington, Long Island, he was still thinking. And driving his car from the station to his home he was still thinking about Tompkins' crafty old face, and worlds of probability, and the fulfillment of desire.

But when he stepped inside his house, those thoughts had to stop. Janet, his wife, wanted him to speak sharply to the maid, who had been drinking again. His son Tommy wanted help with the sloop, which was to be launched tomorrow. And his baby daughter wanted to tell about her day in kindergarten.

Mr. Wayne spoke pleasantly but firmly to the maid. He helped Tommy put the final coat of copper paint on the sloop's bottom, and he listened to Peggy tell about her adventures in the playground.

Later, when the children were in bed and he and Janet were alone in their living room, she asked him if something were wrong.

"Wrong?"

"You seem to be worried about something," Janet said. "Did you have a bad day at the office?"

"Oh, just the usual sort of thing…"

He certainly was not going to tell Janet, or anyone else, that he had taken the day off and gone to see Tompkins in his crazy old Store of the Worlds. Nor was he going to speak about the right every man should have, once in his lifetime, to fulfill his most secret desires. Janet, with her good common sense, would never understand that.

The next days at the office were extremely hectic. All of Wall Street was in a mild panic over events in the Middle East and in Asia, and stocks were reacting accordingly. Mr. Wayne settled down to work. He tried not to think of the fulfillment of desire at the cost of everything he possessed, with ten years of his life thrown in for good measure. It was crazy! Old Tompkins must be insane!

On weekends he went sailing with Tommy. The old sloop was behaving very well, making practically no water through her bottom seams. Tommy wanted a new suit of racing sails, but Mr. Wayne sternly rejected that. Perhaps next year, if the market looked better. For now, the old sails would have to do.

Sometimes at night, after the children were asleep, he and Janet would go sailing. Long Island Sound was quiet then, and cool. Their boat glided past the blinking buoys, sailing toward the swollen yellow moon.

"I *know* something's on your mind," Janet said.

"Darling, please!"

"Is there something you're keeping from me?"

"Nothing!"

"Are you sure? Are you absolutely sure?"

"Absolutely sure."

"Then put your arms around me. That's right..."
And the sloop sailed itself for a while.

Desire and fulfillment...But autumn came, and the sloop had to be hauled. The stock market regained some stability, but Peggy caught the measles. Tommy wanted to know the differences between ordinary bombs, atom bombs, hydrogen bombs, cobalt bombs, and all the other kinds of bombs that were in the news. Mr. Wayne explained to the best of his ability. And the maid quit unexpectedly.

Secret desires were all very well. Perhaps he *did* want to kill someone, or live on a South Seas island. But there were responsibilities to consider. He had two growing children, and a better wife than he deserved.

Perhaps around Christmas time...

But in mid-winter there was a fire in the unoccupied guest bedroom due to defective wiring. The firemen put out the blaze without much damage, and no one was hurt. But it put any thought of Tompkins out of his mind for a while. First the bedroom had to be repaired, for Mr. Wayne was very proud of his gracious old house.

Business was still frantic and uncertain due to the international situation. Those Russians, those Arabs, those Greeks, those Chinese. The intercontinental missiles, the atom bombs, the sputniks...Mr. Wayne spent long days at the office, and sometimes evenings, too. Tommy caught the mumps. A part of the roof had to be re-shingled. And then already it was time to consider the spring launching of the sloop.

A year had passed, and he'd had very little time to think of secret desires. But perhaps next year. In the meantime—

"Well?" said Tompkins. "Are you all right?"

"Yes, quite all right," Mr. Wayne said. He got up from the chair and rubbed his forehead.

"Do you want a refund?" Tompkins asked.

"No. The experience was quite satisfactory."

"They always are," Tompkins said, winking lewdly at the parrot. "Well, what was yours?"

"A world of the recent past," Mr. Wayne said.

"A lot of them are. Did you find out about your secret desire? Was it murder? Or a South Seas island?"

"I'd rather not discuss it," Mr. Wayne said, pleasantly but firmly.

"A lot of people won't discuss it with me," Tompkins said sulkily. "I'll be damned if I know why."

"Because—well, I think the world of one's secret desire feels sacred, somehow. No offense...Do you think you'll ever be able to make it permanent? The world of one's choice, I mean?"

The old man shrugged his shoulders. "I'm trying. If I succeed, you'll hear about it. Everyone will."

"Yes, I suppose so." Mr. Wayne undid his parcel and laid its contents on the table. The parcel contained a pair of army boots, a knife, two coils of copper wire, and three small cans of corned beef.

Tompkins' eyes glittered for a moment. "Quite satisfactory," he said. "Thank you."

"Goodbye," said Mr. Wayne. "And thank *you.*"

Mr. Wayne left the ship and hurried down to the end of the lane of gray rubble. Beyond it, as far as he could see, lay flat fields of rubble, brown and gray and black. Those fields, stretching to every horizon, were made of the twisted corpses of cities, the shattered remnants of trees, and the fine white ash that once was human flesh and bone.

"Well," Mr. Wayne said to himself, "at least we gave as good as we got."

That year in the past had cost him everything he owned, and ten years of life thrown in for good measure. Had it been a dream? It was still worth it! But now he had to put away all thought of Janet and the children. That was finished, unless Tompkins perfected his process. Now he had to think about his own survival.

With the aid of his wrist geiger he found a deactivated lane through the rubble. He'd better get back to the shelter before dark, before the rats came out. If he didn't hurry he'd miss the evening potato ration.

PROSPECTOR'S SPECIAL

The sandcar moved smoothly over the rolling dunes, its six fat wheels rising and falling like the ponderous rumps of tandem elephants. The hidden sun beat down from a dead-white sky, pouring heat into the canvas top, reflecting heat back from the parched sand.

"Stay awake," Morrison told himself, pulling the sandcar back to its compass course.

It was his twenty-first day on Venus's Scorpion Desert, his twenty-first day of fighting sleep while the sandcar rocked across the dunes, forging over humpbacked little waves. Night travel would have been easier, but there were too many steep ravines to avoid, too many house-sized boulders to dodge. Now he knew why men went into the desert in teams; one man drove while the other kept shaking him awake.

"But it's better alone," Morrison reminded himself. "Half the supplies and no accidental murders."

His head was beginning to droop; he snapped himself erect. In front of him, the landscape shimmered and danced through the polaroid windshield. The sandcar lurched and rocked with treacherous gentleness. Morrison rubbed his eyes and turned on the radio.

He was a big, sunburned, rangy young man with close cropped black hair and gray eyes. He had come to Venus with a grubstake of twenty thousand dollars, to find his fortune in the Scorpion Desert as others had done before him. He had outfitted in Presto, the last town on the edge of the wilderness, and spent all but ten dollars on the sandcar and equipment.

In Presto, ten dollars just covered the cost of a drink in the town's only saloon. So Morrison ordered rye and water, drank with the miners and prospectors, and laughed at the oldtimers' yarns about the sandwolf packs and the squadrons of voracious birds that inhabited the interior desert. He knew all about sunblindness, heatstroke and telephone breakdown. He was sure none of it would happen to him.

511

But now, after twenty-one days and eighteen hundred miles, he had learned respect for this waterless waste of sand and stone three times the area of the Sahara. You really *could* die here!

But you could also get rich, and that was what Morrison planned to do.

His radio hummed. At full volume, he could hear the faintest murmur of dance music from Venusborg. Then it faded and only the hum was left.

He turned off the radio and gripped the steering wheel tightly in both hands. He unclenched one hand and looked at his watch. Nine-fifteen in the morning. At ten-thirty he would stop and take a nap. A man had to have rest in this heat. But only a half-hour nap. Treasure lay somewhere ahead of him, and he wanted to find it before his supplies got much lower.

The precious outcroppings of goldenstone *had* to be up ahead! He'd been following traces for two days now. Maybe he would hit a real bonanza, as Kirk did in '89, or Edmonson and Arsler in '93. If so, he would do just what they did. He'd order up a Prospector's Special, and to hell with the cost.

The sandcar rolled along at an even thirty miles an hour, and Morrison tried to concentrate on the heat-blasted yellow-brown landscape. That sandstone patch over there was just the tawny color of Janie's hair.

After he struck it rich, he and Janie would get married; and he'd go back to Earth and buy an ocean farm. No more prospecting. Just one rich strike so he could buy his spread on the deep blue Atlantic. Maybe some people thought fishherding was tame; it was good enough for him.

He could see it now, the mackerel herds drifting along and browsing at the plankton pens, himself and his trusty dolphin keeping an eye out for the silvery flash of a predatory barracuda or a steel-gray shark coming along behind the branching coral...

Morrison felt the sandcar lurch. He woke up, grabbed the steering wheel and turned it hard. During his moments of sleep, the vehicle had crept over the dune's crumbling edge. Sand and pebbles spun under the fat tires as the sandcar fought for traction. The car tilted perilously. The tires shrieked against the sand, gripped, and started to pull the vehicle back up the slope.

Then the whole face of the dune collapsed.

Morrison held onto the steering wheel as the sandcar flipped over on its side and rolled down the slope. Sand filled his mouth and eyes. He spat and held on while the car rolled over again and dropped into emptiness.

For seconds, he was in the air. The sandcar hit bottom squarely on its wheels. Morrison heard a double boom as the two rear tires blew out. Then his head hit the windshield.

When he recovered consciousness, the first thing he did was look at his watch. It read 10:35.

"Time for that nap," Morrison said to himself. "But I guess I'll survey the situation first."

He found that he was at the bottom of a shallow fault strewn with knife-edged pebbles. Two tires had blown on impact, his windshield was gone, and one of the doors was sprung. His equipment was strewn around, but appeared to be intact.

"Could have been worse," Morrison said.

He bent down to examine the tires more carefully.

"It *is* worse," he said.

The two blown tires were shredded beyond repair. There wasn't enough rubber left in them to make a child's balloon. He had used up his spares ten days back crossing Devil's Grill. Used them and discarded them. He couldn't go on without tires.

Morrison unpacked his telephone. He wiped dust from its black plastic face, then dialed Al's Garage in Presto. After a moment, the small video screen lighted up. He could see a man's long, mournful, grease-stained face.

"Al's Garage. Eddie speaking."

"Hi, Eddie. This is Tom Morrison. I bought that GM sandcar from you about a month ago. Remember?"

"Sure I remember you," Eddie said. "You're the guy doing a single into the Southwest Track. How's the bus holding out?"

Fine. Great little car. Reason I called—"

"Hey," Eddie said, "what happened to your face?"

Morrison put his hand to his forehead and felt blood. "Nothing much," he said. "I went over a dune and blew out two tires."

He turned the telephone so that Eddie could see the tires.

"Unrepairable," said Eddie.

"I thought so. And I used up all my spares crossing Devil's Grill. Look, Eddie, I'd like you to 'port me a couple of tires. Retreads are fine. I can't move the sandcar without them."

"Sure," Eddie said, "except I haven't any retreads. I'll have to 'port you new ones at five hundred apiece. Plus four hundred dollars 'porting charges. Fourteen hundred dollars, Mr. Morrison."

"All right."

"Yes, sir. Now if you'll show me the cash, or a money order which you can send back with the receipt, I'll get moving on it."

"At the moment," Morrison said, "I haven't got a cent on me."

"Bank account?"

"Stripped clean."

"Bonds? Property? Anything you can convert into cash?"

"Nothing except this sandcar, which you sold me for eight thousand dollars. When I come back, I'll settle my bill with the sandcar."

"*If* you get back. Sorry, Mr. Morrison. No can do."

"What do you mean?" Morrison asked. "You know I'll pay for the tires."

"And you know the rules on Venus," Eddie said, his mournful face set in obstinate lines. "No credit! Cash and carry!"

"I can't run the sandcar without tires," Morrison said. "Are you going to strand me out here?"

"Who in hell is stranding you?" Eddie asked. "This sort of thing happens to prospectors every day. You know what you have to do now, Mr. Morrison. Call Public Utility and declare yourself a bankrupt. Sign over what's left of the sandcar, equipment, and anything you've found on the way. They'll get you out."

"I'm not turning back," Morrision said. "Look!" He held the telephone close to the ground. "You see the traces, Eddie? See those red and purple flecks? There's precious stuff near here!"

"Every prospector sees traces," Eddie said. "Damn desert is full of traces."

"These are rich," Morrison said. "These are leading straight to big stuff, a bonanza lode. Eddie, I know it's a lot to ask, but if you could stake me to a couple of tires—"

"I can't do it," Eddie said. "I just work here. I can't 'port you any tires, not unless you show me money first. Otherwise I get fired and probably jailed. You know the law."

"Cash and Carry," Morrison said bleakly.

"Right. Be smart and turn back now. Maybe you can try again some other time."

"I spent twelve years getting this stake together," Morrison said. "I'm not going back."

He turned off the telephone and tried to think. Was there anyone else on Venus he could call? Only Max Krandall, jewel broker. But Max couldn't raise fourteen hundred dollars in that crummy two-by-four office near Venusborg's jewel market. Max could barely scrape up his own rent, much less take care of stranded prospectors.

"I can't ask Max for help," Morrison decided. "Not until I've found goldenstone. The real stuff, not just traces. So that leaves it up to me."

He opened the back of the sandcar and began to unload, piling his equipment on the sand. He would have to choose carefully; anything he took would have to be carried on his back.

The telephone had to go with him, and his lightweight testing kit. Food concentrates, revolver, compass. And nothing else but water, all the water he could carry. The rest of the stuff would have to stay behind.

By nightfall, Morrison was ready. He looked regretfully at the twenty cans of water he was leaving. In the desert, water was a man's most precious possession, second only to his telephone. But it couldn't be helped. After drinking his fill, he hoisted his pack and set a southwest course into the desert.

For three days he trekked to the southwest; then on the fourth day he veered to due south, following an increasingly rich trace. The sun, eternally hidden, beat down on him, and the dead-white sky was like a roof of heated iron over his head. Morrison followed the traces, and something followed him.

On the sixth day, he sensed movement just out of the range of his vision. On the seventh day, he saw what was trailing him.

Venus's own brand of wolf, small, lean, with a yellow coat and long, grinning jaws, it was one of the few mammals that made its home in the Scorpion Desert. As Morrison watched, two more sandwolves appeared beside it.

He loosened the revolver in its holster. The wolves made no attempt to come closer. They had plenty of time.

Morrison kept on going, wishing he had brought a rifle with him. But that would have meant eight pounds more, which meant eight pounds less water.

As he was pitching camp at dusk the eighth day, he heard a crackling sound. He whirled around and located its source, about ten feet to his left and above his head. A little vortex had appeared, a tiny mouth in the air like a whirlpool in the sea. It spun, making the characteristic crackling sounds of 'porting.

"Now who could be 'porting anything to me?" Morrison asked, waiting while the whirlpool slowly widened.

Solidoporting from a base projector to a field target was a standard means of moving goods across the vast distances of Venus. Any inanimate object could be 'ported; animate beings couldn't because the process involved certain minor but distressing molecular changes in protoplasm. A few people had found this out the hard way when 'porting was first introduced.

Morrison waited. The aerial whirlpool became a mouth three feet in diameter. From the mouth stepped a chromeplated robot carrying a large sack.

"Oh, it's you," Morrison said.

"Yes, sir," the robot said, now completely clear of the field. "Williams 4 at your service with the Venus Mail."

It was a robot of medium height, thin-shanked and flatfooted, humanoid in appearance, amiable in disposition. For twenty-three years it had been Venus's entire postal service—sorter, deliverer, and dead storage. It had been built to last, and for twenty-three years the mails had always come through.

"Here we are, Mr. Morrison," Williams 4 said. "Only twice-a-month mail call in the desert, I'm sorry to say, but it comes promptly and that's a blessing. This is for you. And this. I think there's one more. Sandcar broke down, eh?"

"It sure did," Morrison said, taking his letters.

Williams 4 went on rummaging through its bag. Although it was a superbly efficient postman, the old robot was known as the worst gossip on three planets.

"There's one more in here somewhere," Williams 4 said. "Too bad about the sandcar. They just don't build 'em like they did in my youth. Take my advice, young man. Turn back if you still have the chance."

Morrison shook his head.

"Foolish, downright foolish," the old robot said. "Pity you don't have my perspective. Too many's the time I've come across you boys lying in the sand in the dried-out sack of your skin, or with your bones gnawed to splinters by the sandwolves and the filthy black kites. Twenty-three years I've been delivering mail to fine-looking young men like you, and each one thinking he's unique and different."

The robot's eyecells became distant with memory. "But they *aren't* different," Williams 4 said. "They're as alike as robots off the assembly line—especially after the wolves get through with them. And then I have to send their letters and personal effects back to their loved ones on Earth."

"I know," Morrison said. "But some get through, don't they?"

"Sure they do," the robot said. "I've seen men make one, two, three fortunes. And then die on the sands trying to make a fourth."

"Not me," Morrison said. "I just want one. Then I'm going to buy me an undersea farm on Earth."

The robot shuddered. "I have a dread of salt water. But to each his own. Good luck, young man."

The robot looked Morrison over carefully—probably to see what he had in the way of personal effects—then climbed back into the aerial whirlpool. In a moment, it was gone. In another moment, the whirlpool had vanished.

Morrison sat down to read his mail. The first letter was from his jewel broker, Max Krandall. It told about the depression that had hit Venusborg, and hinted that Krandall might have to go into bankruptcy if some of his prospectors didn't strike something good.

The second letter was a statement from the Venus Telephone Company. Morrison owed two hundred and ten dollars and eight cents for two months' telephone service. Unless he remitted this sum at once, his telephone was liable to be turned off.

The last letter, all the way from Earth, was from Janie. It was filled with news about his cousins, aunts, and uncles. She told him about the Atlantic farm sites she had looked over, and the wonderful little place she had found near Martinique in the Caribbean. She begged him to give up prospecting if it looked dangerous; they could find another way of financing the farm. She sent all her love and wished him a happy birthday in advance.

"Birthday?" Morrison asked himself. "Let's see, today is July twenty-third. No, it's the twenty-fourth, and my birthday's August first. Thanks for remembering, Janie."

That night he dreamed of Earth and the blue expanse of the Atlantic Ocean. But toward dawn, when the heat of Venus became insistent, he found he was dreaming of mile upon mile of goldenstone, of grinning sandwolves, and the Prospector's Special.

Rock gave way to sand as Morrison plowed his way across the bottom of a long-vanished lake. Then it was rock again, twisted and tortured into a thousand gaunt shapes. Reds, yellows, and browns swam in front of his eyes. In all that desert, there wasn't one patch of green.

He continued his trek into the tumbled stone mazes of the interior desert, and the wolves trekked with him, keeping pace far out on either flank.

Morrison ignored them. He had enough on his mind just to negotiate the sheer cliffs and the fields of broken stone that blocked his way to the south.

By the eleventh day after leaving the sandcar, the traces were almost rich enough for panning. The sandwolves were tracking him still, and his water was almost gone. Another day's march would finish him.

Morrison thought for a moment, then unstrapped his telephone and dialed Public Utility in Venusborg.

The video screen showed a stern, severely dressed woman with iron-gray hair. "Public Utility," she said. "May we be of service?"

"Hi," Morrison said cheerfully. "How's the weather in Venusborg?"

"Hot," the woman said. "How's it out there?"

"I hadn't even noticed," Morrison said, grinning. "Too busy counting my fortune."

"You've found goldenstone?" the woman asked, her expression becoming less severe.

"Sure have," Morrison said. "But don't pass the word around yet. I'm still staking my claim. I think I can use a refill on these."

Smiling easily, he held up his canteens. Sometimes it worked. Sometimes, if you showed enough confidence, Public Utility would fill you up without checking your account. True, it was embezzling, but this was no time for niceties.

"I suppose your account is in order?" asked the woman.

"Of course," Morrison said, feeling his smile grow stiff. "The name's Tom Morrison. You can check—"

"Oh, I don't do that personally," the woman said. "Hold that canteen steady. Here we go."

Gripping the canteen in both hands, Morrison watched as the water 'ported four thousand miles from Venusborg, appeared as a slender crystal stream above the mouth of his canteen. The stream entered the canteen, making a wonderful gurgling sound. Watching it, Morrison found his dry mouth actually was beginning to salivate.

Then the water stopped.

"What's the matter?" Morrison asked.

His video screen went blank. Then it cleared, and Morrison found himself staring into a man's narrow face. The man was seated in front of a large desk. The sign in front of him read *Milton P. Reade, Vice President, Accounts.*

"Mr. Morrison," Read said, "your account is overdrawn. You have been obtaining water under false pretenses. That is a criminal offense."

"I'm going to pay for the water," Morrison said.

"When?"

"As soon as I get back to Venusborg."

"With what," asked Mr. Reade, "do you propose to pay?"

"With goldenstone," Morrison said. "Look around here, Mr. Reade. The traces are rich! Richer than they were for the Kirk claim! I'll be hitting the outcroppings in another day—"

"That's what every prospector thinks," Mr. Reade said. "Every prospector on Venus is only a day from goldenstone. And they all expect credit from Public Utility."

"But in this case—"

"Public Utility," Mr. Reade continued inexorably, "Is not a philanthropic organization. Its charter specifically forbids the extension of credit. Venus is a frontier, Mr. Morrison, a *farflung* frontier. Every manufactured article on Venus must be imported from Earth at outrageous cost. We do have our own water, but locating it, purifying it, then 'porting it is an expensive process. This company, like every other company on Venus, necessarily operates on a very narrow margin of profit, which is invariably plowed back into further expansion. That is why there can be no credit on Venus."

"I know all that," Morrison said. "But I'm telling you, I only need a day or two more—"

"Absolutely impossible. By the rules, we shouldn't even help you out now. The time to report bankruptcy was a week ago, when your sandcar broke down. Your garage man reported, as required by law. But you didn't. We would be within our rights to leave you stranded. Do you understand that?"

"Yes, of course," Morrison said wearily.

"However, the company has decided to stretch a point in your favor. If you turn back immediately, we will keep you supplied with water for the return trip."

"I'm not turning back yet. I'm almost on the real stuff."

"You must turn back! Be reasonable, Morrison! Where would we be if we let every prospector wander over the desert while we supplied his water? There'd be ten thousand men out there, and we'd be out of business inside of a year. I'm stretching the rules now. Turn back."

"No," said Morrison.

"You'd better think about it. If you don't turn back now, Public Utility takes no further responsibility for your water supply."

Morrison nodded. If he went on, he would stand a good chance of dying in the desert. But if he turned back, what then? He would be in Venusborg, penniless and in debt, looking for work in an overcrowded city. He'd sleep in a community shed and eat at a soup kitchen with the other prospectors who had turned back. And how would he be able to raise the fare back to Earth? When would he ever see Janie again?

"I guess I'll keep on going," Morrison said.

"Then Public Utility takes no further responsibility for you," Reade repeated, and hung up.

Morrison packed up his telephone, took a sip from his meager water supply, and went on.

The sandwolves loped along at each side, moving in closer. Overhead, a delta-winged kite found him. It balanced on the updrafts for a day and a night, waiting for the wolves to finish him. Then a flock of small flying scorpions sighted the waiting kite. They drove the big creature upstairs into the cloud bank. For a day the flying reptiles waited. Then they in turn were driven off by a squadron of black kites.

The traces were very rich now, on the fifteenth day since he had left the sandcar. By rights, he should be walking over goldenstone. He should be surrounded by goldenstone. But still he hadn't found any.

Morrison sat down and shook his last canteen. It gave off no wet sound. He uncapped it and turned it up over his mouth. Two drops trickled down his parched throat.

It was about four days since he had talked to Public Utility. He must have used up the last of his water yesterday. Or had it been the day before?

He recapped the empty canteen and looked around at the heat-blasted landscape. Abruptly he pulled the telephone out of his pack and dialed Max Krandall in Venusborg.

Krandall's round, worried face swam into focus on the screen. "Tommy," he said, "you look like hell."

"I'm all right," Morrison said. "A little dried out, that's all. Max, I'm near goldenstone."

"Are you sure?" Krandall asked.

"See for yourself," Morrison said, swinging the telephone around. "Look at the stone formations! Do you see the red and purple markings over there?"

"Traces, all right," Krandall admitted dubiously.

"There's rich stuff just beyond it," Morrison said. "There has to be! Look, Max, I know you're short on money, but I'm going to ask you a favor. Send me a pint of water. Just a pint, so I can go on for another day or two. We can both get rich for the price of a pint of water."

"I can't do it," Krandall said sadly.

"You can't?"

"That's right. Tommy, I'd send you water even if there wasn't anything around you but sandstone and granite. Do you think I'd let you die of thirst if I could help it? But I can't do a thing. Take a look."

Krandall rotated his telephone. Morrison saw that the chairs, table, desk, filing cabinet and safe were gone from the office. All that was left in the room was the telephone. "I don't know why they haven't taken out the phone," Krandall said. "I owe two months on my bill."

"I do too," said Morrison.

"I'm stripped," Krandall said. "I haven't got a dime. Don't get me wrong, I'm not worried about myself. I can always eat at a soup kitchen, But I can't 'port you any water. Not you or Remstaater."

"Jim Remstaater?"

"Yeah. He was following a trace up north past Forgotten River. His sandcar broke an axle last week and he wouldn't turn back. His water ran out yesterday."

"I'd bail him out if I could," said Morrison.

"And he'd bail you out if he could," Krandall said. "But he can't and you can't and I can't. Tommy, you have only one hope."

"What's that?"

"Find goldenstone. Not just traces, find the real thing worth real money. Then phone me. If you really have goldenstone, I'll bring in Wilkes from Tri-Planet Mining and get him to advance us some money. He'll probably want fifty per cent of the claim."

"That's plain robbery!"

"No, it's just the high cost of credit on Venus," Krandall answered. "Don't worry, there'll still be plenty left over. But you have to find goldenstone first."

"OK," Morrison said. "It should be around here somewhere. Max, what's today's date?"

"July thirty-first. Why?"

"Just wondering. I'll call you when I've found something." After hanging up, Morrison sat on a little boulder and stared dully at the sand. July thirty-first. Tomorrow was his birthday. His family would be thinking about him, Aunt Bess in Pasadena, the twins in Laos, Uncle Ted in Durango. And Janie, of course, waiting for him in Tampa.

Morrison realized that tomorrow might be his last birthday unless he found goldenstone.

He got to his feet, strapped the telephone back in his pack beside the empty canteens, and set a course to the south.

He wasn't alone. The birds and beasts of the desert marched with him, Overhead, the silent black kites circled endlessly, The sandwolves crept closer on his flanks, their red tongues lolling out, waiting for the carcass to fall...

"I'm not dead yet!" Morrison shouted at them.

He drew his revolver and fired at the nearest wolf. At twenty feet, he missed. He went down on one knee, held the revolver tightly in both hands and fired again. The wolf yelped in pain. The pack immediately went for the wounded animal, and the kites swooped down for their share. Morrison put the revolver back in its bolster and went on.

He could tell he was in a badly dehydrated state. The landscape jumped and danced in front of him, and his footing was unsure. He discarded the empty canteens, threw away everything but the testing kit, telephone and revolver. Either he was coming out of the desert in style or he wasn't coming out at all.

The traces continued to run rich. But still he came upon no sign of tangible wealth.

That evening he found a shallow cave set into the base of a cliff. He crawled inside and built a barricade of rocks across the entrance. Then he drew his revolver and leaned back against the far wall.

The sandwolves were outside, sniffing and snapping their jaws. Morrison propped himself up and got ready for an all night vigil.

He didn't sleep, but he couldn't stay awake, either. Dreams and visions tormented him. He was back on Earth and Janie was saying to him, "It's the tuna. Something must be wrong with their diet. Every last one of them is sick."

"It's the darnedest thing," Morrison told her. "Just as soon as you domesticate a fish, it turns into a prima donna."

"Are you going to stand there philosophizing," Janie asked, "while your fish are sick?"

"Call the vet."

"I did. He's off at the Blake's place, taking care of their dairy whale."

"All right, I'll go out and take a look." He slipped on his face mask. Grinning, he said, "I don't even have time to dry off before I have to go out again."

His face and chest were wet.

Morrison opened his eyes. His face and chest *were* wet—from perspiration. Staring at the partially blocked mouth of the cave, he could see green eyes, two, four, six, eight.

He fired at them, but they didn't retreat, He fired again, and his bullet ricocheted off the cave wall, stinging him with stone splinters. With his next shots, he succeeded in winging one of the wolves. The pack withdrew.

That emptied the revolver. Morrison searched through his pockets and found five more cartridges. He carefully loaded the gun. Dawn couldn't be far away now.

And then he was dreaming again, this time of the Prospector's Special. He had heard about it in every little saloon that bordered the Scorpion. Bristly-bearded old prospectors told a hundred different stories about it, and the cynical bartenders chimed in with their versions. Kirk had it in '89, ordered up big and special just for him. Edmonson and Arsler received it in '93. That was certain. And other men had had it too, as they sat on their precious goldenstone claims. Or so people said.

But was it real? Was there such a thing as the Prospector's Special? Would he live to see that rainbow-hued wonder, tall as a church steeple, wide as a house, more precious than goldenstone itself?

Sure he would! Why, he could almost see it now…

Morrison shook himself awake. It was morning. Painfully, he crawled out of the cave to face the day.

He stumbled and crawled to the south, escorted closely by wolves, shaded by predatory flying things. His fingers scrabbled along rock and sand. The traces were rich, rich!

But where in all this desolation was the goldenstone?

Where? He was almost past caring. He drove his sunburned, dried-out body, stopping only to fire a single shot when the wolves came too close.

Four bullets left.

He had to fire again when the kites, growing impatient, started diving at his head. A lucky shot tore into the flock, downing two. It gave the wolves something to fight over. Morrison crawled on blindly.

And fell over the edge of a little cliff.

It wasn't a serious fall, but the revolver was knocked from his hand. Before he could find it, the wolves were on him. Only their greed saved Morrison. While they fought over him, he rolled away and retrieved his revolver. Two shots scattered the pack. That left one bullet.

He'd have to save that one for himself, because he was too tired to go on. He sank to his knees. The traces were rich here. Fantastically rich. Somewhere nearby…

"Well, I'll be damned," Morrison said.

The little ravine into which he had fallen was solid goldenstone.

He picked up a pebble. Even in its rough state he could see the deep luminous golden glow, the fiery red and purple flecks deep in the shining stone.

"Make sure," Morrison told himself. "No false alarms, no visions, no wild hopes. Make sure."

He broke off a chunk of rock with the butt of his revolver.

It still looked like goldenstone. He took out his testing kit and spilled a few drops of white solution on the rock. The solution foamed green.

"Goldenstone, sure as sure," Morrison said, looking around at the glowing cliff walls. "Hey, I'm rich!"

He took out his telephone. With trembling fingers he dialed Krandall's number.

"Max!" Morrison shouted. "I've hit it! I've hit the real stuff!"

"My name is not Max," a voice over the telephone said.

"Huh?"

"My name is Boyard," the man said.

The video screen cleared, and Morrison saw a thin, sallow faced man with a hairline mustache.

"I'm sorry, Mr. Boyard," Morrison said. "I must have gotten the wrong number. I was calling—"

"It doesn't matter who you were calling," Mr. Boyard said. "I am District Supervisor of the Venus Telephone Company. Your bill is two months overdue."

"I can pay it now," Morrison said, grinning.

"Excellent," said Mr. Boyard. "As soon as you do, your service will be resumed."

The screen began to fade.

"Wait!" Morrison cried. "I can pay as soon as I reach your office. But I must make one telephone call. Just one call, so that I—"

"Not a chance," Mr. Boyard said decisively. "*After* you have paid your bill, your service will be turned on immediately."

"I've got the money right here!" Morrison said. "Right here in my hand!"

Mr. Boyard paused. "Well, it's unusual, but I suppose we could arrange for a special robot messenger if you are willing to pay the expenses."

"I am!"

"Hm. It's irregular, but I daresay we…Where is the money?"

"Right here," Morrison said. "You recognize it, don't you? It's goldenstone!"

"I am sick and tired of the tricks you prospectors think you can put over on us. Holding up a handful of pebbles—"

"But this is really goldenstone! Can't you see it!"

"I am a businessman," Mr. Boyard said, "not a jeweler. I wouldn't know goldenstone from goldenrod."

The video screen went blank.

Frantically, Morrison tried to reach the operator. There was nothing, not even a dial tone. His telephone was disconnected.

He put the instrument down and surveyed his situation.

The narrow crevice into which he had fallen ran straight for about twenty yards, then curved to the left. No cave was visible in the steep walls, no place where he could build a barricade.

He heard a movement behind him. Whirling around, he saw a huge old wolf in full charge. Without a moment's hesitation, Morrison drew and fired, blasting off the top of the beast's head.

"Damn it," Morrison said. "I was going to save that bullet for myself."

It gave him a moment's grace. He ran down the ravine, looking for an opening in its sides. Goldenstone glowed at him and sparkled red and purple. And the sandwolves loped along behind him.

Then Morrison stopped. In front of him, the curving ravine ended in a sheer wall.

He put his back against it, holding the revolver by its butt. The wolves stopped five feet from him, gathering themselves for a rush. There were ten or twelve of them, and they were packed three deep in the narrow pass. Overhead, the kites circled, waiting for their turn.

At that moment, Morrison heard the crackling sound of 'porting equipment. A whirlpool appeared above the wolves' heads and they backed hastily away.

"Just in time!" Morrison said.

"In time for what?" asked Williams 4, the postman.

The robot climbed out of the Vortex and looked around.

"Well, young man," Williams 4 said, "this is a fine fix you've gotten yourself into. Didn't I warn you? Didn't I advise you to turn back? And now look!"

"You were perfectly right," Morrison said. "What did Max Krandall send me?"

"Max Krandall did not, and could not, send a thing."

"Then why are you here?"

"Because it's your birthday," Williams 4 said. "We of the Postal Department always give special service for birthdays. Here you are."

Williams 4 gave him a handful of mail, birthday greetings from Janie, and from his aunts, uncles and cousins on Earth.

"Something else here," Williams 4 said, rummaging in his bag. "I *think* there was something else here. Let me see...Yes, here it is."

He handed Morrison a small package.

Hastily, Morrison tore off the wrappings. It was a birthday present from his Aunt Mina in New Jersey. He opened it. It was a large box of salt-water taffy, direct from Atlantic City.

"Quite a delicacy, I'm told," said Williams 4, who had been peering over his shoulder. "But not very satisfactory under the circumstances. Well, young man, I hate to see anyone die on his birthday. The best I can wish you is a speedy and painless departure."

The robot began walking toward the vortex.

"Wait!" Morrison cried. "You can't just leave me like this! I haven't had any water in days! And those wolves—"

"I know," Williams 4 said. "Do you think I feel *happy* about it? Even a robot has some feelings!"

"Then help me."

"I can't. The rules of the Postal Department expressly and categorically forbid it. I remember Abner Lathe making much the same request of me in '97. It took three years for a burial party to reach him."

"You have an emergency telephone, haven't you?" Morrison asked.

"Yes. But I can use it only for personal emergencies."

"Can you at least carry a letter for me? A special delivery letter?"

"Of course I can," the robot postman said. "That's what I'm here for. I can even lend you pencil and paper."

Morrison accepted the pencil and paper and tried to think. If he wrote to Max now, special delivery, Max would have the letter in a matter of hours. But how long would Max need to raise some money and send him water and ammunition? A day, two days? Morrison would have to figure out some way of holding out...

"I assume you have a stamp," the robot said.

"I don't," Morrison replied. "But I'll buy one from you. Solidoport special."

"Excellent," said the robot. "We have just put out a new series of Venusborg triangulars. I consider them quite an esthetic accomplishment. They cost three dollars apiece."

"That's fine. Very reasonable. Let me have one."

"There is the question of payment."

"Here," Morrison said, handing the robot a piece of goldenstone worth about five thousand dollars in the rough.

The postman examined the stone, then handed it back.

"I'm sorry, I can accept only cash."

"But this is worth more than a thousand postage stamps!" Morrison said. "This is goldenstone!"

"It may well be," Williams 4 said. "But I have never had any assaying knowledge taped into me. Nor is the Venus Postal Service run on a barter system. I'll have to ask for three dollars in bills or coins."

"I don't have it."

"I am very sorry." Williams 4 turned to go.

"You can't just go and let me die!"

"I can and must," Williams 4 said sadly. "I am only a robot, Mr. Morrison. I was made by men, and naturally I partake of some of their sensibilities. That's as it should be. But I also have my limits, which, in their nature, are similar to the limits most humans have on this harsh planet. And, unlike humans, I cannot transcend my limits."

The robot started to climb into the whirlpool. Morrison stared at him blankly, and saw beyond him the waiting wolfpack. He saw the soft glow of several million dollars' worth of goldenstone shining from the ravine's walls.

Something snapped inside him.

With an inarticulate yell, Morrison dived, tackling the robot around the ankles. Williams 4, half in and half out of the 'porting vortex, struggled and kicked, and almost succeeded in shaking Morrison loose. But with a maniac's strength Morrison held on. Inch by inch he dragged the robot out of the vortex, threw him on the ground and pinned him.

"You are disrupting the mail service," said Williams 4.

"That's not all I'm going to disrupt," Morrison growled. "I'm not afraid of dying. That was part of the gamble. But I'm damned if I'm going to die fifteen minutes after I've struck it rich!"

"You have no choice."

"I do. I'm going to use that emergency telephone of yours."

"You can't," Williams 4 said. "I refuse to extrude it. And you could never reach it without the resources of a machine shop."

"Could be," said Morrison. "I plan to find out." He pulled out his empty revolver.

"What are you going to do?" Williams 4 asked.

"I'm going to see if I can smash you into scrap metal *without* the resources of a machine shop. I think your eye cells would be a logical place to begin."

"They would indeed," said the robot. "I have no personal sense of survival, of course. But let me point out that you would be leaving all Venus without a postman. Many would suffer because of your antisocial action."

"I hope so," Morrison said, raising the revolver above his head.

"Also," the robot said hastily, "you would be destroying government property. That is a serious offense."

Morrison laughed and swung the pistol. The robot moved its head quickly, dodging the blow. It tried to wriggle free, but Morrison's two hundred pounds was seated firmly on its thorax.

"I won't miss this time," Morrison promised, hefting the revolver.

"Stop!" Williams 4 said. "It is my duty to protect government property, even if that property happens to be myself."

"You may use my telephone, Mr. Morrison. Bear in mind that this offense is punishable by a sentence of not more than ten and not less than five years in the Solar Swamp penitentiary."

"Let's have that telephone," Morrison said.

The robot's chest opened and a small telephone extruded. Morrison dialed Max Krandall and explained the situation.

"I see, I see," Krandall said. "All right, I'll try to find Wilkes. But, Tom, I don't know how much I can do. It's after business hours. Most places are closed—"

"Get them open again," said Morrison. "I can pay for it. And get Jim Remstaater out of trouble, too."

"It can't be done just like that. You haven't established any rights to your claim. You haven't even proved that your claim is valuable."

"Look at it." Morrison turned the telephone so that Krandall could see the glowing walls of the ravine.

"Looks real," Krandall said. "But unfortunately, all that glitters is not goldenstone."

"What can we do?" Morrison asked.

"We'll have to take it step by step. I'll 'port you the Public Surveyor. He'll check your claim, establish its limits, and make sure no one else has filed on it. You give him a chunk of goldenstone to take back. A big chunk."

"How can I cut goldenstone? I don't have any tools."

"You'll have to figure out a way. He'll take the chunk back for assaying. If it's rich enough, you're all set."

"And if it isn't?"

"Perhaps we better not talk about that," Krandall said.

"I'll get right to work on this, Tommy. Good luck!"

Morrison signed off. He stood up and helped the robot to its feet.

"In twenty-three years of service," Williams 4 said, "this is the first time anybody has threatened the life of a government postal employee. I must report this to the police authorities at Venusborg, Mr. Morrison. I have no choice."

"I know," Morrison said. "But I guess five or ten years in the penitentiary is better than dying."

"I doubt it. I carry mail there, you know. You will have the opportunity of seeing for yourself in about six months."

"What?" said Morrison, stunned.

"In about six months, after I have completed my mail calls around the planet and returned to Venusborg. A matter like this must be reported in person. But first and foremost, the mails must go through."

"Thanks, Williams. I don't know how—"

"I am simply performing my duty," the robot said as it climbed into the vortex. "If you are still on Venus in six months, I will be delivering your mail to the penitentiary."

"I won't be here," Morrison said. "So long, Williams!" The robot disappeared into the 'porting vortex. Then the vortex disappeared. Morrison was alone in the Venusian twilight.

He found an outcropping of goldenstone larger than a man's head. He chipped at it with his pistol butt, and tiny particles danced and shimmered in the air. After an hour, he had put four dents in his revolver, but he had barely scratched the highly refractory surface of the goldenstone.

The sandwolves began to edge forward. Morrison threw stones at them and shouted in his dry, cracked voice. The wolves retreated.

He examined the outcropping again and found a hairline fault running along one edge. He concentrated his blows along the fault.

The goldenstone refused to crack.

Morrison wiped sweat from his eyes and tried to think. A chisel, he needed a chisel...

He pulled off his belt. Putting the edge of the steel buckle against the crack, he managed to hammer it in a fraction of an inch. Three more blows drove the buckle firmly into the fault. With another blow, the outcropping sheared off cleanly. He had separated a twenty-pound piece from the cliff. At fifty dollars a troy ounce, this lump should I be worth about twelve thousand dollars—if it assayed out as pure as it looked.

The twilight had turned a deep gray when the Public Surveyor 'ported in. It was a short, squat robot with a conservative crackle-black finish.

"Good day, sir," the surveyor said. "You wish to file a claim? A standard unrestricted mining claim?"

"That's right," Morrison said.

"And where is the center of the aforesaid claim?"

"Huh? The center? I guess I'm standing on it."

"Very well," the robot said.

Extruding a steel tape, it walked rapidly away from Morrison. At a distance of two hundred yards, it stopped. More steel tape fluttered as it walked, flew and climbed a square with Morrison at the center. When it had finished, the surveyor stood for a long time without moving.

"What are you doing?" Morrison asked.

"I'm making depth-photographs of the terrain," the robot said. "It's rather difficult in this light. Couldn't you wait till morning?"

"No!"

"Well, I'll just have to cope," the robot said.

It moved and stood, moved and stood, each subterranean exposure taking longer than the last as the twilight deepened.

If it had had pores, it would have sweated.

"There," said the robot at last, "that takes care of it. Do you have a sample for me to take back?"

"Here it is," Morrison said, hefting the slab of goldenstone and handing it to the surveyor. "Is that all?"

"Absolutely all," the robot said. "Except, of course, that you haven't given me the Deed of Search."

Morrison blinked. "I haven't given you the what?"

"The Deed of Search. That is a government document showing that the claim you are filing on is free, as per government order, of fissionable material in excess of fifty per cent of the total mass to a depth of sixty feet. It's a mere formality, but a necessary one."

"I never heard of it," Morrison said.

"It became a requirement last week," explained the surveyor. "You don't have the Deed? Then I'm afraid your standard unrestricted claim is invalid."

"Isn't there anything I can do?"

"Well," the robot said, "you *could* change your standard unrestricted claim to a special restricted claim. That requires no Deed of Search."

"What does the special restricted part mean?"

"It means that in five hundred years all rights revert to the Government of Venus."

"All right!" Morrison shouted. "Fine! Good! Is that all?"

"Absolutely all," the surveyor said. "I shall bring this sample back and have it assayed and evaluated immediately. From it and the depth-photographs we can extrapolate the value and extent of your claim."

"Send me back something to take care of the wolves," Morrison said. "And food. And listen—I want a Prospector's Special."

"Yes, sir. It will all be 'ported to you—if your claim is of sufficient value to warrant the outlay."

The robot climbed into the vortex and vanished.

Time passed, and the wolves edged forward again. They snarled at the rocks Morrison threw, but they didn't retreat. Jaws open and tongues lolling, they crept up the remaining yards between them and the prospector.

Then the leading wolf leaped back and howled. A gleaming vortex had appeared over his head and a rifle had fallen from the vortex, striking him on a forepaw.

The wolves scrambled away. Another rifle fell from the vortex. Then a large box marked *Grenades, Handle With Care.* Then another box marked *Desert Ration K.*

Morrison waited, staring at the gleaming mouth of the vortex. It crossed the sky to a spot a quarter of a mile away and paused there, and then a great round brass base emerged from the vortex, and the mouth widened to allow an even greater bulge of brass to which the base was attached. The bulge grew higher as the base was lowered to the sand. When the last of it appeared, it stood alone in the horizon to-horizon expanse, a gigantic ornate brass punchbowl in the desert. The vortex rose and paused again over the bowl.

Morrison waited, his throat raw and aching. Now a small trickle came out of the vortex and splashed down into the bowl. Still Morrison didn't move.

And then it came. The trickle became a roar that sent the wolves and kites fleeing in terror, and a cataract poured from the vortex to the huge punchbowl.

Morrison began staggering toward it. He should have ordered a canteen, he told himself thirstily, stumbling across the quarter of a mile of sand. But at last he stood beneath the Prospector's Special, higher than a church steeple, wider than a house, filled with water more precious than goldenstone itself. He turned the spigot at the bottom. Water soaked the yellow sands and ran in rivulets down the dune.

He should have ordered a cup or glass, Morrison thought, lying on his back with open mouth.

Shall We Have a Little Talk?

The landing was a piece of cake despite gravitational vagaries produced by two suns and six moons. Low-level cloud cover could have given him some trouble if Jackson had been coming in visually. But he considered that to be kid stuff. It was better and safer to plug in the computer and lean back and enjoy the ride.

The cloud cover broke up at 2,000 feet. Jackson was able to confirm his earlier sighting: there was a city down there, just as sure as sure.

He was in one of the world's loneliest jobs; but his line of work, paradoxically enough, required an extremely gregarious man. Because of this built-in contradiction, Jackson was in the habit of talking to himself. Most of the men in his line of work did. Jackson would talk to anyone, human or alien, no matter what their size or shape or color.

It was what he was paid to do; and what he had to do anyhow. He talked when he was alone on the long interstellar runs, and he talked even more when he was with someone or something that would talk back. He figured he was lucky to be paid for his compulsions.

"And not just *paid,* either," he reminded himself. "*Well* paid, and with a bonus arrangement on top of that. And furthermore, this feels like my lucky planet. I feel like I could get rich on this one—unless they kill me down there, of course."

The lonely flights between the planets and the imminence of death were the only disadvantages of this job; but if the work weren't hazardous and difficult, the pay wouldn't be so good.

Would they kill him? You could never tell. Alien life forms were unpredictable—just like humans, only more so.

"But I don't think they'll kill me," Jackson said. "I just feel downright lucky today."

This simple philosophy had sustained him for years, across the endless lonely miles of space, and in and out of ten, twelve, twenty planets. He saw no reason to change his outlook now.

The ship landed. Jackson switched the status controls to standby.

He checked the analyzer for oxygen and trace-element content in the atmosphere, and took a quick survey of the local microorganisms. The place was viable. He leaned back in his chair and waited. It didn't take long, of course. They—the locals, indigenes, autochthons, whatever you wanted to call them—came out of their city to look at the spaceship. And Jackson looked through the port at them.

"Well now," he said. "Seems like the alien life forms in this neck of the woods are honest-to-Joe humanoids. That means a five-thousand-dollar bonus for old Uncle Jackson."

The inhabitants of the city were bipedal monocephaloids. They had the appropriate number of fingers, noses, eyes, ears and mouths. Their skin was a flesh-colored beige, their lips were a faded red, their hair was black, brown, or red.

"Shucks, they're just like home folks!" Jackson said. "Hell, I ought to get an extra bonus for that. Humanoidissimus, eh?"

The aliens wore clothes. Some of them carried elaborately carved lengths of wood like swagger sticks. The women decorated themselves with carved and enameled ornaments. At a flying guess, Jackson ranked them about equivalent to Late Bronze Age on Earth.

They talked and gestured among themselves. Their language was, of course, incomprehensible to Jackson; but that didn't matter. The important thing was that they *had* a language and that their speech sounds could be produced by his vocal apparatus.

"Not like on that heavy planet last year," Jackson said. "Those supersonic sons of bitches! I had to wear special earphones and mike, and it was 110 in the shade."

The aliens were waiting for him, and Jackson knew it. That first moment of actual contact—it always was a nervous business.

That's when they were most apt to let you have it.

Reluctantly he moved to the hatch, undogged it, rubbed his eyes, and cleared his throat. He managed to produce a smile. He told himself, "Don't get sweaty; 'member, you're just a little old interstellar wanderer—kind of galactic vagabond—to extend the hand of friendship and all that jazz. You've just dropped in for a little talk, nothing more. Keep on believing that, sweety, and the extraterrestrial Johns will believe right along with you. Remember Jackson's Law: All intelligent life forms share the divine faculty of gullibility; which means that the triple-tongued Thung of Orangus V can be conned out of his skin just as Joe Doakes of St. Paul"

And so, wearing a brave, artificial little smile, Jackson swung the port open and stepped out to have a little talk.

"Well now, how y'all?" Jackson asked at once, just to hear the sound of his own voice.

The nearest aliens shrank away from him. Nearly all of them were frowning. Several of the younger ones carried bronze knives in a forearm scabbard. These were clumsy weapons, but as effective as anything ever invented. The aliens started to draw.

"Now take it easy," Jackson said, keeping his voice light and unalarmed.

They drew their knives and began to edge forward. Jackson stood his ground, waiting, ready to bolt through the hatch like a jet-propelled jack-rabbit, hoping he could make it.

Then a third man (might as well call them "men," Jackson decided) stepped in front of the belligerent two. This one was older. He spoke rapidly. He gestured. The two with the knives looked.

"That's right," Jackson said encouragingly. "Take a good look. Heap big spaceship. Plenty strong medicine. Vehicle of great power, fabricated by a real advanced technology. Sort of makes you stop and think, doesn't it?"

It did.

The aliens had stopped; and if not thinking, they were at least doing a great deal of talking. They pointed at the ship, then back at their city.

"You're getting the idea," Jackson told them. "Power speaks a universal language, eh, cousins?"

He had been witness to many of these scenes on many different planets. He could nearly write their dialogue for them. It usually went like this:

Intruder lands in outlandish space vehicle, thereby eliciting (1) curiosity, (2) fear, and (3) hostility. After some minutes of awed contemplation, one autochthon usually says to his friend: "Hey, that damned metal thing packs one hell of a lot of power."

"You're right, Herbie," his friend Fred, the second autochthon, replies.

"You bet I'm right," Herbie says. "And hell, with that much power and technology and stuff, this son of a gun could like *enslave* us. I mean he really could."

"You've hit it, Herbie, that's just exactly what could happen."

"So what I say," Herbie continues, "I say, let's not take any risks. I mean, *sure,* he *looks* friendly enough, but he's just got too damned much *power,* and that's not right. And right now is the best chance we'll ever get to take him on account of he's just standing there waiting for like an ovation or something. So let's put this bastard out of his misery, and then we can talk the whole thing over and see how it stacks up situationwise."

"By Jesus, I'm with you!" cries Fred. Others signify their assent.

"Good for you, lads," cries Herbie. "Let's wade in and take this alien joker like *now!*"

So they start to make their move; but suddenly, at the last second, Old Doc, (the third autochthon) intervenes, saying, "Hold it a minute, boys, we can't do it like that. For one thing, we got laws around here—"

"To hell with that," says Fred (a born troublemaker and somewhat simple to boot).

"—and aside from the laws, it would be just too damned dangerous for *us.*"

"Me 'n' Fred here ain't scared," says valiant Herb. "Maybe you better go take in a movie or something, Doc. Us guys'll handle this."

"I was not referring to a short-range personal danger," Old Doc says scornfully. "What I fear is the destruction of our city, the slaughter of our loved ones, and the annihilation of our culture."

Herb and Fred stop. "What you talking about, Doc? He's just one stinking alien; you push a knife in his guts, he'll bleed like anyone else."

"Fools! *Schlemiels!*" thunders wise Old Doc. "Of course, you can kill him! But what happens after that?"

"Huh?" says Fred, squinting his china-blue pop eyes.

"Idiots! *Cochons!* You think this is the only spaceship these aliens got? You think they don't even know whereabouts this guy has gone? Man, you gotta assume they got *plenty* more ships where this one came from, and you gotta also assume that they'll be damned mad if this ship doesn't show up when it's supposed to, and you gotta assume that when these aliens learn the score, they're gonna be damned sore and buzz back here and stomp on everything and everybody."

"How come I gotta assume that?" asks feeble-witted Fred.

"'Cause it's what *you'd* do in a deal like that, right?"

"I guess maybe I would at that," says Fred with a sheepish grin. "Yeah, I just might do that little thing. But look, maybe *they* wouldn't."

"Maybe, maybe," mimics wise Old Doc. "Well, baby, we can't risk the whole ball game on a goddamned *maybe.* We can't afford to kill this alien joker on the chance that *maybe* his people wouldn't do what any reasonable-minded guy would do, which is, namely, to blow us all to hell."

"Well, I suppose we maybe can't," Herbie says. "But Doc, what *can* we do?"

"Just wait and see what he wants."

II

A scene very much like that, according to reliable reconstruction, had been enacted at least 30 or 40 times. It usually resulted in a policy of wait and see. Occasionally, the contactor from Earth was killed before wise counsel could prevail; but Jackson was paid to take risks like that.

Whenever the contactor was killed, retribution followed with swift and terrible inevitability. Also with regret, of course, because Earth was an extremely civilized place and accustomed to living within the law. No civilized, law-abiding race likes to commit genocide. In fact, the folks on Earth consider genocide a very unpleasant matter, and they don't like to read about it or anything like it in their morning papers. Envoys must be protected, of course, and murder must be punished; everybody knows that. But it still doesn't feel nice to read about a genocide over your morning coffee. News like that can spoil a man's entire day. Three or four genocides and a man just might get angry enough to switch his vote.

Fortunately, there was never much occasion for that sort of mess. Aliens usually caught on pretty fast. Despite the language barrier, aliens learned that you simply *don't* kill Earthmen.

And then, later, bit by bit, they learned all the rest.

The hotheads had sheathed their knives. Everybody was smiling except Jackson, who was grinning like a hyena. The aliens were making graceful arm and leg motions, probably of welcome.

"Well, that's real nice," Jackson said, making a few graceful gestures of his own. "Makes me feel real to-home. And now, suppose you take me to your leader, show me the town, and all that jazz. Then I'll set myself down and figure out that lingo of yours, and we'll have a little talk. And after that, everything will proceed splendidly. *En avant!*"

So saying, Jackson stepped out at a brisk pace in the direction of the city. After a brief hesitation, his new found friends fell into step behind him.

Everything was moving according to plan.

Jackson, like all the other contactors, was a polyglot of singular capabilities. As basic equipment, he had an eidetic memory and an extremely discriminating ear. More important, he possessed a startling aptitude for language and an uncanny intuition for meaning. When Jackson came up against an incomprehensible tongue, he picked out, quickly and unerringly, the significant units, the fundamental building blocks of the language. Quite without effort he sorted vocalizations into cognitive, volitional, and emotional aspects of speech. Grammatical elements presented themselves at once to his practiced ear. Prefixes and suffixes were no trouble; word sequence, pitch, and reduplication were no sweat. He didn't know much about the science of linguistics, but he didn't need to know. Jackson was a natural. Linguistics had been developed to describe and explain things which he knew intuitively.

He had not yet encountered the language which he could not learn. He never really expected to find one. As he often told his friends in the Forked Tongue Club in New York, "Waal, shukins, there just really ain't nuthin *tough* about them alien tongues. Leastwise, not the ones I've run across. I mean that sincerely. I mean to tell you, boys, that the man who can express hisself in Sioux or Khmer ain't going to encounter too much trouble out there amongst the stars."

And so it had been, to date...

Once in the city, there were many tedious ceremonies which Jackson had to endure. They stretched on for three days—about par for the course; it wasn't every day that a traveler from space came in for a visit. So naturally enough every mayor, governor, president, and alderman, *and* their wives, wanted to shake his hand. It was all very understandable, but Jackson resented the waste of his time. He had work to do, some of it not very pleasant, and the sooner he got started, the quicker it would be over.

On the fourth day he was able to reduce the official nonsense to a minimum. That was the day on which he began in earnest to learn the local language.

A language, as any linguist will tell you, is undoubtedly the most beautiful creation one is ever likely to encounter. But with that beauty goes a certain element of danger.

Language might aptly be compared to the sparkling, ever-changing face of the sea. Like the sea, you never know what reefs may be concealed in its pellucid depths. The brightest water hides the most treacherous shoals.

Jackson, well prepared for trouble, encountered none at first. The main language (Hon) of this planet (Na) was spoken by the overwhelming majority of its inhabitants (En-a-To-Na—literally, men of the Na, or Naians, as Jackson preferred to think of them). Hon seemed quite a straightforward affair. It used one term for one concept, and allowed no fusions, juxtapositions, or agglutinations. Concepts were built up by sequences of simple words ("spaceship" was *ho-pa-aie-an*—boat-flying-outer-sky). Thus, Hon was very much like Chinese and Annamite on Earth. Pitch differences were employed not only intentionally to differentiate between homonyms, but also positionally, to denote gradations of "perceived realism," bodily discomfort, and three classes of pleasurable expectation. All of which was mildly interesting but of no particular difficulty to a competent linguist.

To be sure, a language like Hon was rather a bore because of the long word-lists one had to memorize. But pitch and position could be fun, as well as being absolutely essential if one wanted to make any sense out of the sentence units. So, taken all in all, Jackson was not dissatisfied, and he absorbed the language as quickly as it could be given to him.

It was a proud day for Jackson, about a week later, when he could say to his tutor: "A very nice and pleasant good morning to you, most estimable and honored tutor, and how is your blessed health upon this glorious day?"

"Felicitations most *ird wunk!*" the tutor replied with a smile of deep warmth. "Your accent, dear pupil, is superb! Positively *gor nak*, in fact, and your grasp of my dear mother tongue is little short of *ur nak tai.*"

Jackson glowed all over from the gentle old tutor's compliments. He felt quite pleased with himself. Of course, he hadn't recognized several words; *ird wunk* and *ur nak tai* sounded faintly familiar, but *gor nak* was completely unknown. Still, lapses were expected of a beginner in any language. He did know enough to understand the Naians and to make himself understood by them. And that was what his job required.

He returned to his spaceship that afternoon. The hatch had been standing open during his entire stay on Na but he found that not a single article had been stolen. He shook his head ruefully at this, but refused to let it upset him. He loaded his pockets with a variety of objects and sauntered back to the city. He was ready to perform the final and most important part of his job.

III

In the heart of the business district, at the intersection of Um and Alhretto, he found what he was looking for: a real-estate office. He entered and was taken to the office of Mr. Erum, a junior partner of the firm.

"Well, well, well, well!" Erum said, shaking hands heartily. "This is a real honor, sir, a very considerable and genuine privilege. Are you thinking of acquiring a piece of property?"

"That was my intention," Jackson said. "Unless, of course, you have discriminatory laws that forbid your selling to a foreigner."

"No difficulty there," Erum said. "In fact, it'll be a veritable *orai* of a pleasure to have a man from your distant and glorious civilization in our midst."

Jackson restrained a snicker. "The only other difficulty I can imagine is the question of legal tender. I don't have any of your currency, of course; but I have certain quantities of gold, platinum, diamonds, and other objects which are considered valuable on Earth."

"They are considered valuable here, too," Erum said. "Quantities, did you say? My dear sir, we will have no difficulties; not even a *blaggle* shall *mit* or *ows*, as the poet said."

"Quite so," Jackson replied. Erum was using some words he didn't know, but that didn't matter. The main drift was clear enough. "Now, suppose we begin with a nice industrial site. After all, I'll have to do something with my time. And after that, we can pick out a house."

"Most decidedly *prominex*," Erum said gaily. "Suppose I just *raish* through my listings here...Yes, what do you say to a *bromicaine* factory? It's in a first-class condition and could easily be converted to *vor* manufacture or used as it is."

"Is there any real market for *bromicaine?*" Jackson asked.

"Well, bless my *muergentan*, of course there is! *Bromicaine* is indispensable, though its sales are seasonable. You see, refined *bromicaine*, or *ariisi*, is used by the *protigash* devolvers, who of course harvest by the soltice season, except in those branches of the industry that have switched over to *ticothene revature*. Those from a steadily—"

"Fine, fine," Jackson said. He didn't care what a *bromicaine* was and never expected to see one. As long as it was a gainful employment of some kind, it filled his specifications.

"I'll buy it," he said.

"You won't regret it," Erum told him. "A good *bromicaine* factory is a *garveldis hagatis,* and *menijoy* as well."

"Sure," Jackson said, wishing that he had a more extensive Hon vocabulary. "How much?"

"Well, sir, the price is no difficulty. But first you'll have to fill out the *ollanbrit* form. It is just a few *sken* questions which *ny naga* of everyone."

Erum handed Jackson the form. The first question read: "Have you, now or at any past time, *elikated mushkies forsically?* State date of all occurrences. If no occurrences, state the reason for *transgrishal reduct* as found."

Jackson read no farther. "What does it mean," he asked Erum, "to *elikate mushkies forsically?*"

"Mean?" Erum smiled uncertainly. "Why, it means exactly what it says. Or so I would imagine."

"I meant," Jackson said, "that I do not understand the words. Could you explain them to me?"

"Nothing simpler," Erum replied. "To *elikate mushkies* is almost the same as a *bijur probishkai.*"

"I beg your pardon?" Jackson said.

"It means—well, to *elikate* is really rather simple, though perhaps not in the eyes of the law. *Scorbadising* is a form of *elikation,* and so is *manruv garing.* Some say that when we breathe *drorsically* in the evening *subsis,* we are actually *elikating.* Personally, I consider that a bit fanciful."

"Let's try *mushkies,*" Jackson suggested.

"By all means, let's!" Erum replied, with a coarse boom of laughter. "If only one could—eh!" He dug Jackson in the ribs with a sly elbow.

"Hm, yes," Jackson replied coldly. "Perhaps you could tell me what, exactly, a *mushkie* is?"

"Of course. As it happens, there is no such thing," Erum replied. "Not in the singular, at any rate. One mushkie would be a logical fallacy, don't you see?"

"I'll take your word for it. What *are mushkies?*"

"Well, primarily, they're the object of *elikation.* Secondarily, they are half-sized wooden sandals which are used to stimulate erotic fantasies among the Kutor religionists."

"Now we're getting someplace!" Jackson cried.

"Only if your tastes happen to run that way," Erum answered with discernable coldness.

"I meant in terms of understanding the question on the form—"

"Of course, excuse me," Erum said. "But you see, the question asks if you have ever *elikated mushkies forsically.* And that makes all the difference."

"Does it really?"

"Of course! The modification changes the entire meaning."

"I was afraid that it would," Jackson said. "I don't suppose you could explain what *forsically* means?"

"I certainly can!" Erum said. "Our conversation now could—with a slight assist from the *deme* imagination—be termed a *forsically designed* talk.'"

"Ah," said Jackson.

"Quite so," said Erum. *"Forsically* is a mode, a manner. It means 'spiritually-forward-leading-by-way-of-fortuitous-friendship.'"

"That's a little more like it," Jackson said. "In that case, when one *elikates mushkies forsically—*"

"I'm terribly afraid you're on the wrong track," Erum said. "The definition I gave you applies only to conversations. It is something rather different when one speaks of *mushkies.*"

"What does it mean then?"

"Well, it means—or rather it *expresses*—an advanced and intensified case of *mushkie elikidation,* but with a definite *nmogmetic* bias. I consider it a rather unfortunate phraseology, personally."

"How would you put it?"

"I'd lay it on the line and to hell with the fancy talk,"

Erum said toughly. "I'd come right out and say: 'Have you now or at any other time *dunfiglers voc* in illegal, immoral, or *insirtis* circumstances, with or without the aid and/or consent of a *brachniian?* If so, state when and why. If not, state *neugris kris* and why not.'"

"That's how you'd put it, huh?" Jackson said.

"Sure, I would," Erum said defiantly. "These forms are for adults, aren't they? So why not come right out and call a *spigler* a *spigler* a *spey?* Everybody *dunfiglers voc* some of the time, and so what? No one's feelings are ever hurt by it, for heaven's sake. I mean, after all, it simply involves, oneself and a twisted old piece of wood, so why should anyone care?"

"Wood?" Jackson echoed.

"Yes, *wood.* A commonplace, dirty old piece of wood. Or at least that's all it would be if people didn't get their feelings so ridiculously involved."

"What do they do with the wood?" Jackson asked quickly.

"Do with it? Nothing much, when you come right down to it. But the religious aura is simply too much for our so-called intellectuals. They are unable, in my opinion, to isolate the simple primordial fact—*wood*—from the cultural *volturneiss* which surrounds it at *festerhiss,* and to some extent at *uuis,* too."

"That's how intellectuals are," Jackson said. "But *you* can isolate it, and you find—"

"I find it's really nothing to get excited about. I really mean that. I mean to say that a cathedral, viewed correctly, is no more than a pile of rocks and a forest is just an assembly of atoms. Why should we see this case differently? I mean, really, you could *elikate mushkies forsically* without even *using* wood! What do you think of that?"

"I'm impressed," Jackson said.

"Don't get me wrong! I'm not saying it would be *easy*, or natural, or even *right*. But still, you damned well could! Why, you could substitute *cormed grayti* and still come out all right!" Erum paused and chuckled. "You'd look foolish, but you'd still come out all right."

"Very interesting," Jackson said.

"I'm afraid I became a bit vehement," Erum said, wiping his forehead. "Was I talking very loudly? Do you think perhaps I was overheard?"

"Of course not. I found it all very interesting. I must leave just now, Mr. Erum, but I'll be back tomorrow to fill out that form and buy the property."

"I'll hold it for you," Erum said, rising and shaking Jackson's hand warmly. "And I want to thank you. It isn't often that I have the opportunity for this kind of frank, no-holds-barred conversation."

"I found it very instructive," Jackson said. He left Erum's office and walked slowly back to his ship. He was disturbed, upset, and annoyed. Linguistic incomprehension irked him, no matter how comprehensible it might be. He *should* have been able to figure out, somehow, how one went about *elikating mushkies forsically.*

Never mind, he told himself. You'll work it out tonight, Jackson baby, and then you'll go back in there and cannonball through them forms. So don't get het up over it, man.

He'd work it out. He damned well had to work it out, as he had to own a piece of property.

That was the second part of his job.

Earth had come a long way since the bad old days of naked, aggressive warfare. According to the history books, a ruler back in those ancient times could simply send out his troops to seize whatever the ruler wanted. And if any of the folks at home had the temerity to ask why he wanted it, the ruler could have them beheaded or locked up in a dungeon or sewn up in a sack and thrown into the sea. And he wouldn't even feel guilty about doing any of those things because he invariably believed that he was right and they were wrong.

This policy, technically called the *droit de seigneur* was one of the most remarkable features of the *laisser-faire capitalism* which the ancients knew.

But, down the slow passage of centuries, cultural processes were inexorably at work. A new ethic came into the world; and slowly but surely, a sense of fair play and justice was bred into the human race. Rulers came to be chosen by ballot and were responsive to the desires of the electorate. Conceptions of Justice, Mercy, and Pity came to the forefront of men's minds, ameliorating the old law of tooth and talon and amending the savage bestiality of the ancient time of unreconstruction.

The old days were gone forever. Today, no ruler could simply *take;* the voters would never stand for it.

Nowadays one had to have an excuse for taking.

Like for example a Terran citizen who happened to own property all legal and aboveboard on an alien planet, and who urgently needed and requested Terran military assistance in order to protect himself, his home, his means of a legitimate livelihood...

But first he had to own that property. He had to *really* own it, to protect himself from the bleeding-hearts Congressmen and the soft-on-aliens newsmen who always started an investigation whenever Earth took charge of another planet.

To provide a legal basis for conquest—that was what the contactors were for.

"Jackson," Jackson said to himself, "you gonna git yourself that li'l' ole *bromicaine* factory tomorrow and you gonna own it without let or hindrance. You heah me, boy? I mean it sincerely."

On the morrow, shortly before noon, Jackson was back in the city. Several hours of intensive study and a long consultation with his tutor had sufficed to show him where he had gone wrong.

It was simple enough. He had merely been a trifle hasty in assuming an extreme and invariant isolating technique in the Hon use of radicals. He had thought, on the basis of his early studies, that word meaning and word order were the only significant factors required for an understanding of the language. But that wasn't so. Upon further examination, Jackson found that the Hon language had some unexpected resources: affixation, for example, and an elementary form of reduplication. Yesterday he hadn't even been prepared for any morphological inconsistencies; when they had occurred, he had found himself in semantic difficulties.

The new forms were easy enough to learn. The trouble was, they were thoroughly illogical and contrary to the entire spirit of Hon.

One word produced by one sound and bearing one meaning—that was the rule he had previously deduced. But now he discovered 18 important exceptions—compounds produced by a variety of techniques, each of them with a list of modifying suffixes. For Jackson, this was as odd as stumbling across a grove of palm trees in Antarctica.

He learned the 18 exceptions, and thought about the article he would write when he finally got home.

And the next day, wiser and warier, Jackson strode meaningfully back to the city.

IV

In Erum's office, he filled out the government forms with ease. That first question—"Have you, now or at any past time, *elikated mushkies forsically?"*—he could now answer with an honest no. The plural *"mushkies"* in its primary meaning, represented in this context the singular "woman." (The singular *"mushkies"* used similarly would denote an uncorporeal state of femininity.)

Elikation was, of course, the role of sexual termination, unless one employed the modifier *"forsically."* If one did, this quiet term took on a charged meaning in this particular context, tantamount to edematous polysexual advocation.

Thus, Jackson could honestly write that, as he was not a Naian, he had never had that particular urge.

It was as simple as that. Jackson was annoyed at himself for not having figured it out on his own.

He filled in the rest of the questions without difficulty, and handed the paper back to Erum.

"That's really quite *skoe,"* Erum said. "Now, there are just a few more simple items for us to complete. The first we can do immediately. After that, I will arrange a brief official ceremony for the Property Transferral Act, and that will be followed by several other small bits of business. All of it should take no more than a day or so, and then the property will be all yours."

"Sure, kid, that's great," Jackson said. He wasn't bothered by the delays. Quite the contrary, he had expected many more of them. On most planets, the locals caught on quickly to what was happening. It took no great reasoning power to figure out that Earth wanted what she wanted, but wanted it in a legalistic manner.

As for why she wanted it that way—that wasn't too hard to fathom, either. A great majority of Terrans were idealists, and they believed fervently in concepts such as truth, justice, mercy, and the like. And not only did they believe, they also let those noble concepts guide their actions—except when it would be inconvenient or unprofitable. When that happened, they acted expediently, but continued to talk moralistically. This meant that they were "hypocrites"—a term which every race has its counterpart of.

Terrans wanted what they wanted, but they also wanted that what they wanted should look nice. This was a lot to expect sometimes, especially when what they wanted was ownership of someone else's planet. But in one way or another, they usually got it.

Most alien races realized that overt resistance was impossible and so resorted to various stalling tactics.

Sometimes they refused to sell, or they required an infinite multiplicity of forms or the approval of some local official who was always absent. But for each ploy the contactor always had a suitable counterploy.

Did they refuse to sell property on racial grounds? The laws of Earth specifically forbade such practices, and the Declaration of Sentient Rights stated the freedom of all sentients to live and work wherever they pleased. This was a freedom that Terra would fight for, if anyone forced her to.

Were they stalling? The Terran Doctrine of Temporal Propriety would not allow it.

Was the necessary official absent? The Uniform Earth Code Against Implicit Sequestration in Acts of Omission expressly forbade such a practice. And so on and so on. It was a game of wits Earth invariably won, for the strongest is usually judged the cleverest.

But the Naians weren't even *trying* to fight back. Jackson considered that downright despicable.

The exchange of Naian currency for Terran platinum was completed and Jackson was given his change in crisp 50-Vrso bills. Erum beamed with pleasure and said, "Now, Mr. Jackson, we can complete today's business if you will kindly *trombramcthulanchierir* in the usual manner."

Jackson turned, his eyes narrowed and his mouth compressed into a bloodless downward-curving line.

"What did you say?"

"I merely asked you to—"

"I know what you asked! But what does it *mean*?"

"Well, it means—it means—" Erum laughed weakly. "It means exactly what it says. That is to say—*ethybolically* speaking—"

Jackson said in a low, dangerous voice, "Give me a synonym."

"There is no synonym," Erum said.

"Baby, you better come up with one anyhow," Jackson said, his hand closing over Erum's throat.

"Stop! Wait! Ulp!" Erum cried. "Mr. Jackson, I beg of you! How can there be a synonym when there is one and only one term for the thing expressed—if I may so express it?"

"You're putting me on!" Jackson howled. "And you better quit it, on account of we got laws against willful obfuscation, intentional obstructionism, implicit superimposition, and other stuff like you're doing. You hear me?"

"I hear you," Erum trembled.

"Then hear this: *stop agglutinating,* you devious dog!

You've got a perfectly ordinary run-of-the-mill analytical-type language, distinguished only by its extreme isolating tendency. And when you got a language like that, man, then you simply don't agglutinate a lot of big messy compounds. Get me?"

"Yes, yes," Erum cried. "But believe me, I don't intend to *numniscaterate* in the slightest! Not *noniskakkekaki,* and you really must *debruchili* that!"

Jackson drew back his fist, but got himself under control in time. It was unwise to hit aliens if there was any possibility that they were telling the truth. Folks on Terra didn't like it. His pay could be docked; and if, by some unlucky chance, he killed Erum, he could be slapped with a six-month jail sentence.

But still...

"I'll find out if you're lying or not!" Jackson screamed, and stormed out of the office.

He walked for nearly an hour, mingling with the crowds in the slum quarters of Grath-Eth, below the gray, evil-smelling Ungperdis. No one paid any attention to him. To all outward appearances, he could have been a Naian, just as any Naian could have been a Terran.

Jackson located a cheerful saloon on the comer of Niis and Da Streets and went in.

It was quiet and masculine inside. Jackson ordered a local variety of beer. When it was served, he said to the bartender, "Funny thing happened to me the other day."

"Yeah?" said the bartender.

"Yeah, really," Jackson said. "I had this big business deal on, see, and then at the last minute they asked to *trombramcthulanchierir* in the usual manner."

He watched the bartender's face carefully. A faint expression of puzzlement crossed the man's stolid features.

"So why didn't you?" the bartender asked.

"You mean *you* would have?"

"Sure I would have. Hell, it's the standard *cathanpriptiaia,* ain't it?"

"Course it is," one of the loungers at the bar said. "Unless, of course, you suspected they was trying to *numniscaterate.*"

"No, I don't think they were trying anything like that," Jackson said in a flat low, lifeless voice. He paid for his drink and started to leave.

"Hey," the bartender called after him, "You sure they wasn't *noniskakkekaki?*"

"You never know," Jackson said, walking slump-shouldered into the street.

Jackson trusted his instincts, both with languages and with people. His instincts told him now that the Naians were straight and were not practicing an elaborate deception on him. Erum had not been inventing new words for the sake of willful confusion. He had been really speaking the Hon language as he knew it.

But if that were true, then Na was a very strange language. In fact, it was downright eccentric. And its implications were not merely curious. They were disastrous.

V

That evening Jackson went back to work. He discovered a further class of exceptions which he had not known or even suspected. That was a group of 29 multivalued potentiators. These words, meaningless in themselves, acted to elicit a complicated and discordant series of shadings from other words. Their particular type of potentiation varied according to their position in the sentence.

Thus, when Erum had asked him "to *trombramcthulanchierir* in the usual manner," he had merely wanted Jackson to make an obligatory ritual obeisance. This consisted of clasping his hands behind his neck and rocking back on his heels. He was required to perform this action with an expression of definite yet modest pleasure, in accordance with the totality of the situation, and also in accord with the state of his stomach and nerves and with his religion and ethical code, and bearing in mind minor temperamental differences due to fluctuations in heat and humidity, and not forgetting the virtues of patience, similitude, and forgiveness.

It was all quite understandable. And all completely contradictory to everything Jackson had previously learned about Hon.

It was more than contradictory; it was unthinkable, impossible, and entirely out of order. It was as if, having discovered palm trees in frigid Antarctica, he had further found that the fruit of these trees was not coconuts, but muscatel grapes.

It couldn't be—but it was.

Jackson did what was required of him. When he had finished *trombramcthulanchieriring* in the usual manner, he had only to get through the official ceremony and the several small requirements after it.

Erum assured him that it was all quite simple, but Jackson suspected that he might somehow have difficulties.

So, in preparation, he put in three days of hard work acquiring a real mastery of the 29 exceptional potentiators, together with their most common positions and their potentiating effect in each of these positions. He finished, boneweary and with his irritability index risen to 97.3620 on the Grafheimer scale. An impartial observer might have noticed an ominous gleam in his china-blue eyes.

Jackson had had it. He was sick of the Hon language and of all things Naian. He had the vertiginous feeling that the more he learned, the less he knew. It was downright perverse.

"Hokay," Jackson said, to himself and to the universe at large. "I have learned the Naian language, and I have learned a set of completely inexplicable exceptions, *and* I have *also* learned a further and even more contradictory set of exceptions to the exceptions."

Jackson paused and in a very low voice said: "I have learned an *exceptional* number of exceptions. Indeed, an impartial observer might think that this language is composed of nothing *but* exceptions.

"But *that,*" he continued, "is damned well impossible, unthinkable, and unacceptable. A language is by God and by definition *systematic,* which means it's gotta follow some kind of *rules.* Otherwise, nobody can't understand *nobody.* That's the way it works and that's the way it's gotta be. And if anyone thinks they can horse around linguisticwise with Fred C. Jackson—"

Here Jackson paused and drew the blaster from his holster. He checked the charge, snapped off the safety, and replaced the weapon.

"Just better no one give old Jackson no more double-talking," old Jackson muttered. "Because the next alien who tries it is going to get a three-inch circle drilled through his lousy cheating guts."

So saying, Jackson marched back to the city. He was feeling decidedly lightheaded, but absolutely determined. His job was to steal this planet out from under its inhabitants in a legal manner, and in order to do that he had to make sense out of their language. Therefore, in one way or another, he was going to *make* sense. Either that, or he was going to make some corpses.

At this point, he didn't much care which.

Erum was in his office, waiting for him. With him were the mayor, the president of the City Council, the borough president, two aldermen and the director of the Board of Estimates. All of them were smiling affably, albeit nervously. Strong spirits were present on a sideboard, and there was a subdued air of fellowship in the room.

All in all, it looked as if Jackson were being welcomed as a new and highly respected property owner, an adornment to Fakka. Aliens took it that way sometimes: made the best of a bad bargain by trying to ingratiate themselves with the Inevitable Earthman.

"*Mun,*" said Erum, shaking his hand enthusiastically. "Same to you, kid," Jackson said. He had no idea what the word meant. Nor did he care. He had plenty of other Naian words to choose among, and he had the determination to force matters to a conclusion.

"*Mun!*" said the mayor.

"Thanks, pop," said Jackson.

"*Mun!*" declared the other officials.

"Glad you boys feel that way," said Jackson. He turned to Erum. "Well, let's get it over with, okay?" "*Mun-mun-mun,*" Erum replied. "*Mun, mun-*

mun." Jackson stared at him for several seconds. Then he said, in a low, controlled voice, "Erum, baby, just exactly *what* are you trying to say to me?"

"*Mun, mun, mun,*" Erum stated firmly. "*Mun, mun mun mun. Mun mun.*" He paused, and in a somewhat nervous voice asked the mayor: "*Mun, mun?*"

"*Mun...mun mun,*" the mayor replied firmly, and the other officials nodded. They all turned to Jackson.

"*Mun, mun-mun?*" Erum asked him, tremulously, but with dignity...

Jackson was numbed speechless. His face turned a choleric red and a large blue vein started to pulse in his neck. But he managed to speak slowly, calmly, and with infinite menace.

"Just *what,*" he said, "do you lousy third-rate yokels think you're pulling?"

"*Mun-mun?*" the mayor asked Erum.

"*Mun-mun, mun-mun-mun,*" Erum replied quickly, making a gesture of incomprehension.

"You better talk sense," Jackson said. His voice was still low, but the vein in his neck writhed like a firehose under pressure.

"*Mun!*" one of the alderman said quickly to the borough president.

"*Mun mun-mun mun?*" the borough president answered piteously, his voice breaking on the last word.

"So you won't talk sense, huh?"

"*Mun! Mun-mun!*" the mayor cried, his face gone ashen with fright.

The others looked and saw Jackson's hand clearing the blaster and taking aim at Erum's chest.

"Quit horsing around!" Jackson commanded. The vein in his neck pulsed like a python in travail.

"*Mun-mun-mun!*" Erum pleaded, dropping to his knees.

"*Mun-mun-mun!*" the mayor shrieked, rolling his eyes and fainting.

"You get it now," Jackson said to Erum. His finger whitened on the trigger.

Erum, his teeth chattering, managed to gasp out a strangled "*Mun-mun, mun?*" But then his nerves gave way and he waited for death with jaw agape and eyes unfocused.

Jackson took up the last fraction of slack in the trigger. Then, abruptly, he let up and shoved the blaster back in its holster.

"*Mun, mun!*" Erum managed to say.

"Shaddap," Jackson said. He stepped back and glared at the cringing Naian officials.

He would have dearly loved to blast them all. But he couldn't do it. Jackson had to come to a belated acknowledgement of an unacceptable reality.

His impeccable linguist's ear had heard, and his polyglot brain had analyzed. Dismayingly, he had realized that the Naians were not trying to put anything over on him. They were speaking not nonsense, but a true language.

This language was made up at present of the single sound *"mun."* This sound could carry an extensive repertoire of meanings through variations in pitch and pattern, changes in stress and quantity, alteration of rhythm and repetition, and through accompanying gestures and facial expressions.

A language consisting of infinite variations on a single word! Jackson didn't want to believe it, but he was too good a linguist to doubt the evidence of his own trained senses.

He could learn this language, of course.

But by the time he had learned it, what would it have changed into?

Jackson sighed and rubbed his face wearily. In a sense it was inevitable. All languages change. But on Earth and the few dozen worlds she had contacted, the languages changed with relative slowness.

On Na, the rate of change was faster. Quite a bit faster.

The Na language changed as fashions change on Earth, only faster. It changed as prices change or as the weather changes. It changed endlessly and incessantly, in accordance with unknown rules and invisible principles. It changed its form as an avalanche changes its shape. Compared with it, English was like a glacier.

The Na language was, truly and monstrously, a simulacrum of Heraclitus's river. You cannot step into the same river twice, said Heraclitus; for other waters are forever flowing on.

Concerning the language of Na, this was simply and literally true.

That made it bad enough. But even worse was the fact that an observer like Jackson could never hope to fix or isolate even one term out of the dynamic shifting network of terms that composed the Na language. For the observer's action would be gross enough by itself to disrupt and alter the system, causing it to change unpredictably. And so, if the term were isolated, its relationship to the other terms in the system would necessarily be destroyed, and the term itself, by definition, would be false.

By the fact of its change, the language was rendered impervious to codification and control. Through indeterminacy, the Na tongue resisted all attempts to conquer it. And Jackson had gone from Heraclitus to Heisenberg without touching second base. He was dazed and dazzled, and he looked upon the officials with something approaching awe.

"You've done it, boys," he told them. "You've beaten the system. Old Earth could swallow you and never notice the difference; you couldn't do a damned thing about it. But the folks back home like their legalism, and our law says that we must be in a state of communication as a prior condition to any transaction."

"Mun?" Erum asked politely.

"So I guess that means I leave you folks alone," Jackson said. "At least, I do as long as they keep that law on the books. But what the hell, a reprieve is the best anyone can ask for. Eh?"

"Mun mun," the mayor said hesitantly.

"I'll be getting along now," Jackson said. "Fair's fair...But if I ever find out that you Naians were putting one over on me—"

He left the sentence unfinished. Without another word, Jackson turned and went back to his ship.

In half an hour he was spaceworthy, and fifteen minutes after that he was underway.

VI

In Erum's office, the officials watched while Jackson's spaceship glowed like a comet in the dark afternoon sky. It dwindled to a brilliant needlepoint, and then vanished into the vastness of space.

The officials were silent for a moment; then they turned and looked at each other. Suddenly, spontaneously, they burst into laughter. Harder and harder they laughed, clutching their sides while tears rolled down their cheeks.

The mayor was the first to check the hysteria. Getting a grip on himself he said, *"Mun, mun, mun-mun."*

This thought instantly sobered the others. Their mirth died away. Uneasily they contemplated the distant unfriendly sky, and they thought back over their recent adventures.

At last young Erum asked, *"Mun-mun? Mun-mun?"*

Several of the officials smiled at the naïveté of the question. And yet, none could answer that simple yet crucial demand. Why indeed? Did anyone dare hazard even a guess?

It was a perplexity leaving in doubt not only the future but the past as well. And, if a real answer were unthinkable, then no answer at all was surely insupportable.

The silence grew, and Erum's young mouth twisted downward in premature cynicism. He said quite harshly, *"Mun! Mun-mun! Mun?"*

His shocking words were no more than the hasty cruelty of the young; but such a statement could not go unchallenged. And the venerable first alderman stepped forward to essay a reply.

"Mun mun, mun-mun," the old man said, with disarming simplicity. *"Mun mun mun-mun? Mun mun-mun-mun. Mun mun mun; mun mun mun; mun mun. Mun, mun mun mun—mun mun mun. Mun-mun? Mun mun mun mun!"*

This straightforward declaration of faith pierced Erum to the core of his being. Tears sprang unanticipated to his eyes. All postures forgotten, he turned to the sky, clenched his fist and shouted, *"Mun! Mun! Mun-mun!"*

Smiling serenely, the old alderman murmured, *"Mun-mun-mun; mun, mun-mun."*

This was, ironically enough, the marvelous and frightening truth of the situation. Perhaps it was just as well that the others did not hear.

WHAT IS LIFE?

Mortonson relates that while he was out strolling in the foothills of the Himalayas one day, a tremendous voice that seemed to come from everywhere and nowhere said to him, "Hey, you."

"Me?" Mortonson asked.

"Yes, you," the voice boomed. "Can you tell me, what is life?"

Mortonson stood, frozen in midstride, pouring perspiration, aware that he was having a genuine mystical experience, and that a lot was going to depend on how he answered The Question.

"I'm going to need a moment or two for this one," he said.

"Don't take too long," said the voice, reverberating hugely from all sides.

Mortonson sat down on a rock and considered the situation. The god or demon who had asked the question surely knew that Mortonson—a mere mortal and not too fantastic a specimen at that—hadn't the faintest idea of what life was. So his answer should perhaps reveal his understanding of his own mortal limitations, but also show his awareness that it was somehow appropriate for the god or demon to ask this question of a potentially divine creature like Man, here represented by Mortonson with his stooped shoulders, sunburned nose, orange rucksack, and crumpled pack of Marlboros. On the other hand, maybe the implication of the question was that Mortonson himself really *did* know what life was and could spontaneously state in a few well-chosen words. But it was already a bit late for spontaneous wisdom.

"I'll be right with you," Mortonson said.

"Okay," said the tremendous voice, booming off the mountains and rolling through the valleys.

It was really a drag to be put on the line like this spiritually. And it wasn't fair. After all, Mortonson hadn't come to Nepal as a *pilgrim,* he was only there on a thirty-day excursion. He was simply a young American with a sunburned nose chain-smoking Marlboros on a hillside in Nepal where he had come through a combination of restlessness and an

551

unexpected birthday gift of five hundred dollars from his parents. So what could you infer from that, context-wise? Raw American Encounters Immemorial Eastern Wisdom and Fails Miserably To Get With It. A bummer!

Nobody likes to be put on the spot like that. It's embarrassing and potentially ego-damaging to have this vast otherworldly voice come at you with what has to be a trick question. How do you handle it? Avoid the trap, expose the double-bind, reveal your knowledge of the Metagame by playing it in a spirit of frivolity! Tell the voice: *Life is a voice asking a man what life is!* And then roar with cosmic laughter.

But to bring that off you need to be sure that the voice understands the levels of your answer; What if it says, "Yeah, that's what's *happening,* but what is *life?*" And you're left standing there with ectoplasmic egg on your face as that cosmic laughter is directed at *you*—great gusty heroic laughter at your pomposity, your complacency, your arrogance at even attempting to answer the Unanswerable.

"How's it coming?" the voice asked.

"I'm still working on it," Mortonson said.

Obviously, this was one of those spiritual quickies, and Mortonson was still stalling around, and hadn't even gotten around yet to considering what in hell life was. Quickly he reviewed some possibilities: Life is a warm puppy. Life is asymmetry. Life is Chance. Life is Chaos shot through with Fatality (remember that one). Life is just a bowl of cherries. Life is birdcall and windsong (nice). Life is what you make it. Life is Cosmic Dance. Life is a Movie. Life is matter become curious (did Victor Hugo say that?). Life is whatever the hell you want to call it.

"This is really a tough one," Mortonson said.

"That's for sure," the voice said, rolling from peak to peak and filling the air with its presence.

One should always be prepared for this kind of spiritual emergency, Mortonson thought. Why didn't NYU have a course in Normative Attitudes Toward the Unexpected? But college never prepared you for anything important, you just went along learning a little here and there, picking up on Chuang Tzu, Thoreau, Norman Brown, Pajneesh, the Shivapuri Baba and the other Insiders who really knew the score. And all their stuff sounded absolutely right on! But when you closed the book, that was the end of it, and there you were scratching your nose and wishing that someone would invite you to a party where you'd meet a beautiful childlike young woman with long straight hair and upright pointy breasts and long slender legs, but now was no time to get into that because that damned voice was waiting for the answer, the Big Answer, but what in almighty hell was *life?*

"I've almost got it," he said.

What really bugged him was the knowledge that he had a lot to gain if he could only come up with the right answer. It was a really incredible chance for spiritual advancement, an opportunity to skip a few intermediate steps and get right up to Enlightenment, Moksha, Satori! A really together person could solve this and parlay the ensuing insight into guruhood, maybe even into Buddhadom! You could spend a lifetime going to Esalen or a Gurdjieff group and never get near anything like this! But what was life?

Mortonson ground out his cigarette and saw that it was his last. No more until he got back to his pension. Christ! He had to get on with this! Life is hesitation? Desire? Longing? Sorrow? Preparation? Fruition? Coming together? Moving apart?

Mortonson rubbed his forehead and said in a loud but somewhat shaky voice, "Life is conflagration!"

There was an uncanny silence. After what he judged was a proper discretionary wait, Mortonson asked, "Uh, was that right?"

"I'm trying it out," the noble and tremendous voice boomed. "Conflagration is too long. Blaze? Fire! Life is fire! That fits!"

"Fire is what I meant," Mortonson said.

"You really helped me out," the voice said, "I was stuck on that one. Now maybe you can help me with 78 across. I need to know the middle name of the inventor of the frictionless star drive. It's on the tip of my tongue but I can't quite get it. The third letter is D."

Mortonson had been prepared for some freaky revelations, but playing Cosmic Crosswords was not his idea of where anything was at, spiritually speaking. He just couldn't relate to it, even though it was definitely an Extraordinary Experience.

He relates that he thereupon turned and walked away from the voice and the higher mysteries and returned to his pension in Katmandu. Now he has gone back to his job as expeditor in his father's gristle-processing plant in Skowhegan, and he takes his vacations in Majorca.

SARKANGER

Richard Gregor and Frank Arnold sat in the offices of the AAA Ace Interplanetary Decontamination Service filling in the long slow time between customers. Gregor, tall, thin, and lachrymose, was playing a complicated game of solitaire. Arnold, short and plump, with thinning canary yellow hair and china blue eyes, was watching an old Fred Astaire movie on a small TV.

Then, miracle of miracles, a customer walked in.

He was a Sarkanger, a weasel-headed alien from Sarkan II. He was dressed in a white lounge suit and carried an expensive briefcase.

"I have a planet that needs exterminating," the Sarkanger said.

"You've come to the right place," Arnold said. "What seems to be the matter?"

"It's the Meegs," the Sarkanger told him. "We tolerated them as long as they stayed in their burrows. But now they are attacking our saunicus and something must be done."

"What are these Meegs?" Gregor asked.

"They are small, ugly creatures of low intelligence with long claws and matted fur."

"And what is a saunicus?"

"The saunicus is a leafy green vegetable not unlike your terrestrial cabbage. It is the sole diet of the Sarkangers."

"And now the Meegs are eating your vegetables?"

"Not eating them. Mutilating them. Wantonly destroying them."

"For what reason?"

"Who can understand why a Meeg does anything?"

"True enough," Arnold said, laughing. "Yes sir, that's certainly true! Well, sir, I think we can help you. There's really only one problem."

Gregor gave his partner a look of alarm.

"The question is," Arnold said, "whether we can fit you into our schedule."

He opened his appointment book. The pages were crowded with names and dates which Arnold had written in hoping for just such a chance as this.

"That's a bit of luck," he said. "We have an open slot this weekend. All we need do is arrange the fee and be on our way. I have our standard contract form right here."

"I have brought my own," the Sarkanger said, taking a document from his briefcase and giving it to Arnold. "You will notice that a very substantial fee is already filled in."

"Why yes," Arnold said, signing with a flourish, "I did notice that."

Gregor studied the paper. "You've also doubled the penalty clause in case of failure to complete our work."

"That's why I made the fee so substantial," the Sarkanger said. "We need results now, before the end of the planting season."

Gregor didn't like it. But his partner gave him a hard look compounded of unpaid bills and overdue bank loans. With reluctance Gregor scribbled his signature.

Four days later their ship popped out of subspace in the vicinity of the red dwarf star Sarkan. A few hours later they had landed on Sarkan II, home of the Sarkangers and their pests, the Meegs.

There was no one to greet them at Sarkan's largest city, Sulkers. The entire population had gone to the satellite Ulvis Minor for a vacation, at considerable expense despite mass bookings, to wait in gaily colored cabanas until their planet was cleansed.

The partners toured Sulkers and were unimpressed by the mud wall architecture. They set up their base camp outside of the city, on the edge of a saunicus field. Just as the Sarkanger had told them, many of the cabbages had been rended, ripped, slashed, filleted, and generally messed about.

They would begin exterminating in the morning. Arnold had discovered that Meegs were susceptible to papayin, an enzyme of the papaya plant. Exposed to concentrations as low as twenty parts in a million, Meegs went into a coma from which they could be revived only by the immediate application of cold compresses. It was not a bad way to go when you consider the many less pleasant ways the galaxy has for killing people. They had brought a sufficient supply of canned, fresh, frozen, and desiccated papayas to wipe out several planetfuls of Meegs.

They set up tents and deck chairs, built a campfire, and watched Sarkan's red dwarf sun sink into a sculptured frieze of sunset clouds.

They had just finished a dinner of reconstituted chili and beans when they heard a rustling sound in the bushes nearby. A small creature stepped out cautiously. It was about the size and shape of a cat, with thick orange-brown fur.

Gregor said to Arnold, "Do you think that might be a Meeg?"

The creature said, "Of course I am a Meeg. And you gentlemen are the AAA Ace Decontamination Service?"

"That is correct," Gregor said.

"Wonderful! Then you've come about the Sarkangers!"

"Not exactly," Arnold said.

"You mean you didn't get our letter? I knew we should have sent it spacemail special delivery…But why are you here?"

"This is a little embarrassing," Gregor said. "We didn't know you Meegs spoke English."

"Not all of us do," the Meeg said. "But I happen to be a graduate of your Cornell University."

"Look," Gregor said, "the fact is, a Sarkanger came to our office a few days ago and paid us to rid his planet of vermin."

"Vermin?" the Meeg said. "What was he referring to?"

"You," Arnold said.

"Me? Us? Vermin? A Sarkanger called us that? I know we've had our disagreements, but that's carrying matters a bit too far. And he paid you to kill us? And you took his money?"

"Frankly," Arnold said, "we had expected Meegs to be more—rudimentary. More verminlike, if you know what I mean."

"But this is preposterous!" the Meeg cried. "*They* are the vermin! *We* are civilized!"

"I'm not so sure about that," Gregor said. "What about the way you tear apart saunicus?"

"You should not comment ignorantly on the religious practices of an alien people."

"What's religious about rending cabbage?" Arnold demanded.

"It's not the act itself," the Meeg explained. "It's the meaning attached to it. Ever since Meeg Gh'tan, known as the Great Feline, discovered supreme enlightenment in the simple act of shredding cabbage, we his followers reenact the rite every year."

"But you tear apart the Sarkangers' cabbages," Gregor pointed out. "Why not tear apart your own?"

"The Sarkangers refused to let us cultivate the saunicus because of some silly religion they have. Of course we'd prefer to tear apart our own cabbages. Wouldn't anyone?"

"The Sarkangers didn't mention that," Arnold said.

"Puts matters in a different light, doesn't it?"

"It doesn't change the fact that we have a contract with the Sarkangers."

"A contract for murder!"

"I understand how you feel," Arnold said, "and I do sympathize. But you see, if we don't fulfill our contract, it will mean bankruptcy for us. That's a kind of death, too, you know."

"Suppose," the Meeg said, "we Meegs were to offer you a new contract."

"We have a prior agreement with the Sarkangers," Gregor said. "It wouldn't be legal."

"It would be perfect legal in any Meeg court," the Meeg said. "A basic principle of Meeg jurisprudence is that no contract with a Sarkanger is binding."

"My partner and I will have to think about it," Arnold said. "It's a difficult position."

"I appreciate that," the Meeg said. "I'll give you a chance to think it over. Just remember that the Sarkangers deserve to be exterminated and that you'll make a handsome profit as well as earning the undying gratitude of a race of intelligent and not, I think, unlikable cats."

After the Meeg had left, Gregor said, "Let's just get out of here. This is not a very nice business."

"We can't just up and leave," Arnold said. "Non-fulfillment of contract is a serious matter. We're going to have to exterminate one race or the other."

"I won't do it," Gregor said.

"You don't seem to understand our extremely precarious legal position," Arnold told him. "The courts will crucify us if we don't wipe out the Meegs as we promised. But if we exterminate the Sarkangers we could at least claim an honest mistake."

"It's morally complicated," Gregor said. "I don't like problems like that."

"It gets even more complicated," a voice said behind them.

Arnold jumped as though touched by an electric wire. Gregor went into a state of frozen immobility.

"I'm over here," the voice said.

They looked around. There was nobody there. Only a large saunicus cabbage on the ground all by itself at the edge of their camp. Somehow this saunicus looked more intelligent that most of the ones they had seen. But could it have spoken?

"Yes, yes," said the saunicus. "I spoke to you. Telepathically, of course, since vegetables—in whose family I am proud to consider myself a member—have no organs of articulation."

"But vegetables can't telepathize," Arnold said. "They have no brains or other organs to telepathize with. Excuse me, I don't mean to be offensive."

"We don't need organs," the saunicus said. "Don't you know that all matter with a sufficiently complex degree of organization possesses intelligence? Communication is the inevitable concomitant of intelligence. Only the higher vegetables such as myself can telepathize. Saunicus intelligence is being studied at your Harvard University. We have even applied for observer status at your United Planets. Under the circumstances, I think we should have a say in this matter of who gets exterminated."

"True, it's only fair," Gregor said. "After all, it's you the Meegs and the Sarkangers are fighting over."

"To be more precise," the saunicus said, "they are fighting over which race will have the exclusive right to rend, tear, and mutilate us. Or do I state the case unfairly?"

"No, that seems to sum it up," Gregor said. "Which one do you vote for?"

"As you might expect, I am in favor of neither. Both those races are contemptible vermin. I vote for an entirely different solution."

"I was afraid of that," Arnold said. "What did you have in mind?"

"Simple enough. Sign a contract with me to rid my planet of both Meegs and Sarkangers."

"Oh, no," Gregor said.

"We are, after all, much the earliest inhabitants of this planet. We arrived not long after the lichens, before animal life had even developed. We are peaceful, indigenous, and threatened by barbarous newcomers. It seems to me that your moral duty is clear."

Arnold sighed. "Morality is all very well. But there are practical considerations, too."

"I am aware of that," the saunicus said. "Aside from your satisfaction for doing a good job, we would be prepared to sign a contract and pay you double what the others have offered."

"Look," Arnold said, "it's difficult for me to believe that a vegetable has a bank account."

"Intelligence, no matter what form it comes in, can always get money. Working through our holding company, Saunicus Entertainment Modalities, we publish books and tapes and compile databases on a variety of subjects. We impart our knowledge telepathically to Terran authors whom we hire at a flat rate per page. Our gardening section is especially profitable: only a vegetable can be a true expert on growing plants. I think you will find our Dun & Bradstreet rating more than adequate."

The saunicus went to a distant part of the field to give the partners a chance to talk it over. When he was fifty yards away—outside of telepathic range—Arnold said, "I didn't much like that cabbage. He seemed too smart for his own good, if you know what I mean."

"Yeah, it was like he was trying to prove something," Gregor said. "But the Meeg—didn't you sense something untrustworthy about him?"

Arnold nodded. "And the Sarkanger who began all this—he seemed like a thoroughly unscrupulous character."

Gregor said, "It's difficult to decide which race to exterminate on such short acquaintance. I wish we knew them a little better."

"Let's just exterminate somebody, anybody," Arnold said, "and get finished with this job. But which?"

"We'll flip a coin. Then no one can accuse us of being prejudiced."

"But there are three parties to choose from."

"So we draw straws. I just don't know what else to do."

Just at that moment a tremendous clap of thunder came rolling off the nearby mountains. The sky, previously a light azure, now turned dark and ominous. Massive, quick-moving cumulus bubbled and frothed across the horizon. From the vast vault of the heavens there came a tremendous voice:

"I can stand for this no longer!"

"Oh my God," Gregor said, "we've offended somebody!"

"To whom are we speaking?" Arnold said, looking up at the sky.

"I am the voice of this planet which you know as Sarkan."

"I never knew planets could talk," Gregor mumbled under his breath. But the being or whoever it was picked it up at once.

"In general," the voice said, "we planets do not bother communicating with the tiny creatures who crawl across our surfaces. We are content with our own thoughts, and with the company of our own kind. The occasional comet brings us news of distant places, and that's enough for us. We try to ignore the nonsense that goes on on our surfaces. But sometimes it gets to be too much. These murderous Sarkangers, Meegs, and saunicus which inhabit me are simply too vile to be tolerated any longer. I am about to take an appropriate and long overdue action."

"What are you going to do?" Arnold asked.

"I shall flood myself to a mean depth of ten meters, thus disposing of Sarkangers, Meegs, *and* saunicus. A few innocent species will also suffer, but what the hell, that's the way it goes. You two have one hour to get out of here. After that, I can't be held responsible for your safety."

The partners packed up quickly and returned to their spaceship.

"Thanks for the warning," Gregor said just before they took off.

"It's not out of any fondness for you," the planet replied. "As far as I'm concerned you're vermin just like the others. But you're vermin from another planet. If word ever got out that I wiped you out, others of your species would come with their atom bombs and laser cannons and destroy me as a rogue planet. So get out of here while I'm still in a good mood."

Several hours later, in orbit above Sarkan, Arnold and Gregor watches scenes of fantastic destruction take place before their eyes.

When it was over Gregor set a course for home.

"I suppose," he said to Arnold, "that this is the end of AAA Ace. We've forfeited our contract. The Sarkangers' lawyers will nail us."

Arnold looked up. He had been studying the contract. "No," he said, "Oddly enough, I think we're in the clear. Read that last paragraph."

Gregor read it and scratched his head. "I see what you mean. But do you think it'll hold up in court?"

"Sure it will. Floods are always considered Acts of God. And if we don't tell and the planet doesn't tell, who's ever going to know different?"

DUKAKIS AND THE ALIENS

Dukakis had always known that the first day in the White House was going to be weird. But he could never have guessed how weird. The strangeness began as soon as he was alone in the Oval Office. He sat down in the big presidential command chair and closed his eyes, just for a moment, to dream again the dream that had come true—himself, President, sitting in the Oval Office, the highest office on the planet, and almost certainly the whole solar system with all its asteroids and comets...

"Mr. President, sir?"

Dukakis's eyes snapped open. He hadn't even heard anyone come in. Rubber-soled shoes, he supposed. But he hadn't even heard the door open. He'd left word everyone was to leave him alone until he called for them. And now here was this guy, early thirties, balding, leaning anxiously over him. The guy's dark hair was cut short and parted on the left. He wore a dark blue suit. There was a small white flower in his buttonhole.

"Yes, what is it?" Dukakis asked. "Who are you?"

"I'm Watkins, sir," the man said. "One of your new Secret Service guards."

"Yes, Watkins, what can I do for you?"

"Sir, there are certain matters of state secrecy that we members of the presidential bodyguard are sworn to divulge to the new president as soon as he is physically inside the Oval Office."

"Must that be right now?" Dukakis asked, rubbing his eyes.

"You can understand our hurry, Mr. President. There are matters of highest importance of which the public is not really informed. Not even the inner circle of advisors and experts knows everything, and certainly not all the details. The only person who knows it all is the president. He is the final arbiter, the place where the buck stops, the man who has to at last decide what should be done."

"Done about what?" Dukakis asked.

"That is for you to decide, sir, after I have divulged to you what is arguably the biggest secret of this or any administration in the past or even into the foreseeable future."

Dukakis laughed. "What is it? Are you going to introduce me to little green aliens?"

Watkins paled visibly. "Has someone already gotten to you?"

"What are you talking about?" Dukakis said, "I was making a joke."

"The aliens are no joke," Watkins said. "Come with me, sir, and I'll take you to them."

"I beg your pardon?"

"The aliens, sir. I'm taking you now to meet them."

"Not now," Dukakis said. "I'm really not up for aliens. And I'm supposed to meet the President of Nigeria in fifteen minutes."

Watkins made an expression of concern. "I had hoped, sir, that we could do this expeditiously."

"What about next Tuesday, between ten and eleven, for the aliens?" Dukakis asked.

"I'm afraid that won't be soon enough for them," Watkins said.

Dukakis laughed, then noticed that Watkins was not laughing. Dukakis's face resumed its familiar lugubrious non-smiling lines. He asked, jokingly, but in a tone that one could take seriously, too, if one wanted to, "What do we care what will or will not be soon enough for them?"

"I'm afraid we care very much," Watkins said. "This is a matter of the utmost urgency. Please come with me, Mr. President. There are some people you need to meet. I suppose 'people' is the correct word."

Dukakis stirred uneasily. This first Secret Service briefing wasn't going the way he had anticipated. Why hadn't anyone told him about this alien thing? He felt out of his depth.

"I'd like to call in my advisors," Dukakis said.

"We'd prefer you didn't," Watkins said. "Not yet. You can consult with them after you've learned about the alien matter. But not before. You must be briefed first so that you can decide how much to tell your advisors."

"I don't understand what it is I'm being briefed on," Dukakis said.

"You will very shortly," Watkins said. "If we may just proceed..."

The Secret Service man seemed to be familiar with the Oval Office. He walked to a tall closet and unlocked it with a key from his pocket. Dukakis looked in over his shoulder. There was a long row of suits hanging on a rack. Watkins pushed them aside, revealing, behind them, the open-framed ironwork of a small elevator.

"I didn't know this was here," Dukakis said.

Watkins smiled. "You weren't supposed to. Not until now."

Watkins opened the gate. Dukakis walked into the elevator. Watkins came in behind him and closed the gate. Dukakis went to the switchboard. There were four floors listed.

"Which one should I press?" Dukakis asked.

"None of them," Watkins said. "These just go to the parking garages under the White House."

"Where are we going?"

"You'll see." Using a Swiss Army knife, Watkins pried at the panel. It came loose. Behind it was a single red button caged in a wire holder. Watkins took off the wire container.

"Now you can press it," he said to Dukakis.

Dukakis pressed the red button. There was a soft hum of machinery. The elevator began to move down, then sideways. It picked up speed alarmingly.

"What's powering this thing?" Dukakis asked.

"Tesla coil," Watkins said.

"Never heard of it," Dukakis said.

"The full technology has never been released to the public."

"Why not, if it's so good?"

"That's part of what we'll be explaining to you, sir."

"Where are we going?" Dukakis asked.

"To the secret installation under Dulces, New Mexico."

"New Mexico? But that's thousands of miles away!"

"Two thousand and seven miles from Washington, to be exact. But magnetic induction travel like we're doing is very rapid."

"You said 'the secret base'?"

"Yes, sir."

"I didn't know we had any secret base there."

"We don't, strictly speaking. We have an air force base. The aliens, however, have a secret base under ours."

"Underneath? You mean under the ground?"

"Yes, sir. There are nine underground levels to it."

"That's a big underground city," Dukakis said.

"Yes, it is, sir."

Watkins felt along the wall of the elevator, pressed two small buttons. Cushioned seats unfolded into existence. A secret bar opened from the wall.

"You've got everything in here!" Dukakis said admiringly.

"Even a fax machine. Though we're traveling so fast as to make use of one unnecessary."

Dukakis made himself comfortable. Watkins opened one of the floor panels and took out lunch. Dukakis thought the turkey sandwiches were a little dry, but they were pretty tasty; real turkey breast, not that pressed stuff. A bottle of High Sierra beer washed it down nicely. Whoever stocked this place knew his beer, Dukakis decided.

There were current newspapers in a little rack. Dukakis read for a while, then tried to figure out the rate of speed they were traveling at. But he couldn't work it out. Looking at his watch, he saw they had been in the elevator for almost two hours.

He looked at Watkins. Watkins, seated opposite him, had his hands clasped behind his neck and was rocking gently back and forth.

Dukakis was not amused by the whole situation. But he had begun to wonder if this might be some sort of plot. He thought about old political rivalries. He thought about the Soviets, and the Mafia. Was someone out to get him? Was he being paranoid? Where did paranoia end and prudence begin?

At last the elevator came to a stop. Watkins opened the door. Outside there was a long corridor.

"Now we walk," Watkins said. "I'm sorry about that, but this part of the transportation system hasn't been completed yet. I don't need to tell you who's behind the delay."

Dukakis didn't know what Watkins was talking about but decided not to ask. "Where are we?" he asked.

"Dulces, New Mexico. Underneath it, I mean. In the topmost level of the alien underground base."

"But what are we here for?"

"They need to know your decision, Mr. President."

"On what?"

"Well, sir, that's what the briefing will be all about."

They walked down a tunnel-like corridor. It had curving sides, and there were lights recessed into the ceiling. The walls seemed to be made of polished aluminum. There was a soft hum, as of machinery somewhere behind the walls.

Dukakis was getting a little more nervous now. He knew he shouldn't have come out here without a bodyguard. And he ought to have checked up on Watkins before following him blindly like this, all the way to New Mexico. If only he'd had a day or two in office to accustom himself to command! He hoped he didn't end up paying for being too easygoing.

They continued down the long tubular hallway with the little lights spaced at three-foot intervals in the ceiling. Neither was saying anything.

After a while Dukakis could see a door at the end of the hall. There was a guard standing in front of it. The guard was very tall and he was dressed in a dark blue uniform with crimson and gold epaulets. Dukakis made a mental note to find out what branch of the service the guard belonged to. His uniform was not familiar. Dukakis noted also that the man's face was a featureless blank.

"Who is that guy?" Dukakis asked in a whisper.

"Oh, he's one of the Synthetics," Watkins said. "Don't worry, he's on our side."

They stopped in front of the guard.

"May we pass?" Watkins asked.

"Just a minute," the guard said. He was holding an odd-shaped handgun with a flaring bell-shaped muzzle. "Papers, please."

Watkins took two plastic-enclosed folders from one of his inside pockets and handed them to the guard.

The guard glanced at them, nodded. "Now I must perform the physical inspection."

"Certainly not!" Watkins said. "Not on him. He's the President!"

"I have my orders," the guard said. "You know what they say: in the Goblin Universe, anyone can wear anyone's face."

"But this place is fully shielded against intrusion."

"That's what they thought at Ada, Oklahoma," the guard said.

"Oh," Watkins said. "I had forgotten."

"Please, sir, don't make me use force."

"Oh, very well." Watkins turned to Dukakis, "It's just a formality, sir. He needs to look up your nostrils with a little instrument."

"I don't entirely understand—" Dukakis gasped as the guard seized him, pulled him forward. It seemed best not to resist. The guard tilted Dukakis's head back with one hand and shone a small light up his nostrils with the other. He peered into both nostrils, then turned off his light and released Dukakis.

"You may proceed," the guard said.

Dukakis was still stunned. Watkins pulled him down the corridor. The two men walked along in silence for a while, until the guard was out of sight.

"What was that all about?" Dukakis asked.

"He was looking for implants, sir," Watkins said.

"What are implants?"

"Controlling devices put directly into the brain. They insert them up the nostril, sir, into an area near the optic nerve. Implanted subjects have no control over their actions."

Dukakis frowned. "I do not believe the nostril connects directly with the optic nerve area."

"I realize that, sir. They have to drill a tiny laser hole and then put in the insert."

"Who is this 'They'? Who does this?"

"We're not entirely sure," Watkins said. "At first we thought it was the Zeta Reticulis Grays, but now we're not. We suspect the implanting to be the work of advance elements of reptiloids from Draco. There's still a chance it's being done by the Grays, however, since no one has seen a reptiloid on Earth and lived to report it."

"Who are these Grays?" Dukakis asked.

Watkins smiled ironically. "We used to think they were our friends. Now some us are having second thoughts about working with them. But please don't tell them I said so." Watkins glanced at his watch. "Damn! We're really late! And there's miles of corridor ahead. But I think there's a shortcut around here somewhere…"

Watkins felt along the wall, found a place, pushed it. A section of the wall slid out, revealing another, smaller passageway.

It was dark inside. Dukakis looked at Watkins questioningly. "Please don't balk now," Watkins said. "We simply have to do it." Dukakis grimaced, shrugged, and followed Watkins into the hole.

They walked along in the dark for a while. Then the corridor widened out and there were low lights set into the walls. By this dim glow Dukakis could make out that they were in a large room furnished with big vats, bathtubs, and stone tables.

"What sort of place is this?" Dukakis asked.

"Well, it's a sort of workshop," Watkins said. "I'm sorry I have to bring you through here, sir, but we *are* in a hurry."

As Dukakis's eyes became accustomed to the darkness, he saw there were hooks set into the low stone ceiling. From those hooks hung chunks of meat, still dripping with blood. Dukakis could see coils of entrails hanging over several hooks. Some of the chunks of meat were entire torsos, thighs, hams, buttocks. All or most of them appeared to be human. As he became aware of this, the rank, rotting smell of the meat rose up and assailed his nostrils.

"Ugh!" cried Dukakis.

"I'm sorry, sir," Watkins said, handing the president a handkerchief that had been impregnated with a strong perfume.

"Those dripping things hanging from the hooks…"

"I know, sir. It doesn't look good. I'm sorry we had to come this way."

They came to a row of white porcelain bathtubs. Each was filled with what seemed to be a noisome and horrific experiment. In one, there was a headless male torso, and from the region of its stomach a hand was growing. The other tubs contained similar necrotic apparitions.

"Gawk," Dukakis said, retching.

Watkins shook his head and in a grim voice said, "It is what comes of aliens using the Earth as a dumping ground for genetic engineering projects from all over the galaxy for all these years. We've complained about it, sir."

Farther on they passed a big vat seven feet deep, ten yards long by five yards wide. In it were hunks of meat, both animal and human—haunches, shoulders, hands. Splashing around among the hunks of meat were small gray men. They seemed to be having a good time. They were playing a sort of volleyball with human heads.

Dukakis mastered himself. "Who is responsible for this atrocity?"

Watkins said grimly, "It seems to be the work of the Short Grays of Zeta Reticuli. The other Grays, the tall ones, rely on glandular secretions and follow a much less messy procedure. It's those damned Short Grays who like to bathe in the stuff, even though it is isn't strictly necessary for their survival."

"It's not?" Dukakis said.

"No, sir. They could take care of their bodily needs much more quietly by a mincing of human and animal parts painted onto their vital organs with a fine-haired brush. But no, they insist on bathing with the human parts."

"But why?" Dukakis asked.

"They give many reasons, but the chief thing seems to be to serve their perverted sense of humor."

"You mean they find this sort of thing funny?" Dukakis asked.

"Yes, sir. I'm afraid so. They start giggling as soon as they get into the vat. When they push the first floating parts aside, they begin to get their first bursts of hysterical laughter."

"But that's horrible!"

"It is a sure sign of their alienness," Watkins said. "Aliens don't have much regard for things that are sacred to us humans, like our bodies."

Dukakis and Watkins walked on and at last came out of the dark passageway and into a brightly lit area.

Dukakis thought it looked quite like an immense airplane hangar at night. It was lit brilliantly. Several 747s were parked in corners of the hangar. Big as they were, they were dwarfed by the size of the structure itself.

An open-sided bus came out of a passageway and speeded toward Dukakis and Watkins. At the last moment it skidded to a halt. A door opened in the bus. A man came out and said to Watkins, "Is that the new president there?"

"Yes, Budkins," Watkins said. "He's here."

"We need to confer with him at Central Planning at once."

"I'm afraid there's no time for that," Watkins said. "He's seen the feeding vats. I think I'd better get him back to Washington immediately."

"Couldn't he just come to the meeting and tell us what he thinks about Evacuation Plan Craven B?"

"My dear fellow," Watkins said, "he's only just learned about the alien conspiracy. There's been no time to brief him on the evacuation plan."

"Even a snap judgment would be useful."

"Out of the question," Watkins said.

"No, wait a moment," Dukakis said. "I want to hear this. What is the evacuation plan, Mr. Budkins?"

Budkins said, "The proposition, Mr. President, was that in the event of attack and takeover of America by aliens, all male government officials from the level of GSC 04 and higher would be led to the secret spaceships and taken to our secret Mars colony."

"What about their families?" Dukakis asked.

"No time for that, sir. Sometimes it's better to begin again. On Mars the male government personnel would begin a program of breeding, using for that purpose the bodies of secretarial female personnel who would be transported to Mars for that purpose."

"I'm not sure what I think of that," Dukakis said. "Government officials should stick to their posts, even if the ship is sinking."

At that moment a diminutive figure with a bald head, standing about three and a half feet high, wearing a black uniform with silver markings, and carrying on his back a small backpack, stepped out of the wall, crossed the corridor, and stepped into the wall on the opposite side, disappearing into (or perhaps behind) it.

"What was that?" Dukakis asked, startled.

"I didn't get a good look," Watkins said, "but I think it was one of the Very Short Grays from Belletrix. What they call the Small Men from Belletrix."

"But he walked through the walls!"

"Yes, sir. It was made possible by that special backpack you might have noticed he was wearing. I sure wish we could get our hands on a couple of those things."

"What could you do with them?"

"They'd enable us to search the aliens out and find out for ourselves just what they're up to. It's very confusing not knowing for sure."

At that moment Dukakis suddenly had had enough. "I gotta get out of here," he said. He looked at Watkins and Budkins. Their faces were pale, fanatical, inhuman. Budkins raised a hand in which there was something white and soft and ugly. Dukakis turned and ran. He heard a splintering explosion behind him. He continued running, turned a corner, and found a branching of the ways. He chose the left branch and continued down the polished steel tube.

Ten minutes later they had Dukakis cornered. He turned to face them. Suddenly a smile broke out across his glum face. He raised one hand. In it was a Wand of Power.

"My God!" cried Watkins. "Where did he get that?"

"More to the point," Budkins said, "who is he, really?"

"No time to find out," Watkins said. "Have you got your laser cane?"

"Of course." Budkins took the small rod out of his righthand jacket pocket. Pressing the expansion stud, he caused the rod to extend to its full three feet. Watkins had done the same.

"Ready?" Watkins asked.

"Ready!" Budkins said.

"Then let's fire!"

Caught in the intersecting laser beams, the figure of Dukakis leaped and kicked, transfixed by the twin beams like a bug on a pin. He struggled and writhed, but he did not fall. His face changed, lengthened, whitened, became unfamiliar. His hands grew, changed color from hairy brown to glassy green. Those hands grasped the twin laser beams, and their touch seemed to render the energy beams palpable. Dukakis's hands twisted, and the laser beams fell apart like shattered glowing glass-strands. Dukakis straightened and turned toward Watkins and Budkins, his body hunched over in a posture of aggression. He started toward them and they cowered back. Budkins dropped his laser rod and pulled out a .45. He fired and the slug recoiled from Dukakis's chest. Laughing horribly, Dukakis reached out with his terrible hooked hands....

And at that moment Watkins pulled out a strange-looking handgun. He squeezed the firing stud. A white light shot out, touched Dukakis, and instantly covered him with coruscating energy. Dukakis screamed as his body fluids boiled off. His body moisture boiled away, and the paper-dry nerves and flesh flared up briefly and died away. A few wisps of black ash floated to the floor.

"Are you all right?" Watkins asked.

"Yes, I think so," Budkins said. "But who or what *was* that?"

"Something or someone we hadn't anticipated," Watkins said.

"A new player in the Earth game?" Budkins asked.

"Yes," said Watkins. "There always was the possibility that the Teal Greens of Aldebaran, who have hitherto shown no interest in Earth, would take a hand."

"As if we didn't have enough problems," Watkins said. "Now the Teal Greens!"

"But I think we can still do something about it," Budkins said. "You must contact the Master Programmer at once. Tell her it's essential she take a couple of months off the Earth Main Sequence Time Clock and reset for a Bush victory."

Watkins wasn't sure. "You know how she hates to redo human history. You know what she says: too many anomalies spoil the construct."

"She's got to do it," Budkins said. "The time-line of the Bush presidency is now the only available one that doesn't have the Teal Greens taking over. It'll give us a breathing-space to mount a defense against them."

"All right," Watkins said. "I'll do it. But you know the time-line forecast: with Bush we get the Kuwait invasion and the Persian Gulf War."

"I know," Budkins said, "but what can we do? It's either that or the Teal Greens."

"All right." He went to the door, then turned. "What do you want us to do about Dukakis in this new time-line?"

"Don't worry about him. It's Bush we have to worry about now."

THE NEW ENGLAND
SCIENCE FICTION ASSOCIATION (NESFA)
AND NESFA PRESS

Selected books from NESFA Press:

- *Once Upon a Time (She Said)* by Jane Yolen $26
- *Dimensions of Sheckley* by Robert Sheckley $29
- *Once More* With Footnotes* by Terry Pratchett $25
- *Dancing Naked* by William Tenn $29
- *Immodest Proposals* (Vol. 1) by William Tenn $29
- *Here Comes Civilization* (Vol. 2) by William Tenn $29
- *With Stars in My Eyes* by Peter Weston $23
- *Fancestral Voices* by Jack Speer $17
- *A Star Above It* by Chad Oliver (Vol. 1) $24
- *Far From This Earth* by Chad Oliver (Vol. 2) $24
- *The Rediscovery of Man* by Cordwainer Smith $25
- *Nostrilia* by Cordwainer Smith $22
- *Silverlock* by John Myers Myers $26
- *Ingathering: The Complete People Stories* by Zenna Henderson $25
- *Homecalling and Other Stories* by Judith Merril $29
- *Years in the Making* by L. Sprague de Camp $25

Details and many more books available online at: www.nesfa.org/press

Books may be ordered online or by writing to:
NESFA Press
PO Box 809
Framingham, MA 01701

We accept checks, Visa, or MasterCard. Please add $3 postage and handling per order.

The New England Science Fiction Association:

NESFA is an all-volunteer, non-profit organization of science fiction and fantasy fans. Besides publishing, our activities include running Boskone (New England's oldest SF convention) in February each year, producing a semi-monthly newsletter, holding discussion groups relating to the field, and hosting a variety of social events. If you are interested in learning more about us, we'd like to hear from you. Write to our address above!

ACKNOWLEDGMENTS

Advice & Encouragement: Seth Breidbart, Gay Ellen Dennett, Deb Geisler, David Grubbs, Dan Kimmel, Suford Lewis, Tony Lewis, Mark Olson, Priscilla Olson

Scanning: Lis Carey, Rick Katze

Proofing: Ann Broomhead, Tom Courtney, Crispen Cullen, Gay Ellen Dennett, Dale Farmer, Pam Fremon, David Grubbs, Lisa Hertel, Mark Hertel, Suford Lewis, Tony Lewis, Paula Lieberman, Mark Olson, Sheila Perry, Joe Ross, Davey Snyder, Geri Sullivan, Asa Swain, Tim Szczesuil, Persis Thorndike

Dedicated to George Flynn—*requiescat in pacem*

—Sharon L. Sbarsky
May, 2005